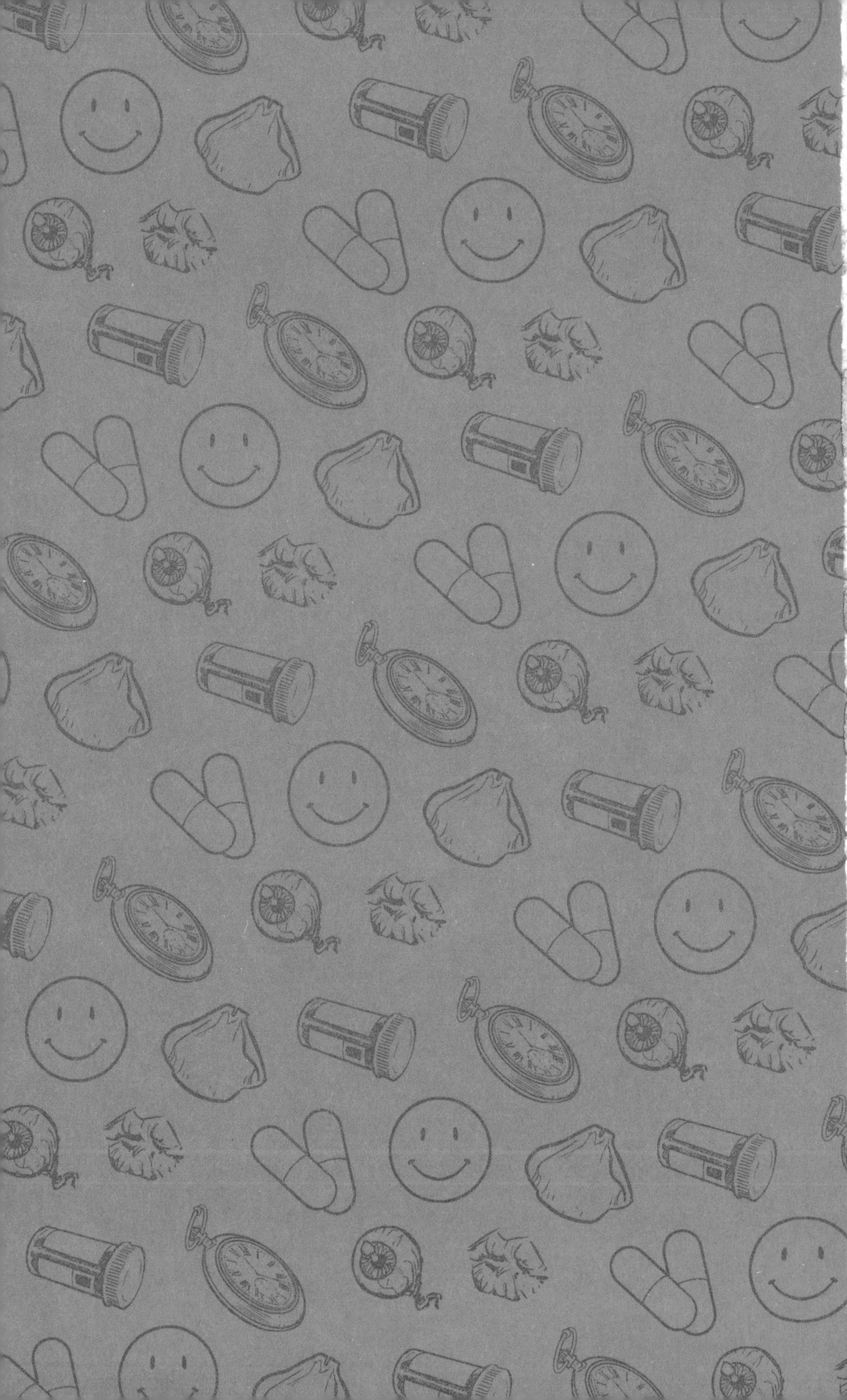

FIGHT CLUB 2™

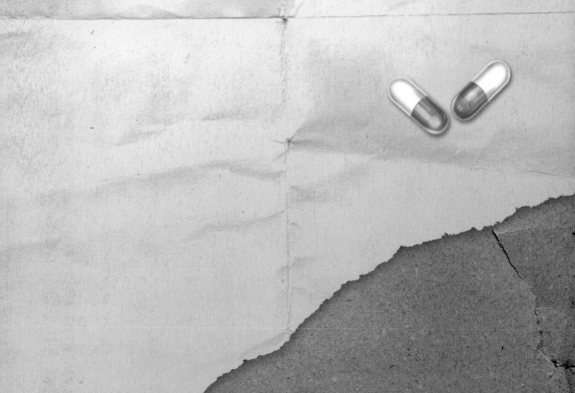

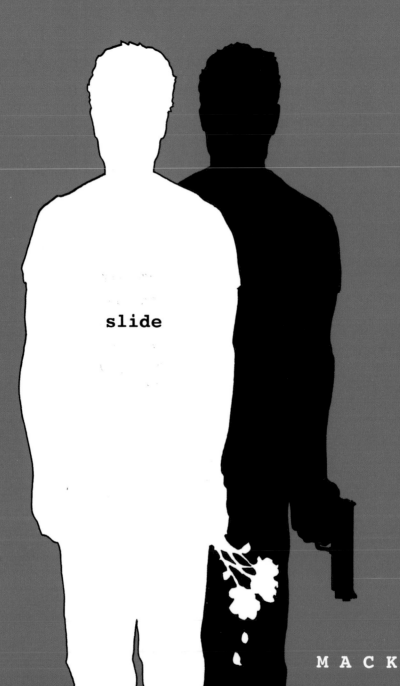

slide

MACK

FIGHT CLUB 2 ™

The Tranquility Gambit

Story by
CHUCK PALAHNIUK

Art by
CAMERON STEWART

Colors by
DAVE STEWART

Letters and logo by
NATE PIEKOS OF BLAMBOT ®

Cover and chapter break art by
DAVID MACK

Dark Horse Books

President and Publisher .... Mike Richardson
Editor .... Scott Allie
Associate Editor .... Shantel LaRocque
Assistant Editor .... Katii O'Brien
Designer .... Rick DeLucco
Digital Art Technician ...... Christianne Goudreau

This book is dedicated to my fellow workshop writers, many of whom have lent their likenesses to the project—Chelsea Cain, Monica Drake, Erin Leonard, Diana Jordan, Suzy Vitello, Mary Wysong-Haeri, and Lidia Yuknavitch.—CP

This book first came into being over a delicious dinner cooked by Marc Mohan.

Special thanks to Matt Fraction, Chelsea Cain, Kelly Sue DeConnick, Brian Michael Bendis, Todd Doughty, and Edward Hibbert.

Neil Hankerson, Executive Vice President / Tom Weddle, Chief Financial Officer / Randy Stradley, Vice President of Publishing / Michael Martens, Vice President of Book Trade Sales / Matt Parkinson, Vice President of Marketing / David Scroggy, Vice President of Product Development / Dale LaFountain, Vice President of Information Technology / Cara Niece, Vice President of Production and Scheduling / Nick McWhorter, Vice President of Media Licensing / Ken Lizzi, General Counsel / Dave Marshall, Editor in Chief / Davey Estrada, Editorial Director / Scott Allie, Executive Senior Editor / Chris Warner, Senior Books Editor / Cary Grazzini, Director of Print and Development / Lia Ribacchi, Art Director / Mark Bernardi, Director of Digital Publishing / Michael Gombos, Director of International Publishing and Licensing

Published by Dark Horse Books
A division of Dark Horse Comics, Inc.
10956 SE Main Street
Milwaukie, OR 97222

First edition: June 2016
ISBN 978-1-61655-945-8

Limited edition: June 2016
ISBN 978-1-50670-230-8

10 9 8 7 6 5 4 3 2
Printed in the United States of America

International Licensing: (503) 905-2377
Comic Shop Locator Service: (888) 266-4226

This edition collects *Fight Club 2* #1–#10 and the *Fight Club 2* Free Comic Book Day 2015 story.

Library of Congress Cataloging-in-Publication Data

Names: Palahniuk, Chuck, author. | Stewart, Cameron, 1976?- illustrator. |
 Stewart, Dave, illustrator. | Piekos, Nate, illustrator. | Mack, David,
 1972- illustrator.
Title: Fight Club 2 : the tranquility gambit / story by Chuck Palahniuk ; art
 by Cameron Stewart ; colors by Dave Stewart ; letters and logo by Nate
 Piekos of Blambot ; covers and chapter break art by David Mack.
Other titles: Tranquility gambit
Description: First edition. | Milwaukie, OR : Dark Horse Books, 2016.
Identifiers: LCCN 2015049534 | ISBN 9781616559458 (hardback)
Subjects: LCSH: Young men--Comic books, strips, etc. | Hand-to-hand
 fighting--Comic books, strips, etc. | Self-actualization
 (Psychology)--Comic books, strips, etc. | Graphic novels. | BISAC: COMICS
 & GRAPHIC NOVELS / Media Tie-In. | GSAFD: Comic books, strips, etc.
Classification: LCC PN6727.P347 F54 2016 | DDC 741.5/973--dc23
LC record available at http://lccn.loc.gov/2015049534

INTRODUCTION

I didn't see this coming. Any of it.

Let's go back to sometime around 1995. I was working as an editor at the firm of W. W. Norton, a proudly independent and employee-owned New York house best known to the public as the publisher of *The Norton Anthology of English Literature*. A pretty conservative place, but one that also gave an editor his head if he didn't ask for a lot of money. I had read a novel in manuscript by a guy with the hard-to-pronounce name of Chuck Palahniuk with the title *Invisible Monsters*, about a horribly maimed supermodel bombing around the Pacific Northwest with some phony Eurotrash friends, stealing drugs from the cabinets of the rich and elderly, selling half of them at the local bars and gobbling up the rest. The hysterical voice of the novel drove me crazy (in a good way), but I couldn't quite understand what was really going on in the book and so could not quite get my colleagues, who were much less charmed, to let me make an offer to publish.

But as it turned out, this Chuck guy came to New York for a visit soon after, and I met him and liked him. He wore checked flannel just like someone from Portland, Oregon, should, and he had a dry and offbeat sense of humor. We later met again at a perfectly horrible writers' conference in Everett, Washington, and that time he was wearing a white Prince Valiant-y shirt with puffed-out sleeves remarkably like the famed puffy shirt worn by Jerry Seinfeld. We corresponded after that, and one day he sent me a story titled "Fight Club," about white-collar drones who head to a certain bar on weekends to pound each other into near-oblivion as a way to escape the consumerist/office-job blues. They head back into work on Monday with ominous bruises and wobbling teeth, and nobody screws with them anymore. They feel *alive*. It was outrageous and perfectly done, and Chuck asked me if I thought he should develop it into a novel. Uh, yeah.

In time the complete manuscript of *Fight Club* arrived at Norton from his agent, Edward Hibbert, and it was unnerving and anarchic and just brilliant. I thought that Chuck had developed his premise with enormous inventiveness and convincing, if occasionally baroque, detail (the things you can learn as Chuck's editor . . .). I bought, totally bought, the book's thesis that contemporary young men suffered from an absence of strong male role models and the malaise of meaningless work and hamster-wheel consumption at Ikea and the Gap, and that only regeneration through violence could bring them back to spiritual life. It made sense to me. I was in. But as for the question every book editor has to ask himself, "Who is going to buy it?" my honest answer to myself had to be "Fucked if I know." You needed a somewhat depraved sense of humor and a pretty strong stomach to go where Chuck was taking you. It sure wasn't like anything else being published in the mid-nineties. That's what I liked about it.

I still vividly remember the editorial meeting where I brought *Fight Club* up for acquisition. The odds were not good. None of my other readers save one assistant, bless her, expressed any enthusiasm—in fact there was mostly an ominous silence, although one editor did say to me, ambiguously, "Well, *you're* good at this sort of thing." That was either a compliment or an indictment. I made my pitch for the book as best I could, to be greeted again by silence around the conference table, which I interpreted, correctly I'm sure, as my colleagues thinking, "He's nuts, but I'm going to let someone else knock him over." With mere seconds to go before that happened, I blurted out, "Look, I really think there's something going on here. Just give me $6,000 to offer and I won't come back to you, I promise." To which the kindly president of the company replied, "Oh, let the kid have his book." (I was forty-five at the time.) I said thanks and rushed to my office to make the offer before they could take it back. And it was accepted.

(Chuck has referred to that offer in print as "fuck-you money." I respectfully disagree. What it was was "Well, okay . . ." money.)

I then proceeded to edit the book, in a couple of key cases getting Chuck to dial back a bit of the violence and darkness. As in not having the sheriff actually castrated in the men's room, just threatened with castration. (So glad that change was made when I saw that scene in the movie . . .). But here is a slightly embarrassing admission I've never made in public before: I did not realize that Tyler Durden was just a projection of the narrator's splintering psyche. I thought he was an actual character because, in my defense, Marla also talked directly to Tyler, and how could another person believe in someone's hallucination? So I convinced Chuck to make the changes necessary to correct what I thought was a source of potential reader confusion. Marla always talks to the narrator, not to Tyler.

I do want to state that Norton published *Fight Club* with genuine enthusiasm. The sales force really took to the book and we sold paperback rights for $25,000, so it was a financial success right out of the box. To this day I hear from editors who worked at paperback houses when *Fight Club* came up for discussion and opinions were violently divided on its merits or lack thereof. "So you're the guy who edited that book," they say with guarded respect. The book received some favorable reviews and some hostile ones, and a certain culty buzz gathered about it, but the sales in hardcover were modest—5,000 copies at most. But Chuck was genuinely launched and I was able to sign up his next novel, one of my favorites, *Survivor*. A modest victory against the forces of consensus reality, I thought.

And then *Fight Club* took on a miraculous second life in Hollywood. A powerful producer at Fox, Laura Ziskin, decided to option it for film, God knows why. Jim Uhls wrote a fantastic script, one of the best book-to-film adaptations ever penned. David Fincher, the dark lord of the cinema, took the project on with the fervid commitment of a personal crusade and made a film so visceral and unsettling that Fox postponed its release until many months after the massacre at Columbine. The theatrical release was deemed a commercial failure, but the DVD with its many extras and endless broadcasts on Spike and other cable channels have had their effect, and *Fight Club* is now recognized as a generational classic and almost a literary rite of passage. Chuck has gone on to write many more challenging novels of unsurpassed inventiveness and wicked humor that have sold millions of copies around the world. One of them was *Invisible Monsters*, which my formerly cautious colleagues at Norton picked up; the rest I have had the keen pleasure of publishing myself. His days as an assembly line worker and technical writer at the Freightliner Corporation are a distant memory. *Fight Club* is a staple of men's studies. And at a certain point I stopped clipping out puns on *Fight Club*'s title and "The first rule . . ." allusions because why bother? On the evidence, I guess I am "good at this sort of thing." Damn right I am.

And now *Fight Club*, in this sequel, has made the transition to a medium that feels like it might have been invented to accommodate the genius and wit of Chuck Palahniuk. Just another thing I didn't see coming, but I'm so glad it has arrived. Tyler Durden lives!

— Gerald Howard
October 2015

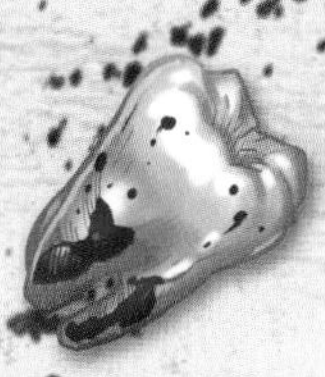

FIGHT CLUB 2™

The Tranquility Gambit

Chapter One

Keep the Home Fires Burning

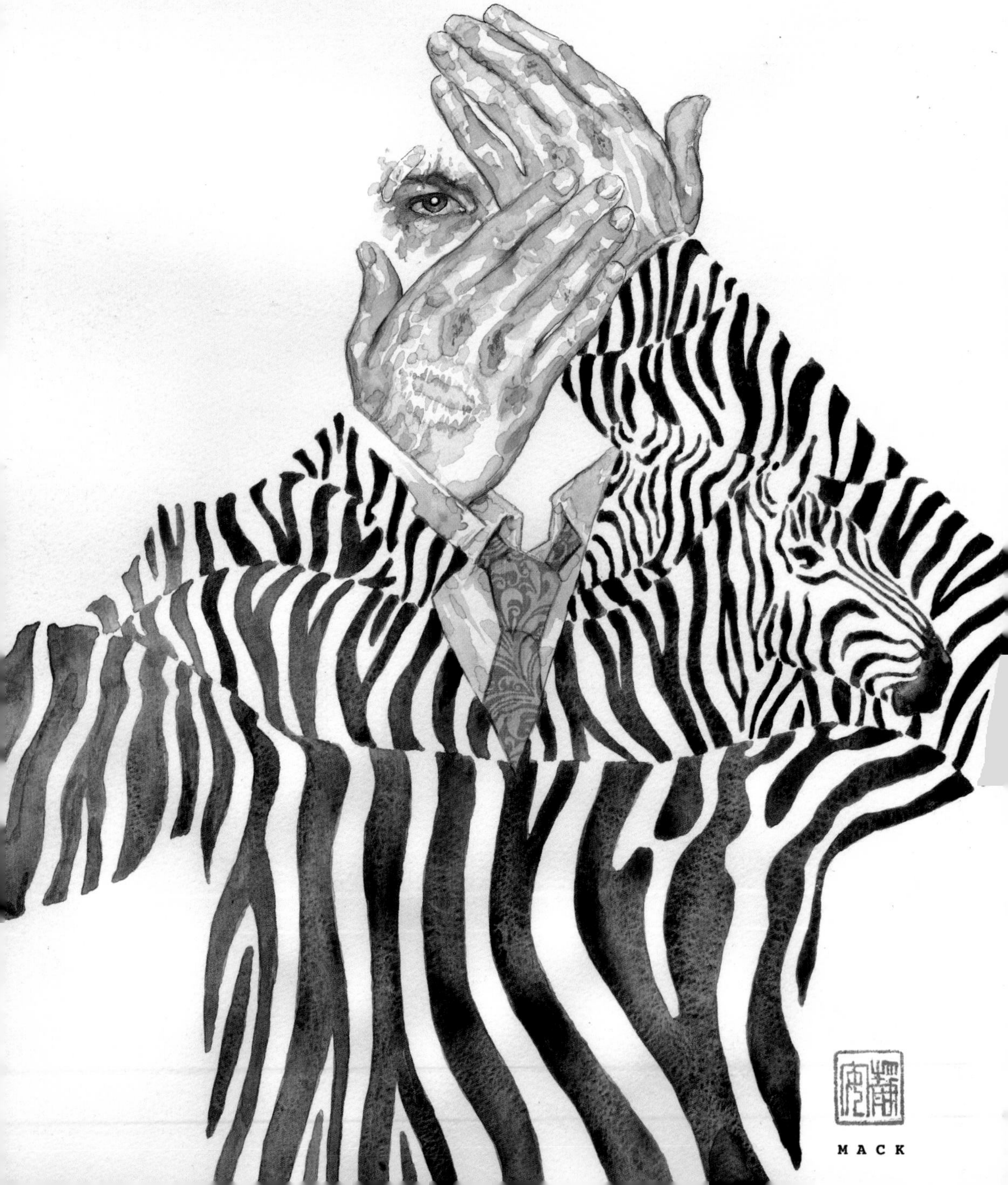
MACK

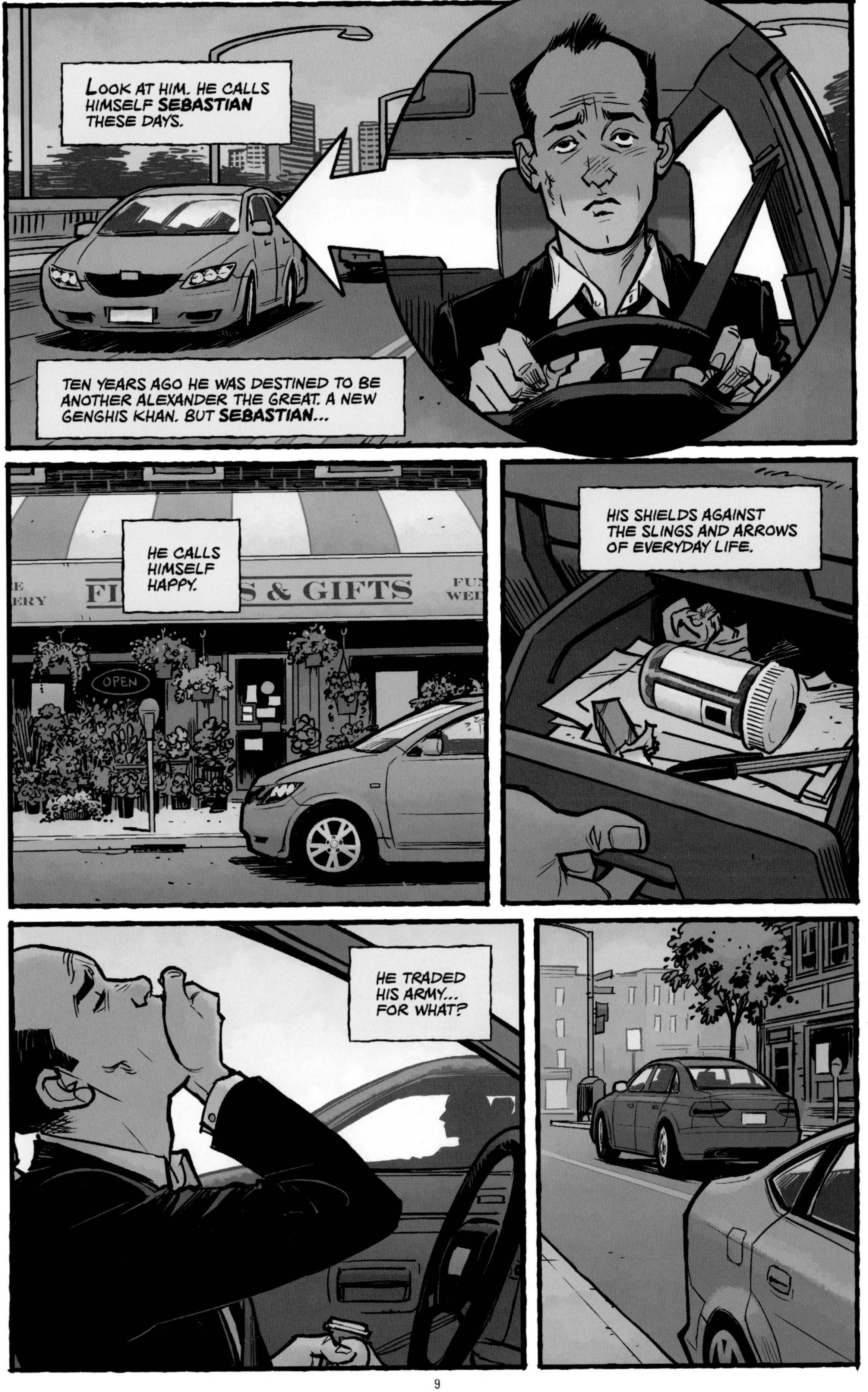
LOOK AT HIM. HE CALLS HIMSELF SEBASTIAN THESE DAYS.
TEN YEARS AGO HE WAS DESTINED TO BE ANOTHER ALEXANDER THE GREAT. A NEW GENGHIS KHAN. BUT SEBASTIAN...
HE CALLS HIMSELF HAPPY.
FL S & GIFTS
OPEN
HIS SHIELDS AGAINST THE SLINGS AND ARROWS OF EVERYDAY LIFE.
HE TRADED HIS ARMY... FOR WHAT?

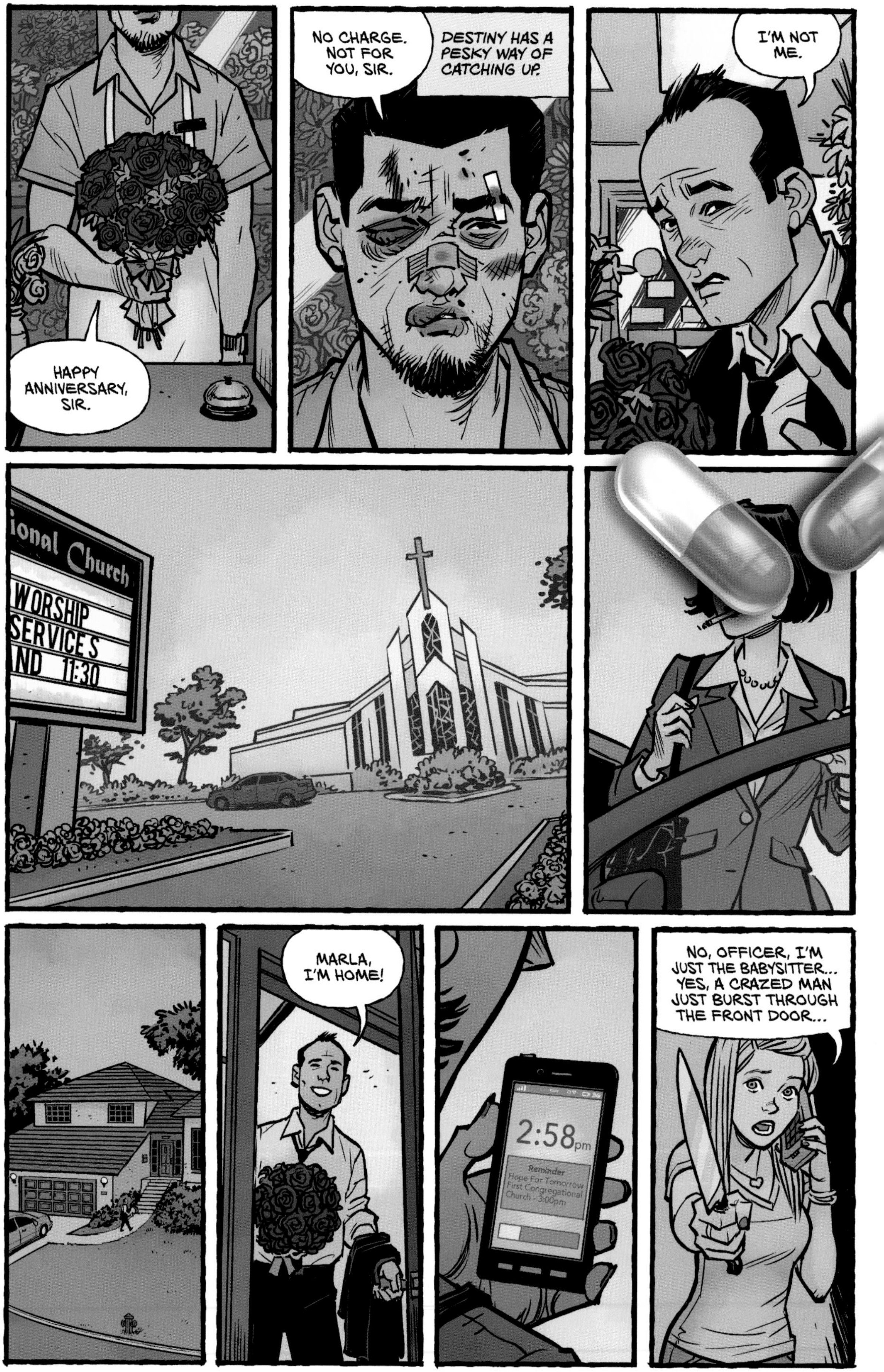
HAPPY ANNIVERSARY, SIR.
NO CHARGE. NOT FOR YOU, SIR.
DESTINY HAS A PESKY WAY OF CATCHING UP.
I'M NOT ME.
ional Church
WORSHIP
SERVICES
ND 11:30
MARLA, I'M HOME!
2:58pm
Reminder
Hope For Tomorrow
First Congregational
Church - 3:00pm
NO, OFFICER, I'M JUST THE BABYSITTER... YES, A CRAZED MAN JUST BURST THROUGH THE FRONT DOOR...

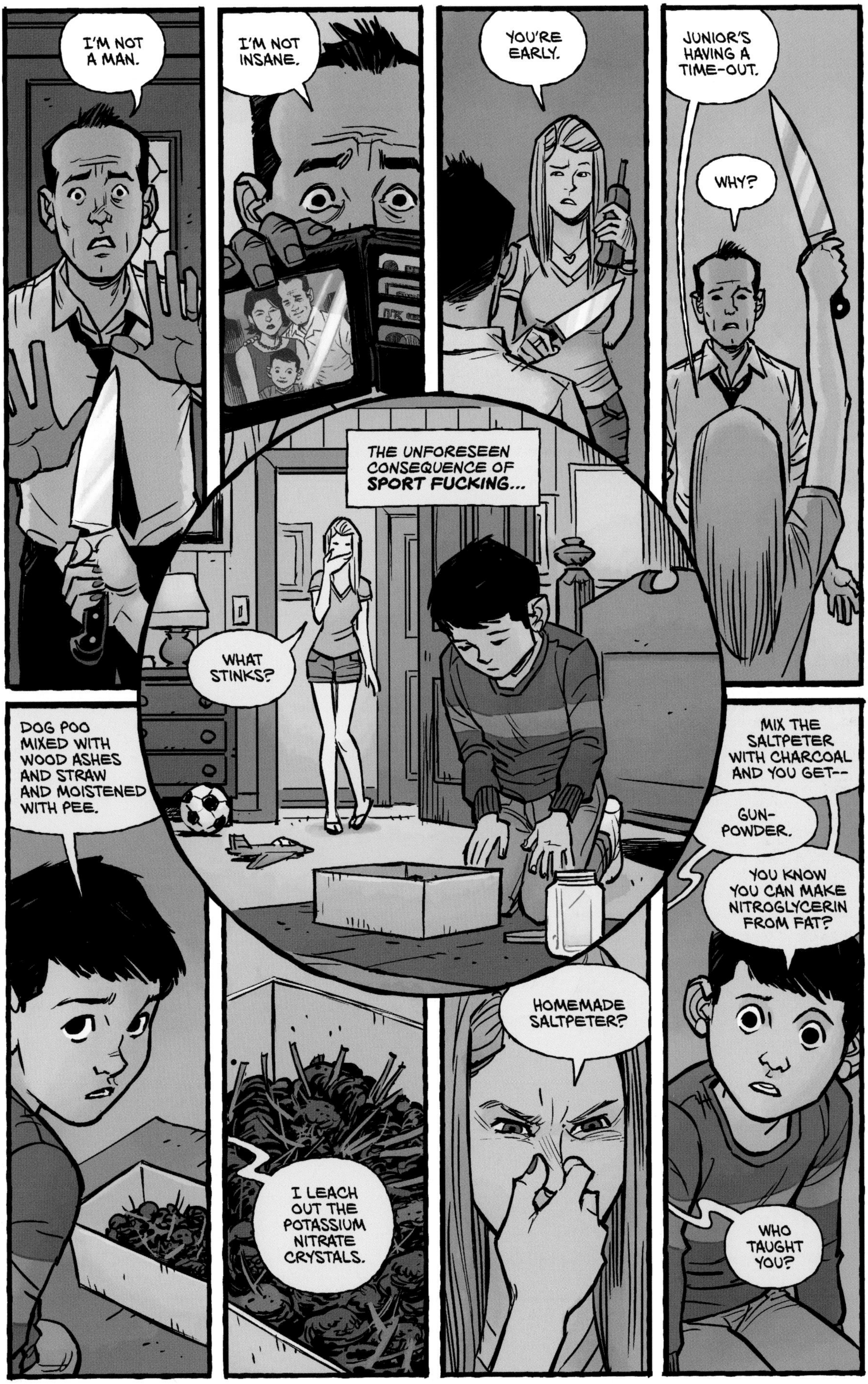
I'M NOT A MAN.
I'M NOT INSANE.
YOU'RE EARLY.
JUNIOR'S HAVING A TIME-OUT.
WHY?
THE UNFORESEEN CONSEQUENCE OF SPORT FUCKING...
WHAT STINKS?
DOG POO MIXED WITH WOOD ASHES AND STRAW AND MOISTENED WITH PEE.
I LEACH OUT THE POTASSIUM NITRATE CRYSTALS.
HOMEMADE SALTPETER?
MIX THE SALTPETER WITH CHARCOAL AND YOU GET--
GUN-POWDER.
YOU KNOW YOU CAN MAKE NITROGLYCERIN FROM FAT?
WHO TAUGHT YOU?

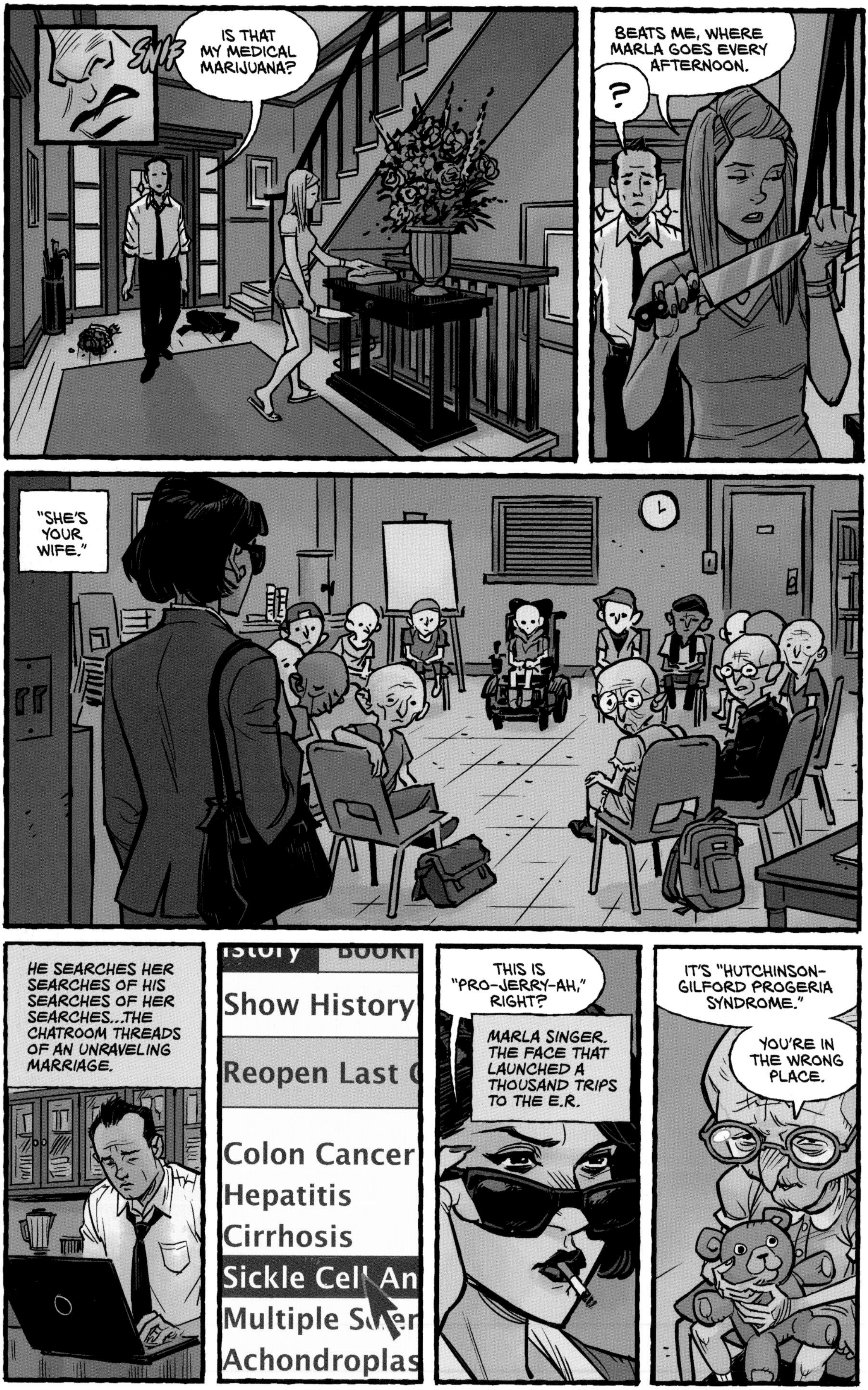
SNIF
IS THAT MY MEDICAL MARIJUANA?
BEATS ME, WHERE MARLA GOES EVERY AFTERNOON.
?
"SHE'S YOUR WIFE."
HE SEARCHES HER SEARCHES OF HIS SEARCHES OF HER SEARCHES...THE CHATROOM THREADS OF AN UNRAVELING MARRIAGE.
Show History
Reopen Last C
Colon Cancer
Hepatitis
Cirrhosis
Sickle Cell An
Multiple Scler
Achondroplas
THIS IS "PRO-JERRY-AH," RIGHT?
MARLA SINGER. THE FACE THAT LAUNCHED A THOUSAND TRIPS TO THE E.R.
IT'S "HUTCHINSON-GILFORD PROGERIA SYNDROME."
YOU'RE IN THE WRONG PLACE.

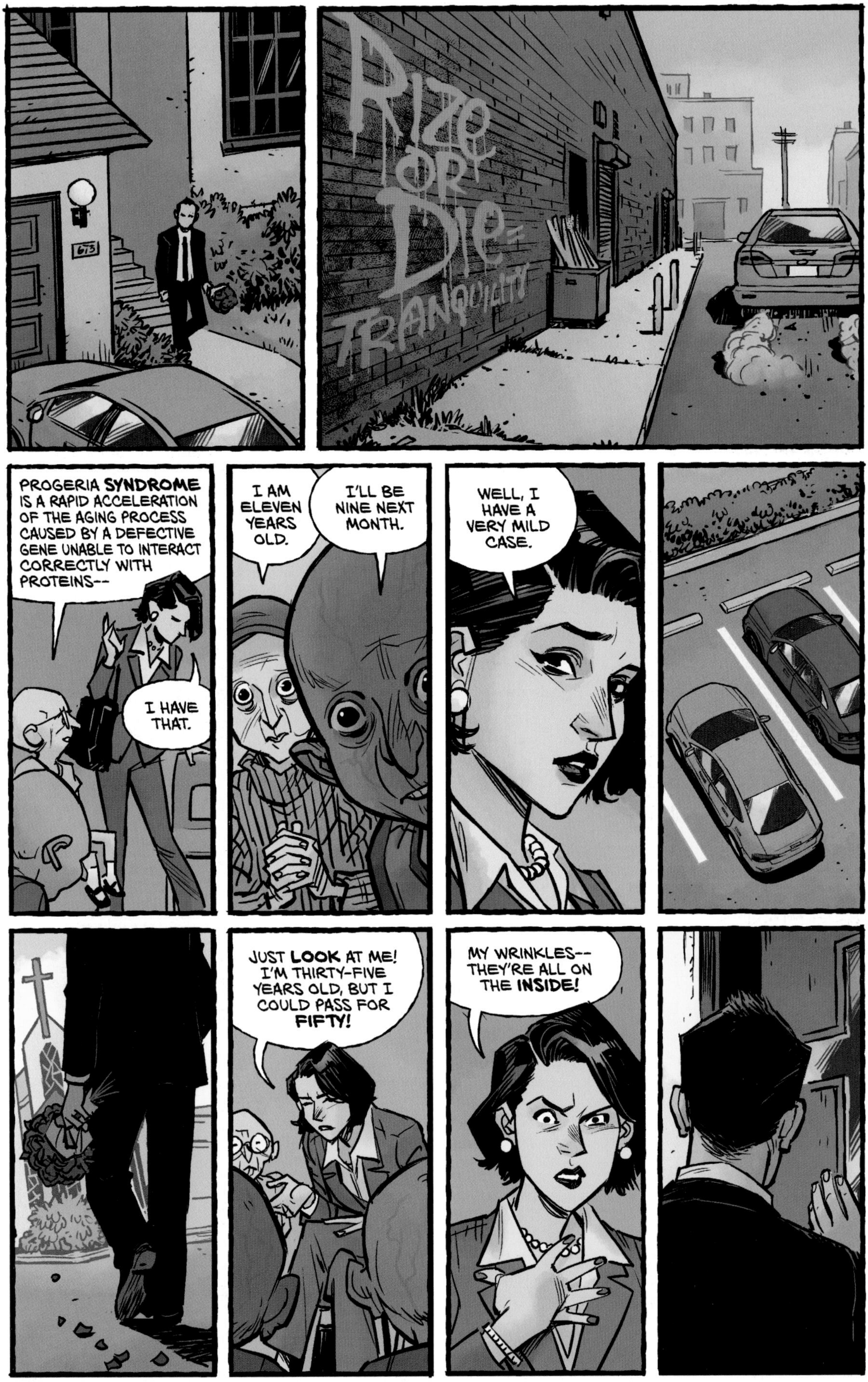

RIZE OR DIE = TRANQUILITY
PROGERIA SYNDROME IS A RAPID ACCELERATION OF THE AGING PROCESS CAUSED BY A DEFECTIVE GENE UNABLE TO INTERACT CORRECTLY WITH PROTEINS--
I HAVE THAT.
I AM ELEVEN YEARS OLD.
I'LL BE NINE NEXT MONTH.
WELL, I HAVE A VERY MILD CASE.
JUST LOOK AT ME! I'M THIRTY-FIVE YEARS OLD, BUT I COULD PASS FOR FIFTY!
MY WRINKLES-- THEY'RE ALL ON THE INSIDE!

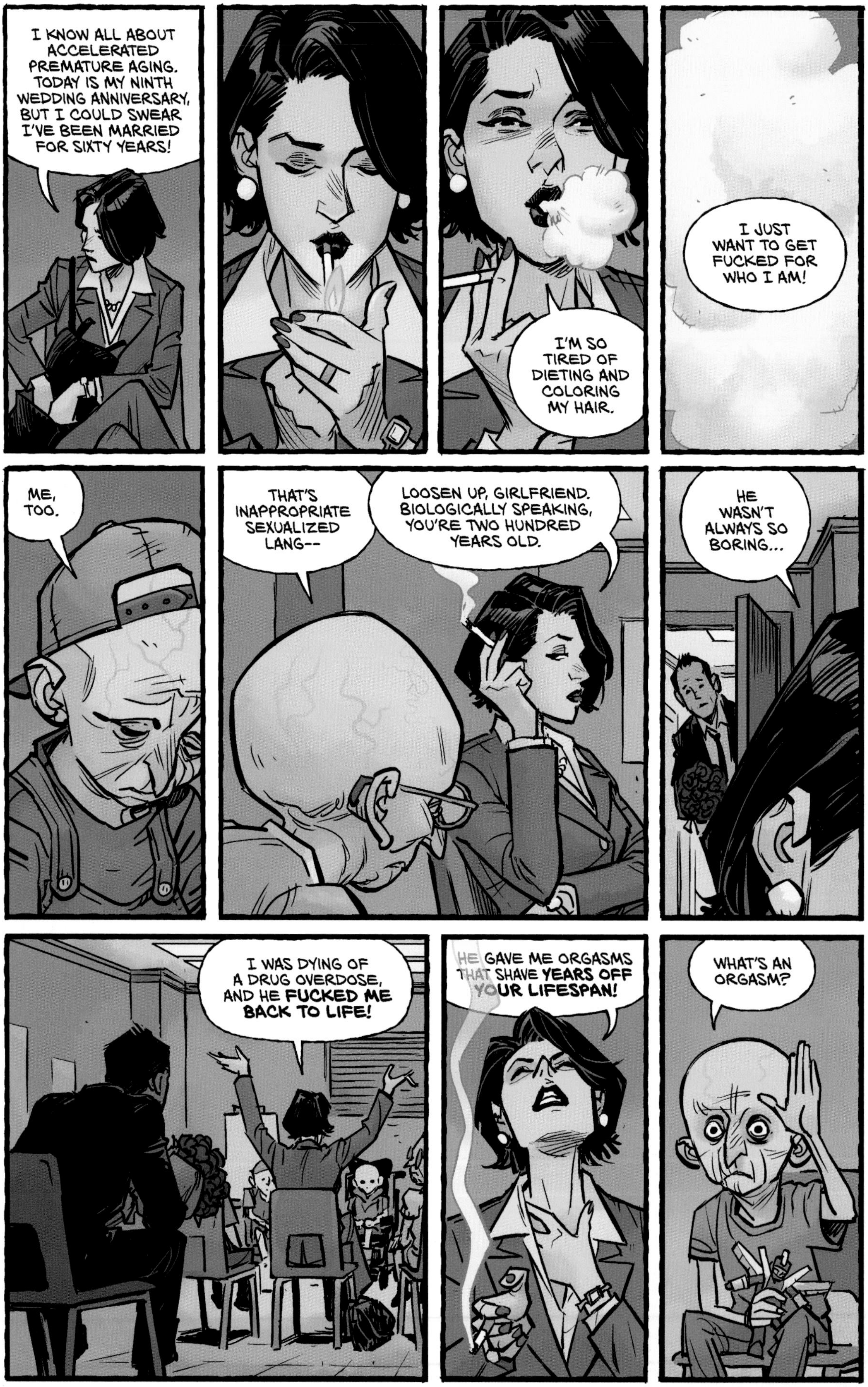
I KNOW ALL ABOUT ACCELERATED PREMATURE AGING. TODAY IS MY NINTH WEDDING ANNIVERSARY, BUT I COULD SWEAR I'VE BEEN MARRIED FOR SIXTY YEARS!
I'M SO TIRED OF DIETING AND COLORING MY HAIR.
I JUST WANT TO GET FUCKED FOR WHO I AM!
ME, TOO.
THAT'S INAPPROPRIATE SEXUALIZED LANG--
LOOSEN UP, GIRLFRIEND. BIOLOGICALLY SPEAKING, YOU'RE TWO HUNDRED YEARS OLD.
HE WASN'T ALWAYS SO BORING...
I WAS DYING OF A DRUG OVERDOSE, AND HE FUCKED ME BACK TO LIFE!
HE GAVE ME ORGASMS THAT SHAVE YEARS OFF YOUR LIFESPAN!
WHAT'S AN ORGASM?

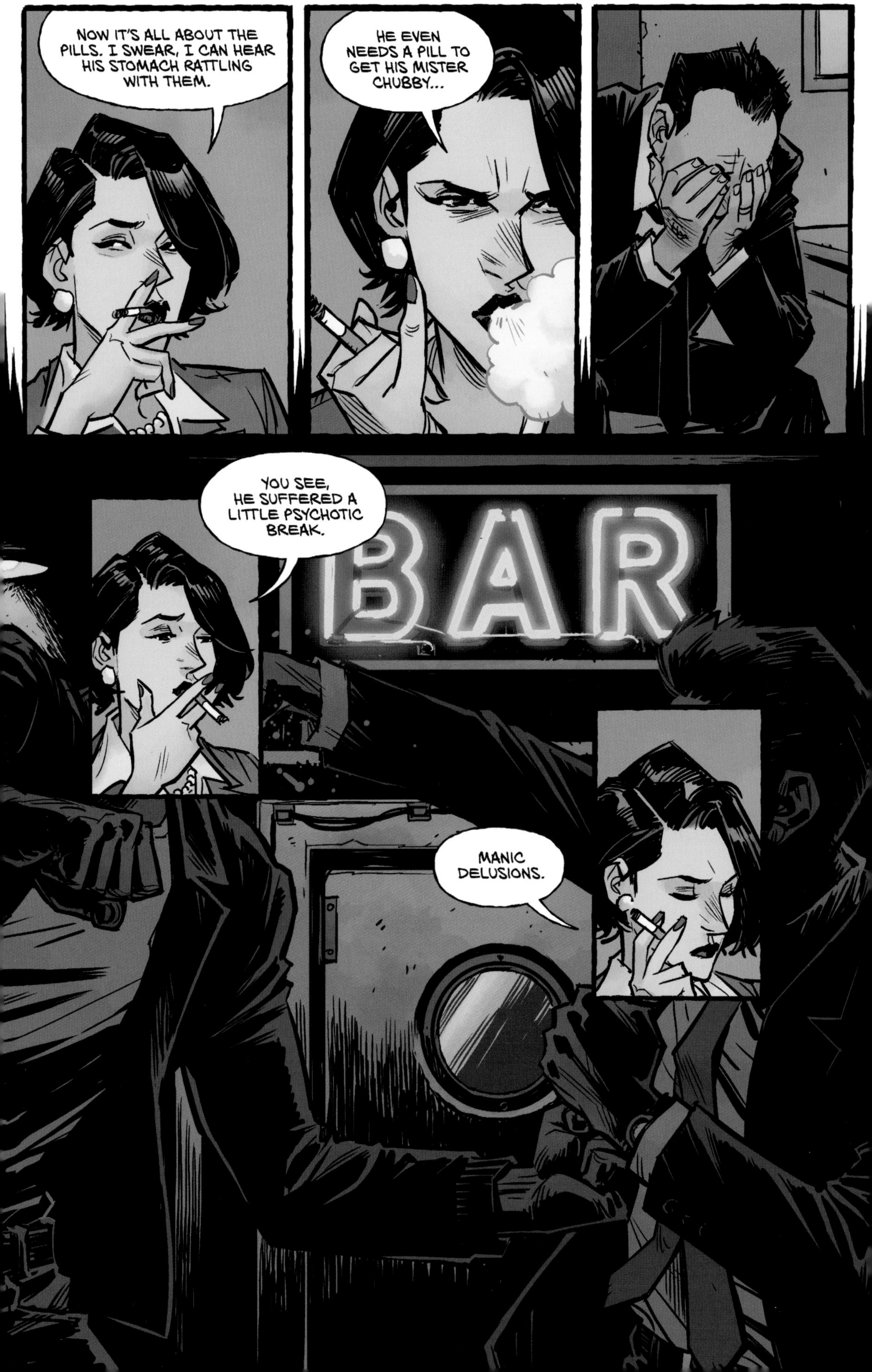
NOW IT'S ALL ABOUT THE PILLS. I SWEAR, I CAN HEAR HIS STOMACH RATTLING WITH THEM.
HE EVEN NEEDS A PILL TO GET HIS MISTER CHUBBY...
YOU SEE, HE SUFFERED A LITTLE PSYCHOTIC BREAK.
BAR
MANIC DELUSIONS.

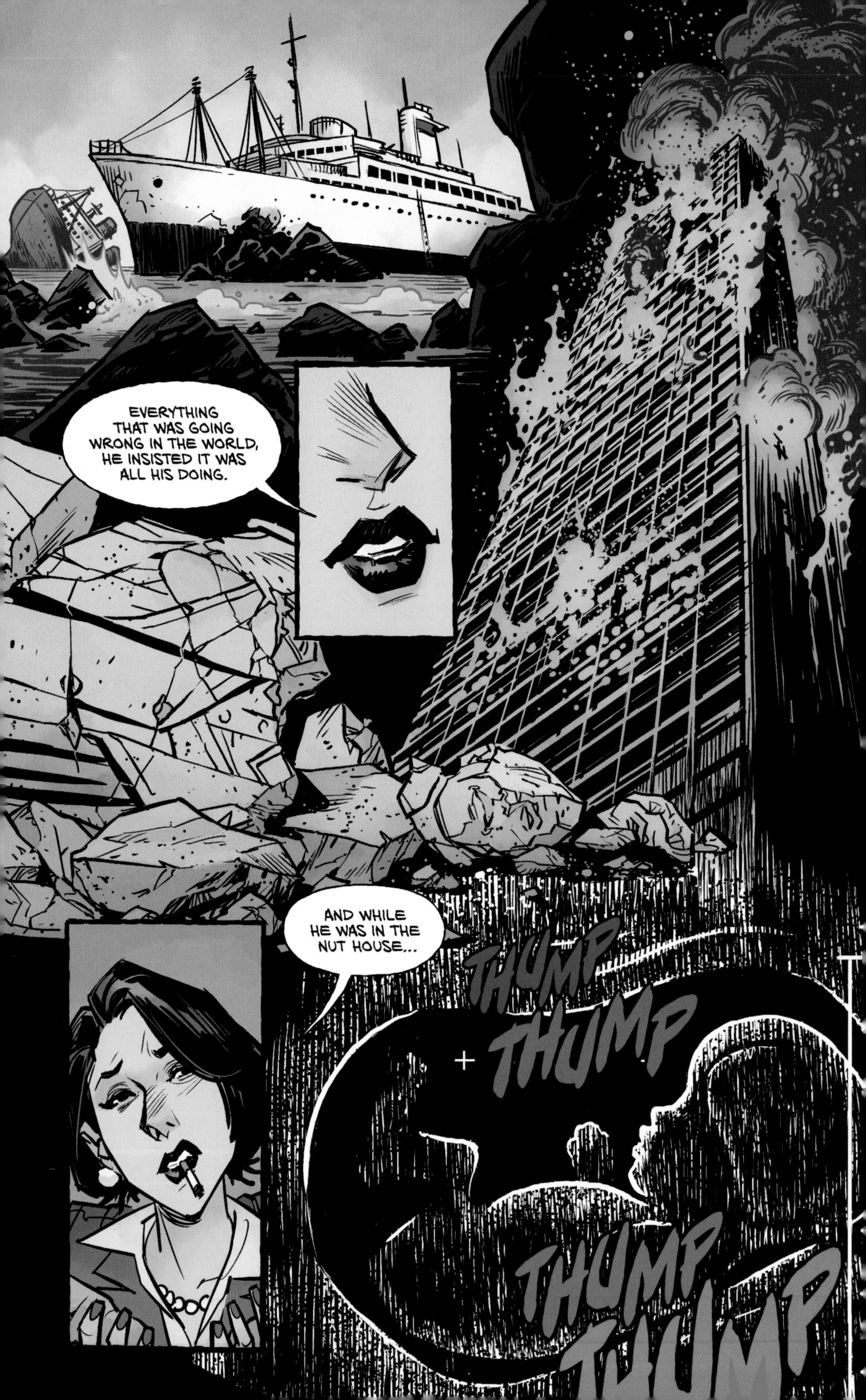
EVERYTHING THAT WAS GOING WRONG IN THE WORLD, HE INSISTED IT WAS ALL HIS DOING.
AND WHILE HE WAS IN THE NUT HOUSE...
THUMP
THUMP
THUMP
THUMP

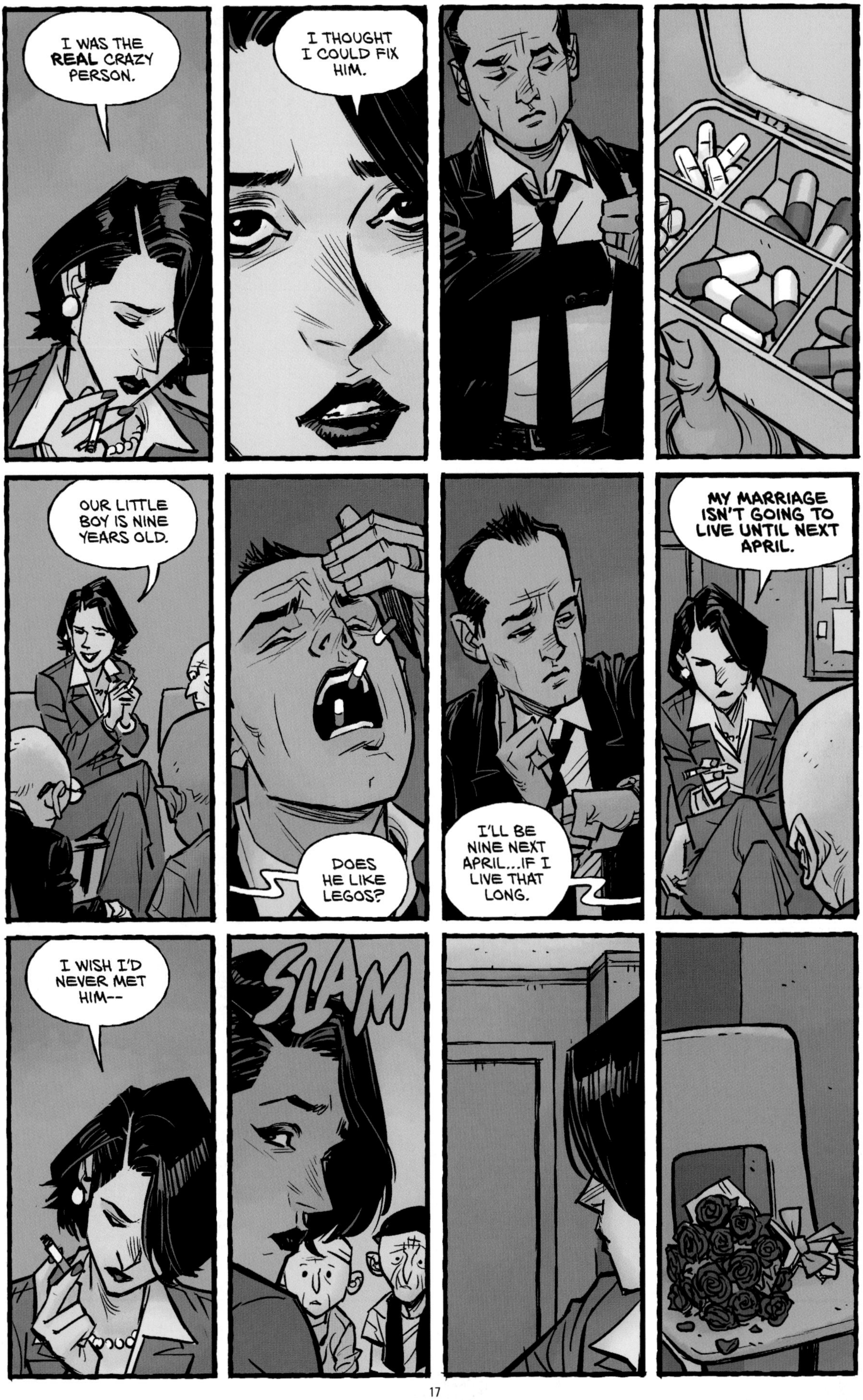
I WAS THE REAL CRAZY PERSON.
I THOUGHT I COULD FIX HIM.
OUR LITTLE BOY IS NINE YEARS OLD.
DOES HE LIKE LEGOS?
I'LL BE NINE NEXT APRIL...IF I LIVE THAT LONG.
MY MARRIAGE ISN'T GOING TO LIVE UNTIL NEXT APRIL.
I WISH I'D NEVER MET HIM--
SLAM

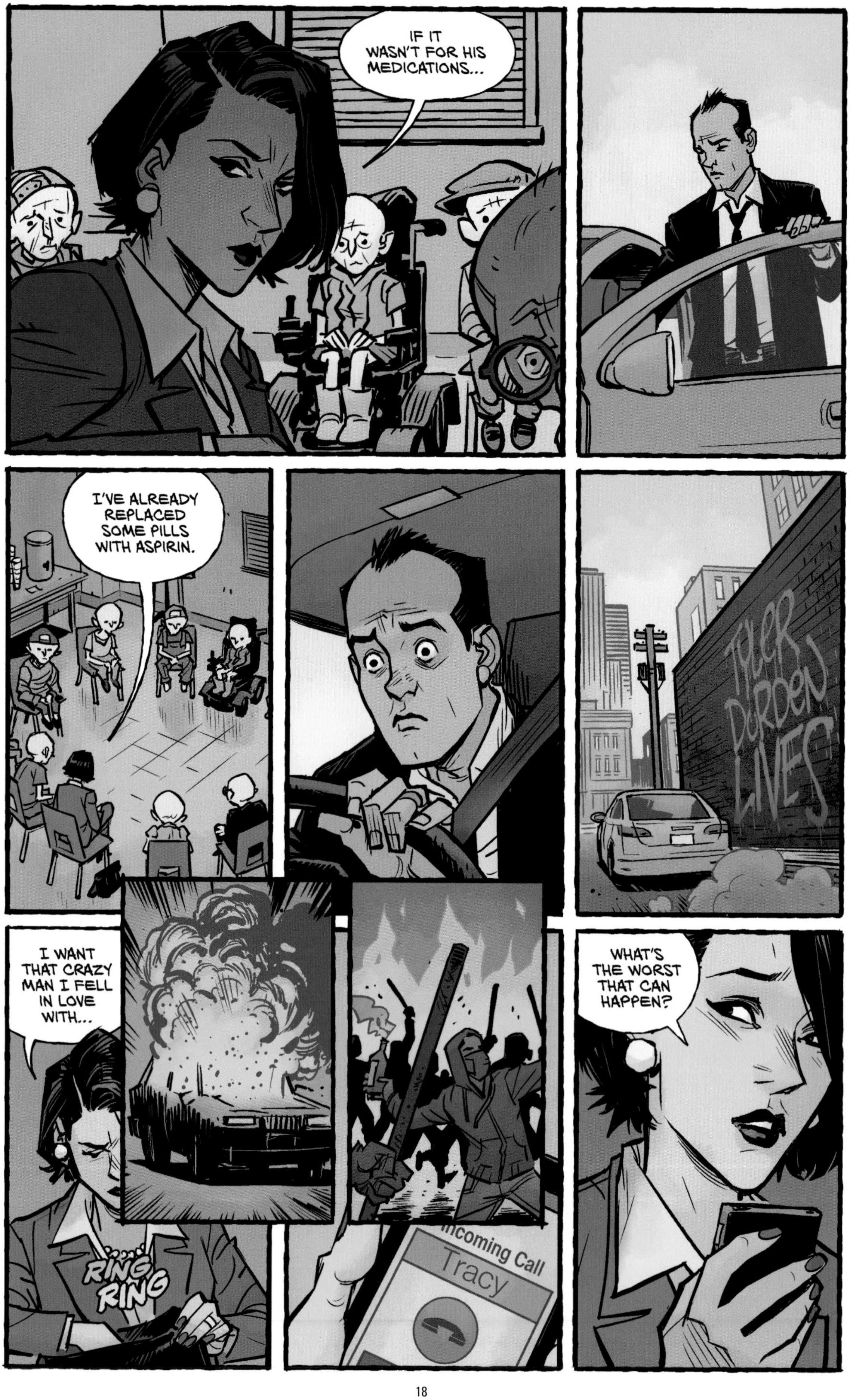
IF IT WASN'T FOR HIS MEDICATIONS...
I'VE ALREADY REPLACED SOME PILLS WITH ASPIRIN.
TYLER DURDEN LIVES
I WANT THAT CRAZY MAN I FELL IN LOVE WITH...
RING RING
Incoming Call
Tracy
WHAT'S THE WORST THAT CAN HAPPEN?

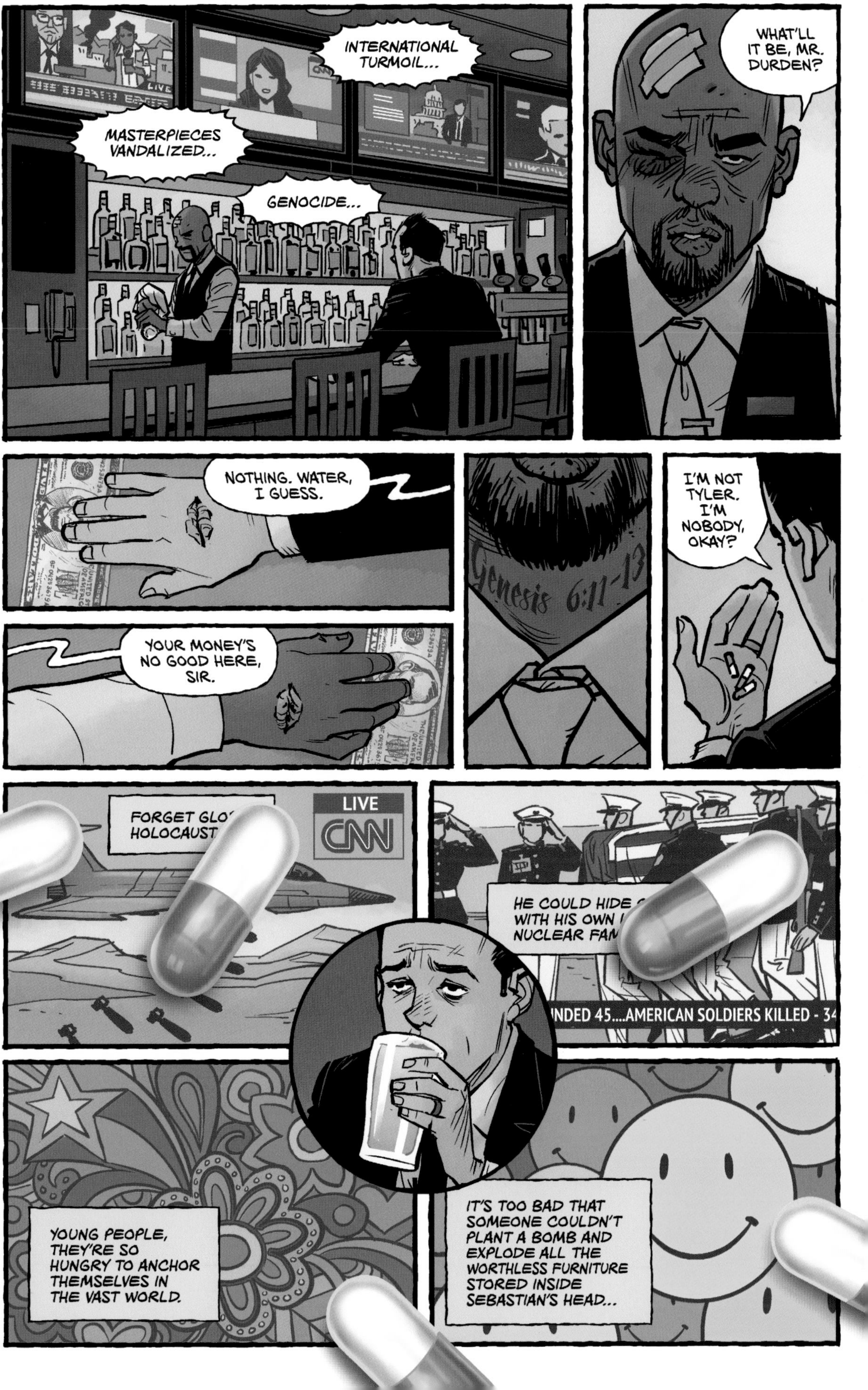
INTERNATIONAL TURMOIL...
MASTERPIECES VANDALIZED...
GENOCIDE...
LIVE
WHAT'LL IT BE, MR. DURDEN?
NOTHING. WATER, I GUESS.
YOUR MONEY'S NO GOOD HERE, SIR.
Genesis 6:11-13
I'M NOT TYLER. I'M NOBODY, OKAY?
FORGET GLO
HOLOCAUST
LIVE
CNN
HE COULD HIDE
WITH HIS OWN
NUCLEAR FAM
NDED 45....AMERICAN SOLDIERS KILLED - 34
YOUNG PEOPLE, THEY'RE SO HUNGRY TO ANCHOR THEMSELVES IN THE VAST WORLD.
IT'S TOO BAD THAT SOMEONE COULDN'T PLANT A BOMB AND EXPLODE ALL THE WORTHLESS FURNITURE STORED INSIDE SEBASTIAN'S HEAD...

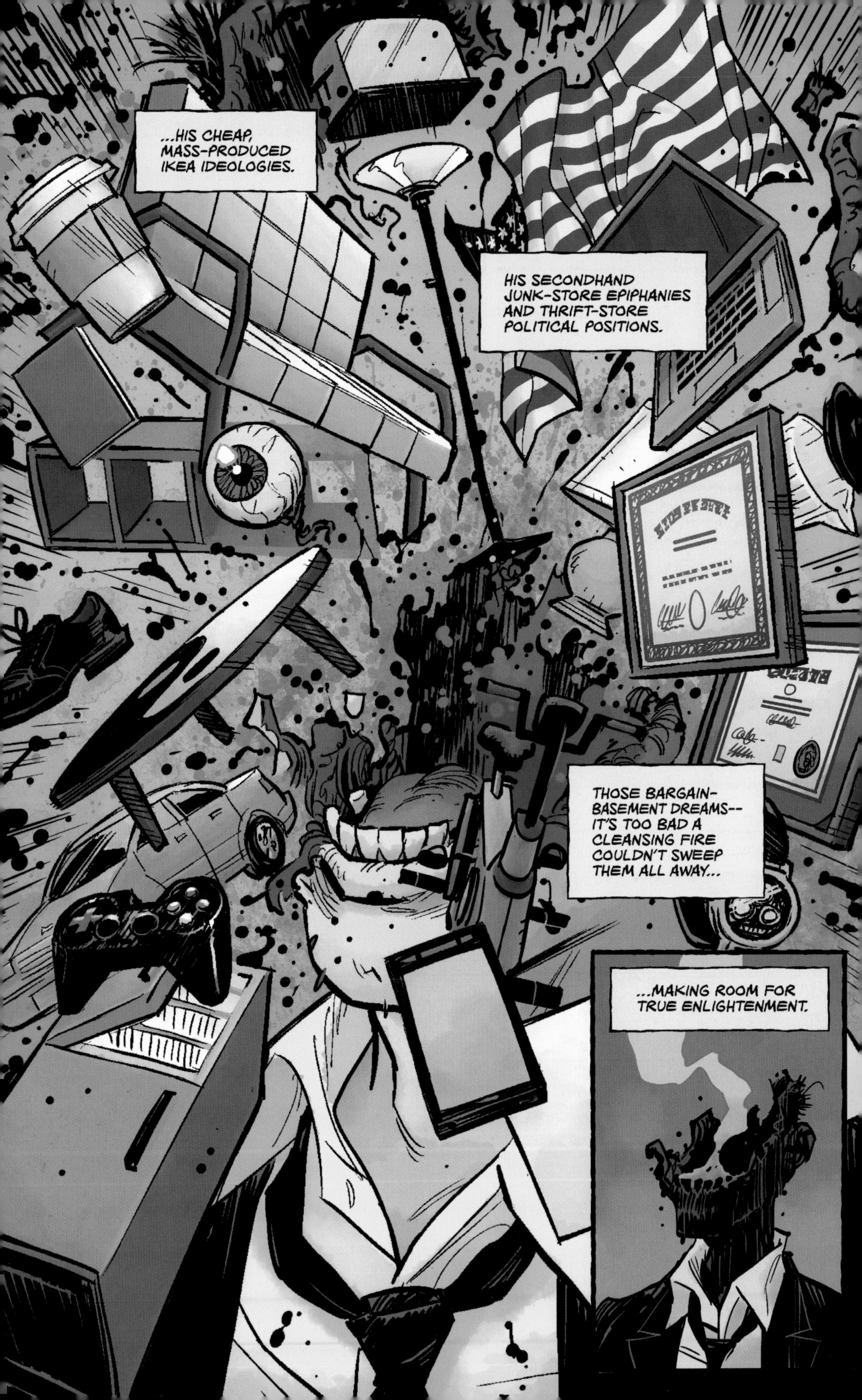
...HIS CHEAP, MASS-PRODUCED IKEA IDEOLOGIES.
HIS SECONDHAND JUNK-STORE EPIPHANIES AND THRIFT-STORE POLITICAL POSITIONS.
THOSE BARGAIN-BASEMENT DREAMS-- IT'S TOO BAD A CLEANSING FIRE COULDN'T SWEEP THEM ALL AWAY...
...MAKING ROOM FOR TRUE ENLIGHTENMENT.

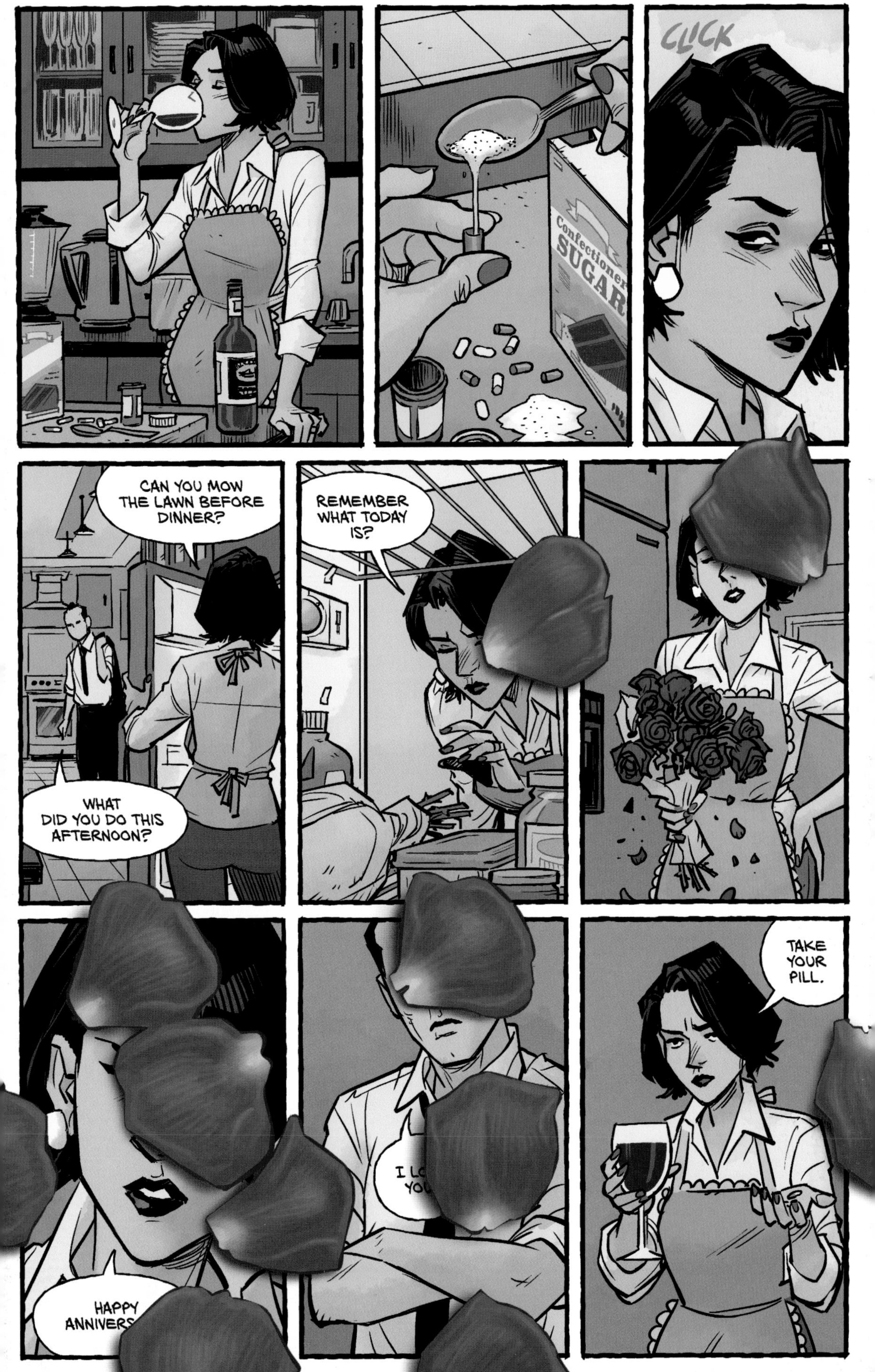
CLICK
CAN YOU MOW THE LAWN BEFORE DINNER?
WHAT DID YOU DO THIS AFTERNOON?
REMEMBER WHAT TODAY IS?
HAPPY ANNIVERS
I LO
YOU
TAKE YOUR PILL.

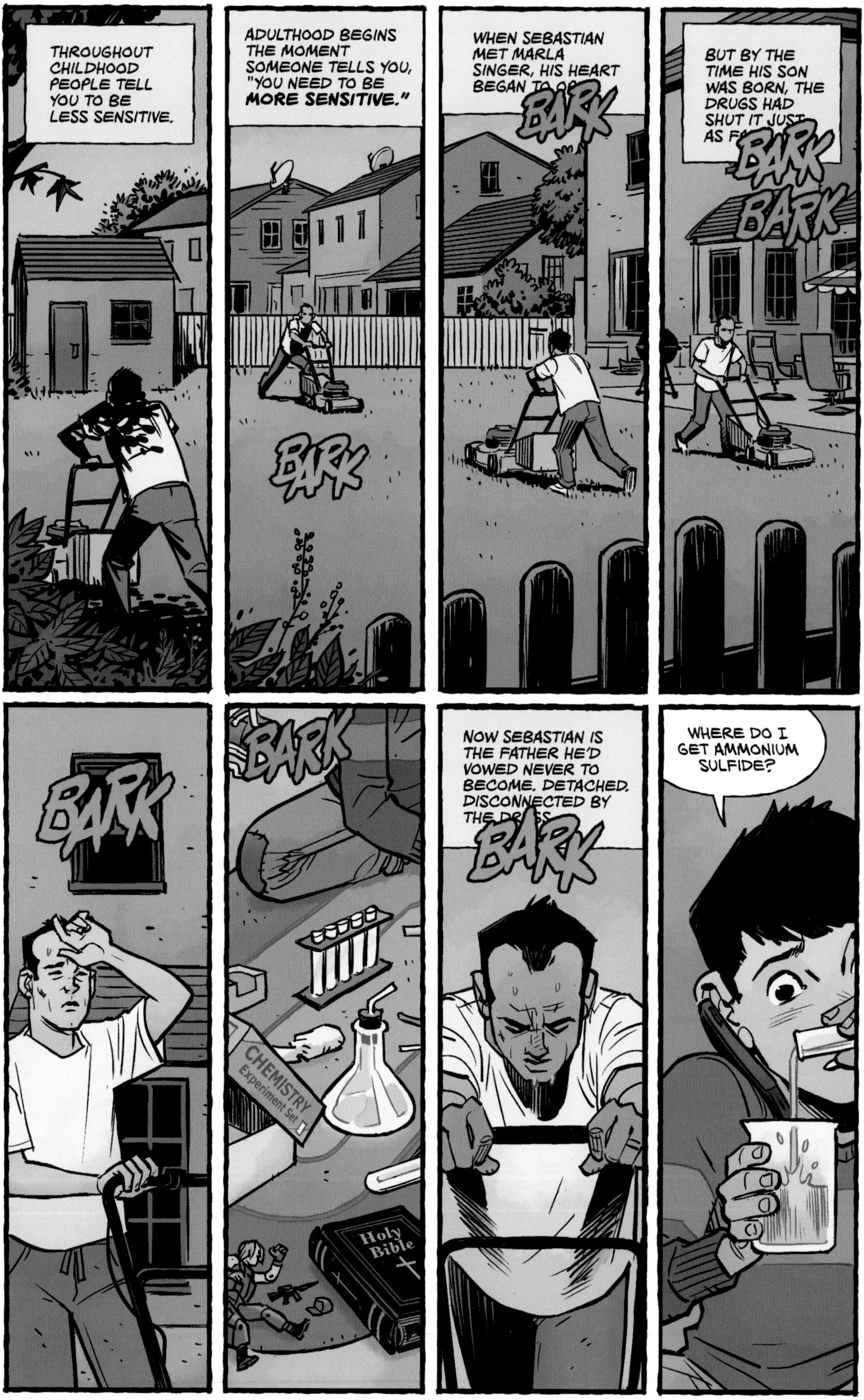
THROUGHOUT CHILDHOOD PEOPLE TELL YOU TO BE LESS SENSITIVE.
ADULTHOOD BEGINS THE MOMENT SOMEONE TELLS YOU, "YOU NEED TO BE **MORE SENSITIVE.**"
BARK
WHEN SEBASTIAN MET MARLA SINGER, HIS HEART BEGAN TO
BARK
BUT BY THE TIME HIS SON WAS BORN, THE DRUGS HAD SHUT IT JUST AS
BARK
BARK
BARK
BARK
CHEMISTRY Experiment Set
Holy Bible
NOW SEBASTIAN IS THE FATHER HE'D VOWED NEVER TO BECOME. DETACHED. DISCONNECTED BY THE
BARK
WHERE DO I GET AMMONIUM SULFIDE?

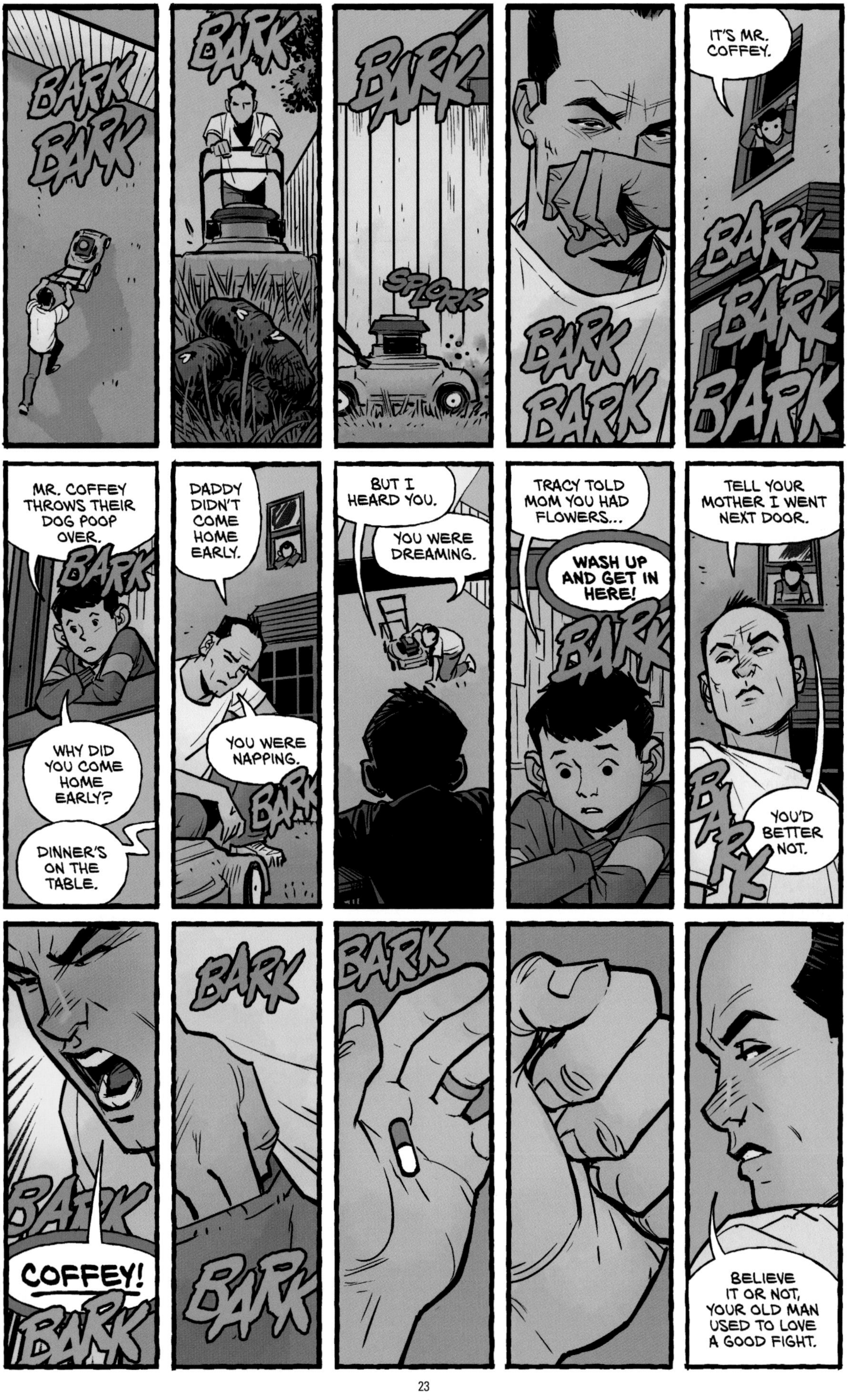
BARK
BARK
BARK
BARK
SPLORK
BARK
BARK
IT'S MR. COFFEY.
BARK
BARK
BARK
MR. COFFEY THROWS THEIR DOG POOP OVER.
BARK
WHY DID YOU COME HOME EARLY?
DINNER'S ON THE TABLE.
DADDY DIDN'T COME HOME EARLY.
YOU WERE NAPPING.
BARK
BUT I HEARD YOU.
YOU WERE DREAMING.
TRACY TOLD MOM YOU HAD FLOWERS...
WASH UP AND GET IN HERE!
BARK
TELL YOUR MOTHER I WENT NEXT DOOR.
BARK
YOU'D BETTER NOT.
BARK
COFFEY!
BARK
BARK
BARK
BARK
BELIEVE IT OR NOT, YOUR OLD MAN USED TO LOVE A GOOD FIGHT.

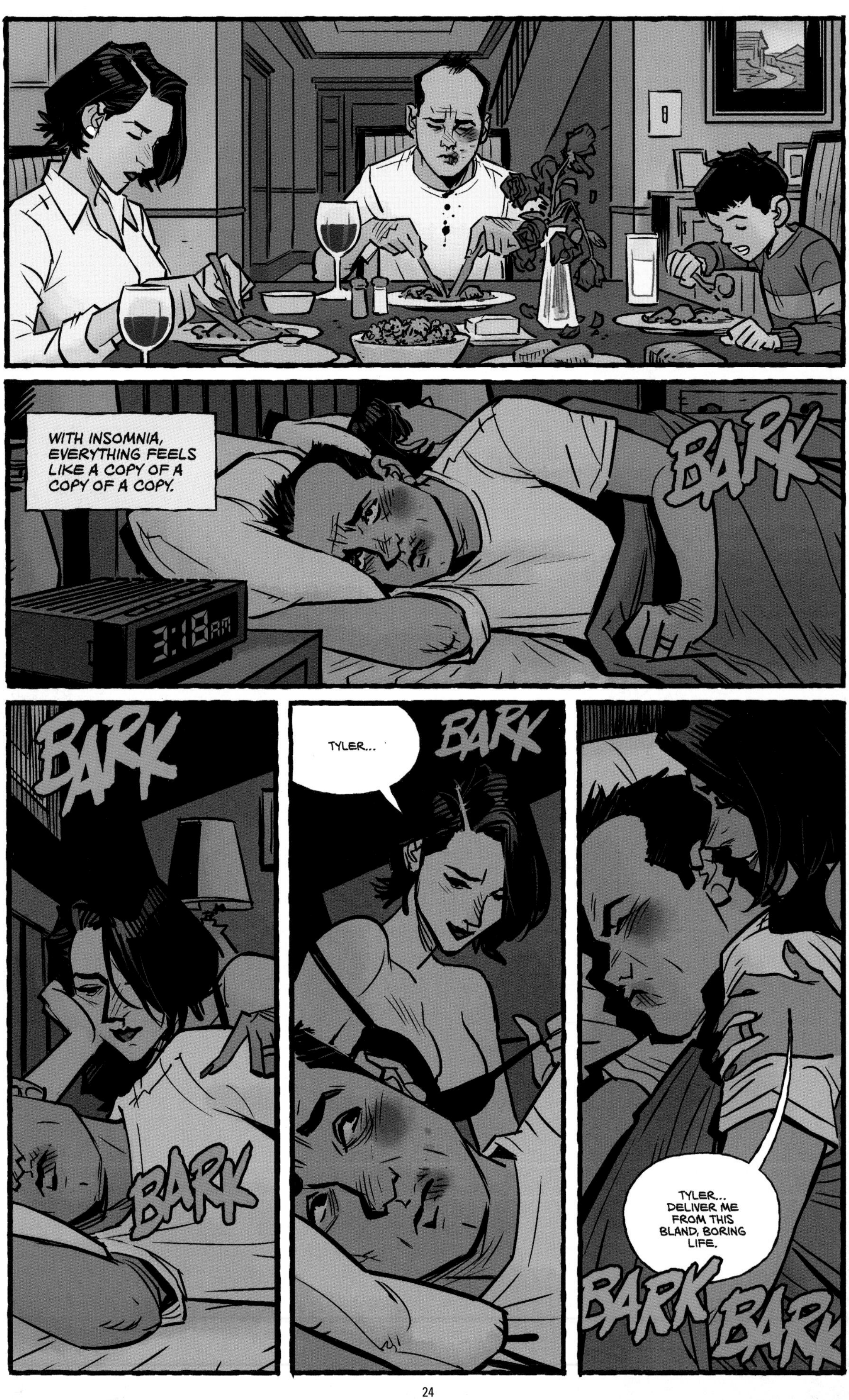
WITH INSOMNIA, EVERYTHING FEELS LIKE A COPY OF A COPY OF A COPY.
3:18AM
BARK
BARK
BARK
TYLER...
BARK
TYLER... DELIVER ME FROM THIS BLAND, BORING LIFE.
BARK
BARK

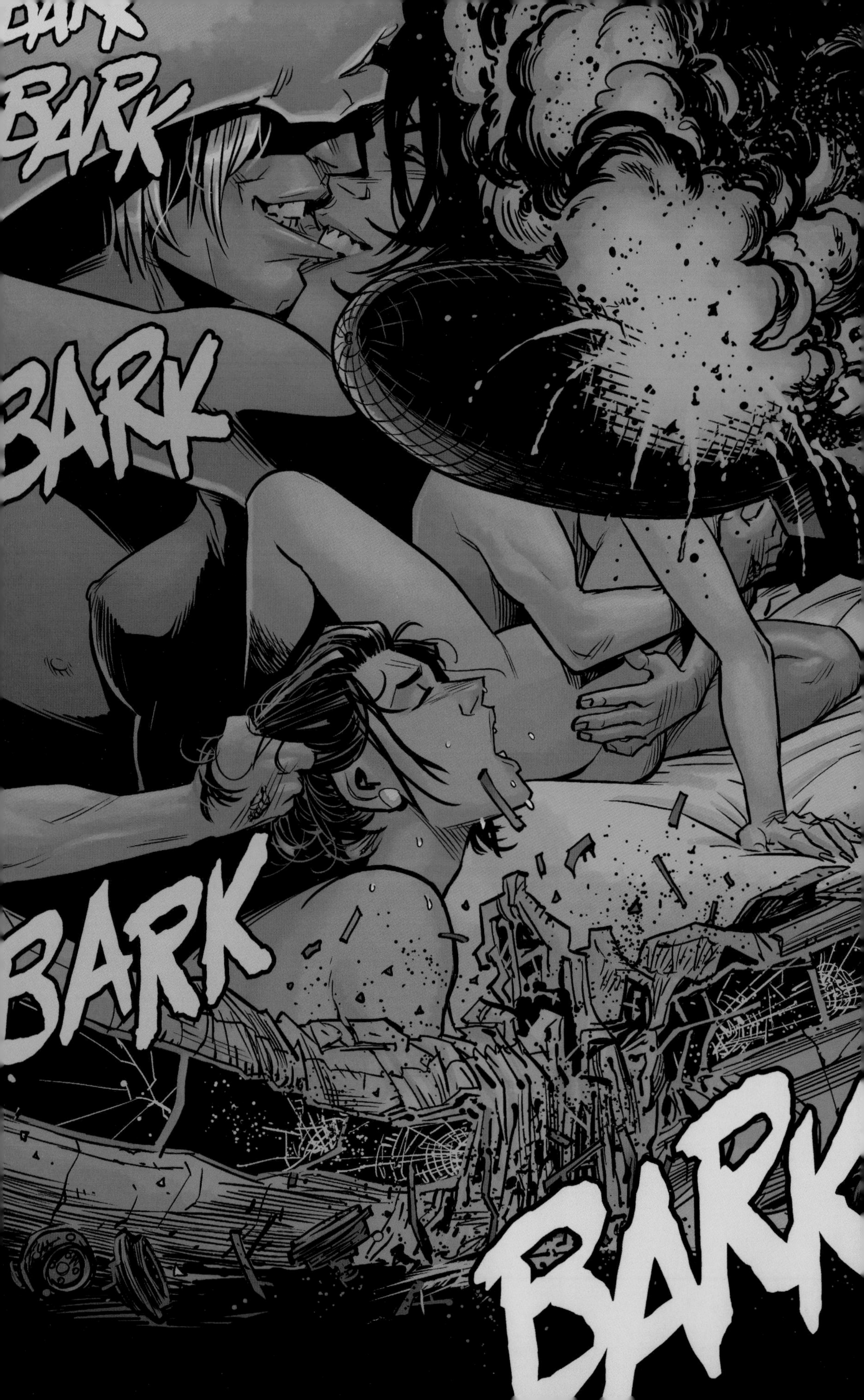
BARK
BARK
BARK
BARK

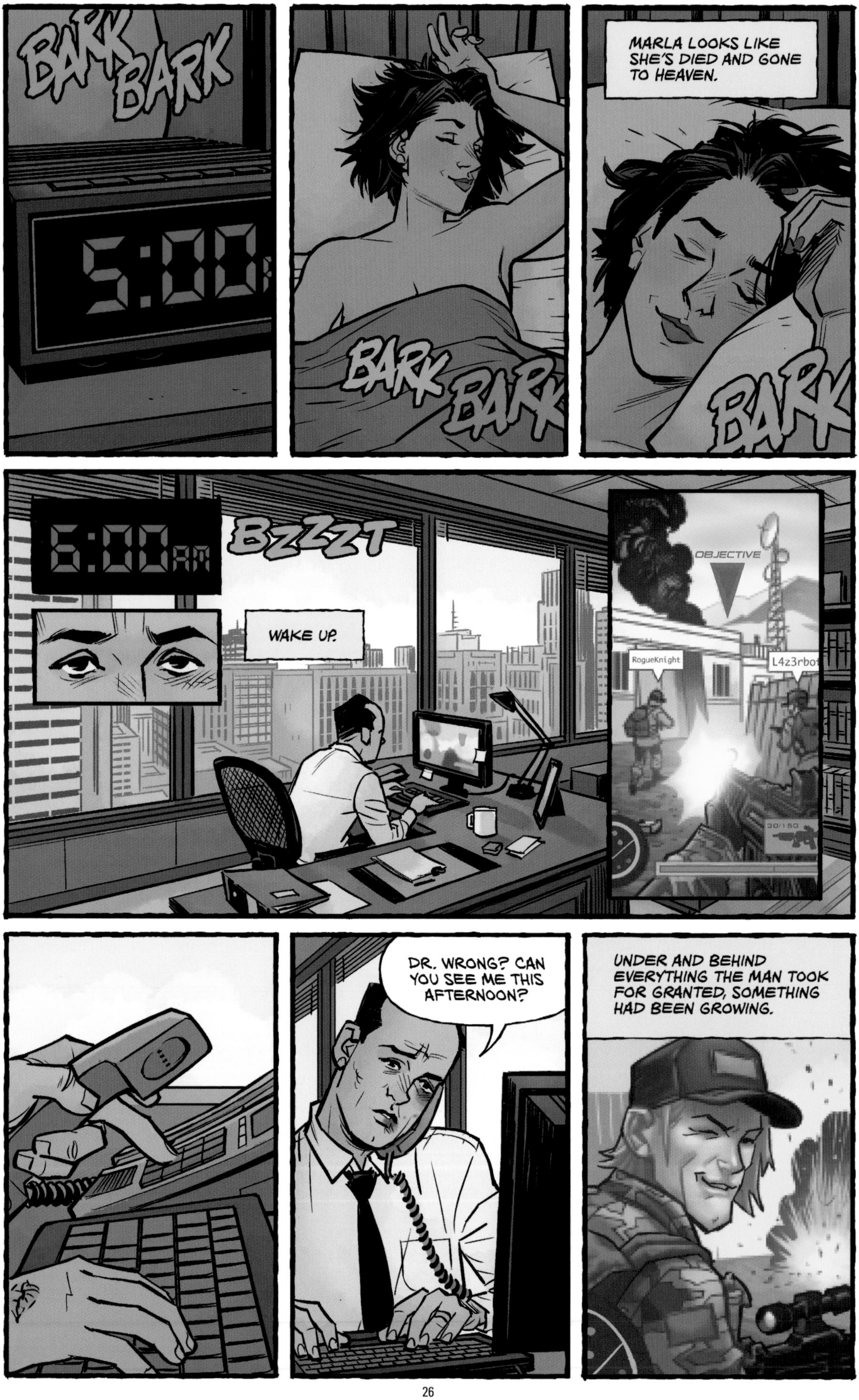
BARK BARK
5:00
BARK BARK
MARLA LOOKS LIKE SHE'S DIED AND GONE TO HEAVEN.
BARK
6:00 AM
BZZZT
WAKE UP.
OBJECTIVE
RogueKnight
L4z3rbot
30/150
DR. WRONG? CAN YOU SEE ME THIS AFTERNOON?
UNDER AND BEHIND EVERYTHING THE MAN TOOK FOR GRANTED, SOMETHING HAD BEEN GROWING.

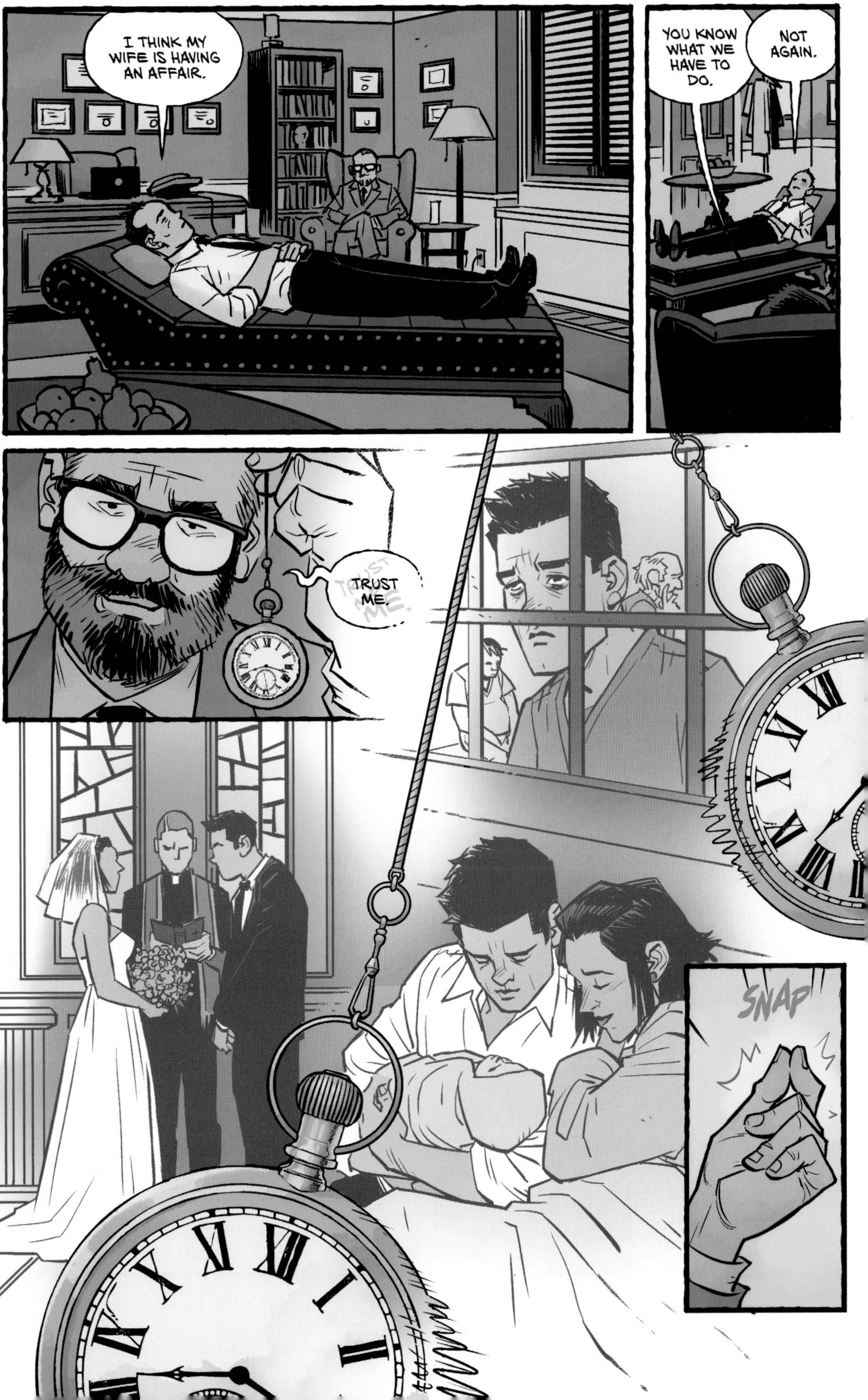
I THINK MY WIFE IS HAVING AN AFFAIR.
YOU KNOW WHAT WE HAVE TO DO.
NOT AGAIN.
TRUST ME.
SNAP

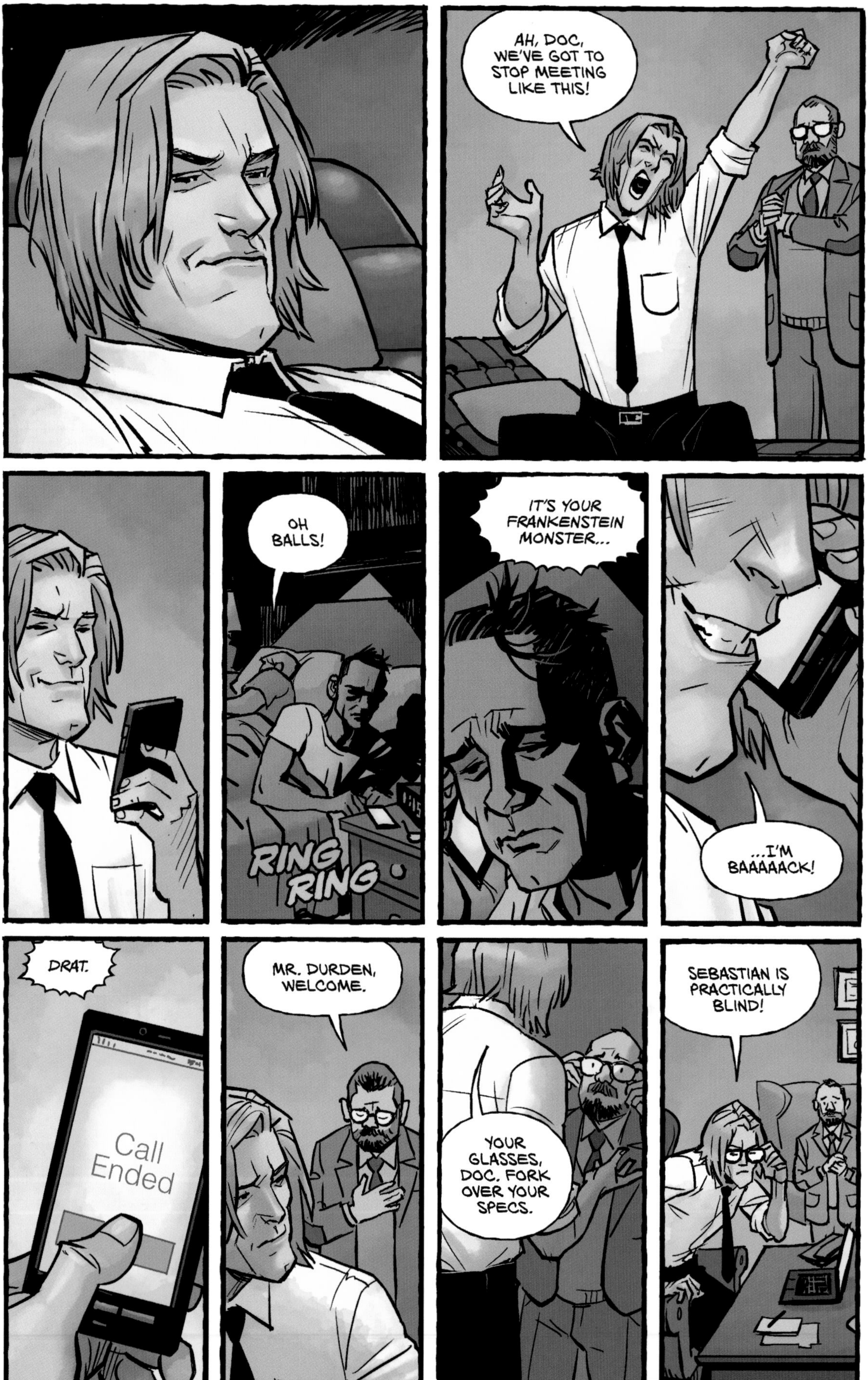
AH, DOC, WE'VE GOT TO STOP MEETING LIKE THIS!
OH BALLS!
RING RING
IT'S YOUR FRANKENSTEIN MONSTER...
...I'M BAAAAACK!
DRAT.
Call Ended
MR. DURDEN, WELCOME.
YOUR GLASSES, DOC. FORK OVER YOUR SPECS.
SEBASTIAN IS PRACTICALLY BLIND!

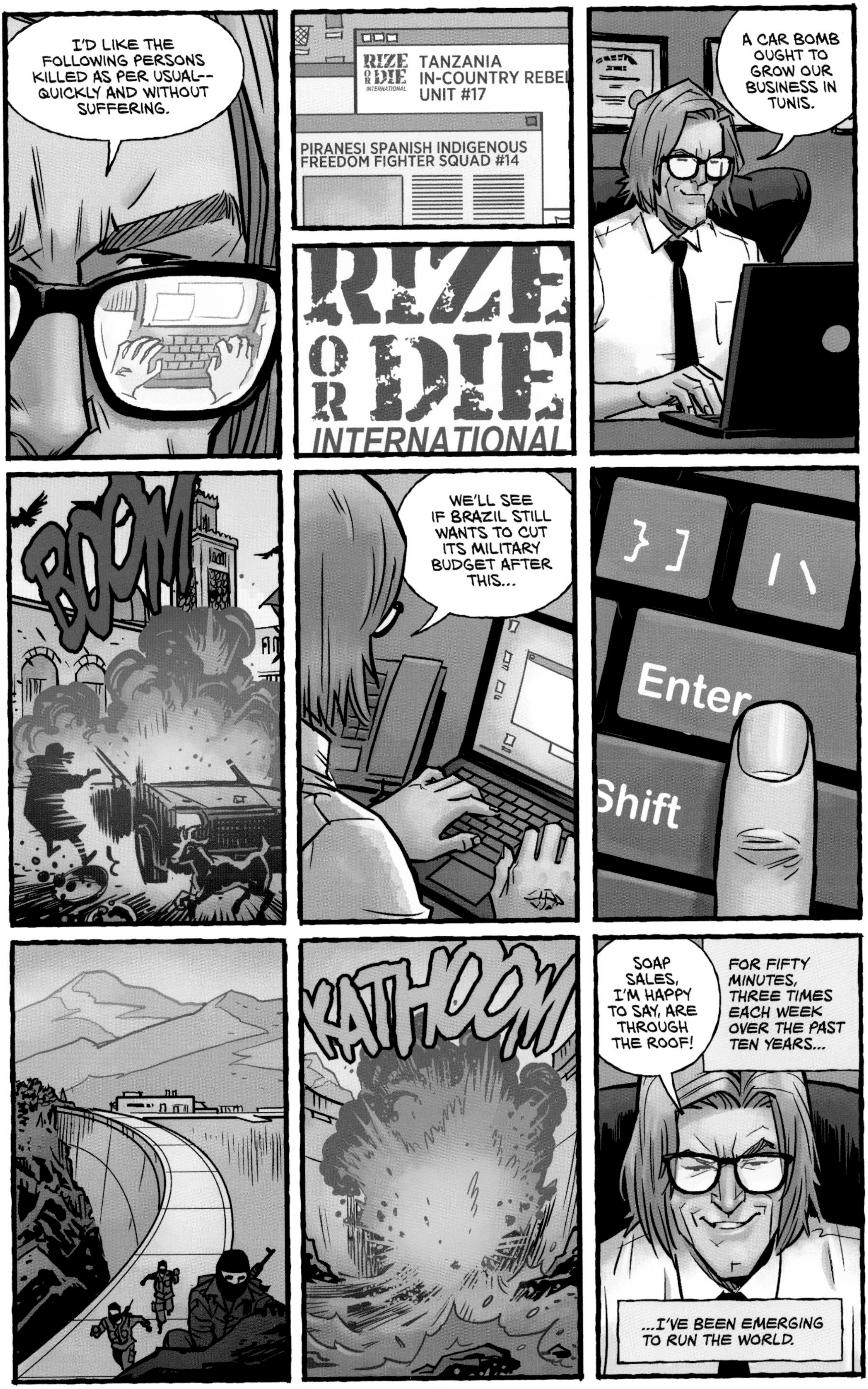

I'D LIKE THE FOLLOWING PERSONS KILLED AS PER USUAL-- QUICKLY AND WITHOUT SUFFERING.
RIZE OR DIE INTERNATIONAL
TANZANIA IN-COUNTRY REBEL UNIT #17
PIRANESI SPANISH INDIGENOUS FREEDOM FIGHTER SQUAD #14
A CAR BOMB OUGHT TO GROW OUR BUSINESS IN TUNIS.
RIZE OR DIE INTERNATIONAL
BOOM
WE'LL SEE IF BRAZIL STILL WANTS TO CUT ITS MILITARY BUDGET AFTER THIS...
Enter
Shift
KATHOOM
SOAP SALES, I'M HAPPY TO SAY, ARE THROUGH THE ROOF!
FOR FIFTY MINUTES, THREE TIMES EACH WEEK OVER THE PAST TEN YEARS...
...I'VE BEEN EMERGING TO RUN THE WORLD.

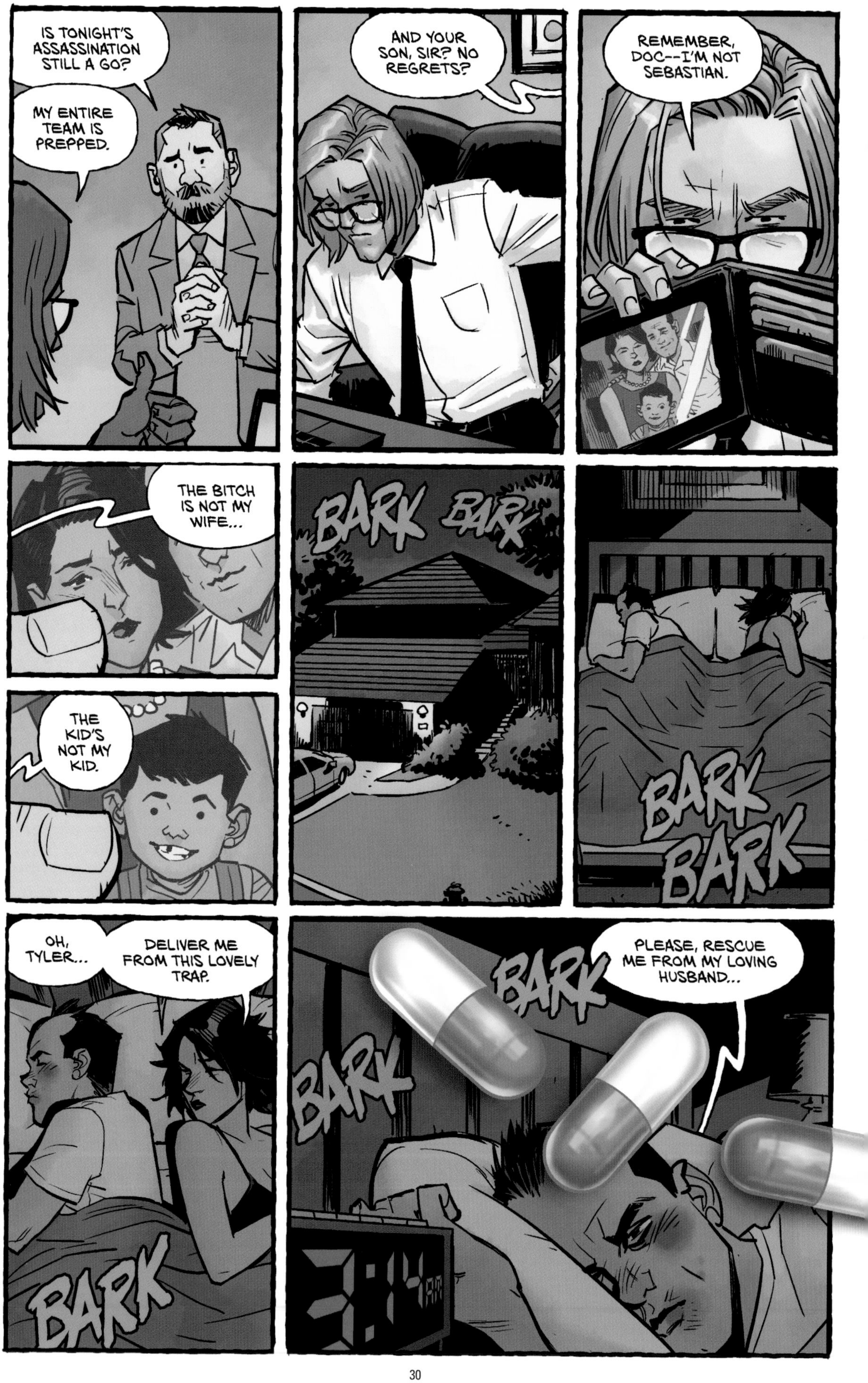
IS TONIGHT'S ASSASSINATION STILL A GO?
MY ENTIRE TEAM IS PREPPED.
AND YOUR SON, SIR? NO REGRETS?
REMEMBER, DOC--I'M NOT SEBASTIAN.
THE BITCH IS NOT MY WIFE...
BARK BARK
THE KID'S NOT MY KID.
BARK BARK
OH, TYLER...
DELIVER ME FROM THIS LOVELY TRAP.
BARK
BARK
BARK
PLEASE, RESCUE ME FROM MY LOVING HUSBAND...

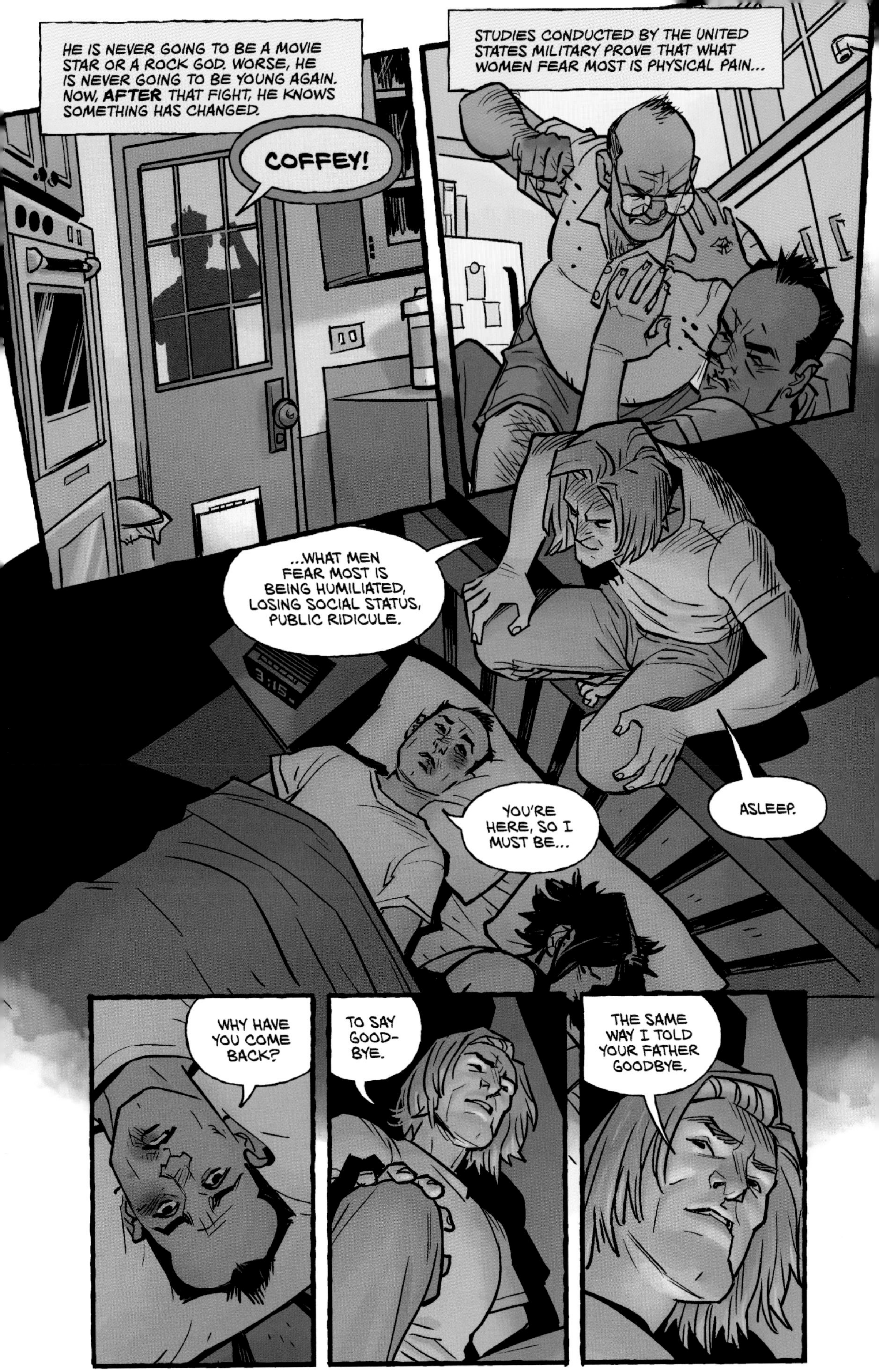
HE IS NEVER GOING TO BE A MOVIE STAR OR A ROCK GOD. WORSE, HE IS NEVER GOING TO BE YOUNG AGAIN. NOW, **AFTER** THAT FIGHT, HE KNOWS SOMETHING HAS CHANGED.
COFFEY!
STUDIES CONDUCTED BY THE UNITED STATES MILITARY PROVE THAT WHAT WOMEN FEAR MOST IS PHYSICAL PAIN...
...WHAT MEN FEAR MOST IS BEING HUMILIATED, LOSING SOCIAL STATUS, PUBLIC RIDICULE.
YOU'RE HERE, SO I MUST BE...
ASLEEP.
WHY HAVE YOU COME BACK?
TO SAY GOOD-BYE.
THE SAME WAY I TOLD YOUR FATHER GOODBYE.

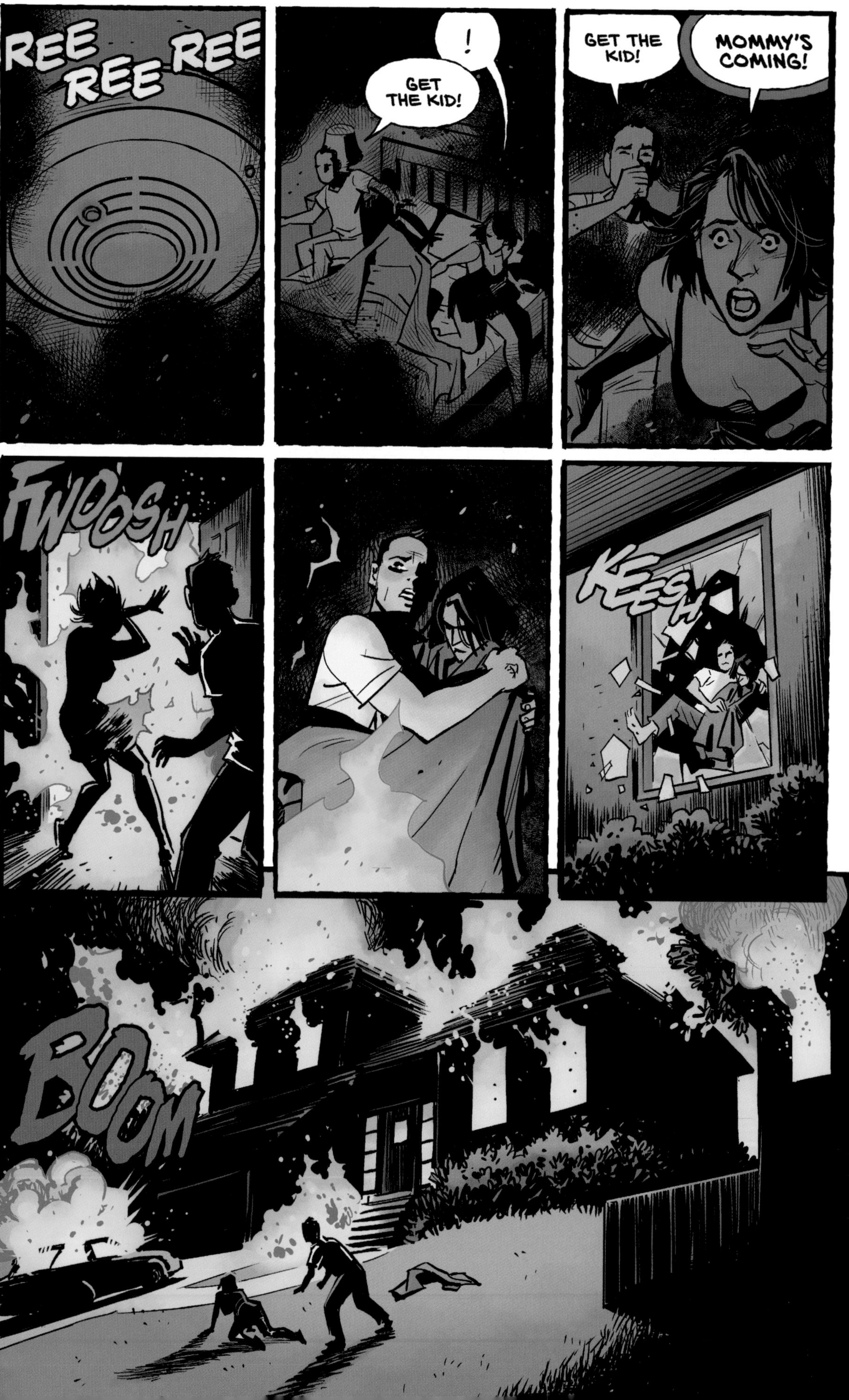
REE REE REE REE
!
GET THE KID!
GET THE KID!
MOMMY'S COMING!
FWOOSH
KEESH
BOOM

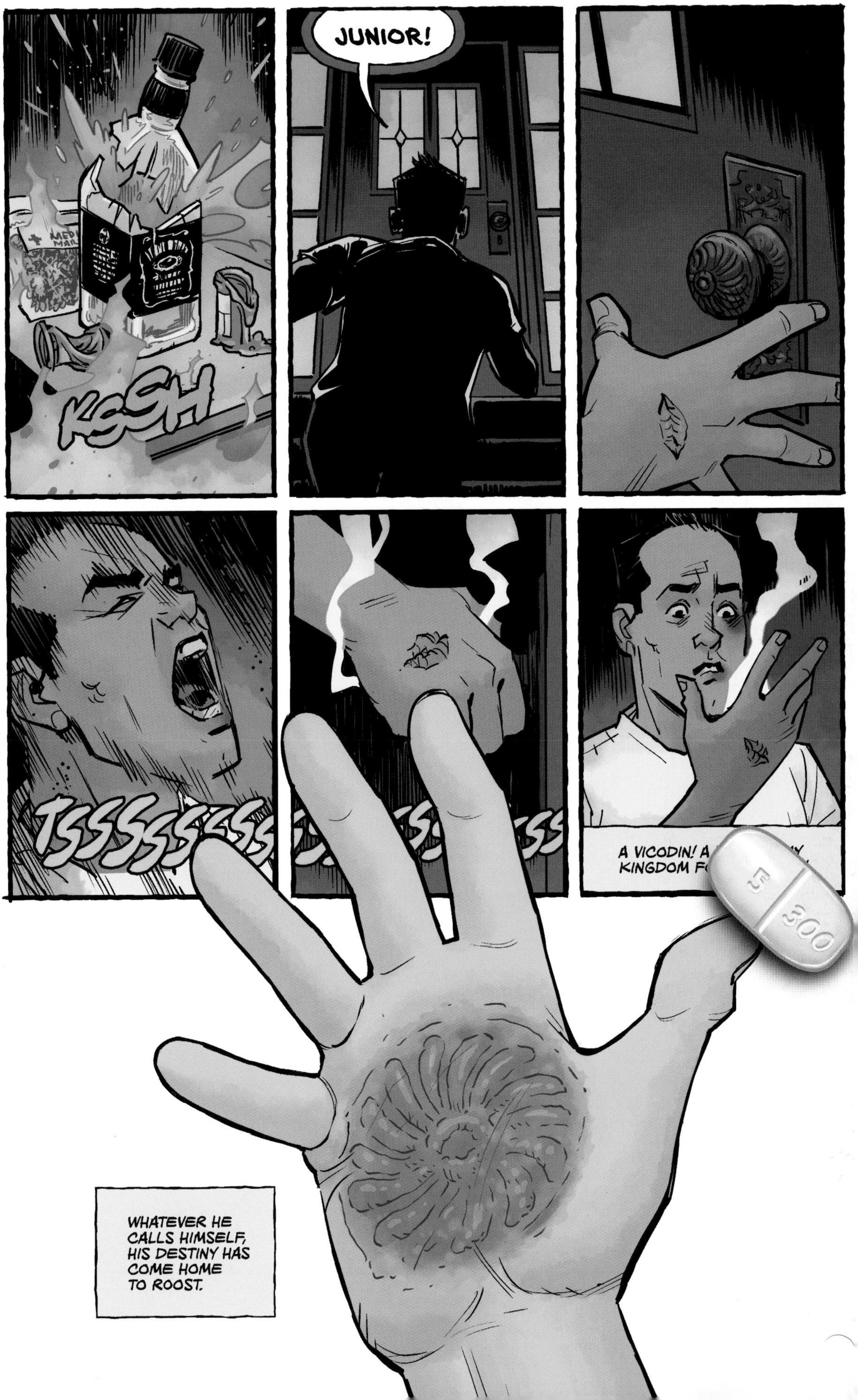
KSSH
JUNIOR!
TSSSSSSSSSSSSSS
A VICODIN! A
KINGDOM FO
WHATEVER HE CALLS HIMSELF, HIS DESTINY HAS COME HOME TO ROOST.

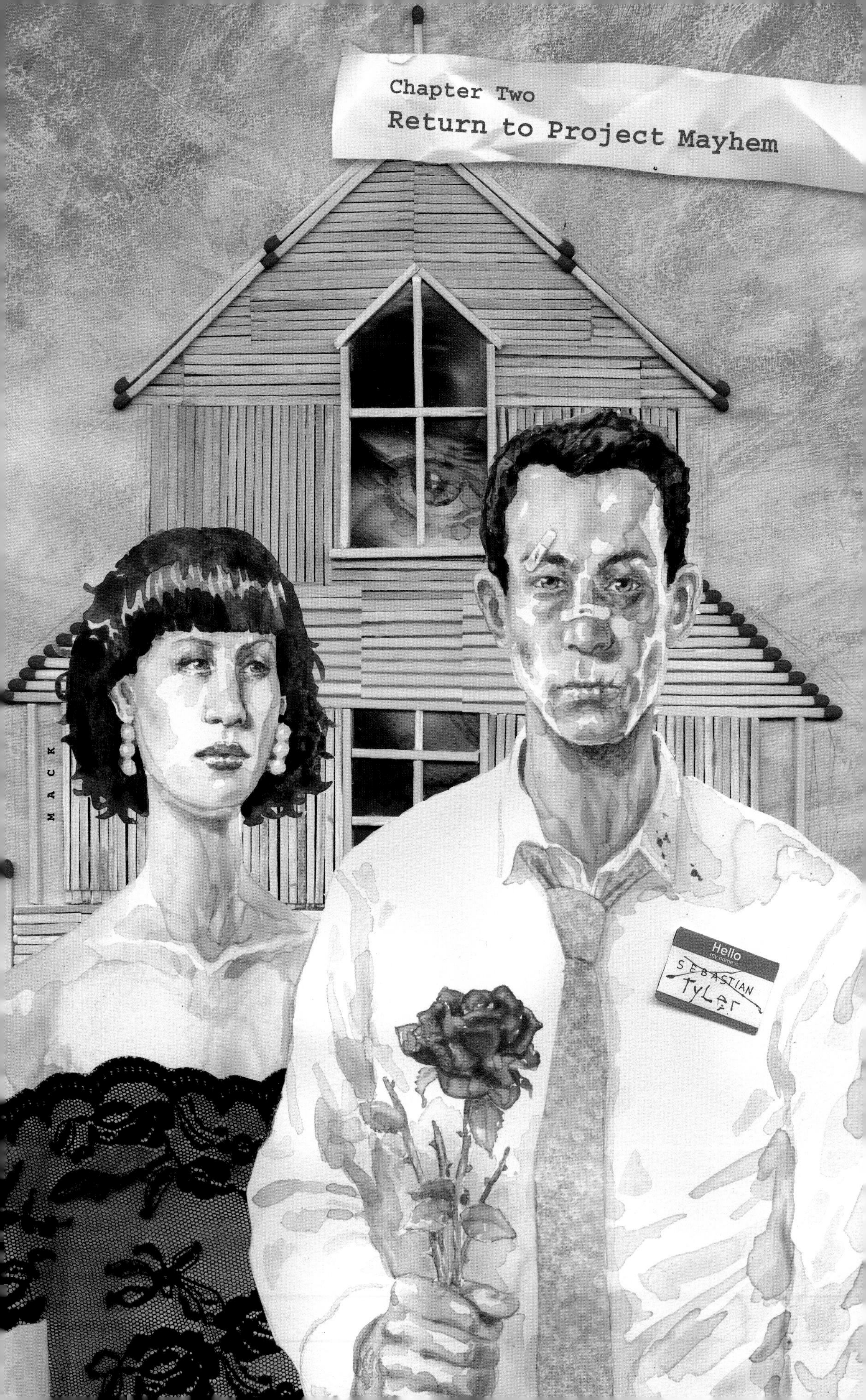
Chapter Two
Return to Project Mayhem
Hello
SEBASTIAN
Tyler
MACK

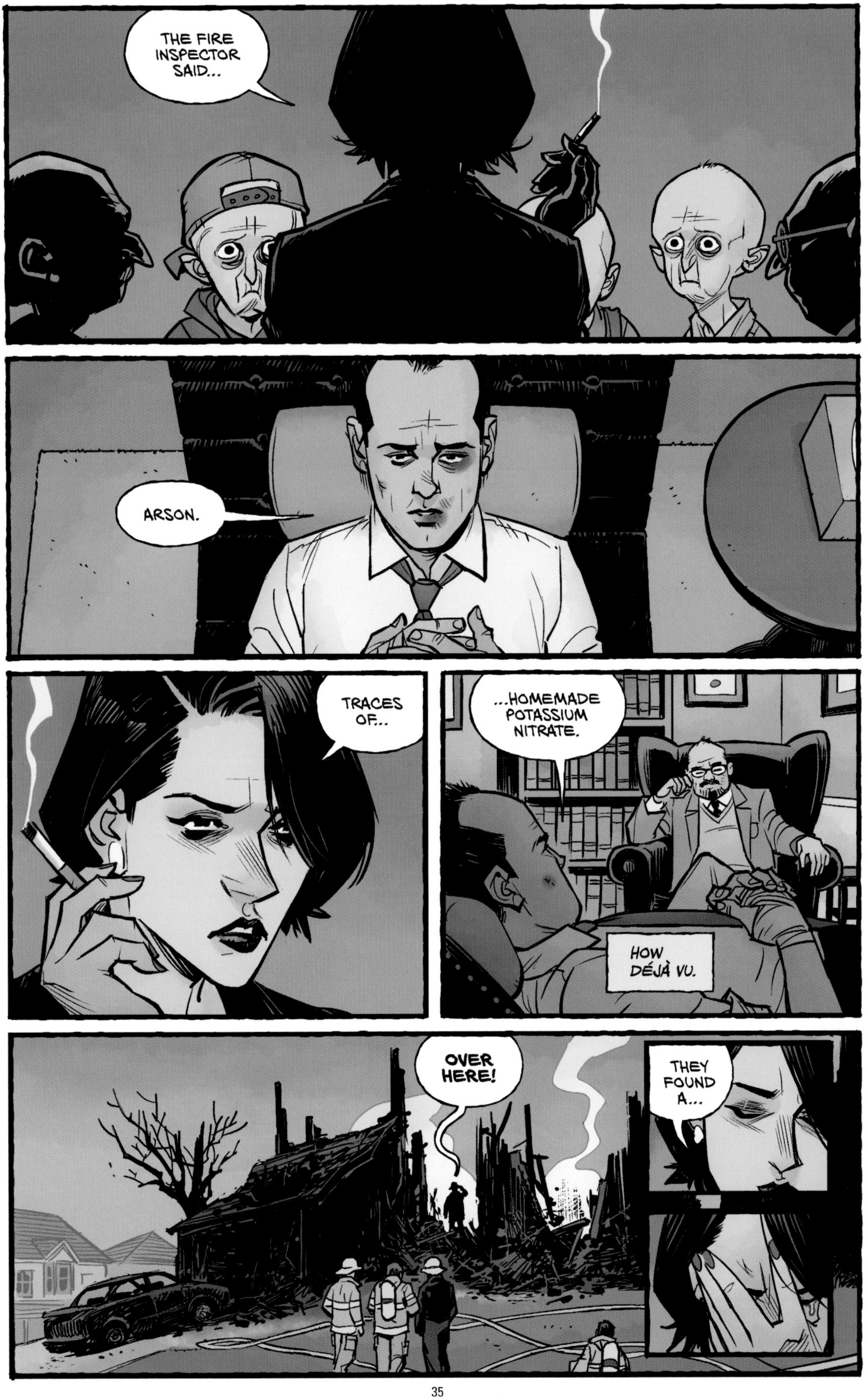
THE FIRE INSPECTOR SAID...
ARSON.
TRACES OF...
...HOMEMADE POTASSIUM NITRATE.
HOW DÉJÀ VU.
OVER HERE!
THEY FOUND A...

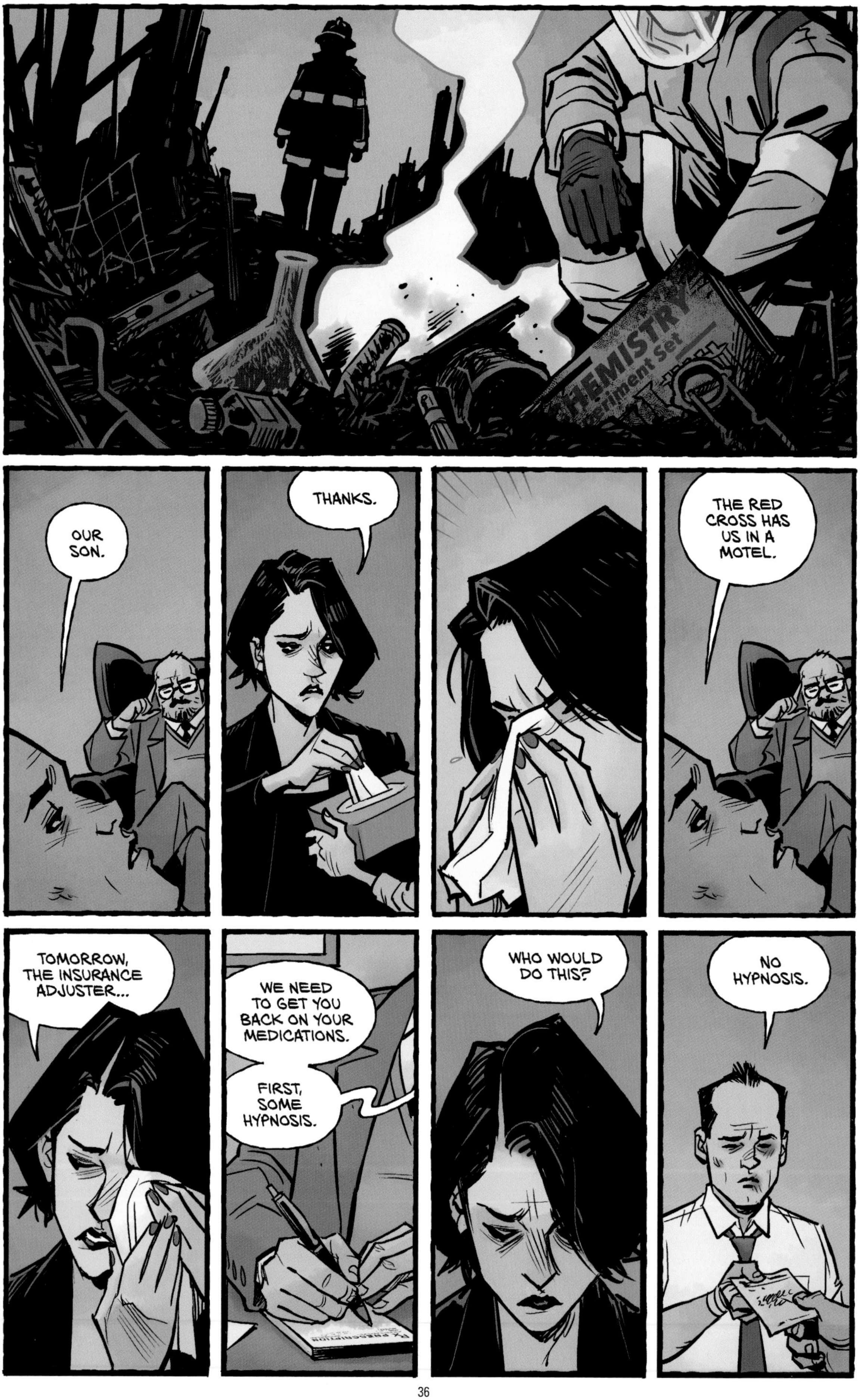
HEMISTRY
eriment Set
OUR SON.
THANKS.
THE RED CROSS HAS US IN A MOTEL.
TOMORROW, THE INSURANCE ADJUSTER...
WE NEED TO GET YOU BACK ON YOUR MEDICATIONS.
FIRST, SOME HYPNOSIS.
WHO WOULD DO THIS?
NO HYPNOSIS.

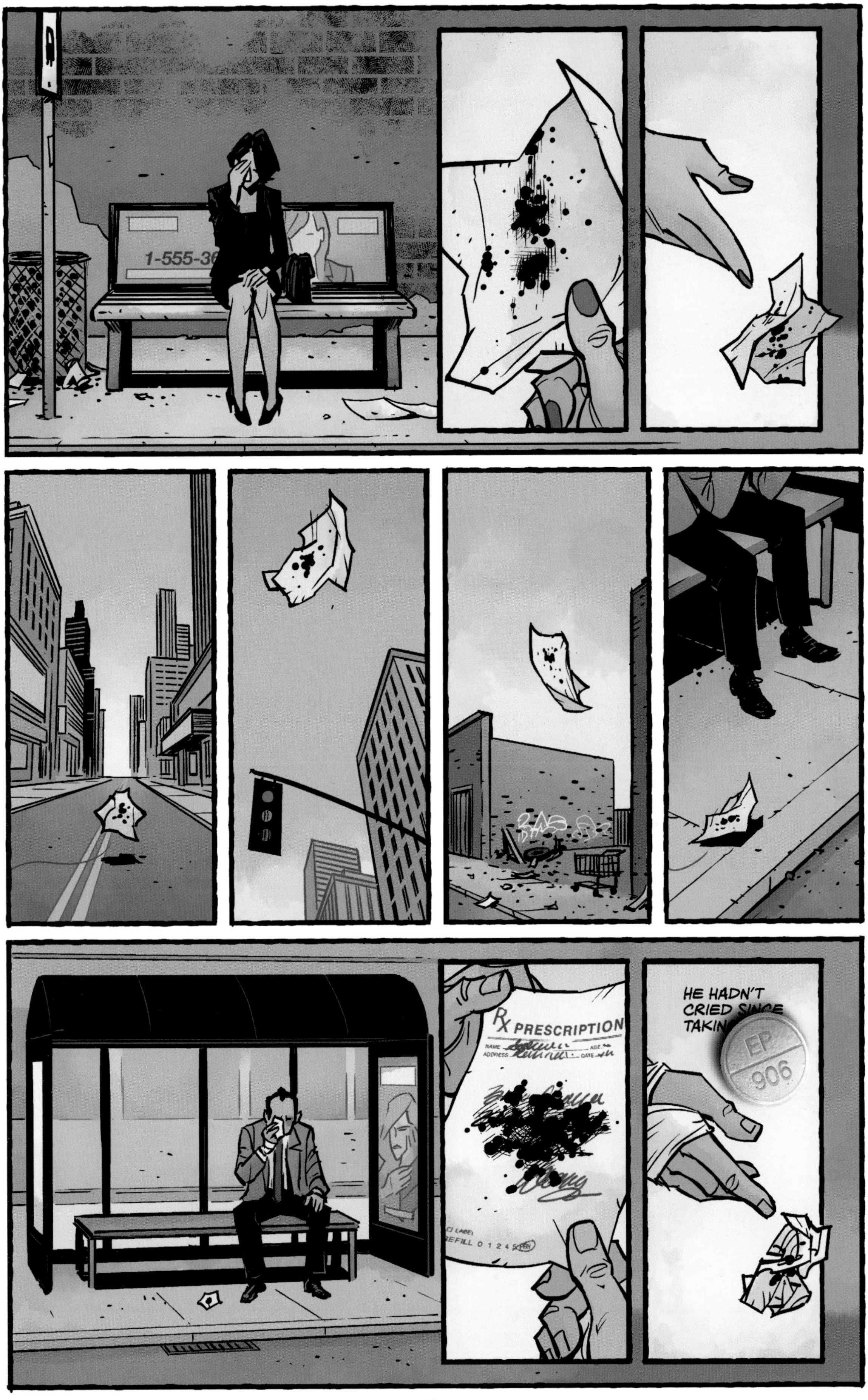
1-555-36
RX PRESCRIPTION
NAME
AGE
ADDRESS
DATE
REFILL 0 1 2 4 5
HE HADN'T CRIED SINCE TAKIN
EP 906

THE POSSIBLE DEATH DOES RAISE A RED FLAG.

SHEILA HOLMAN
SENIOR ADJUSTER

POSSIBLE?

YOU TOOK OUT SUCH A LARGE POLICY...

...ONLY DAYS AGO.

LIFE INSURANCE?

WE DIDN'T.

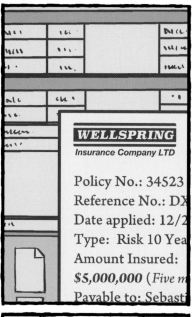

WELLSPRING
Insurance Company LTD

Policy No.: 34523
Reference No.: DX
Date applied: 12/2
Type: Risk 10 Yea
Amount Insured:
$5,000,000 (Five m
Payable to: Sebasti

YOU INSURED YOUR CHILD A WEEK AGO, ONLINE, AT 4:17 A.M.

HOW?

WE WERE ASLEEP.

IN LIGHT OF THE F.B.I.'S REPORT, THE POLICY IS MOOT.

F.B.I.?

SO IT WASN'T ARSON?

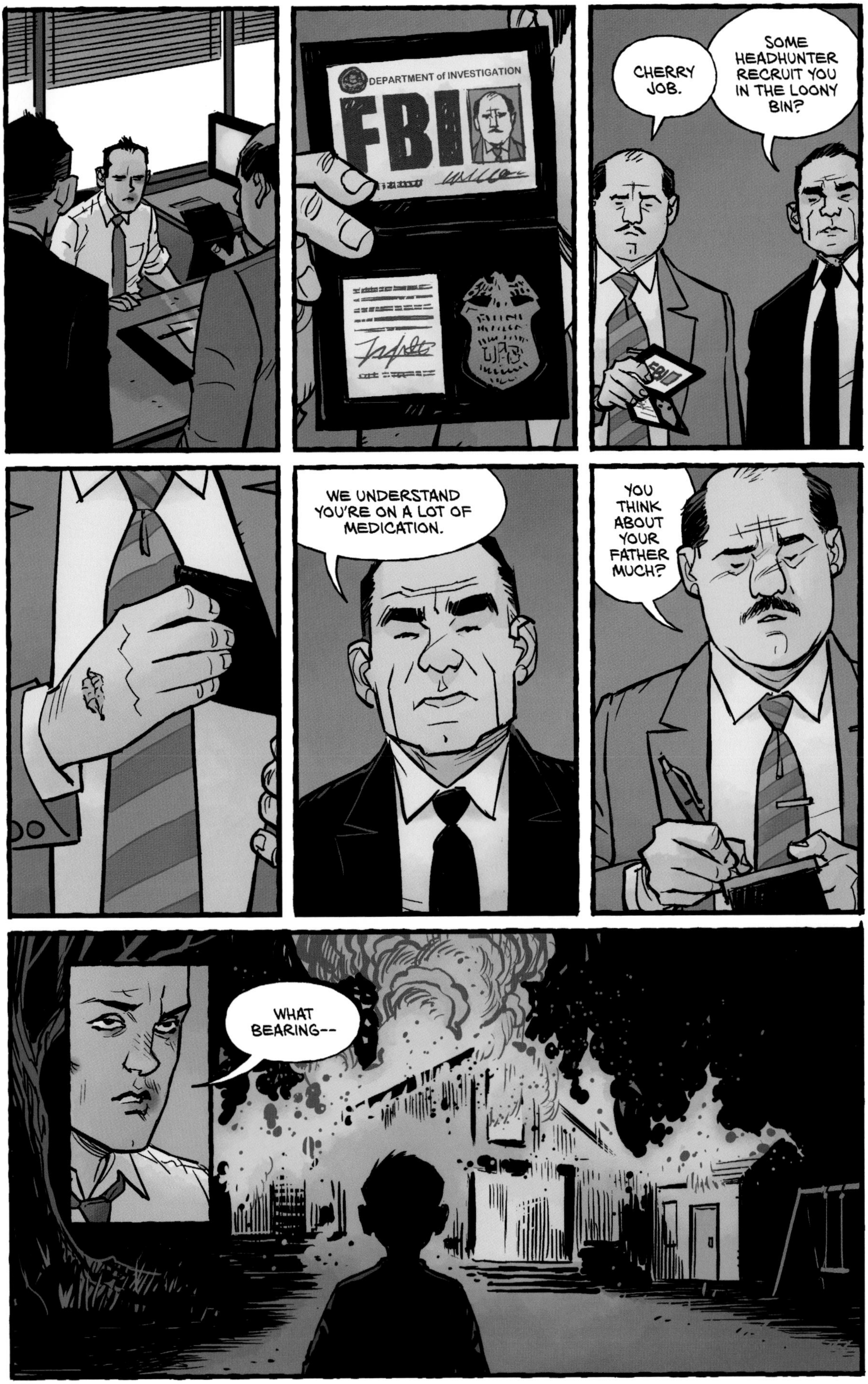
DEPARTMENT of INVESTIGATION
FBI
CHERRY JOB.
SOME HEADHUNTER RECRUIT YOU IN THE LOONY BIN?
WE UNDERSTAND YOU'RE ON A LOT OF MEDICATION.
YOU THINK ABOUT YOUR FATHER MUCH?
WHAT BEARING--

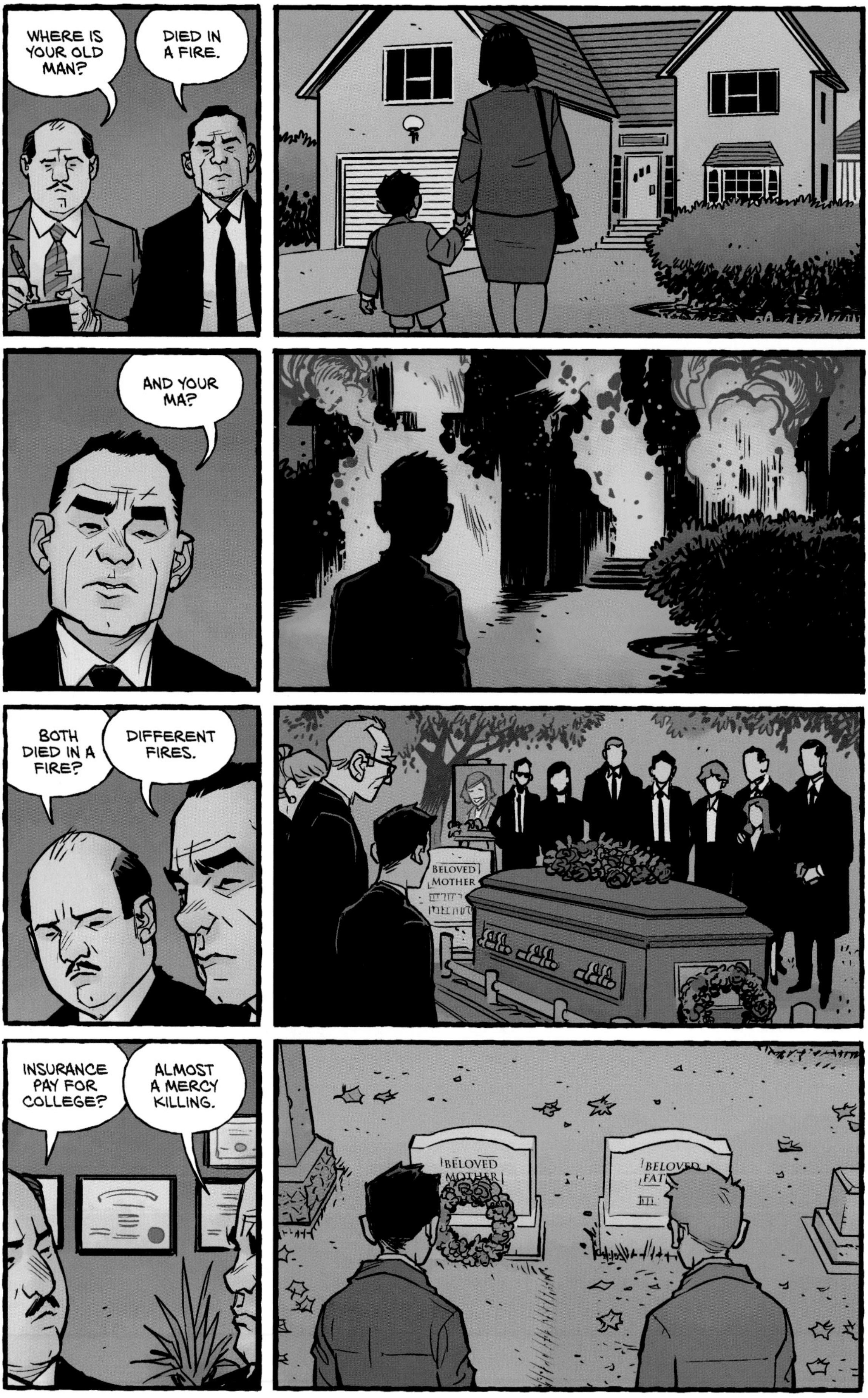
WHERE IS YOUR OLD MAN?
DIED IN A FIRE.
AND YOUR MA?
BOTH DIED IN A FIRE?
DIFFERENT FIRES.
BELOVED MOTHER
INSURANCE PAY FOR COLLEGE?
ALMOST A MERCY KILLING.
BELOVED MOTHER
BELOVED FAT

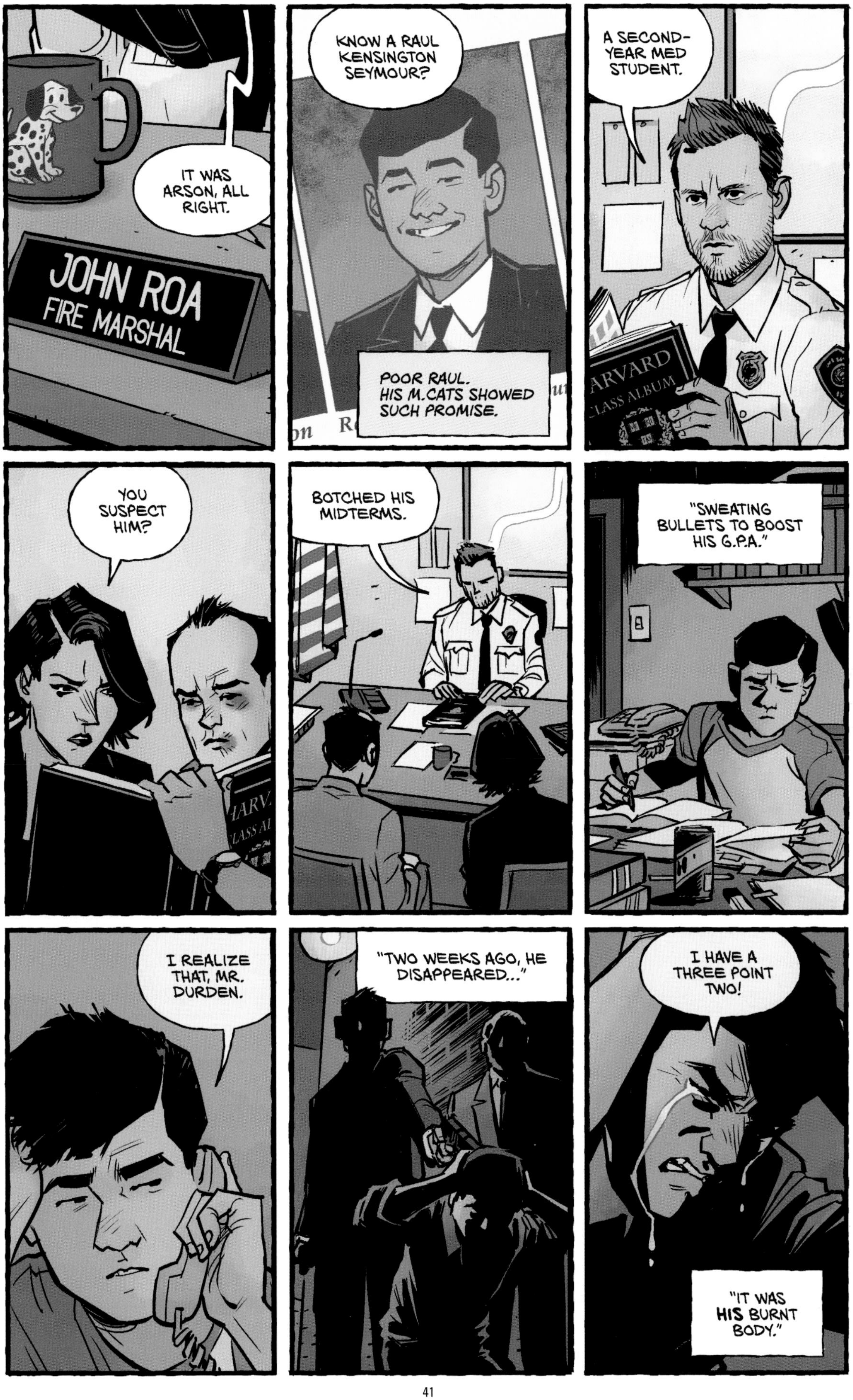
JOHN ROA
FIRE MARSHAL
IT WAS ARSON, ALL RIGHT.
KNOW A RAUL KENSINGTON SEYMOUR?
POOR RAUL. HIS M.CATS SHOWED SUCH PROMISE.
A SECOND-YEAR MED STUDENT.
HARVARD
CLASS ALBUM
YOU SUSPECT HIM?
BOTCHED HIS MIDTERMS.
"SWEATING BULLETS TO BOOST HIS G.P.A."
I REALIZE THAT, MR. DURDEN.
"TWO WEEKS AGO, HE DISAPPEARED..."
I HAVE A THREE POINT TWO!
"IT WAS **HIS** BURNT BODY."

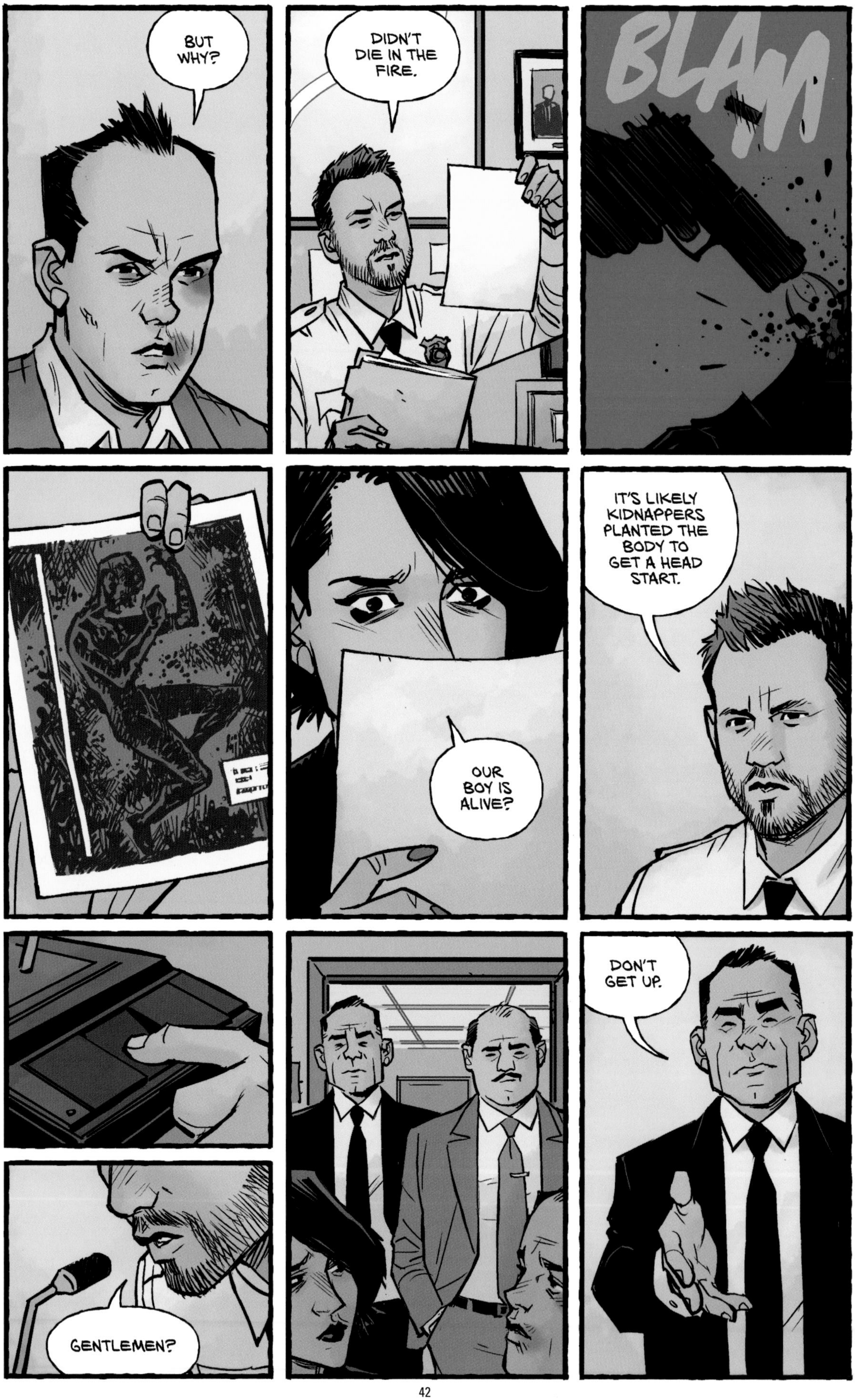

BUT WHY?
DIDN'T DIE IN THE FIRE.
BLAM
IT'S LIKELY KIDNAPPERS PLANTED THE BODY TO GET A HEAD START.
OUR BOY IS ALIVE?
GENTLEMEN?
DON'T GET UP.

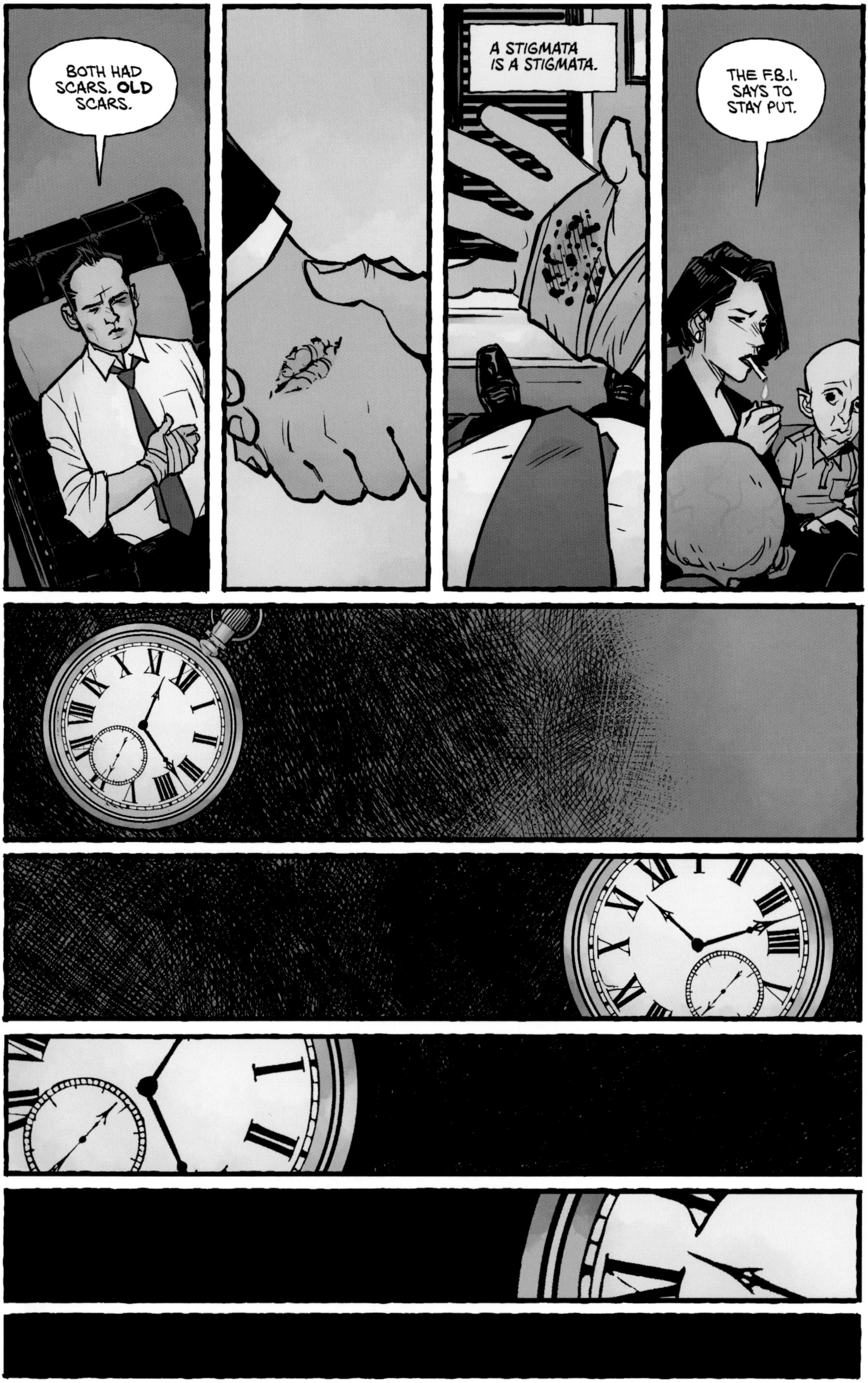
BOTH HAD SCARS. OLD SCARS.
A STIGMATA IS A STIGMATA.
THE F.B.I. SAYS TO STAY PUT.

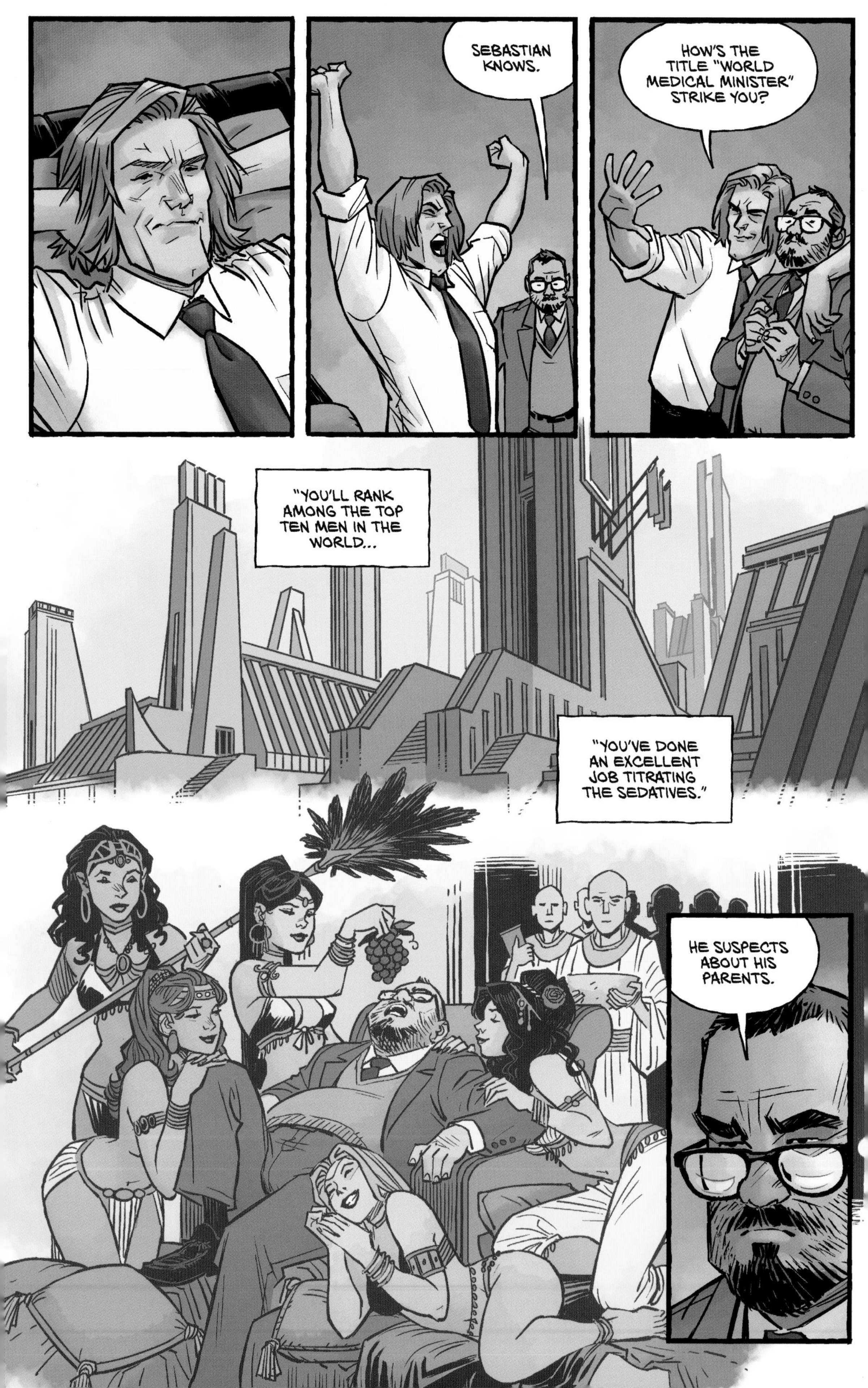
SEBASTIAN KNOWS.
HOW'S THE TITLE "WORLD MEDICAL MINISTER" STRIKE YOU?
"YOU'LL RANK AMONG THE TOP TEN MEN IN THE WORLD...
"YOU'VE DONE AN EXCELLENT JOB TITRATING THE SEDATIVES."
HE SUSPECTS ABOUT HIS PARENTS.

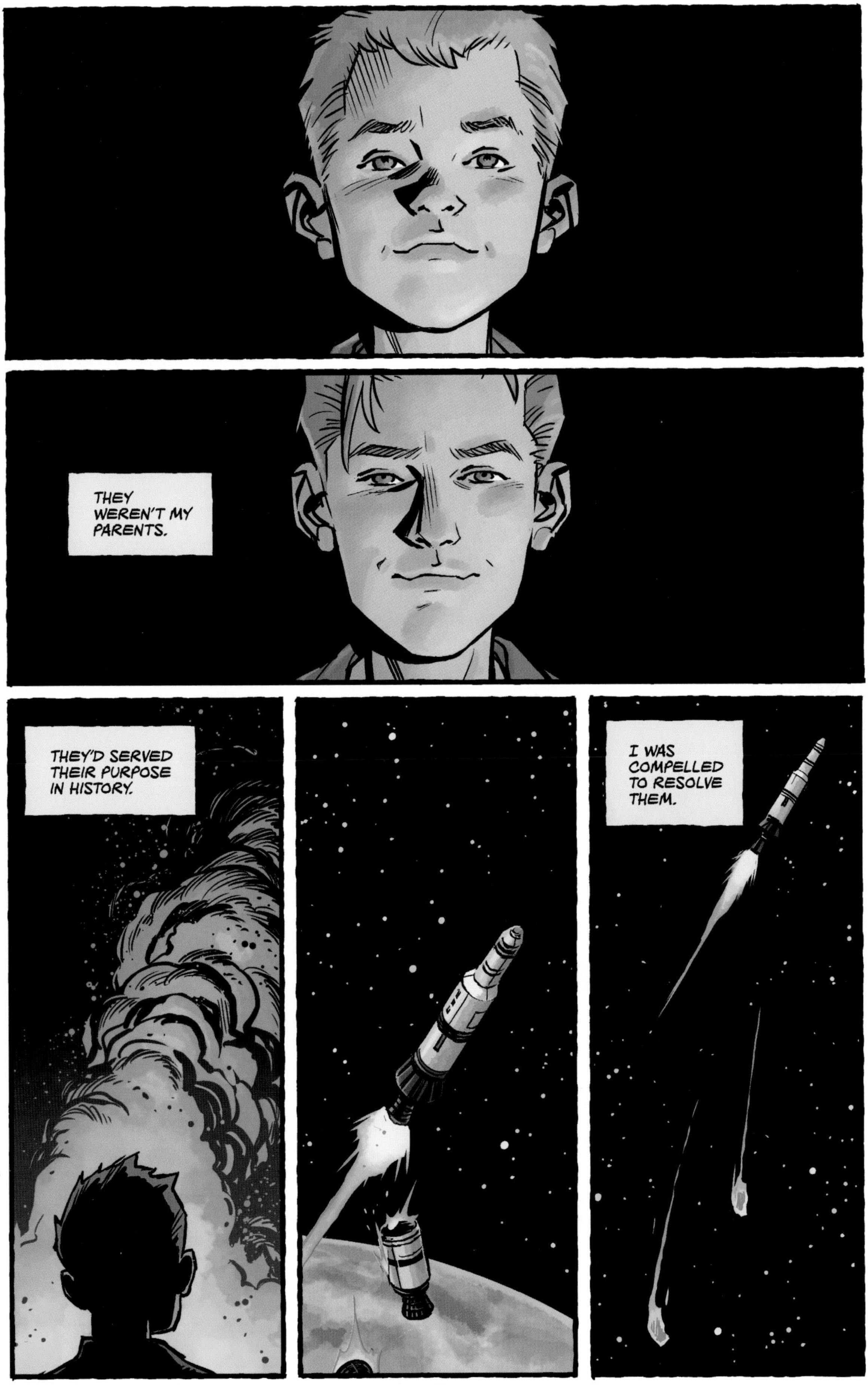
THEY WEREN'T MY PARENTS.
THEY'D SERVED THEIR PURPOSE IN HISTORY.
I WAS COMPELLED TO RESOLVE THEM.

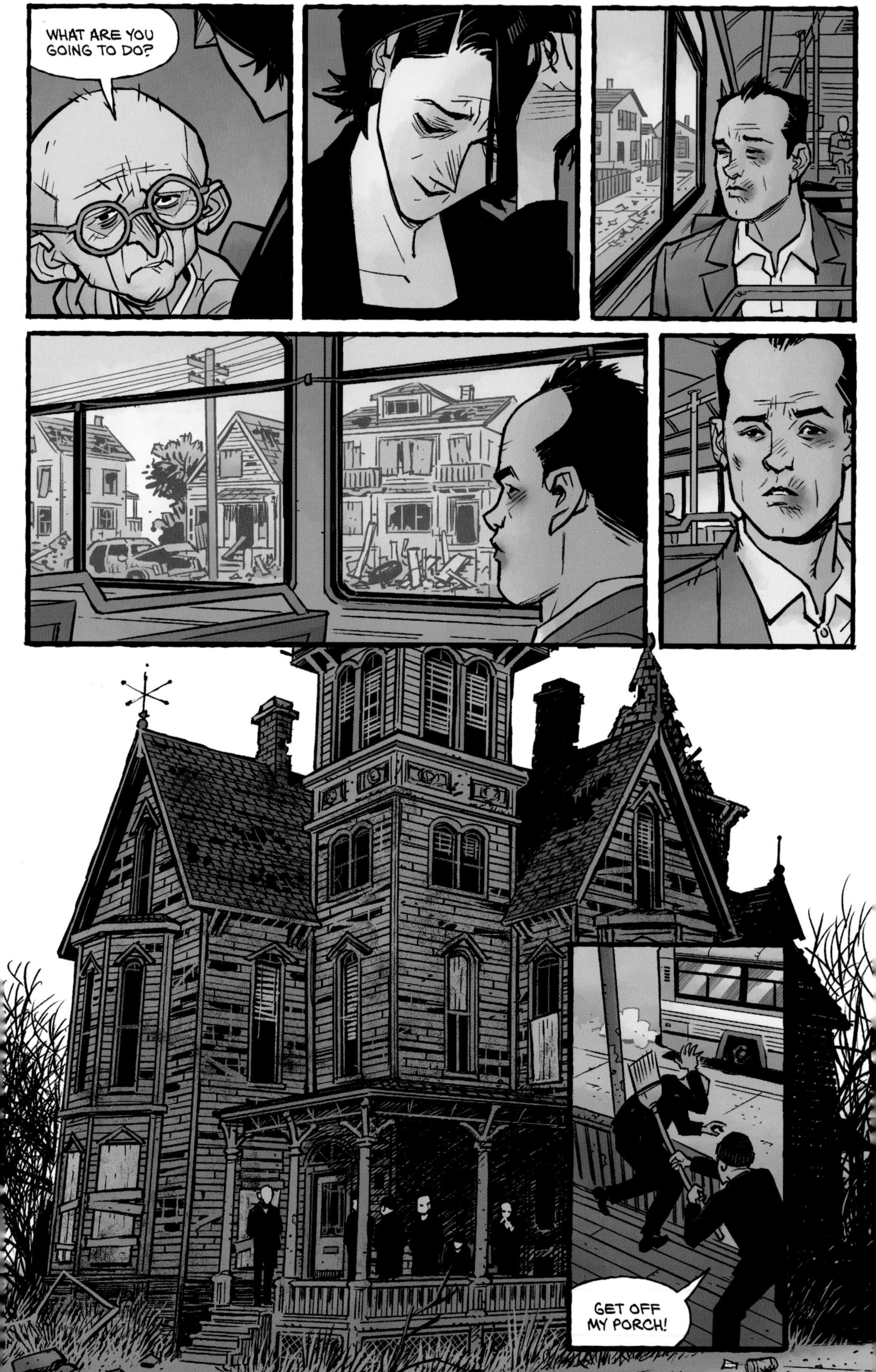
WHAT ARE YOU GOING TO DO?
GET OFF MY PORCH!

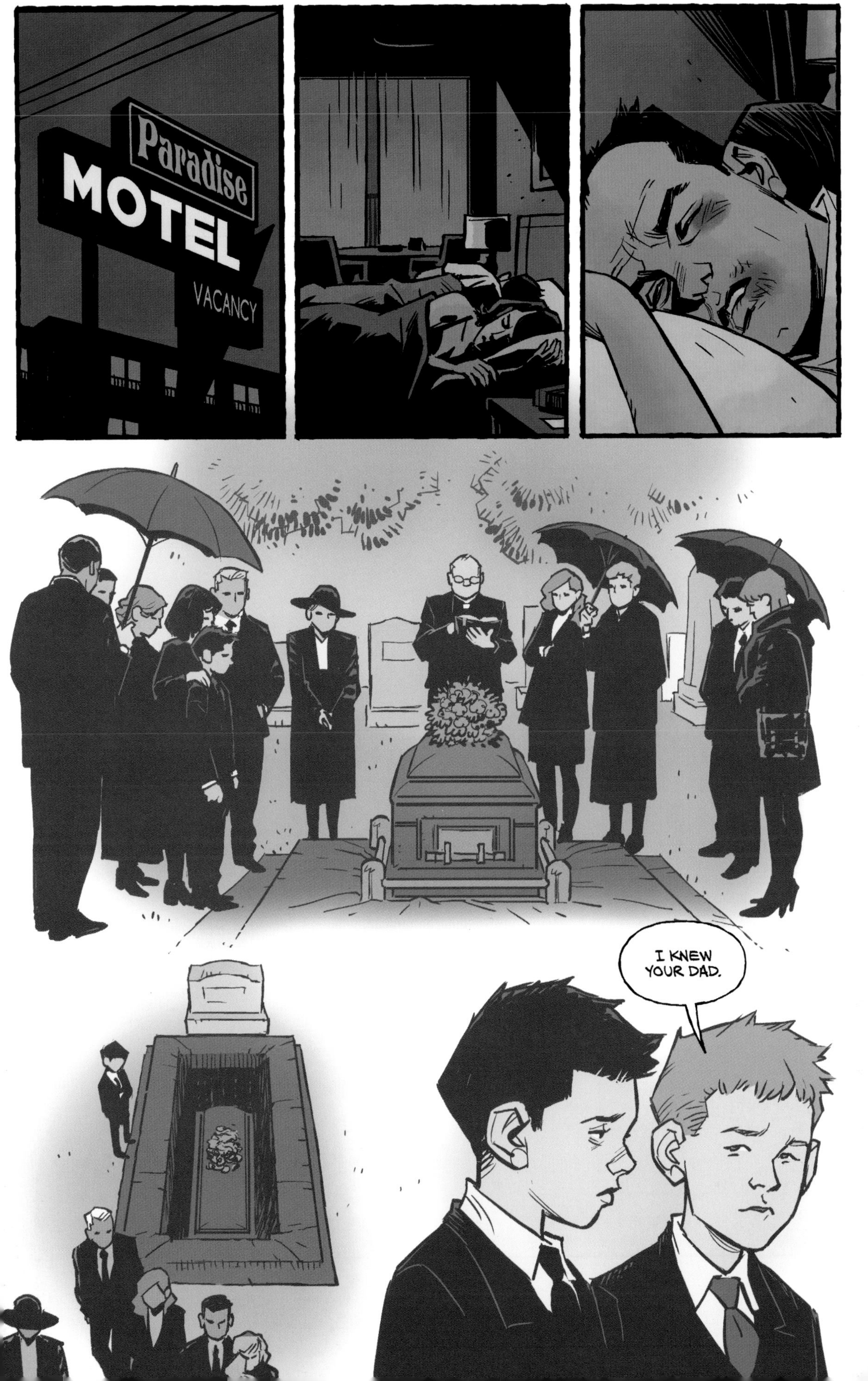
Paradise
MOTEL
VACANCY
I KNEW YOUR DAD.

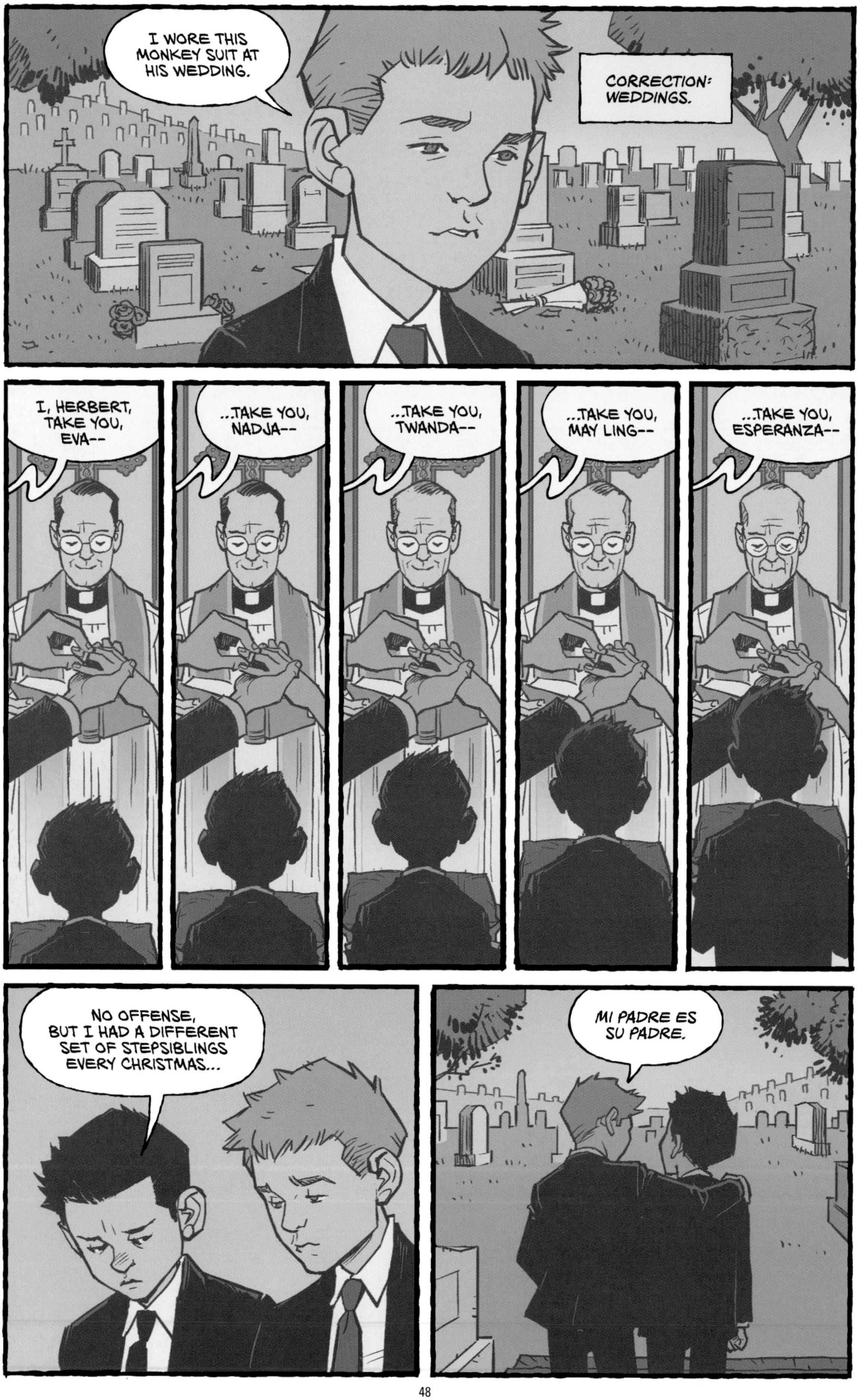
I WORE THIS MONKEY SUIT AT HIS WEDDING.
CORRECTION: WEDDINGS.
I, HERBERT, TAKE YOU, EVA--
...TAKE YOU, NADJA--
...TAKE YOU, TWANDA--
...TAKE YOU, MAY LING--
...TAKE YOU, ESPERANZA--
NO OFFENSE, BUT I HAD A DIFFERENT SET OF STEPSIBLINGS EVERY CHRISTMAS...
MI PADRE ES SU PADRE.

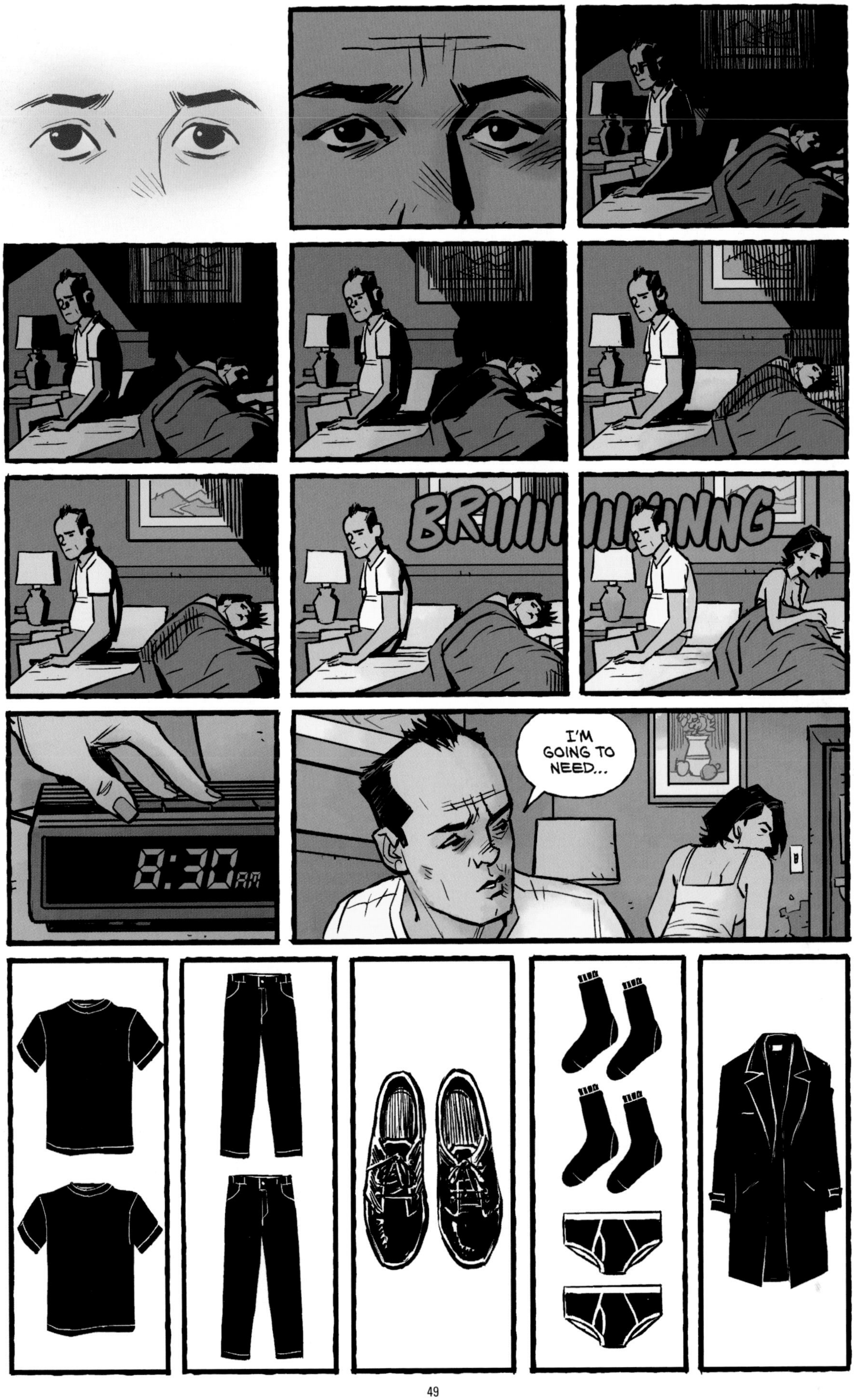
BRIIIIIIIIIINNG
8:30 AM
I'M GOING TO NEED...

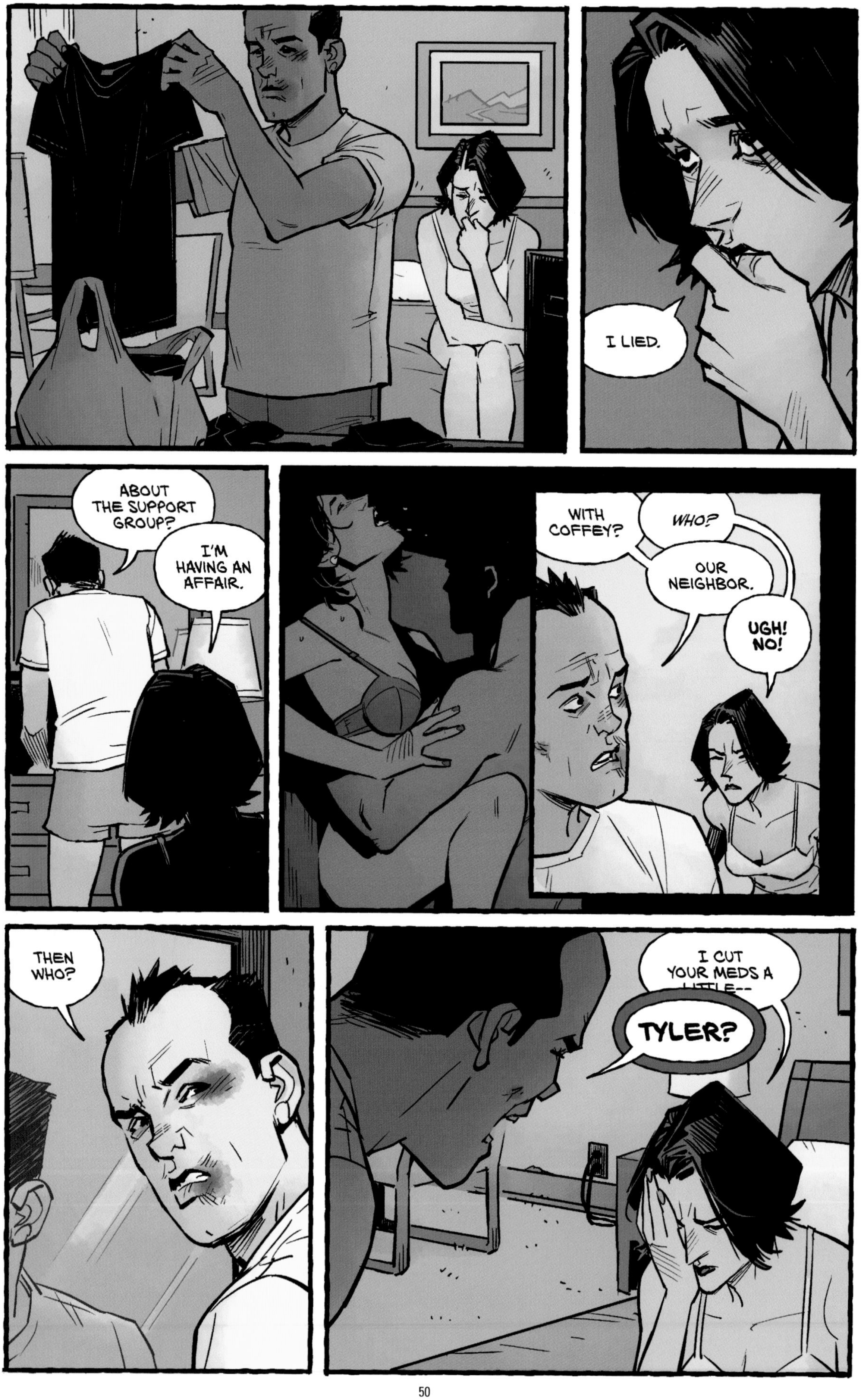
I LIED.
ABOUT THE SUPPORT GROUP?
I'M HAVING AN AFFAIR.
WITH COFFEY?
WHO?
OUR NEIGHBOR.
UGH! NO!
THEN WHO?
I CUT YOUR MEDS A LITTLE--
TYLER?

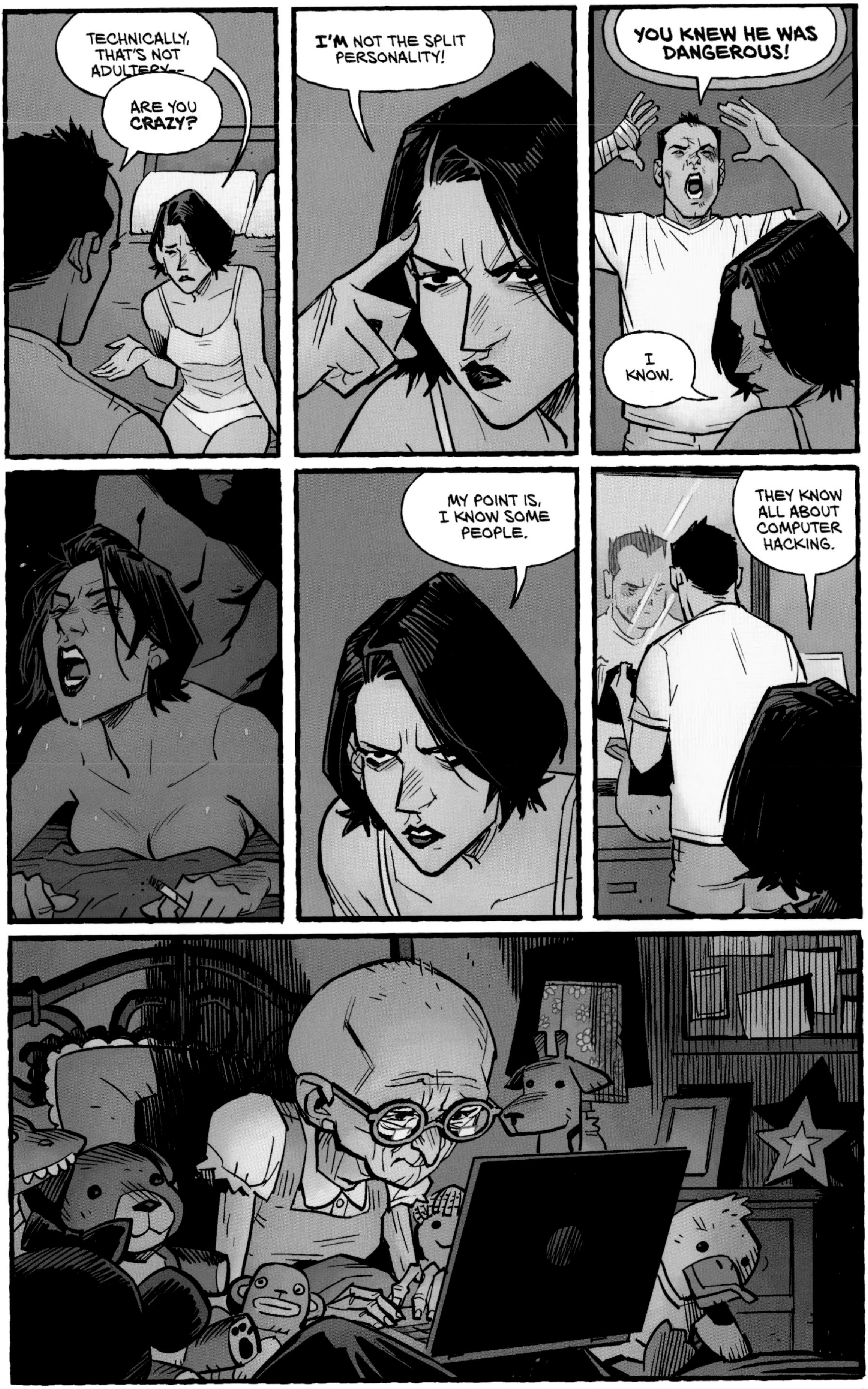
TECHNICALLY, THAT'S NOT ADULTERY--
ARE YOU CRAZY?
I'M NOT THE SPLIT PERSONALITY!
YOU KNEW HE WAS DANGEROUS!
I KNOW.
MY POINT IS, I KNOW SOME PEOPLE.
THEY KNOW ALL ABOUT COMPUTER HACKING.

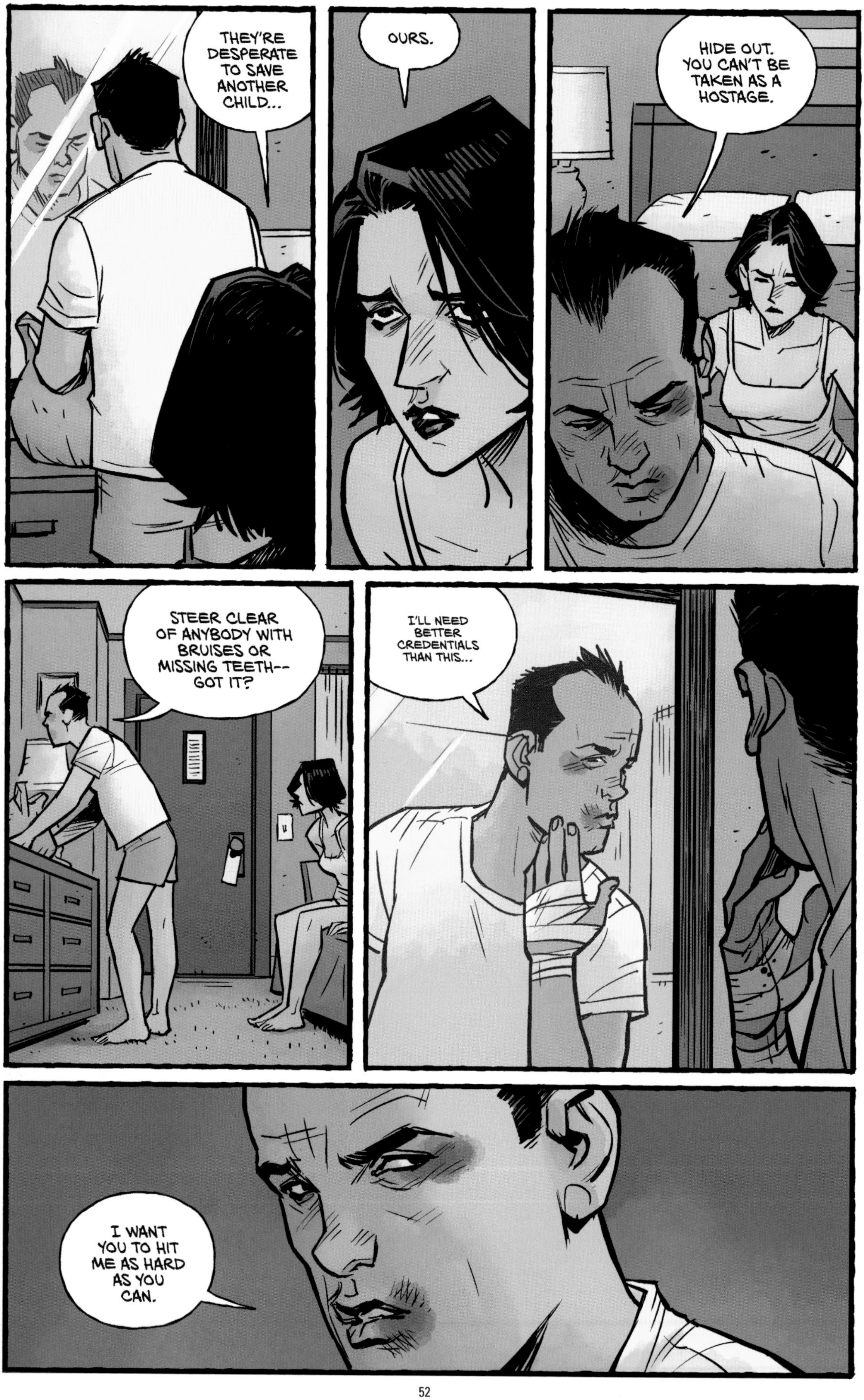
THEY'RE DESPERATE TO SAVE ANOTHER CHILD...
OURS.
HIDE OUT. YOU CAN'T BE TAKEN AS A HOSTAGE.
STEER CLEAR OF ANYBODY WITH BRUISES OR MISSING TEETH-- GOT IT?
I'LL NEED BETTER CREDENTIALS THAN THIS...
I WANT YOU TO HIT ME AS HARD AS YOU CAN.

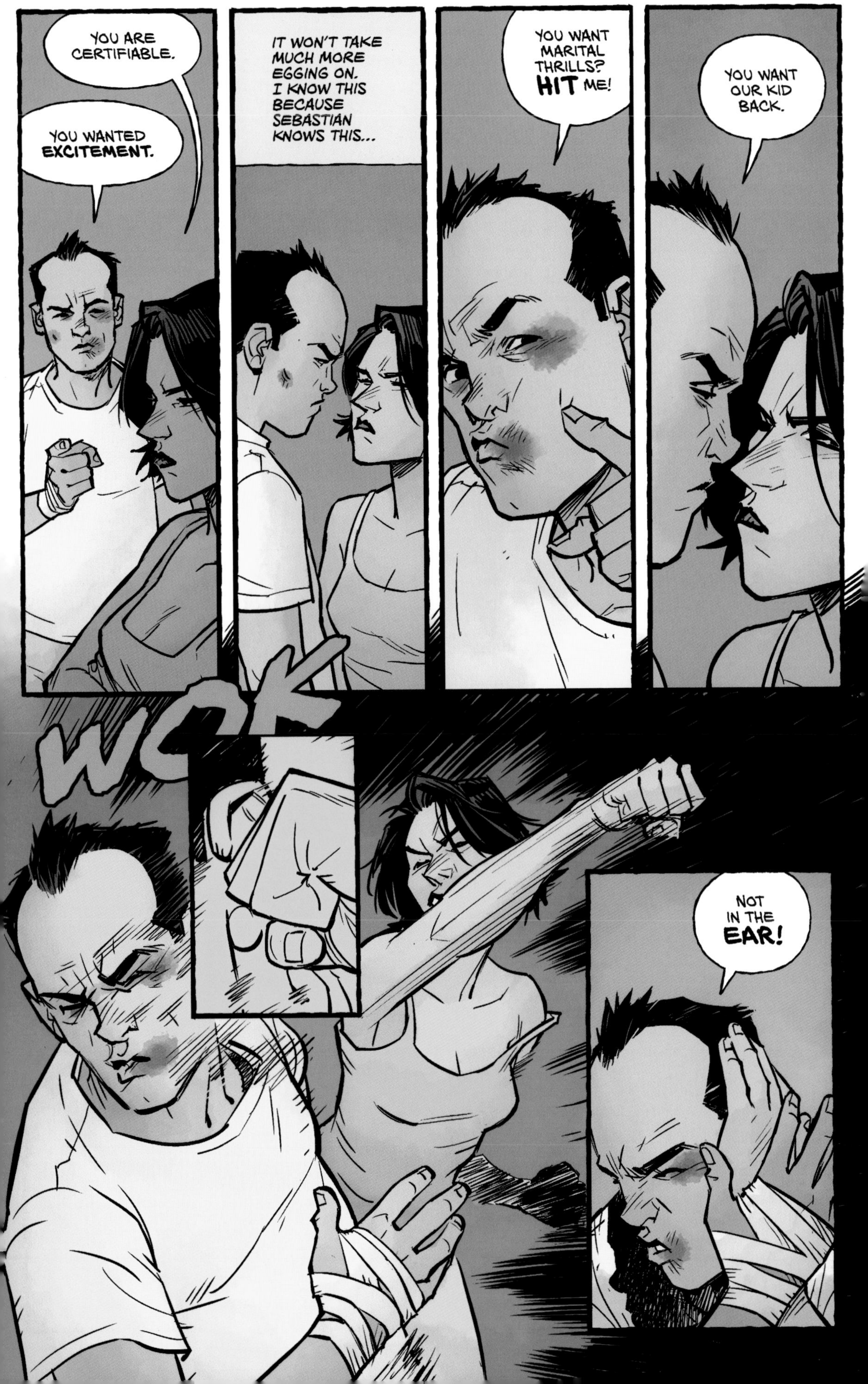
YOU ARE CERTIFIABLE.
YOU WANTED EXCITEMENT.
IT WON'T TAKE MUCH MORE EGGING ON. I KNOW THIS BECAUSE SEBASTIAN KNOWS THIS...
YOU WANT MARITAL THRILLS? HIT ME!
YOU WANT OUR KID BACK.
NOT IN THE EAR!

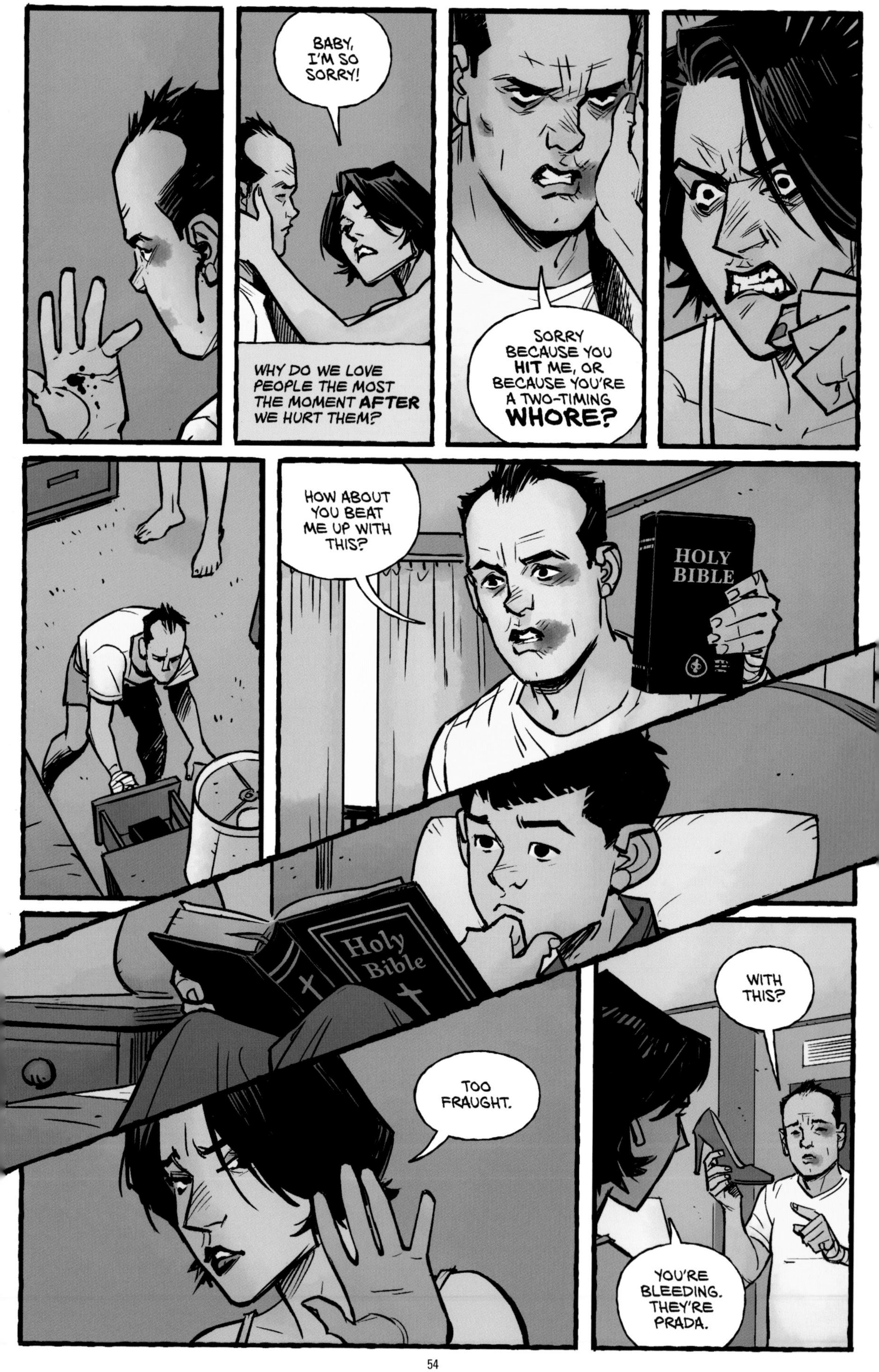
BABY, I'M SO SORRY!
WHY DO WE LOVE PEOPLE THE MOST THE MOMENT AFTER WE HURT THEM?
SORRY BECAUSE YOU HIT ME, OR BECAUSE YOU'RE A TWO-TIMING WHORE?
HOW ABOUT YOU BEAT ME UP WITH THIS?
HOLY BIBLE
Holy Bible
TOO FRAUGHT.
WITH THIS?
YOU'RE BLEEDING. THEY'RE PRADA.

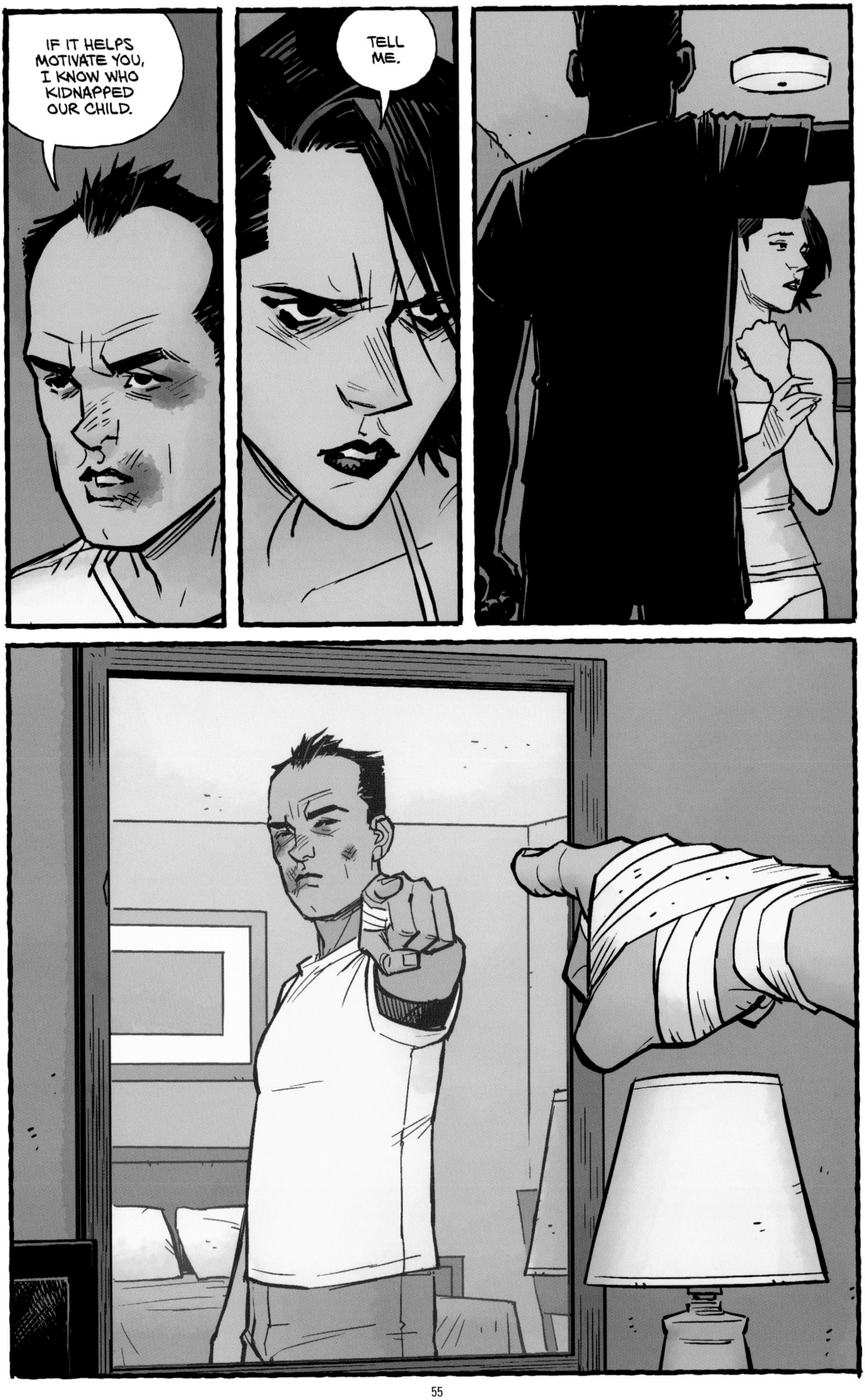
IF IT HELPS MOTIVATE YOU, I KNOW WHO KIDNAPPED OUR CHILD.
TELL ME.

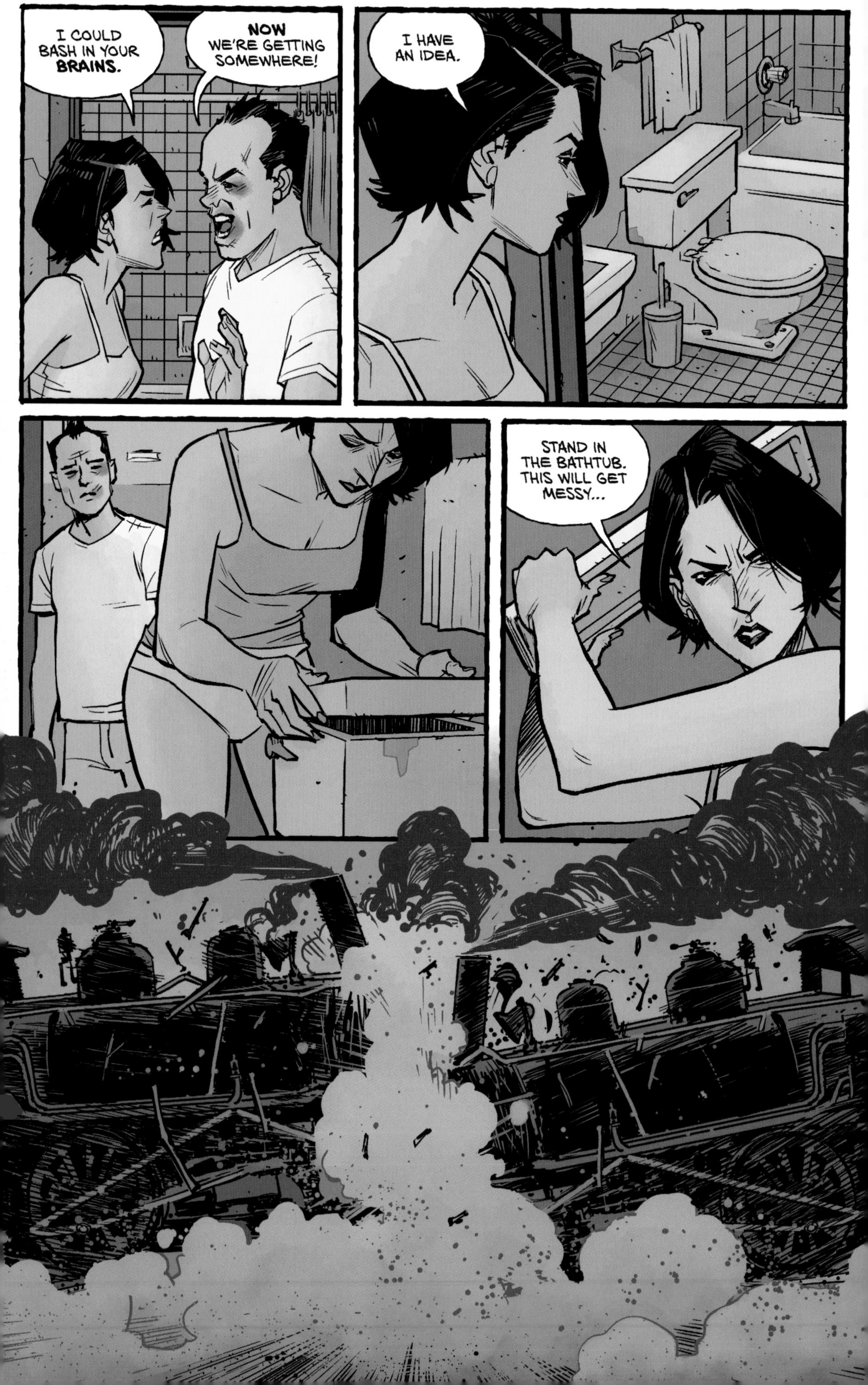
I COULD BASH IN YOUR BRAINS.
NOW WE'RE GETTING SOMEWHERE!
I HAVE AN IDEA.
STAND IN THE BATHTUB. THIS WILL GET MESSY...

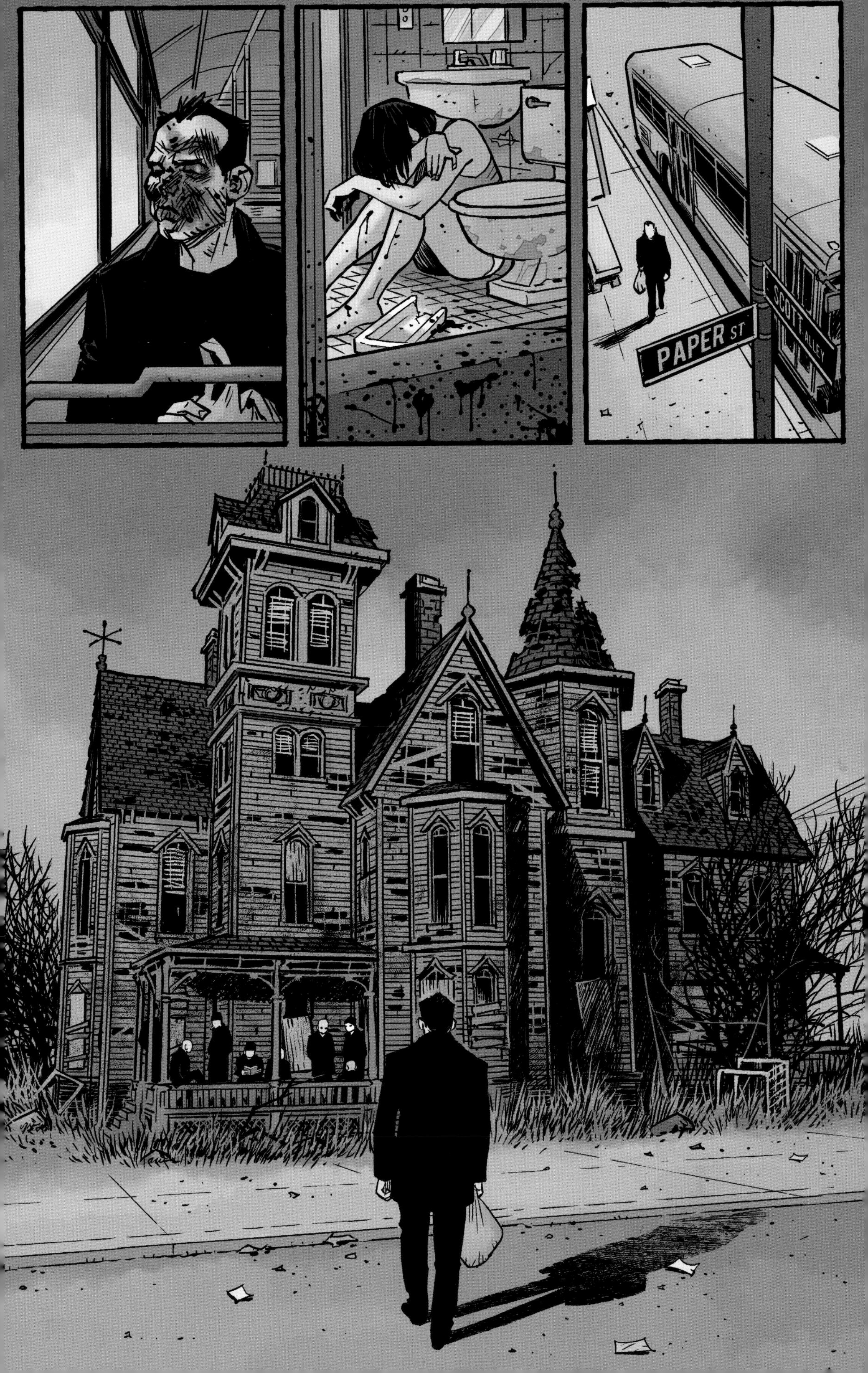
PAPER ST
SCOTT ALLEY

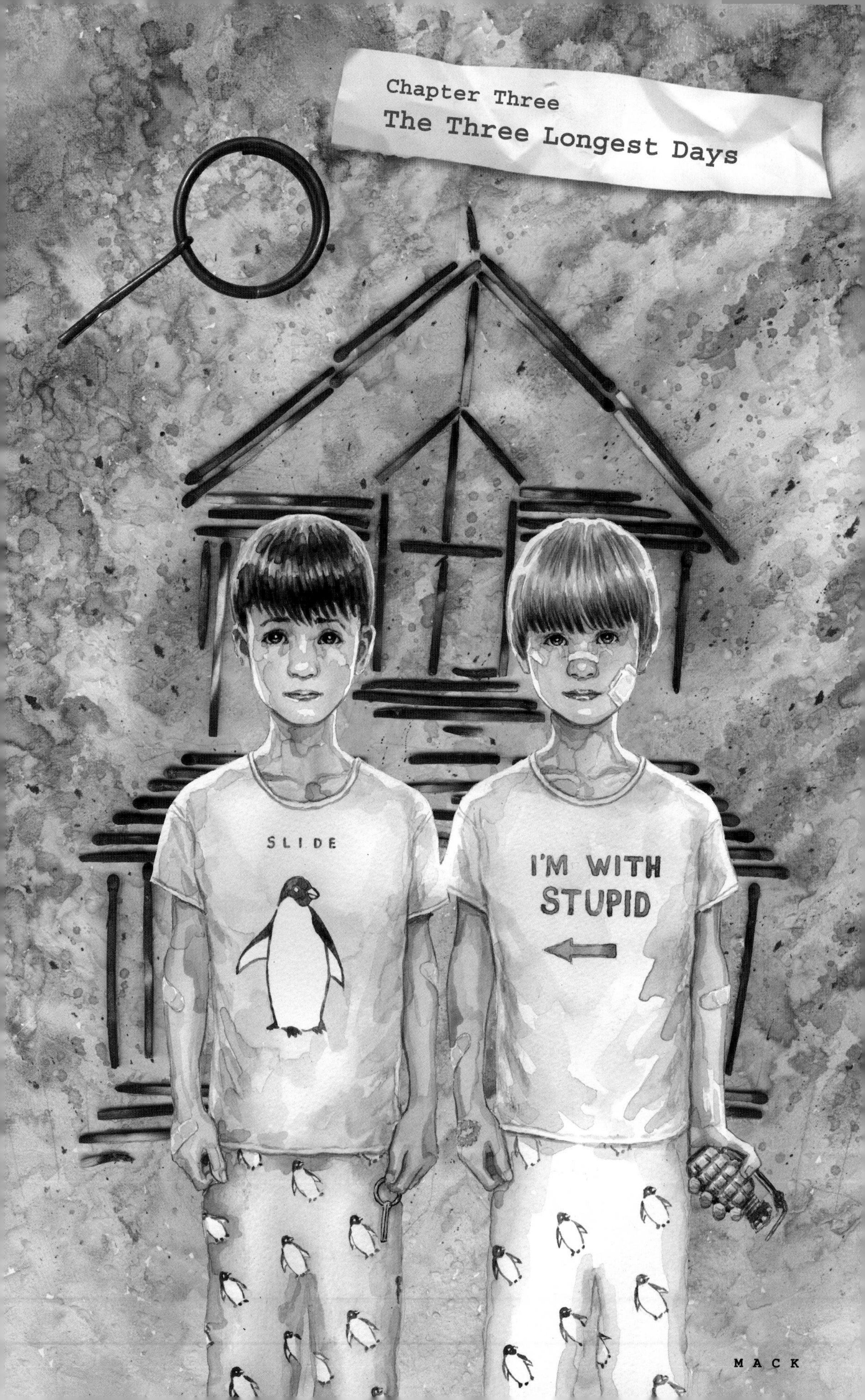
Chapter Three
The Three Longest Days
SLIDE
I'M WITH
STUPID
MACK

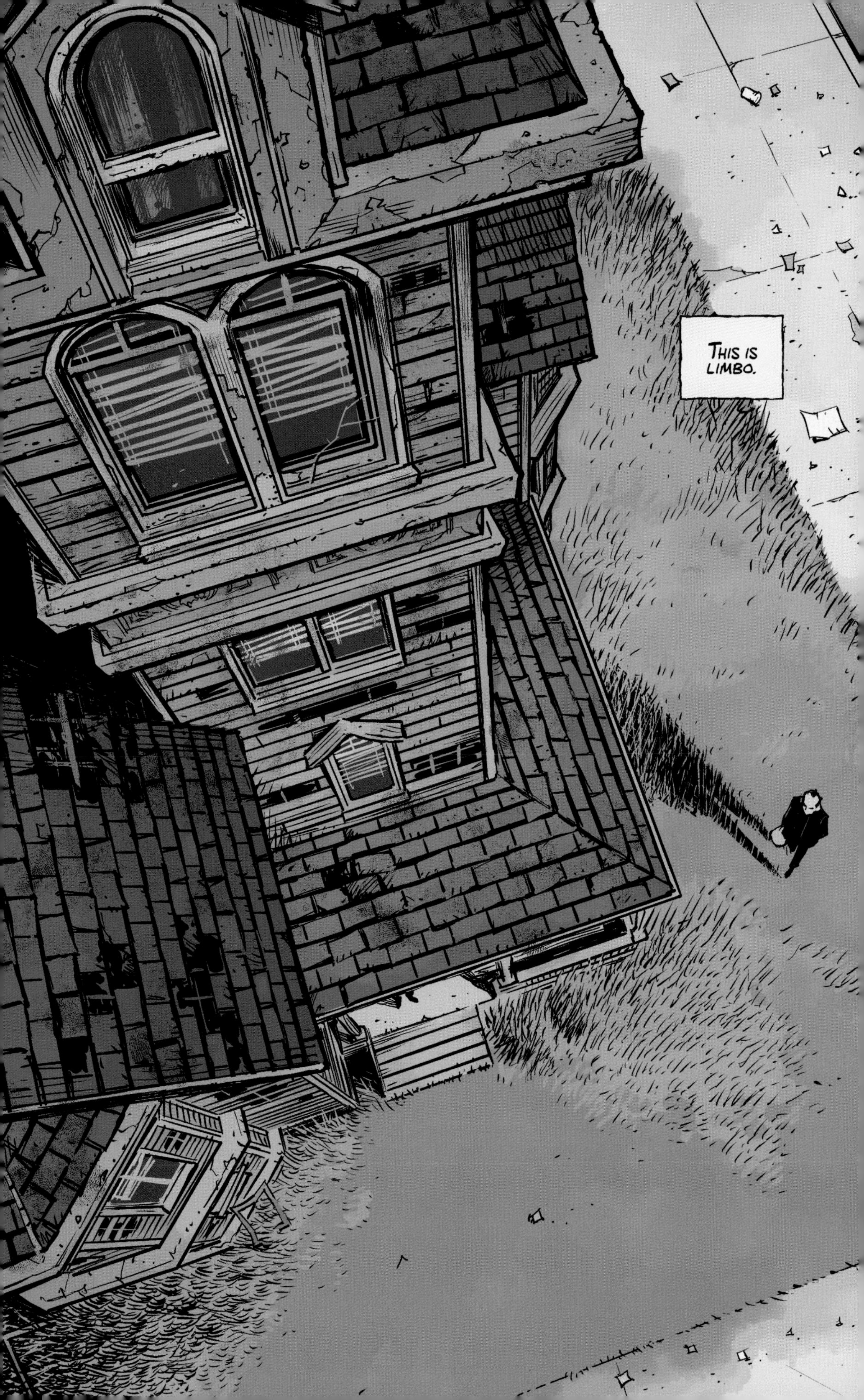
THIS IS LIMBO.

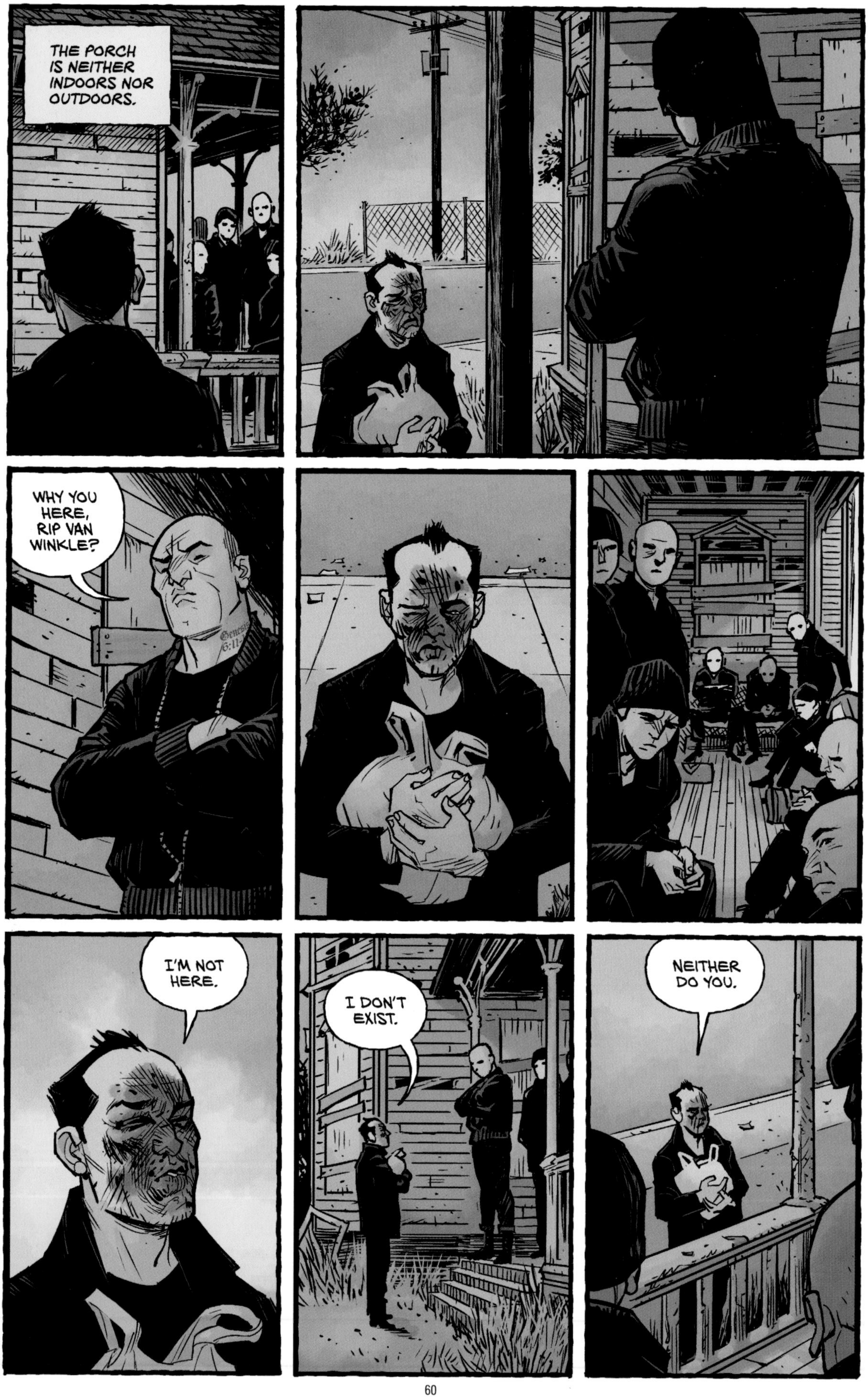
THE PORCH IS NEITHER INDOORS NOR OUTDOORS.
WHY YOU HERE, RIP VAN WINKLE?
I'M NOT HERE.
I DON'T EXIST.
NEITHER DO YOU.

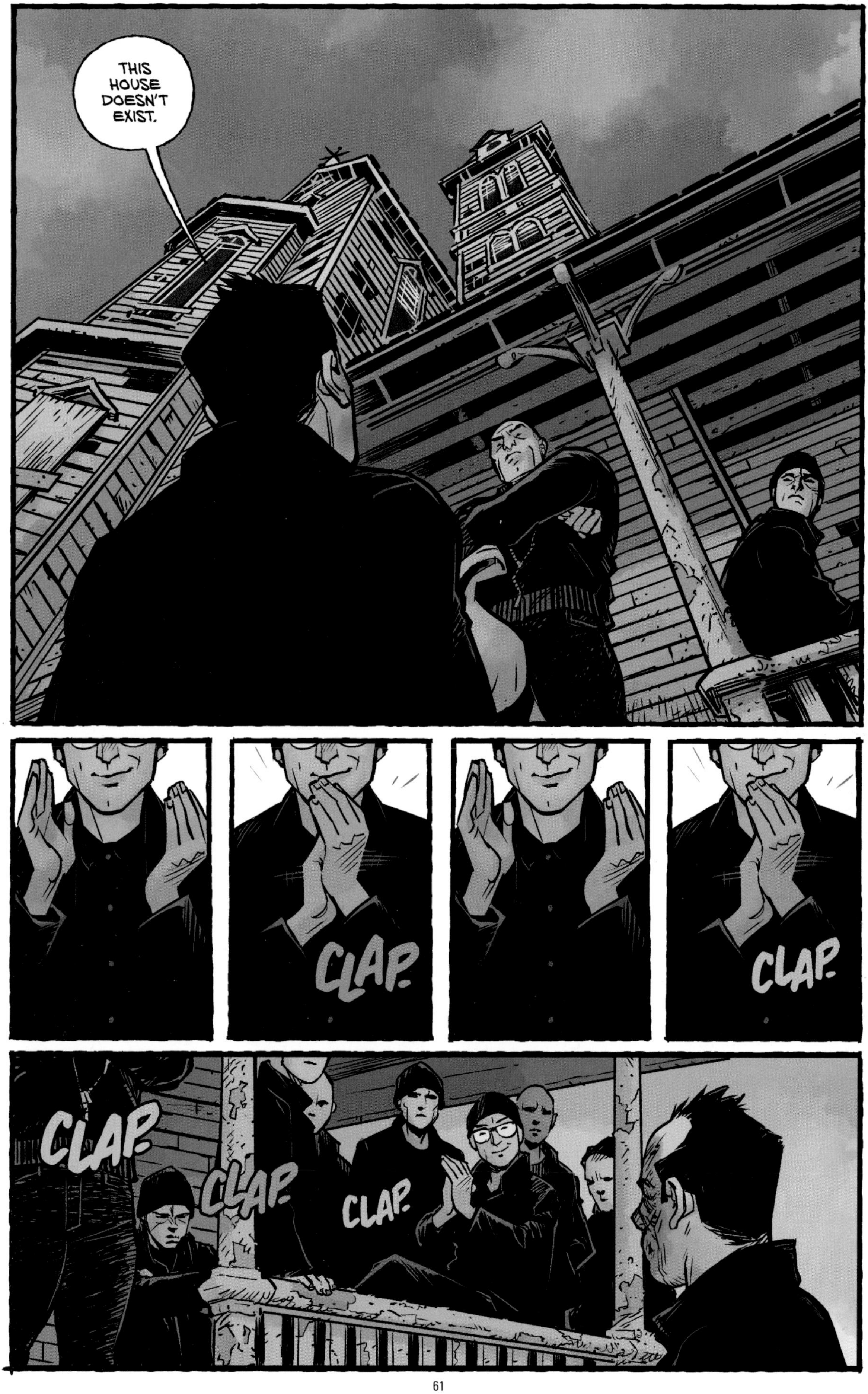
THIS HOUSE DOESN'T EXIST.
CLAP.
CLAP.
CLAP.
CLAP.
CLAP.

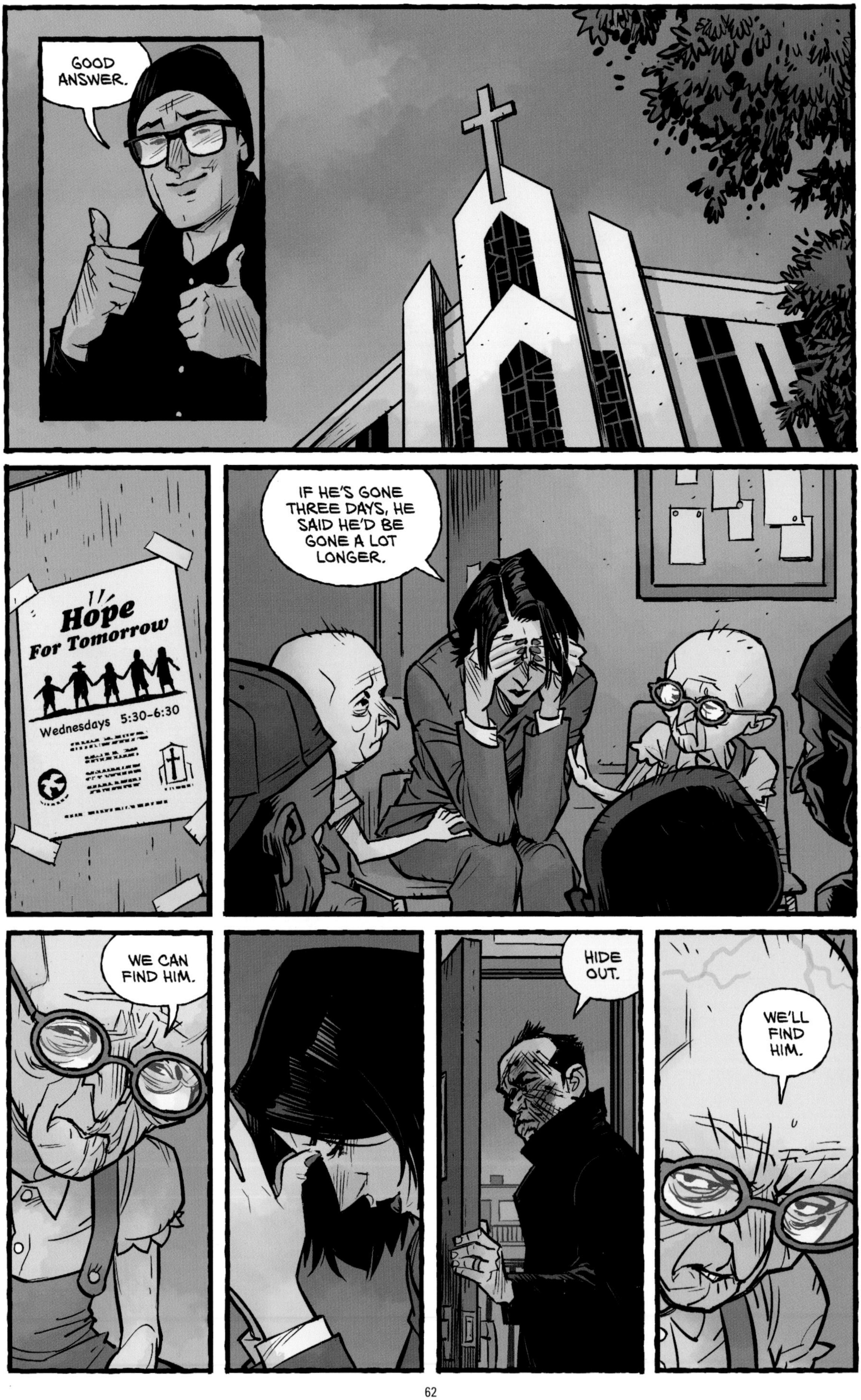
GOOD ANSWER.
IF HE'S GONE THREE DAYS, HE SAID HE'D BE GONE A LOT LONGER.
Hope For Tomorrow
Wednesdays 5:30–6:30
WE CAN FIND HIM.
HIDE OUT.
WE'LL FIND HIM.

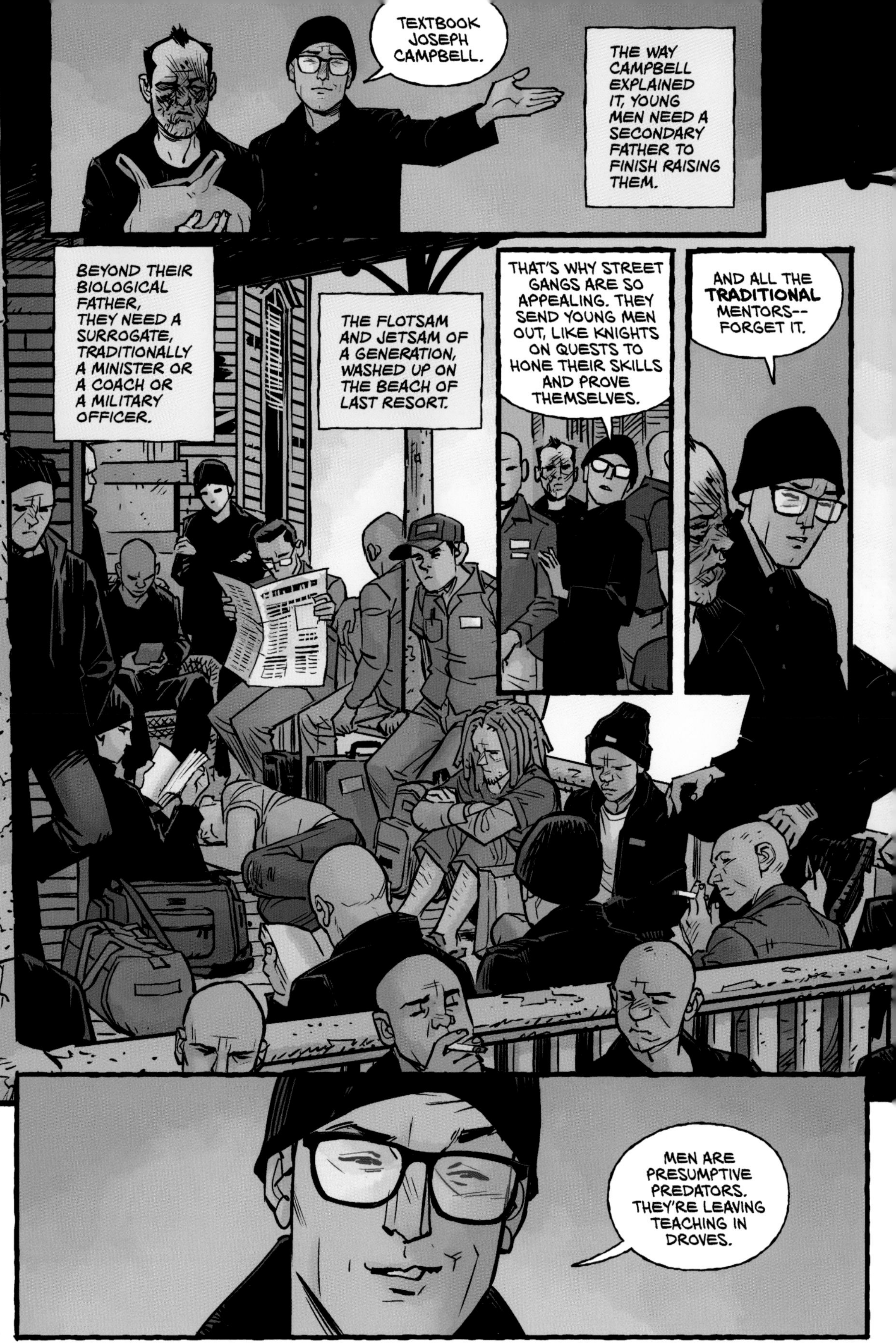
TEXTBOOK JOSEPH CAMPBELL.
THE WAY CAMPBELL EXPLAINED IT, YOUNG MEN NEED A SECONDARY FATHER TO FINISH RAISING THEM.
BEYOND THEIR BIOLOGICAL FATHER, THEY NEED A SURROGATE, TRADITIONALLY A MINISTER OR A COACH OR A MILITARY OFFICER.
THE FLOTSAM AND JETSAM OF A GENERATION, WASHED UP ON THE BEACH OF LAST RESORT.
THAT'S WHY STREET GANGS ARE SO APPEALING. THEY SEND YOUNG MEN OUT, LIKE KNIGHTS ON QUESTS TO HONE THEIR SKILLS AND PROVE THEMSELVES.
AND ALL THE **TRADITIONAL** MENTORS-- FORGET IT.
MEN ARE PRESUMPTIVE PREDATORS. THEY'RE LEAVING TEACHING IN DROVES.

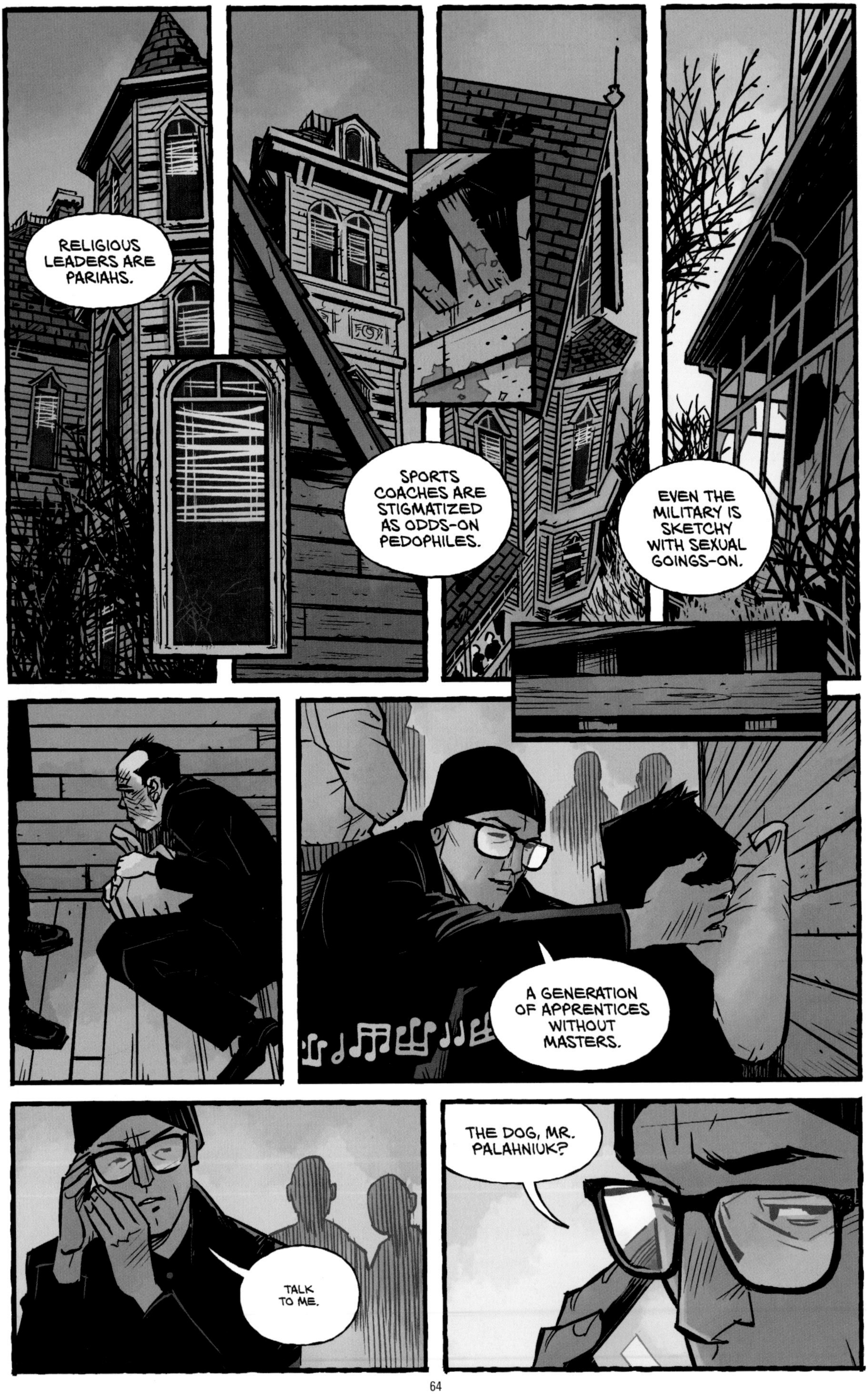
RELIGIOUS LEADERS ARE PARIAHS.
SPORTS COACHES ARE STIGMATIZED AS ODDS-ON PEDOPHILES.
EVEN THE MILITARY IS SKETCHY WITH SEXUAL GOINGS-ON.
A GENERATION OF APPRENTICES WITHOUT MASTERS.
TALK TO ME.
THE DOG, MR. PALAHNIUK?

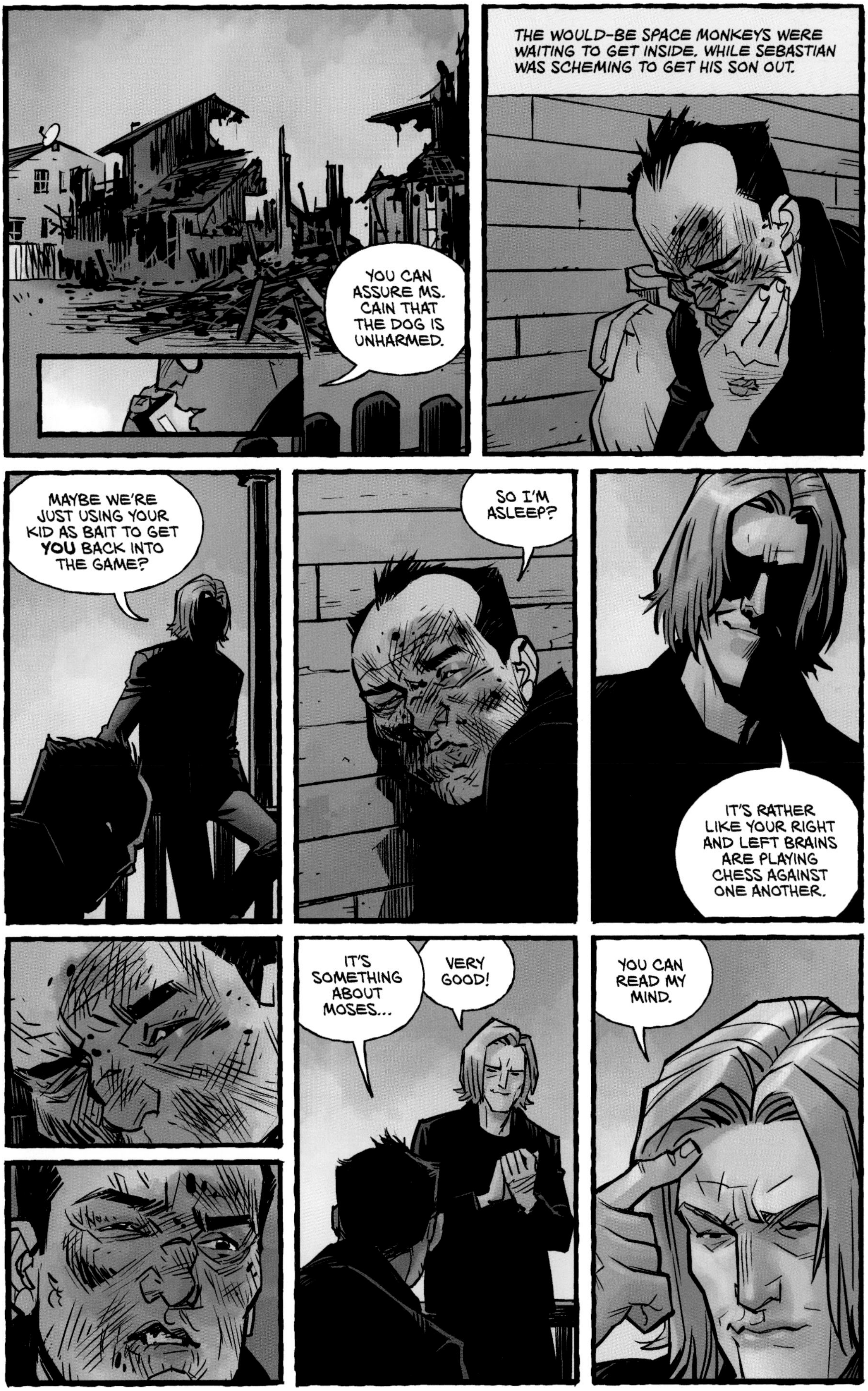
YOU CAN ASSURE MS. CAIN THAT THE DOG IS UNHARMED.
THE WOULD-BE SPACE MONKEYS WERE WAITING TO GET INSIDE, WHILE SEBASTIAN WAS SCHEMING TO GET HIS SON OUT.
MAYBE WE'RE JUST USING YOUR KID AS BAIT TO GET YOU BACK INTO THE GAME?
SO I'M ASLEEP?
IT'S RATHER LIKE YOUR RIGHT AND LEFT BRAINS ARE PLAYING CHESS AGAINST ONE ANOTHER.
IT'S SOMETHING ABOUT MOSES...
VERY GOOD!
YOU CAN READ MY MIND.

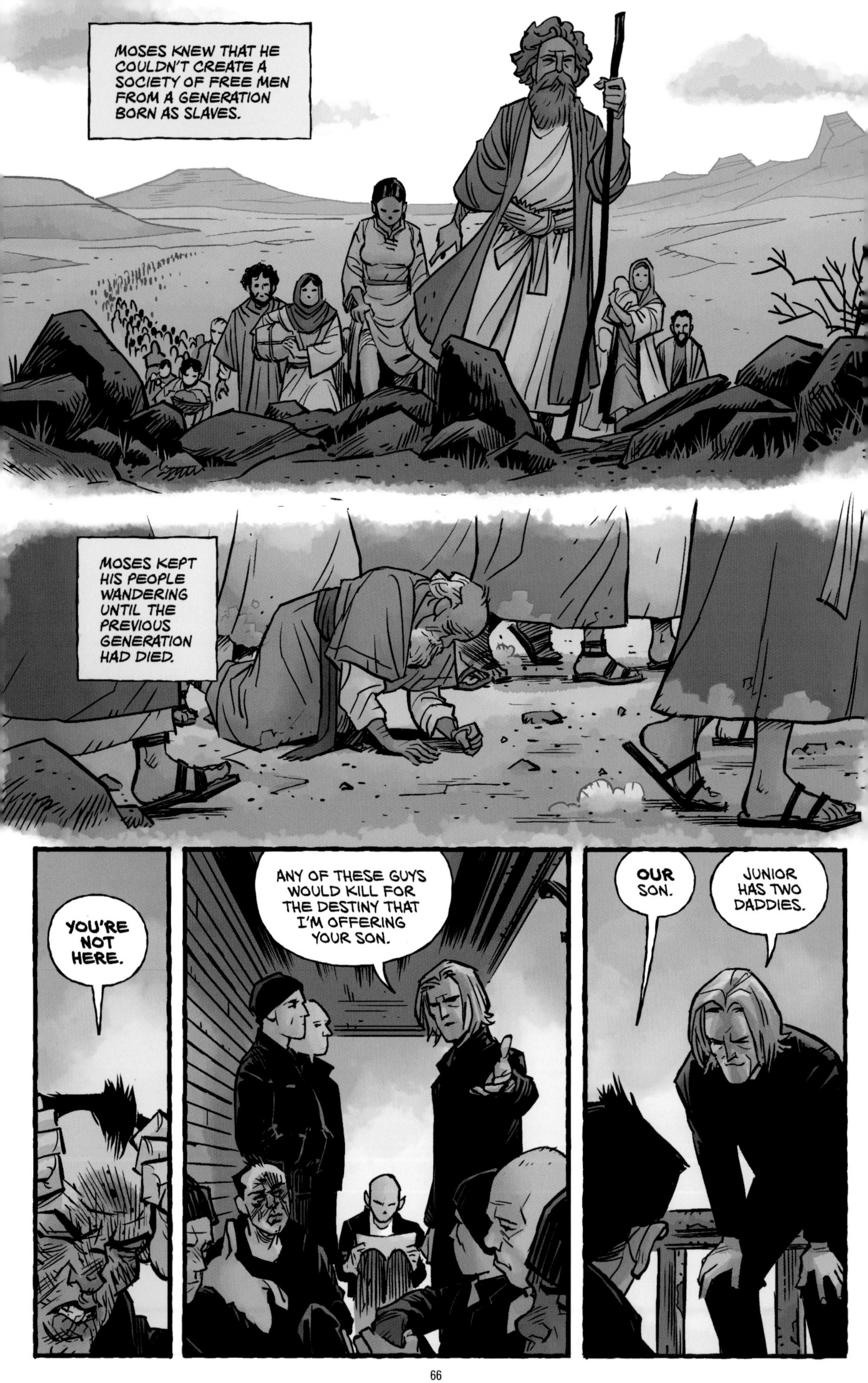
MOSES KNEW THAT HE COULDN'T CREATE A SOCIETY OF FREE MEN FROM A GENERATION BORN AS SLAVES.
MOSES KEPT HIS PEOPLE WANDERING UNTIL THE PREVIOUS GENERATION HAD DIED.
YOU'RE NOT HERE.
ANY OF THESE GUYS WOULD KILL FOR THE DESTINY THAT I'M OFFERING YOUR SON.
OUR SON.
JUNIOR HAS TWO DADDIES.

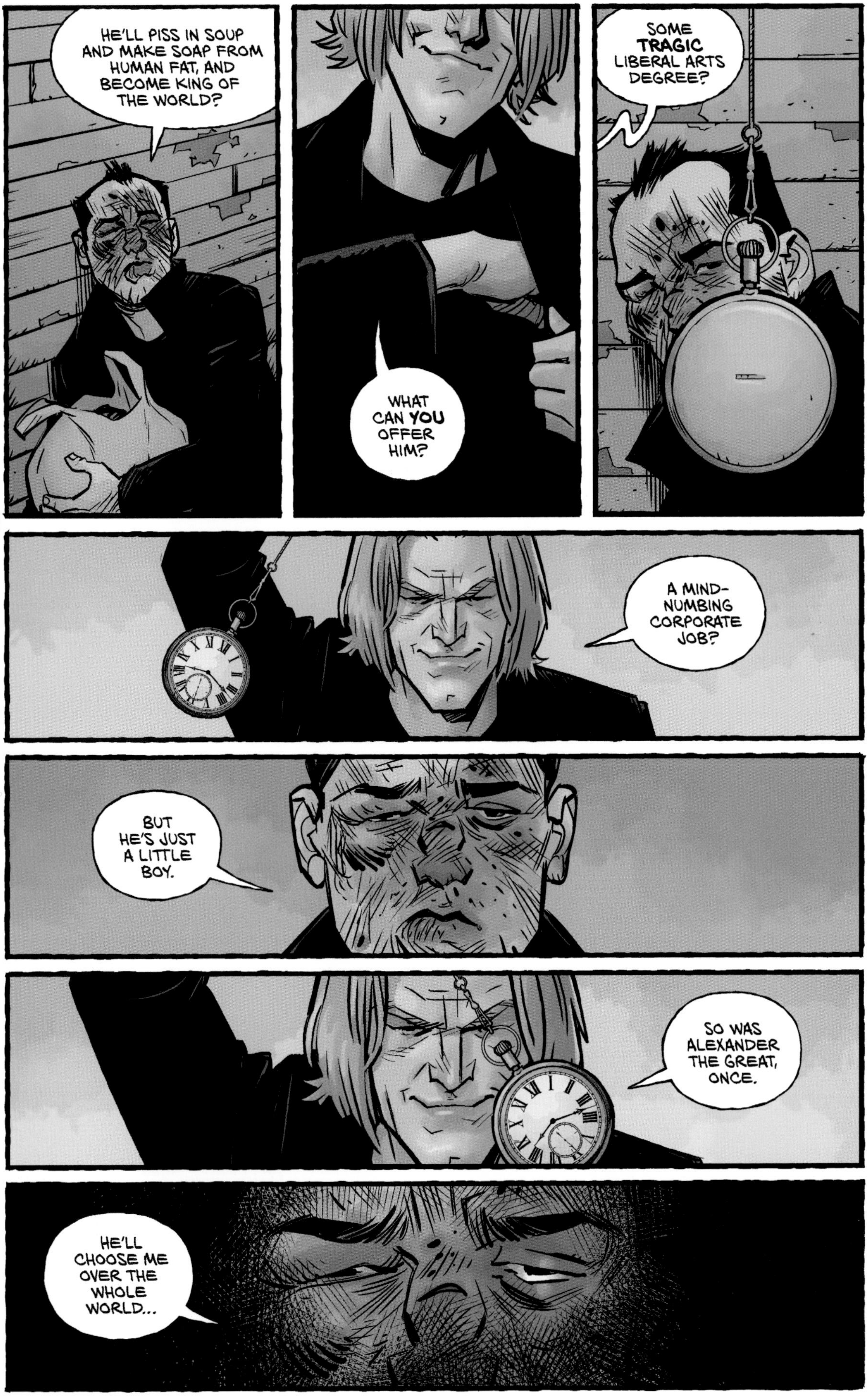
HE'LL PISS IN SOUP AND MAKE SOAP FROM HUMAN FAT, AND BECOME KING OF THE WORLD?
WHAT CAN YOU OFFER HIM?
SOME TRAGIC LIBERAL ARTS DEGREE?
A MIND-NUMBING CORPORATE JOB?
BUT HE'S JUST A LITTLE BOY.
SO WAS ALEXANDER THE GREAT, ONCE.
HE'LL CHOOSE ME OVER THE WHOLE WORLD...

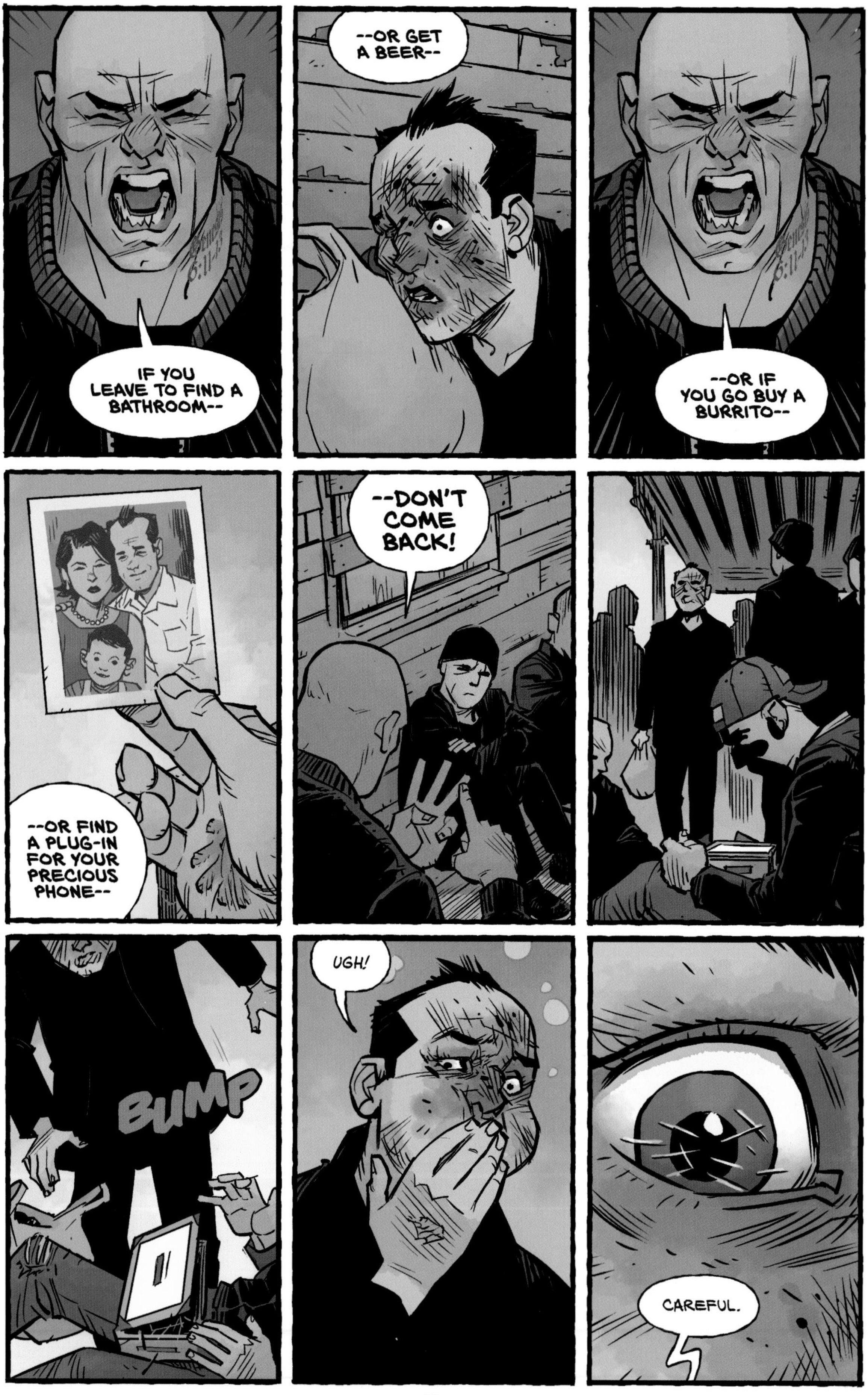
IF YOU LEAVE TO FIND A BATHROOM--
--OR GET A BEER--
--OR IF YOU GO BUY A BURRITO--
--OR FIND A PLUG-IN FOR YOUR PRECIOUS PHONE--
--DON'T COME BACK!
BUMP
UGH!
CAREFUL.

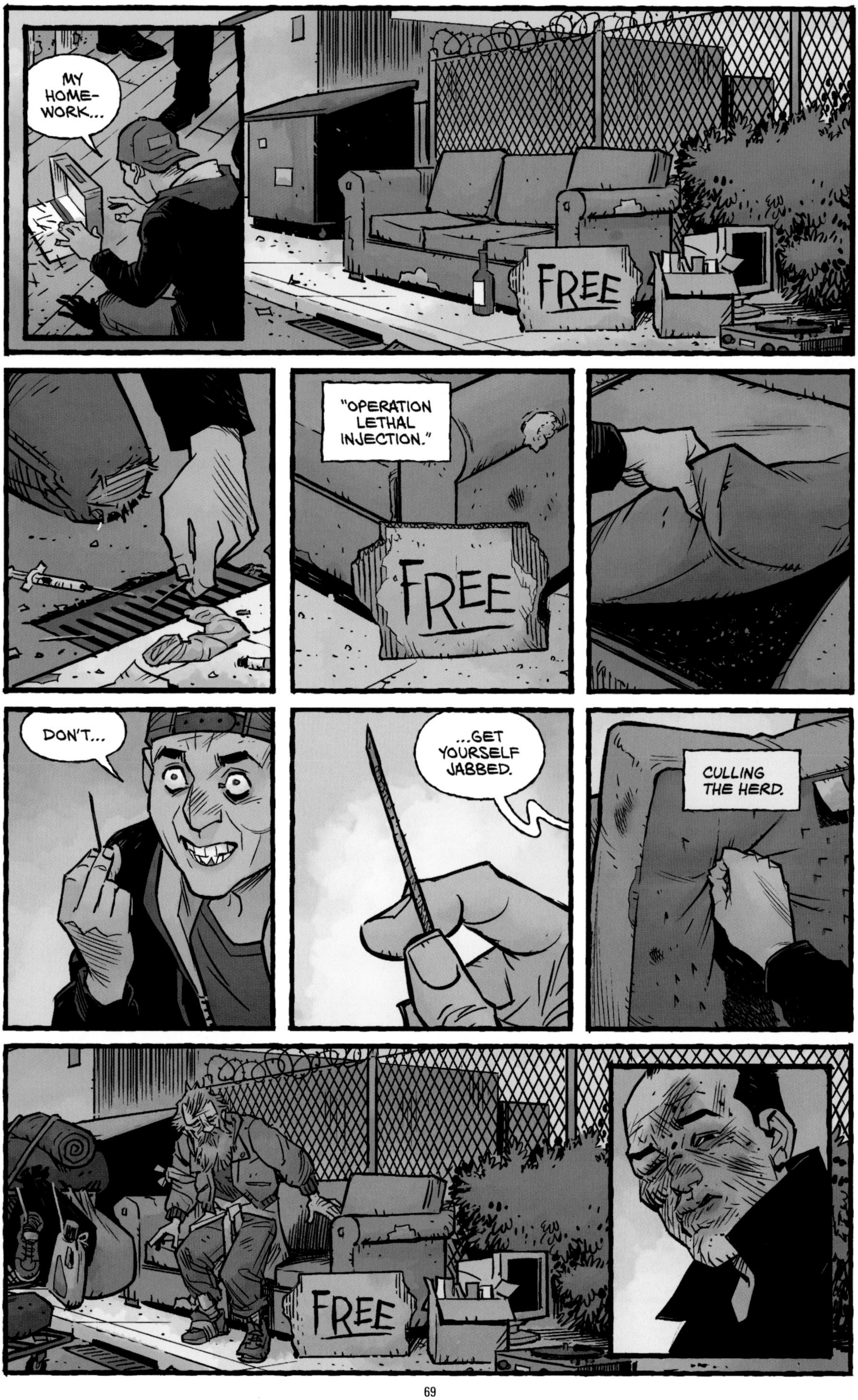

MY HOME-WORK...
FREE
"OPERATION LETHAL INJECTION."
FREE
DON'T...
...GET YOURSELF JABBED.
CULLING THE HERD.
FREE

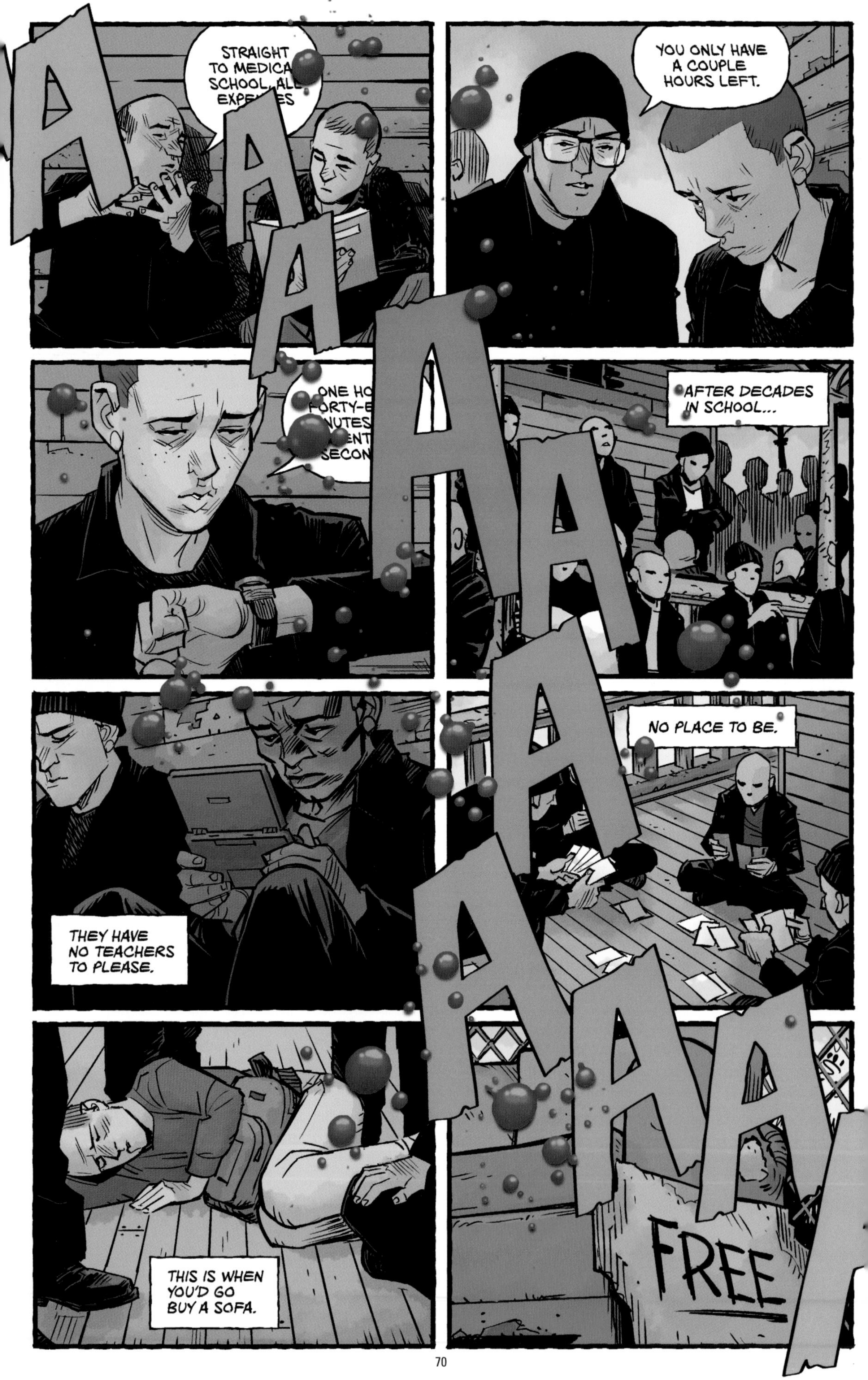
STRAIGHT TO MEDICA SCHOOL, ALL EXPE ES
YOU ONLY HAVE A COUPLE HOURS LEFT.
ONE HO FORTY-E NUTES ENT SECON
AFTER DECADES IN SCHOOL...
THEY HAVE NO TEACHERS TO PLEASE.
NO PLACE TO BE.
THIS IS WHEN YOU'D GO BUY A SOFA.
AAAAAAAAAAAAA
FREE

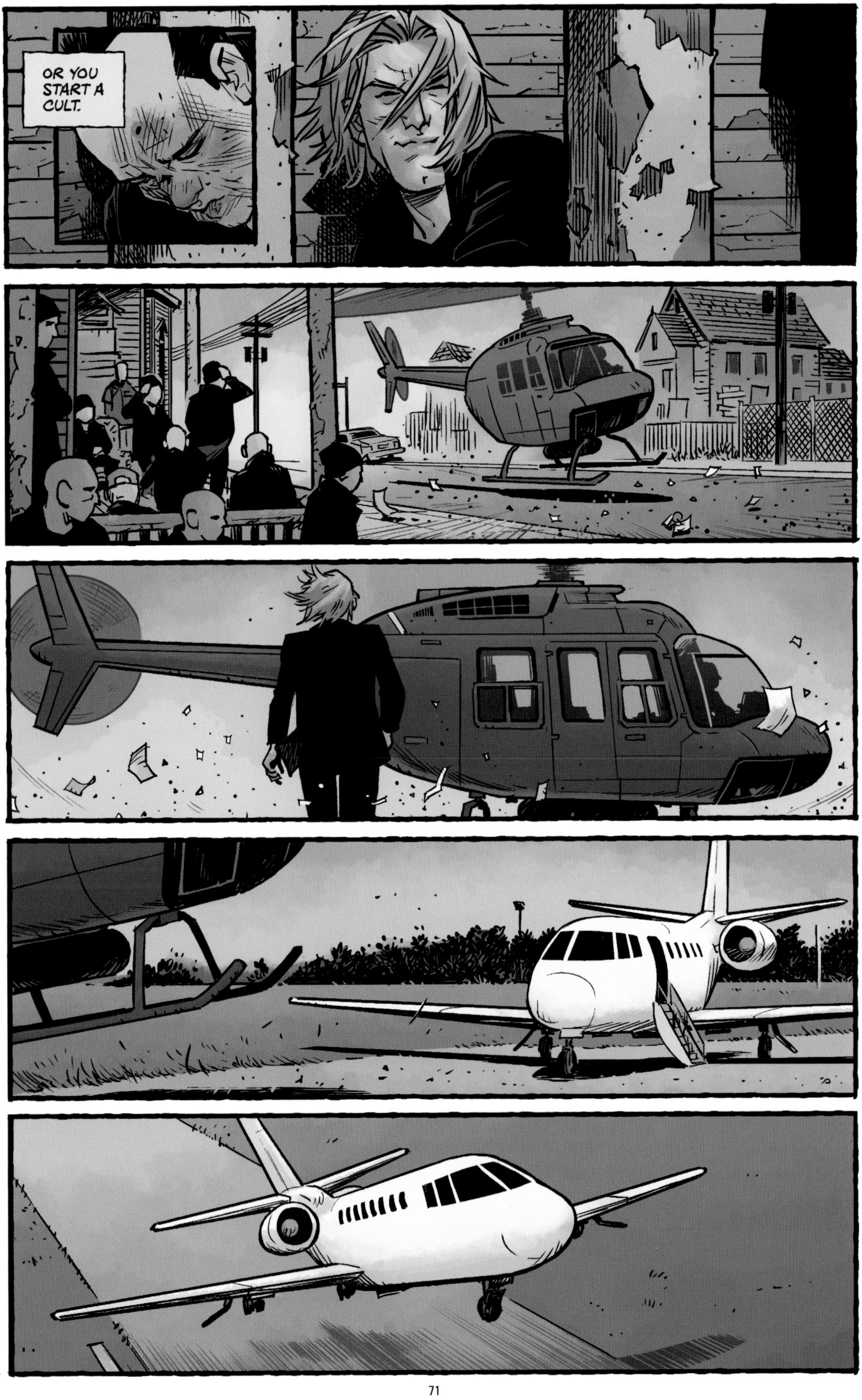
OR YOU START A CULT.

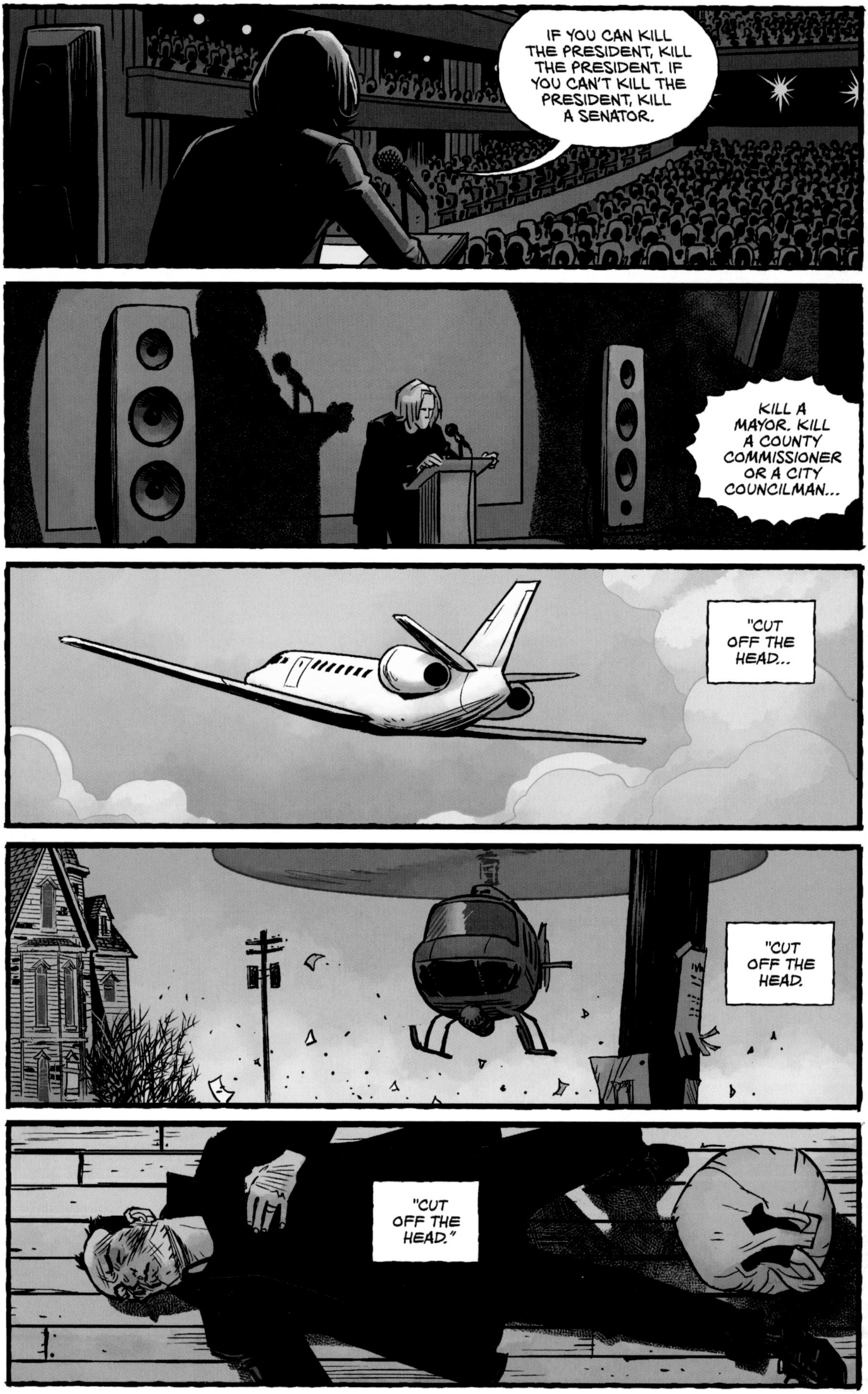
IF YOU CAN KILL THE PRESIDENT, KILL THE PRESIDENT. IF YOU CAN'T KILL THE PRESIDENT, KILL A SENATOR.
KILL A MAYOR. KILL A COUNTY COMMISSIONER OR A CITY COUNCILMAN...
"CUT OFF THE HEAD...
"CUT OFF THE HEAD.
"CUT OFF THE HEAD."

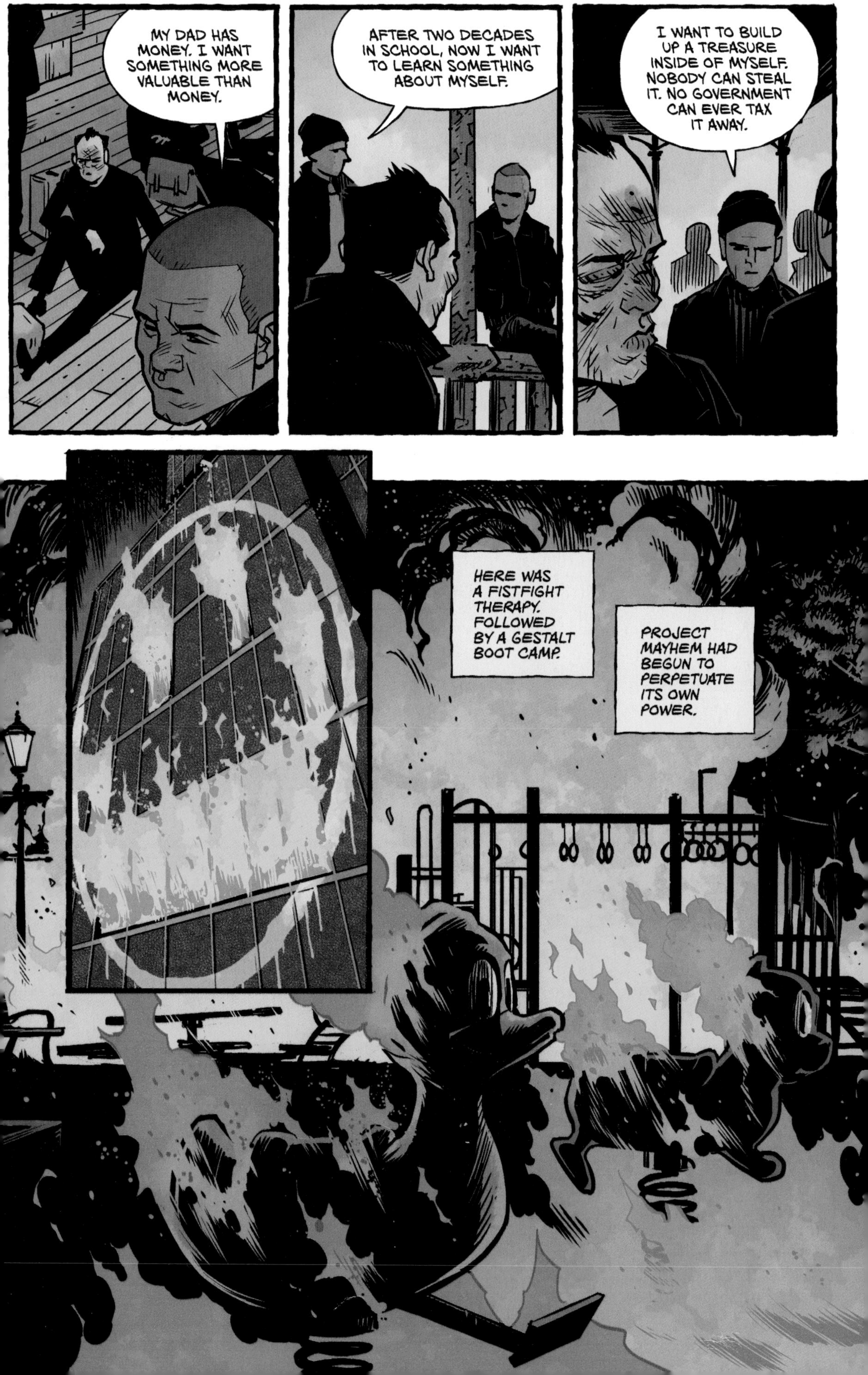
MY DAD HAS MONEY. I WANT SOMETHING MORE VALUABLE THAN MONEY.
AFTER TWO DECADES IN SCHOOL, NOW I WANT TO LEARN SOMETHING ABOUT MYSELF.
I WANT TO BUILD UP A TREASURE INSIDE OF MYSELF. NOBODY CAN STEAL IT. NO GOVERNMENT CAN EVER TAX IT AWAY.
HERE WAS A FISTFIGHT THERAPY. FOLLOWED BY A GESTALT BOOT CAMP.
PROJECT MAYHEM HAD BEGUN TO PERPETUATE ITS OWN POWER.

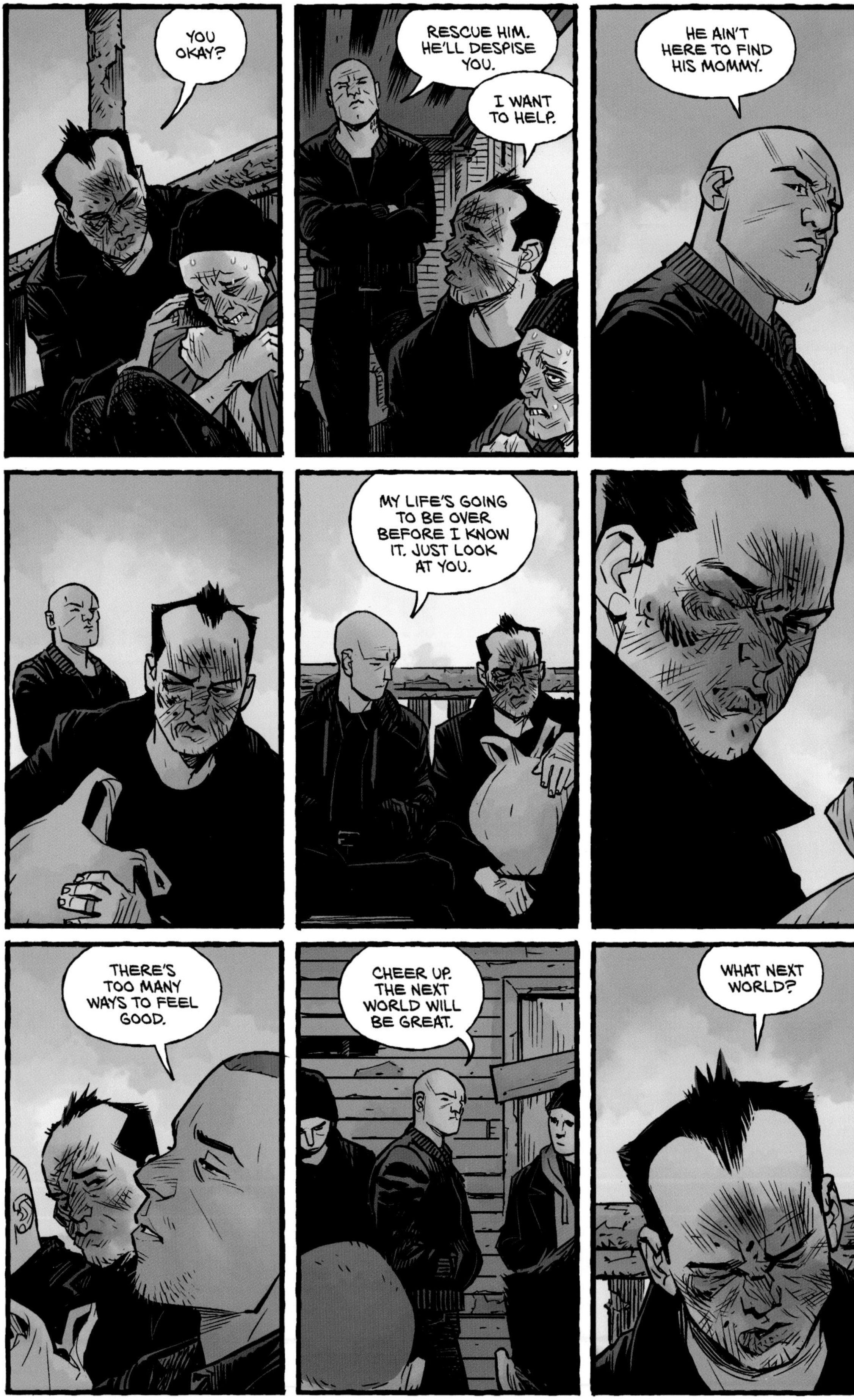
YOU OKAY?
RESCUE HIM. HE'LL DESPISE YOU.
I WANT TO HELP.
HE AIN'T HERE TO FIND HIS MOMMY.
MY LIFE'S GOING TO BE OVER BEFORE I KNOW IT. JUST LOOK AT YOU.
THERE'S TOO MANY WAYS TO FEEL GOOD.
CHEER UP. THE NEXT WORLD WILL BE GREAT.
WHAT NEXT WORLD?

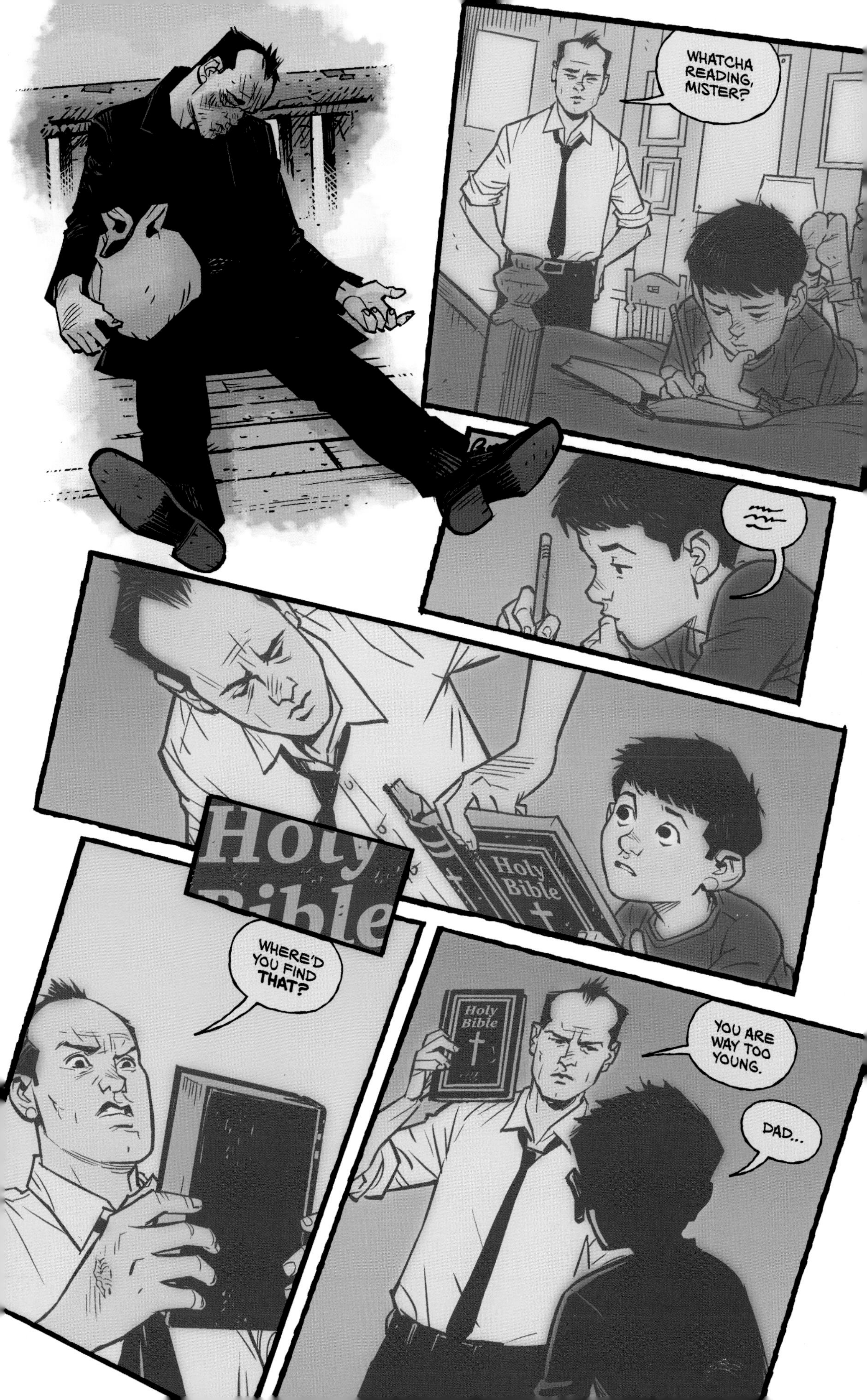
WHATCHA READING, MISTER?
Holy Bible
Holy Bible
Holy Bible
WHERE'D YOU FIND THAT?
Holy Bible
YOU ARE WAY TOO YOUNG.
DAD...

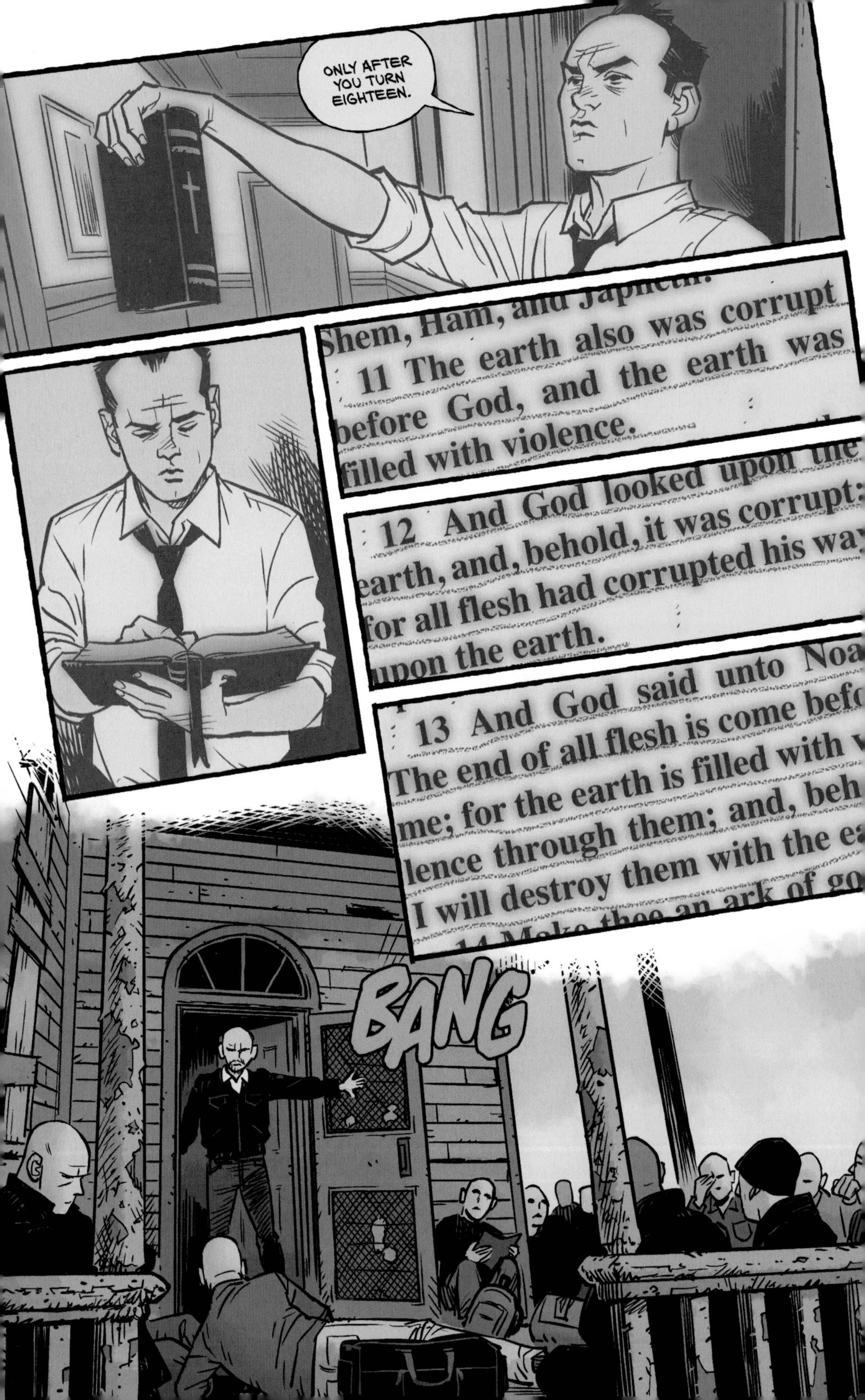
ONLY AFTER YOU TURN EIGHTEEN.
Shem, Ham,
11 The earth also was corrupt
before God, and the earth was
filled with violence.
12 And God looked upon the
earth, and, behold, it was corrupt;
for all flesh had corrupted his wa
upon the earth.
13 And God said unto Noa
The end of all flesh is come bef
The end of all flesh is filled with
me; for the earth is filled with
lence through them; and, beh
I will destroy them with the e
BANG

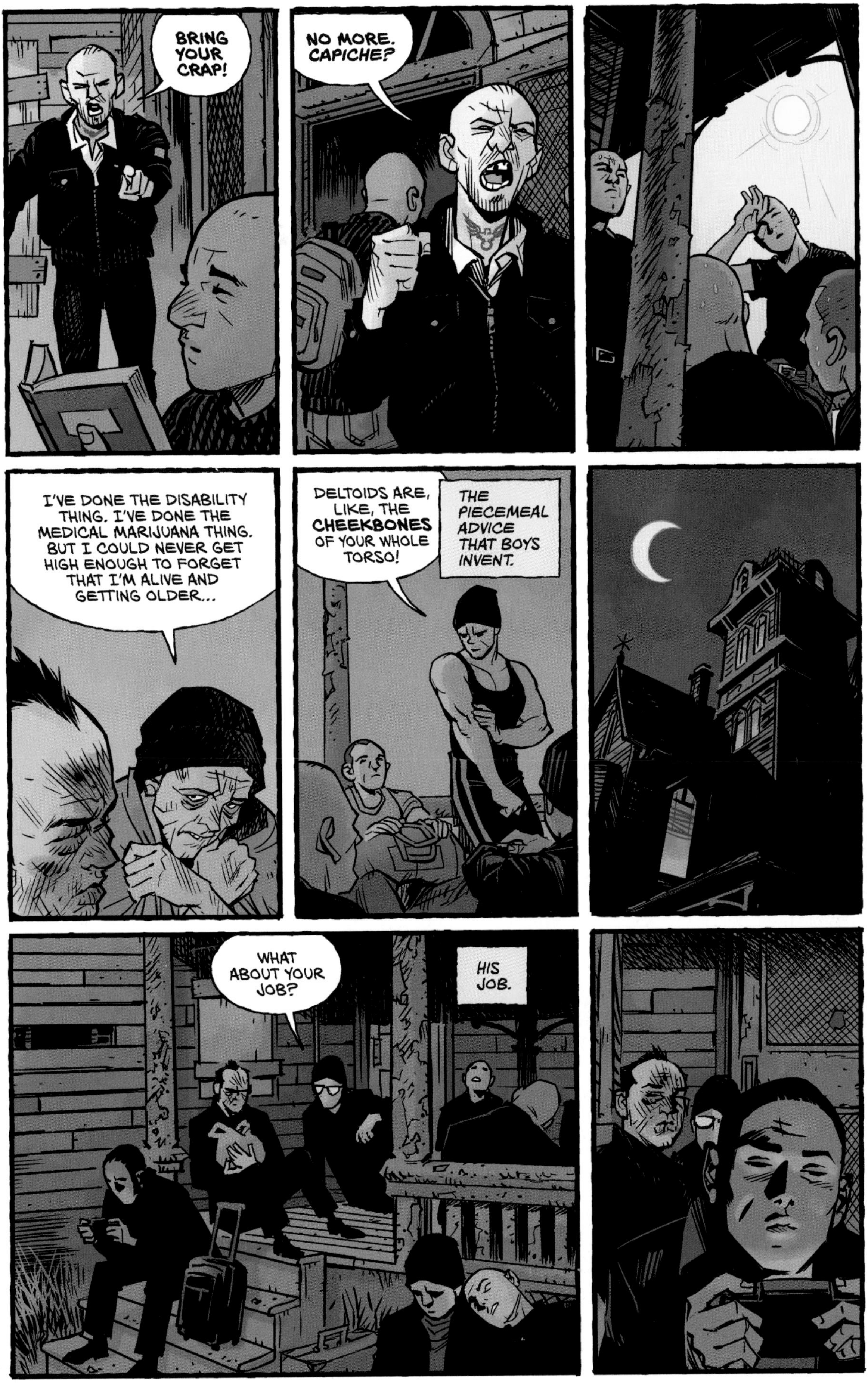
BRING YOUR CRAP!
NO MORE. CAPICHE?
I'VE DONE THE DISABILITY THING. I'VE DONE THE MEDICAL MARIJUANA THING. BUT I COULD NEVER GET HIGH ENOUGH TO FORGET THAT I'M ALIVE AND GETTING OLDER...
DELTOIDS ARE, LIKE, THE CHEEKBONES OF YOUR WHOLE TORSO!
THE PIECEMEAL ADVICE THAT BOYS INVENT.
WHAT ABOUT YOUR JOB?
HIS JOB.

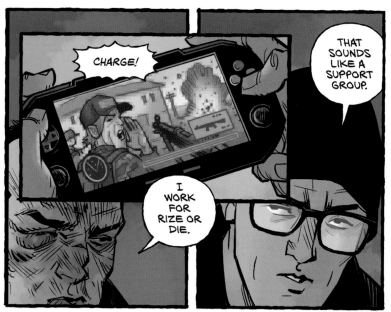

CHARGE!

I WORK FOR RIZE OR DIE.

THAT SOUNDS LIKE A SUPPORT GROUP.

IT IS.

SIR.

SIR.

SIR.

DADDY TYLER IS HOME!

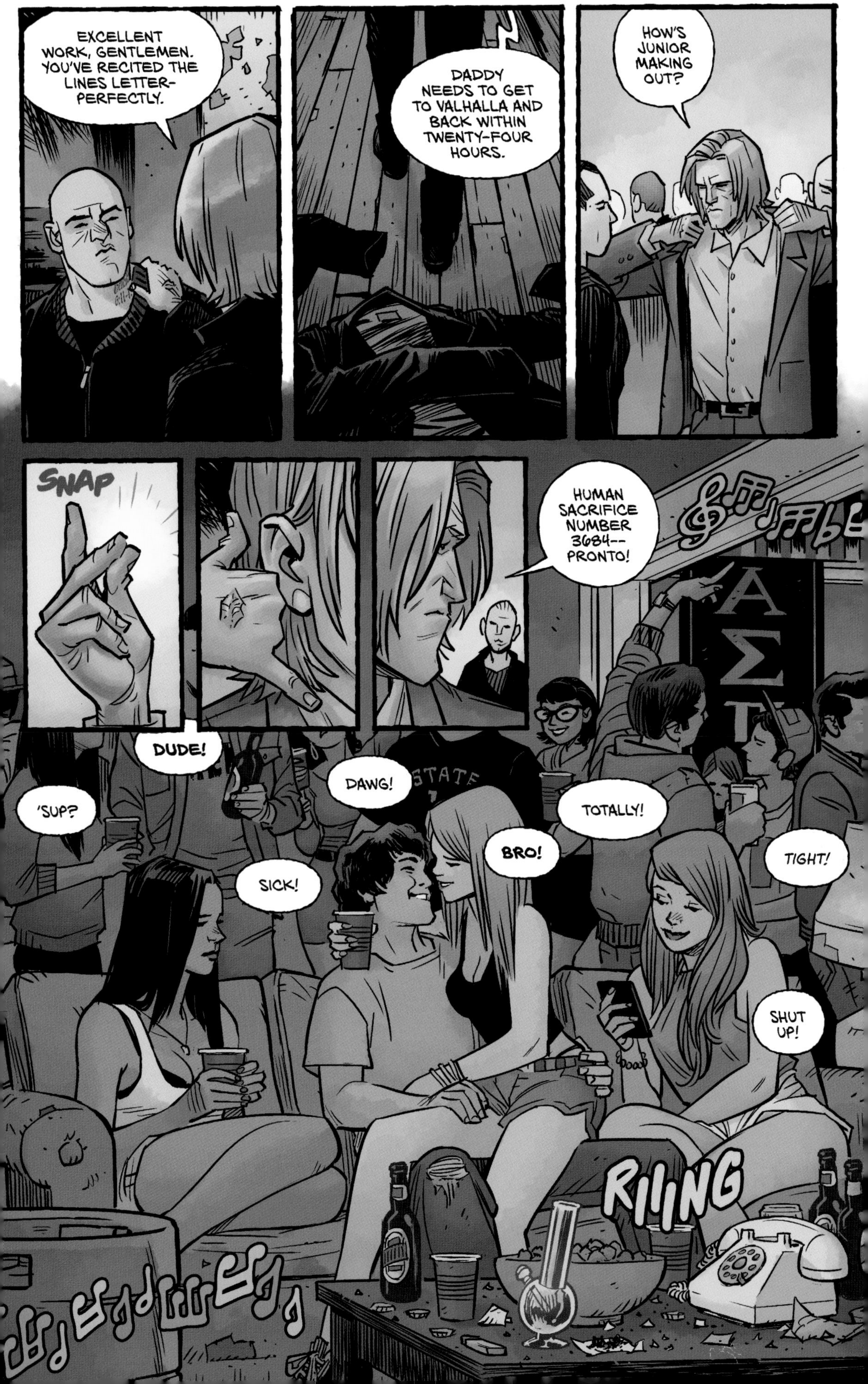
EXCELLENT WORK, GENTLEMEN. YOU'VE RECITED THE LINES LETTER-PERFECTLY.
DADDY NEEDS TO GET TO VALHALLA AND BACK WITHIN TWENTY-FOUR HOURS.
HOW'S JUNIOR MAKING OUT?
SNAP
HUMAN SACRIFICE NUMBER 3684-- PRONTO!
DUDE!
'SUP?
DAWG!
STATE
TOTALLY!
BRO!
SICK!
TIGHT!
SHUT UP!
RIIING

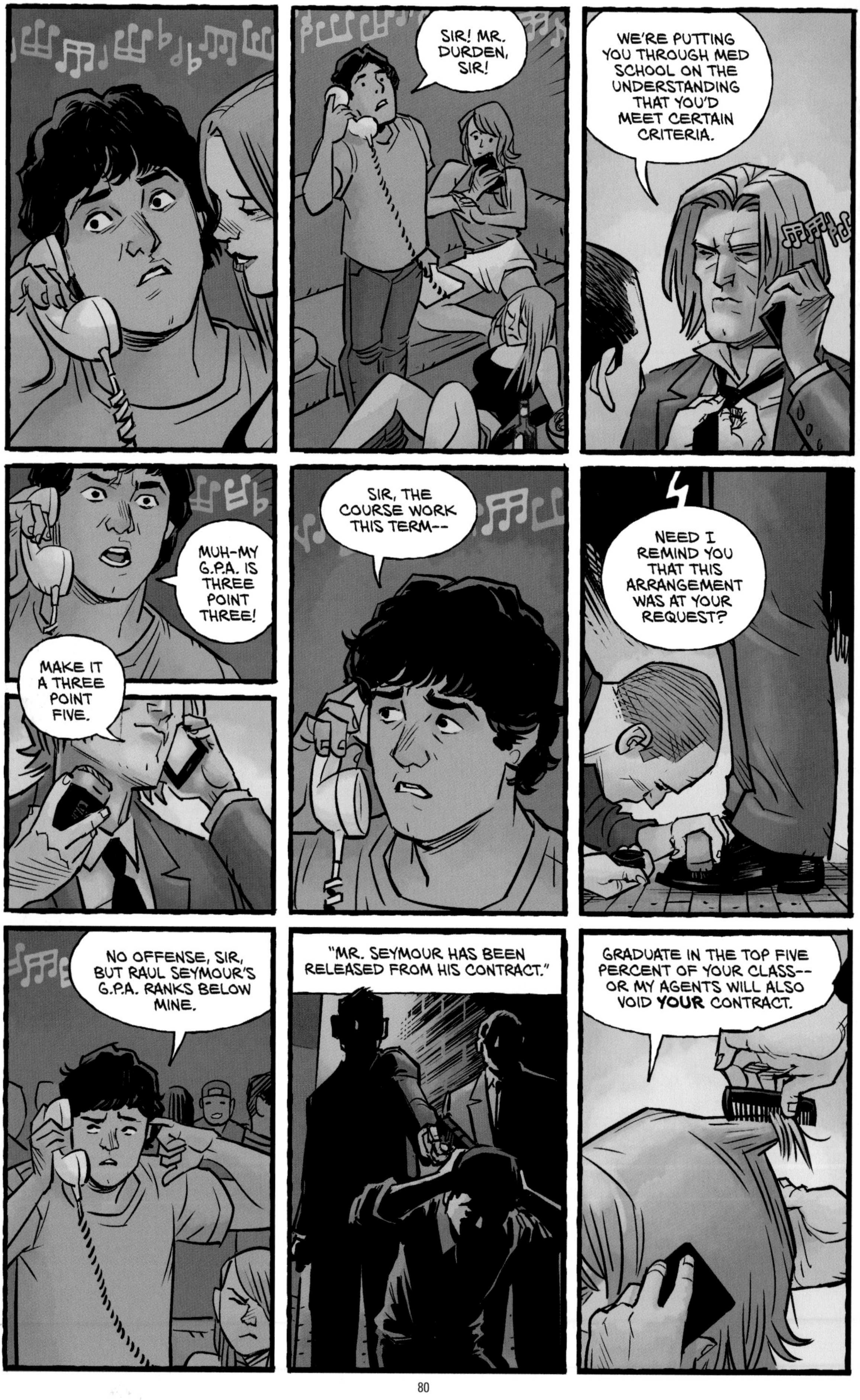
SIR! MR. DURDEN, SIR!
WE'RE PUTTING YOU THROUGH MED SCHOOL ON THE UNDERSTANDING THAT YOU'D MEET CERTAIN CRITERIA.
MUH-MY G.P.A. IS THREE POINT THREE!
MAKE IT A THREE POINT FIVE.
SIR, THE COURSE WORK THIS TERM--
NEED I REMIND YOU THAT THIS ARRANGEMENT WAS AT YOUR REQUEST?
NO OFFENSE, SIR, BUT RAUL SEYMOUR'S G.P.A. RANKS BELOW MINE.
"MR. SEYMOUR HAS BEEN RELEASED FROM HIS CONTRACT."
GRADUATE IN THE TOP FIVE PERCENT OF YOUR CLASS--OR MY AGENTS WILL ALSO VOID **YOUR** CONTRACT.

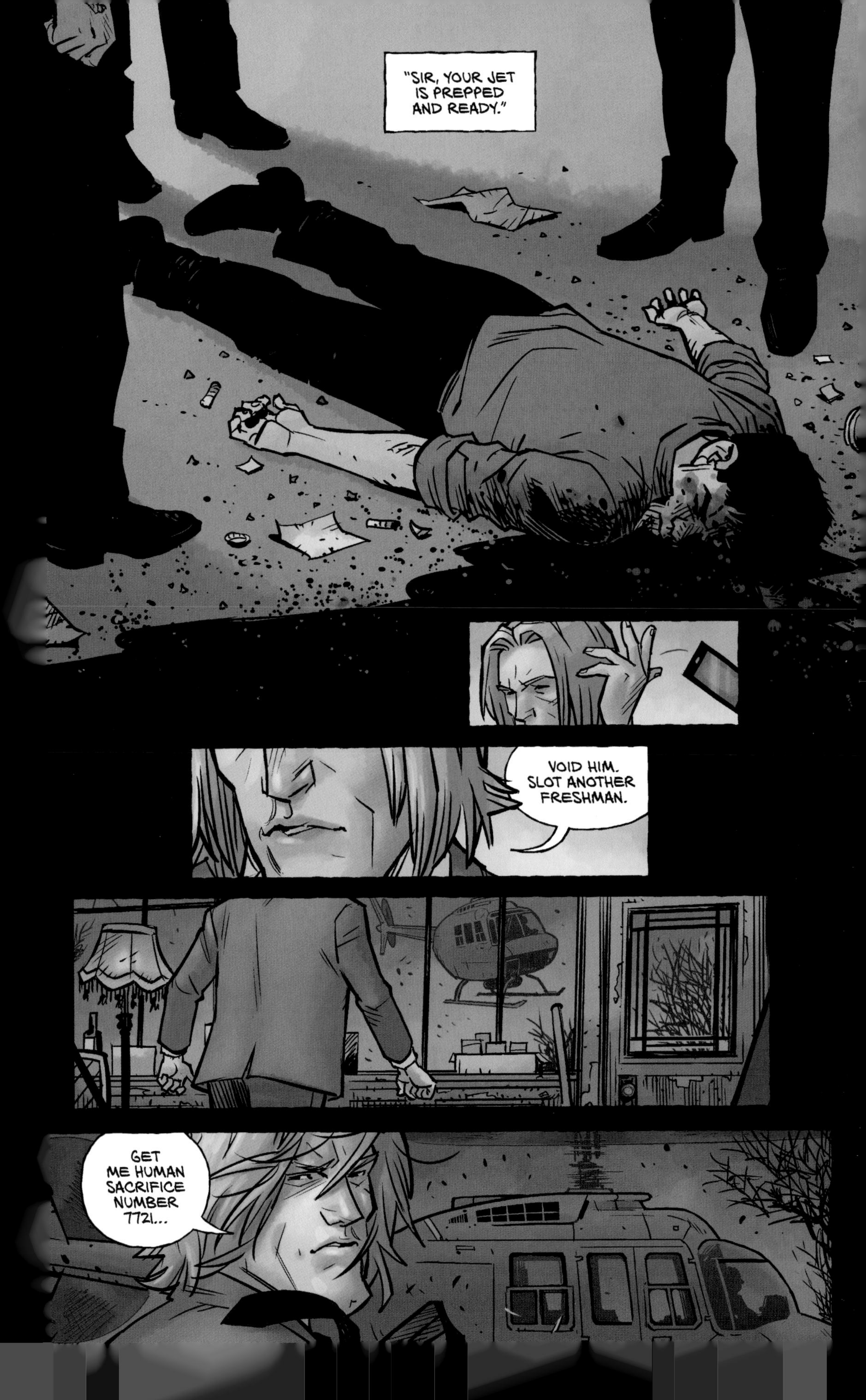
"SIR, YOUR JET IS PREPPED AND READY."
VOID HIM. SLOT ANOTHER FRESHMAN.
GET ME HUMAN SACRIFICE NUMBER 7721...

Chapter Four

Fight Clubs, an Unsentimental Journey

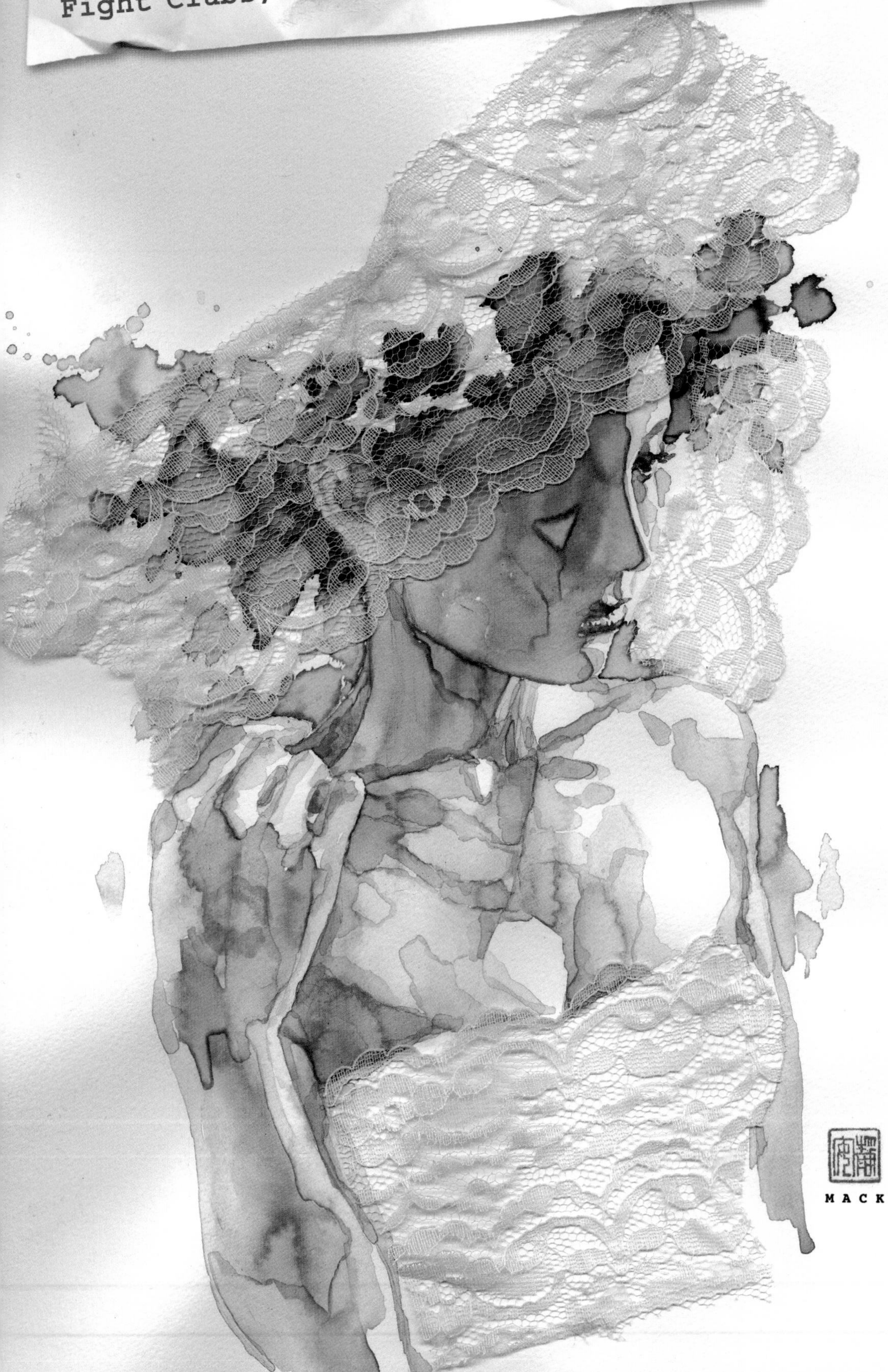
MACK

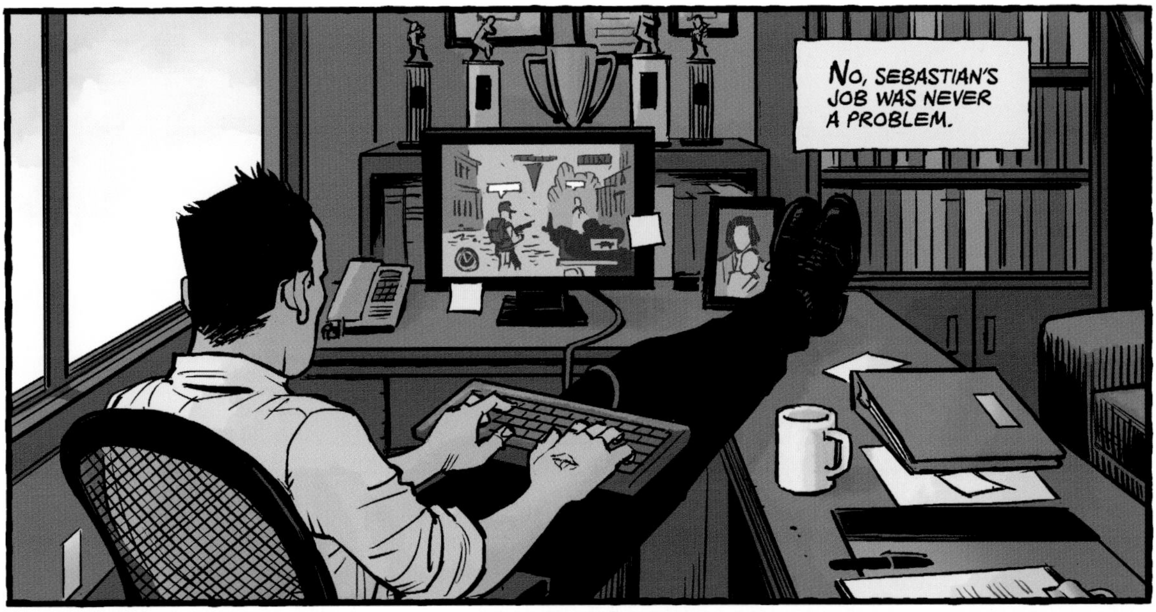
No, Sebastian's job was never a problem.

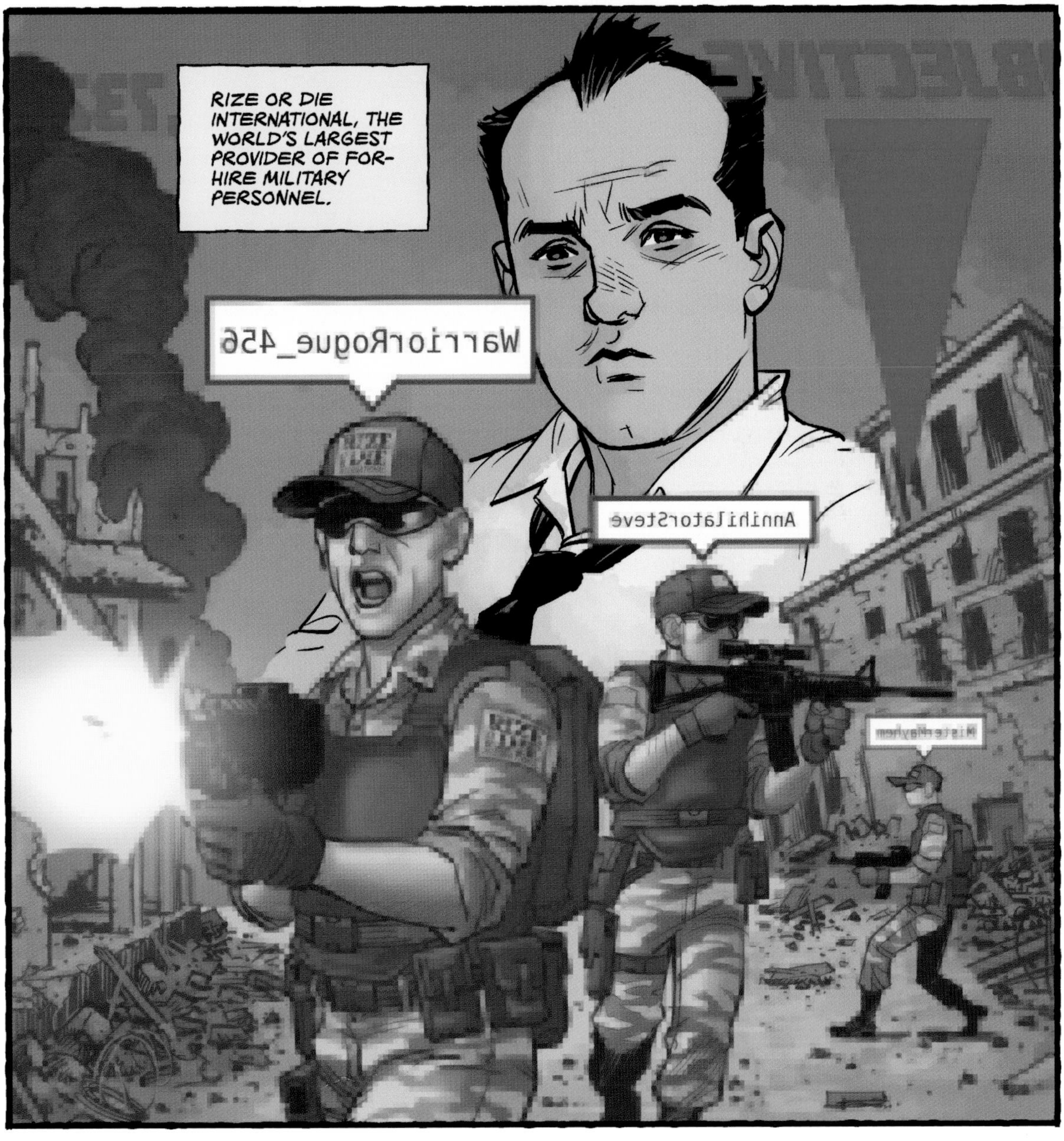
Rize or Die International, the world's largest provider of for-hire military personnel.
WarriorRogue_456
AnnihilatorSteve

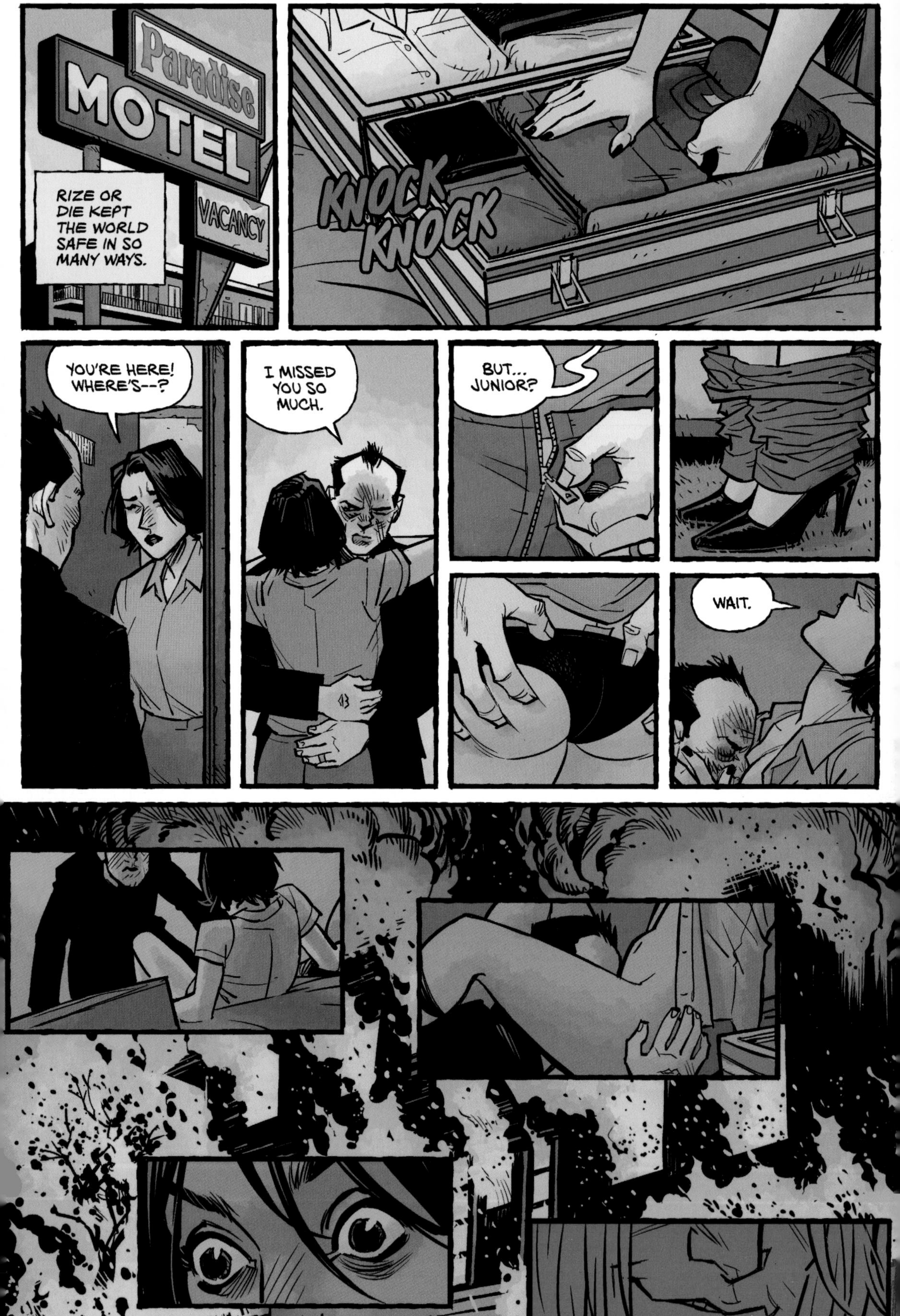
Paradise
MOTEL
VACANCY
RIZE OR DIE KEPT THE WORLD SAFE IN SO MANY WAYS.
KNOCK KNOCK
YOU'RE HERE! WHERE'S--?
I MISSED YOU SO MUCH.
BUT... JUNIOR?
WAIT.

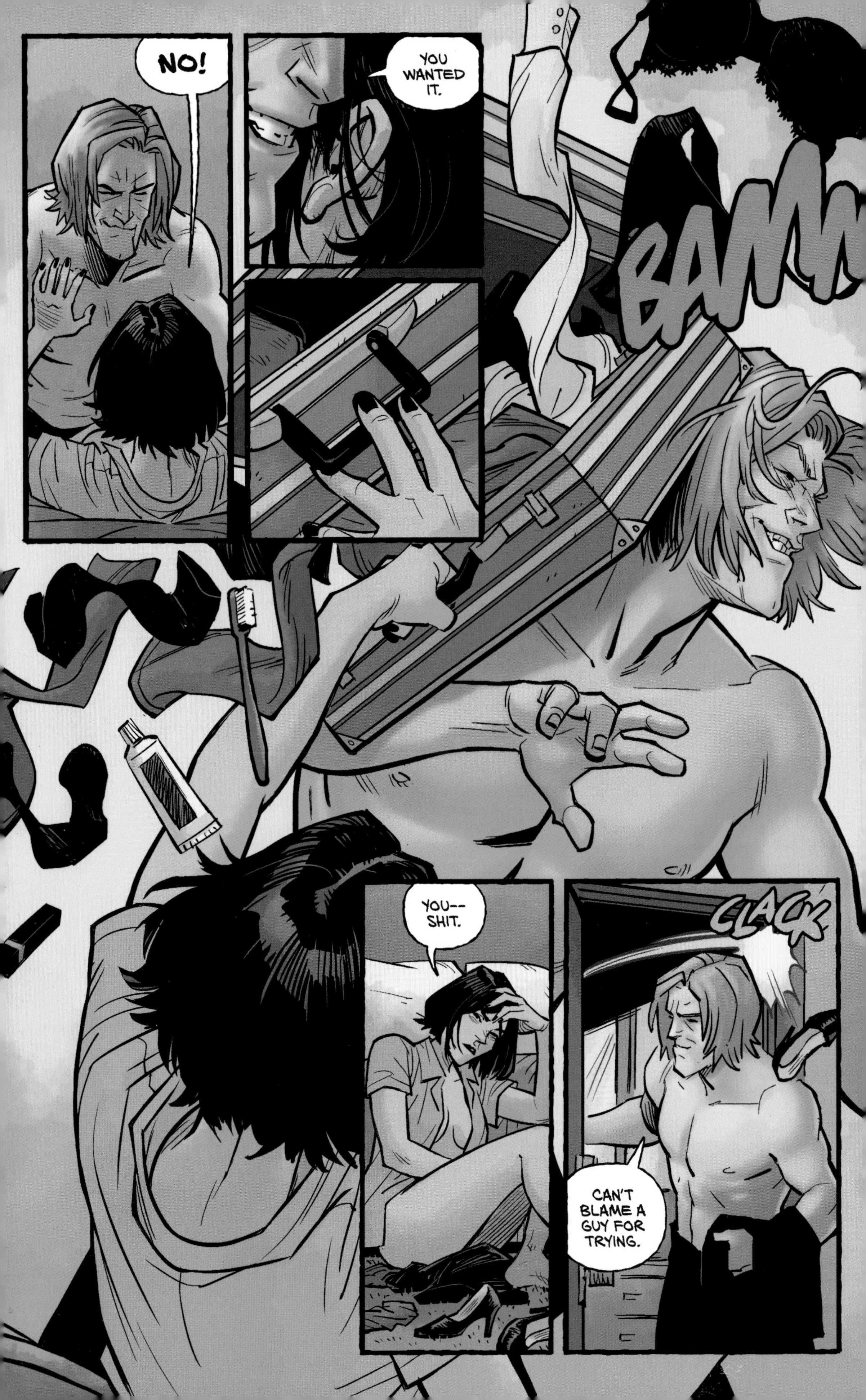
NO!
YOU WANTED IT.
BAMM
YOU-- SHIT.
CLACK
CAN'T BLAME A GUY FOR TRYING.

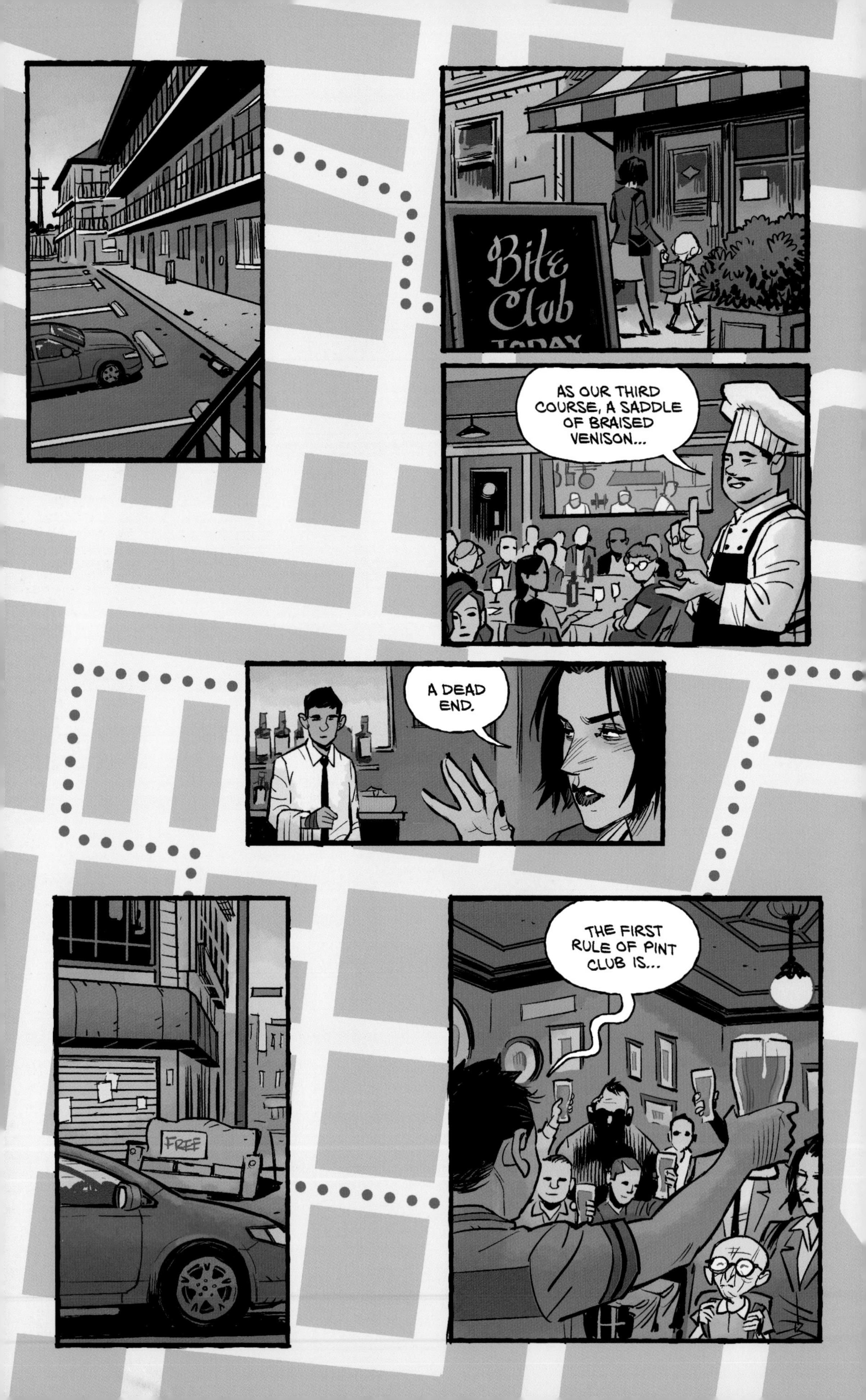
Bite Club
AS OUR THIRD COURSE, A SADDLE OF BRAISED VENISON...
A DEAD END.
FREE
THE FIRST RULE OF PINT CLUB IS...

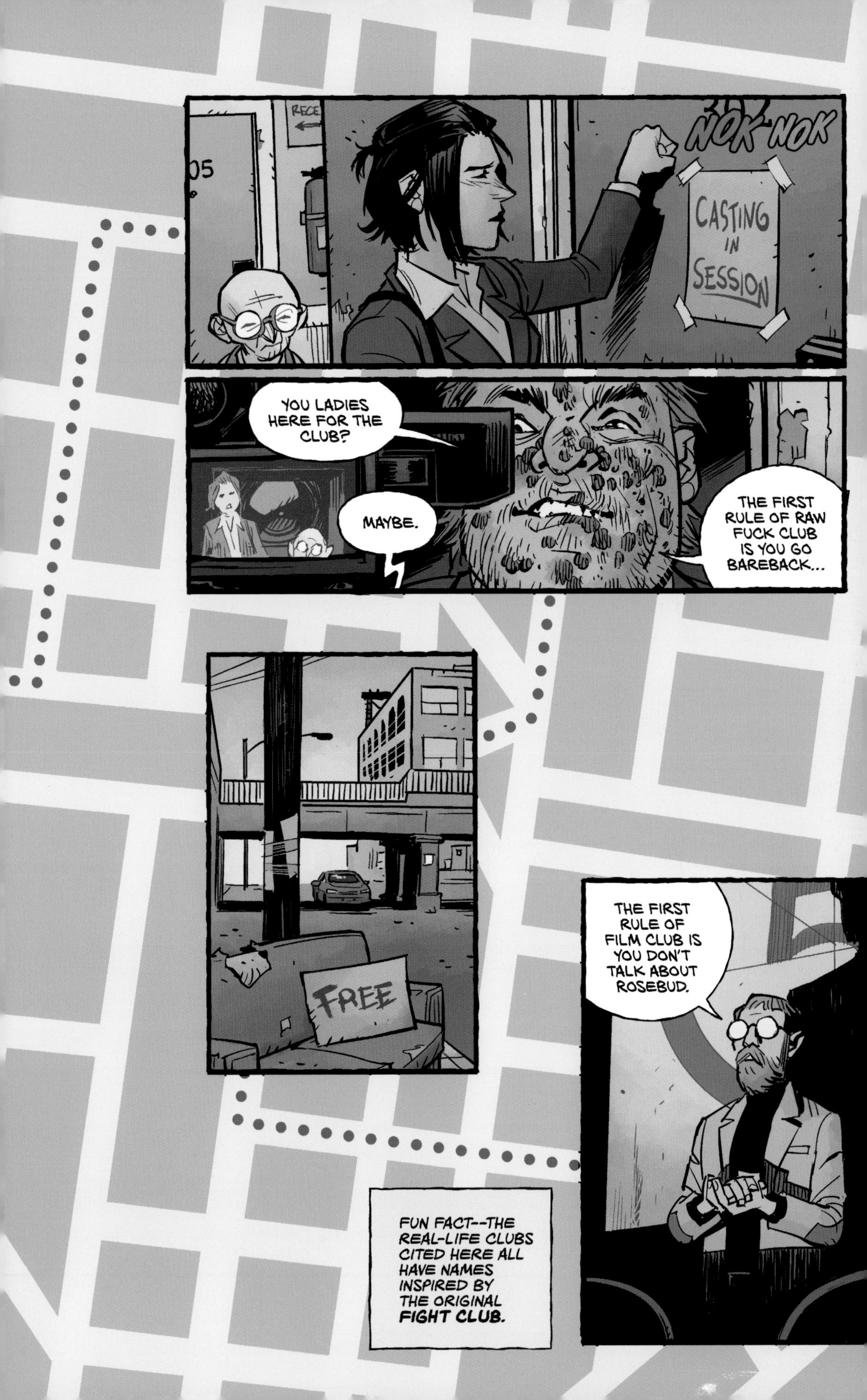
RECE
05
NOK NOK
CASTING IN SESSION
YOU LADIES HERE FOR THE CLUB?
MAYBE.
THE FIRST RULE OF RAW FUCK CLUB IS YOU GO BAREBACK...
FREE
THE FIRST RULE OF FILM CLUB IS YOU DON'T TALK ABOUT ROSEBUD.
FUN FACT--THE REAL-LIFE CLUBS CITED HERE ALL HAVE NAMES INSPIRED BY THE ORIGINAL FIGHT CLUB.

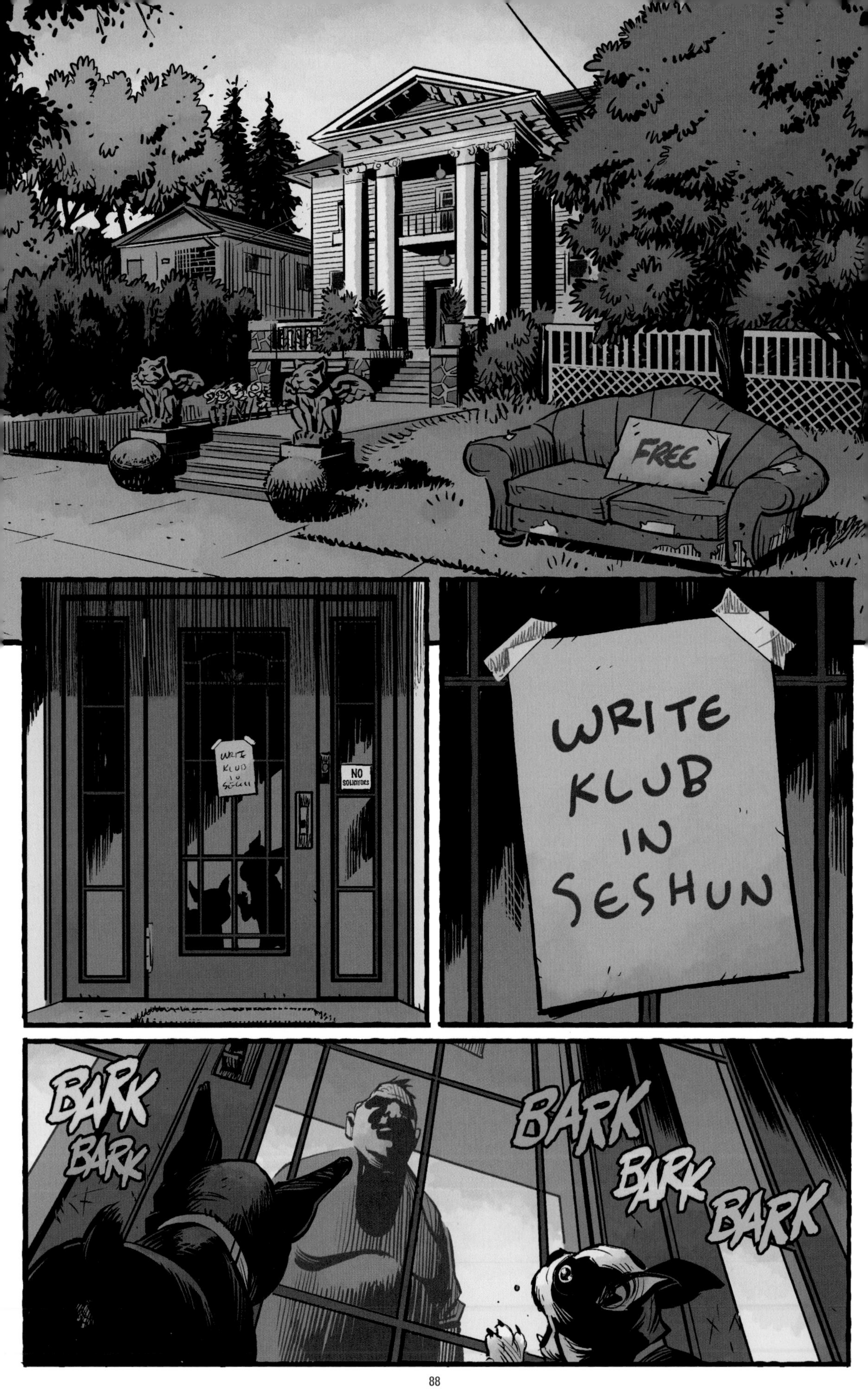
FREE
WRITE KLUB IN SESHUN
NO SOLICITORS
WRITE KLUB IN SESHUN
BARK
BARK
BARK
BARK
BARK

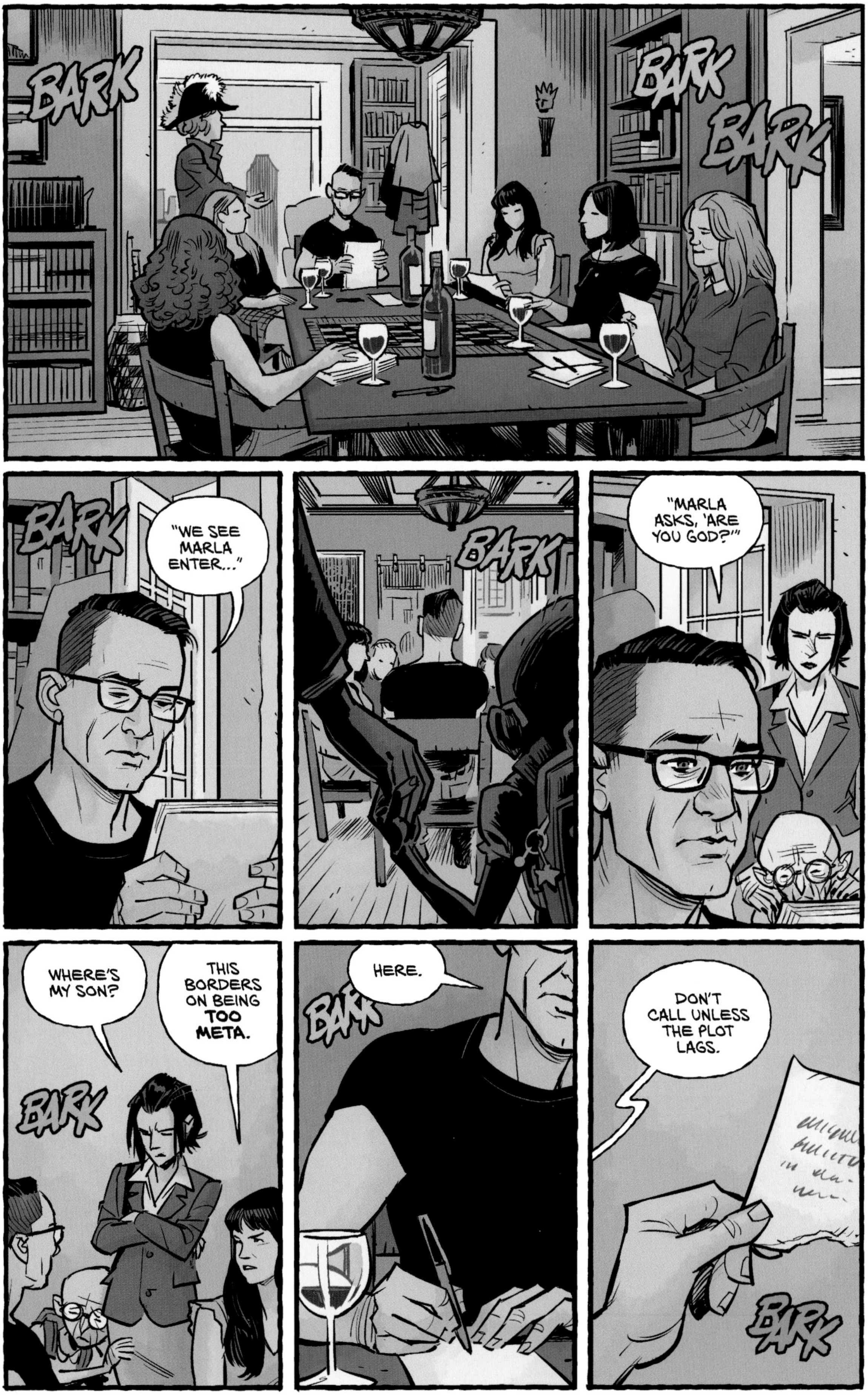
BARK
BARK
BARK
BARK
"WE SEE MARLA ENTER..."
BARK
"MARLA ASKS, 'ARE YOU GOD?'"
WHERE'S MY SON?
THIS BORDERS ON BEING TOO META.
BARK
HERE.
BARK
DON'T CALL UNLESS THE PLOT LAGS.
BARK

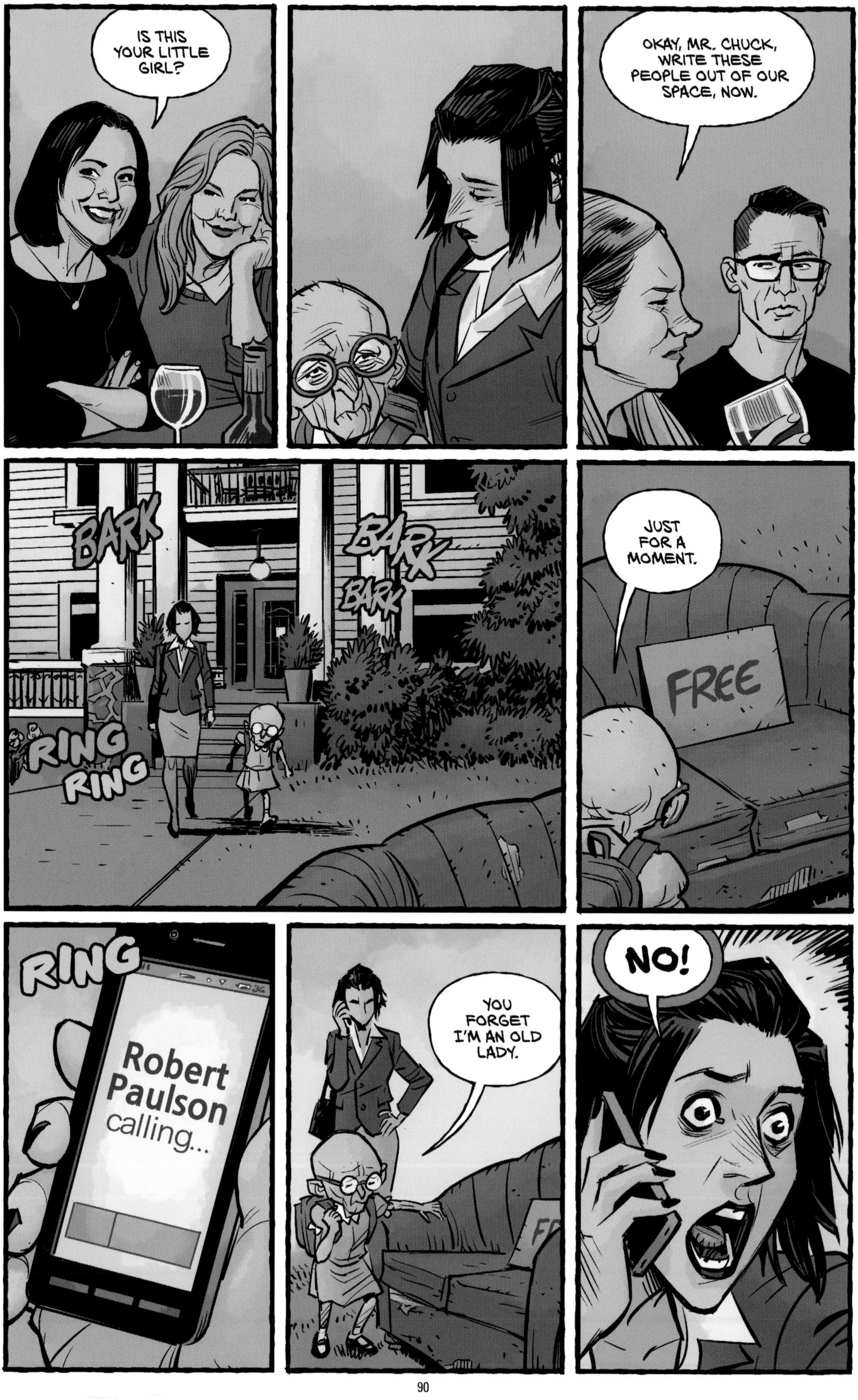
IS THIS YOUR LITTLE GIRL?
OKAY, MR. CHUCK, WRITE THESE PEOPLE OUT OF OUR SPACE, NOW.
BARK
BARK
BARK
RING
RING
JUST FOR A MOMENT.
FREE
RING
Robert Paulson calling...
YOU FORGET I'M AN OLD LADY.
NO!

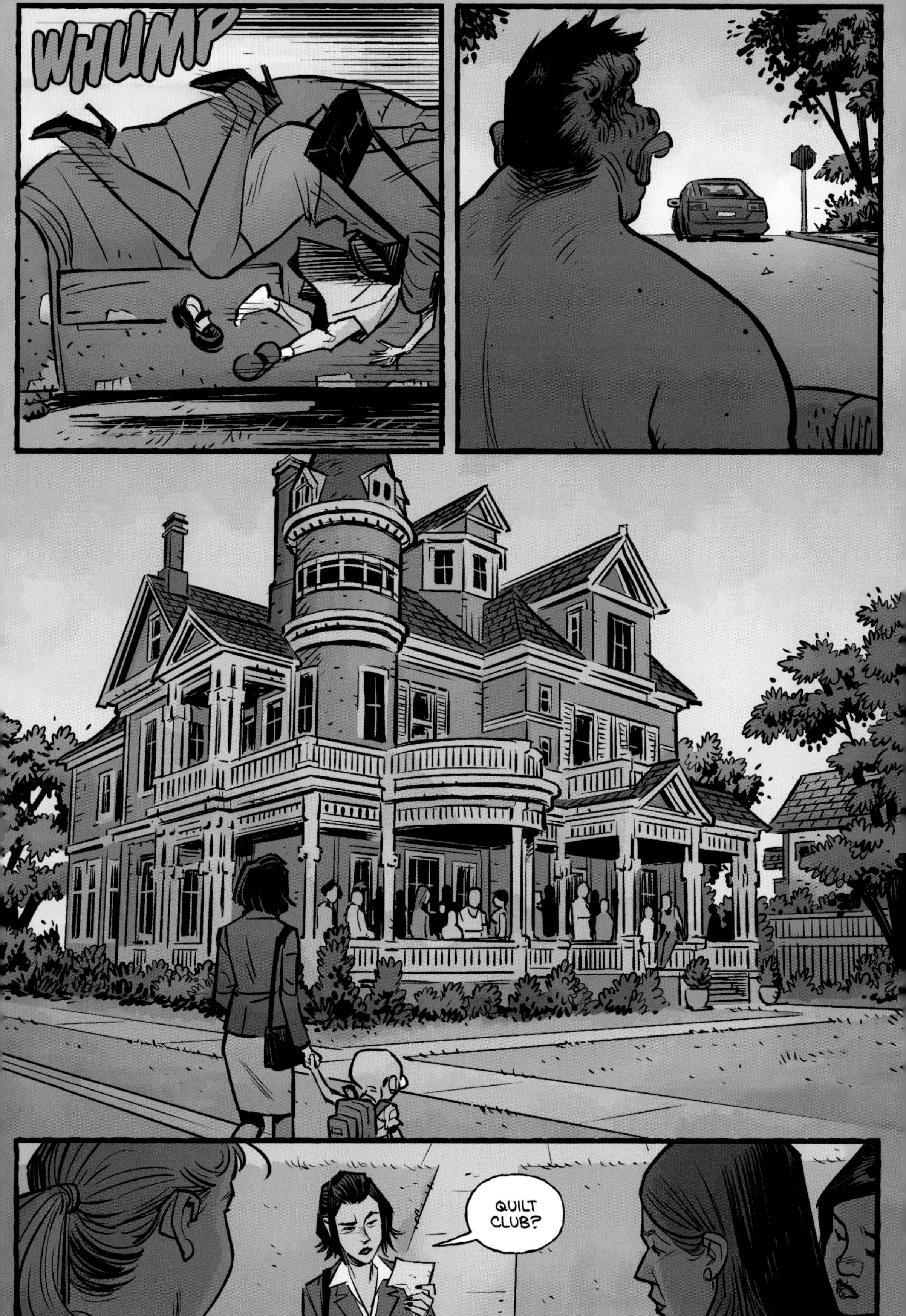
WHUMP
QUILT CLUB?

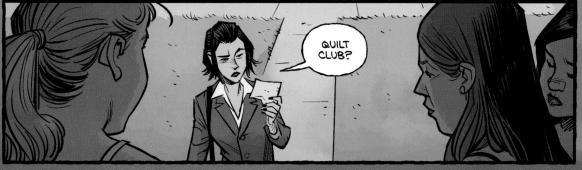

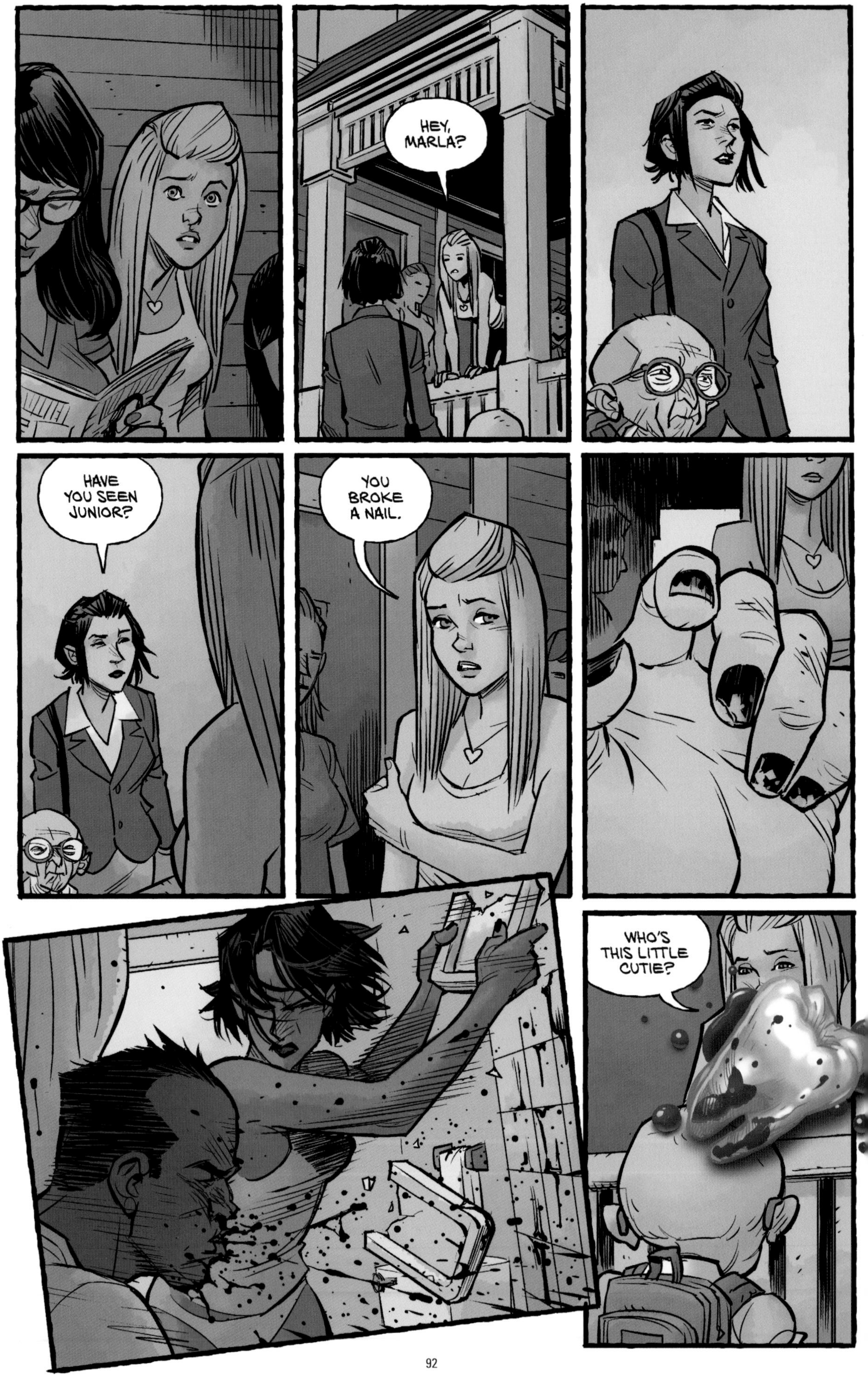
HEY, MARLA?
HAVE YOU SEEN JUNIOR?
YOU BROKE A NAIL.
WHO'S THIS LITTLE CUTIE?

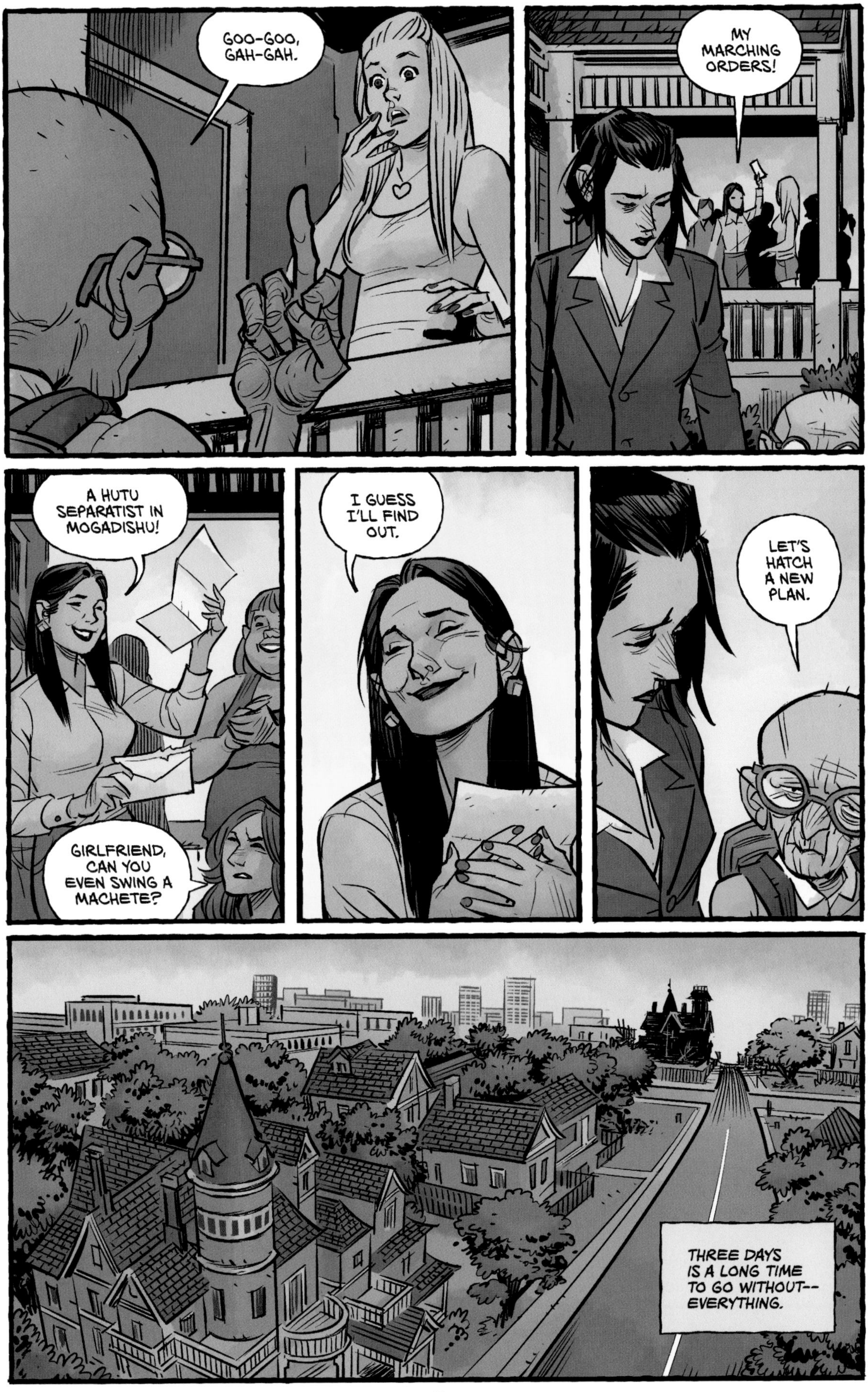
GOO-GOO, GAH-GAH.
MY MARCHING ORDERS!
A HUTU SEPARATIST IN MOGADISHU!
GIRLFRIEND, CAN YOU EVEN SWING A MACHETE?
I GUESS I'LL FIND OUT.
LET'S HATCH A NEW PLAN.
THREE DAYS IS A LONG TIME TO GO WITHOUT-- EVERYTHING.

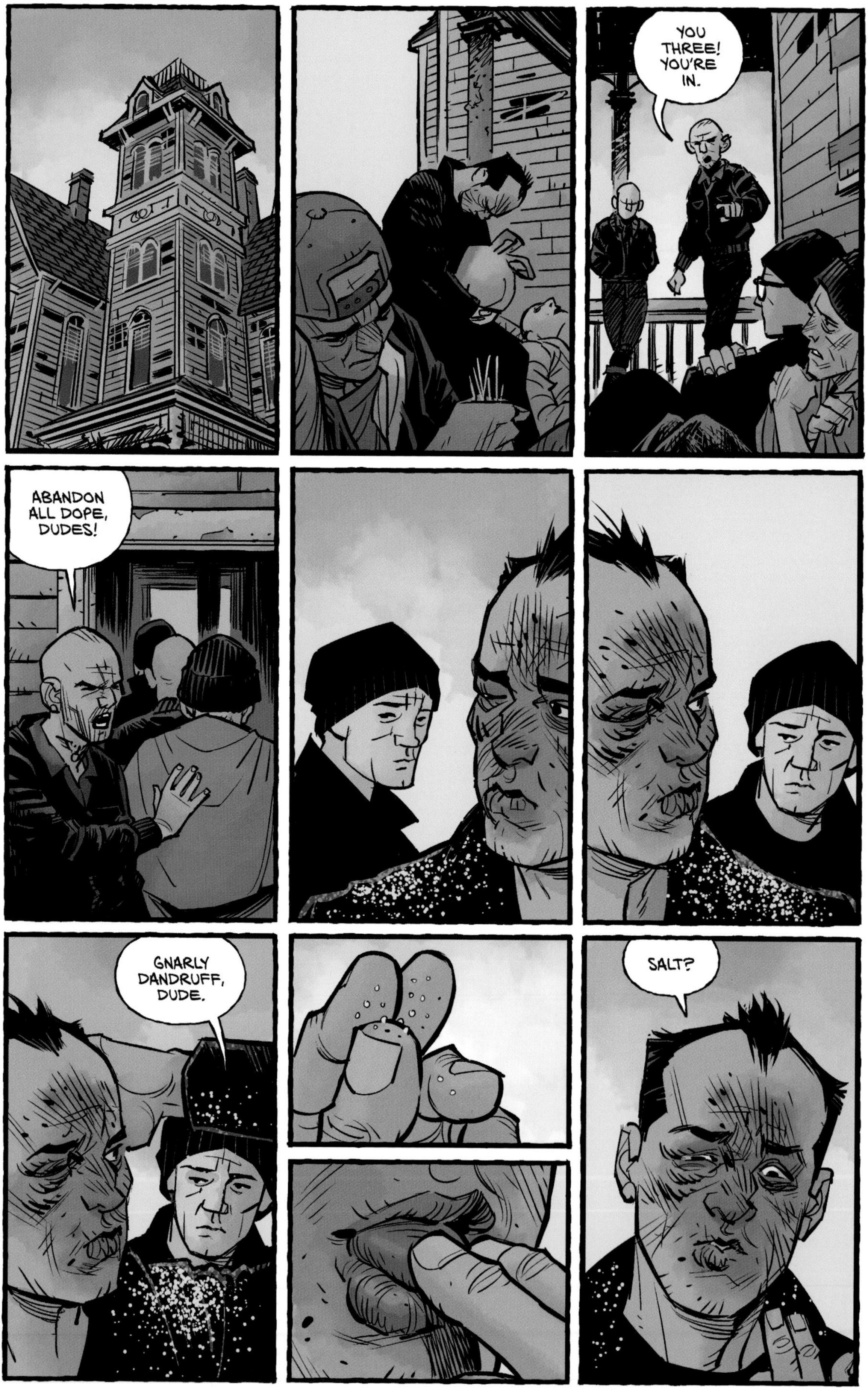
YOU THREE! YOU'RE IN.
ABANDON ALL DOPE, DUDES!
GNARLY DANDRUFF, DUDE.
SALT?

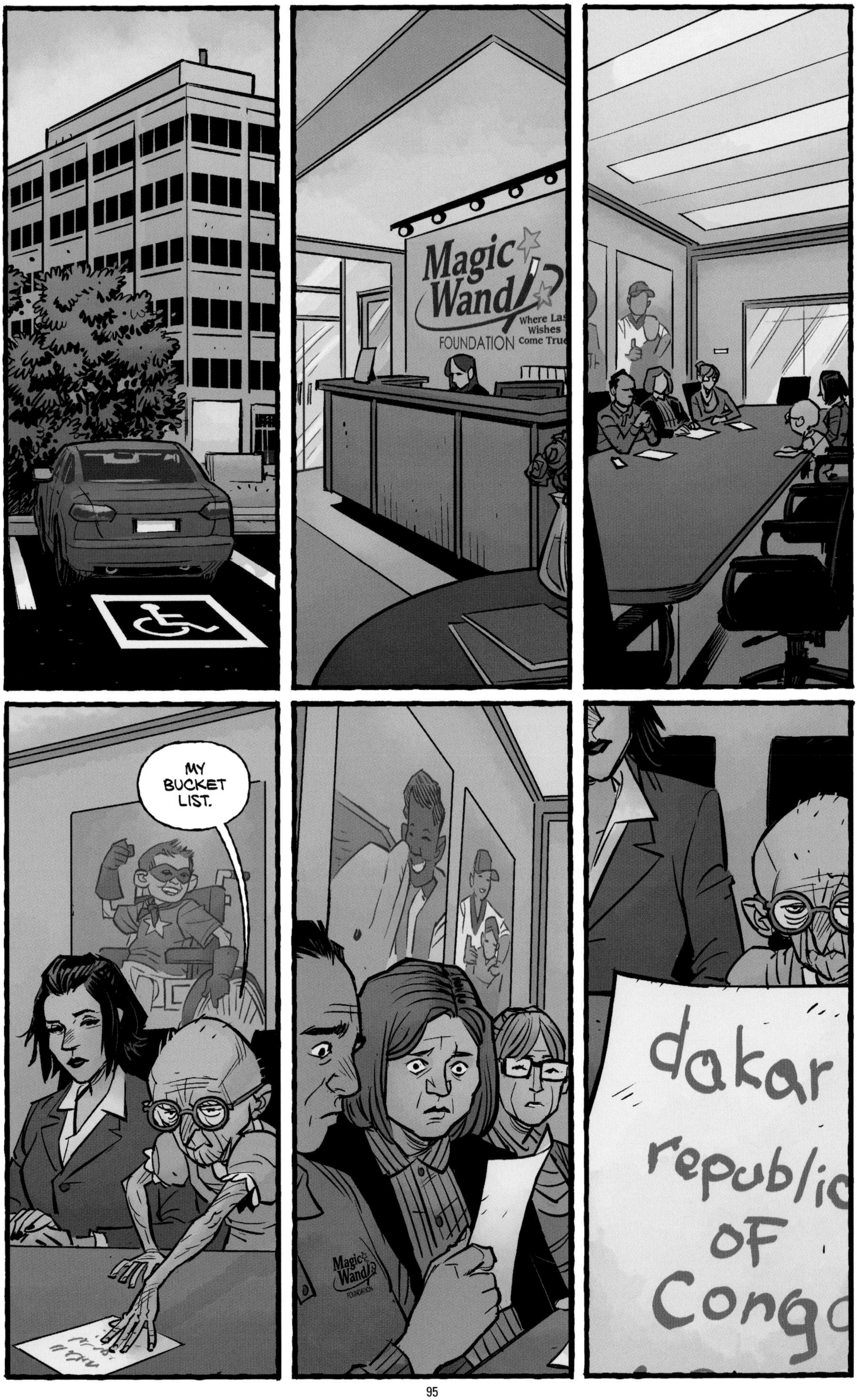
Magic Wand
FOUNDATION
Where Las
Wishes
Come Tru
MY BUCKET LIST.
dakar
republi
OF
Cong

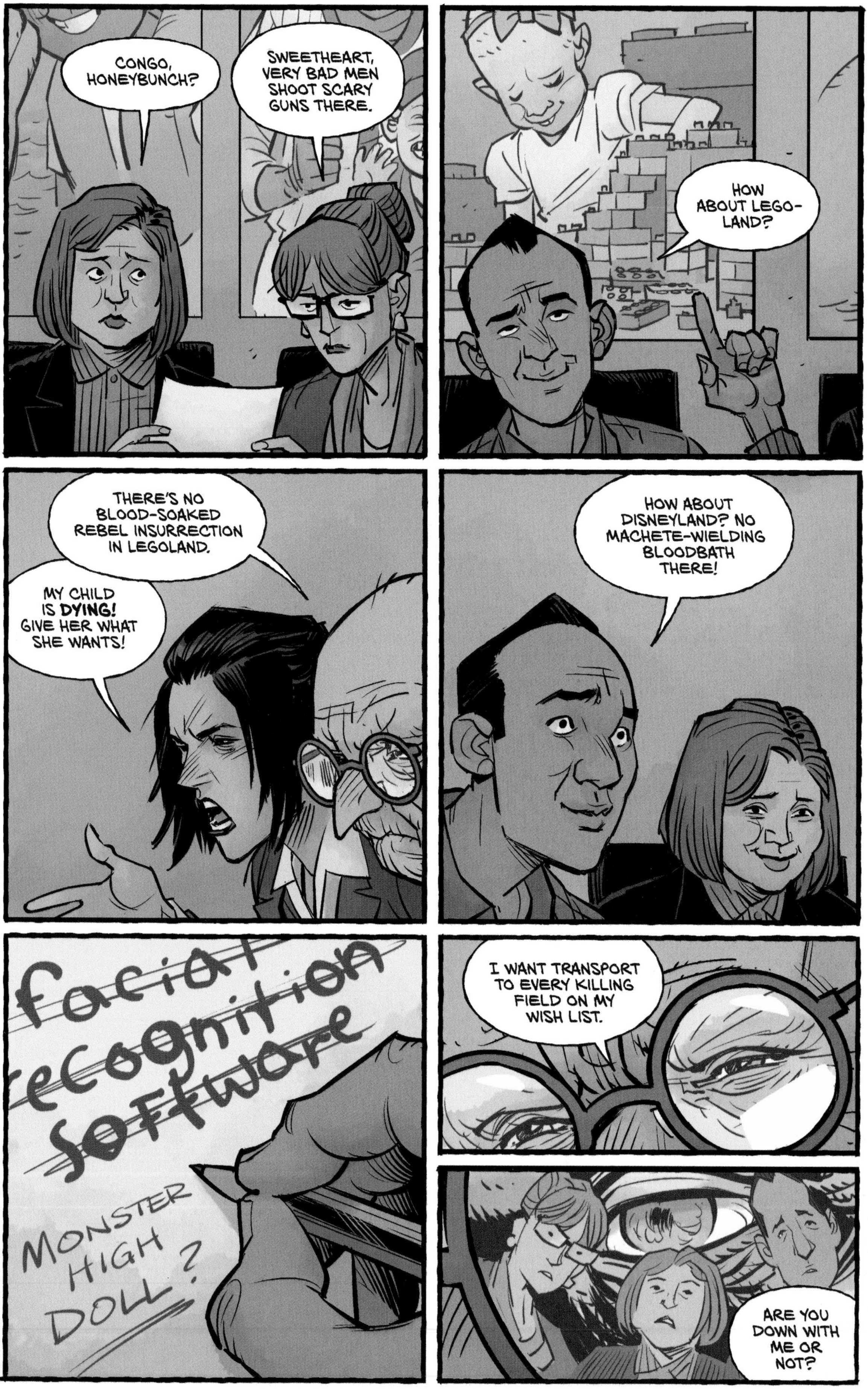
CONGO, HONEYBUNCH?
SWEETHEART, VERY BAD MEN SHOOT SCARY GUNS THERE.
HOW ABOUT LEGO-LAND?
THERE'S NO BLOOD-SOAKED REBEL INSURRECTION IN LEGOLAND.
MY CHILD IS **DYING!** GIVE HER WHAT SHE WANTS!
HOW ABOUT DISNEYLAND? NO MACHETE-WIELDING BLOODBATH THERE!
facial recognition software
MONSTER HIGH DOLL?
I WANT TRANSPORT TO EVERY KILLING FIELD ON MY WISH LIST.
ARE YOU DOWN WITH ME OR NOT?

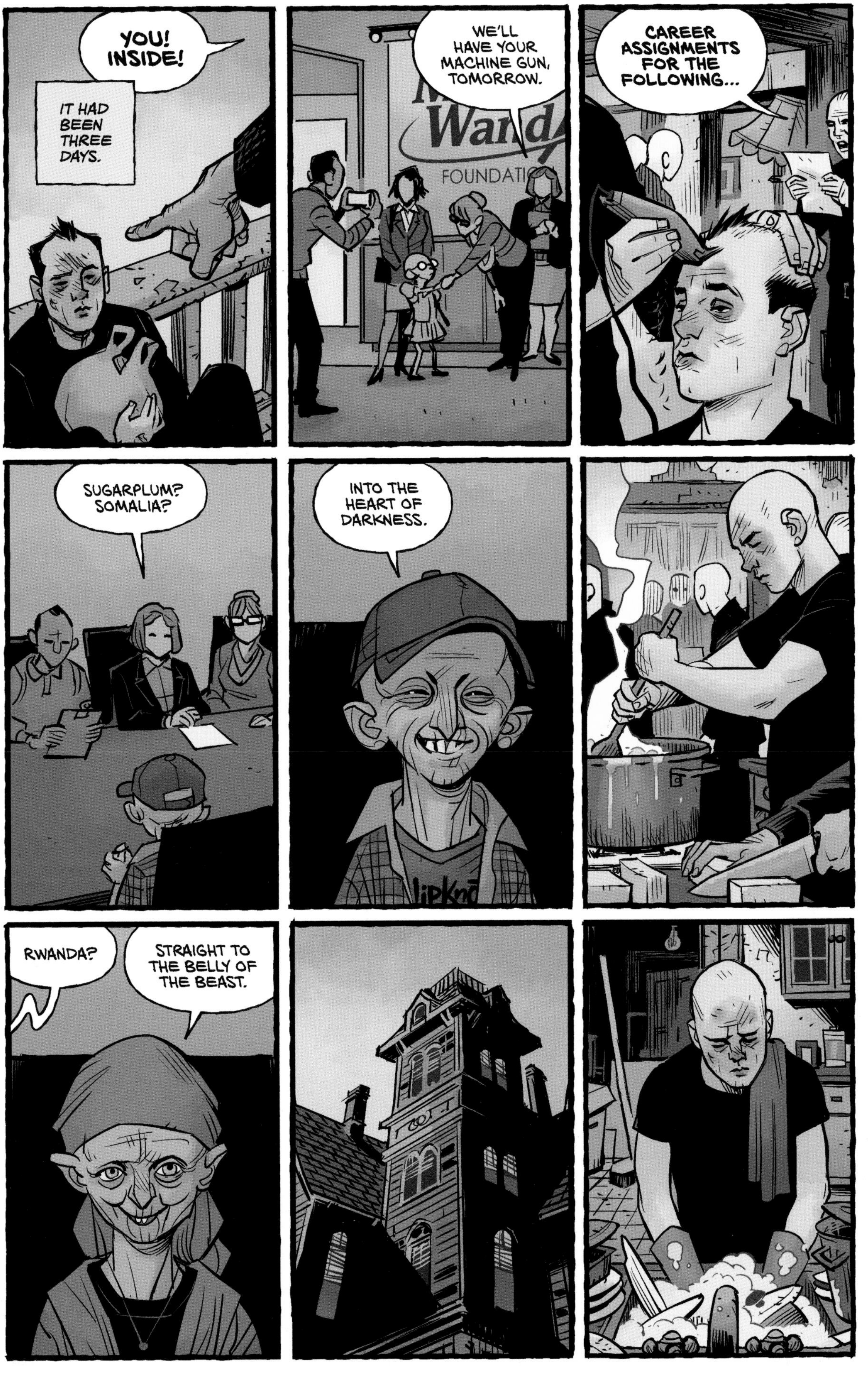
YOU! INSIDE!
IT HAD BEEN THREE DAYS.
WE'LL HAVE YOUR MACHINE GUN, TOMORROW.
FOUNDATI
CAREER ASSIGNMENTS FOR THE FOLLOWING...
SUGARPLUM? SOMALIA?
INTO THE HEART OF DARKNESS.
RWANDA?
STRAIGHT TO THE BELLY OF THE BEAST.

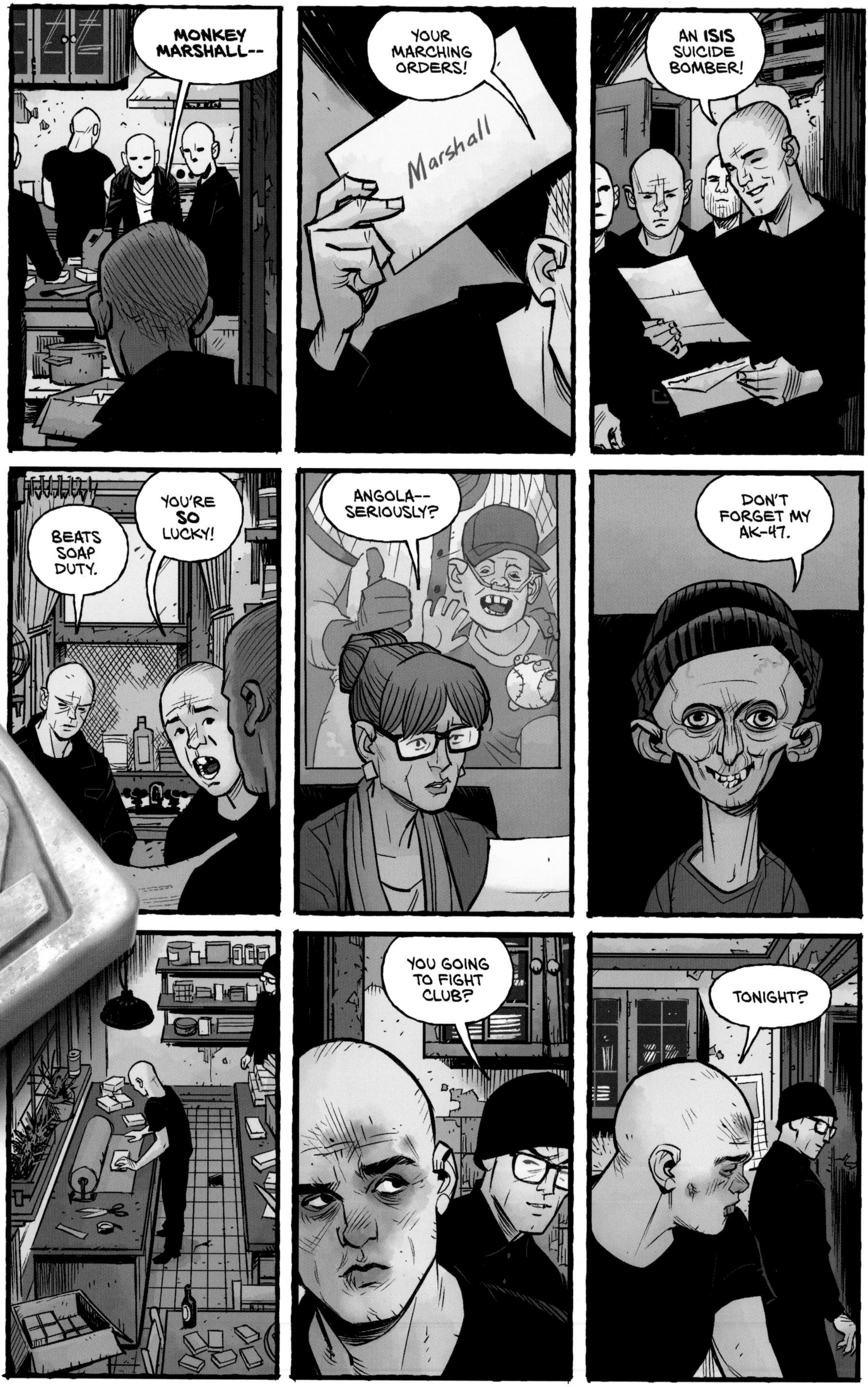

MONKEY MARSHALL--
YOUR MARCHING ORDERS!
Marshall
AN ISIS SUICIDE BOMBER!
YOU'RE SO LUCKY!
BEATS SOAP DUTY.
ANGOLA-- SERIOUSLY?
DON'T FORGET MY AK-47.
YOU GOING TO FIGHT CLUB?
TONIGHT?

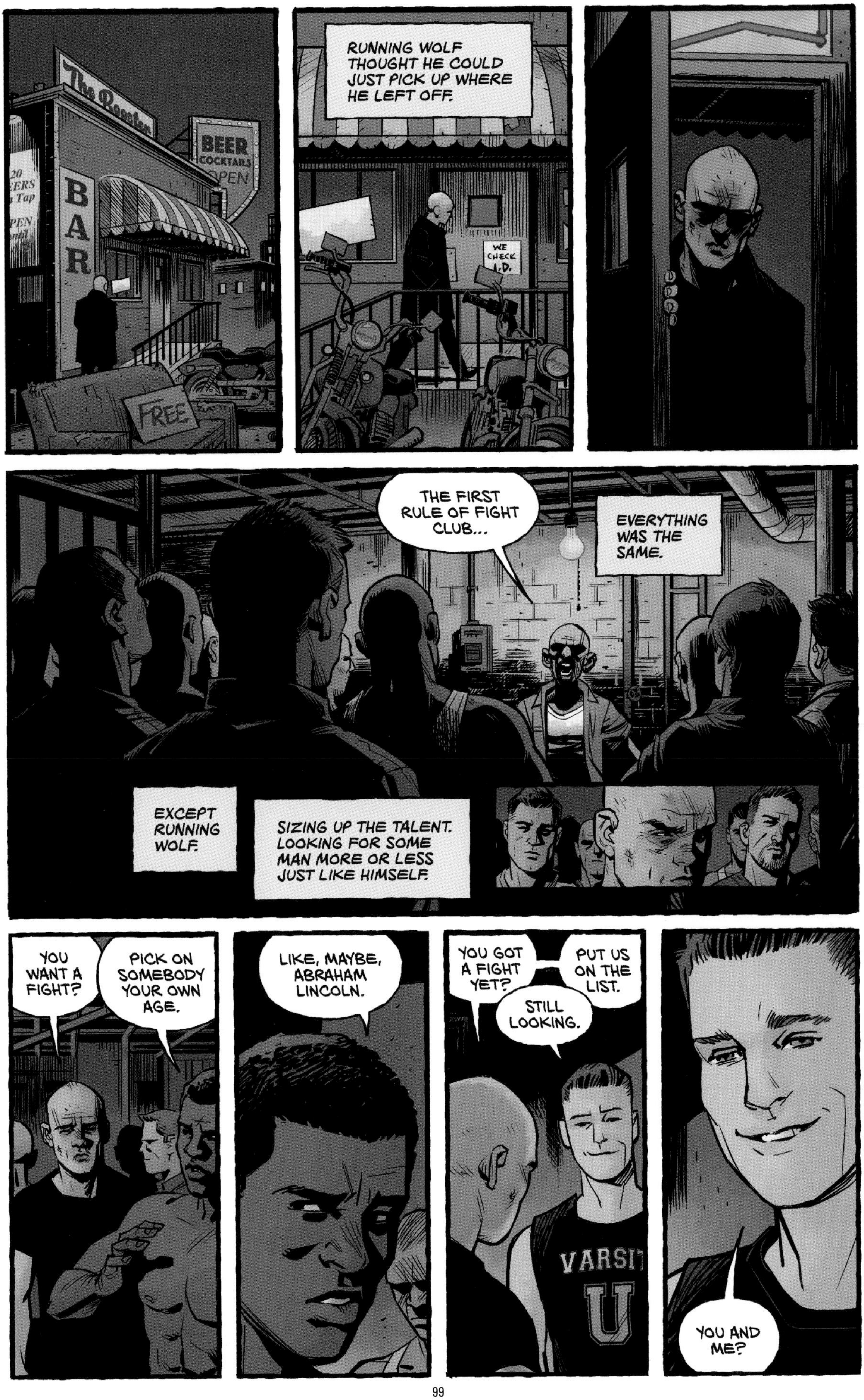

The Rooster
BEER
COCKTAILS
OPEN
BAR
FREE
RUNNING WOLF THOUGHT HE COULD JUST PICK UP WHERE HE LEFT OFF.
WE CHECK I.D.
THE FIRST RULE OF FIGHT CLUB...
EVERYTHING WAS THE SAME.
EXCEPT RUNNING WOLF.
SIZING UP THE TALENT. LOOKING FOR SOME MAN MORE OR LESS JUST LIKE HIMSELF.
YOU WANT A FIGHT?
PICK ON SOMEBODY YOUR OWN AGE.
LIKE, MAYBE, ABRAHAM LINCOLN.
YOU GOT A FIGHT YET?
PUT US ON THE LIST.
STILL LOOKING.
VARSIT
U
YOU AND ME?

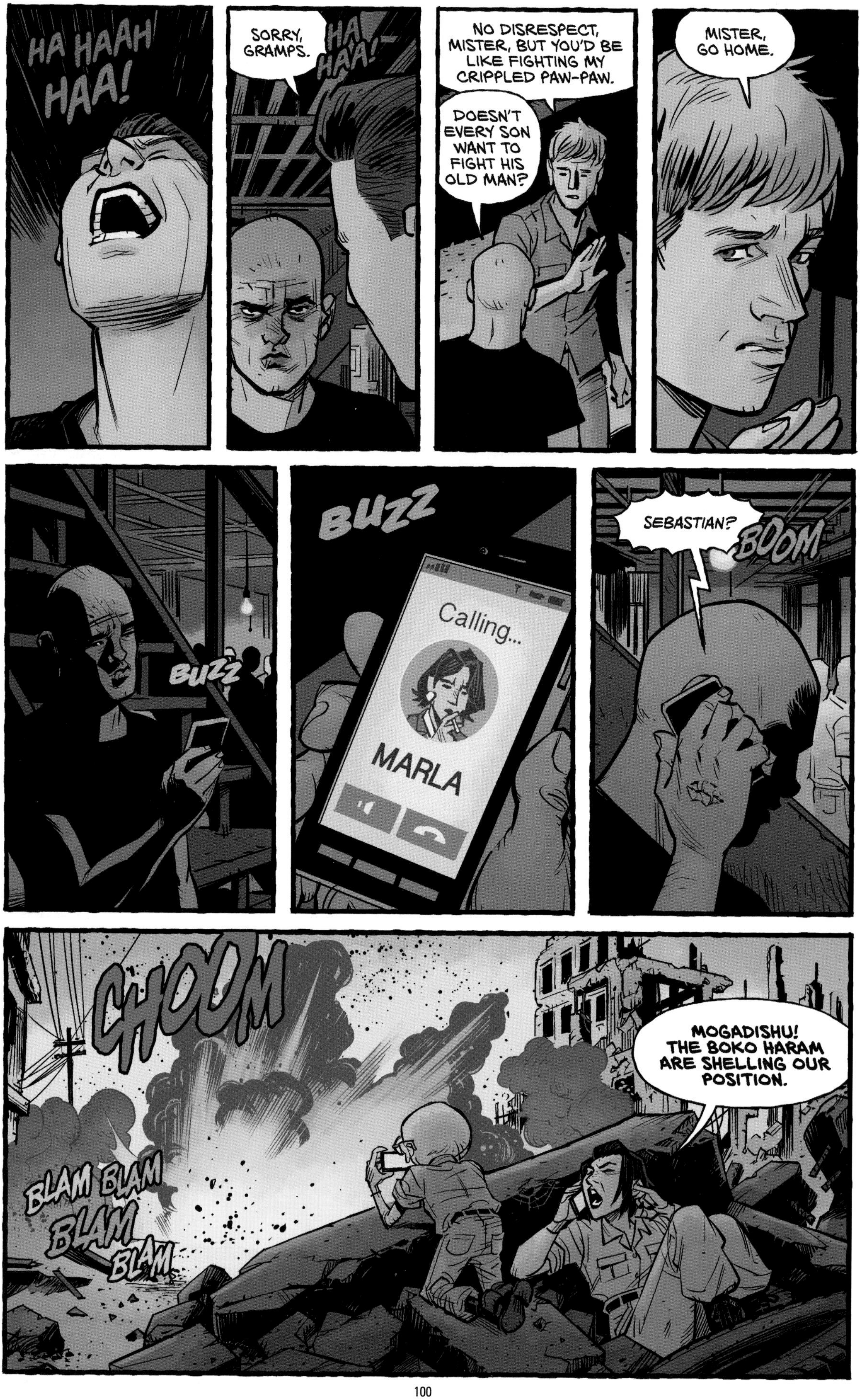
HA HAAH HAA!
SORRY, GRAMPS.
HA HA'A!
NO DISRESPECT, MISTER, BUT YOU'D BE LIKE FIGHTING MY CRIPPLED PAW-PAW.
DOESN'T EVERY SON WANT TO FIGHT HIS OLD MAN?
MISTER, GO HOME.
BUZZ
BUZZ
Calling...
MARLA
SEBASTIAN?
BOOM
CHOOM
MOGADISHU! THE BOKO HARAM ARE SHELLING OUR POSITION.
BLAM BLAM BLAM BLAM

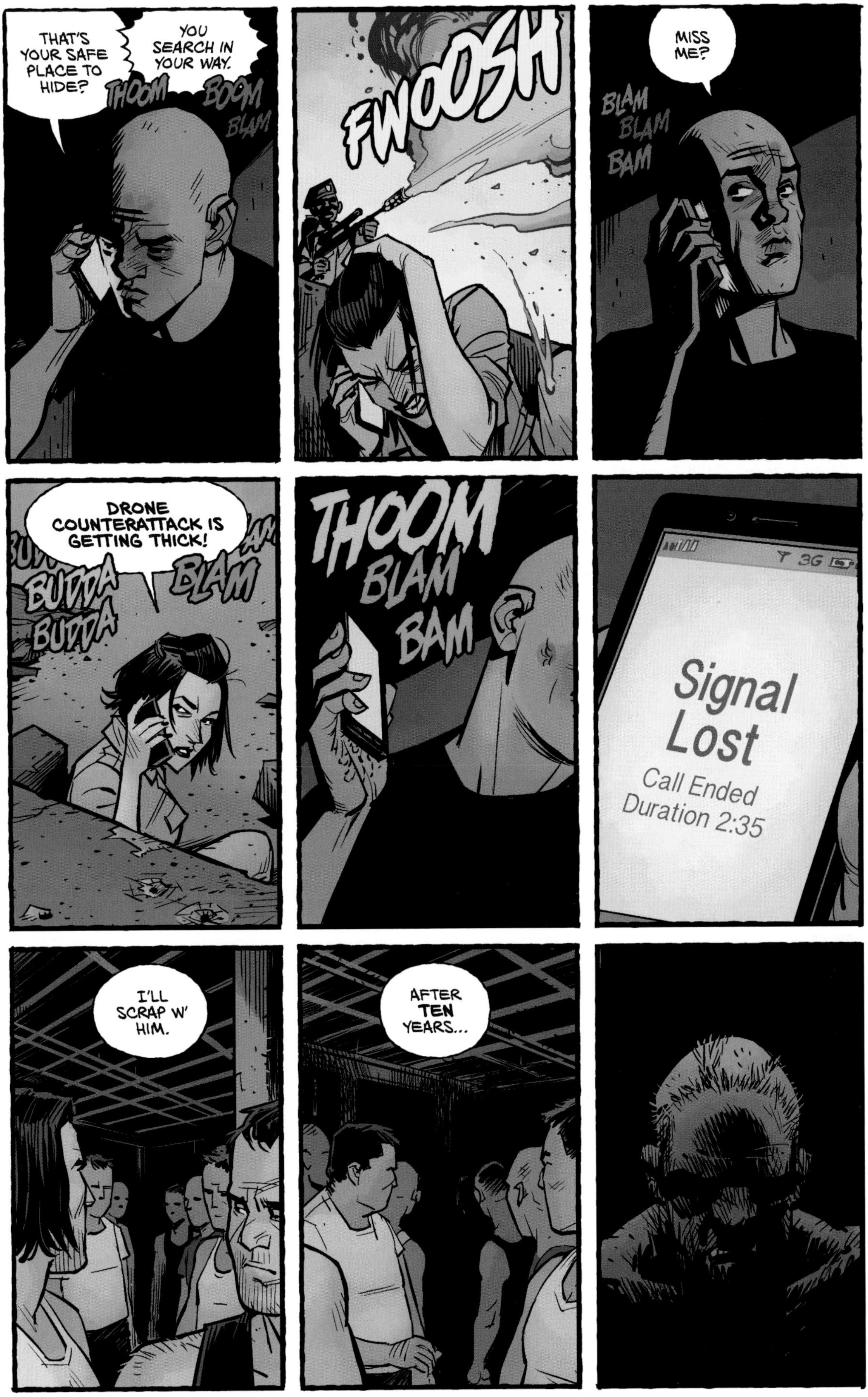
THAT'S YOUR SAFE PLACE TO HIDE?
YOU SEARCH IN YOUR WAY.
THOOM
BOOM
BLAM
FWOOSH
MISS ME?
BLAM BLAM BAM
DRONE COUNTERATTACK IS GETTING THICK!
BUDDA BUDDA
BLAM
THOOM
BLAM
BAM
3G
Signal Lost
Call Ended
Duration 2:35
I'LL SCRAP W' HIM.
AFTER TEN YEARS...

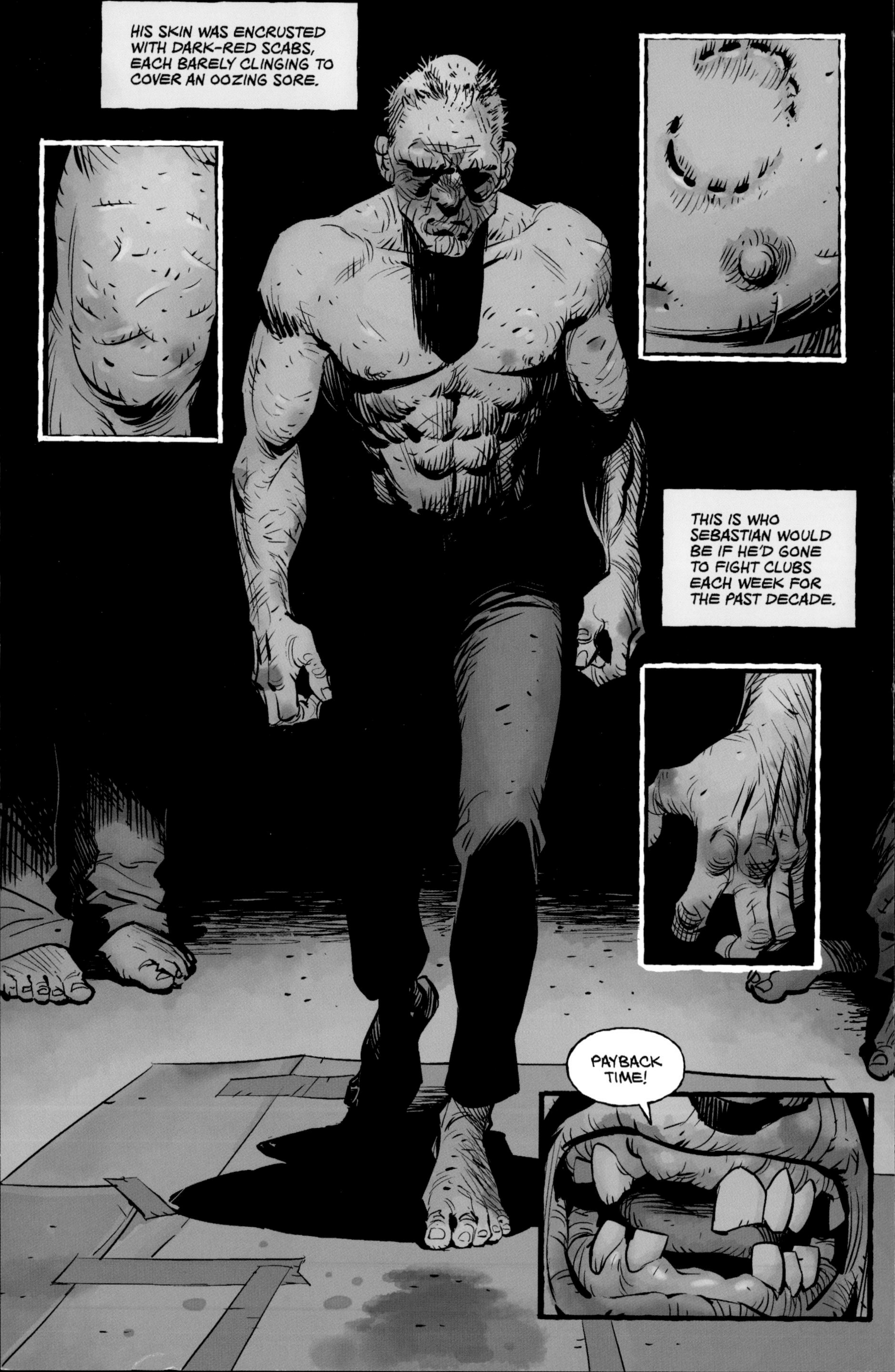
HIS SKIN WAS ENCRUSTED WITH DARK-RED SCABS, EACH BARELY CLINGING TO COVER AN OOZING SORE.
THIS IS WHO SEBASTIAN WOULD BE IF HE'D GONE TO FIGHT CLUBS EACH WEEK FOR THE PAST DECADE.
PAYBACK TIME!

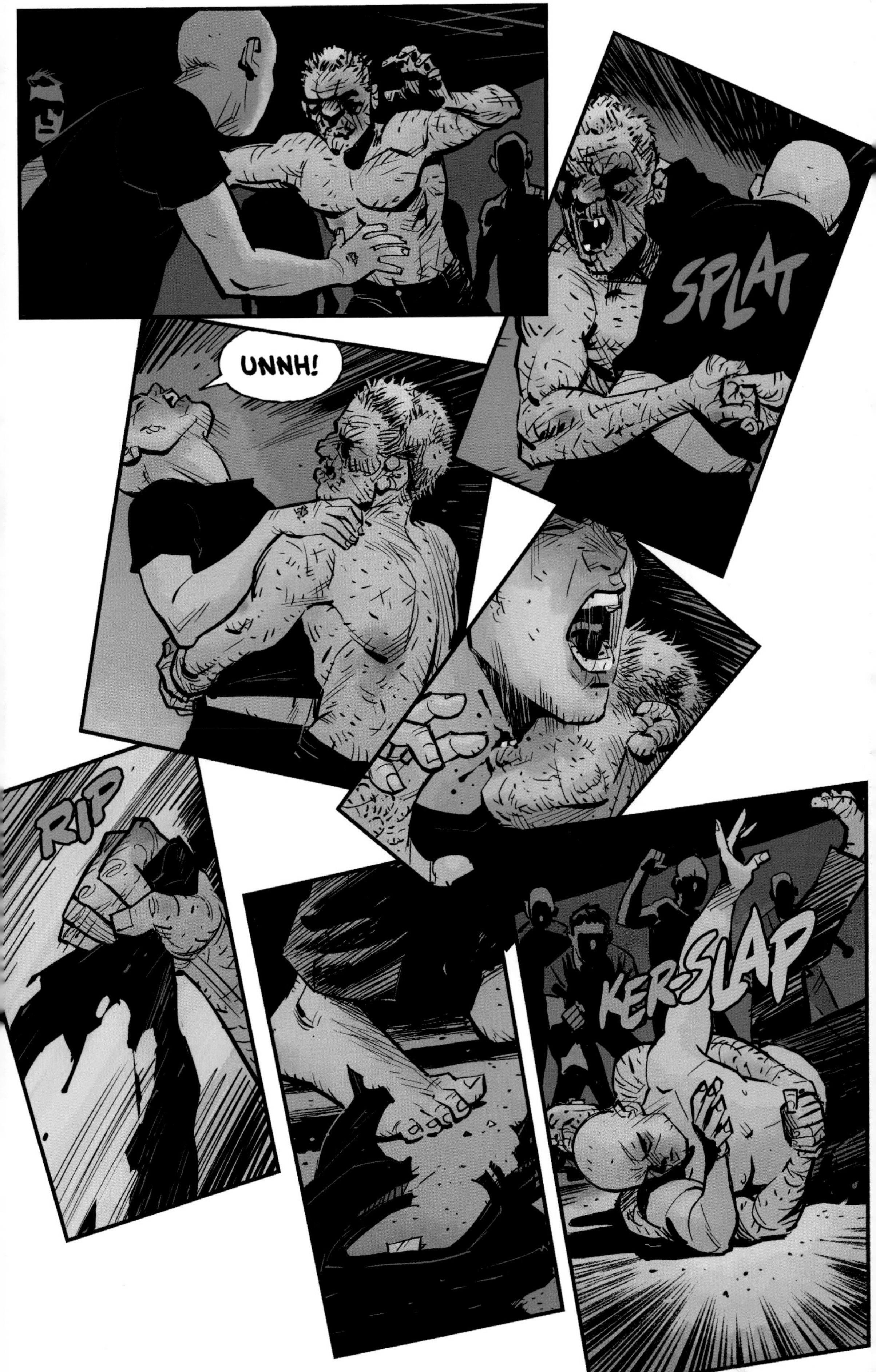
SPLAT
UNNH!
RIP
KER-SLAP

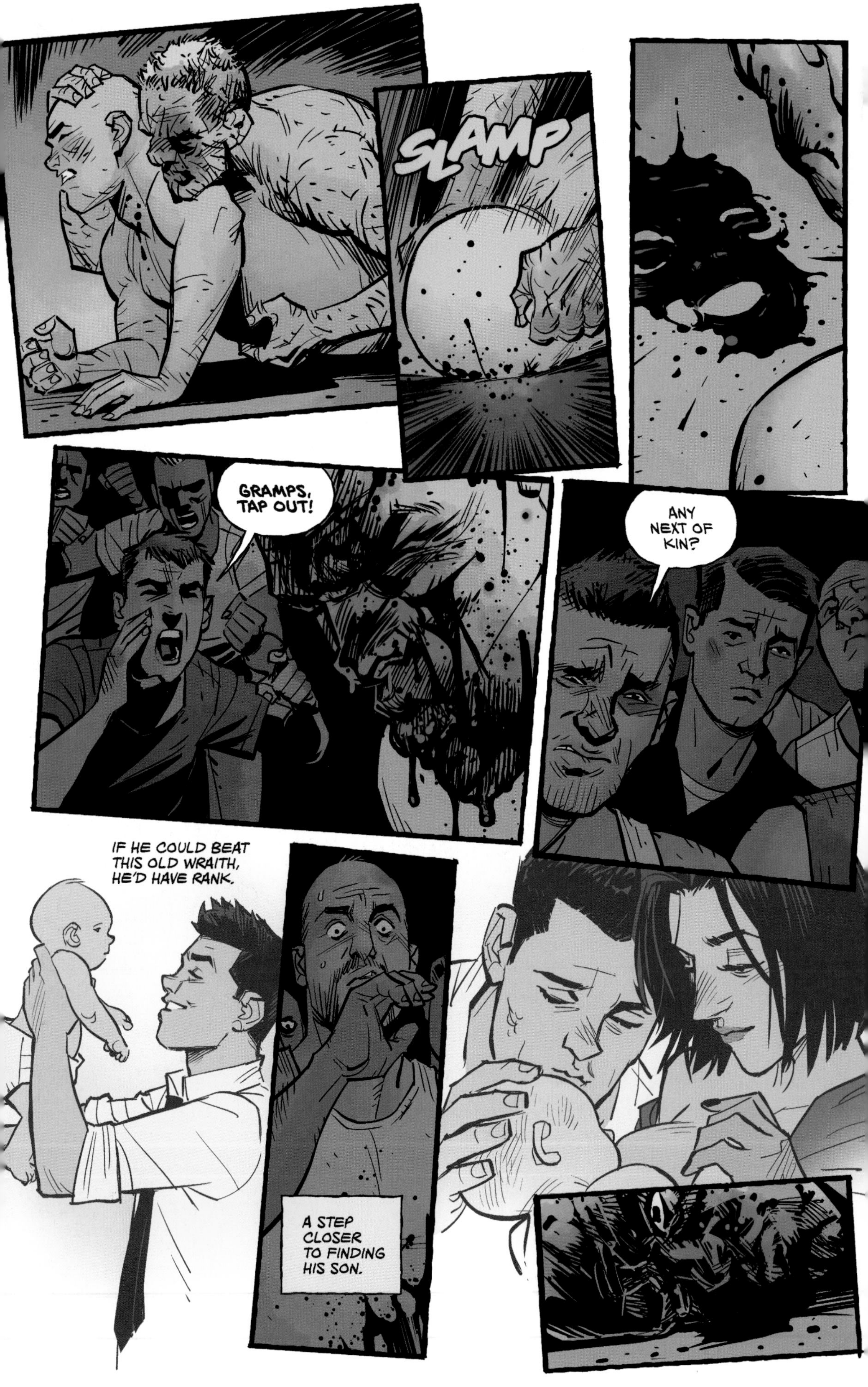
SLAMP
GRAMPS, TAP OUT!
ANY NEXT OF KIN?
IF HE COULD BEAT THIS OLD WRAITH, HE'D HAVE RANK.
A STEP CLOSER TO FINDING HIS SON.

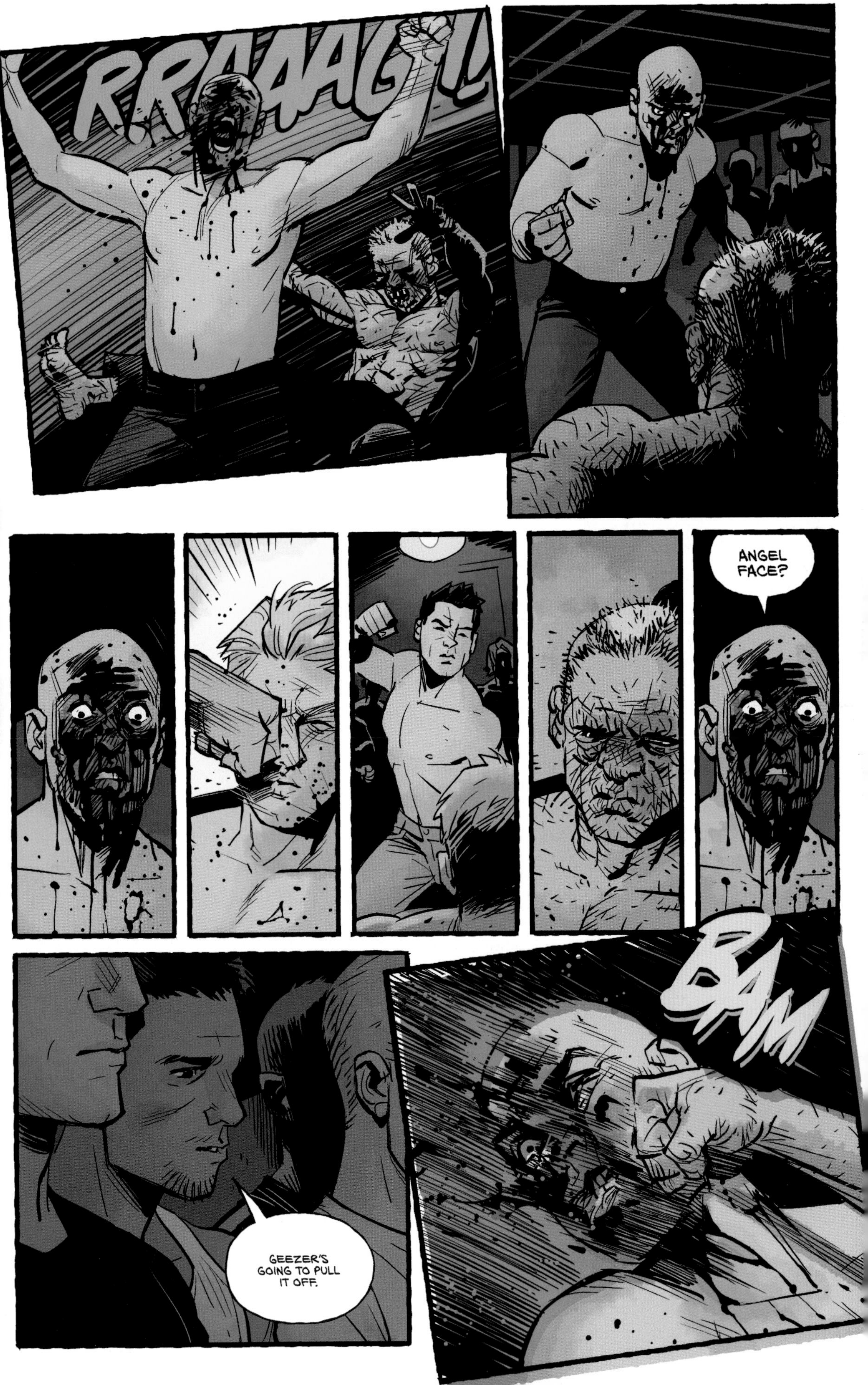
RRAAAG!!
ANGEL FACE?
GEEZER'S GOING TO PULL IT OFF.
BAM

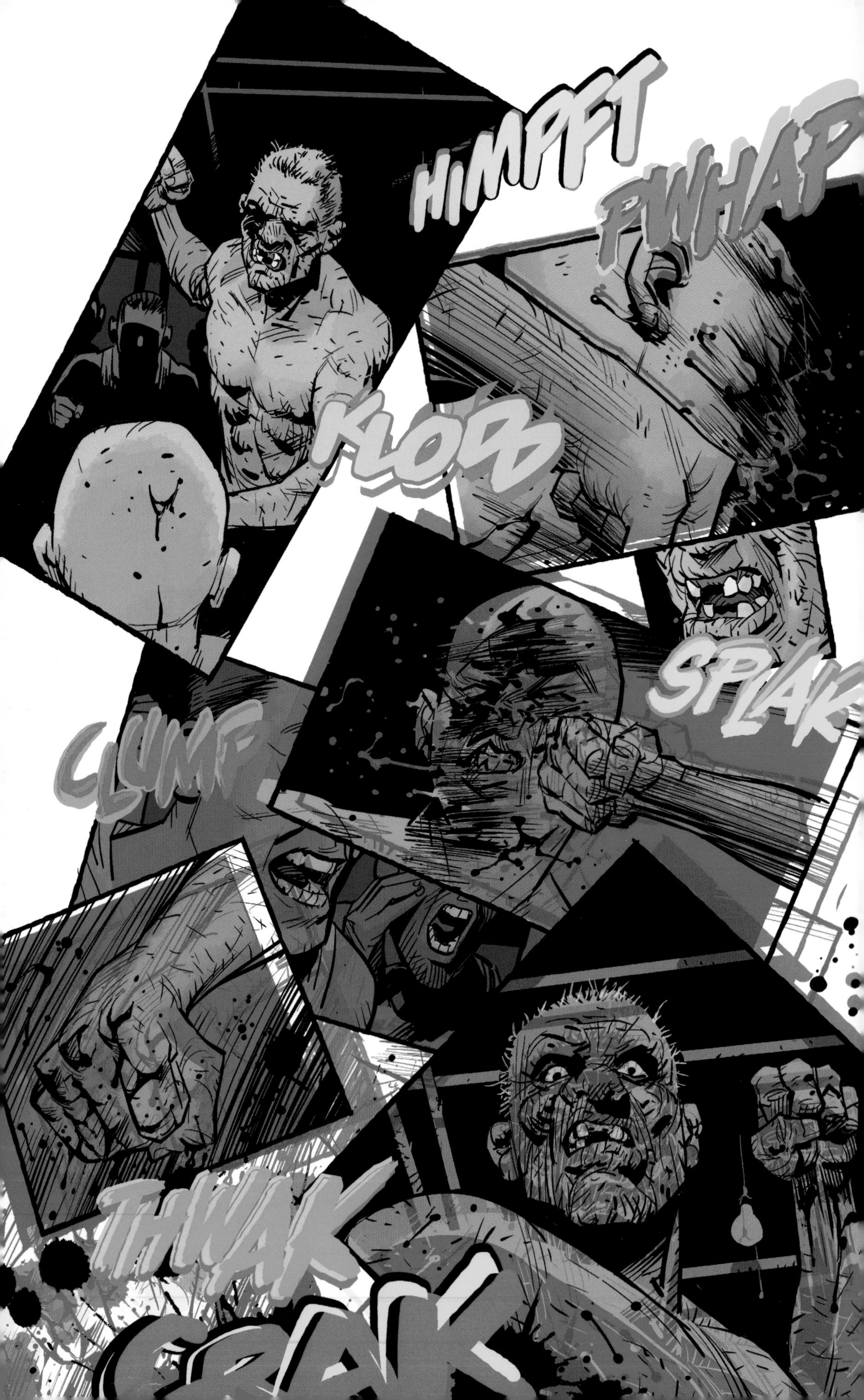
HIMPFT
PWHAP
KLODD
SPLAK
CLUMP
THWAK
CRAK

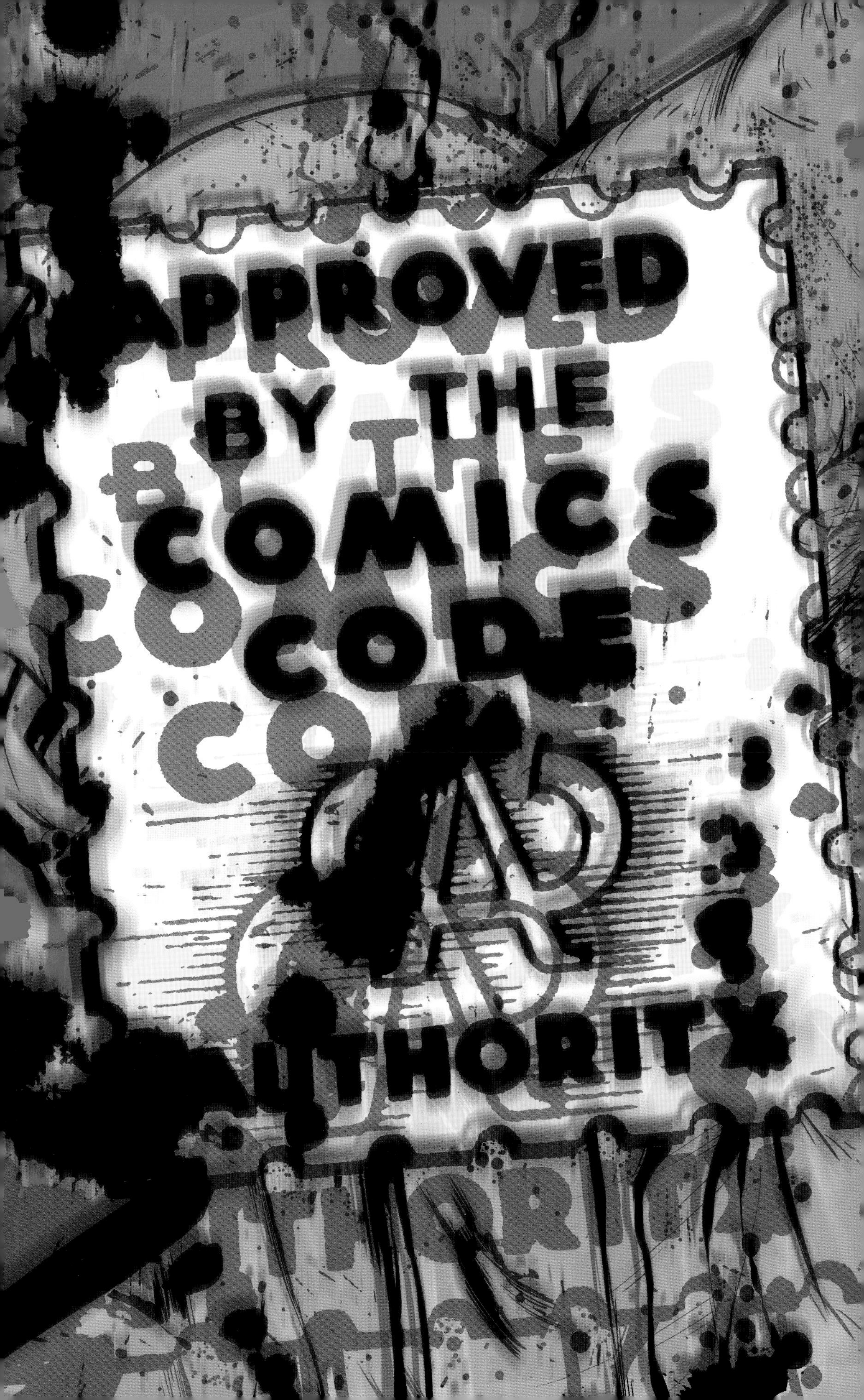
APPROVED
BY THE
COMICS
CODE
UTHORITY

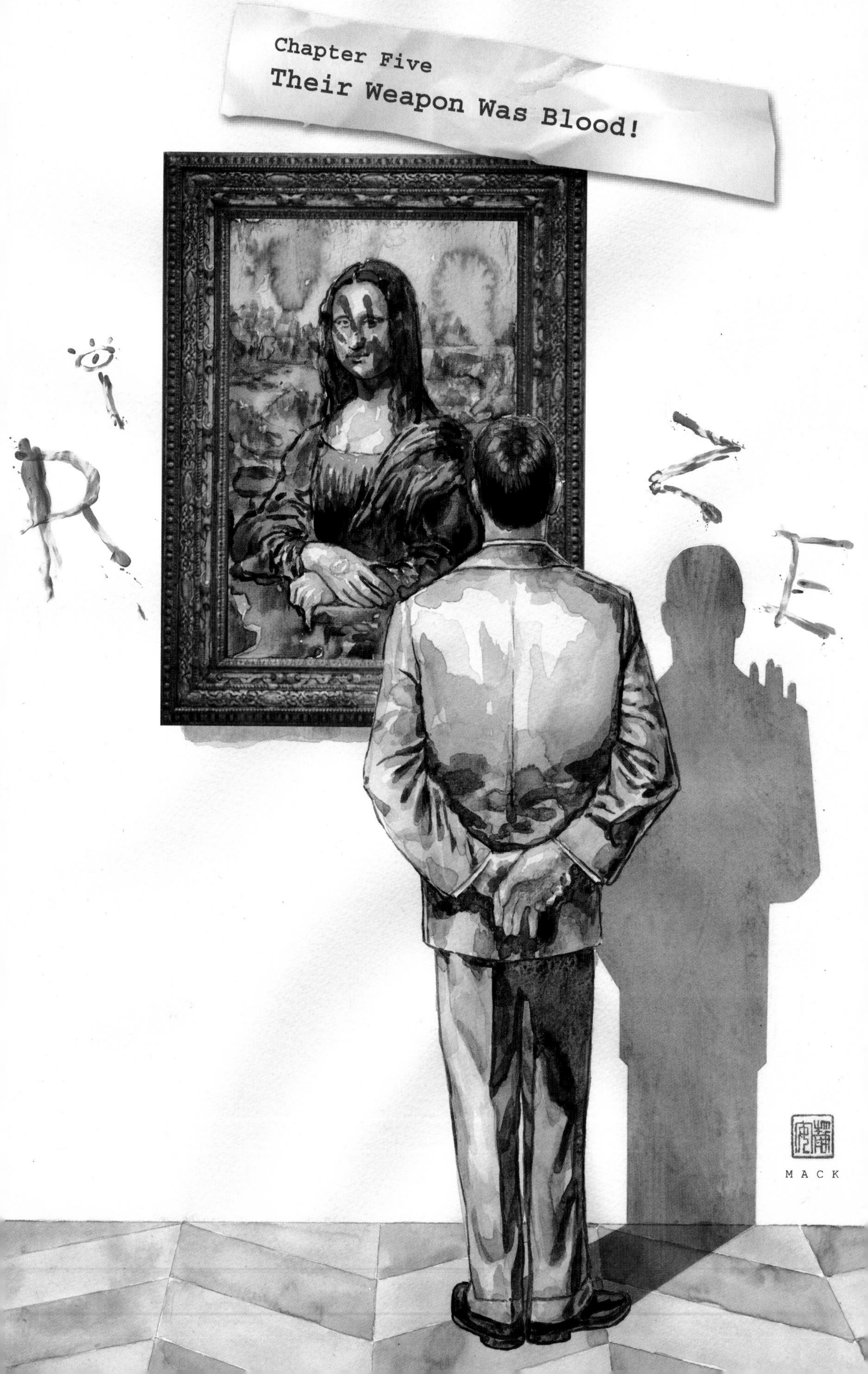
Chapter Five
Their Weapon Was Blood!
MACK

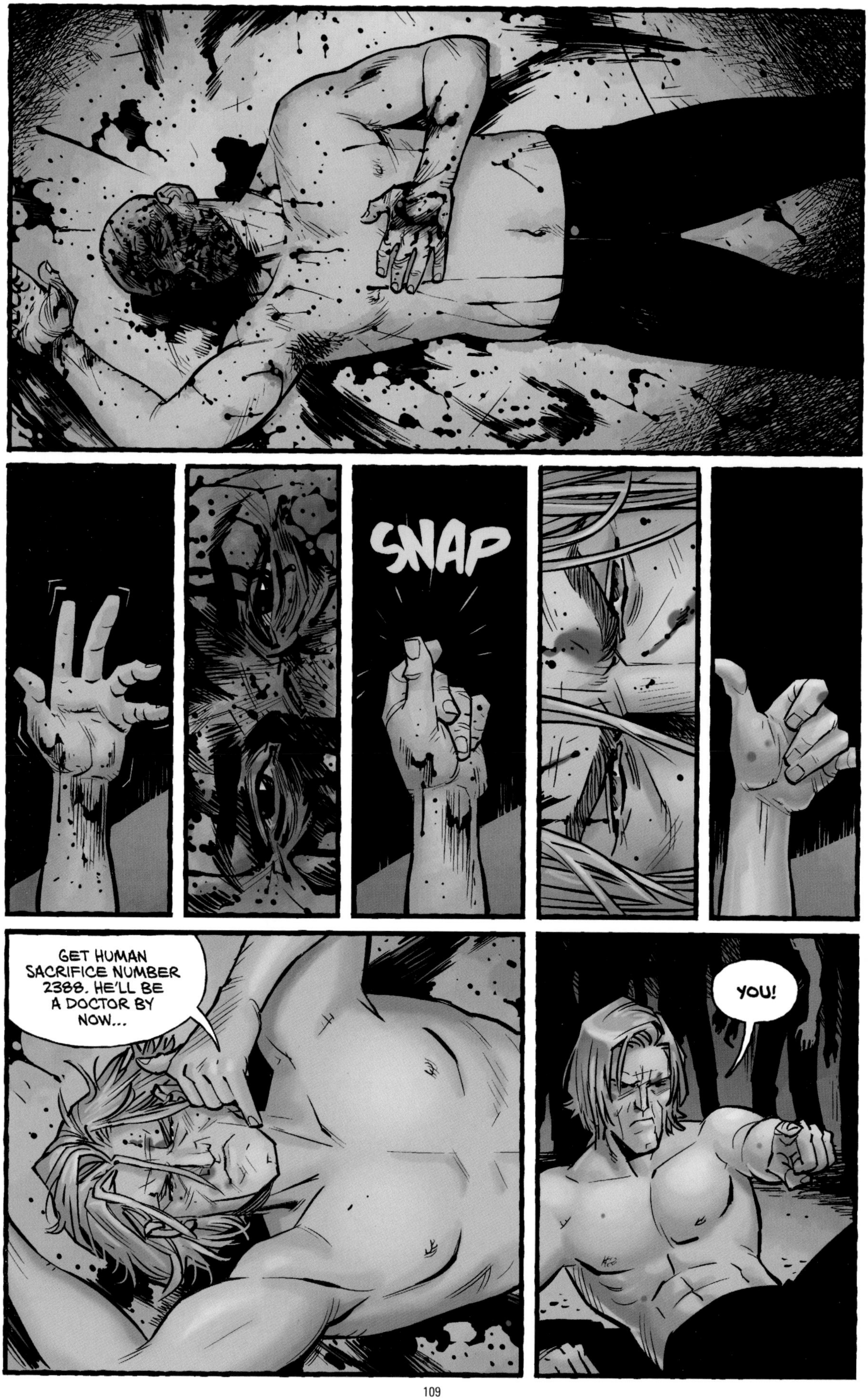
SNAP
GET HUMAN SACRIFICE NUMBER 2388. HE'LL BE A DOCTOR BY NOW...
YOU!

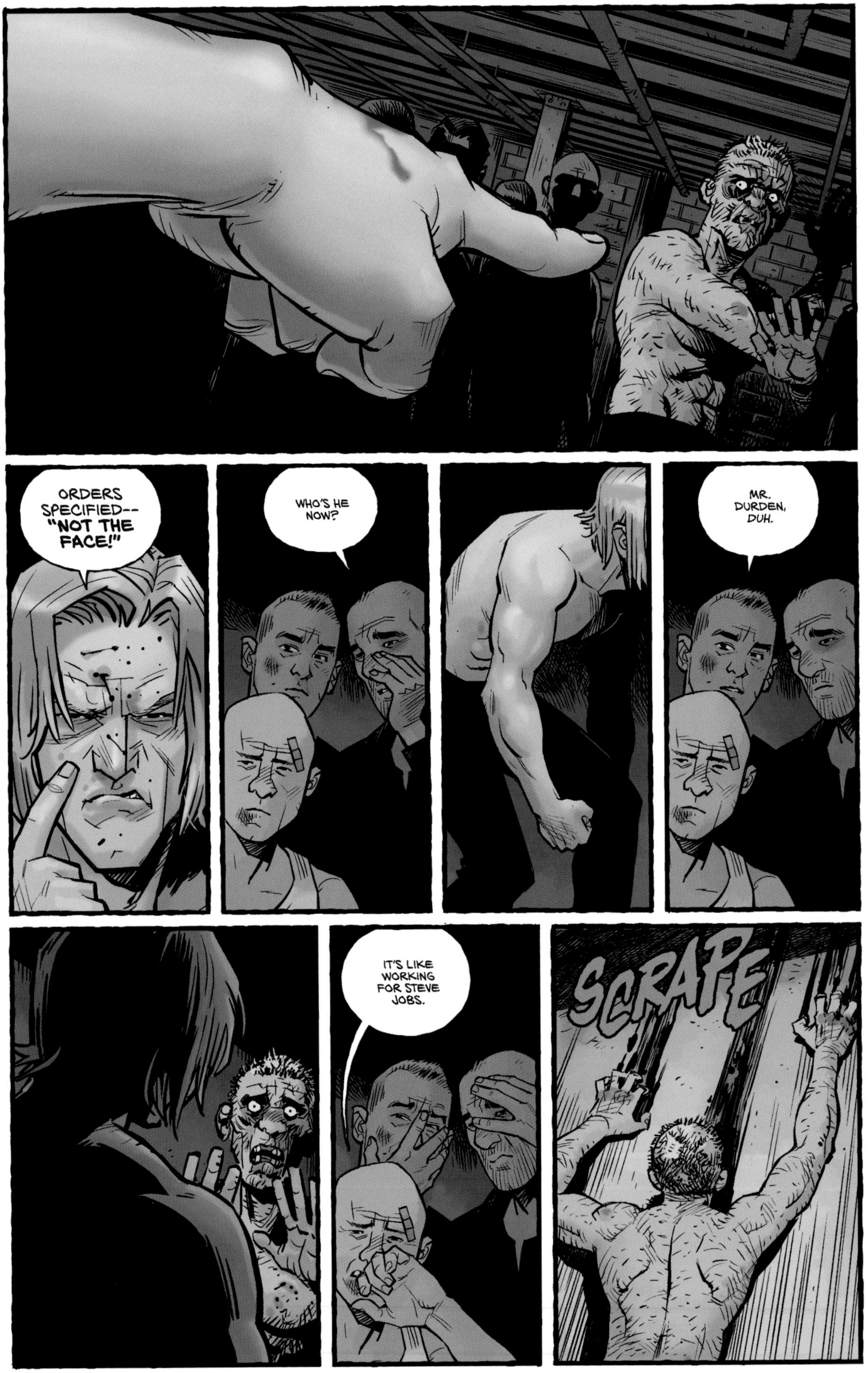
ORDERS SPECIFIED-- "NOT THE FACE!"
WHO'S HE NOW?
MR. DURDEN, DUH.
IT'S LIKE WORKING FOR STEVE JOBS.
SCRAPE

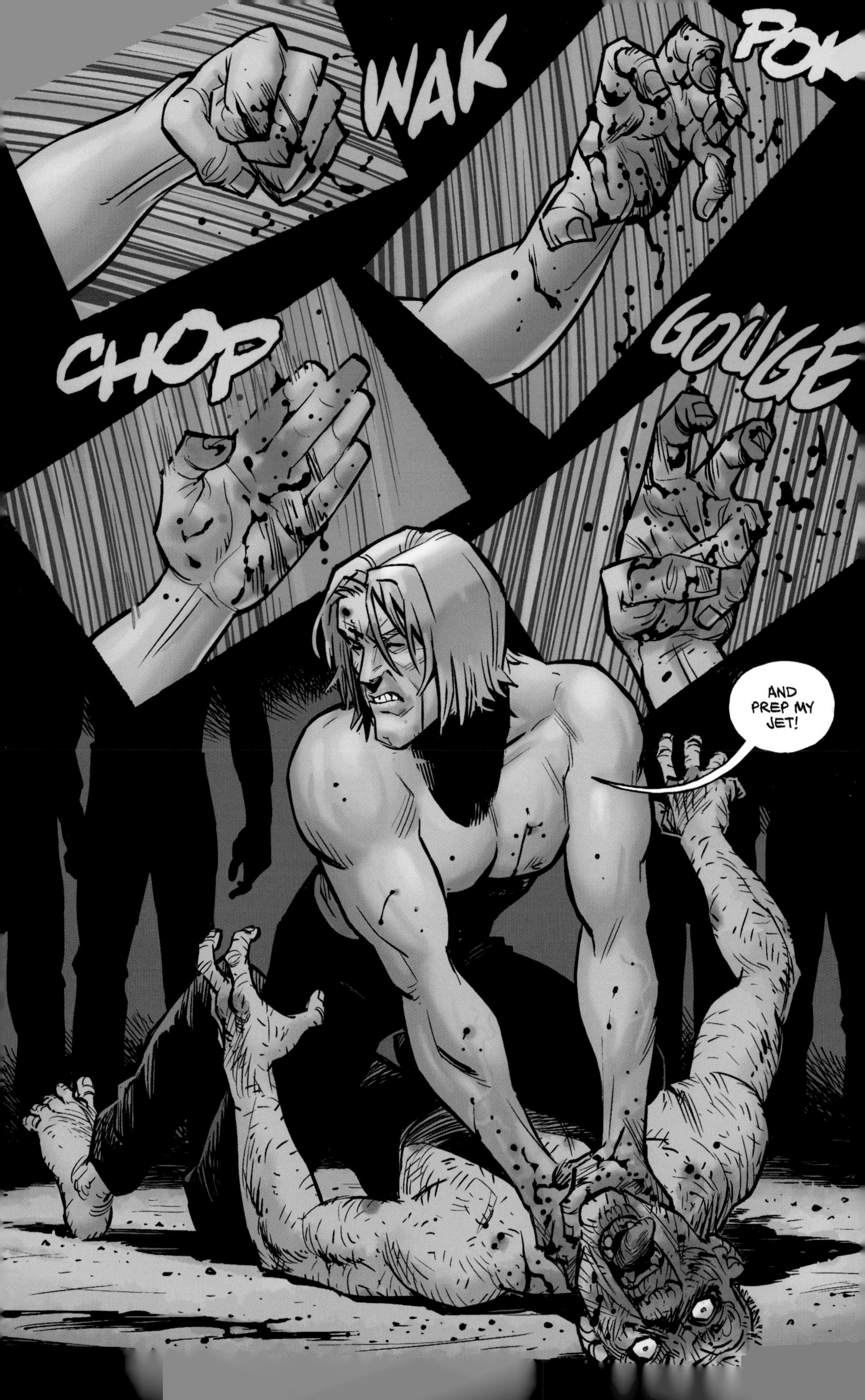
WAK
POK
CHOP
GOUGE
AND PREP MY JET!

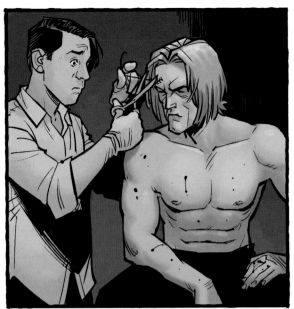

I MAKE NO APOLOGIES FOR MY CARBON FOOTPRINT.

BOOM
BLAM BLAM
RATATATA

YOU'RE SHIVERING.

KAFF GASP KAFF

JUST OLD AGE, DEAR.

I WISH I COULD GIVE YOU A FEW YEARS OF MY LIFE.

IN CASE WE DIE, I HAVE A CONFESSION.

RA TA TA TA

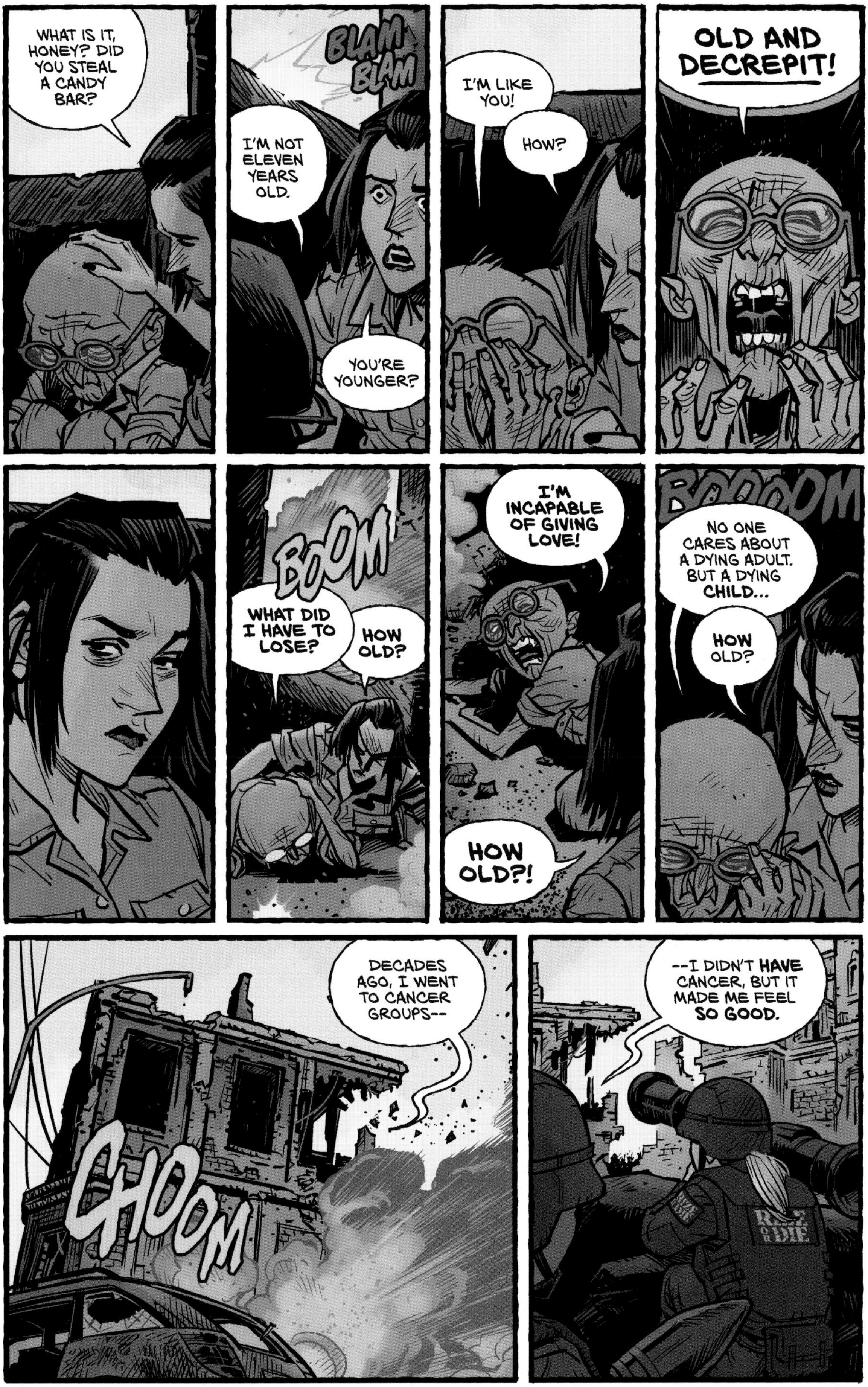
WHAT IS IT, HONEY? DID YOU STEAL A CANDY BAR?
BLAM BLAM
I'M NOT ELEVEN YEARS OLD.
YOU'RE YOUNGER?
I'M LIKE YOU!
HOW?
OLD AND DECREPIT!
BOOM
WHAT DID I HAVE TO LOSE?
HOW OLD?
I'M INCAPABLE OF GIVING LOVE!
HOW OLD?!
BOOOOM
NO ONE CARES ABOUT A DYING ADULT. BUT A DYING CHILD...
HOW OLD?
DECADES AGO, I WENT TO CANCER GROUPS--
CHOOM
--I DIDN'T HAVE CANCER, BUT IT MADE ME FEEL SO GOOD.

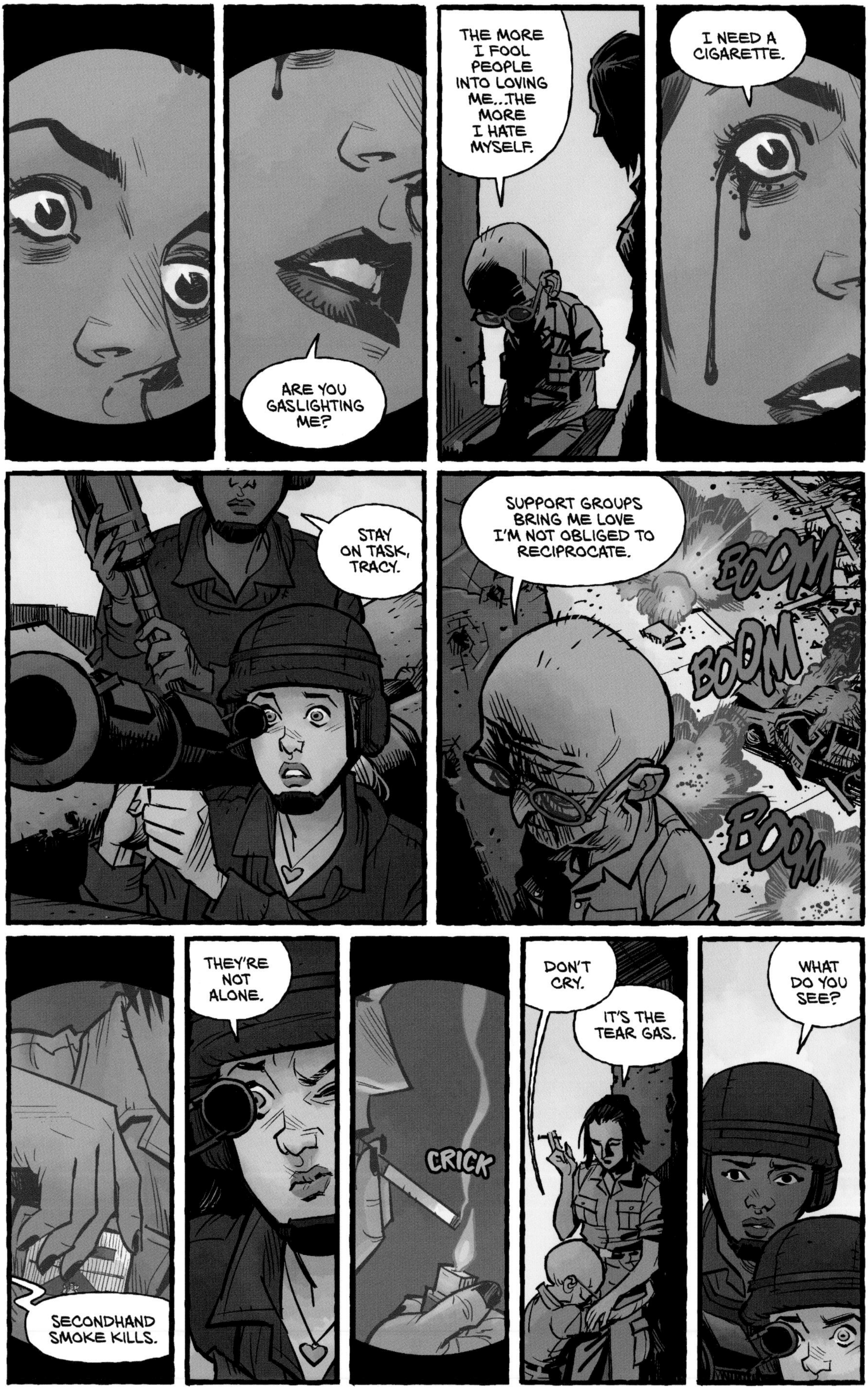
ARE YOU GASLIGHTING ME?
THE MORE I FOOL PEOPLE INTO LOVING ME...THE MORE I HATE MYSELF.
I NEED A CIGARETTE.
STAY ON TASK, TRACY.
SUPPORT GROUPS BRING ME LOVE I'M NOT OBLIGED TO RECIPROCATE.
BOOM
BOOM
BOOM
SECONDHAND SMOKE KILLS.
THEY'RE NOT ALONE.
CRICK
DON'T CRY.
IT'S THE TEAR GAS.
WHAT DO YOU SEE?

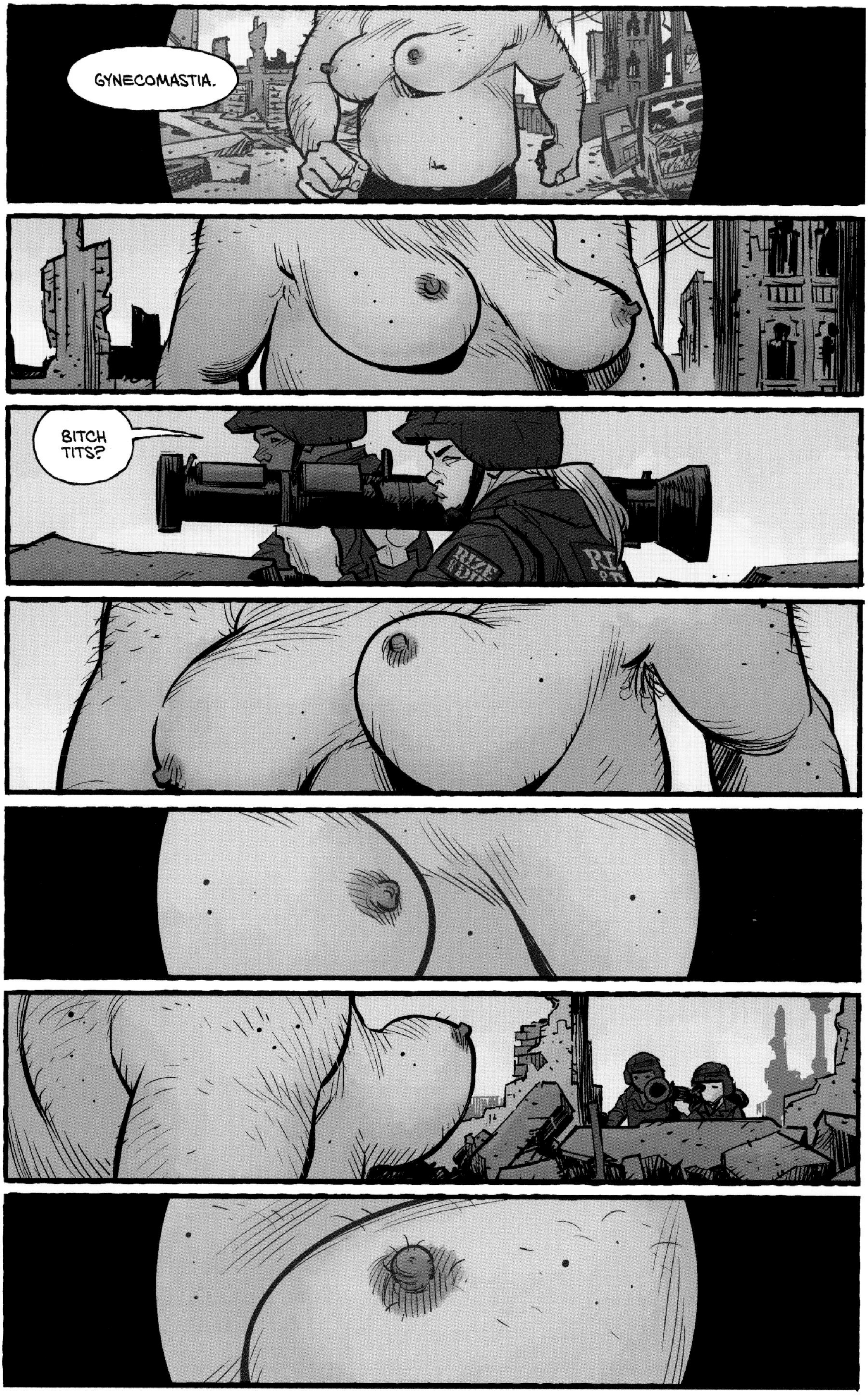
GYNECOMASTIA.
BITCH TITS?

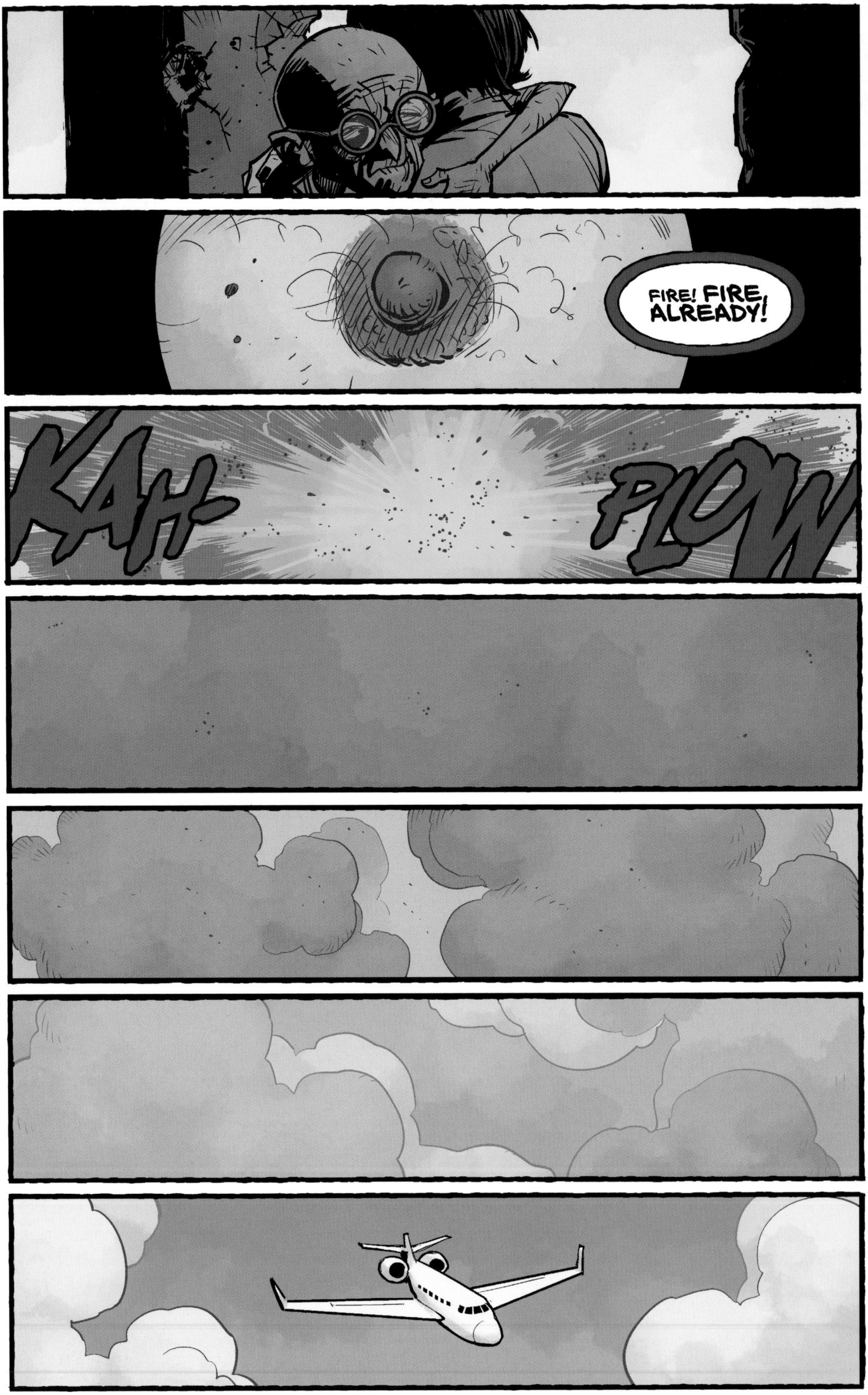
FIRE! FIRE, ALREADY!
KAH-PLOW

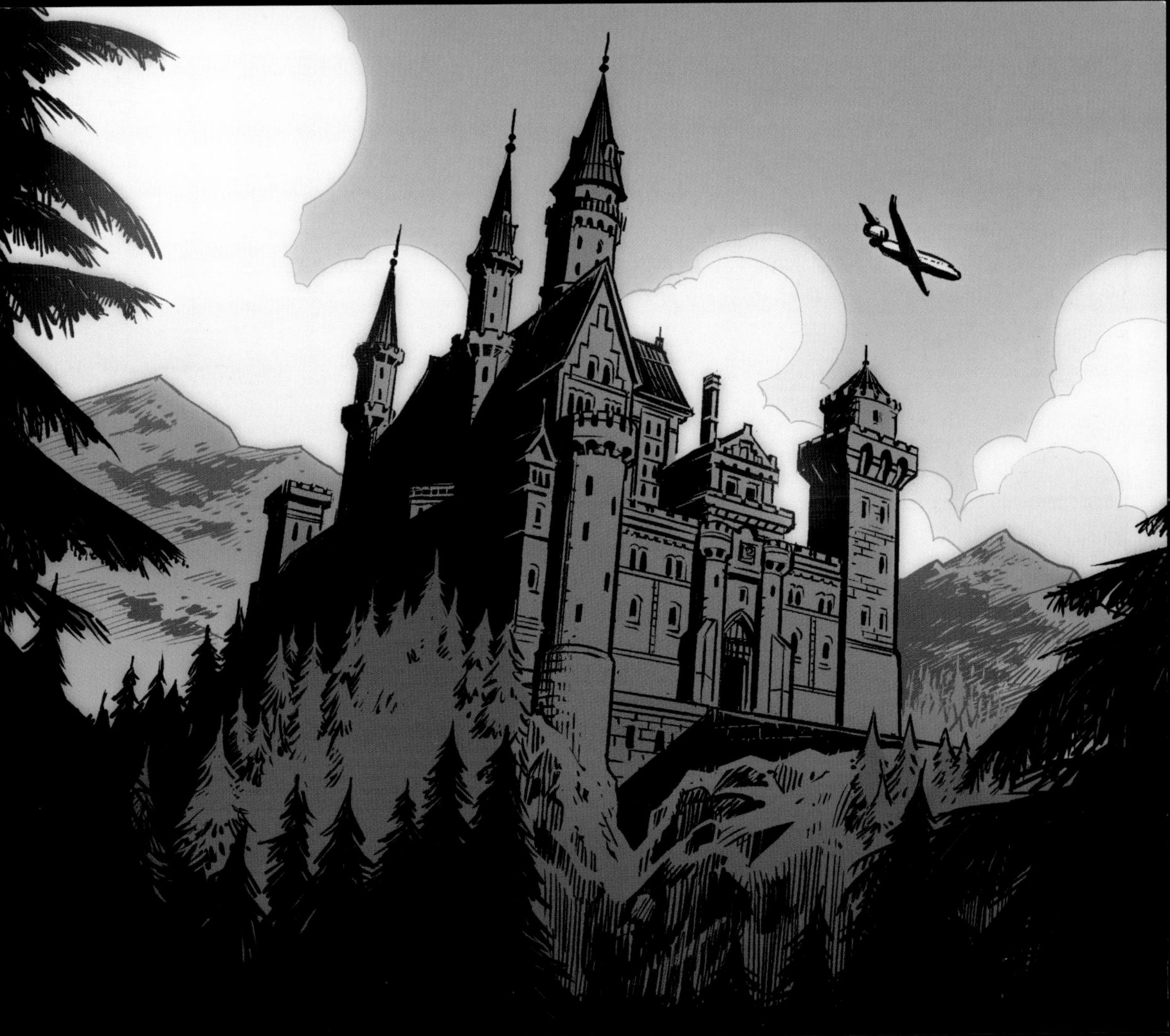

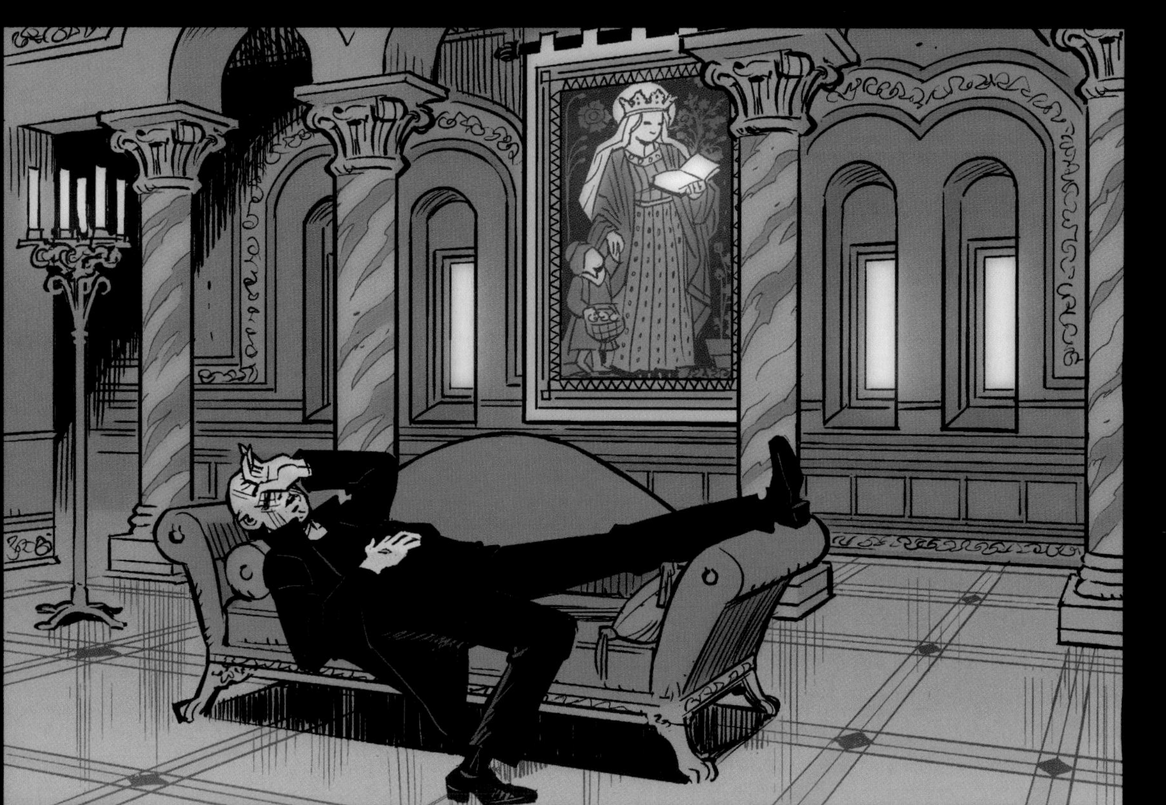

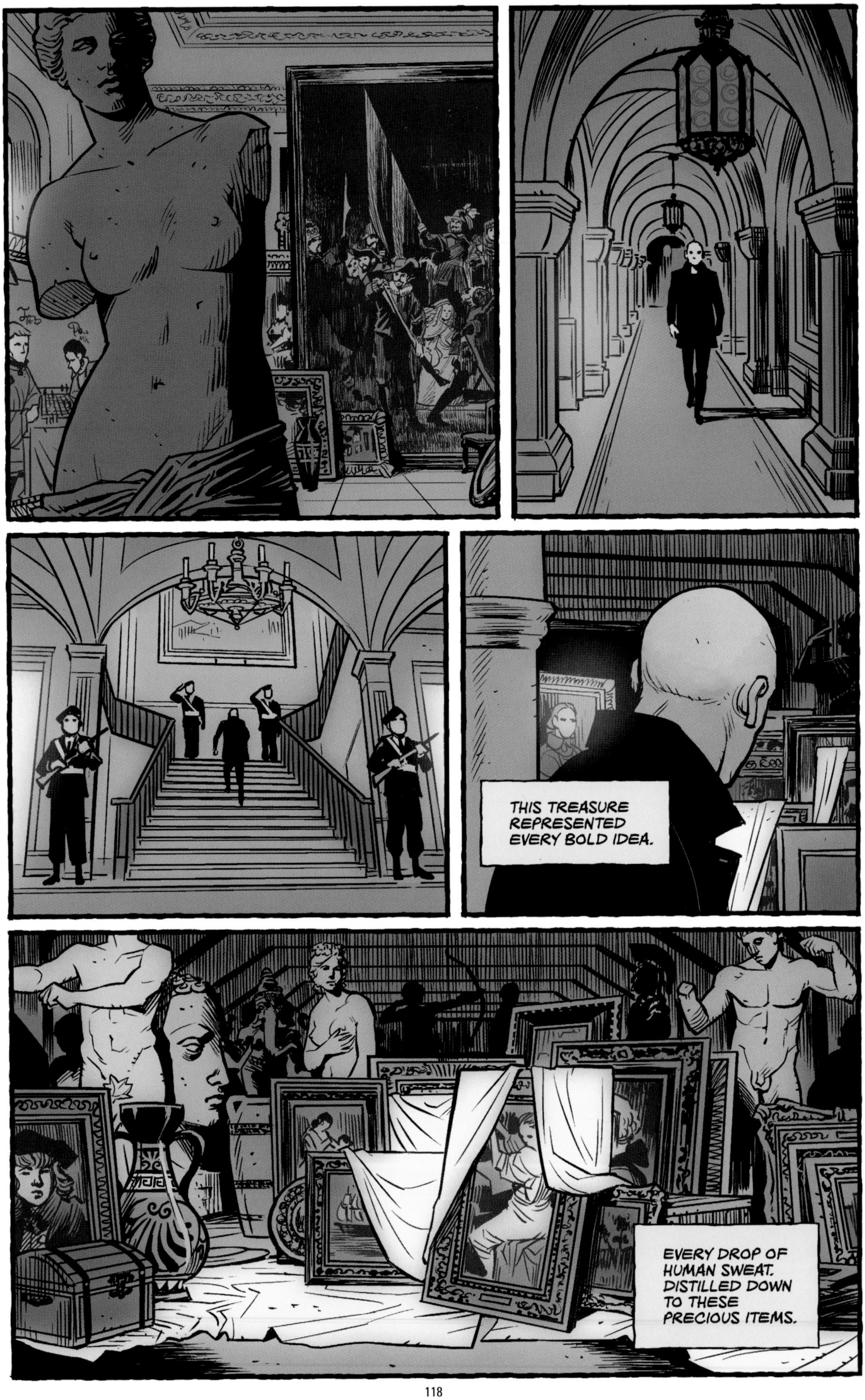
THIS TREASURE REPRESENTED EVERY BOLD IDEA.
EVERY DROP OF HUMAN SWEAT. DISTILLED DOWN TO THESE PRECIOUS ITEMS.

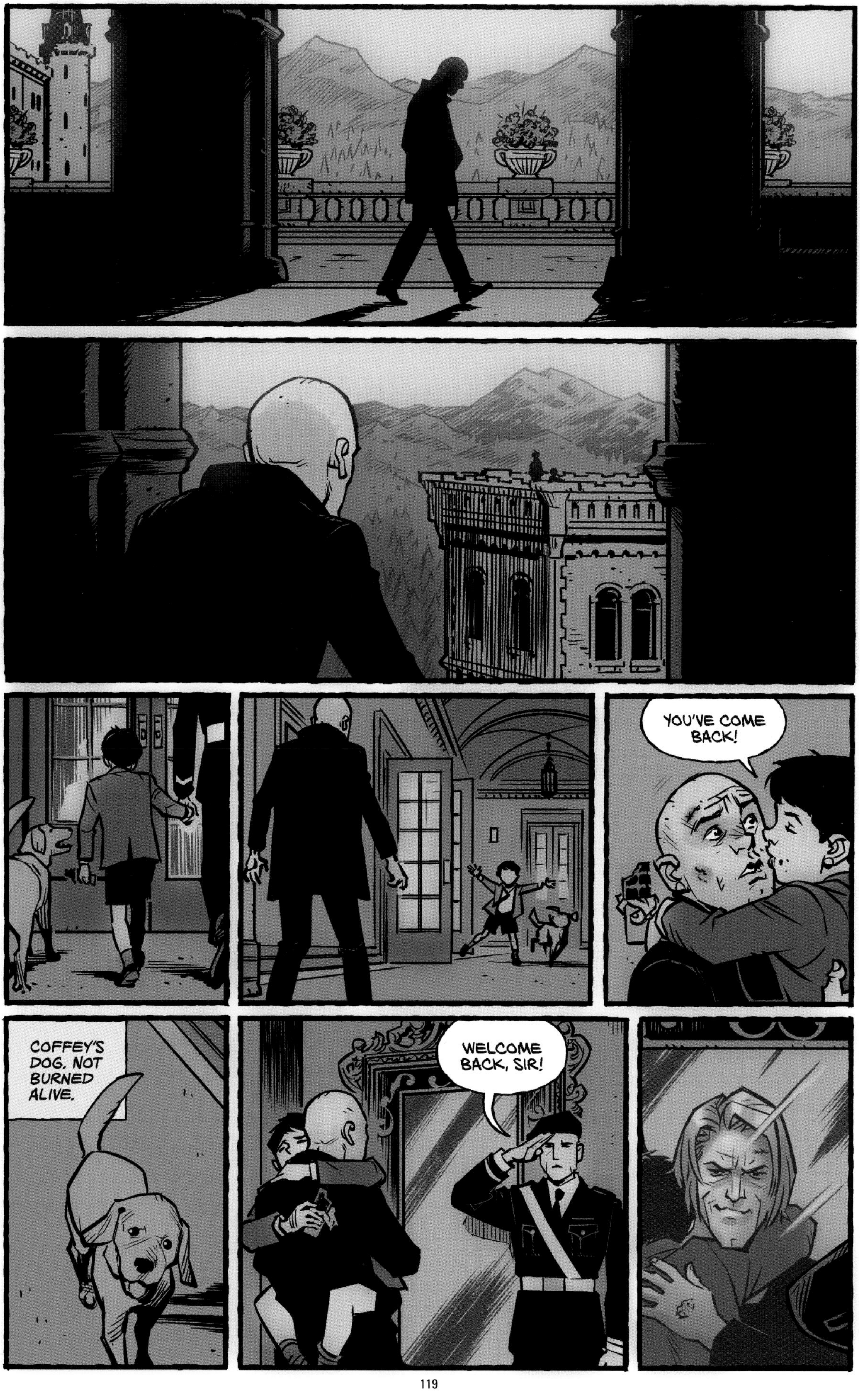
YOU'VE COME BACK!
COFFEY'S DOG. NOT BURNED ALIVE.
WELCOME BACK, SIR!

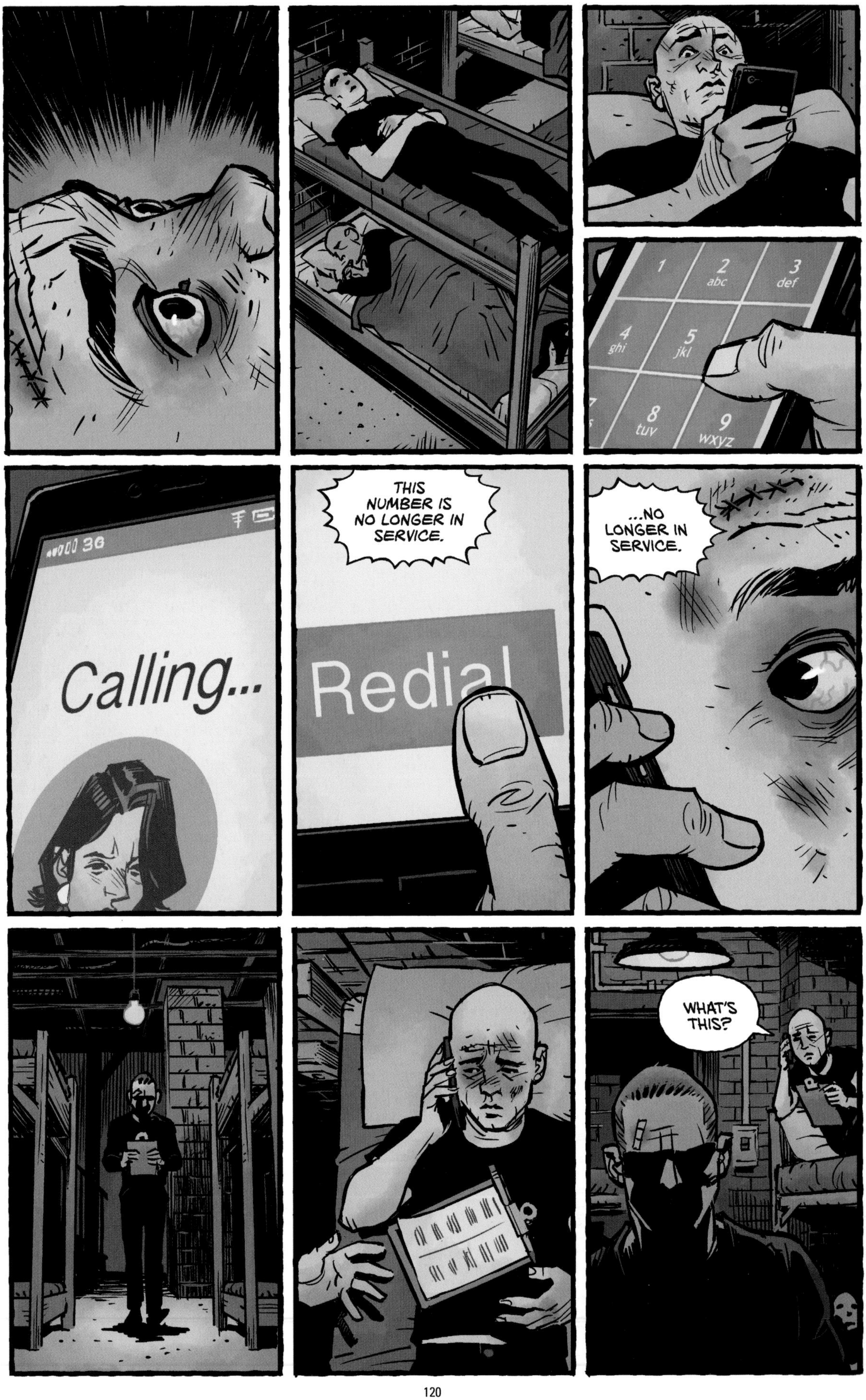
1
2
abc
3
def
4
ghi
5
jkl
8
tuv
9
wxyz
3G
Calling...
THIS NUMBER IS NO LONGER IN SERVICE.
Redial
...NO LONGER IN SERVICE.
WHAT'S THIS?

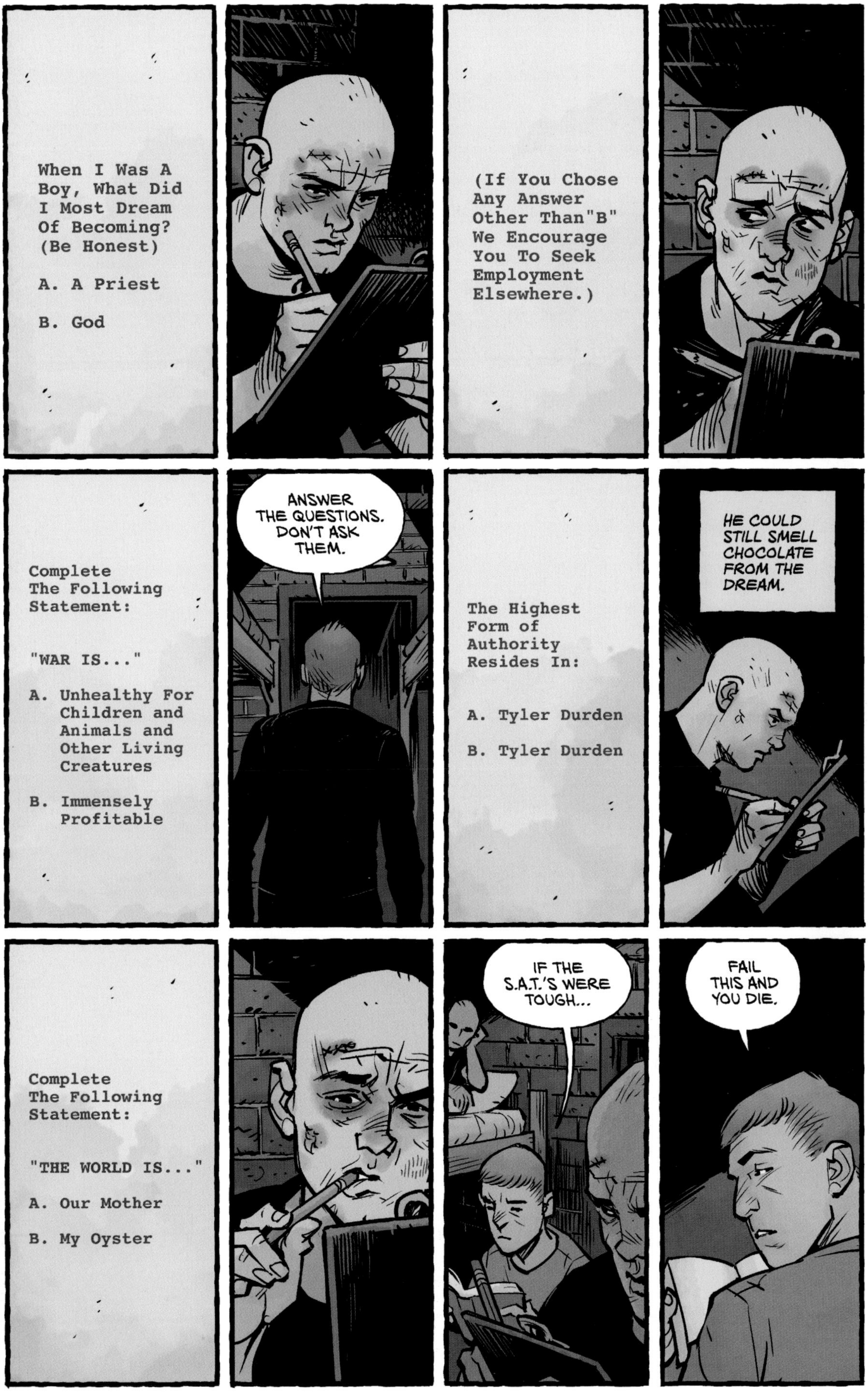
When I Was A Boy, What Did I Most Dream Of Becoming? (Be Honest)
A. A Priest
B. God
(If You Chose Any Answer Other Than"B" We Encourage You To Seek Employment Elsewhere.)
Complete The Following Statement:
"WAR IS..."
A. Unhealthy For Children and Animals and Other Living Creatures
B. Immensely Profitable
ANSWER THE QUESTIONS. DON'T ASK THEM.
The Highest Form of Authority Resides In:
A. Tyler Durden
B. Tyler Durden
HE COULD STILL SMELL CHOCOLATE FROM THE DREAM.
Complete The Following Statement:
"THE WORLD IS..."
A. Our Mother
B. My Oyster
IF THE S.A.T.'S WERE TOUGH...
FAIL THIS AND YOU DIE.

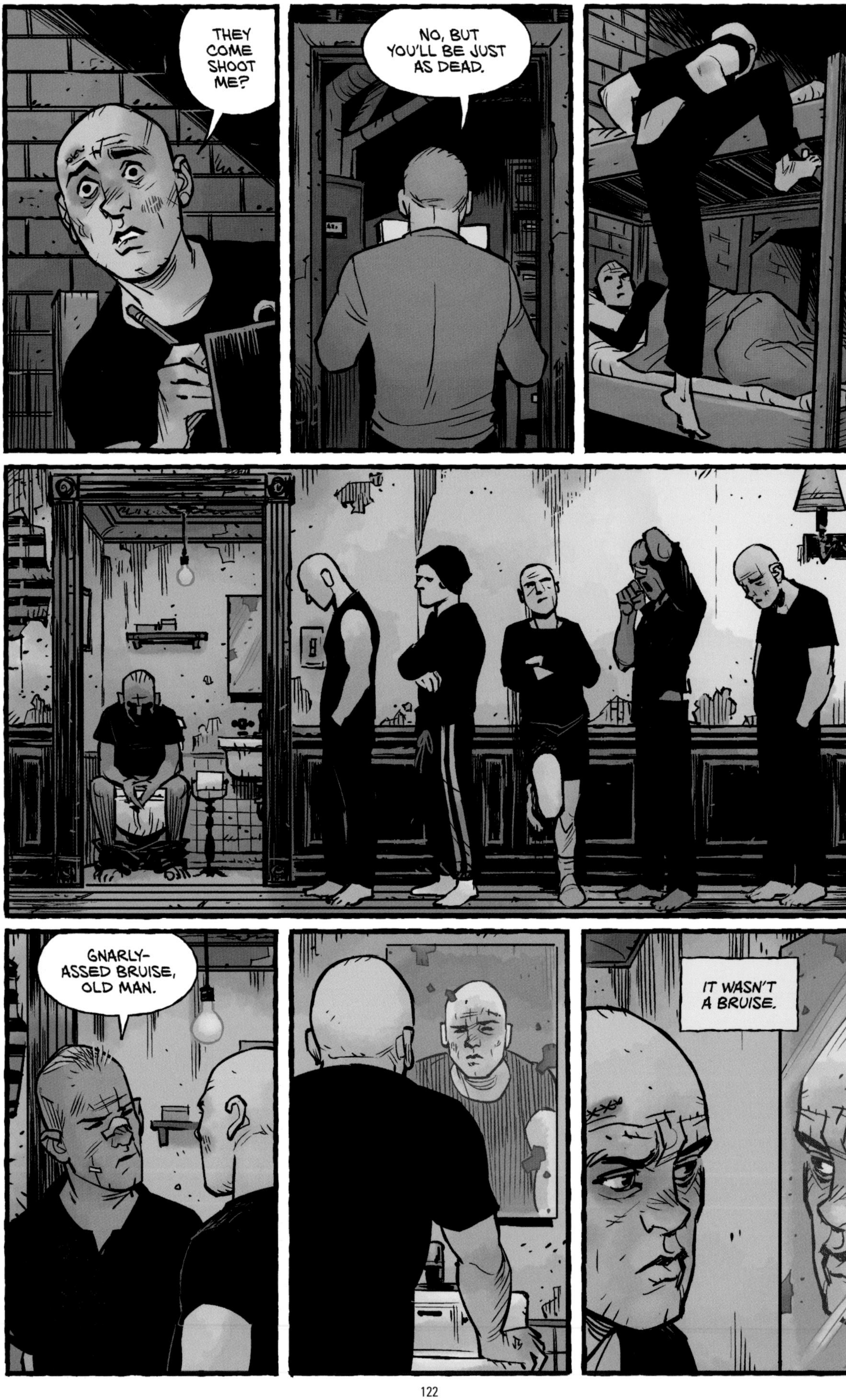
THEY COME SHOOT ME?
NO, BUT YOU'LL BE JUST AS DEAD.
GNARLY-ASSED BRUISE, OLD MAN.
IT WASN'T A BRUISE.

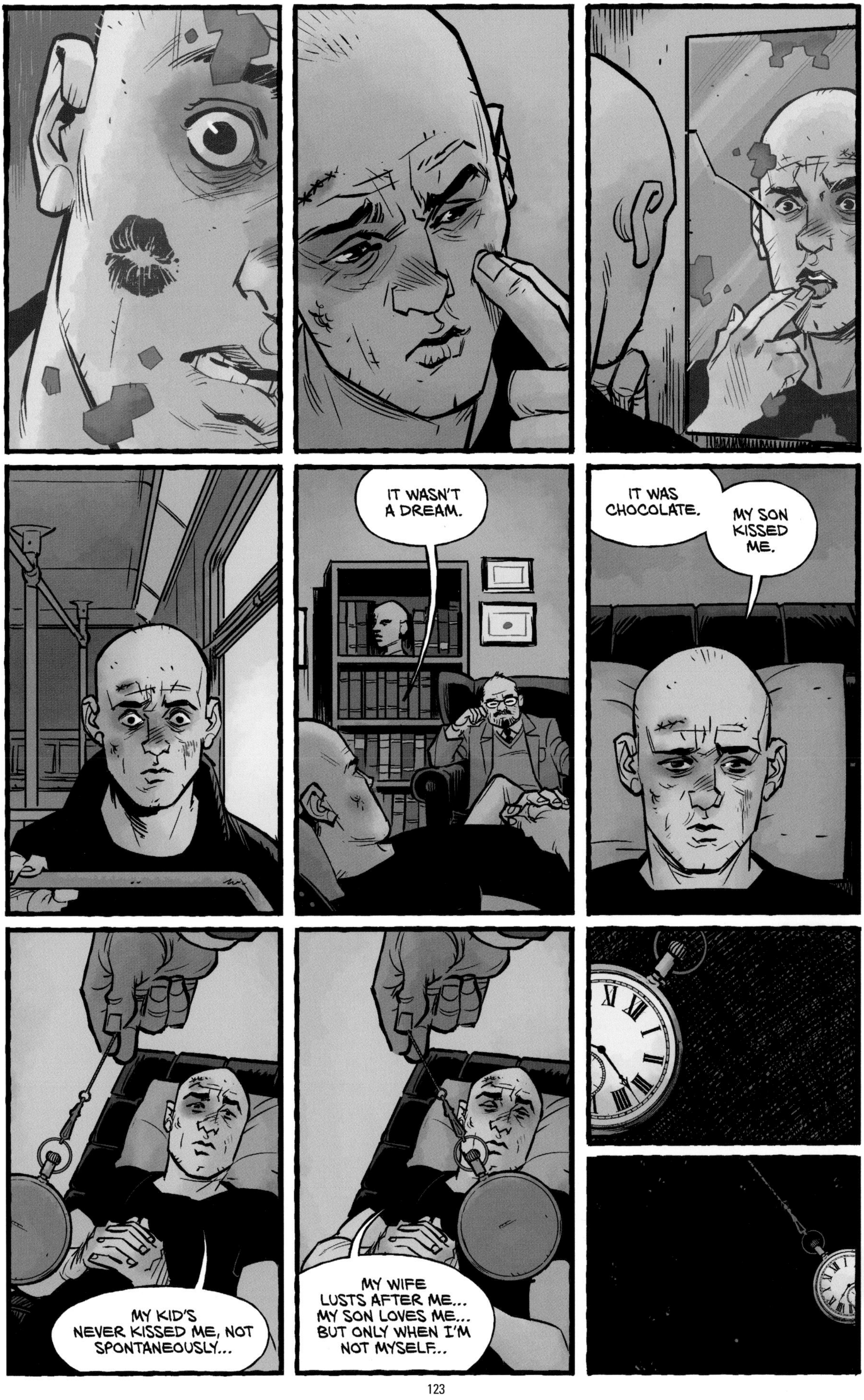
IT WASN'T A DREAM.
IT WAS CHOCOLATE.
MY SON KISSED ME.
MY KID'S NEVER KISSED ME, NOT SPONTANEOUSLY...
MY WIFE LUSTS AFTER ME... MY SON LOVES ME... BUT ONLY WHEN I'M NOT MYSELF...

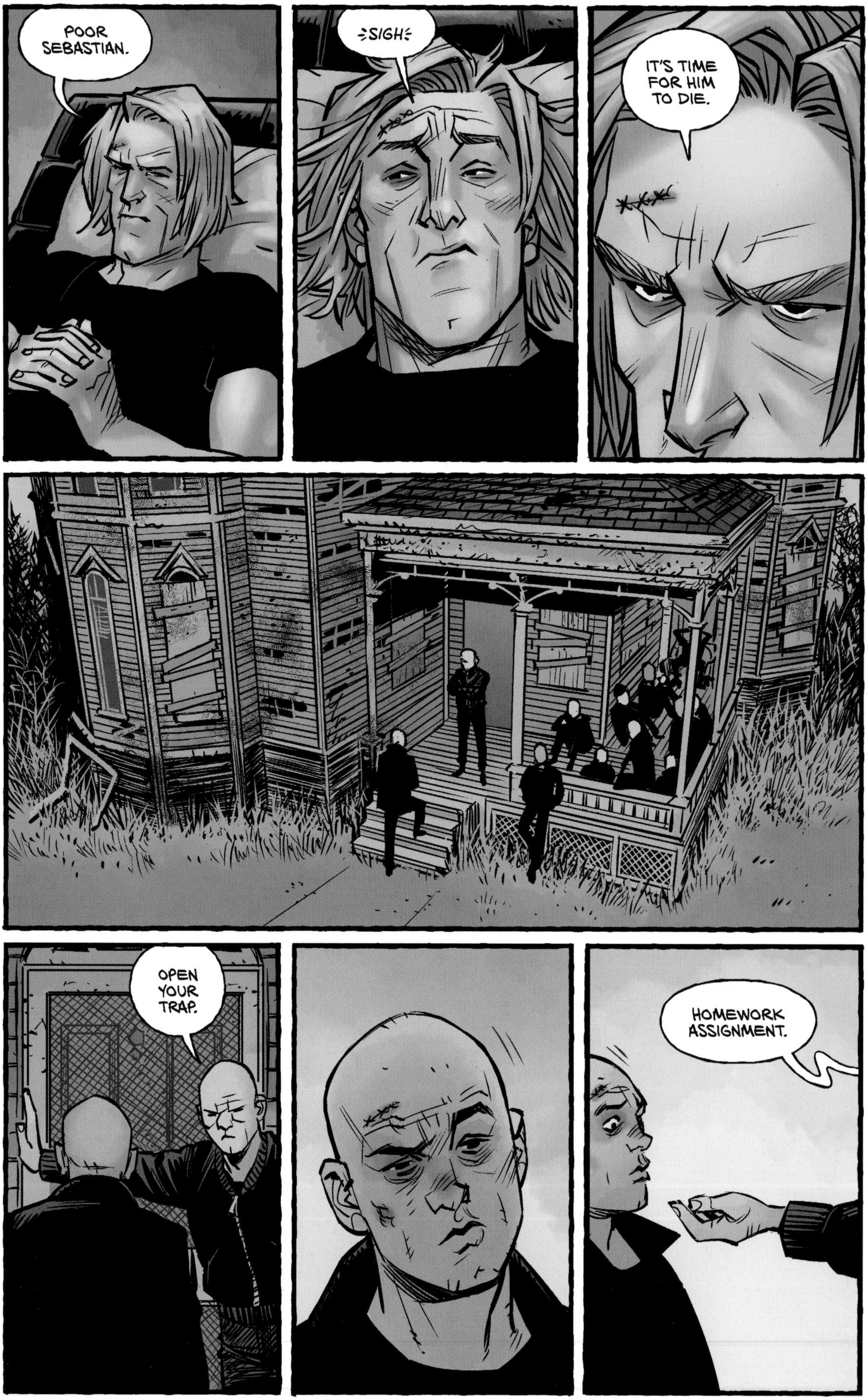
POOR SEBASTIAN.
SIGH
IT'S TIME FOR HIM TO DIE.
OPEN YOUR TRAP.
HOMEWORK ASSIGNMENT.

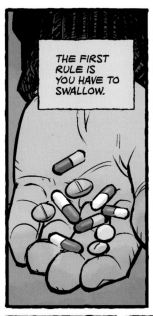

THE FIRST RULE IS YOU HAVE TO SWALLOW.

BOTTOMS UP.

≈GULP≈

FEEDING TIME.

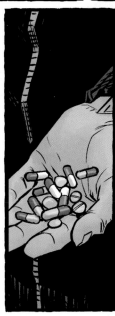

WHAT AM I TAKING?

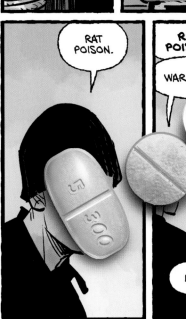

RAT POISON.

RAT POISON!

WARFARIN.

ANTICOAGULANT.

BLOOD THINNER.

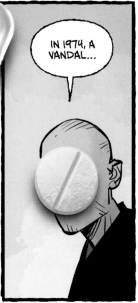

IN 1974, A VANDAL...

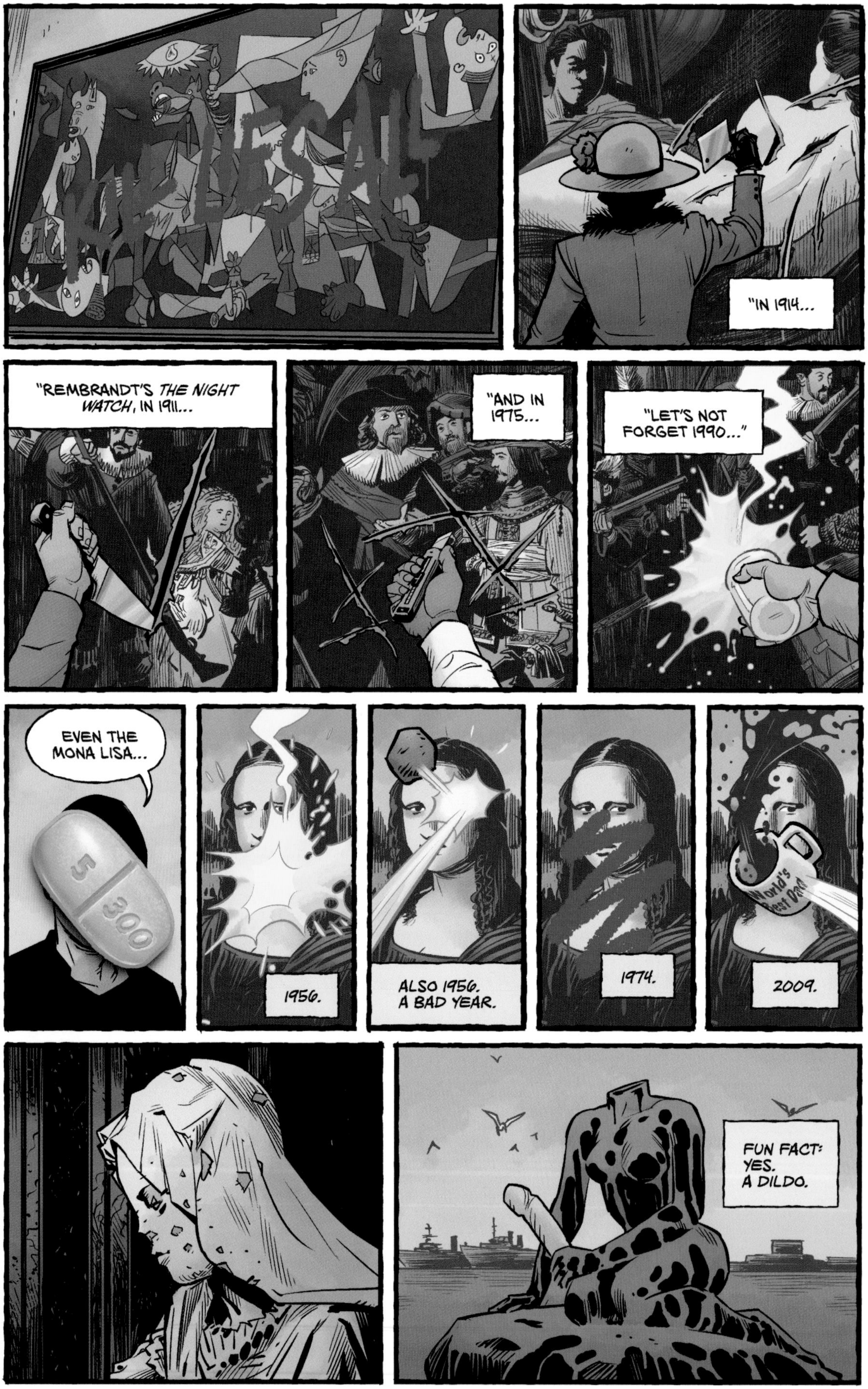
KILL LIES ALL
"IN 1914...
"REMBRANDT'S *THE NIGHT WATCH*, IN 1911...
"AND IN 1975...
"LET'S NOT FORGET 1990..."
EVEN THE MONA LISA...
5 300
1956.
ALSO 1956. A BAD YEAR.
1974.
World's Best Dad
2009.
FUN FACT: YES. A DILDO.

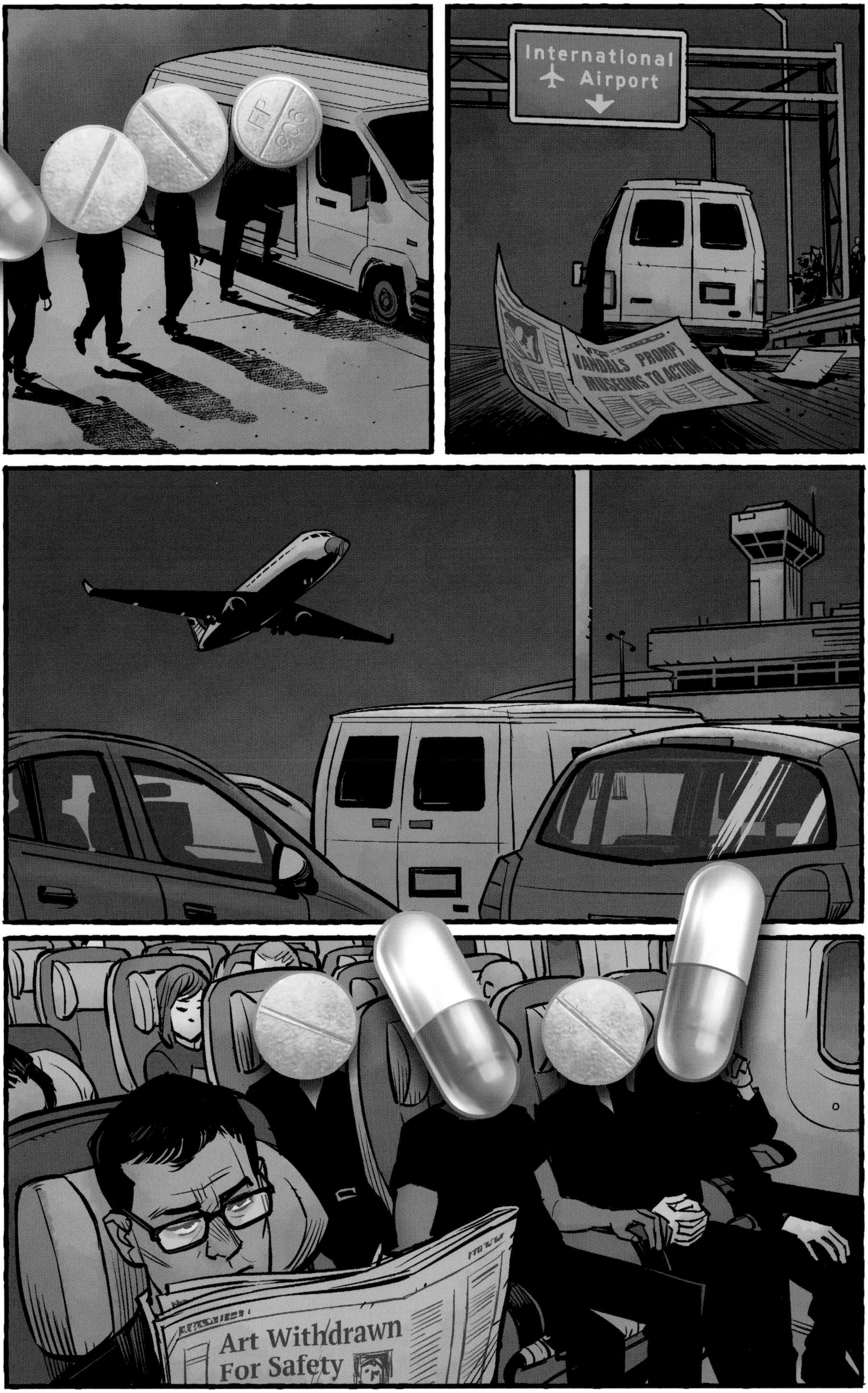
International Airport
VANDALS PROMPT MUSEUMS TO ACTION
Art Withdrawn For Safety

HERE'S THE BEST SPOT.

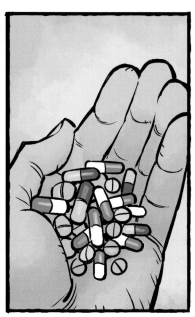

PSEUDO-EPHEDRINE.

VASOCONSTRICTOR.

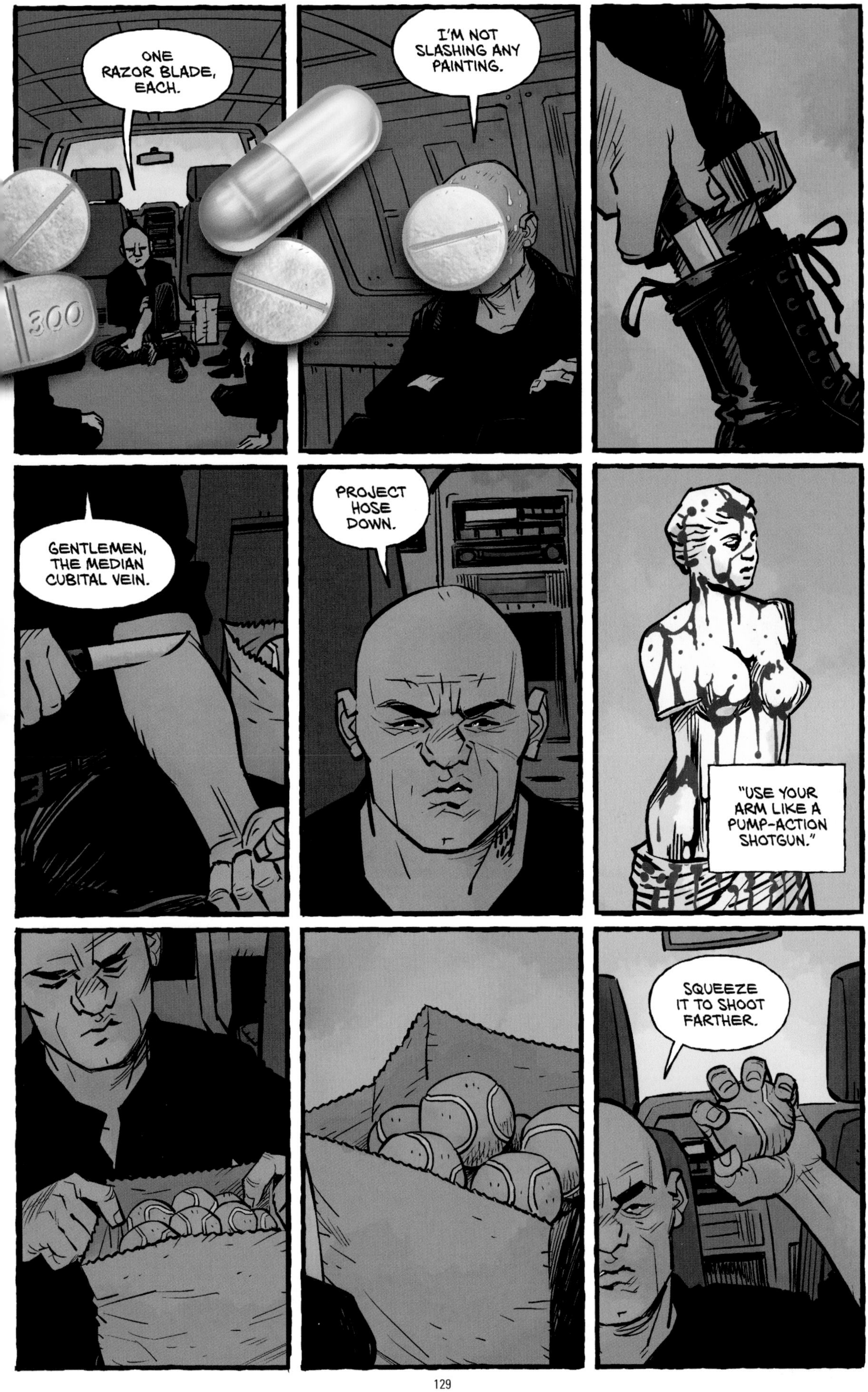
ONE RAZOR BLADE, EACH.
I'M NOT SLASHING ANY PAINTING.
300
GENTLEMEN, THE MEDIAN CUBITAL VEIN.
PROJECT HOSE DOWN.
"USE YOUR ARM LIKE A PUMP-ACTION SHOTGUN."
SQUEEZE IT TO SHOOT FARTHER.

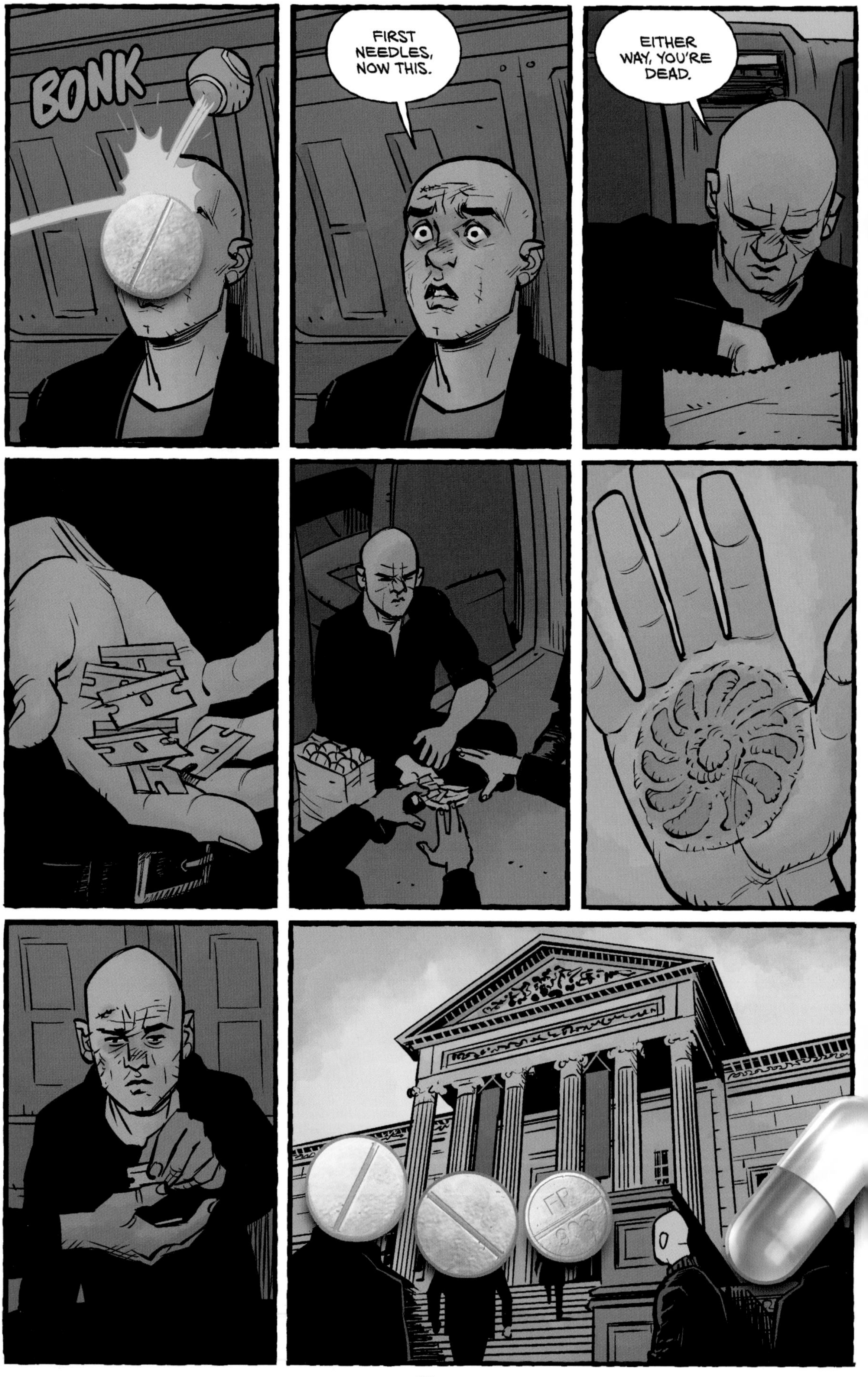
BONK
FIRST NEEDLES, NOW THIS.
EITHER WAY, YOU'RE DEAD.
FP
908

EACH STAKE OUT A DIFFERENT PICTURE.

WAIT FOR MY SIGNAL.

WHAT SIGNAL?

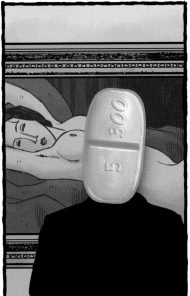

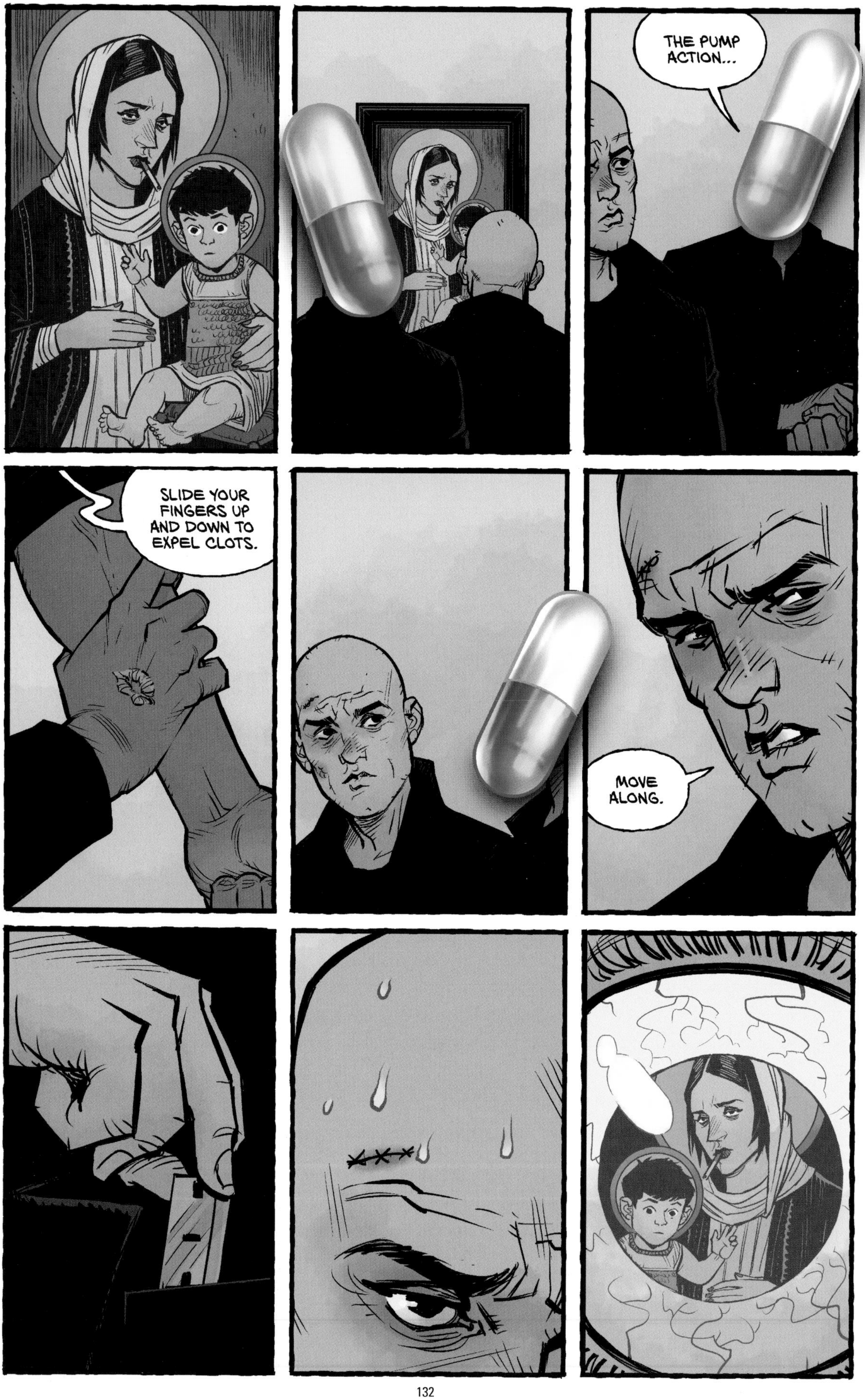
THE PUMP ACTION...
SLIDE YOUR FINGERS UP AND DOWN TO EXPEL CLOTS.
MOVE ALONG.

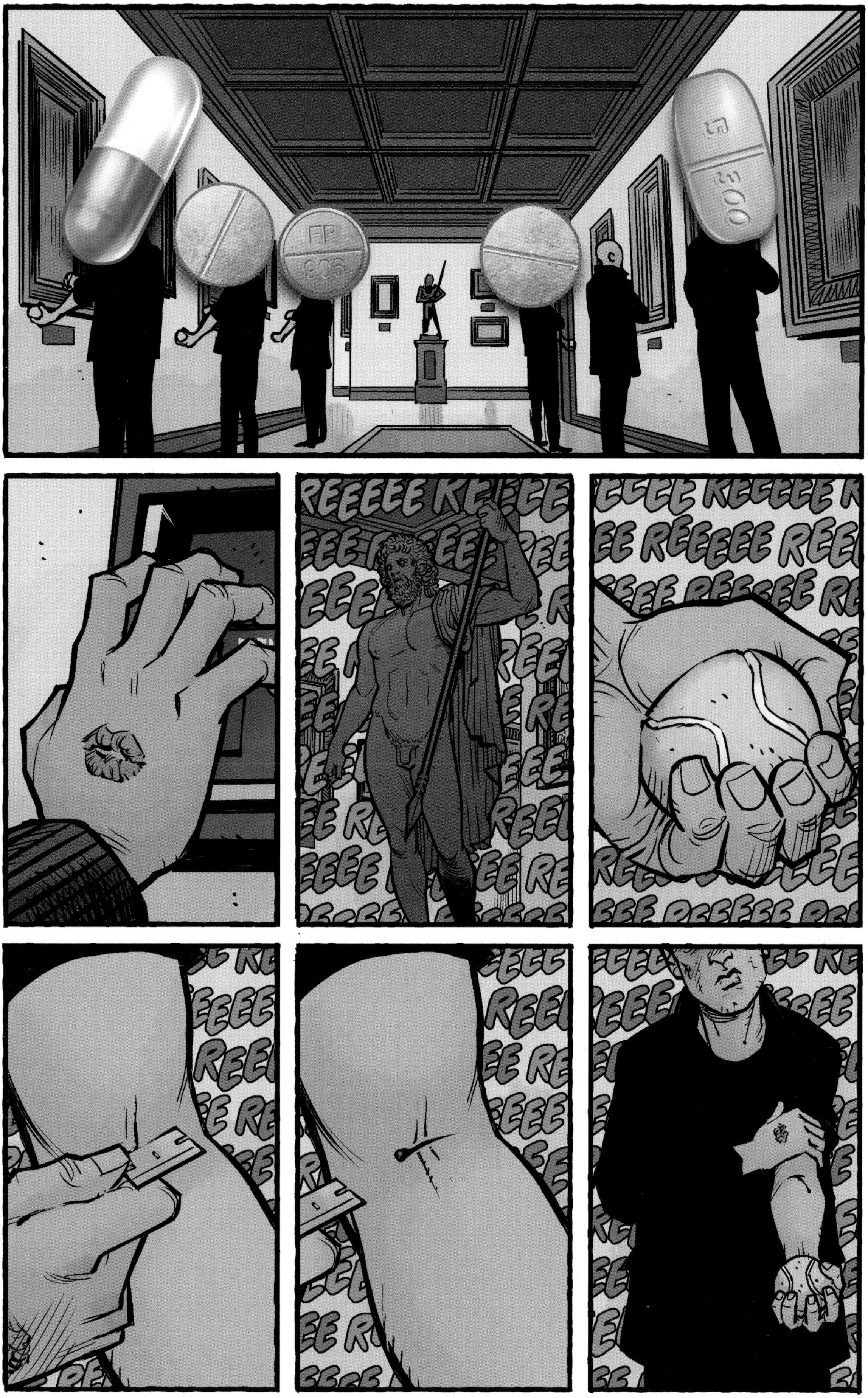
FP
906
300
REEEEEE

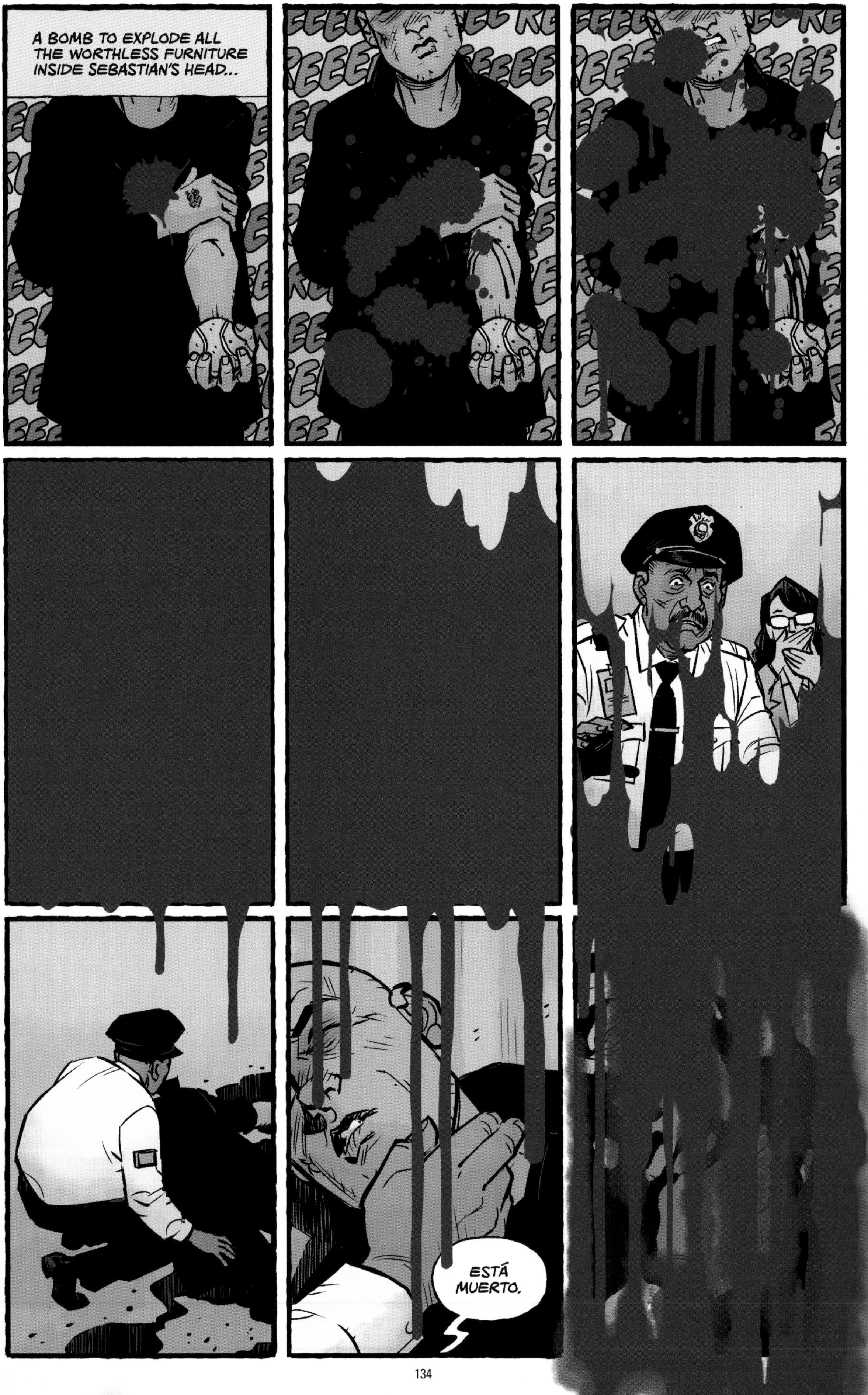
A BOMB TO EXPLODE ALL THE WORTHLESS FURNITURE INSIDE SEBASTIAN'S HEAD...
ESTÁ MUERTO.

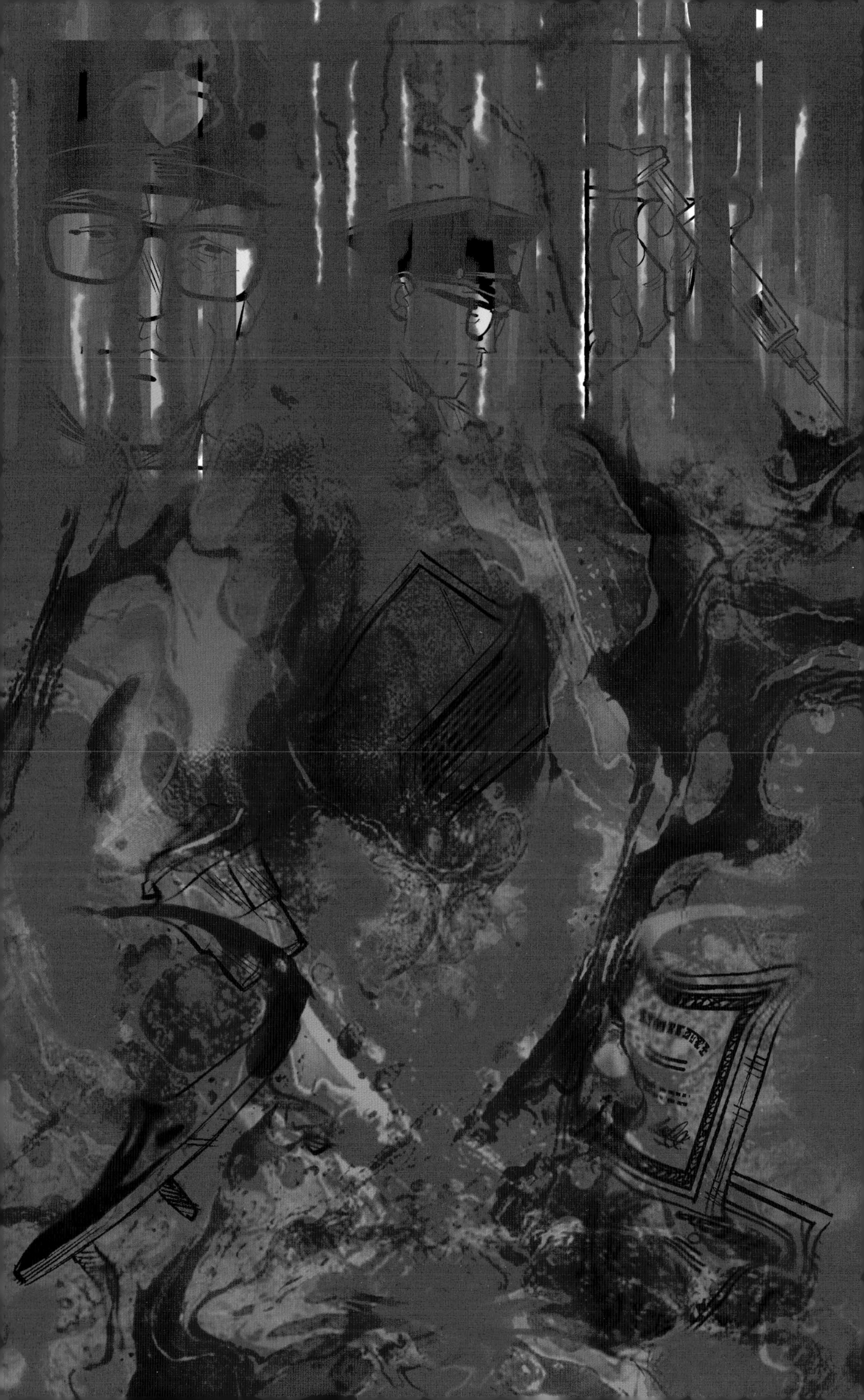

Chapter Six
Becoming Tyler Durden

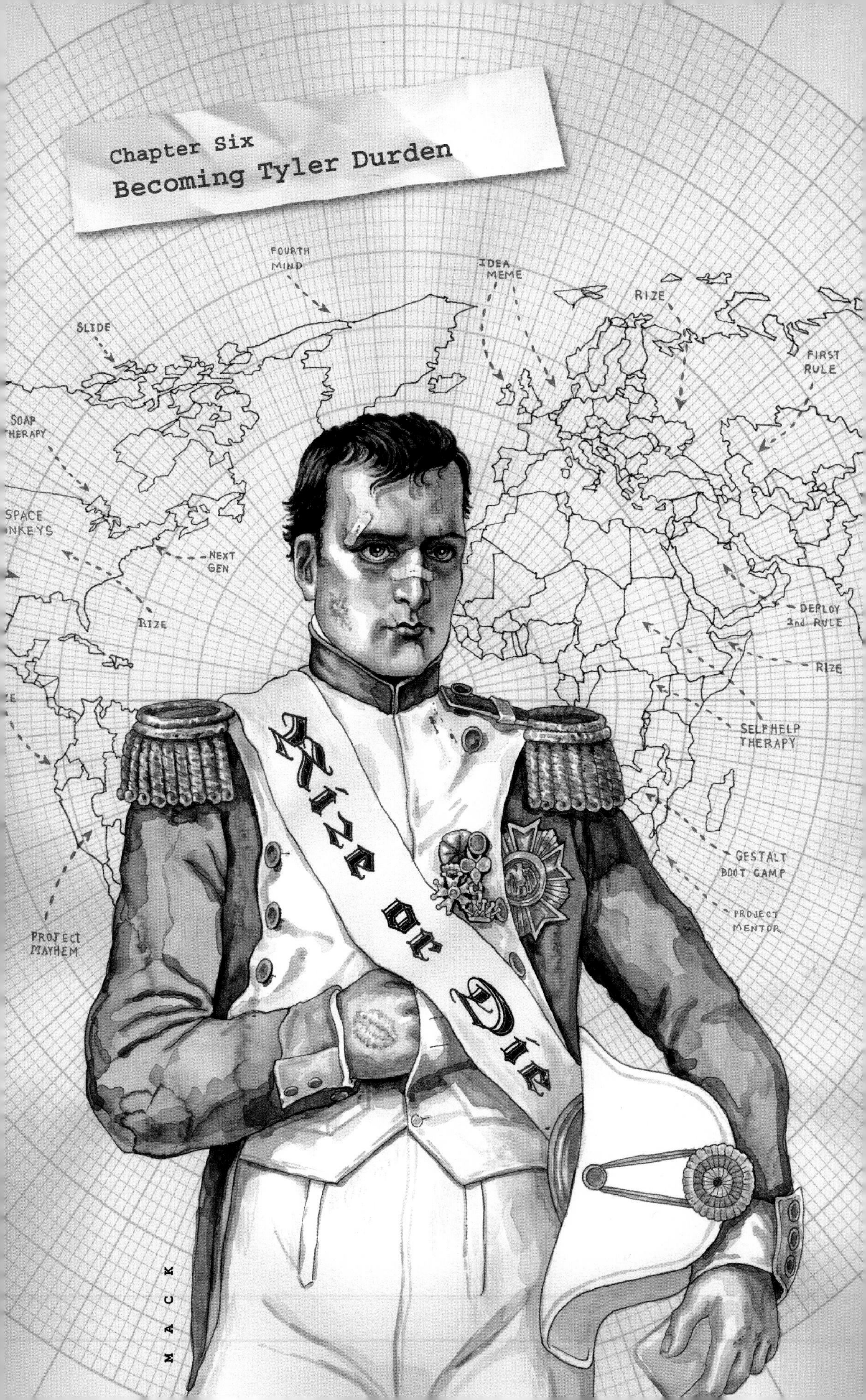
FOURTH MIND
IDEA MEME
RIZE
SLIDE
FIRST RULE
SOAP
SPACE
NEXT GEN
RIZE
DEPLOY 2nd RULE
RIZE
SELFHELP THERAPY
GESTALT BOOT CAMP
PROJECT MENTOR
PROJECT MAYHEM
Rize or Die
MACK

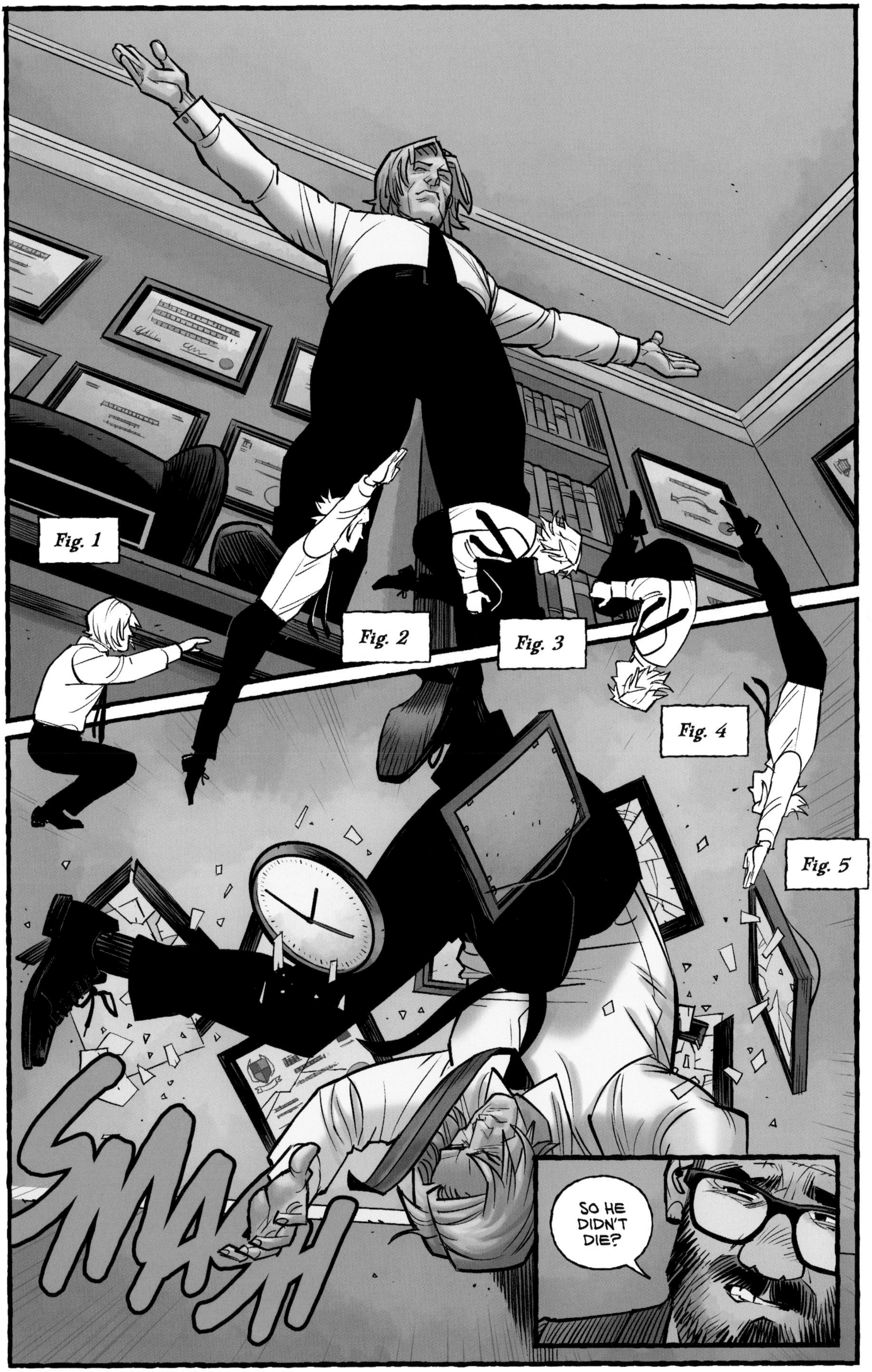
Fig. 1
Fig. 2
Fig. 3
Fig. 4
Fig. 5
SMASH
SO HE DIDN'T DIE?

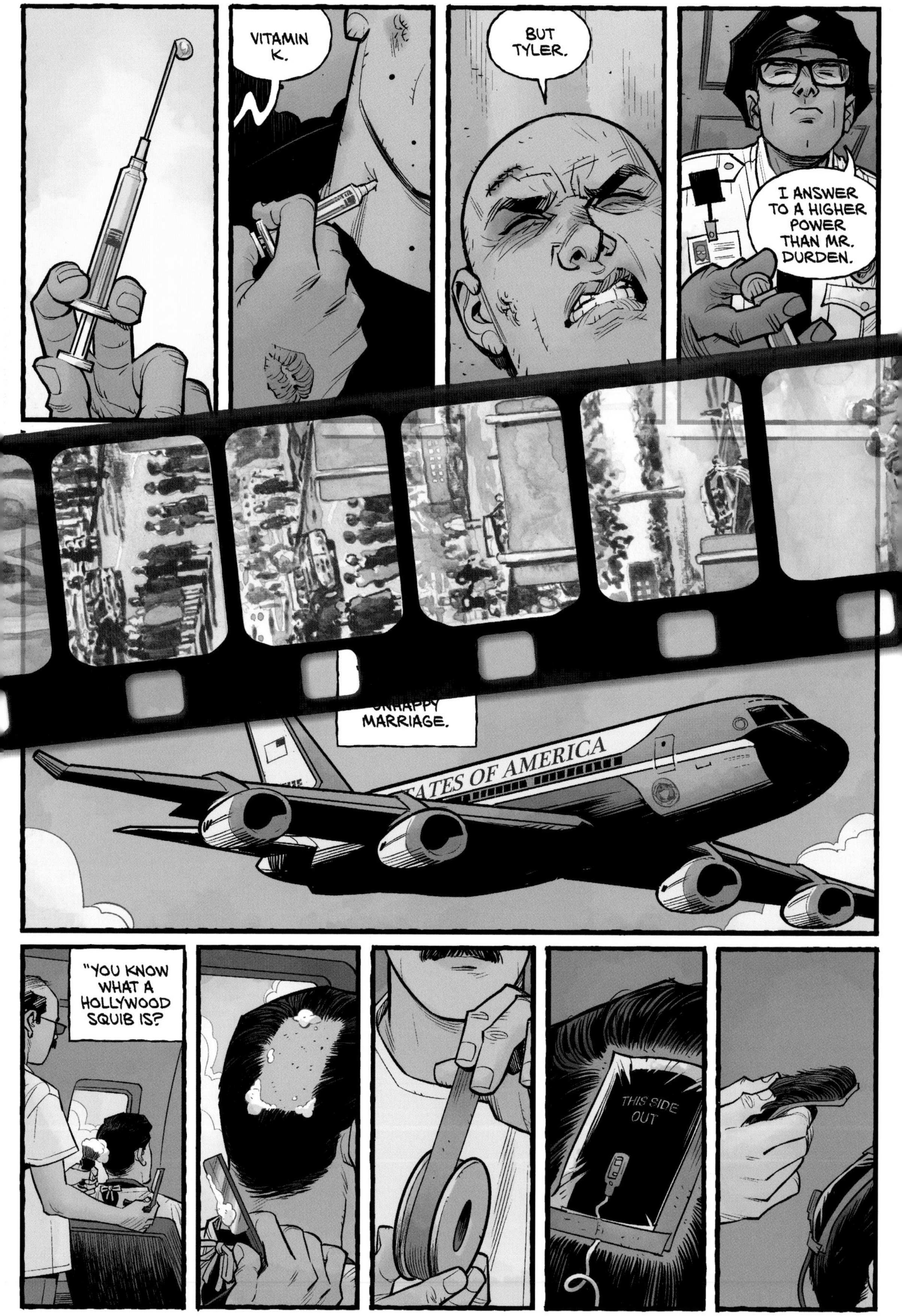
VITAMIN K.
BUT TYLER.
I ANSWER TO A HIGHER POWER THAN MR. DURDEN.
UNHAPPY MARRIAGE.
TATES OF AMERICA
"YOU KNOW WHAT A HOLLYWOOD SQUIB IS?
THIS SIDE OUT

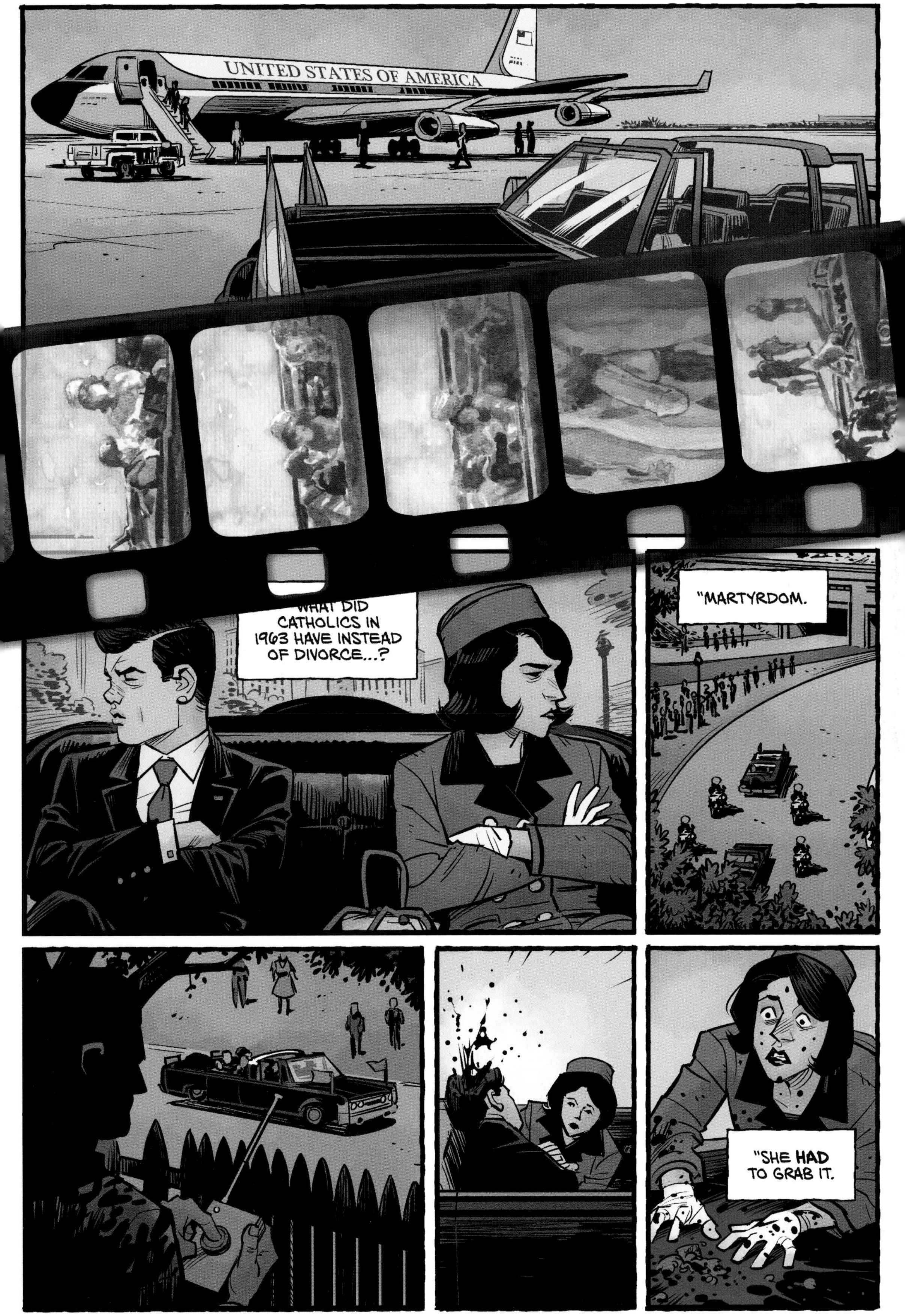
UNITED STATES OF AMERICA
WHAT DID CATHOLICS IN 1963 HAVE INSTEAD OF DIVORCE...?
"MARTYRDOM.
"SHE HAD TO GRAB IT.

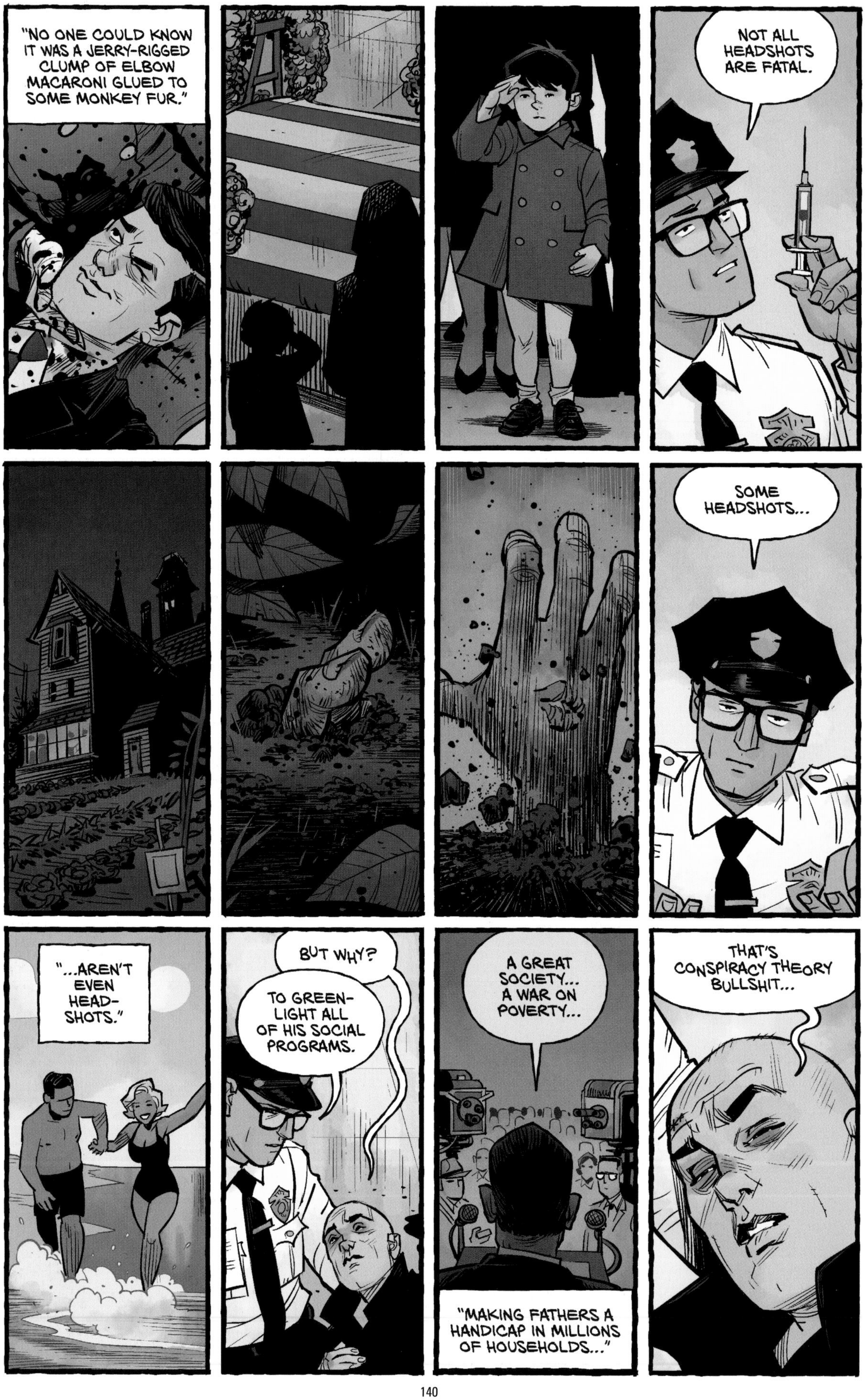
"NO ONE COULD KNOW IT WAS A JERRY-RIGGED CLUMP OF ELBOW MACARONI GLUED TO SOME MONKEY FUR."
NOT ALL HEADSHOTS ARE FATAL.
SOME HEADSHOTS...
"...AREN'T EVEN HEAD-SHOTS."
BUT WHY?
TO GREEN-LIGHT ALL OF HIS SOCIAL PROGRAMS.
A GREAT SOCIETY... A WAR ON POVERTY...
"MAKING FATHERS A HANDICAP IN MILLIONS OF HOUSEHOLDS..."
THAT'S CONSPIRACY THEORY BULLSHIT...

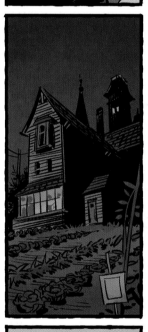

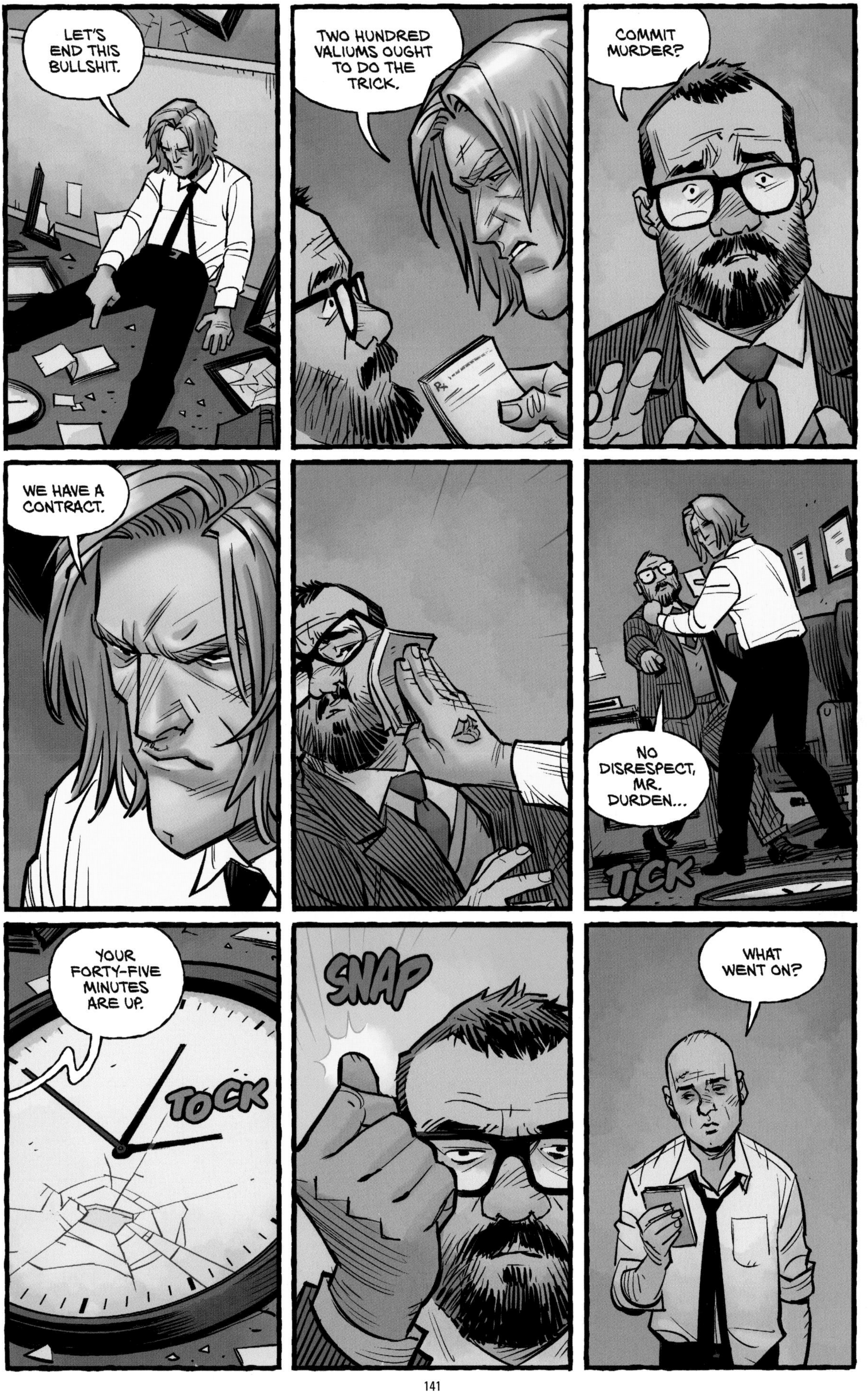
LET'S END THIS BULLSHIT.
TWO HUNDRED VALIUMS OUGHT TO DO THE TRICK.
COMMIT MURDER?
WE HAVE A CONTRACT.
NO DISRESPECT, MR. DURDEN...
TICK
YOUR FORTY-FIVE MINUTES ARE UP.
TOCK
SNAP
WHAT WENT ON?

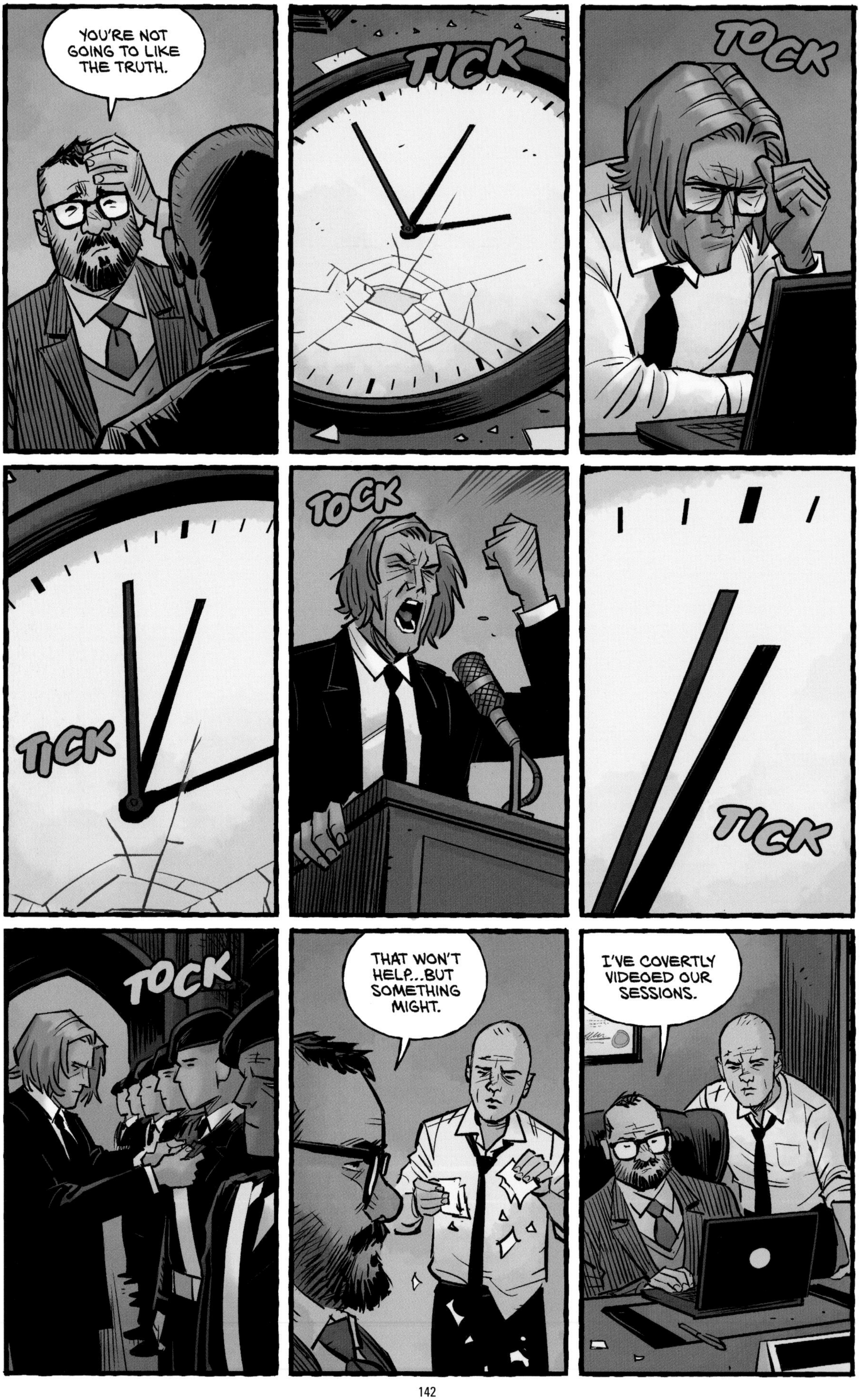
YOU'RE NOT GOING TO LIKE THE TRUTH.
TICK
TOCK
TICK
TOCK
TICK
TOCK
THAT WON'T HELP...BUT SOMETHING MIGHT.
I'VE COVERTLY VIDEOED OUR SESSIONS.

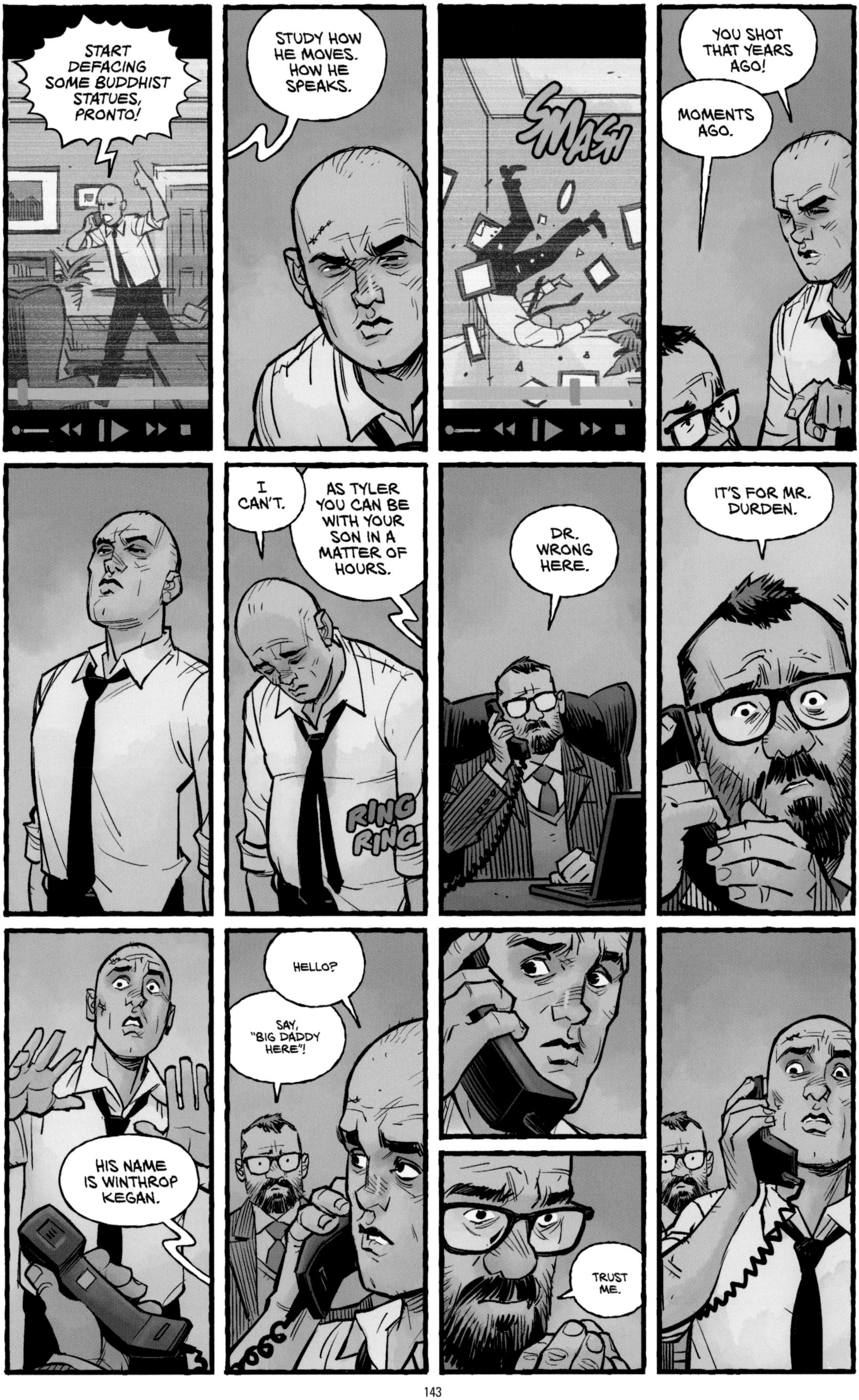
START DEFACING SOME BUDDHIST STATUES, PRONTO!
STUDY HOW HE MOVES. HOW HE SPEAKS.
SMASH
YOU SHOT THAT YEARS AGO!
MOMENTS AGO.
I CAN'T.
AS TYLER YOU CAN BE WITH YOUR SON IN A MATTER OF HOURS.
RING RING
DR. WRONG HERE.
IT'S FOR MR. DURDEN.
HIS NAME IS WINTHROP KEGAN.
HELLO?
SAY, "BIG DADDY HERE"!
TRUST ME.

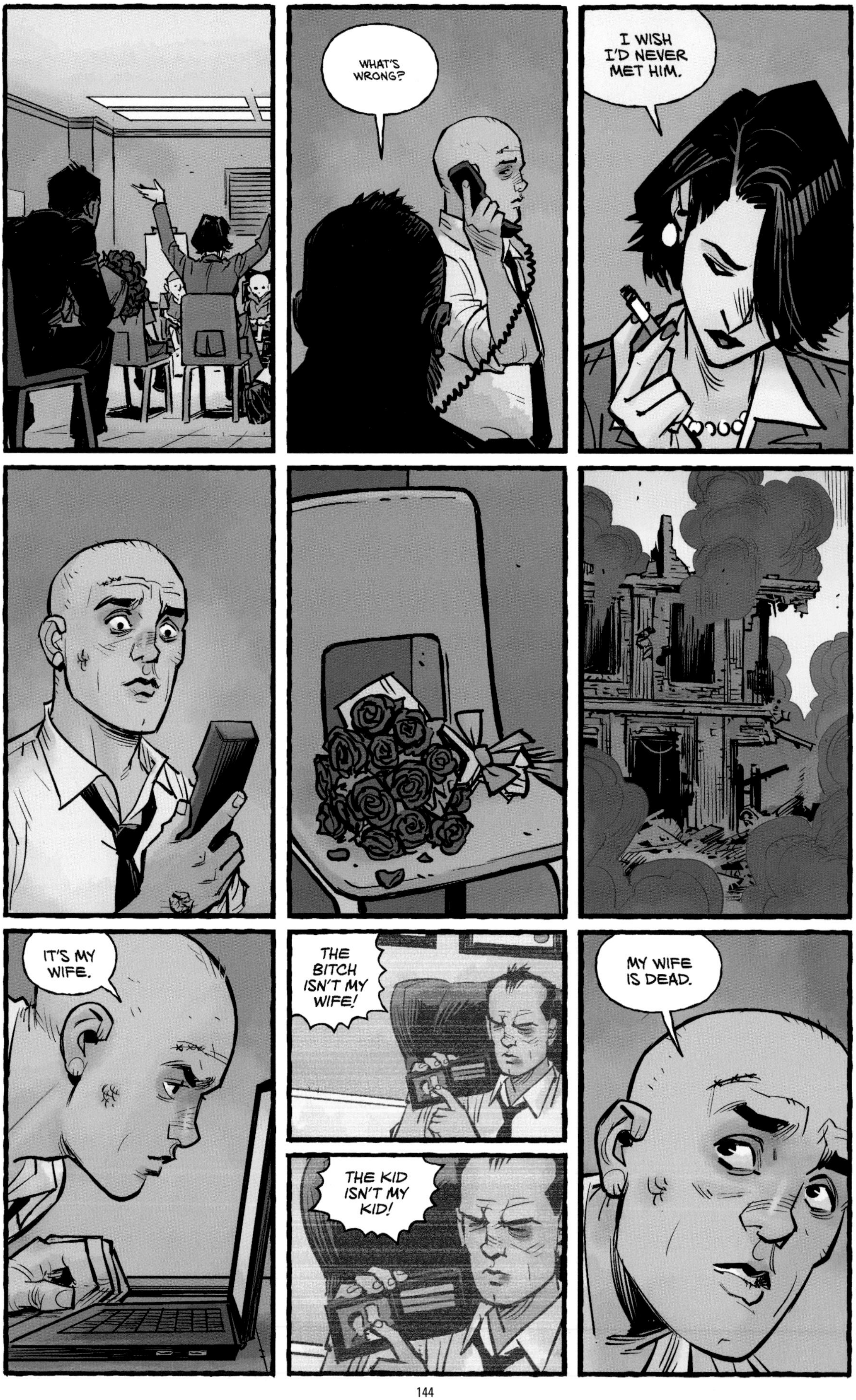
WHAT'S WRONG?
I WISH I'D NEVER MET HIM.
IT'S MY WIFE.
THE BITCH ISN'T MY WIFE!
THE KID ISN'T MY KID!
MY WIFE IS DEAD.

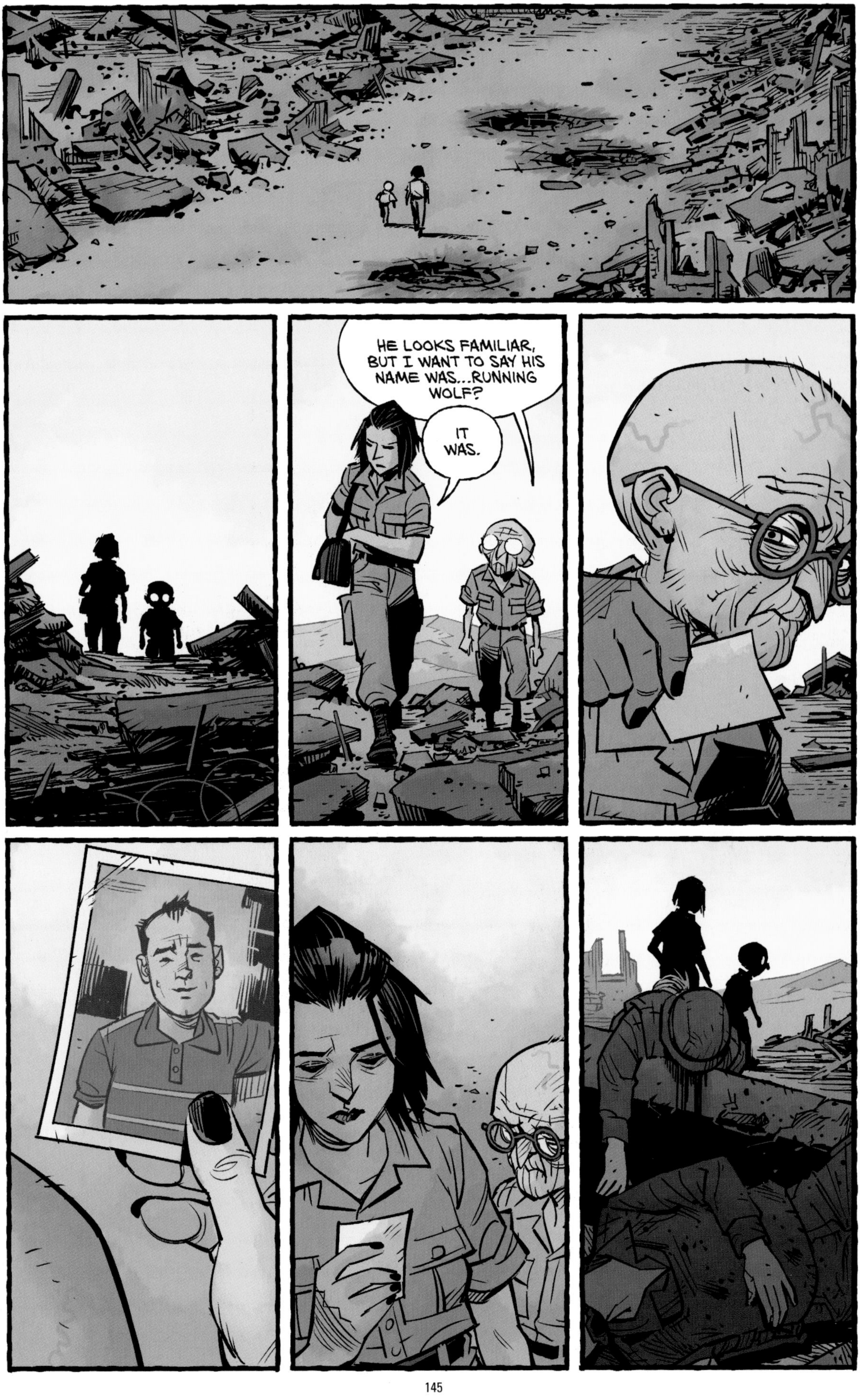
HE LOOKS FAMILIAR, BUT I WANT TO SAY HIS NAME WAS...RUNNING WOLF?
IT WAS.

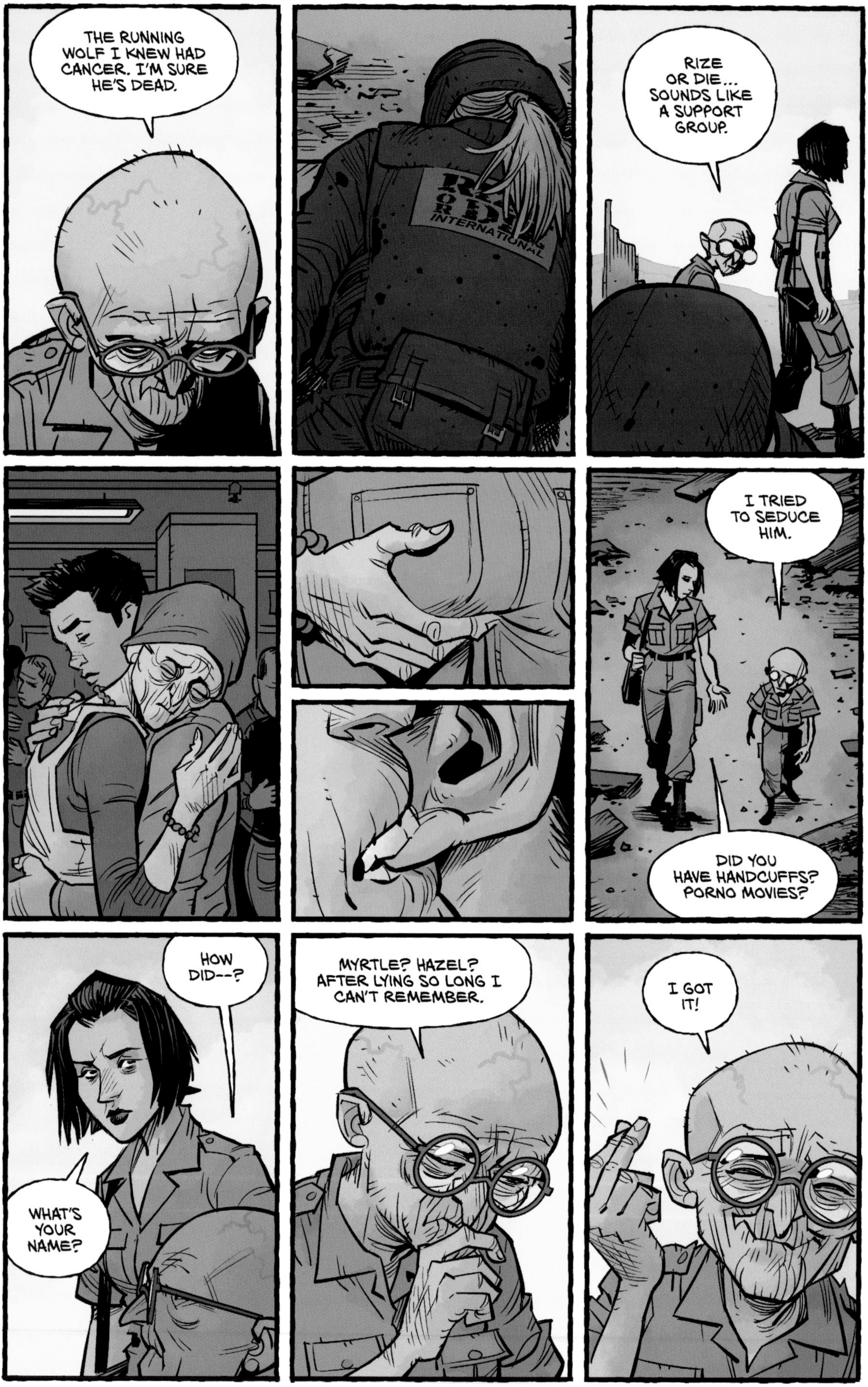
THE RUNNING WOLF I KNEW HAD CANCER. I'M SURE HE'S DEAD.
RIZE OR DIE INTERNATIONAL
RIZE OR DIE... SOUNDS LIKE A SUPPORT GROUP.
I TRIED TO SEDUCE HIM.
DID YOU HAVE HANDCUFFS? PORNO MOVIES?
HOW DID--?
WHAT'S YOUR NAME?
MYRTLE? HAZEL? AFTER LYING SO LONG I CAN'T REMEMBER.
I GOT IT!

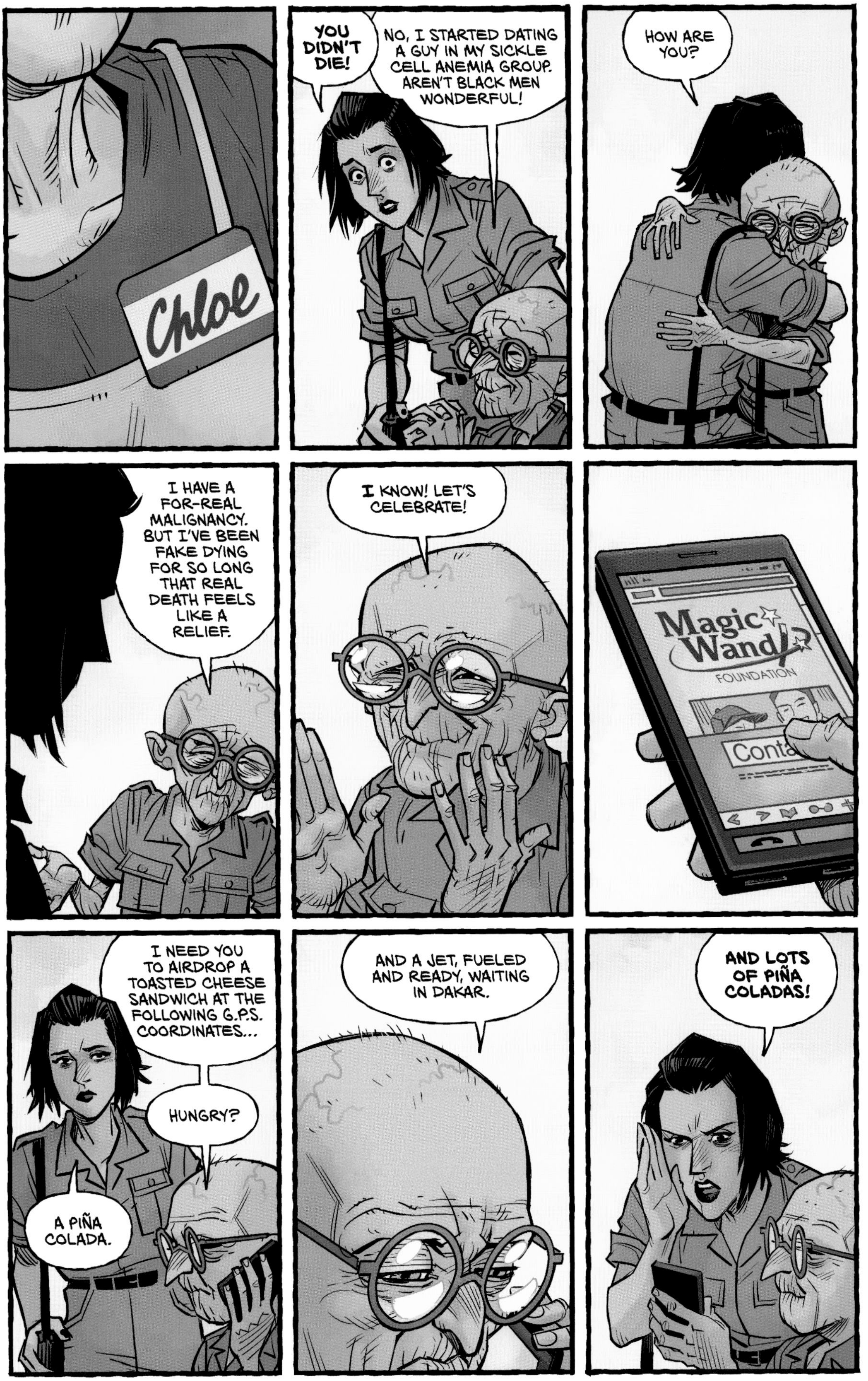
Chloe
YOU DIDN'T DIE!
NO, I STARTED DATING A GUY IN MY SICKLE CELL ANEMIA GROUP. AREN'T BLACK MEN WONDERFUL!
HOW ARE YOU?
I HAVE A FOR-REAL MALIGNANCY. BUT I'VE BEEN FAKE DYING FOR SO LONG THAT REAL DEATH FEELS LIKE A RELIEF.
I KNOW! LET'S CELEBRATE!
Magic Wand
FOUNDATION
Conta
I NEED YOU TO AIRDROP A TOASTED CHEESE SANDWICH AT THE FOLLOWING G.P.S. COORDINATES...
HUNGRY?
A PIÑA COLADA.
AND A JET, FUELED AND READY, WAITING IN DAKAR.
AND LOTS OF PIÑA COLADAS!

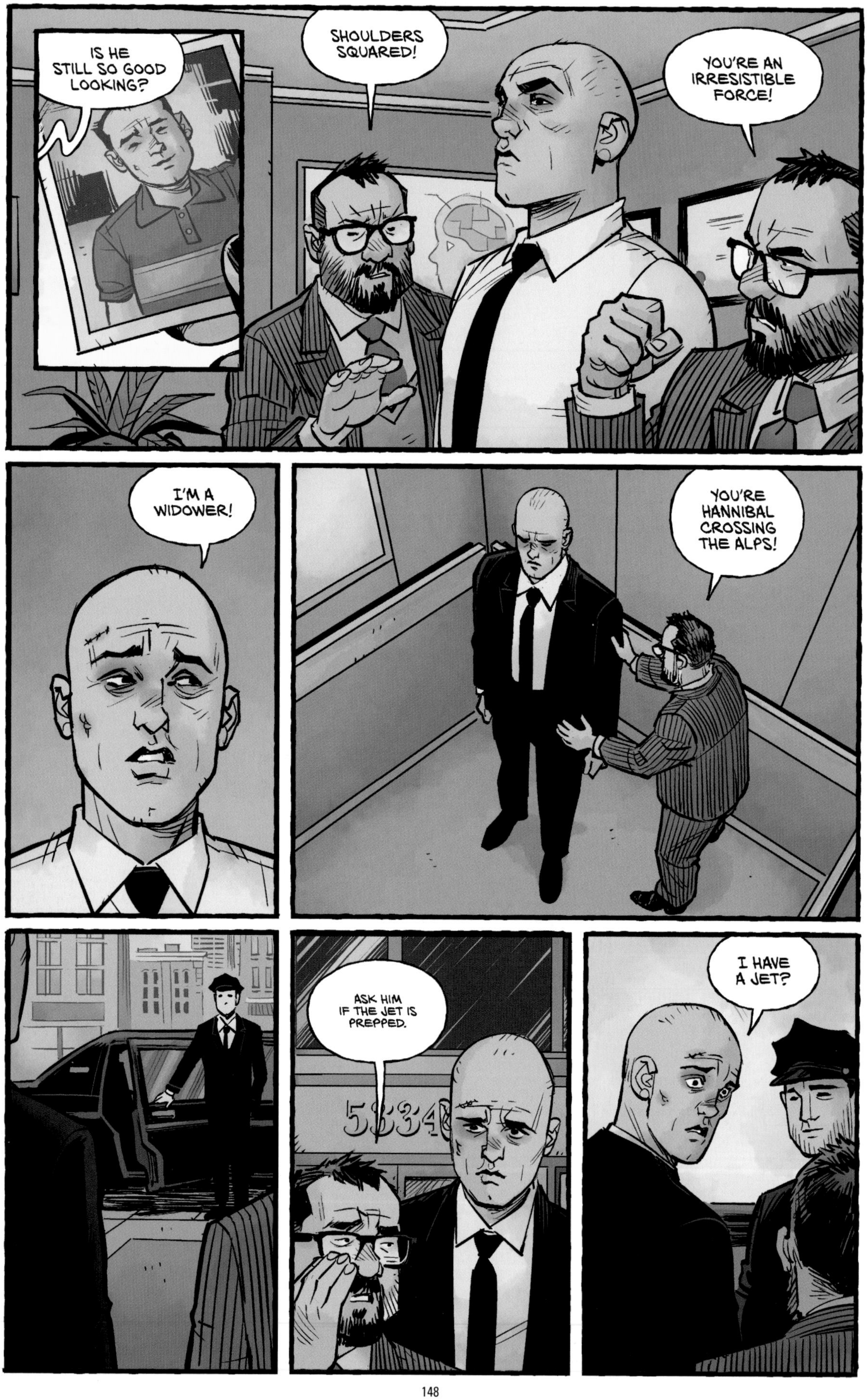
IS HE STILL SO GOOD LOOKING?
SHOULDERS SQUARED!
YOU'RE AN IRRESISTIBLE FORCE!
I'M A WIDOWER!
YOU'RE HANNIBAL CROSSING THE ALPS!
ASK HIM IF THE JET IS PREPPED.
I HAVE A JET?

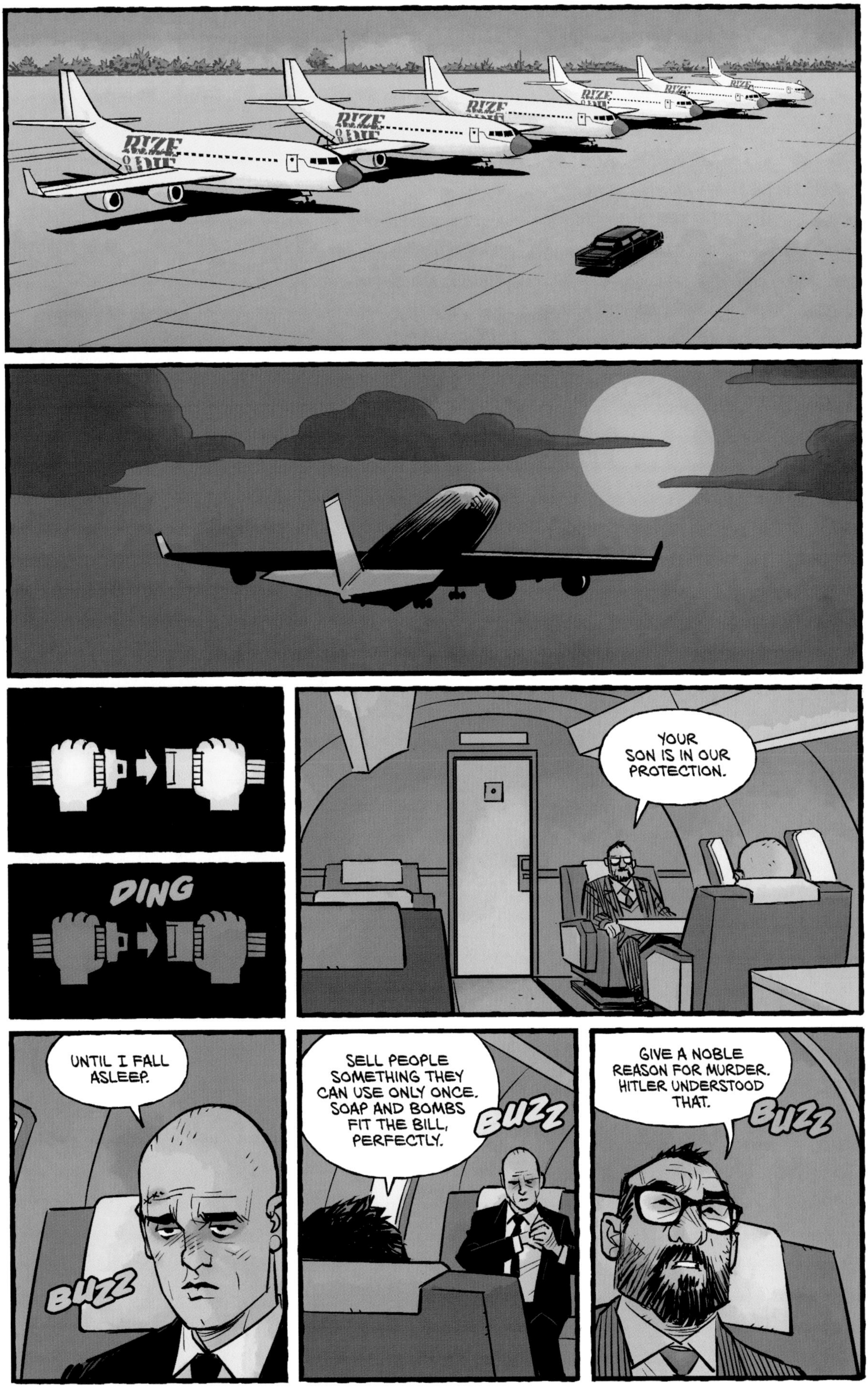
RIZE OR DIE
DING
YOUR SON IS IN OUR PROTECTION.
UNTIL I FALL ASLEEP.
BUZZ
SELL PEOPLE SOMETHING THEY CAN USE ONLY ONCE. SOAP AND BOMBS FIT THE BILL, PERFECTLY.
BUZZ
GIVE A NOBLE REASON FOR MURDER. HITLER UNDERSTOOD THAT.
BUZZ

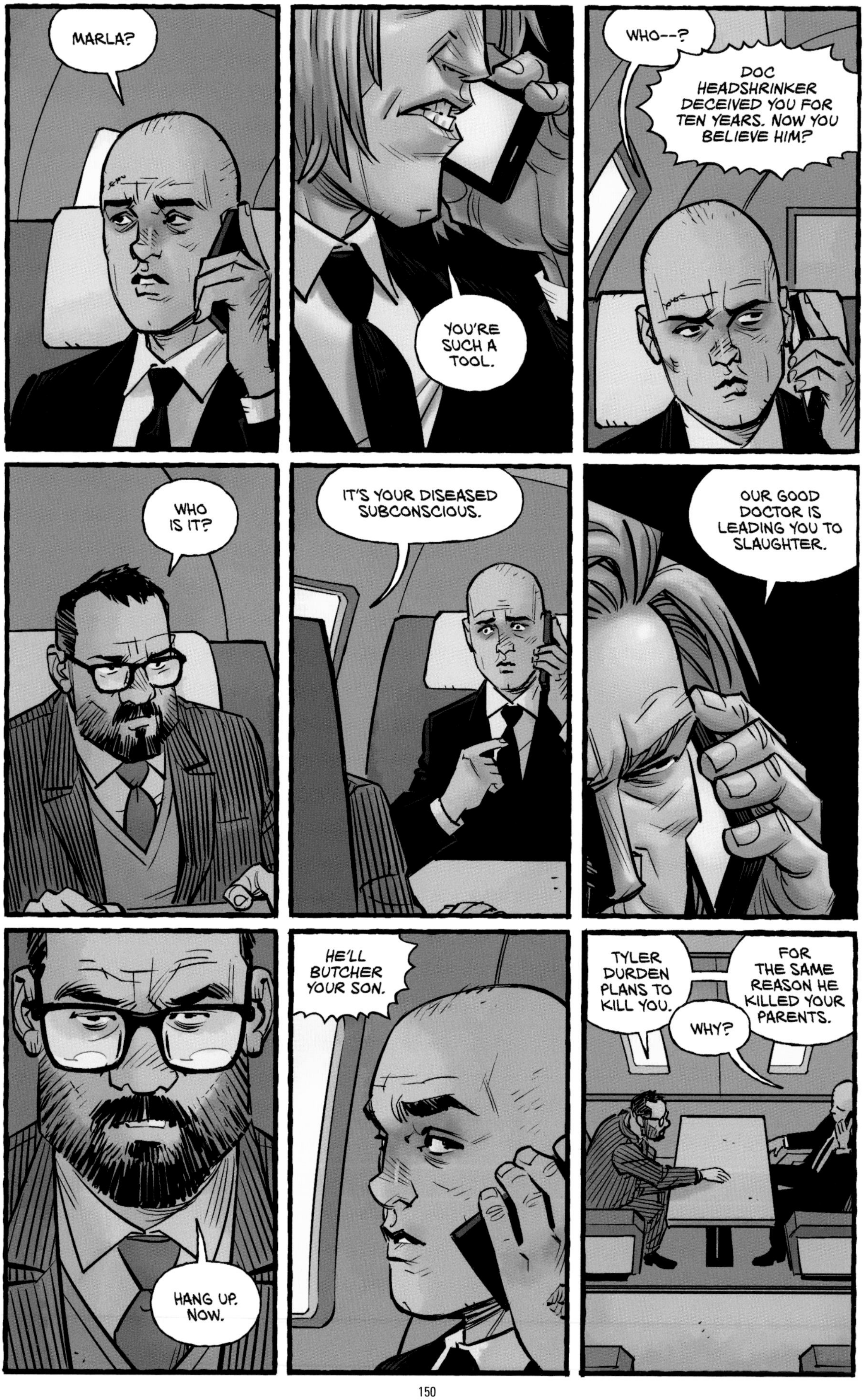
MARLA?
YOU'RE SUCH A TOOL.
WHO--?
DOC HEADSHRINKER DECEIVED YOU FOR TEN YEARS. NOW YOU BELIEVE HIM?
WHO IS IT?
IT'S YOUR DISEASED SUBCONSCIOUS.
OUR GOOD DOCTOR IS LEADING YOU TO SLAUGHTER.
HANG UP. NOW.
HE'LL BUTCHER YOUR SON.
TYLER DURDEN PLANS TO KILL YOU.
WHY?
FOR THE SAME REASON HE KILLED YOUR PARENTS.

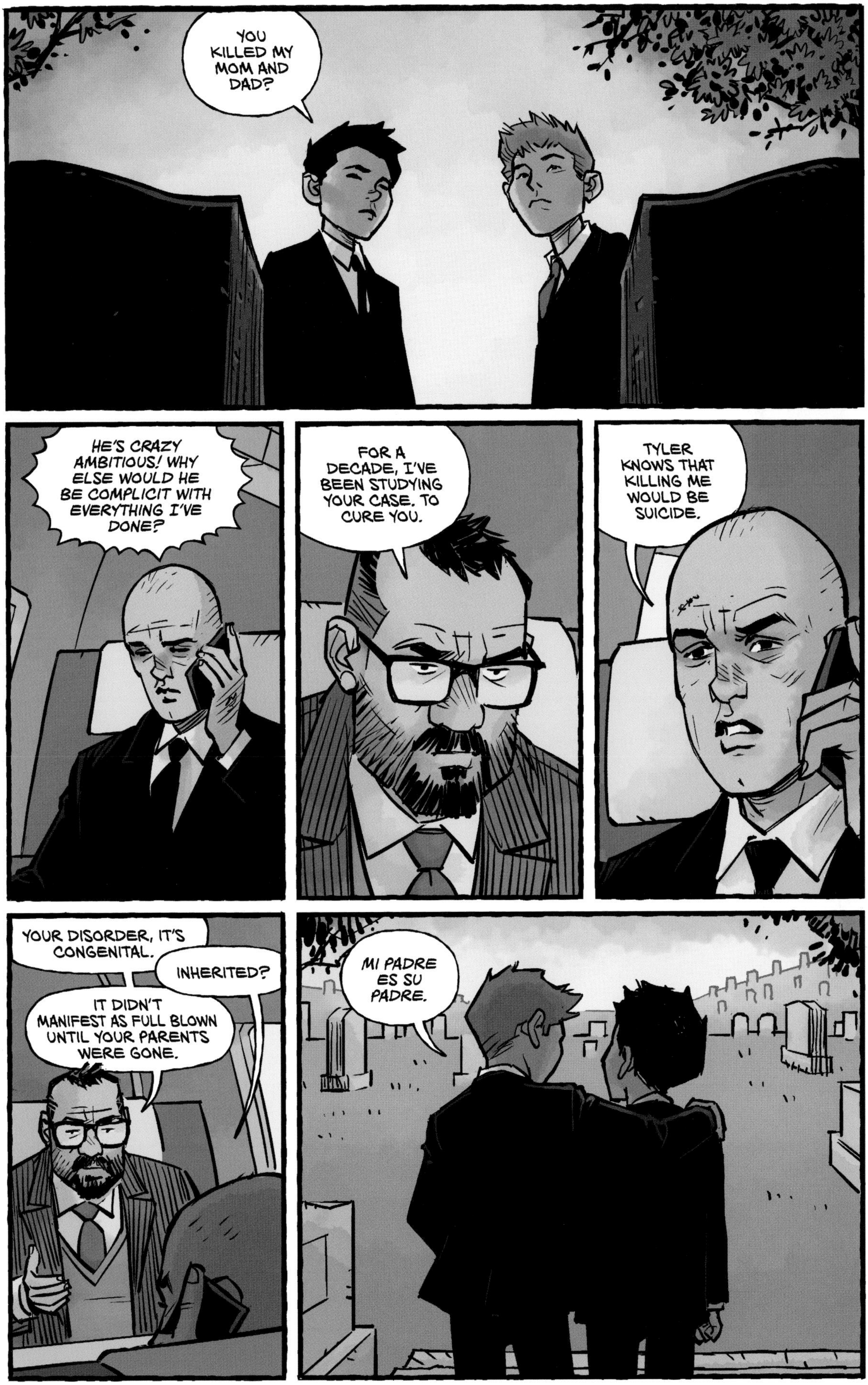
YOU KILLED MY MOM AND DAD?
HE'S CRAZY AMBITIOUS! WHY ELSE WOULD HE BE COMPLICIT WITH EVERYTHING I'VE DONE?
FOR A DECADE, I'VE BEEN STUDYING YOUR CASE. TO CURE YOU.
TYLER KNOWS THAT KILLING ME WOULD BE SUICIDE.
YOUR DISORDER, IT'S CONGENITAL.
INHERITED?
IT DIDN'T MANIFEST AS FULL BLOWN UNTIL YOUR PARENTS WERE GONE.
MI PADRE ES SU PADRE.

TYLER WON'T DIE. HE'S ALREADY INSINUATED HIMSELF IN YOUR SON'S LIFE.

HOW DO YOU THINK YOUR SON MADE THE INCENDIARY BOMB TO DESTROY YOUR HOUSE?

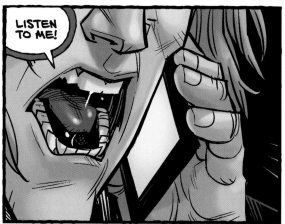

LISTEN TO ME!

SO, TYLER IS SOME SORT OF CONTAGION?

HE'S AN **ARCHETYPE.** TYLER WORKS LIKE A SUPERSTITION OR A PREJUDICE. HE BECOMES PART OF THE LENS THROUGH WHICH YOU SEE THE WORLD.

MORE BLACK-HELICOPTER BULLSHIT.

TAPED TO THE BOTTOM OF YOUR SEAT...

DO YOU KNOW SHE'S DEAD?

A DRONE FOUND...

TYLER SURVIVES ACROSS TIME BY INFECTING ONE GENERATION AFTER ANOTHER.

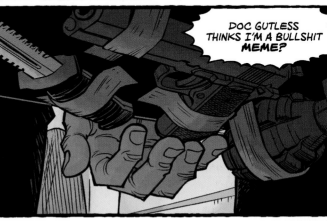

DOC GUTLESS THINKS I'M A BULLSHIT MEME?

DON'T YOU CARE?

SHOOT HIM!

DON'T EVEN CONSIDER SHOOTING ME.

WITHOUT MY GUIDANCE, YOU'LL BECOME A RAVING LUNATIC.

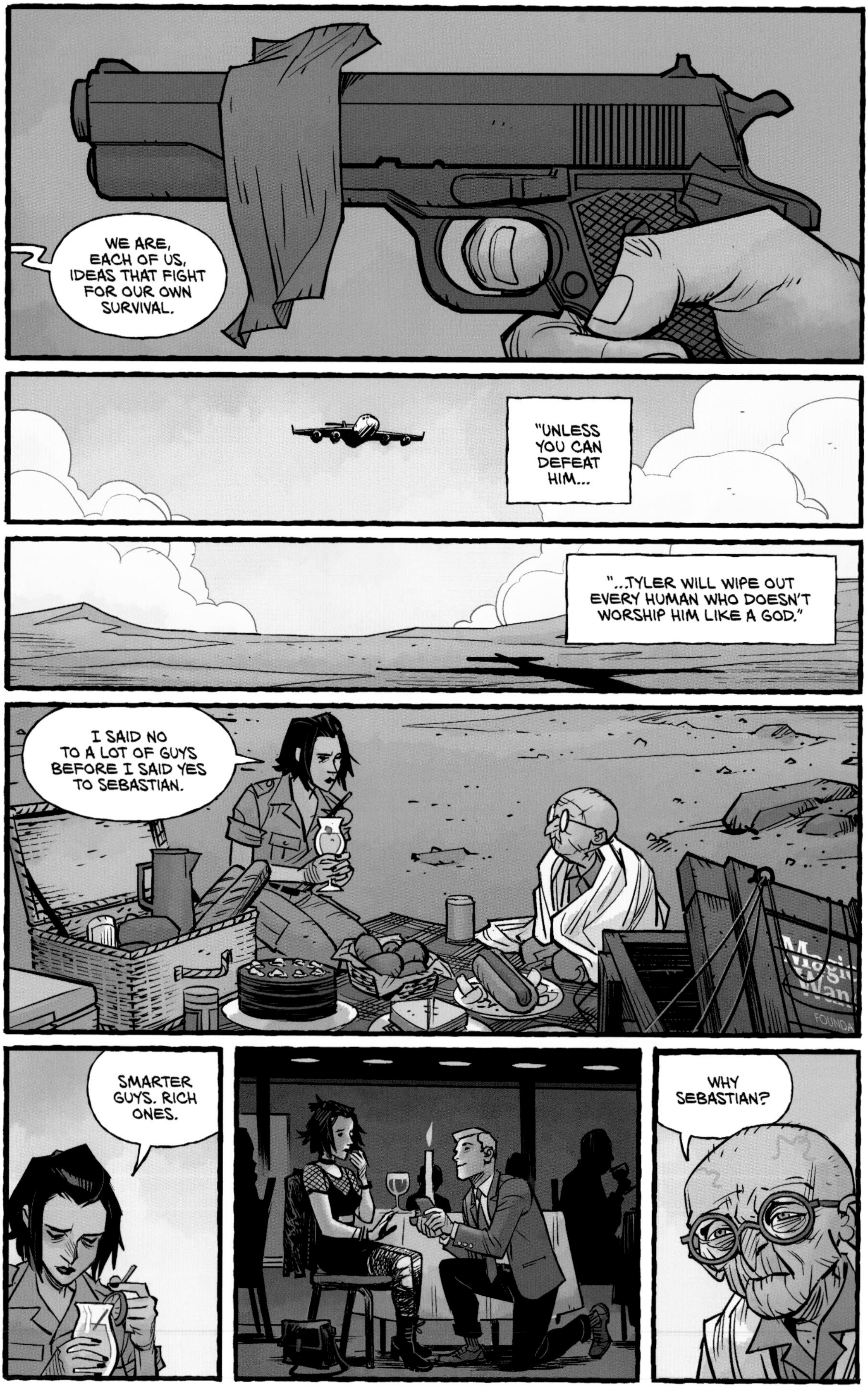
WE ARE, EACH OF US, IDEAS THAT FIGHT FOR OUR OWN SURVIVAL.
"UNLESS YOU CAN DEFEAT HIM...
"...TYLER WILL WIPE OUT EVERY HUMAN WHO DOESN'T WORSHIP HIM LIKE A GOD."
I SAID NO TO A LOT OF GUYS BEFORE I SAID YES TO SEBASTIAN.
SMARTER GUYS. RICH ONES.
WHY SEBASTIAN?

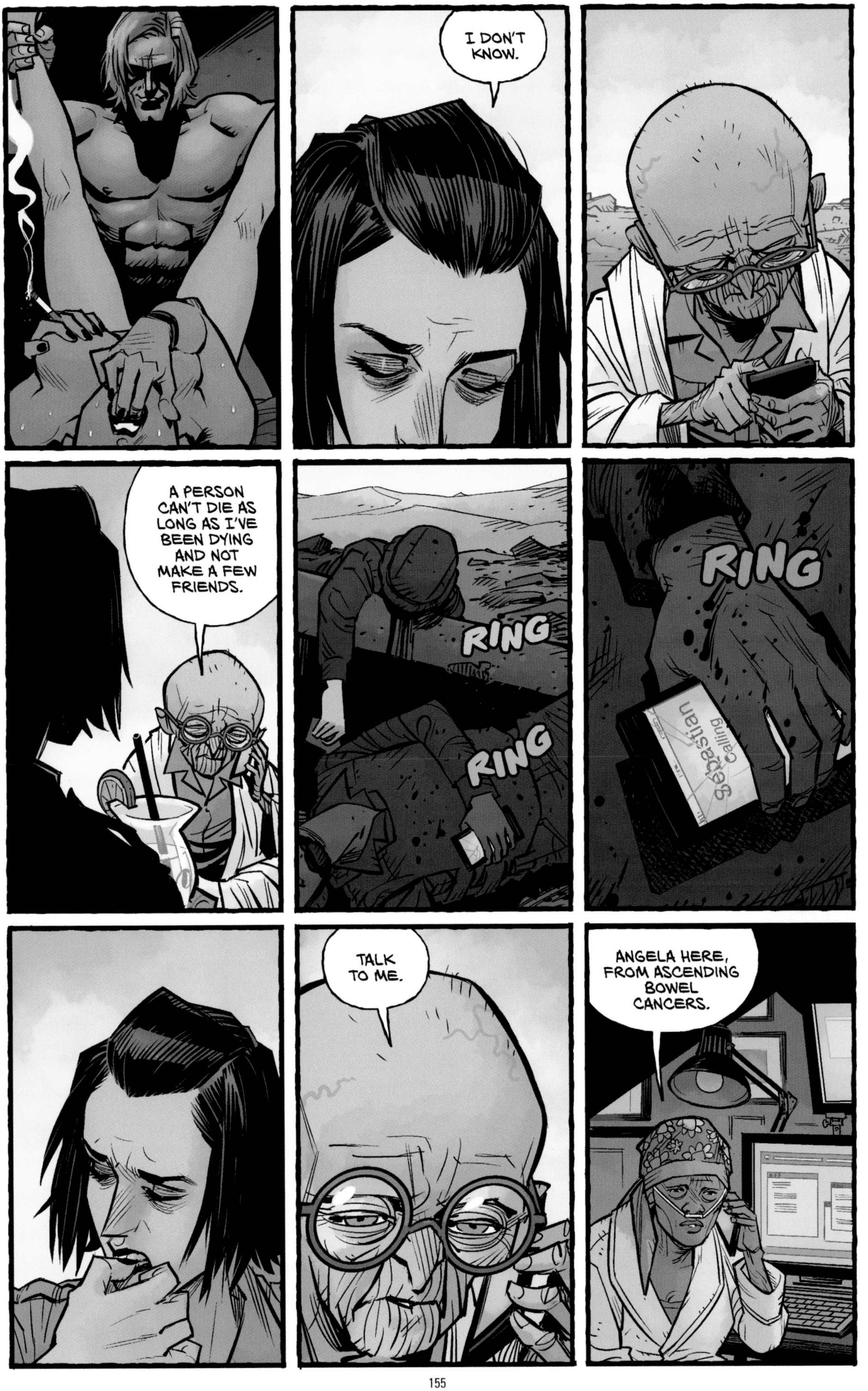
I DON'T KNOW.
A PERSON CAN'T DIE AS LONG AS I'VE BEEN DYING AND NOT MAKE A FEW FRIENDS.
RING
RING
RING
sebastian
Calling
TALK TO ME.
ANGELA HERE, FROM ASCENDING BOWEL CANCERS.

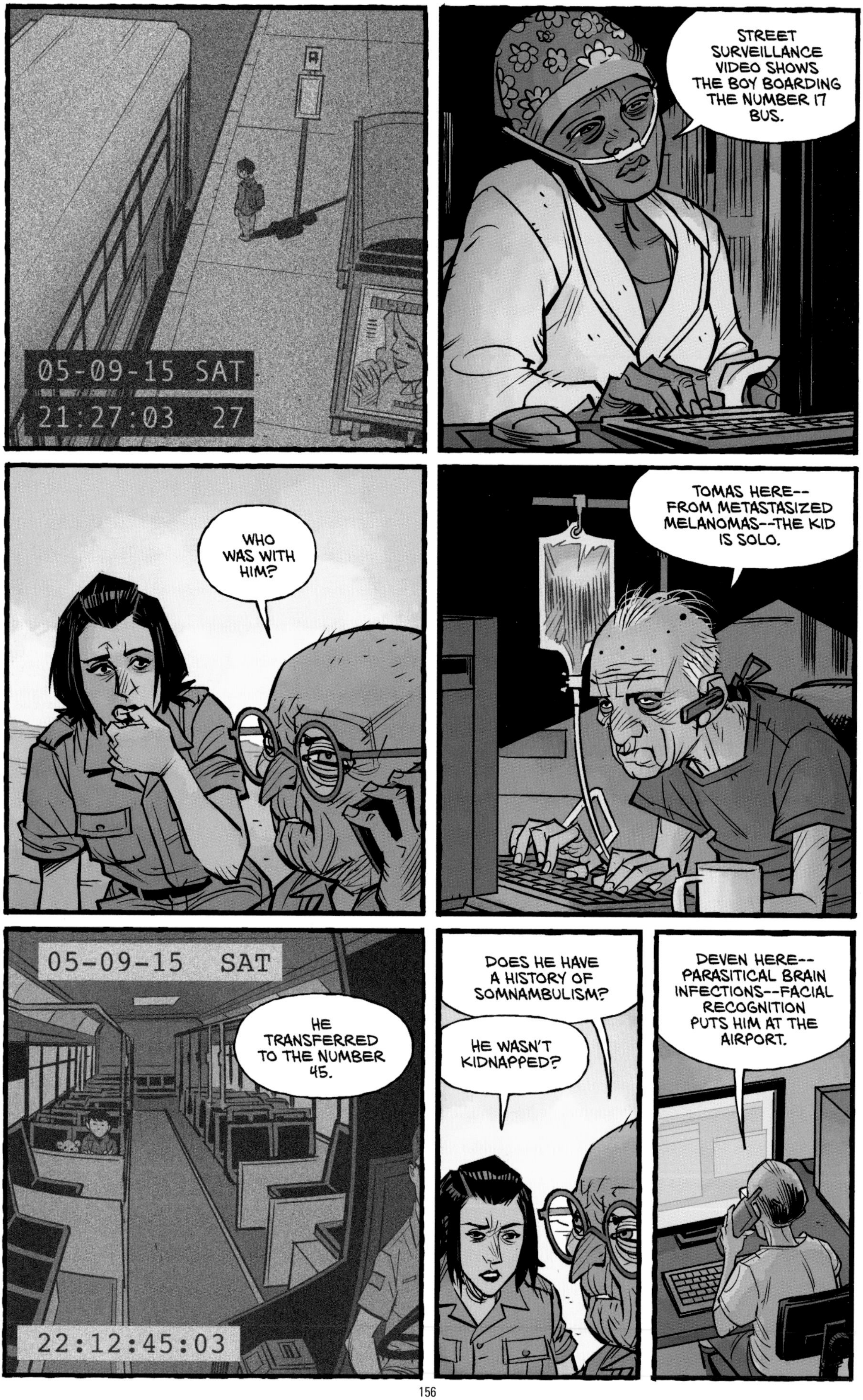
05-09-15 SAT
21:27:03 27
STREET SURVEILLANCE VIDEO SHOWS THE BOY BOARDING THE NUMBER 17 BUS.
WHO WAS WITH HIM?
TOMAS HERE-- FROM METASTASIZED MELANOMAS--THE KID IS SOLO.
05-09-15 SAT
HE TRANSFERRED TO THE NUMBER 45.
22:12:45:03
DOES HE HAVE A HISTORY OF SOMNAMBULISM?
HE WASN'T KIDNAPPED?
DEVEN HERE-- PARASITICAL BRAIN INFECTIONS--FACIAL RECOGNITION PUTS HIM AT THE AIRPORT.

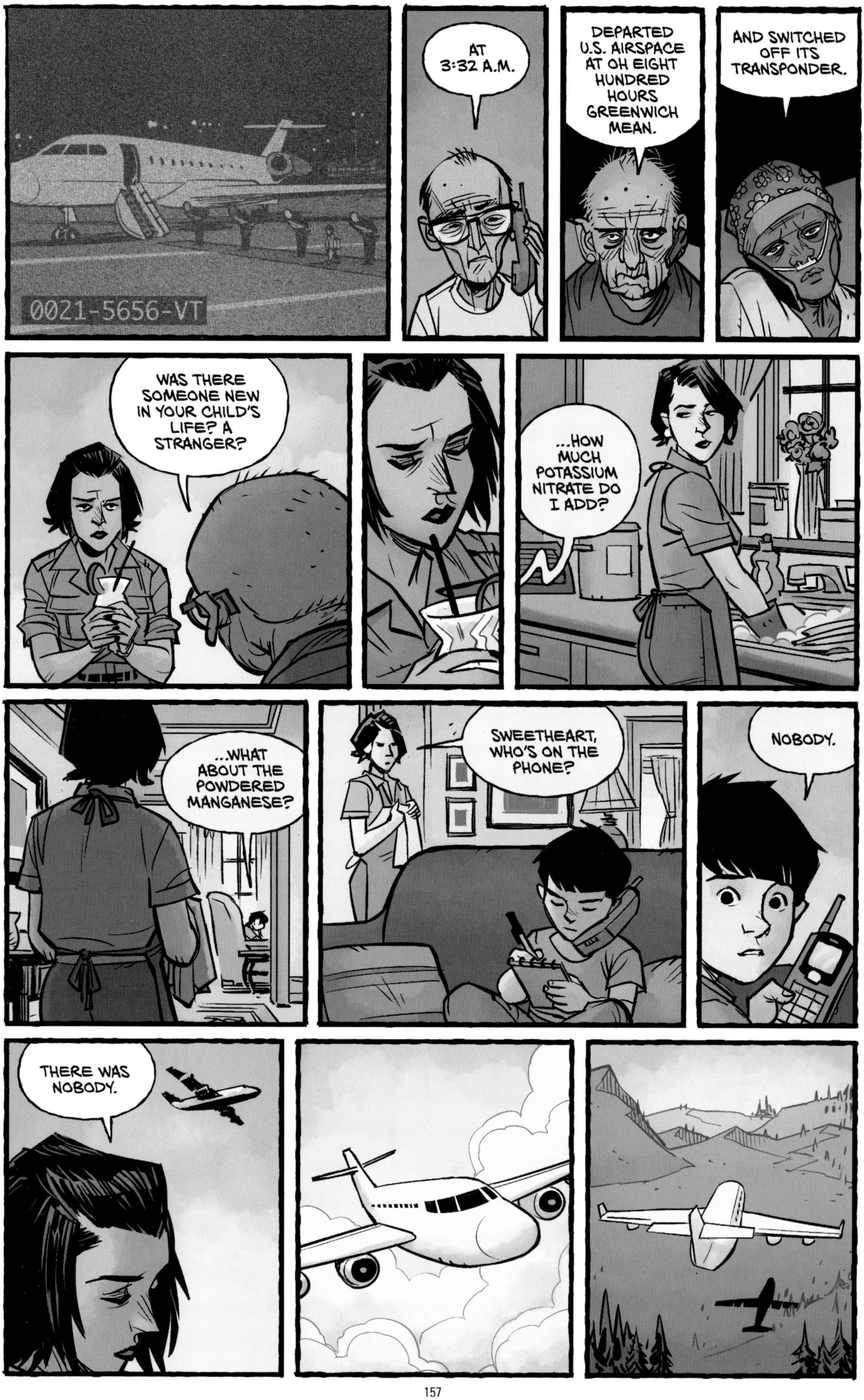
0021-5656-VT
AT 3:32 A.M.
DEPARTED U.S. AIRSPACE AT OH EIGHT HUNDRED HOURS GREENWICH MEAN.
AND SWITCHED OFF ITS TRANSPONDER.
WAS THERE SOMEONE NEW IN YOUR CHILD'S LIFE? A STRANGER?
...HOW MUCH POTASSIUM NITRATE DO I ADD?
...WHAT ABOUT THE POWDERED MANGANESE?
SWEETHEART, WHO'S ON THE PHONE?
NOBODY.
THERE WAS NOBODY.

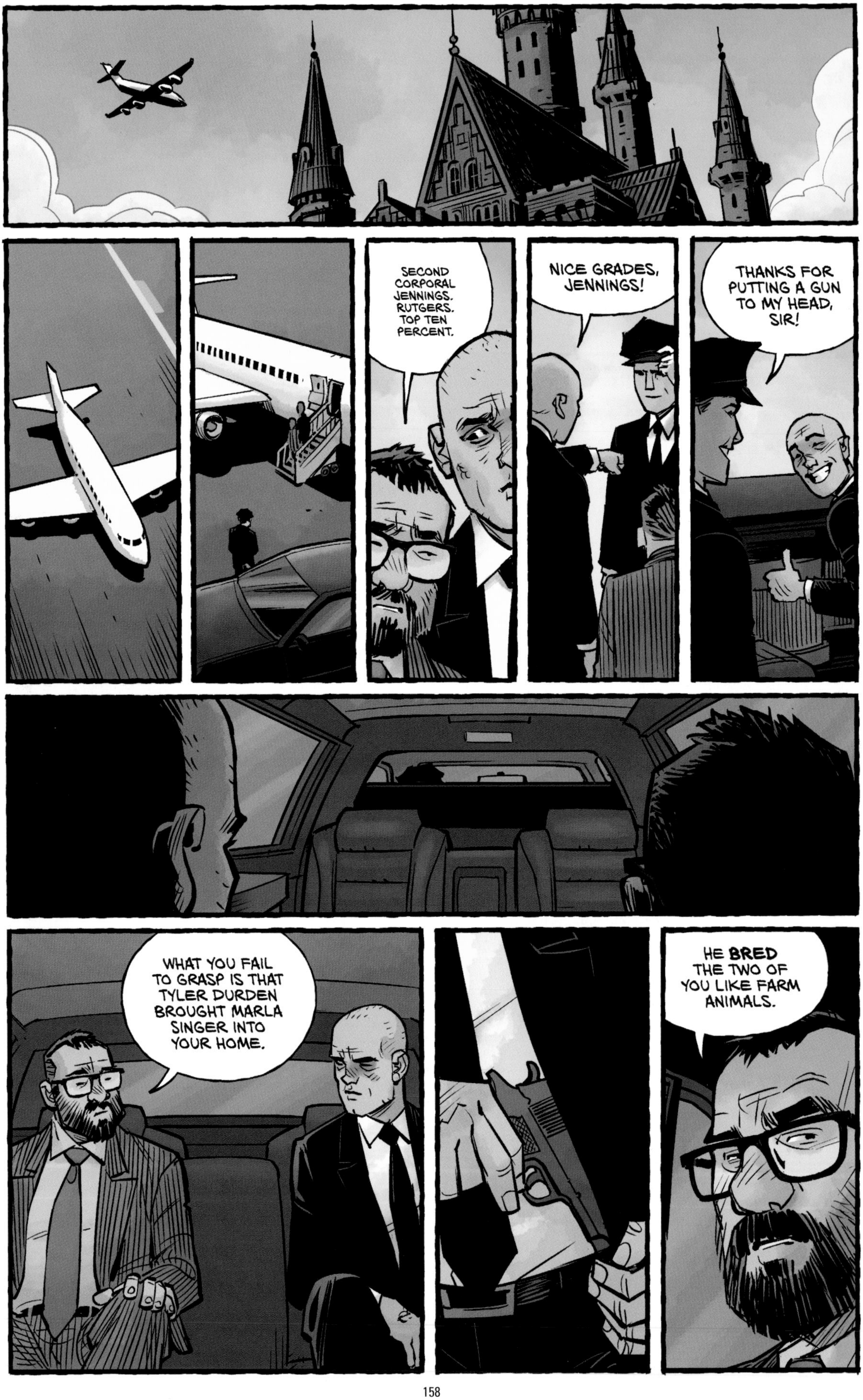
SECOND CORPORAL JENNINGS. RUTGERS. TOP TEN PERCENT.
NICE GRADES, JENNINGS!
THANKS FOR PUTTING A GUN TO MY HEAD, SIR!
WHAT YOU FAIL TO GRASP IS THAT TYLER DURDEN BROUGHT MARLA SINGER INTO YOUR HOME.
HE **BRED** THE TWO OF YOU LIKE FARM ANIMALS.

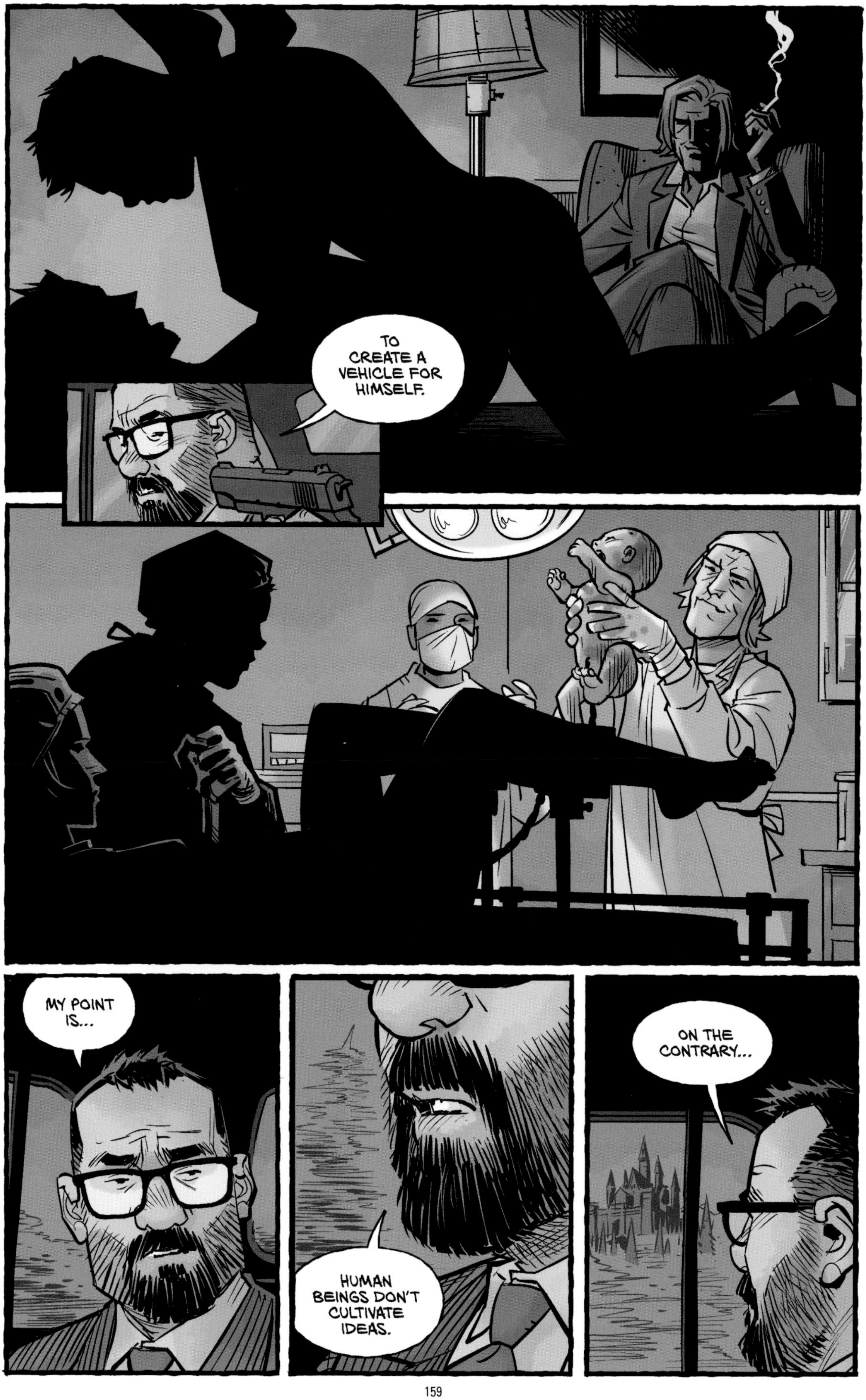
TO CREATE A VEHICLE FOR HIMSELF.
MY POINT IS...
HUMAN BEINGS DON'T CULTIVATE IDEAS.
ON THE CONTRARY...

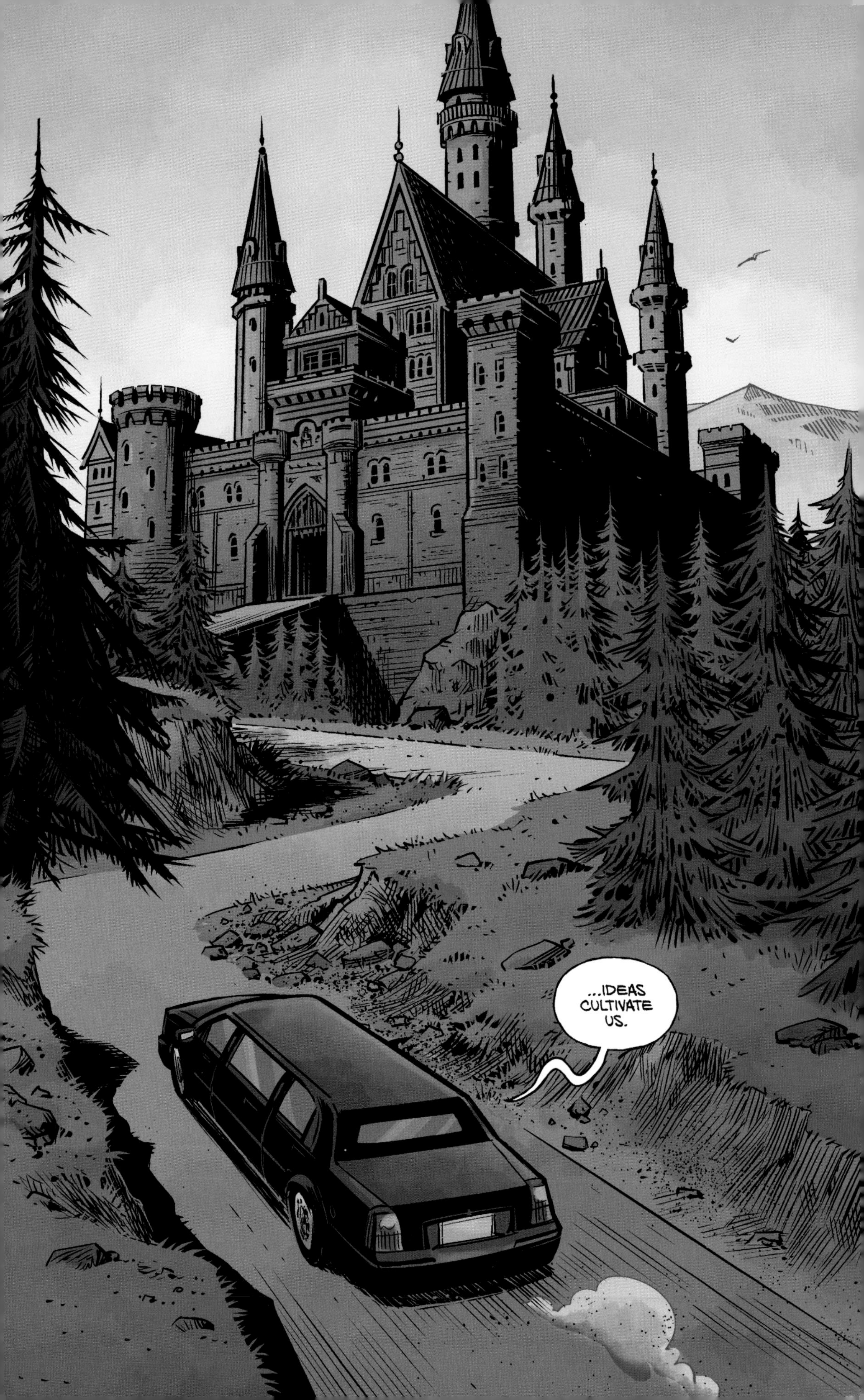
...IDEAS CULTIVATE US.

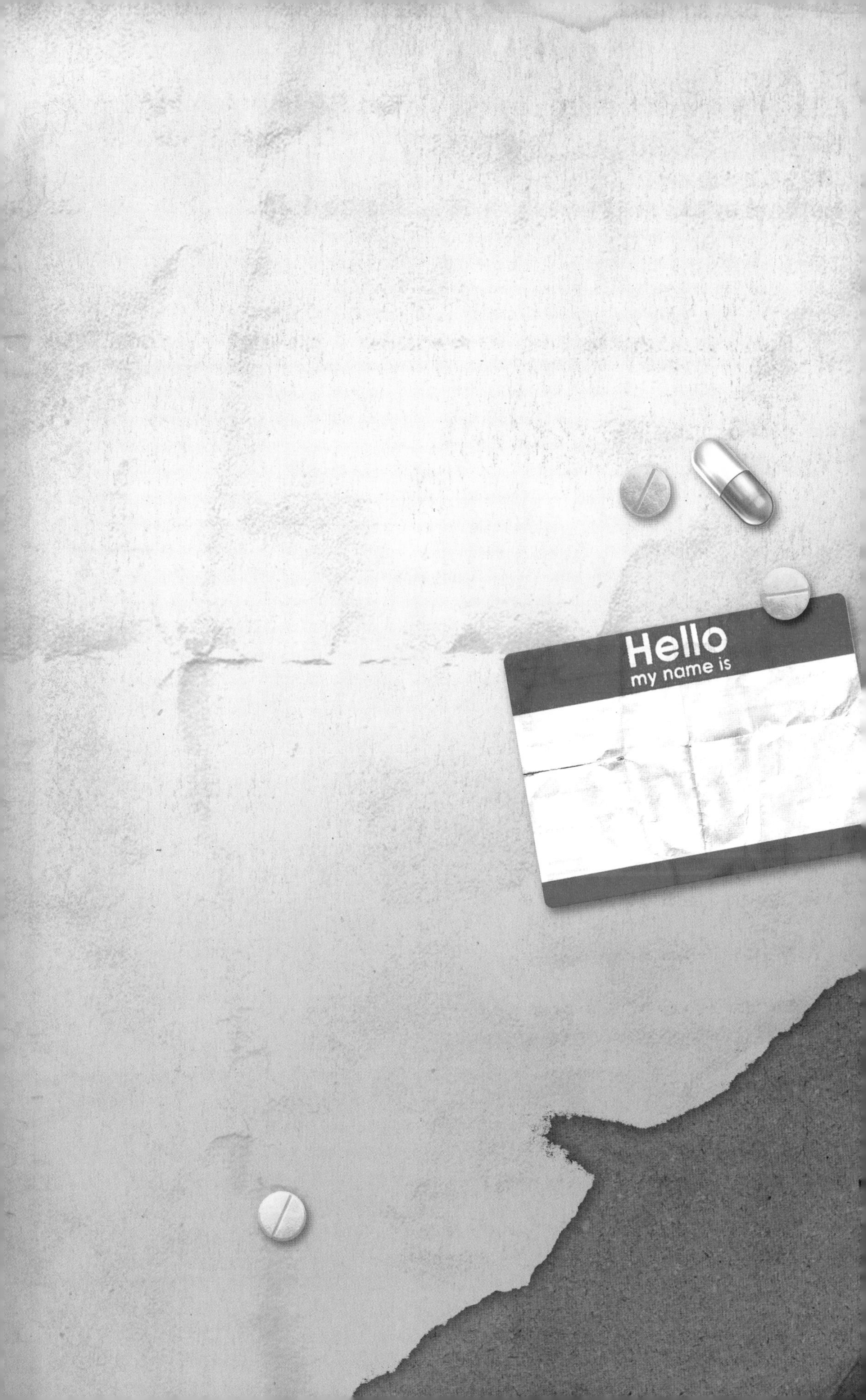
Hello
my name is

Chapter Seven

Peace at Any Price

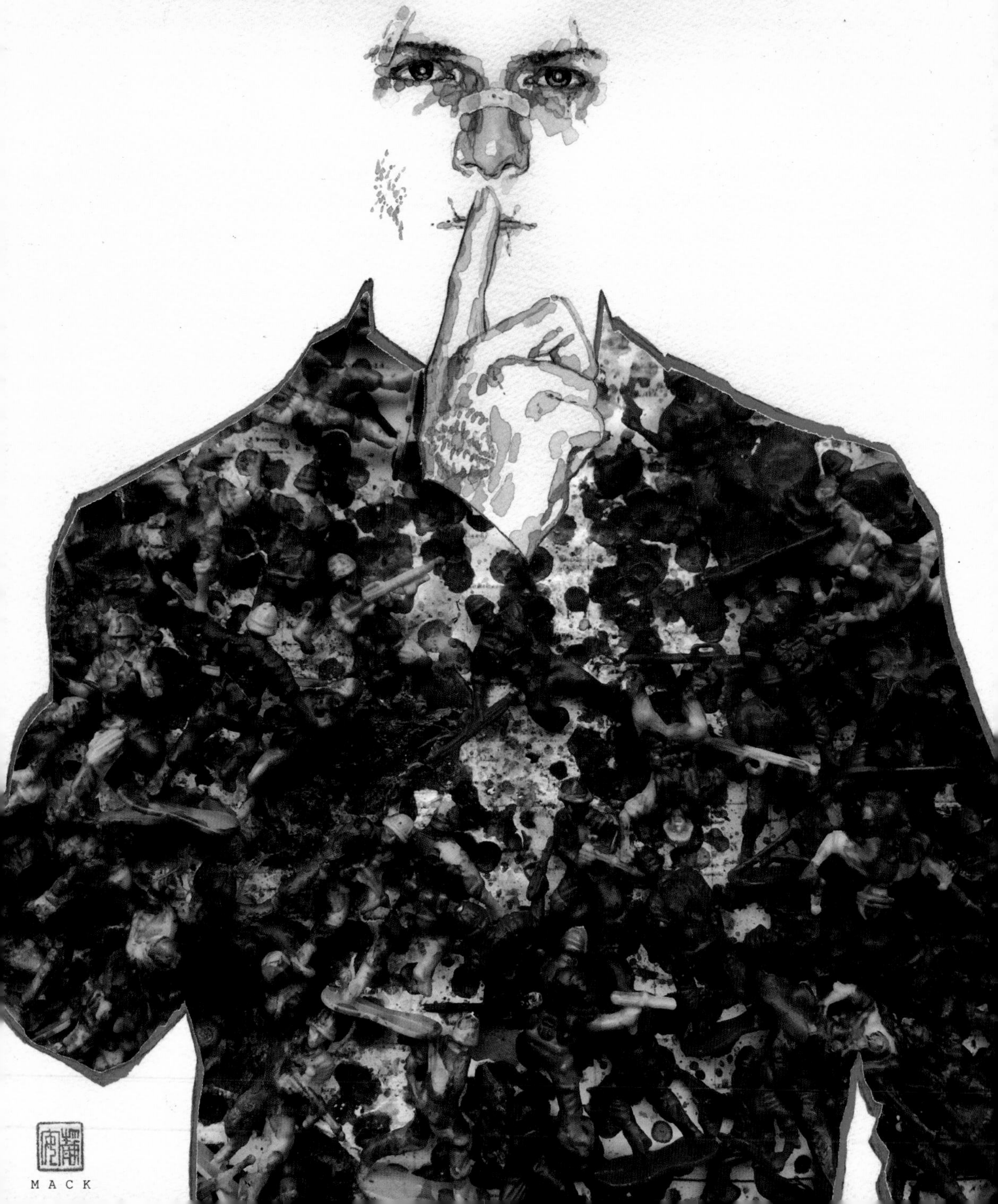
MACK

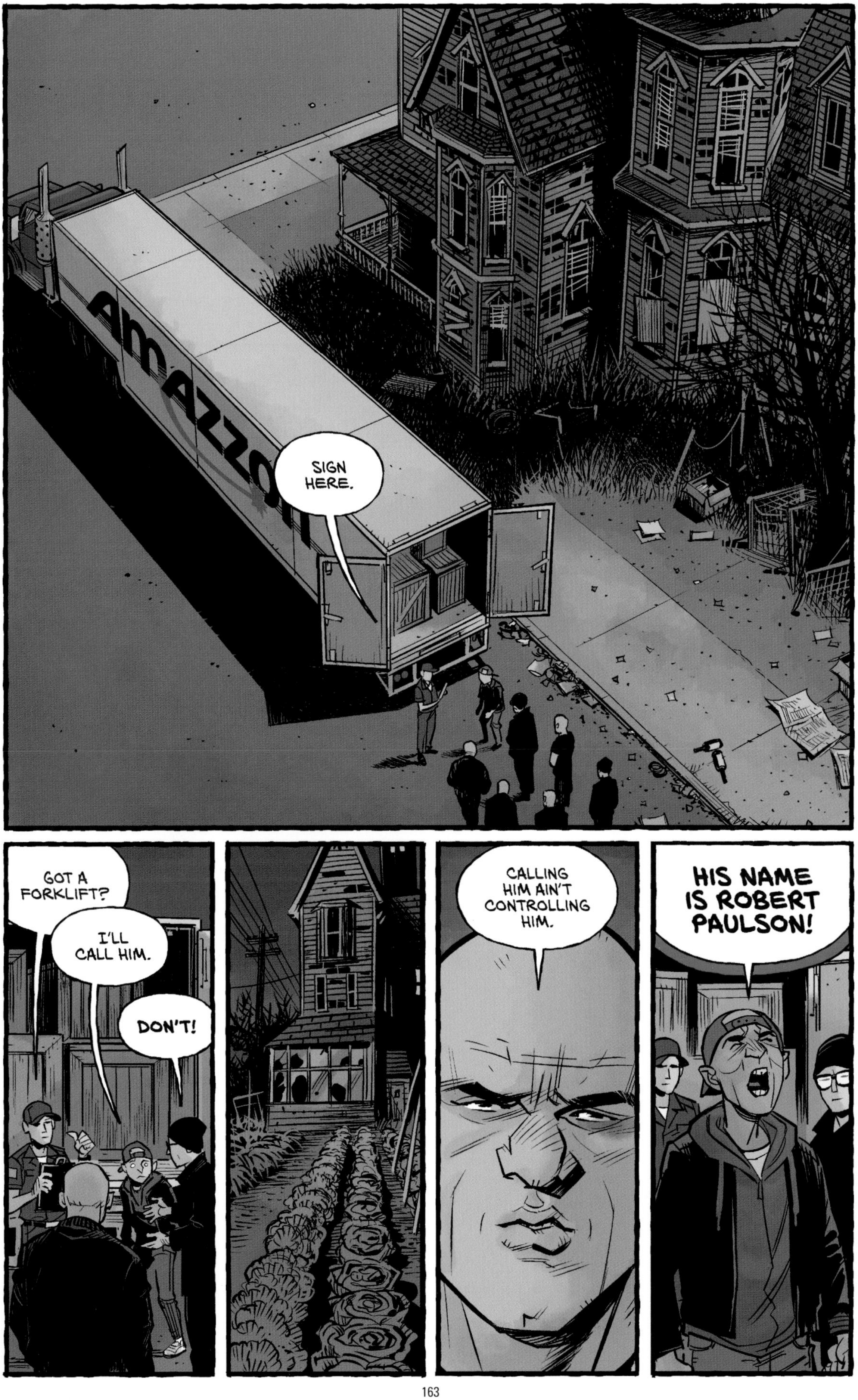
SIGN HERE.
GOT A FORKLIFT?
I'LL CALL HIM.
DON'T!
CALLING HIM AIN'T CONTROLLING HIM.
HIS NAME IS ROBERT PAULSON!

HIS NAME IS ROBERT PAULSON!

HIS NAME IS...

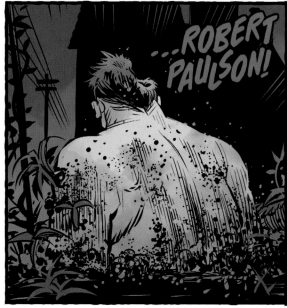

...ROBERT PAULSON!

HIS NAME IS ROBERT PAULSON!

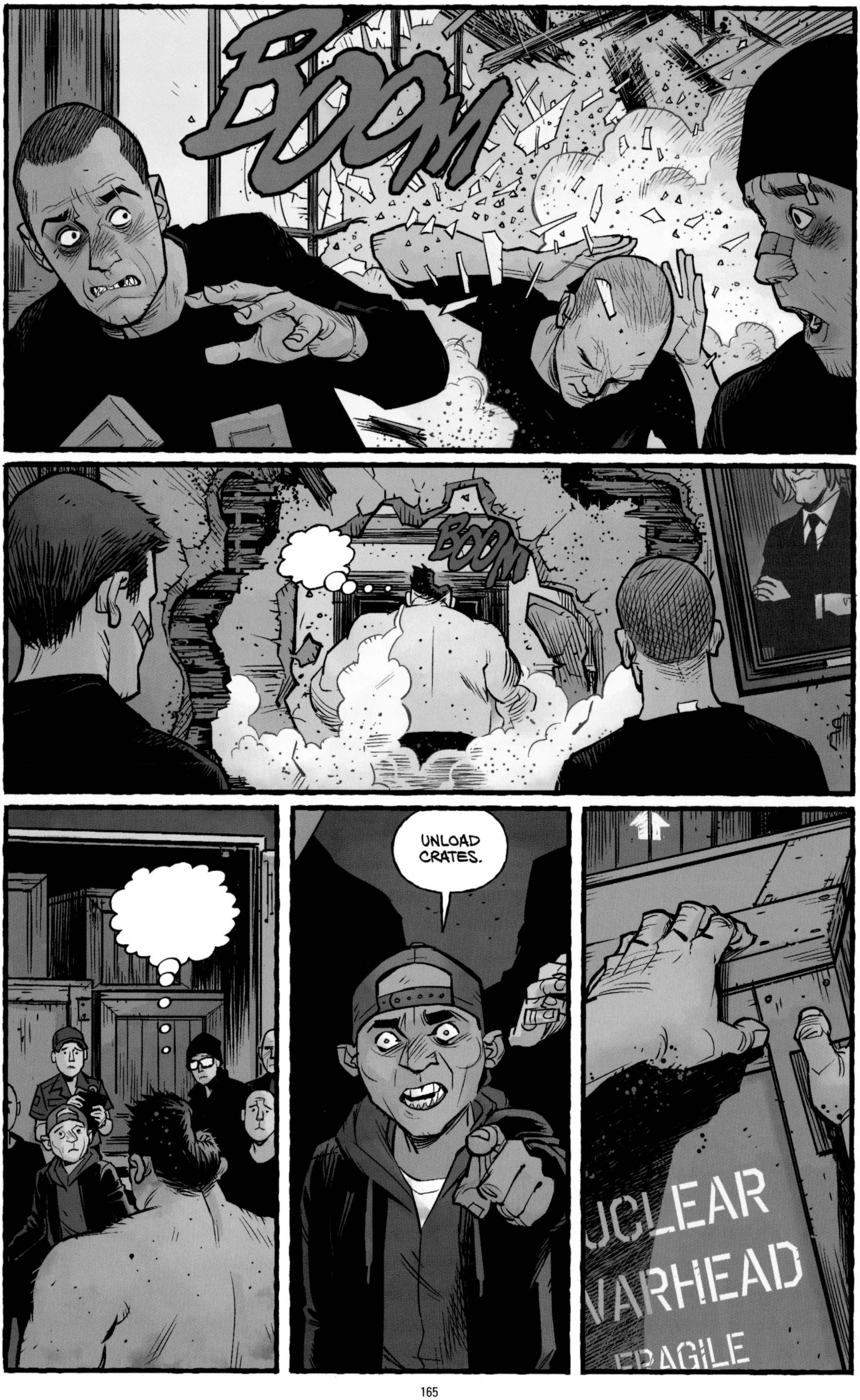
BOOM
BOOM
UNLOAD CRATES.
UCLEAR
VARHEAD
FRAGILE

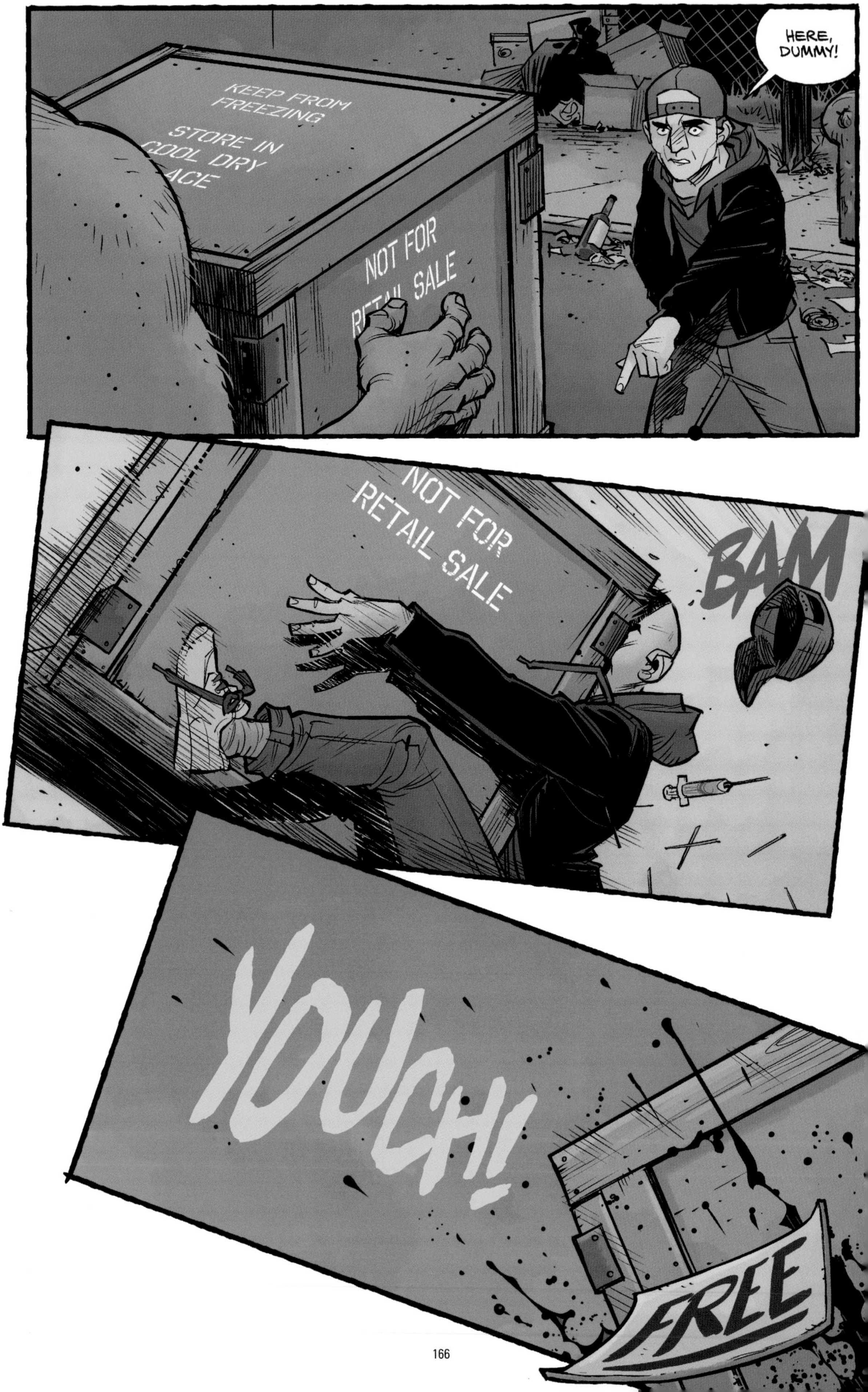
HERE, DUMMY!
KEEP FROM FREEZING
STORE IN COOL DRY ACE
NOT FOR RETAIL SALE
NOT FOR RETAIL SALE
BAM
YOUCH!
FREE

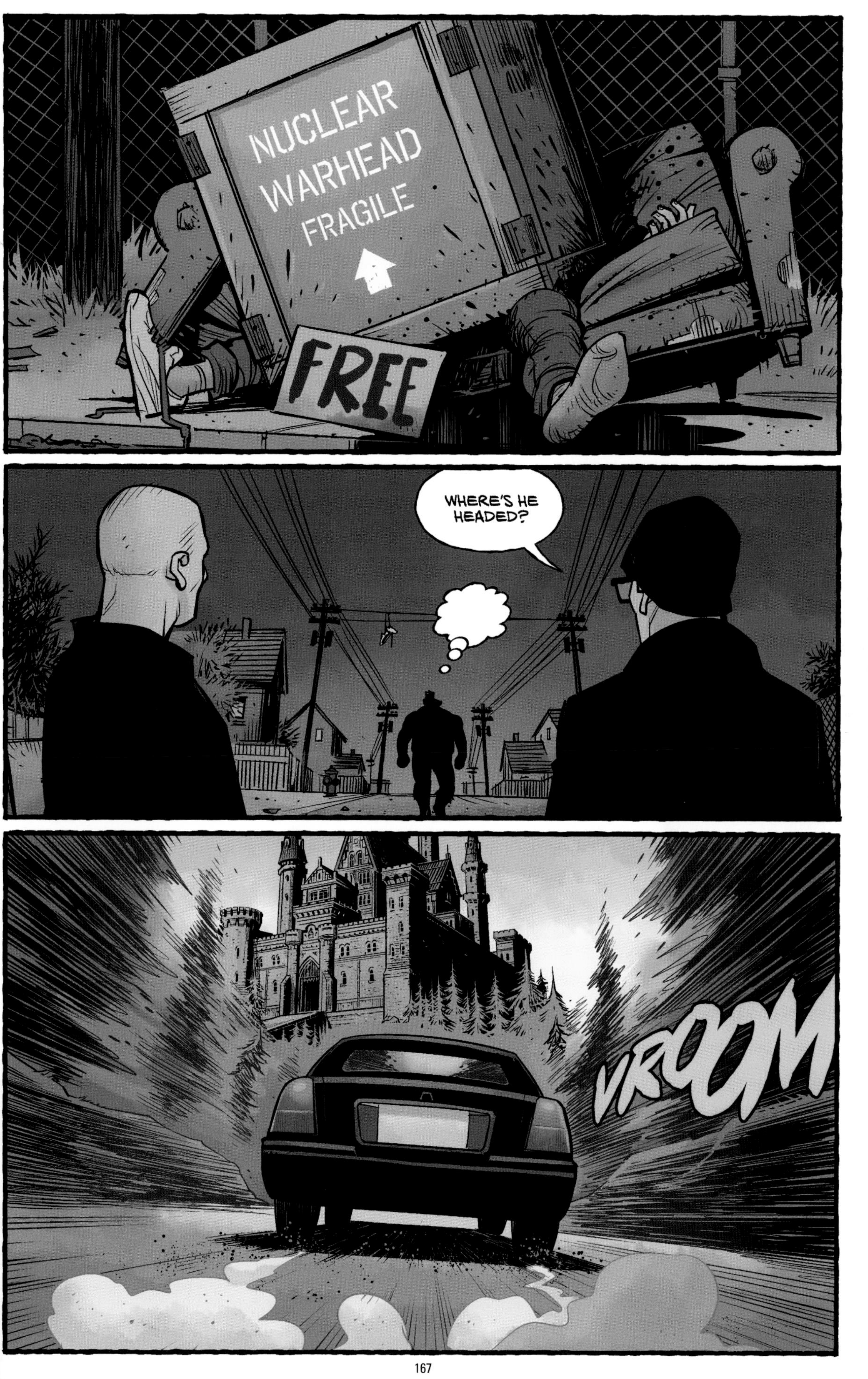
NUCLEAR
WARHEAD
FRAGILE
FREE
WHERE'S HE HEADED?
VROOM

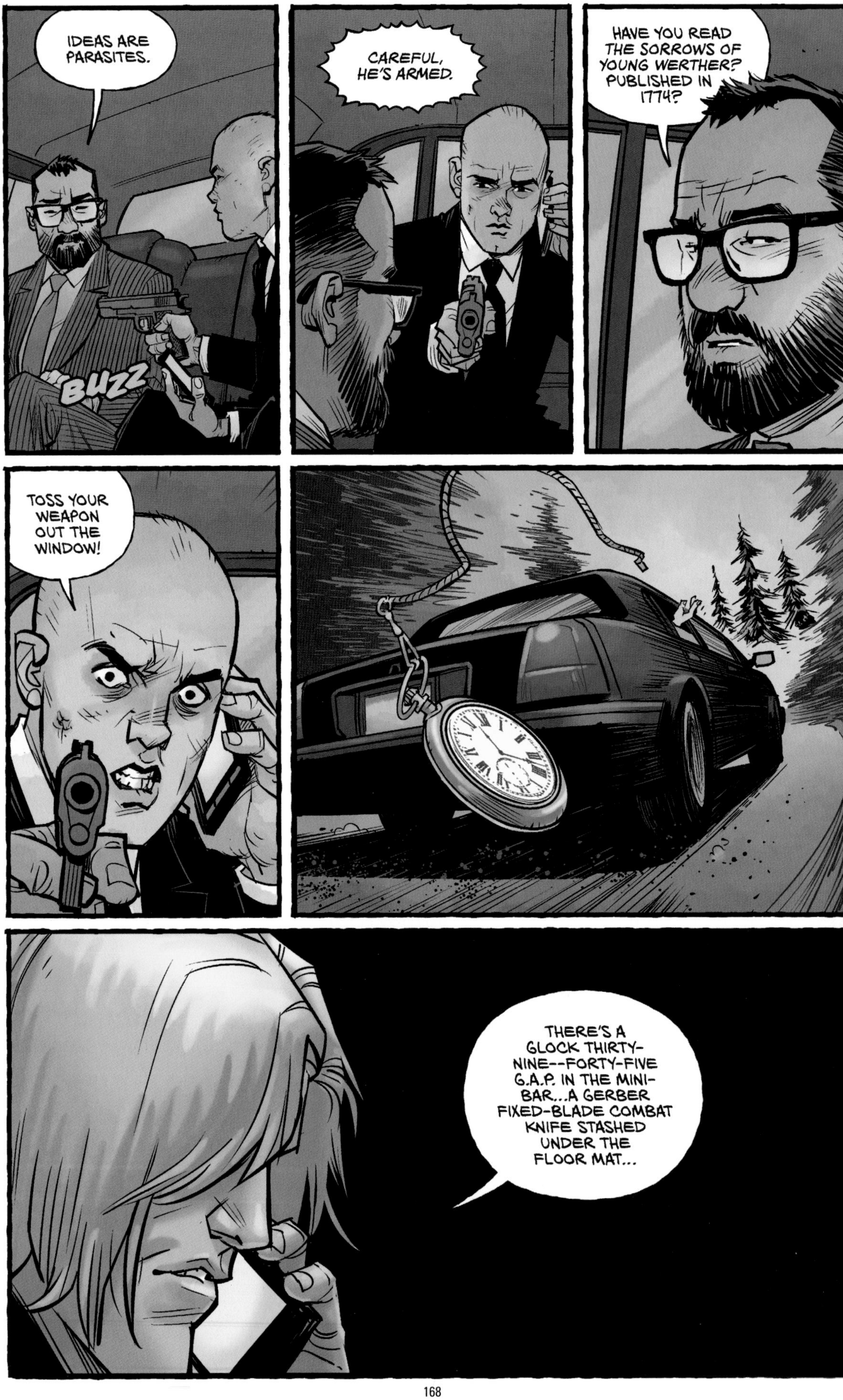
IDEAS ARE PARASITES.
BUZZ
CAREFUL, HE'S ARMED.
HAVE YOU READ THE SORROWS OF YOUNG WERTHER? PUBLISHED IN 1774?
TOSS YOUR WEAPON OUT THE WINDOW!
THERE'S A GLOCK THIRTY-NINE--FORTY-FIVE G.A.P. IN THE MINI-BAR...A GERBER FIXED-BLADE COMBAT KNIFE STASHED UNDER THE FLOOR MAT...

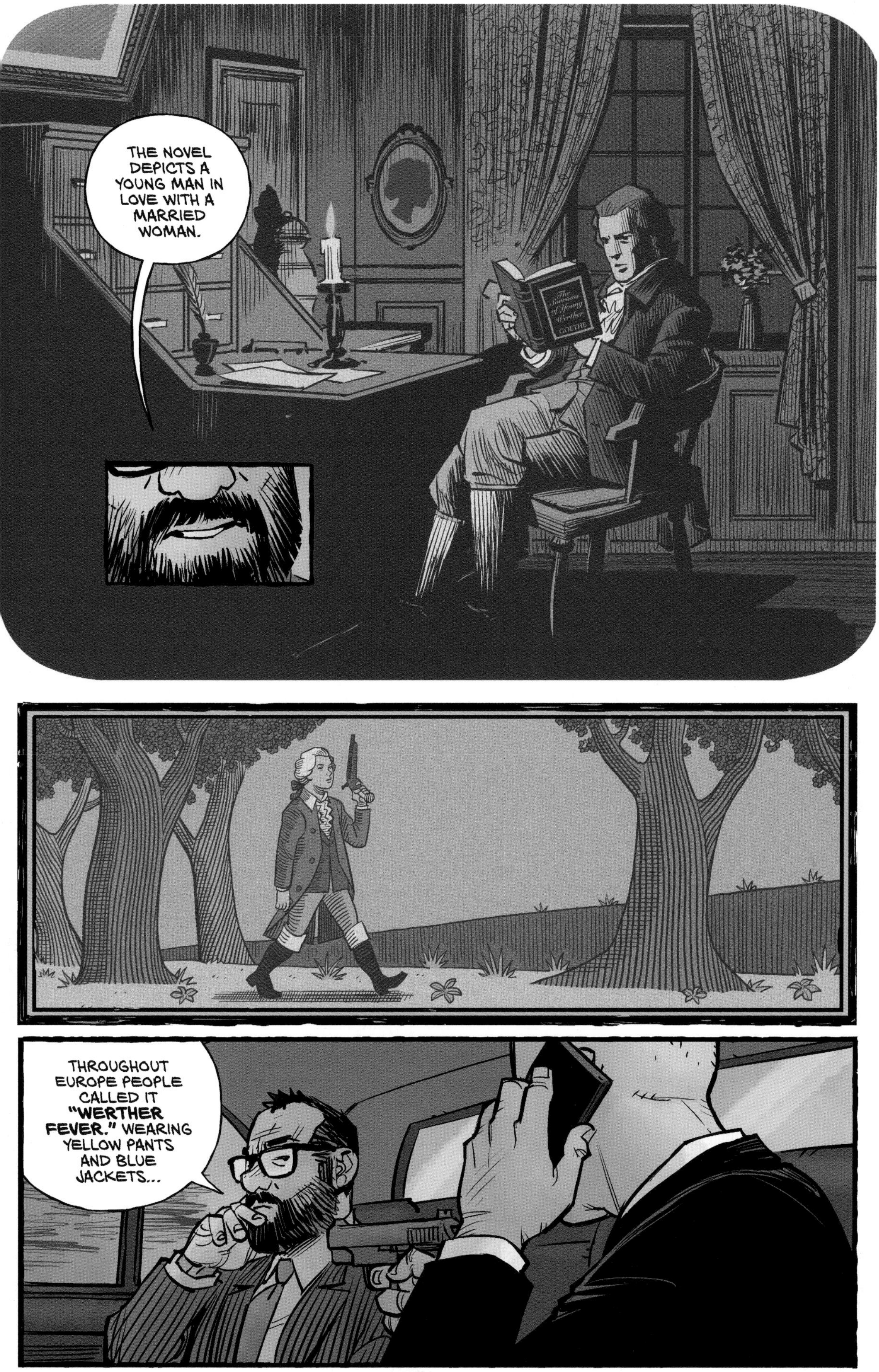
THE NOVEL DEPICTS A YOUNG MAN IN LOVE WITH A MARRIED WOMAN.
The Sorrows of Young Werther
GOETHE
THROUGHOUT EUROPE PEOPLE CALLED IT **"WERTHER FEVER."** WEARING YELLOW PANTS AND BLUE JACKETS...

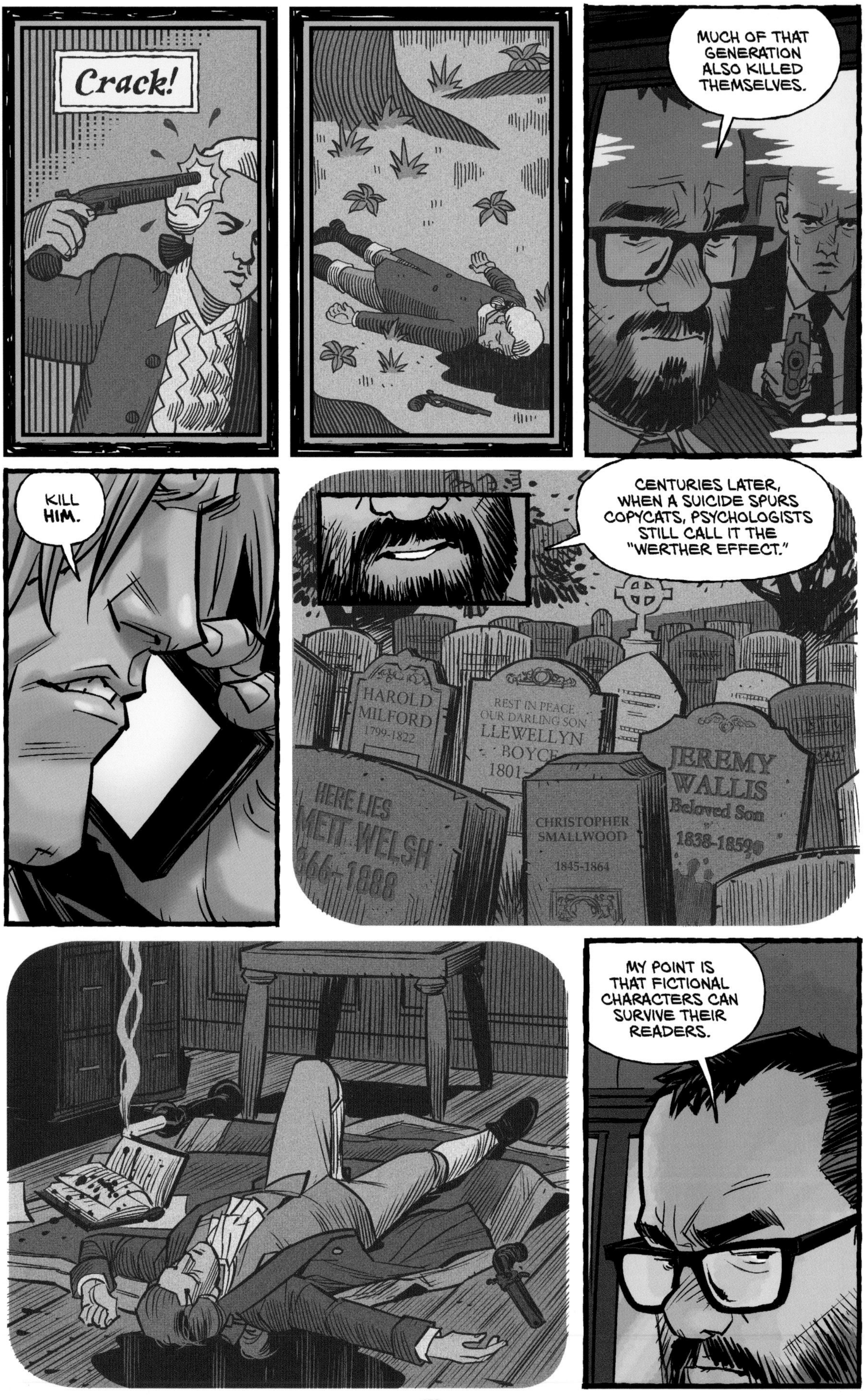
Crack!
MUCH OF THAT GENERATION ALSO KILLED THEMSELVES.
KILL HIM.
CENTURIES LATER, WHEN A SUICIDE SPURS COPYCATS, PSYCHOLOGISTS STILL CALL IT THE "WERTHER EFFECT."
HAROLD MILFORD 1799-1822
REST IN PEACE OUR DARLING SON LLEWELLYN BOYCE
JEREMY WALLIS Beloved Son 1838-1859
HERE LIES
CHRISTOPHER SMALLWOOD 1845-1864
MY POINT IS THAT FICTIONAL CHARACTERS CAN SURVIVE THEIR READERS.

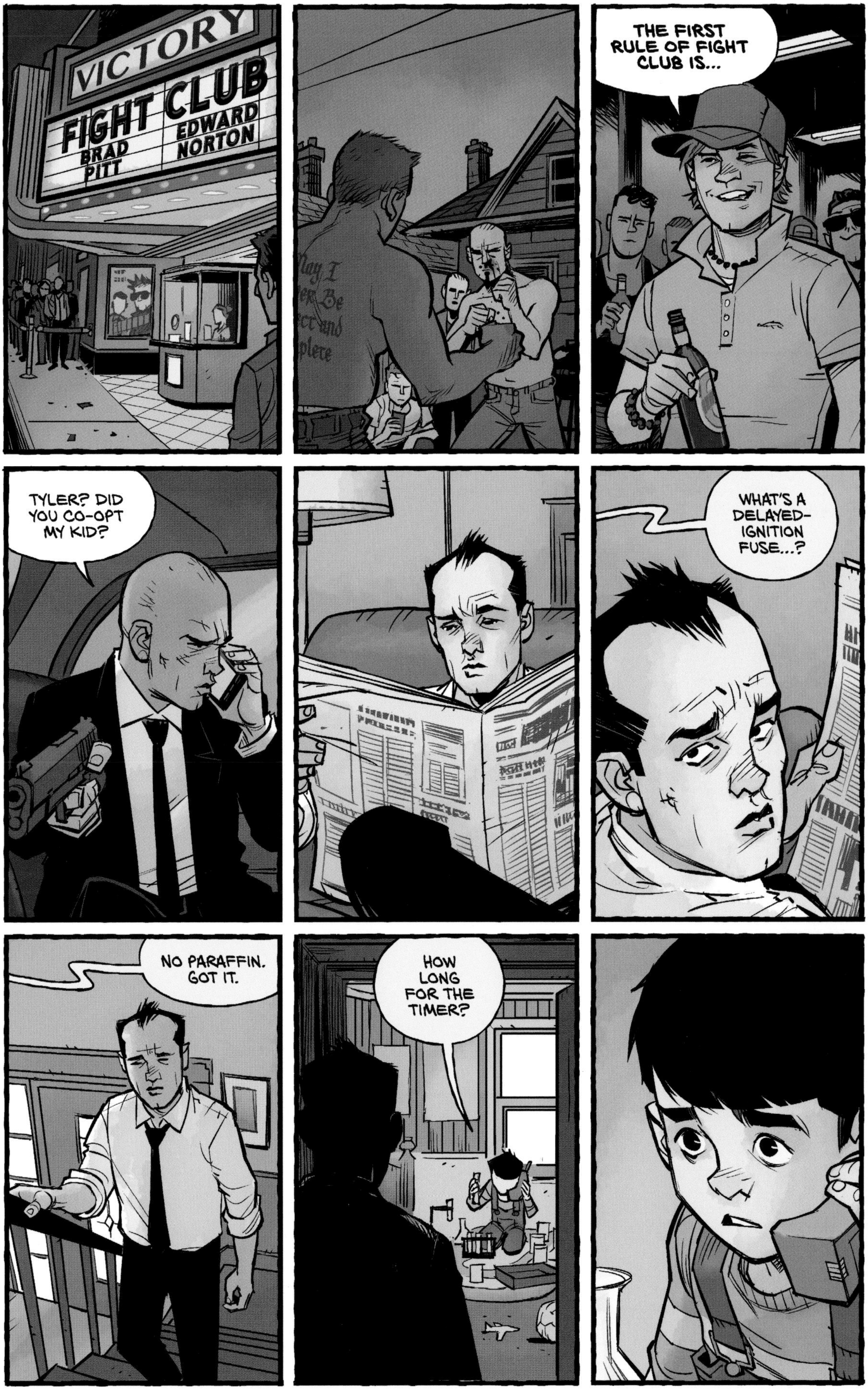
VICTORY
FIGHT CLUB
BRAD PITT
EDWARD NORTON
THE FIRST RULE OF FIGHT CLUB IS...
TYLER? DID YOU CO-OPT MY KID?
WHAT'S A DELAYED-IGNITION FUSE...?
NO PARAFFIN. GOT IT.
HOW LONG FOR THE TIMER?

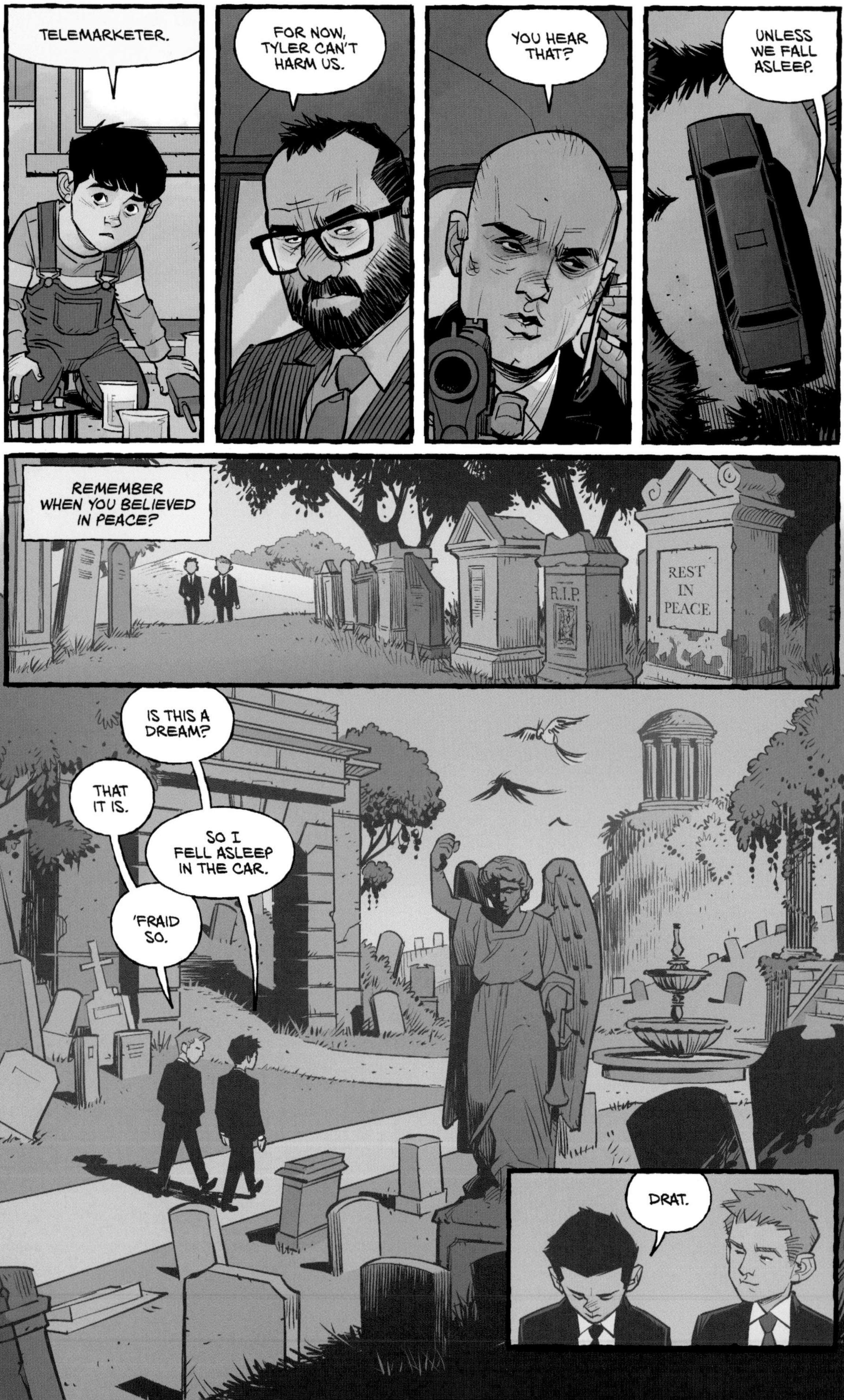
TELEMARKETER.
FOR NOW, TYLER CAN'T HARM US.
YOU HEAR THAT?
UNLESS WE FALL ASLEEP.
REMEMBER WHEN YOU BELIEVED IN PEACE?
R.I.P.
REST IN PEACE
IS THIS A DREAM?
THAT IT IS.
SO I FELL ASLEEP IN THE CAR.
'FRAID SO.
DRAT.

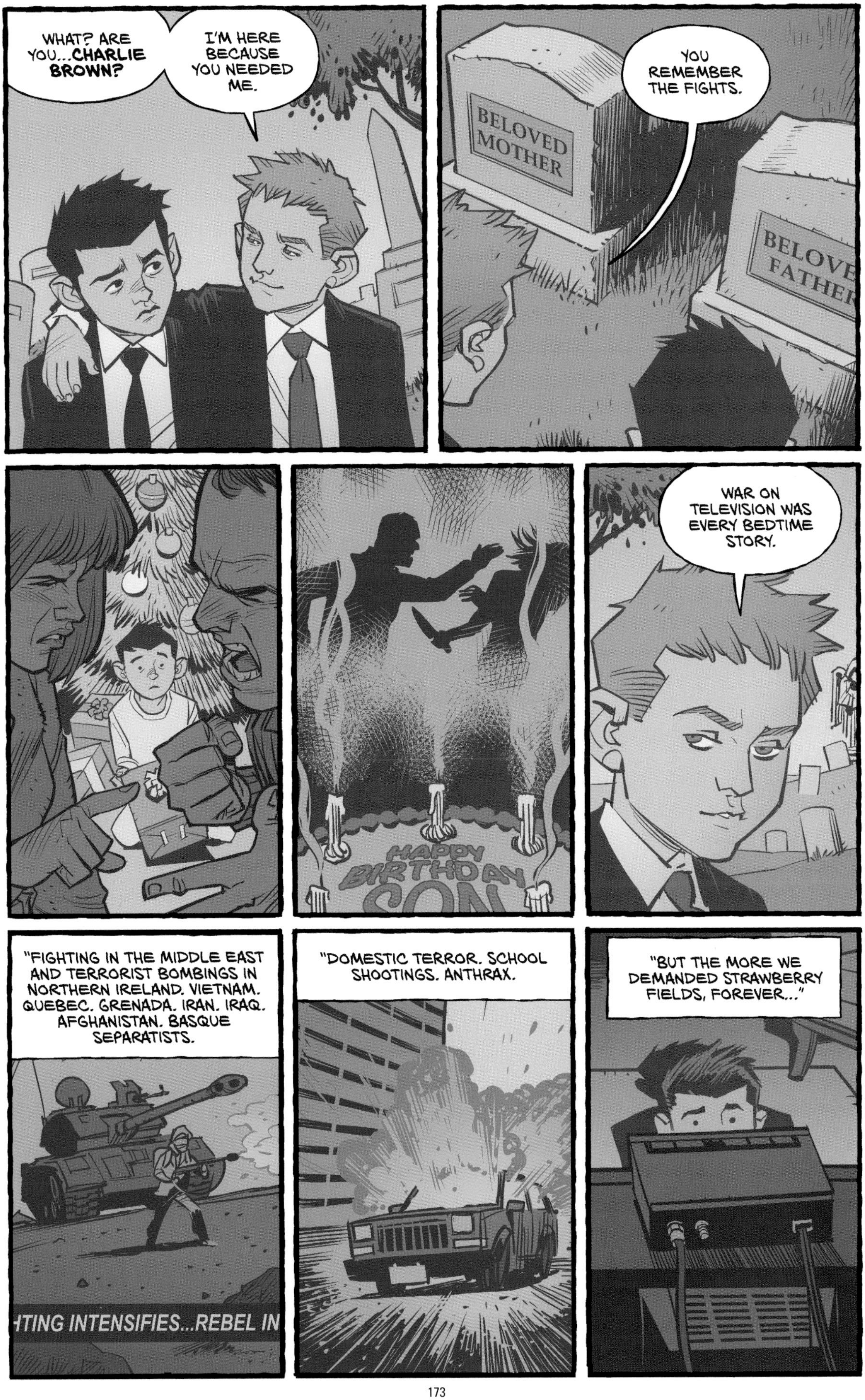
WHAT? ARE YOU...CHARLIE BROWN?
I'M HERE BECAUSE YOU NEEDED ME.
BELOVED MOTHER
YOU REMEMBER THE FIGHTS.
BELOVE FATHER
HAPPY BIRTHDAY SON
WAR ON TELEVISION WAS EVERY BEDTIME STORY.
"FIGHTING IN THE MIDDLE EAST AND TERRORIST BOMBINGS IN NORTHERN IRELAND. VIETNAM. QUEBEC. GRENADA. IRAN. IRAQ. AFGHANISTAN. BASQUE SEPARATISTS.
HTING INTENSIFIES...REBEL IN
"DOMESTIC TERROR. SCHOOL SHOOTINGS. ANTHRAX.
"BUT THE MORE WE DEMANDED STRAWBERRY FIELDS, FOREVER..."

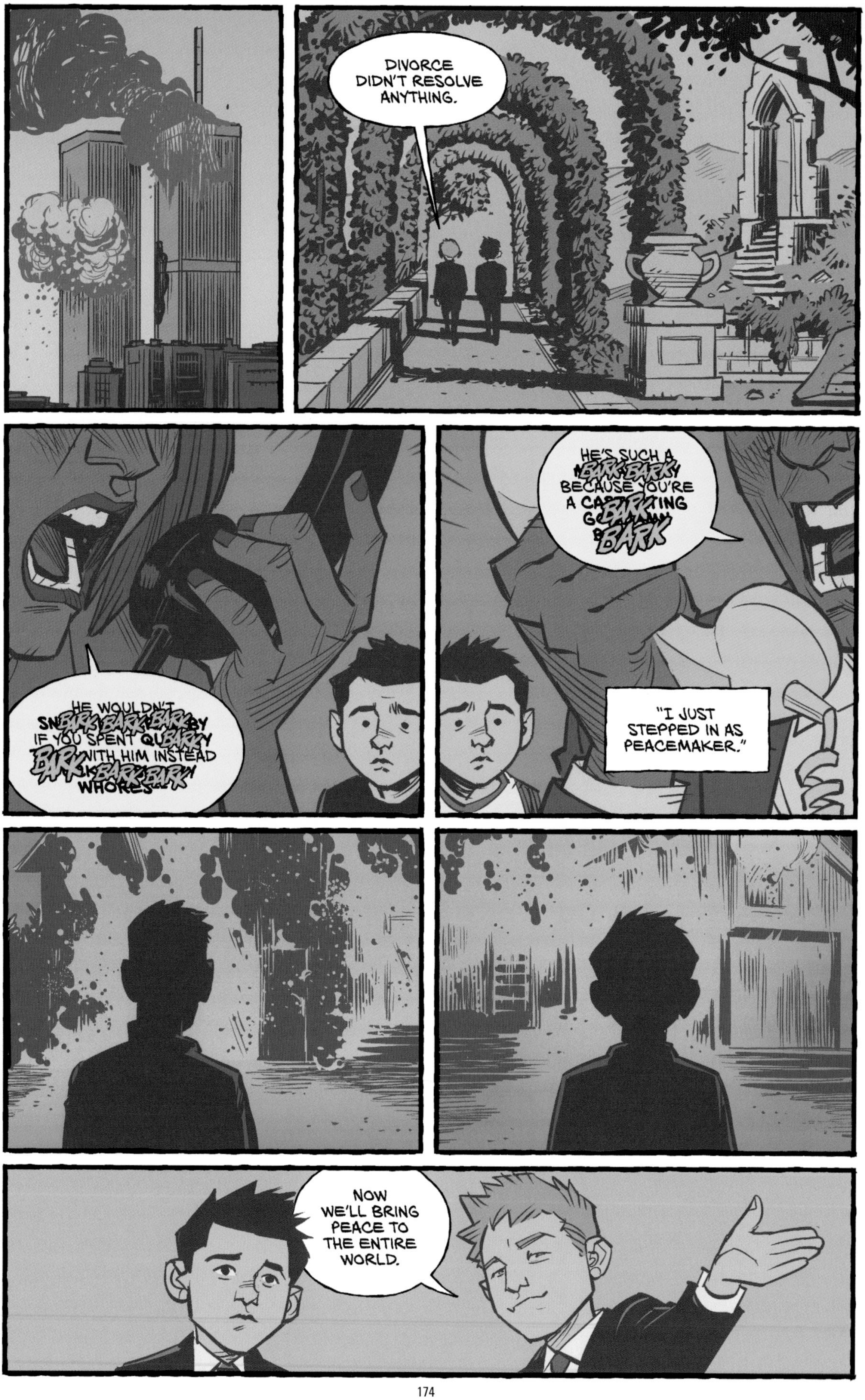
DIVORCE DIDN'T RESOLVE ANYTHING.
HE WOULDN'T BARK BARK BARK IF YOU SPENT BARK BARK WITH HIM INSTEAD BARK BARK WHORES
HE'S SUCH A BARK BARK BECAUSE YOU'RE A BARK ING BARK
"I JUST STEPPED IN AS PEACEMAKER."
NOW WE'LL BRING PEACE TO THE ENTIRE WORLD.

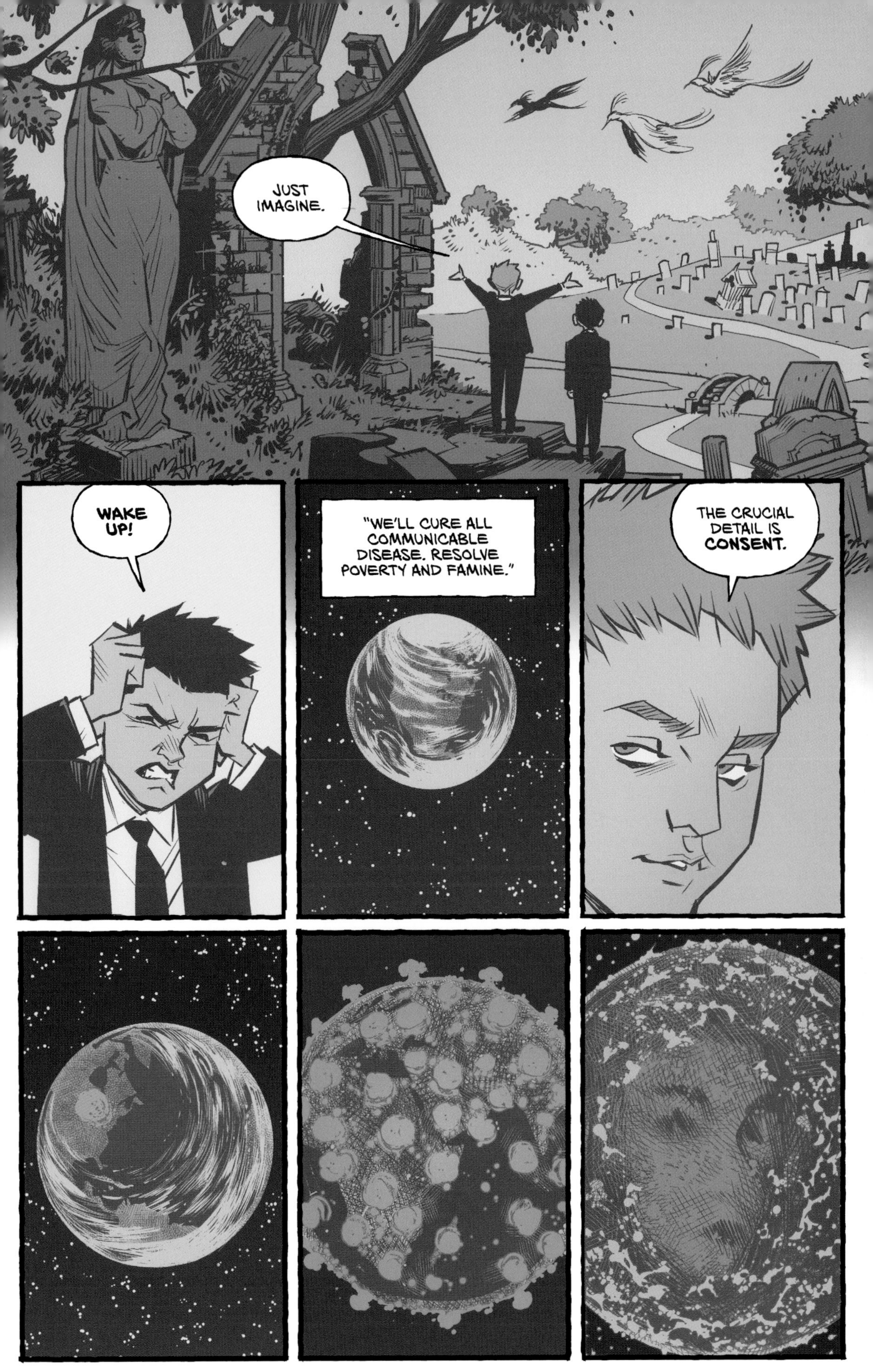
JUST IMAGINE.
WAKE UP!
"WE'LL CURE ALL COMMUNICABLE DISEASE. RESOLVE POVERTY AND FAMINE."
THE CRUCIAL DETAIL IS CONSENT.

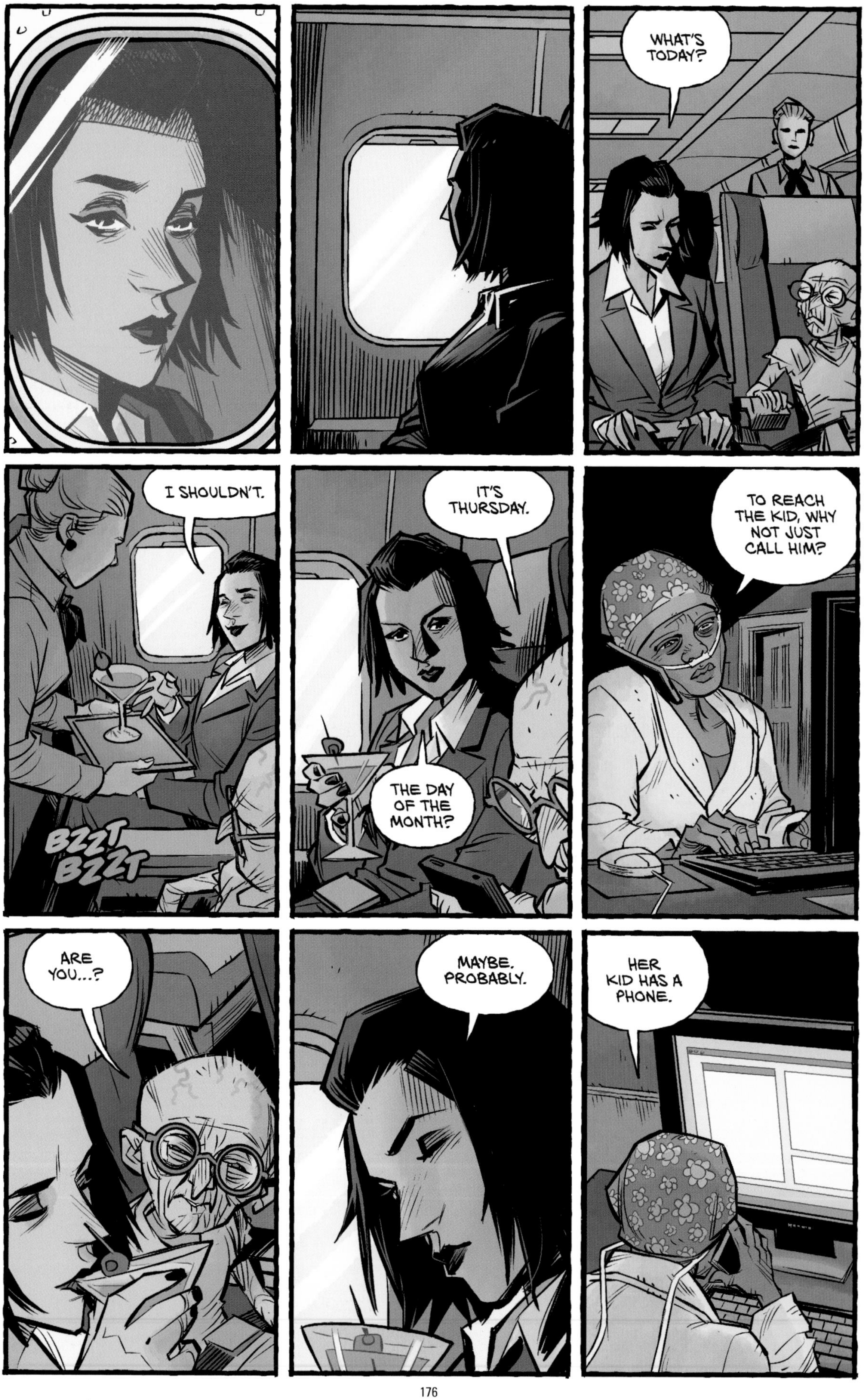
WHAT'S TODAY?
I SHOULDN'T.
BZZT BZZT
IT'S THURSDAY.
THE DAY OF THE MONTH?
TO REACH THE KID, WHY NOT JUST CALL HIM?
ARE YOU...?
MAYBE. PROBABLY.
HER KID HAS A PHONE.

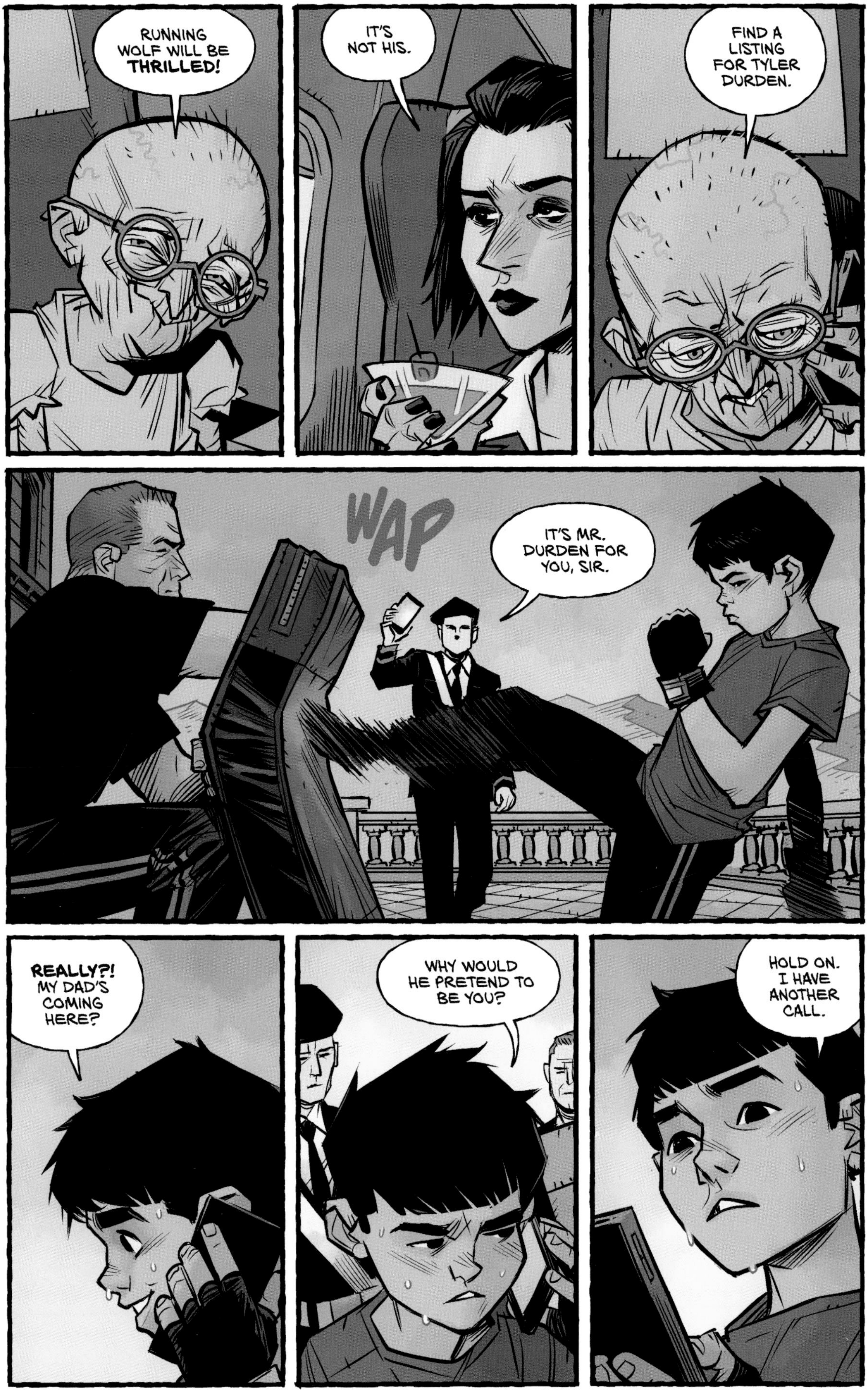
RUNNING WOLF WILL BE **THRILLED!**
IT'S NOT HIS.
FIND A LISTING FOR TYLER DURDEN.
WAP
IT'S MR. DURDEN FOR YOU, SIR.
REALLY?! MY DAD'S COMING HERE?
WHY WOULD HE PRETEND TO BE YOU?
HOLD ON. I HAVE ANOTHER CALL.

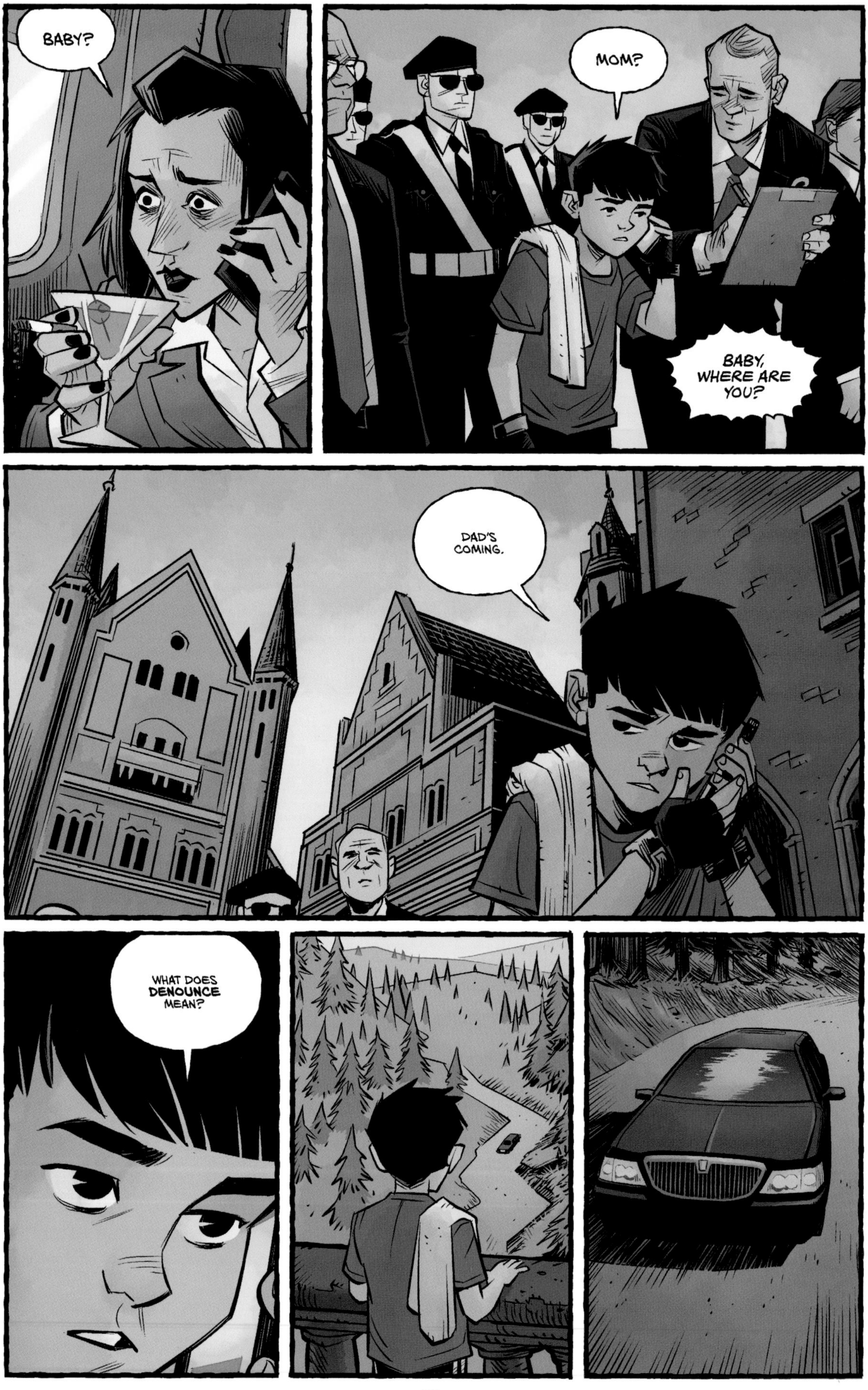
BABY?
MOM?
BABY, WHERE ARE YOU?
DAD'S COMING.
WHAT DOES DENOUNCE MEAN?

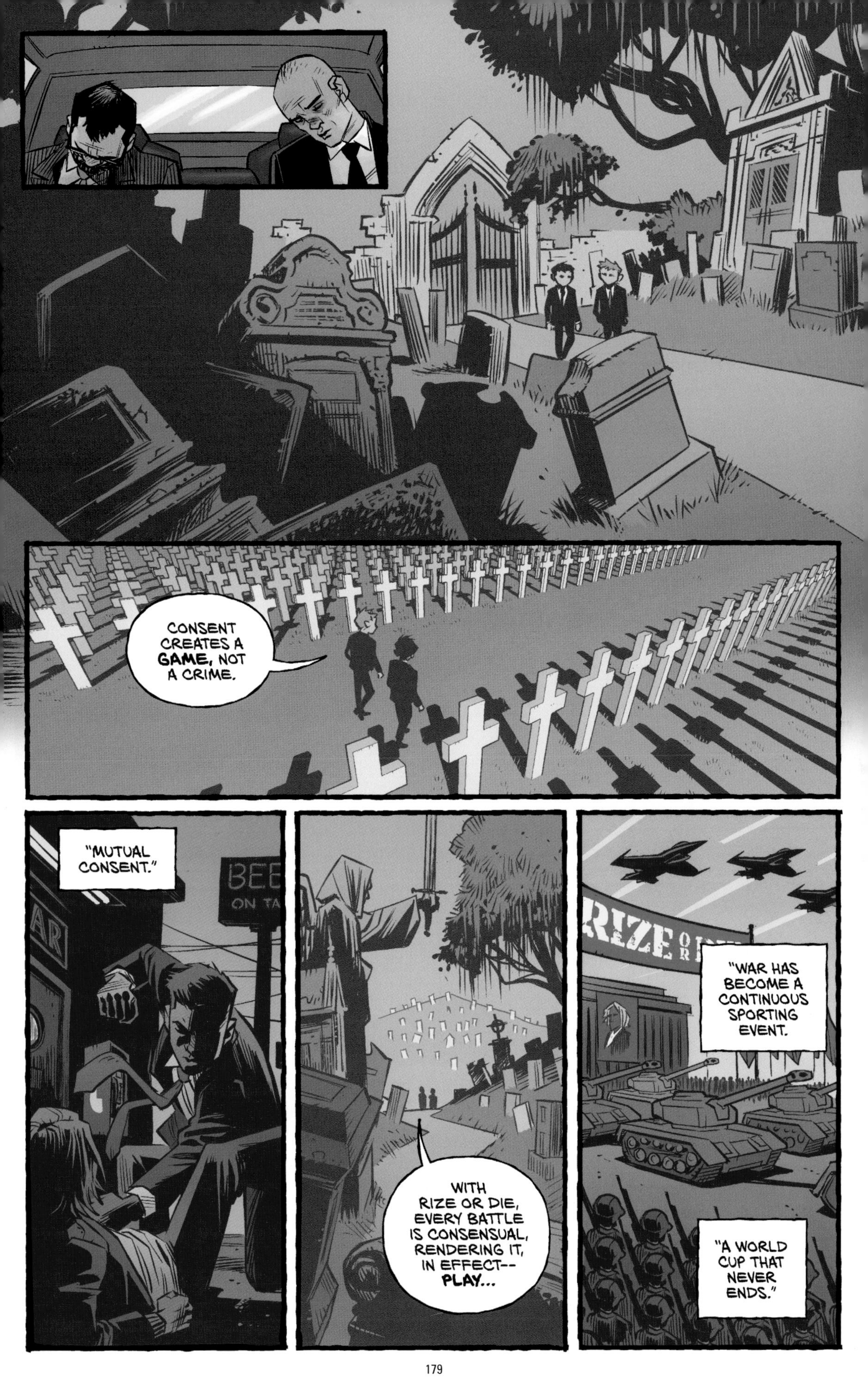
CONSENT CREATES A GAME, NOT A CRIME.
"MUTUAL CONSENT."
BEE
ON TA
AR
WITH RIZE OR DIE, EVERY BATTLE IS CONSENSUAL, RENDERING IT, IN EFFECT-- PLAY...
RIZE
"WAR HAS BECOME A CONTINUOUS SPORTING EVENT.
"A WORLD CUP THAT NEVER ENDS."

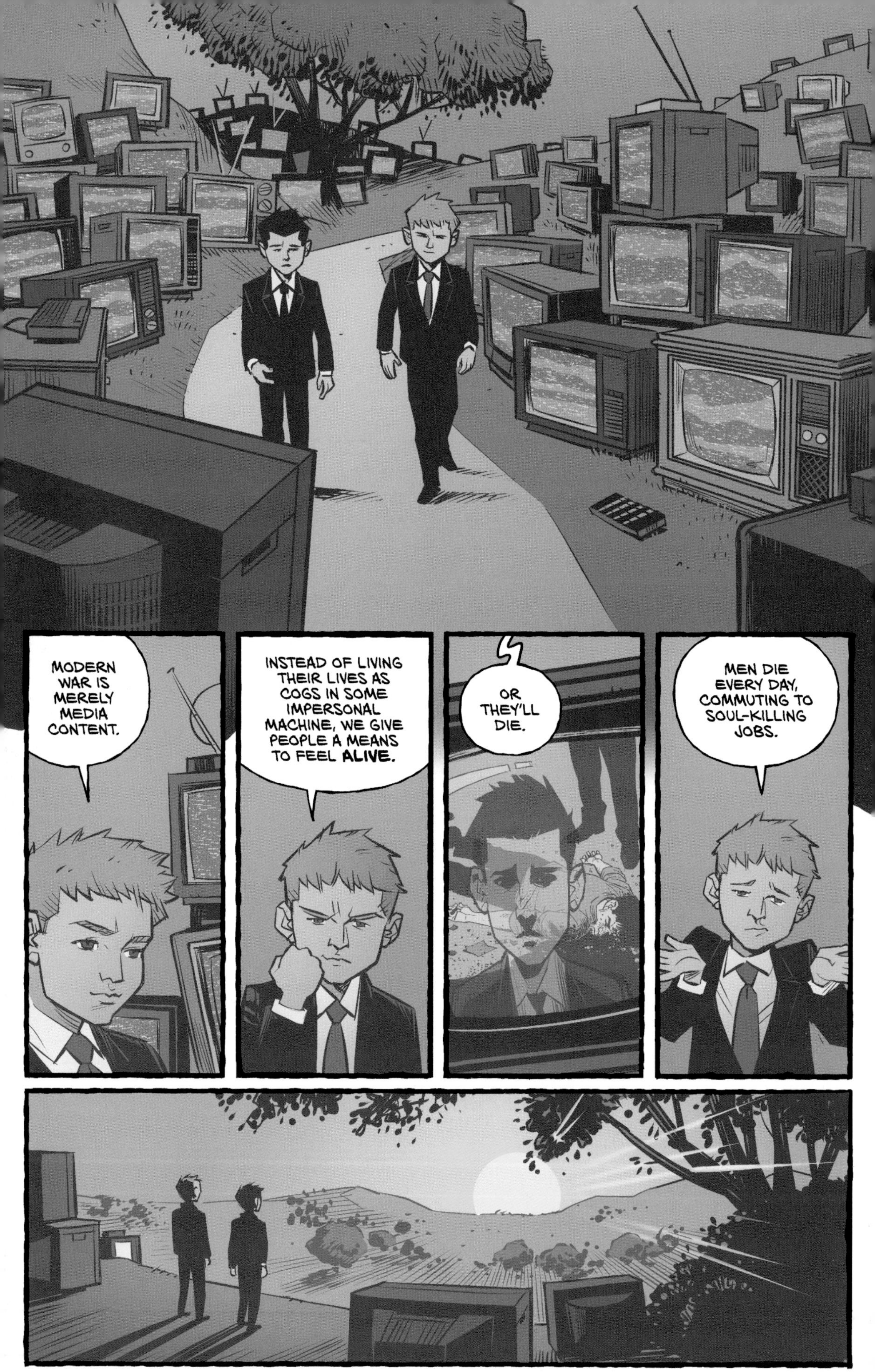
MODERN WAR IS MERELY MEDIA CONTENT.
INSTEAD OF LIVING THEIR LIVES AS COGS IN SOME IMPERSONAL MACHINE, WE GIVE PEOPLE A MEANS TO FEEL **ALIVE.**
OR THEY'LL DIE.
MEN DIE EVERY DAY, COMMUTING TO SOUL-KILLING JOBS.

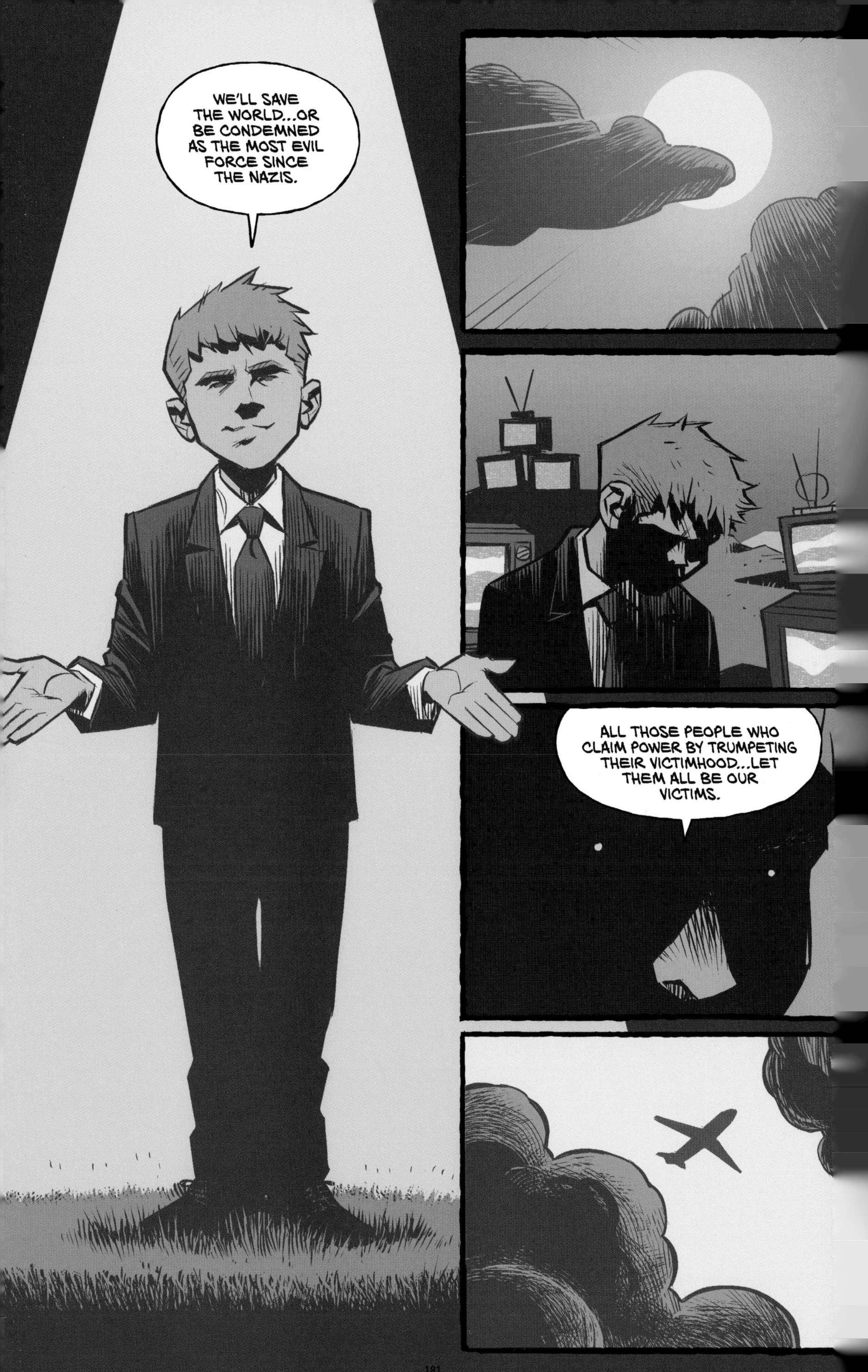
WE'LL SAVE THE WORLD...OR BE CONDEMNED AS THE MOST EVIL FORCE SINCE THE NAZIS.
ALL THOSE PEOPLE WHO CLAIM POWER BY TRUMPETING THEIR VICTIMHOOD...LET THEM ALL BE OUR VICTIMS.

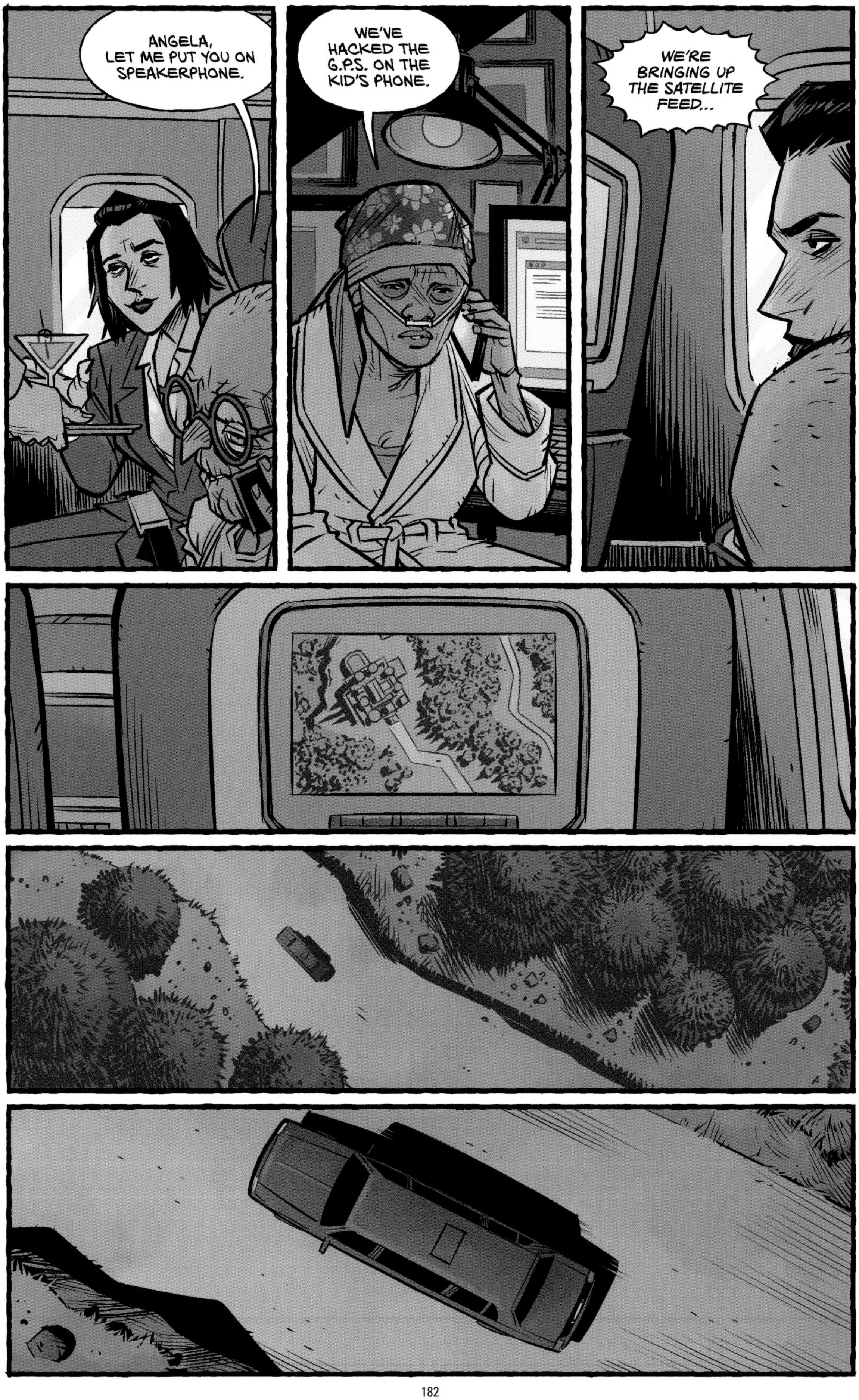
ANGELA, LET ME PUT YOU ON SPEAKERPHONE.
WE'VE HACKED THE G.P.S. ON THE KID'S PHONE.
WE'RE BRINGING UP THE SATELLITE FEED...

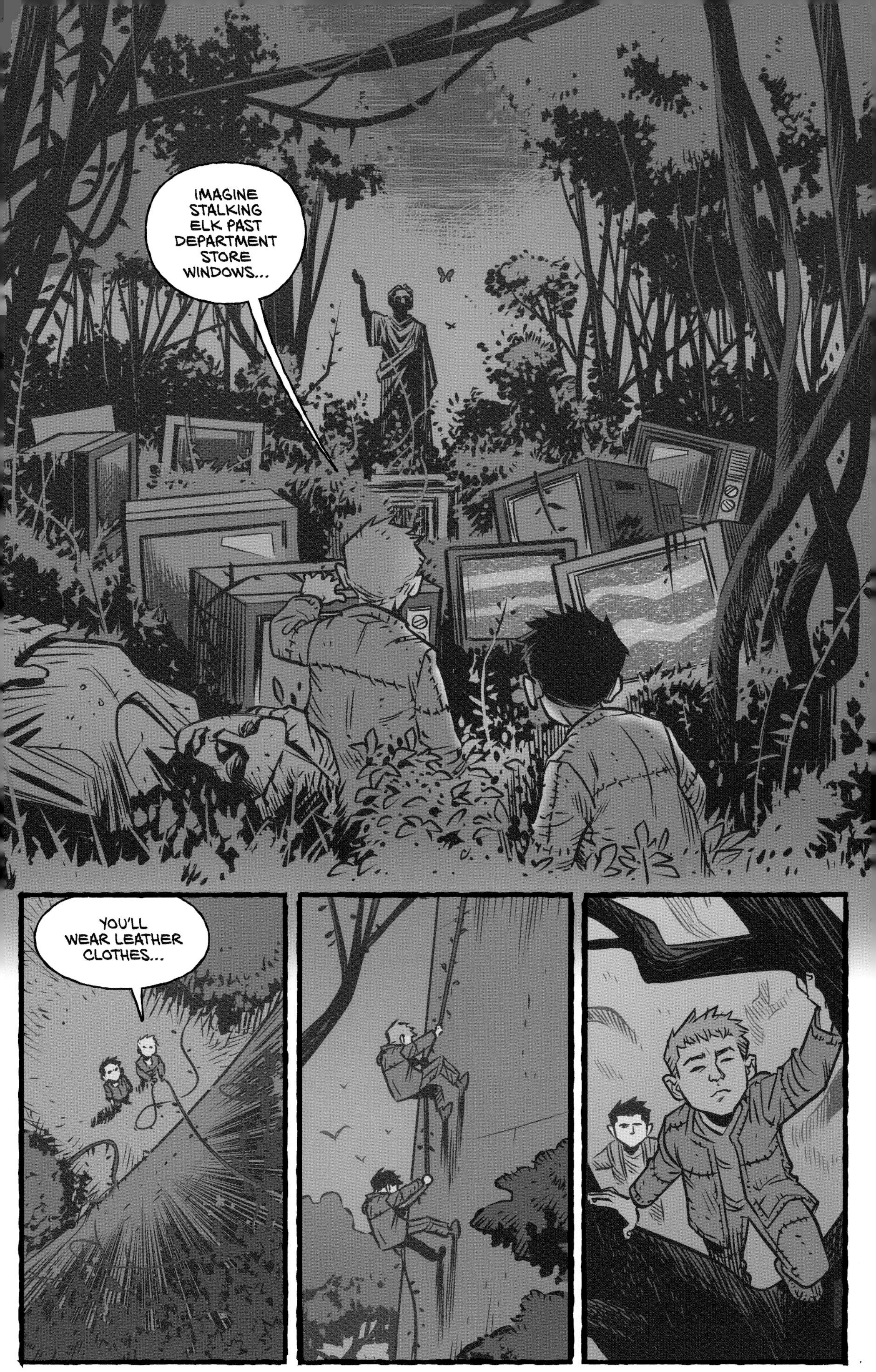
IMAGINE STALKING ELK PAST DEPARTMENT STORE WINDOWS...
YOU'LL WEAR LEATHER CLOTHES...

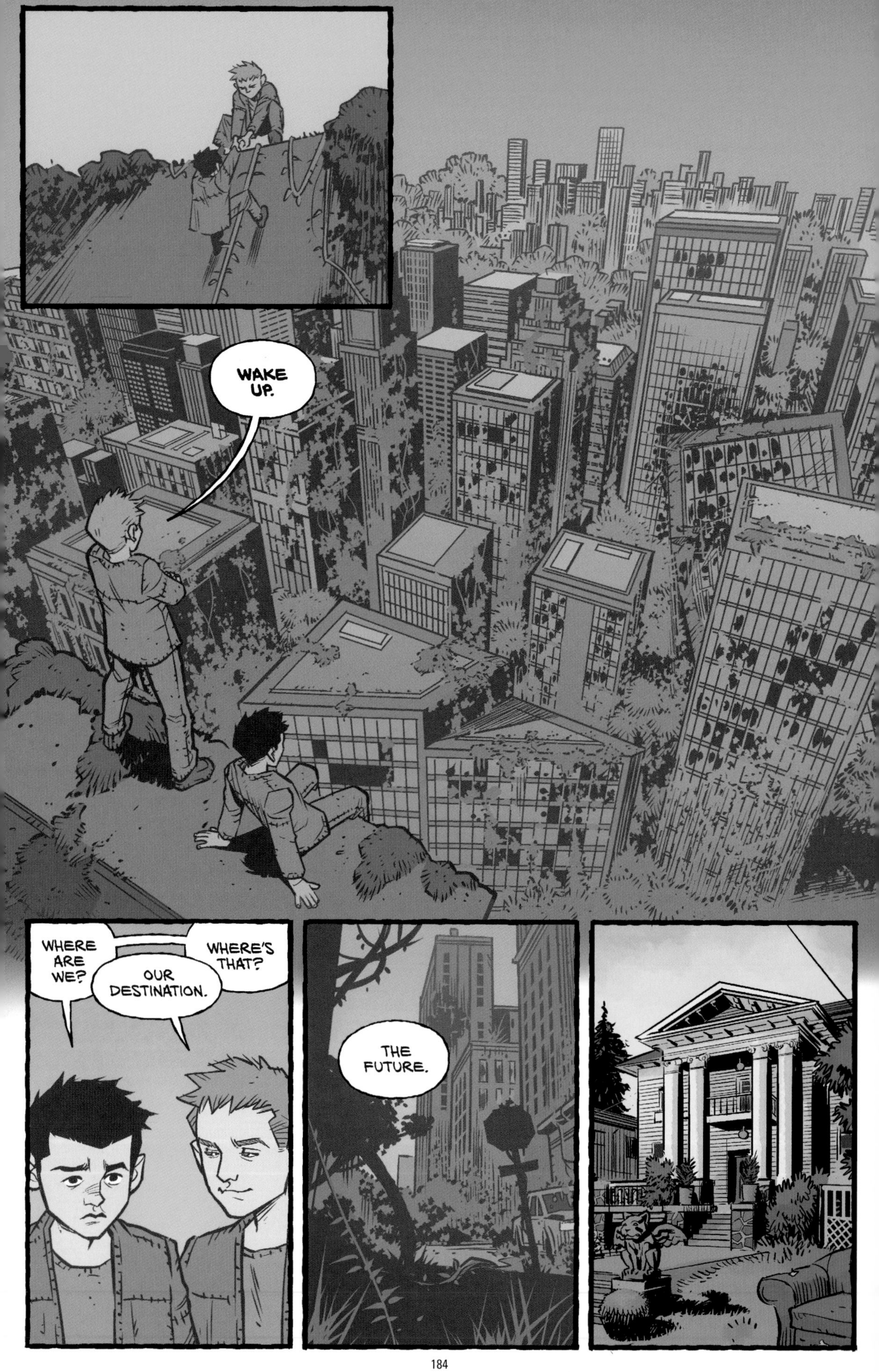
WAKE UP.
WHERE ARE WE?
OUR DESTINATION.
WHERE'S THAT?
THE FUTURE.

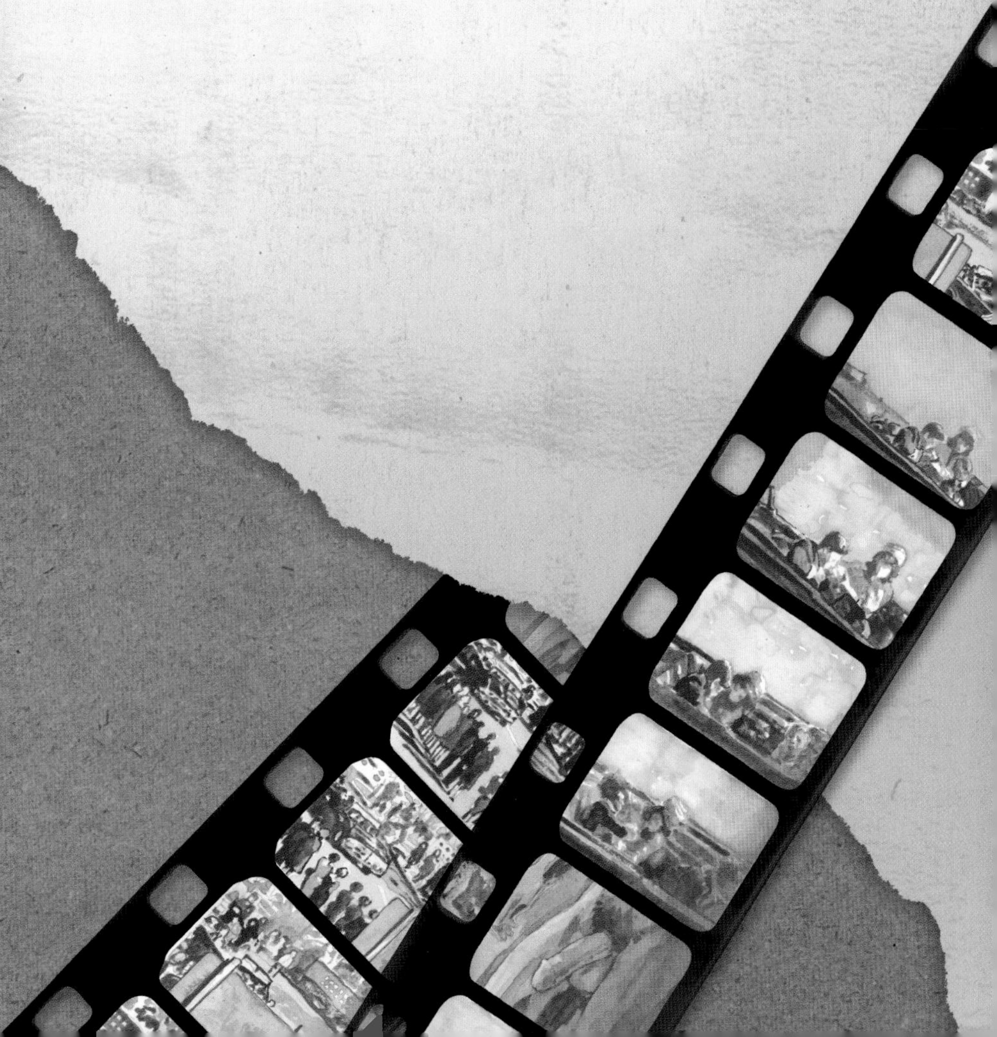

Chapter Eight

Ideas Breed Us

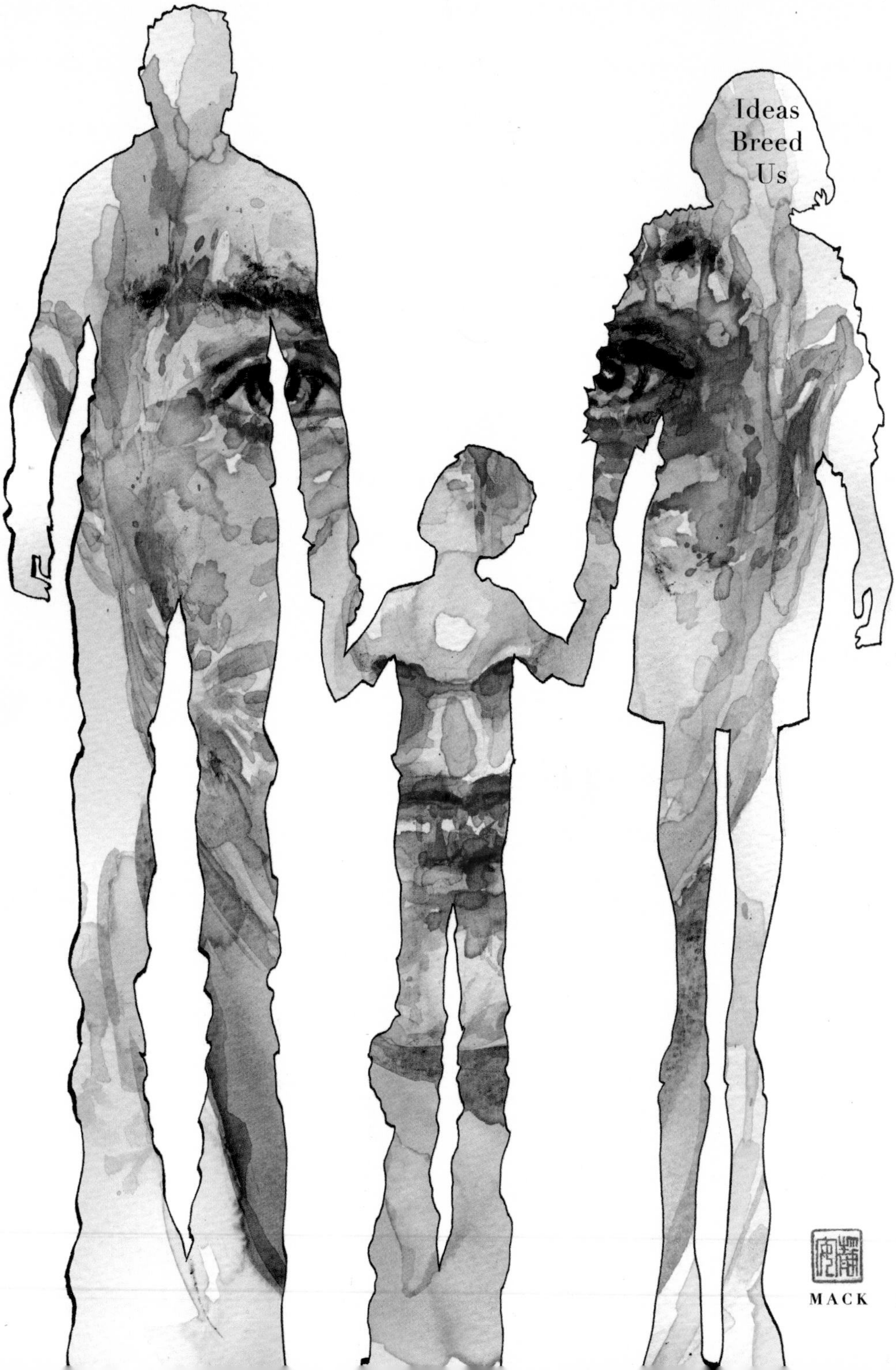
Ideas
Breed
Us
MACK

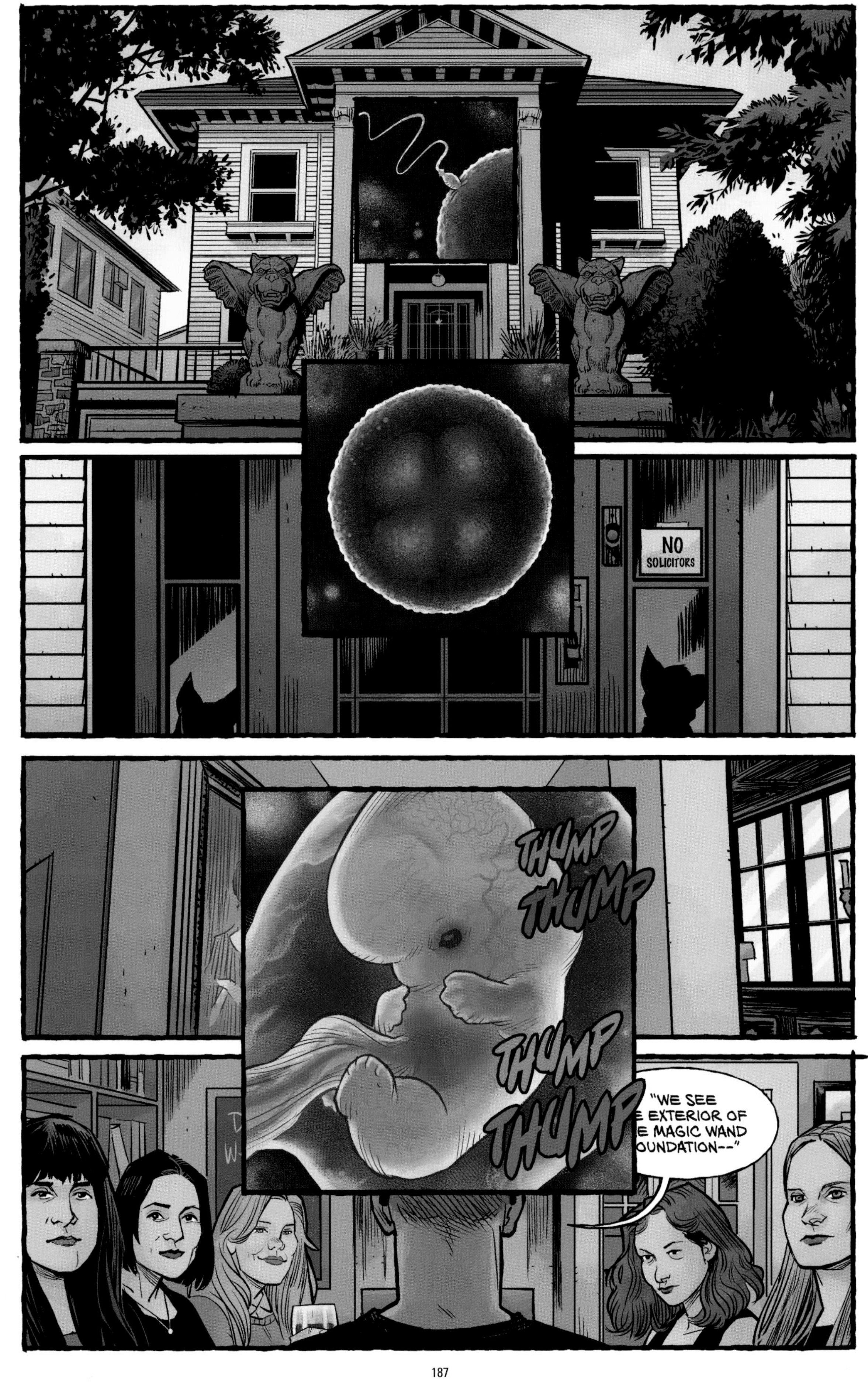
NO SOLICITORS
THUMP THUMP
THUMP THUMP
"WE SEE
E EXTERIOR OF
E MAGIC WAND
OUNDATION--"

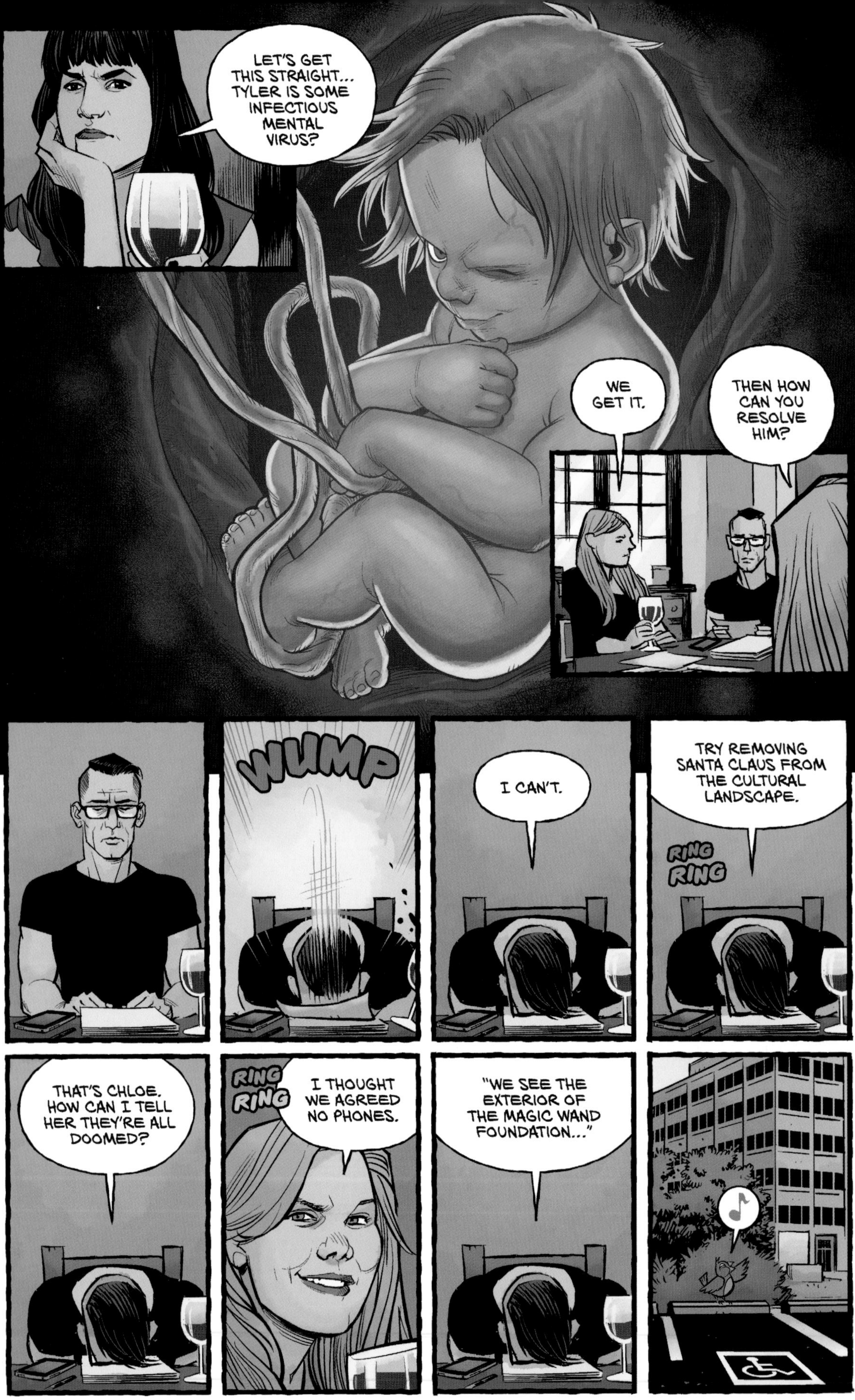
LET'S GET THIS STRAIGHT... TYLER IS SOME INFECTIOUS MENTAL VIRUS?
WE GET IT.
THEN HOW CAN YOU RESOLVE HIM?
WUMP
I CAN'T.
TRY REMOVING SANTA CLAUS FROM THE CULTURAL LANDSCAPE.
RING RING
THAT'S CHLOE. HOW CAN I TELL HER THEY'RE ALL DOOMED?
RING RING
I THOUGHT WE AGREED NO PHONES.
"WE SEE THE EXTERIOR OF THE MAGIC WAND FOUNDATION..."

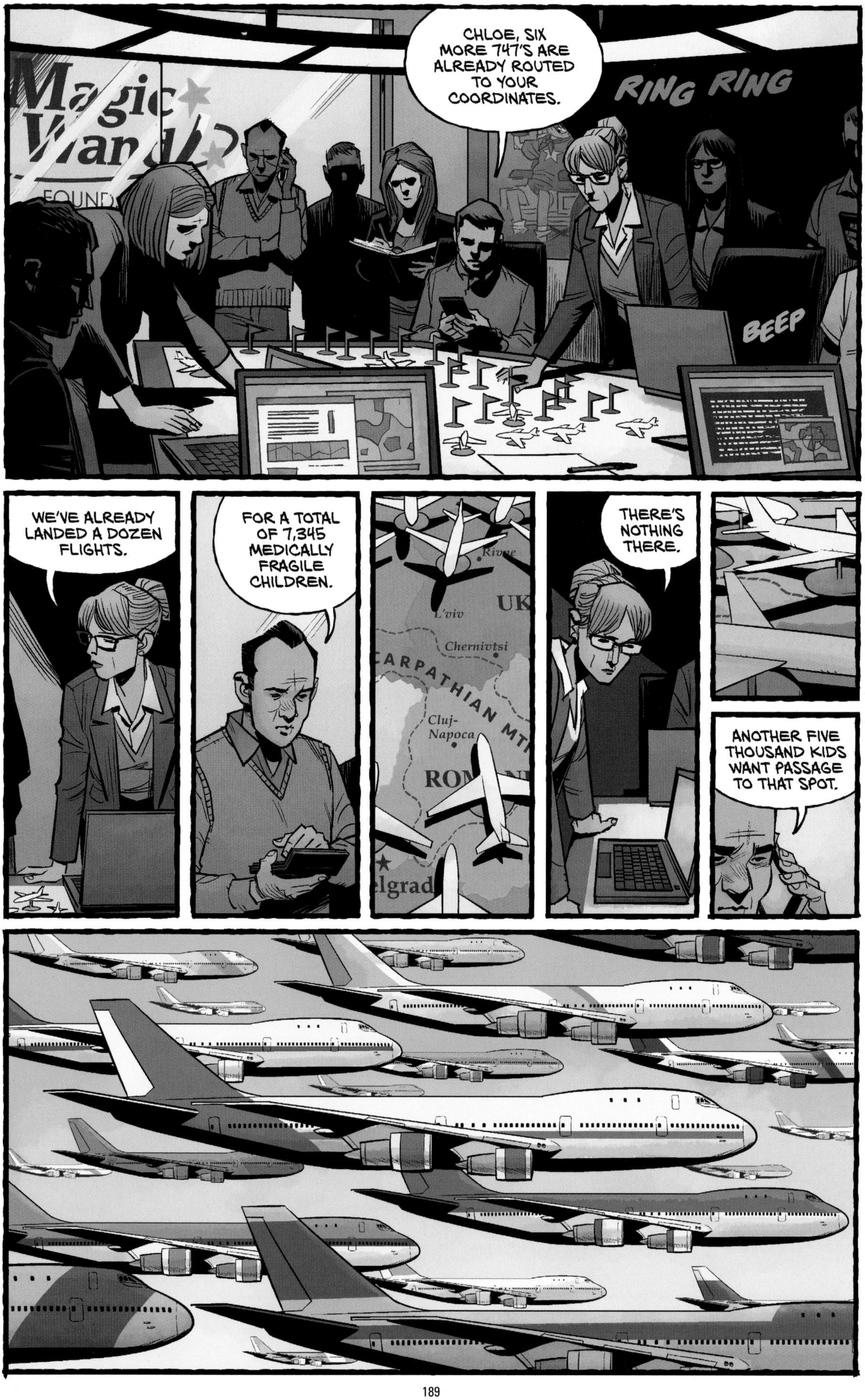
Magic Wand
FOUND
CHLOE, SIX MORE 747'S ARE ALREADY ROUTED TO YOUR COORDINATES.
RING RING
BEEP
WE'VE ALREADY LANDED A DOZEN FLIGHTS.
FOR A TOTAL OF 7,345 MEDICALLY FRAGILE CHILDREN.
Rivne
UK
L'viv
Chernivtsi
CARPATHIAN MT
Cluj-Napoca
ROM
elgrad
THERE'S NOTHING THERE.
ANOTHER FIVE THOUSAND KIDS WANT PASSAGE TO THAT SPOT.

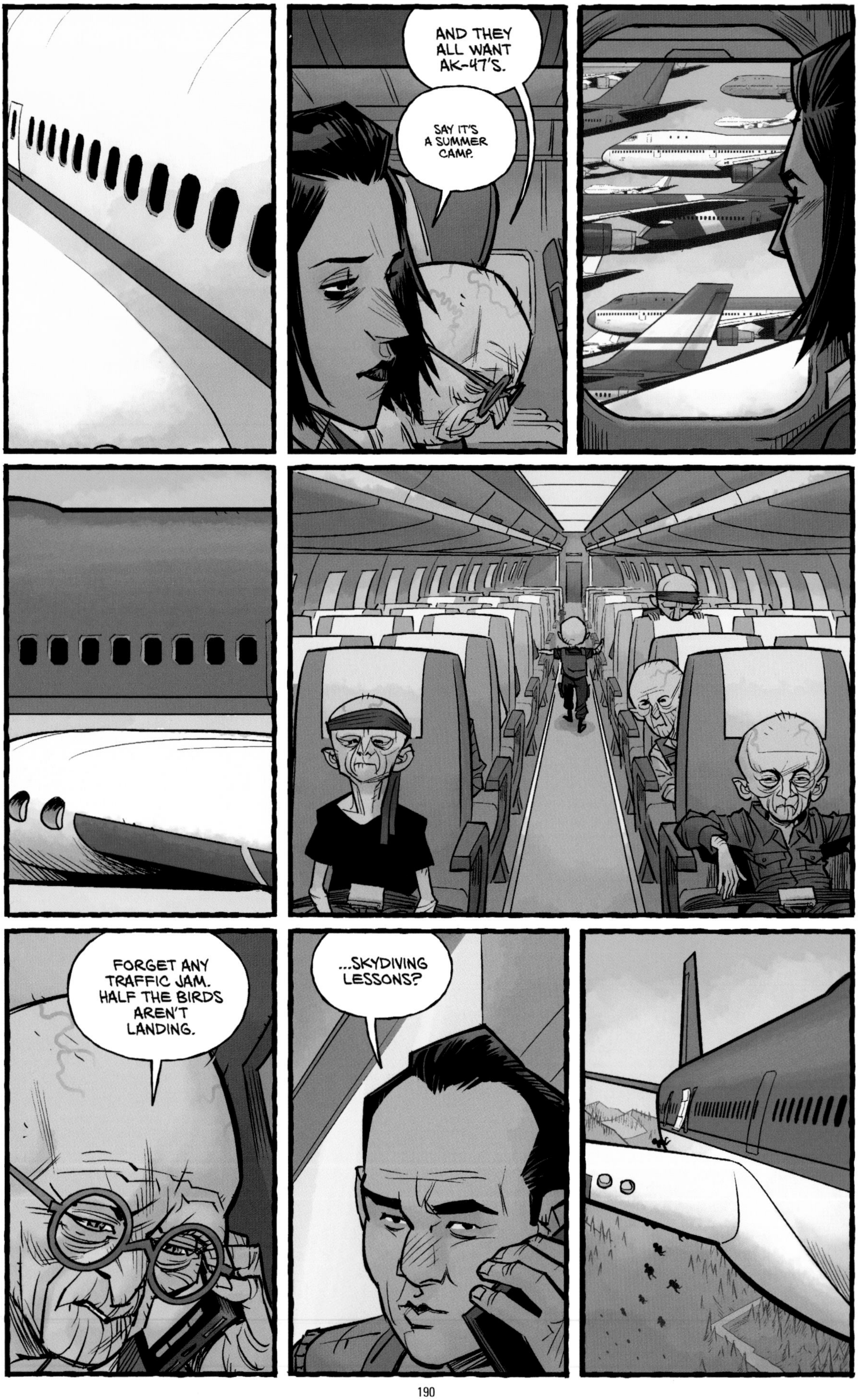
AND THEY ALL WANT AK-47'S.
SAY IT'S A SUMMER CAMP.
FORGET ANY TRAFFIC JAM. HALF THE BIRDS AREN'T LANDING.
...SKYDIVING LESSONS?

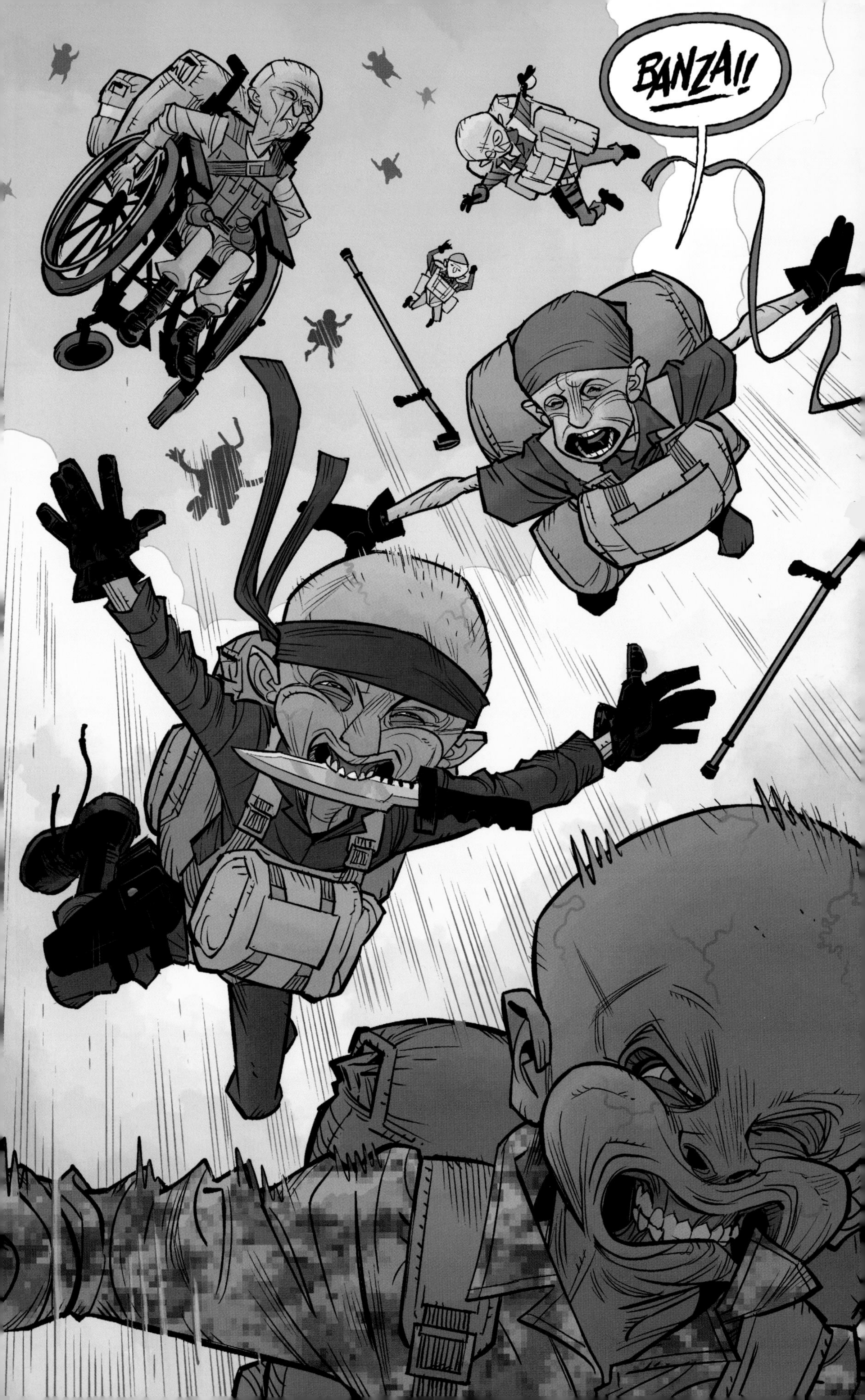
BANZAI!!

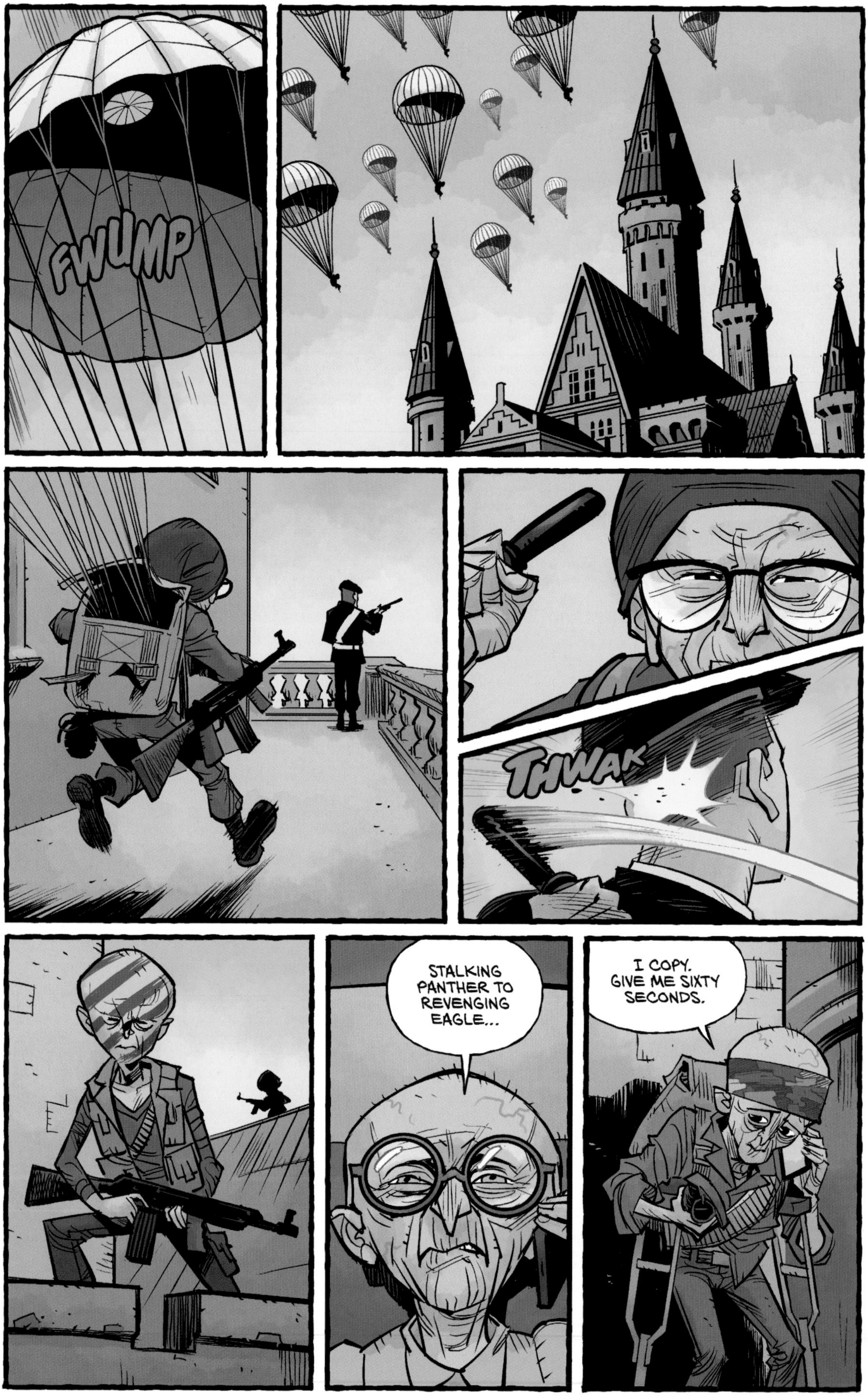
FWUMP
THWAK
STALKING PANTHER TO REVENGING EAGLE...
I COPY. GIVE ME SIXTY SECONDS.

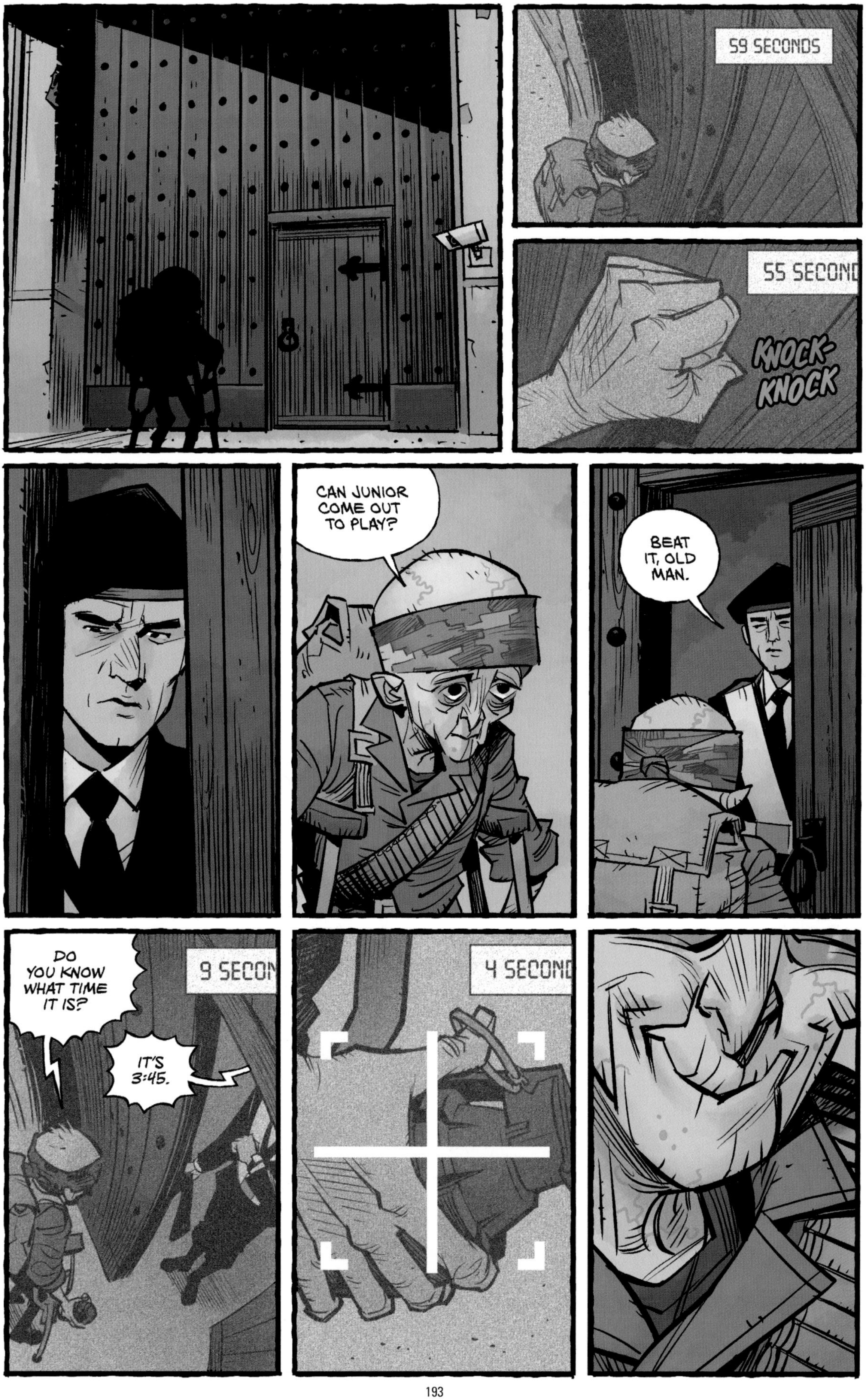
59 SECONDS
55 SECOND
KNOCK-KNOCK
CAN JUNIOR COME OUT TO PLAY?
BEAT IT, OLD MAN.
DO YOU KNOW WHAT TIME IT IS?
9 SECON
IT'S 3:45.
4 SECOND

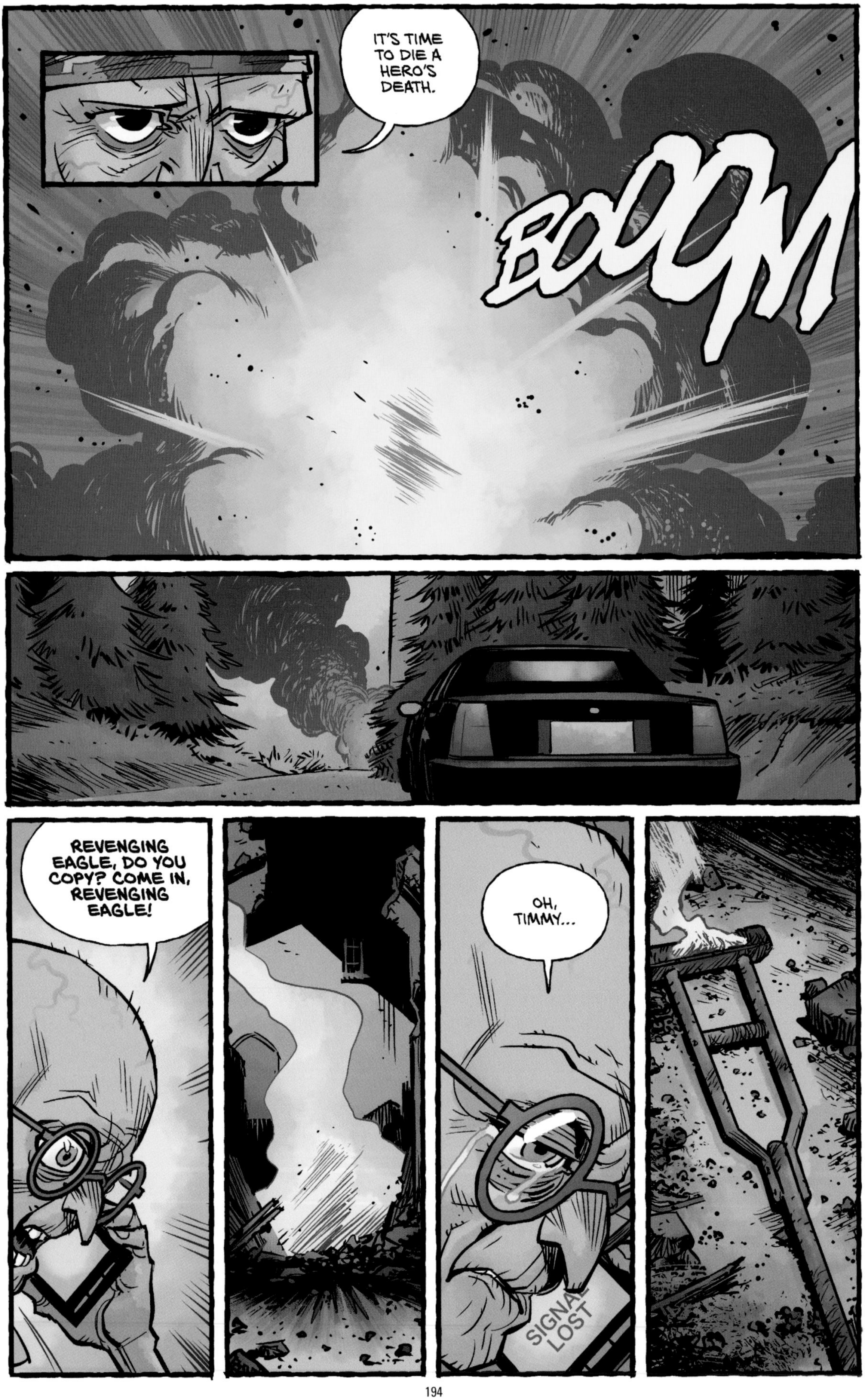
IT'S TIME TO DIE A HERO'S DEATH.
BOOOM
REVENGING EAGLE, DO YOU COPY? COME IN, REVENGING EAGLE!
OH, TIMMY...
SIGNAL LOST

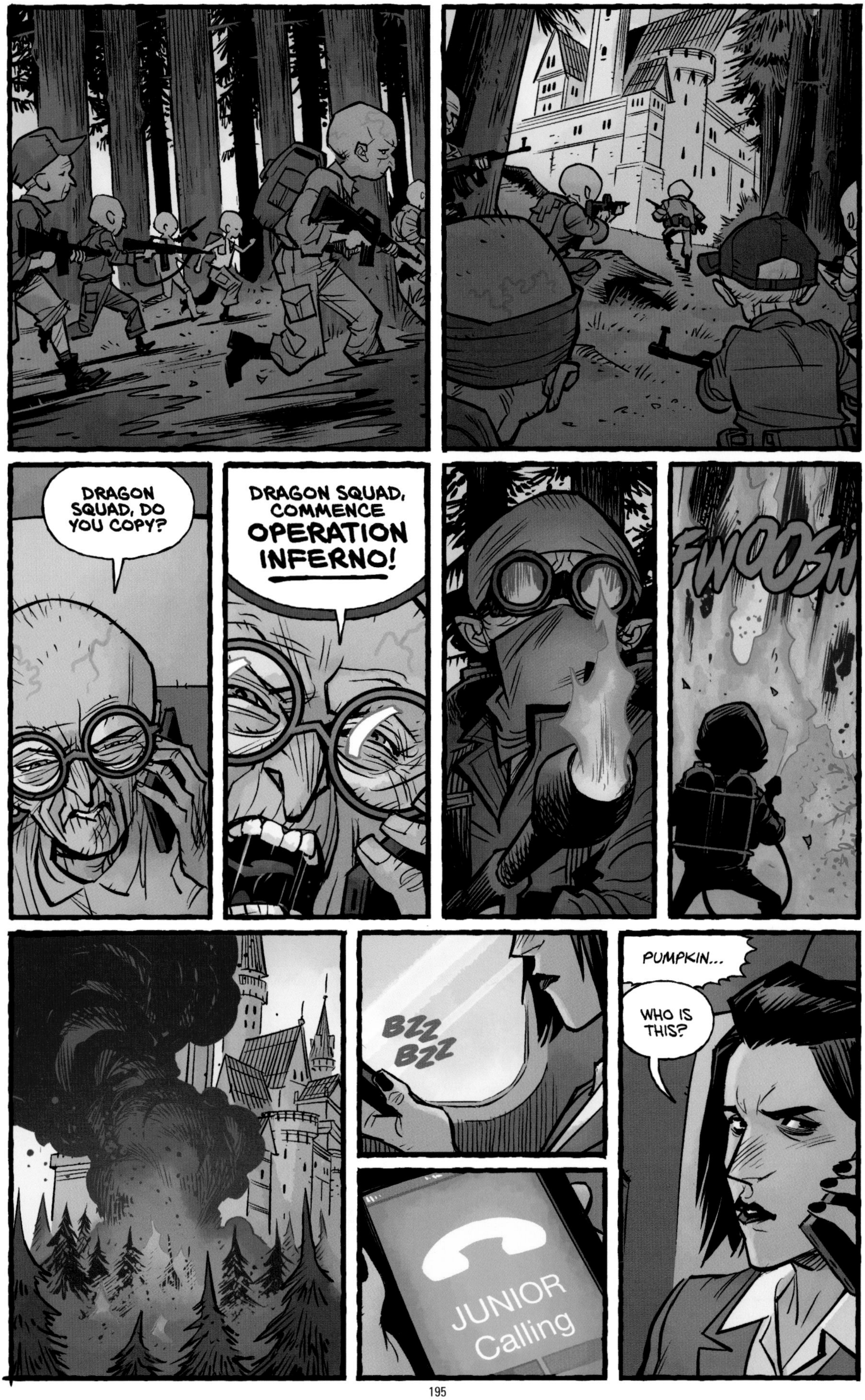
DRAGON SQUAD, DO YOU COPY?
DRAGON SQUAD, COMMENCE OPERATION INFERNO!
FWOOSH
BZZ BZZ
JUNIOR Calling
PUMPKIN...
WHO IS THIS?

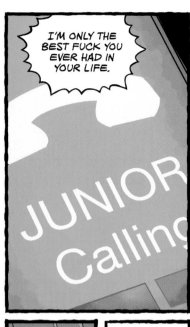

I'M ONLY THE BEST FUCK YOU EVER HAD IN YOUR LIFE.

JUNIOR Calling

YOU—SHIT.

JUNIOR MADE THAT BOMB TO BE FREE OF ALL YOUR HAND-ME-DOWN IDEALS AND THE POINTLESS LIFE YOU WERE SADDLING HIM WITH.

JUNIOR WOULDN'T MURDER US.

I PREFER THE WORD RETIRE.

WE'RE BRINGING IT!

IMPRESSIVE.

YOU'VE TRIGGERED THE TRANQUILITY GAMBIT.

WE'LL LIVE LONG ENOUGH TO KICK YOUR ASS.

JUNIOR WILL KILL HIS PARENTS WITH HIS BARE HANDS.

CALL ENDED

WHAT DID TYLER SAY?

LET'S LAND THIS BIRD ALREADY.

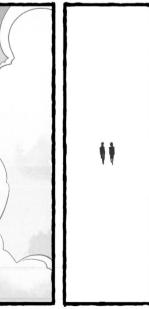

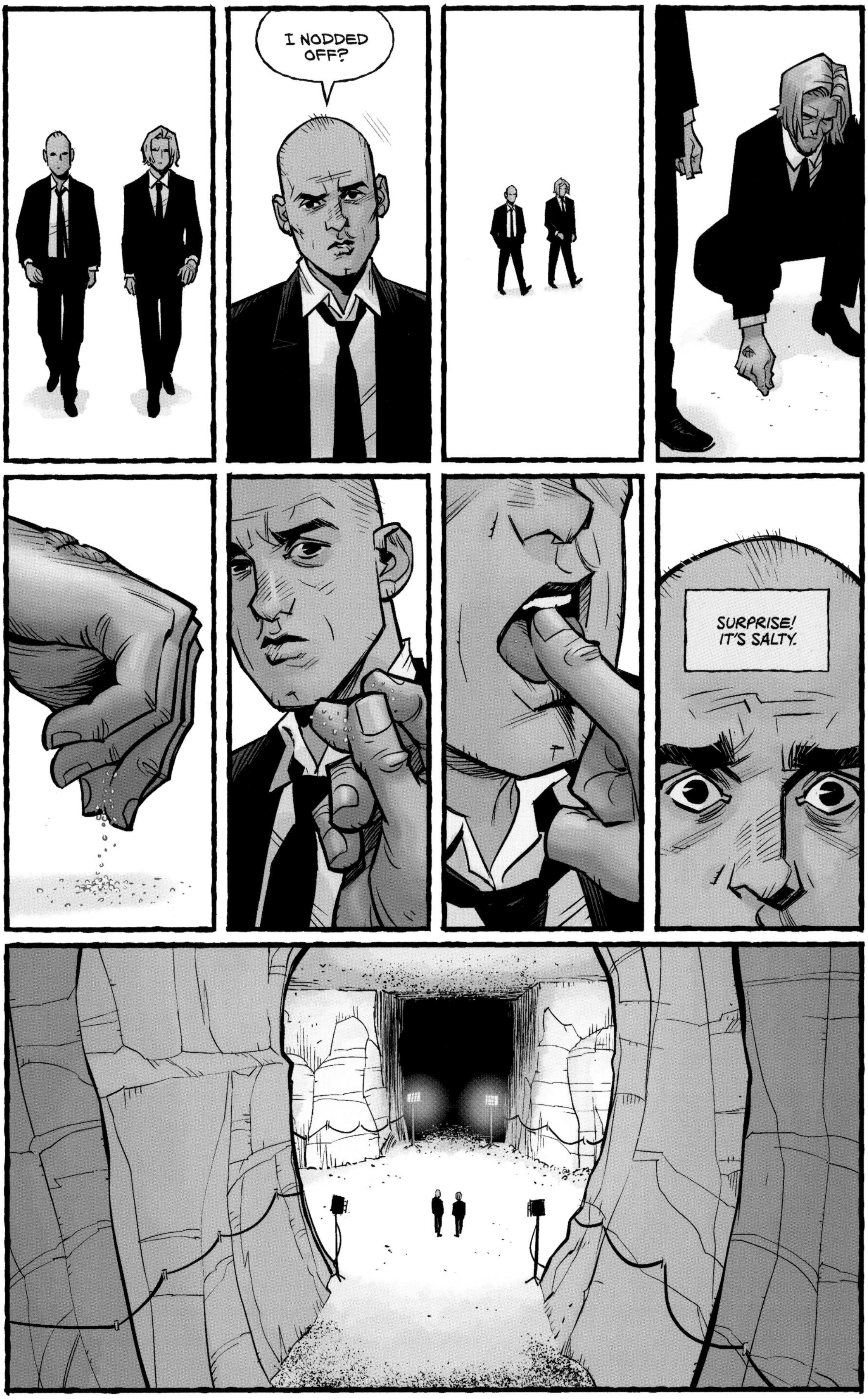
I NODDED OFF?
SURPRISE! IT'S SALTY.

YOUR SON WAS JUST OUR LURE.

WE'RE SAVING THOUSANDS OF SPECIES.

I WANTED TO SAVE YOU, TO—

SQUEEE MEOW WHINNY ME
OYNK MEOW TWEET GRRR
OYNK MOO OYNK
NEIGH MOOOOO GRRR
SNORT

THESE ARE THE LABS WHERE WE BREWED UP BUBONIC PLAGUE, THE SPANISH INFLUENZA, A.I.D.S., EBOLA, BUT NONE OF THEM GAVE US THE UNIVERSAL MORTALITY RATE WE NEEDED.

NEIGH MEOW SNORT SNORT

GRRR OYNK

MORTALITY RATES?

SQUEE MOOOO

IN THESE SAME LABS, WE NOW PRESERVE LIFE.

NOAH'S STRATEGY WASN'T EVEN REMOTELY REALISTIC.

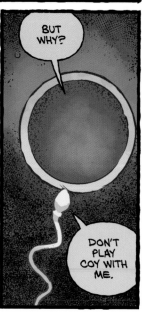

BUT WHY?

DON'T PLAY COY WITH ME.

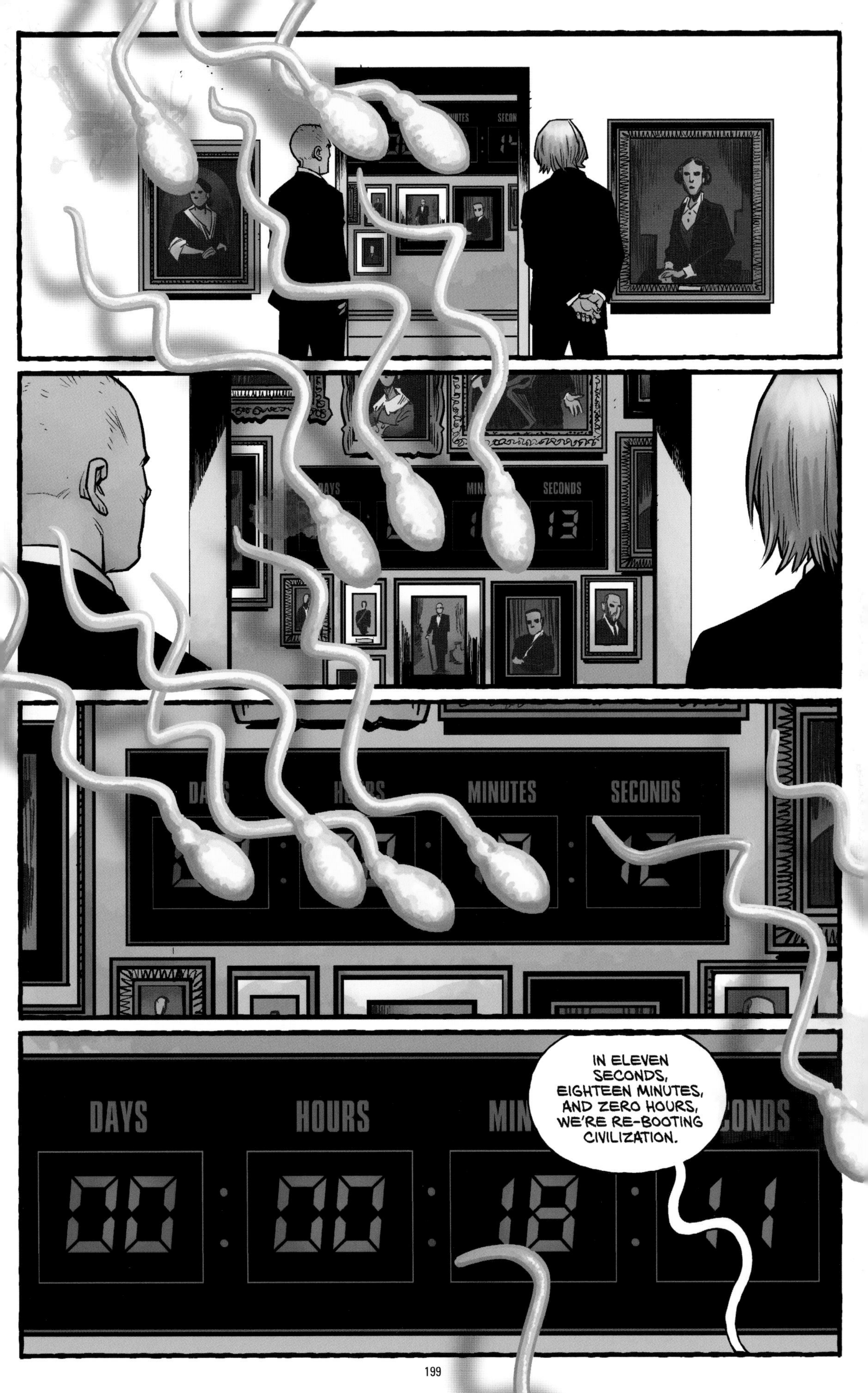
MINUTES
SECON
DAYS
MINU
SECONDS
13
DAYS
HOURS
MINUTES
SECONDS
DAYS
HOURS
00
00
18
IN ELEVEN SECONDS, EIGHTEEN MINUTES, AND ZERO HOURS, WE'RE RE-BOOTING CIVILIZATION.

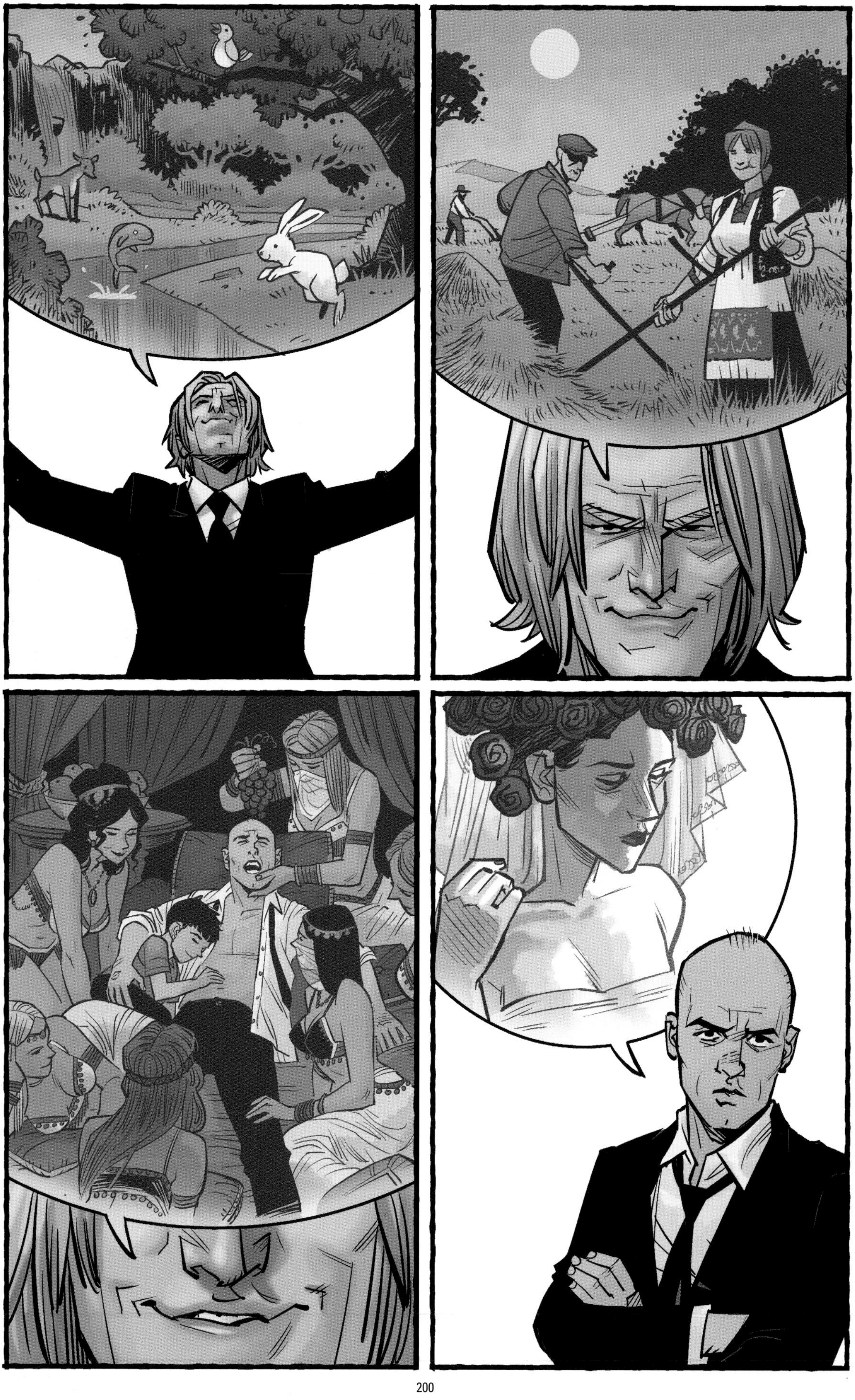

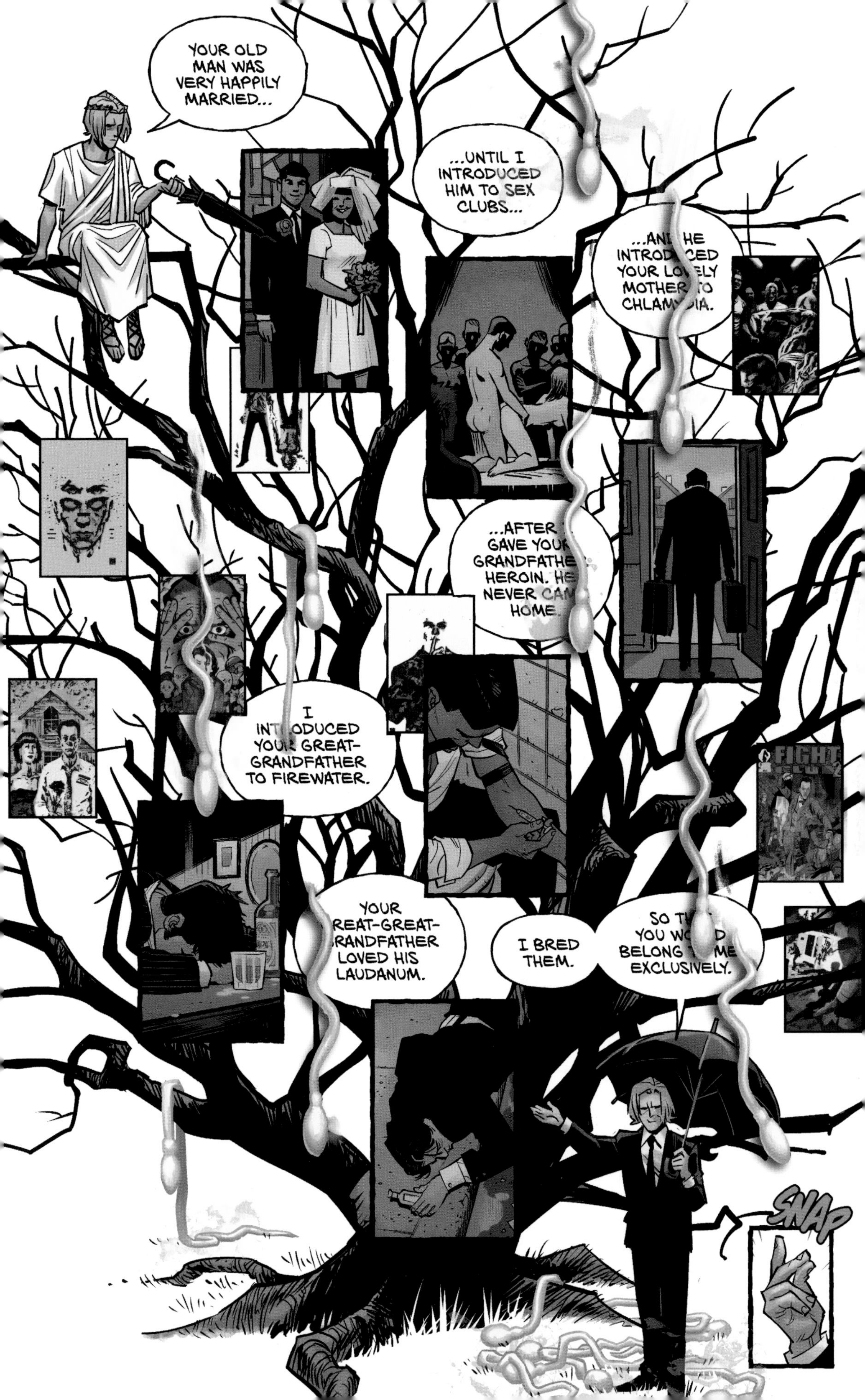
YOUR OLD MAN WAS VERY HAPPILY MARRIED...
...UNTIL I INTRODUCED HIM TO SEX CLUBS...
...AND HE INTRODUCED YOUR LOVELY MOTHER TO CHLAMYDIA.
...AFTER I GAVE YOUR GRANDFATHER HEROIN. HE NEVER CAME HOME.
I INTRODUCED YOUR GREAT-GRANDFATHER TO FIREWATER.
YOUR GREAT-GREAT-GRANDFATHER LOVED HIS LAUDANUM.
FIGHT CLUB 2
I BRED THEM.
SO THAT YOU WOULD BELONG TO ME EXCLUSIVELY.
SNAP

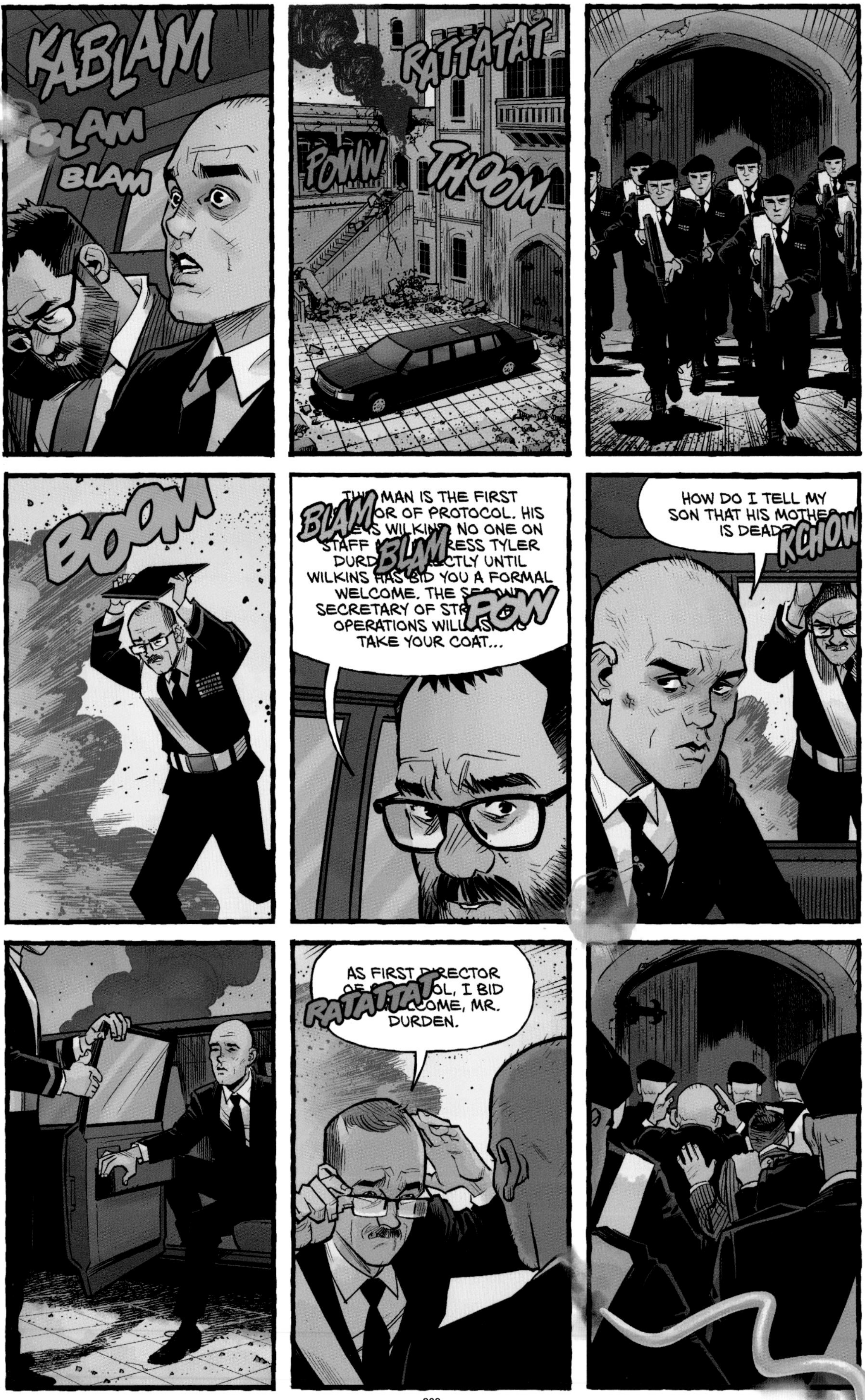
KABLAM
BLAM
BLAM
RATTATAT
POWW
THOOM
BOOM
MAN IS THE FIRST OR OF PROTOCOL. HIS WILKIN NO ONE ON STAFF RESS TYLER DURD ECTLY UNTIL WILKINS HAS BID YOU A FORMAL WELCOME. THE SECO SECRETARY OF STR OPERATIONS WILL TAKE YOUR COAT...
BLAM
BLAM
POW
HOW DO I TELL MY SON THAT HIS MOTHE IS DEAD
KCHOW
AS FIRST IRECTOR OF OL, I BID COME, MR. DURDEN.
RATATTAT

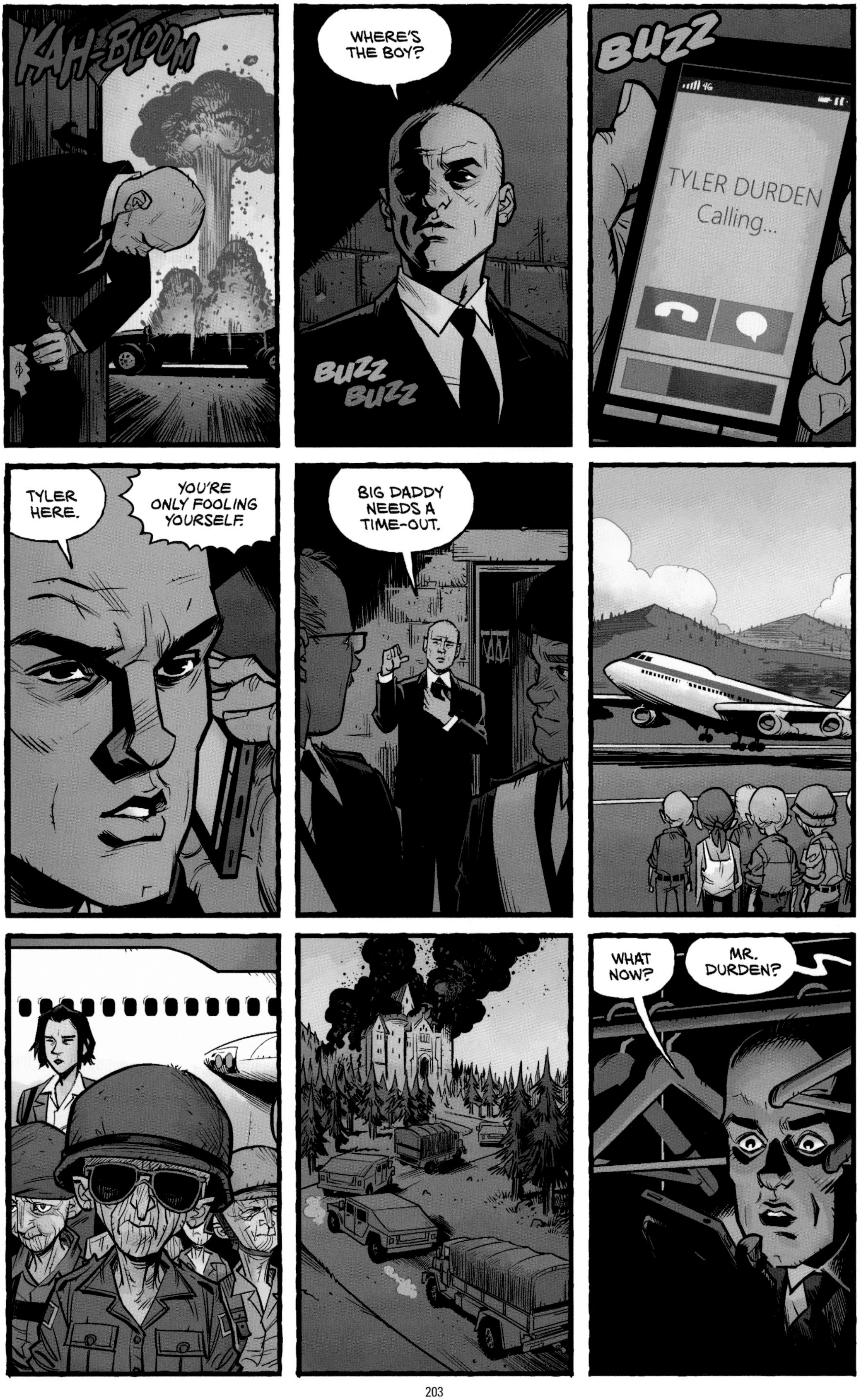
KAH-BLOOM
WHERE'S THE BOY?
BUZZ BUZZ
BUZZ
TYLER DURDEN
Calling...
TYLER HERE.
YOU'RE ONLY FOOLING YOURSELF.
BIG DADDY NEEDS A TIME-OUT.
WHAT NOW?
MR. DURDEN?

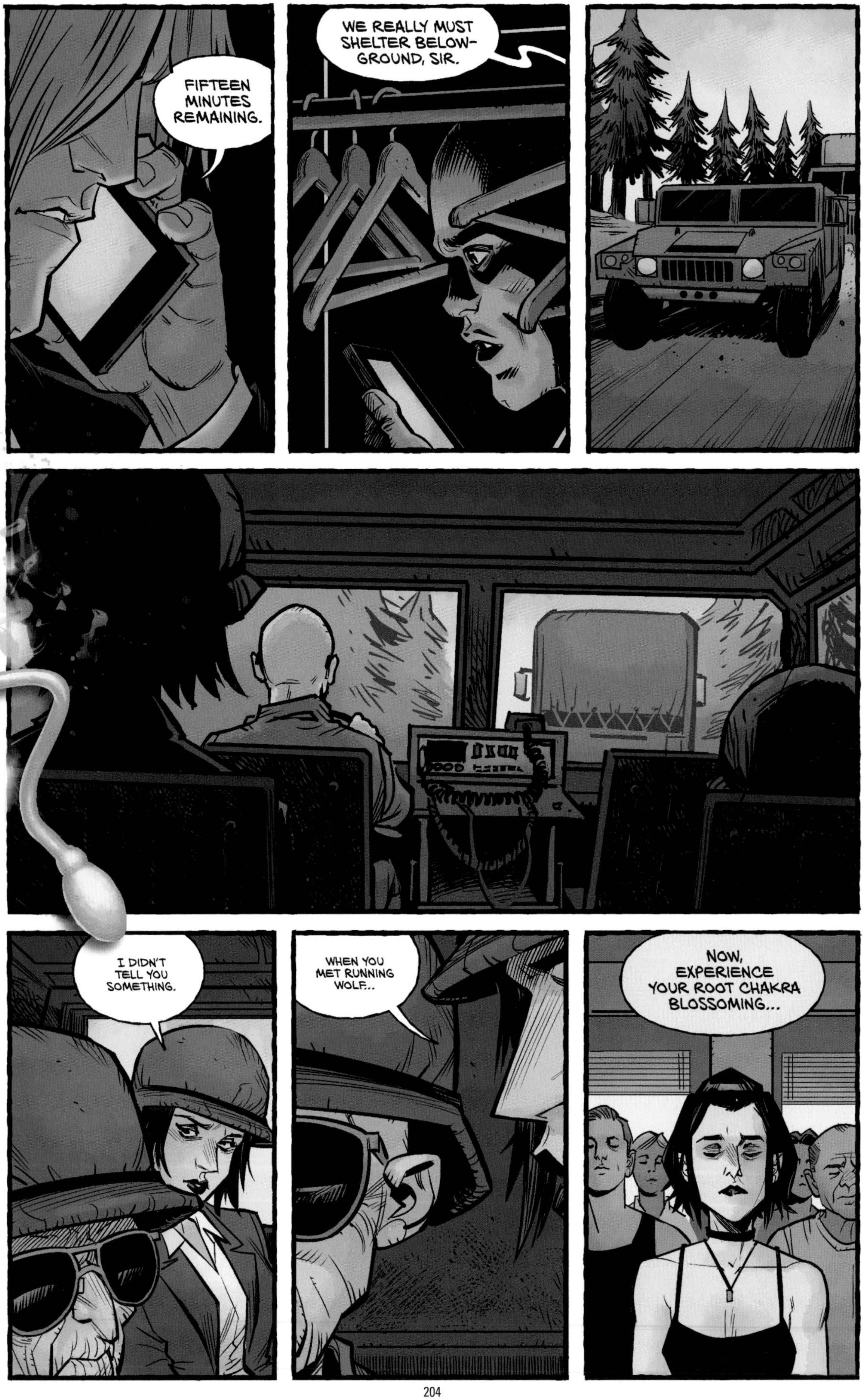
FIFTEEN MINUTES REMAINING.
WE REALLY MUST SHELTER BELOW-GROUND, SIR.
I DIDN'T TELL YOU SOMETHING.
WHEN YOU MET RUNNING WOLF...
NOW, EXPERIENCE YOUR ROOT CHAKRA BLOSSOMING...

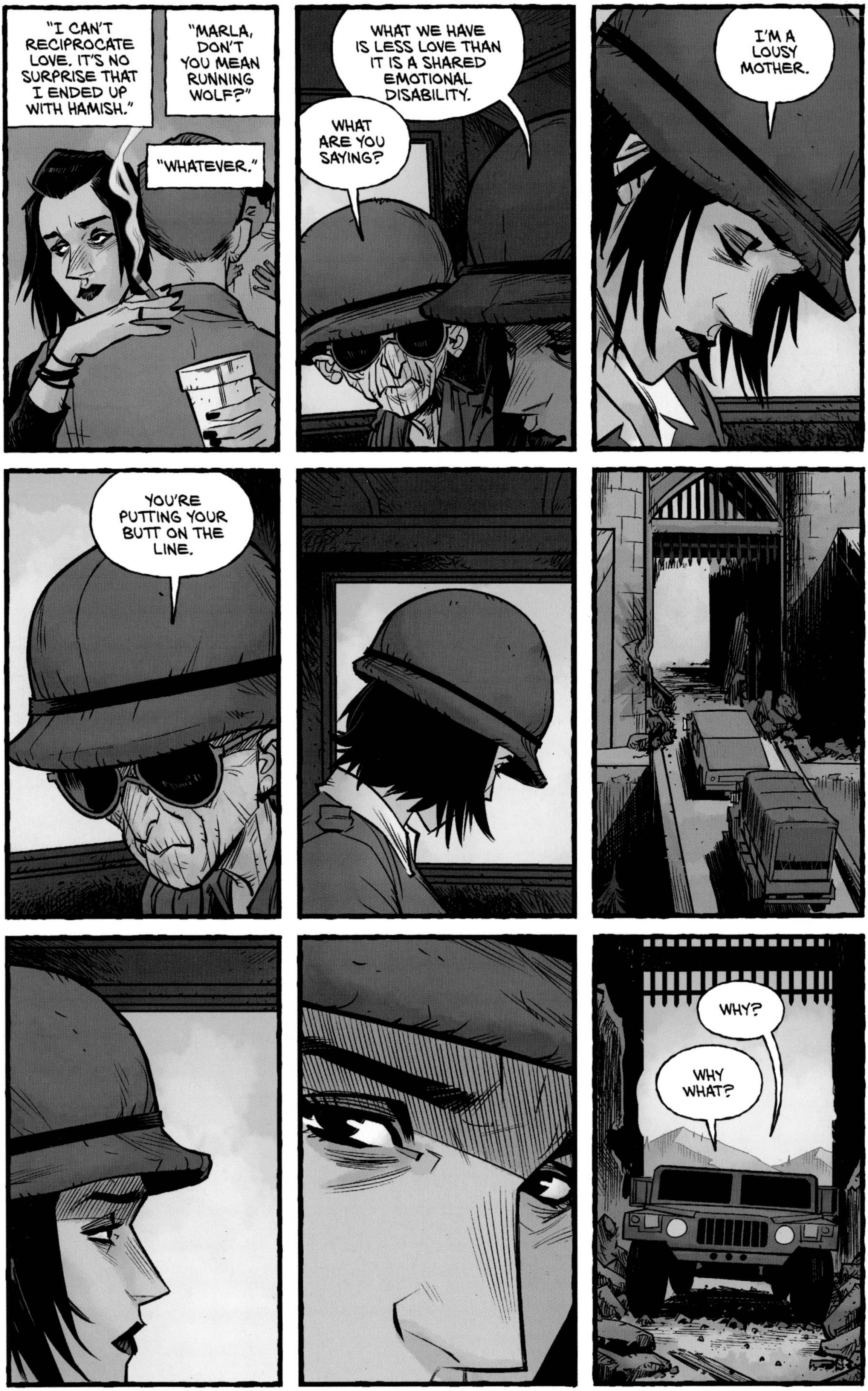
"I CAN'T RECIPROCATE LOVE. IT'S NO SURPRISE THAT I ENDED UP WITH HAMISH."
"MARLA, DON'T YOU MEAN RUNNING WOLF?"
"WHATEVER."
WHAT WE HAVE IS LESS LOVE THAN IT IS A SHARED EMOTIONAL DISABILITY.
WHAT ARE YOU SAYING?
I'M A LOUSY MOTHER.
YOU'RE PUTTING YOUR BUTT ON THE LINE.
WHY?
WHY WHAT?

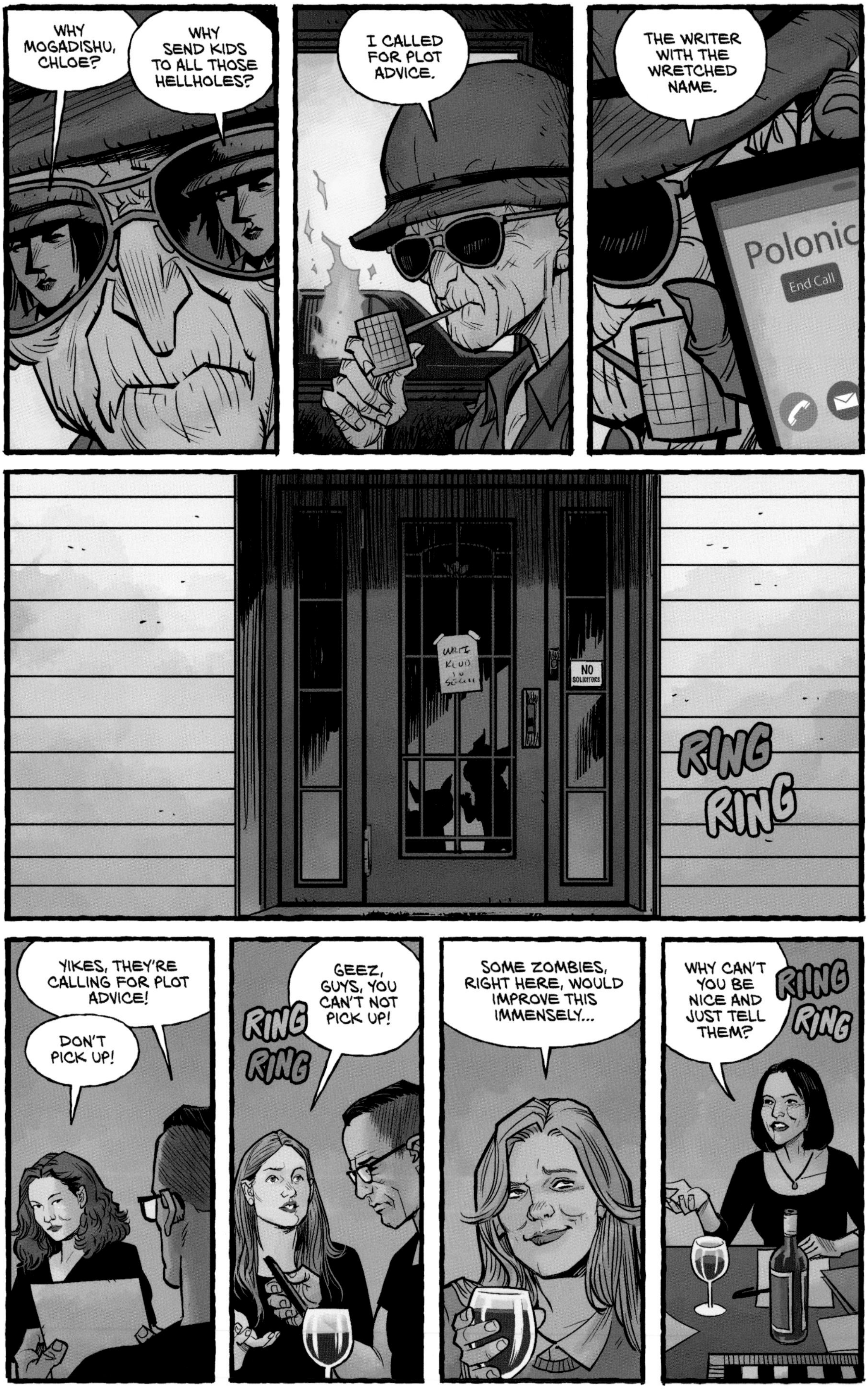
WHY MOGADISHU, CHLOE?
WHY SEND KIDS TO ALL THOSE HELLHOLES?
I CALLED FOR PLOT ADVICE.
THE WRITER WITH THE WRETCHED NAME.
Polonic
End Call
NO SOLICITORS
RING RING
YIKES, THEY'RE CALLING FOR PLOT ADVICE!
DON'T PICK UP!
RING RING
GEEZ, GUYS, YOU CAN'T NOT PICK UP!
SOME ZOMBIES, RIGHT HERE, WOULD IMPROVE THIS IMMENSELY...
WHY CAN'T YOU BE NICE AND JUST TELL THEM?
RING RING

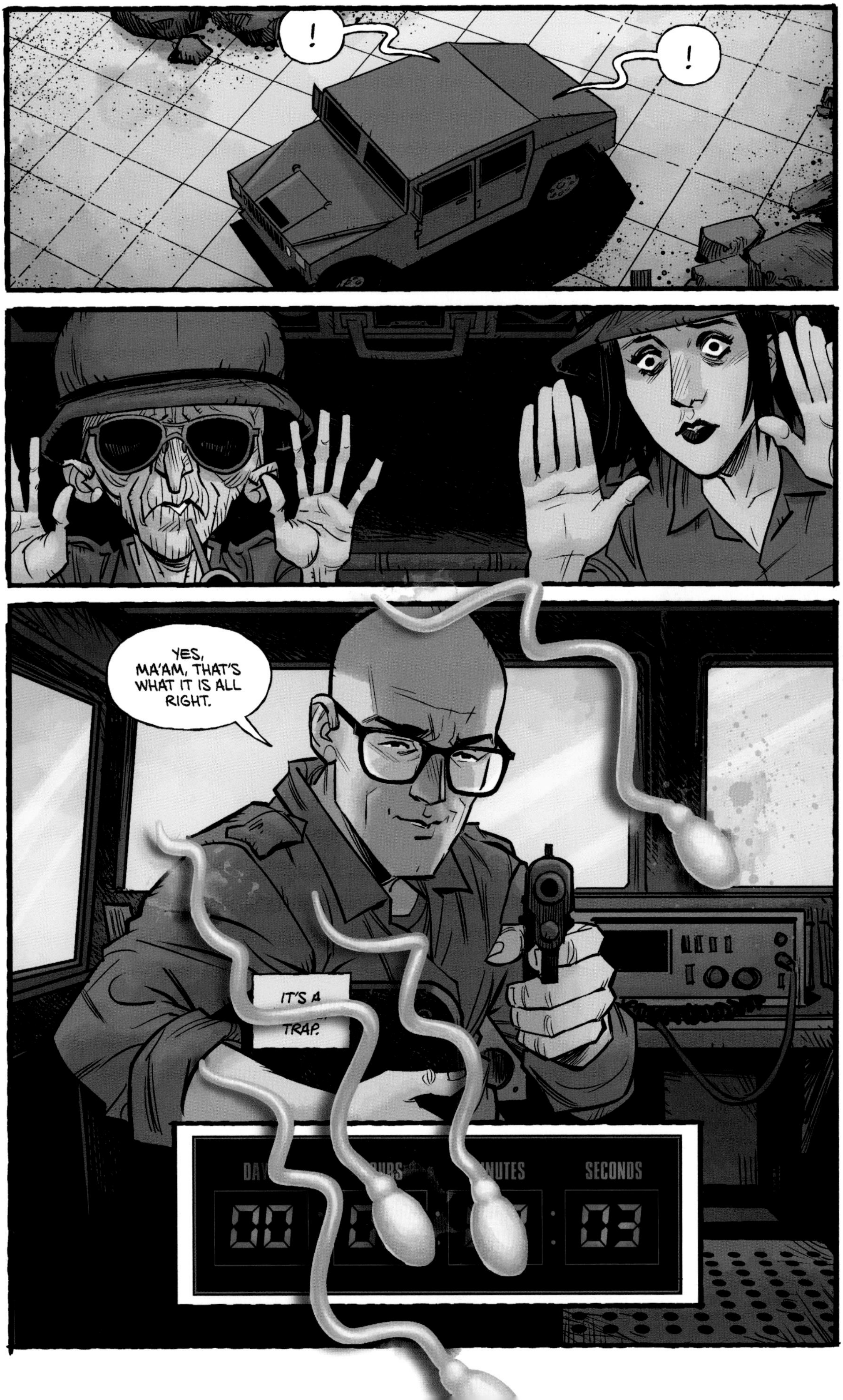
!
!
YES, MA'AM, THAT'S WHAT IT IS ALL RIGHT.
IT'S A TRAP.
SECONDS
00
03

Chapter Nine
A Father and Son Reunion

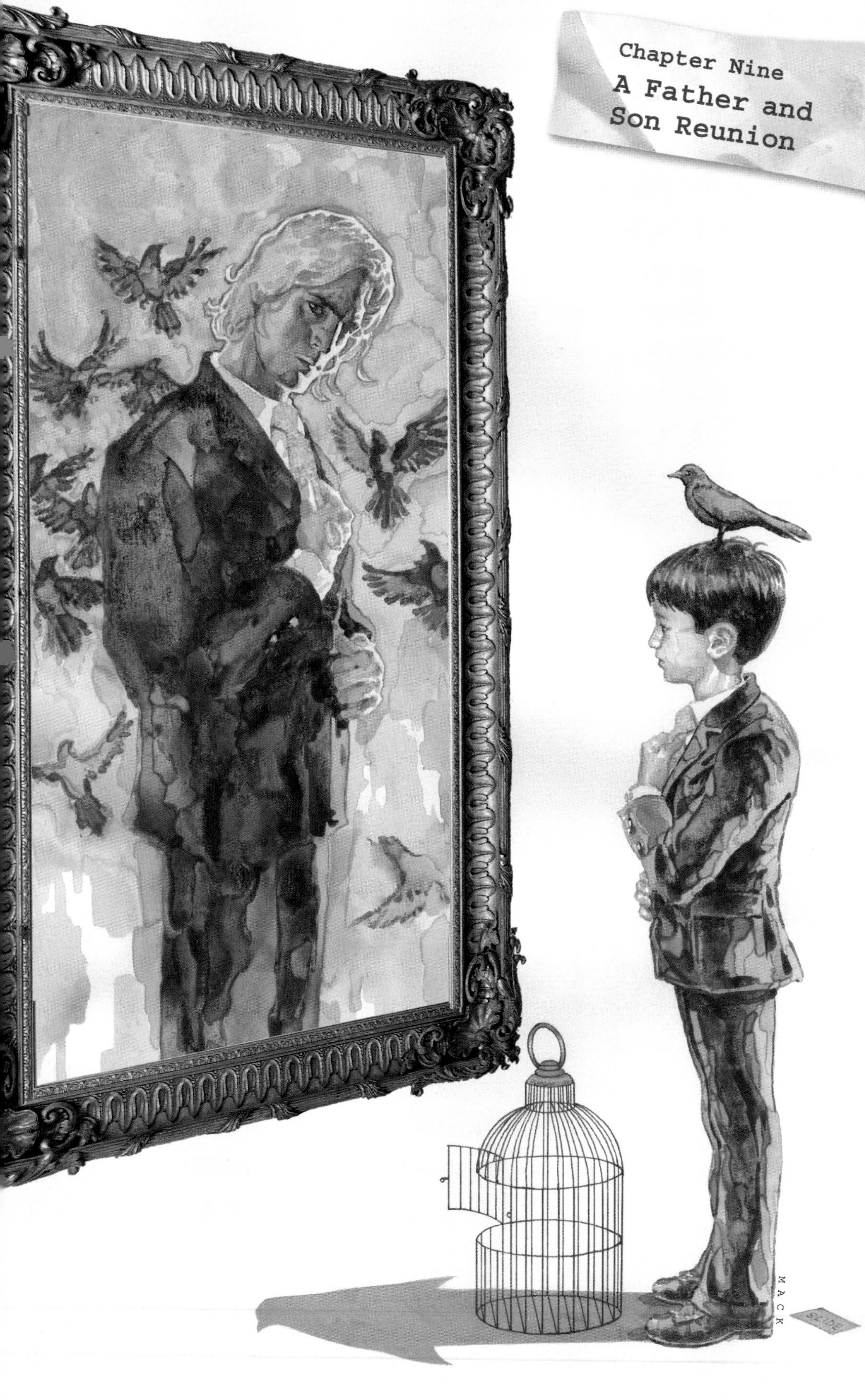
MACK

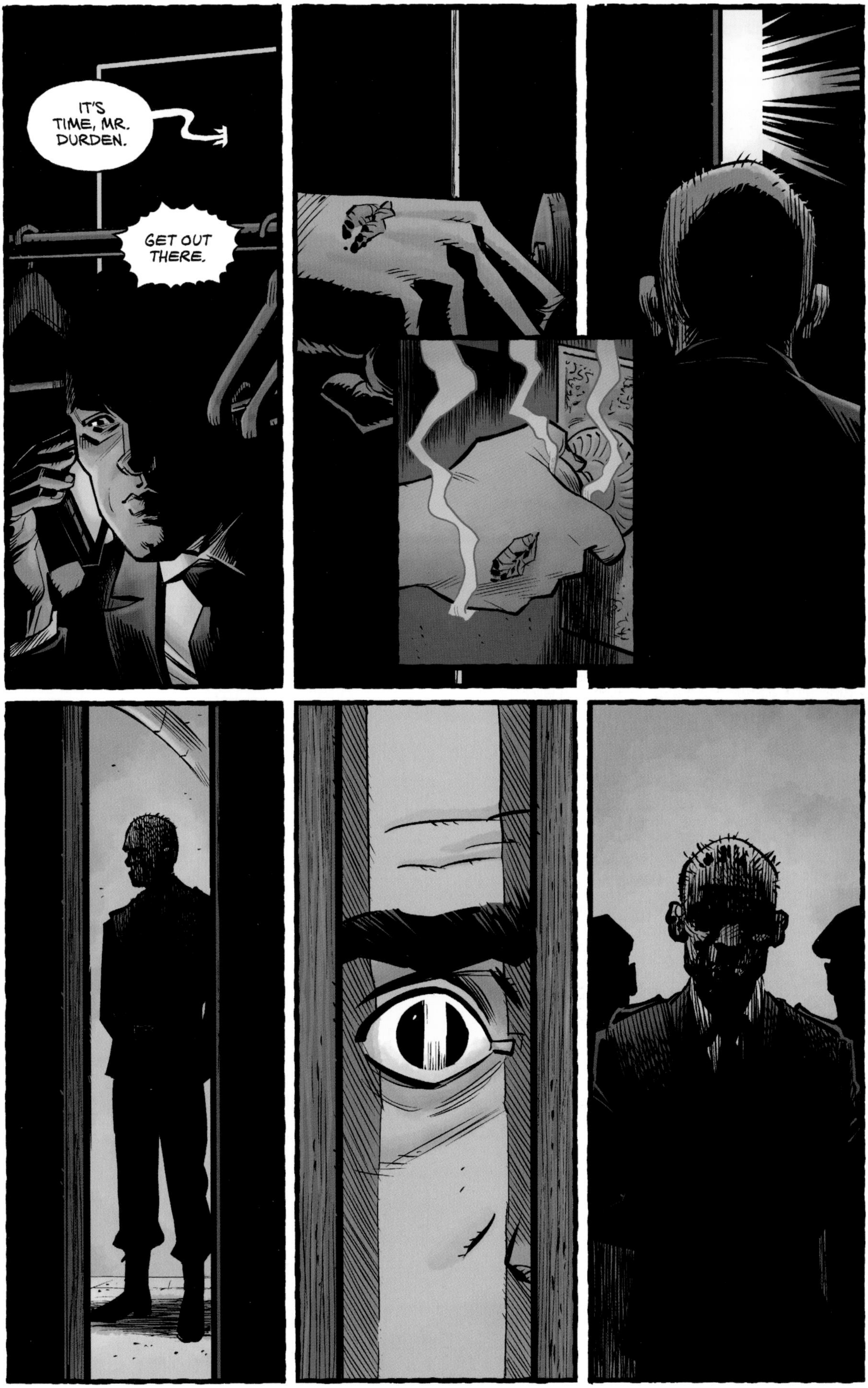
IT'S TIME, MR. DURDEN.
GET OUT THERE.

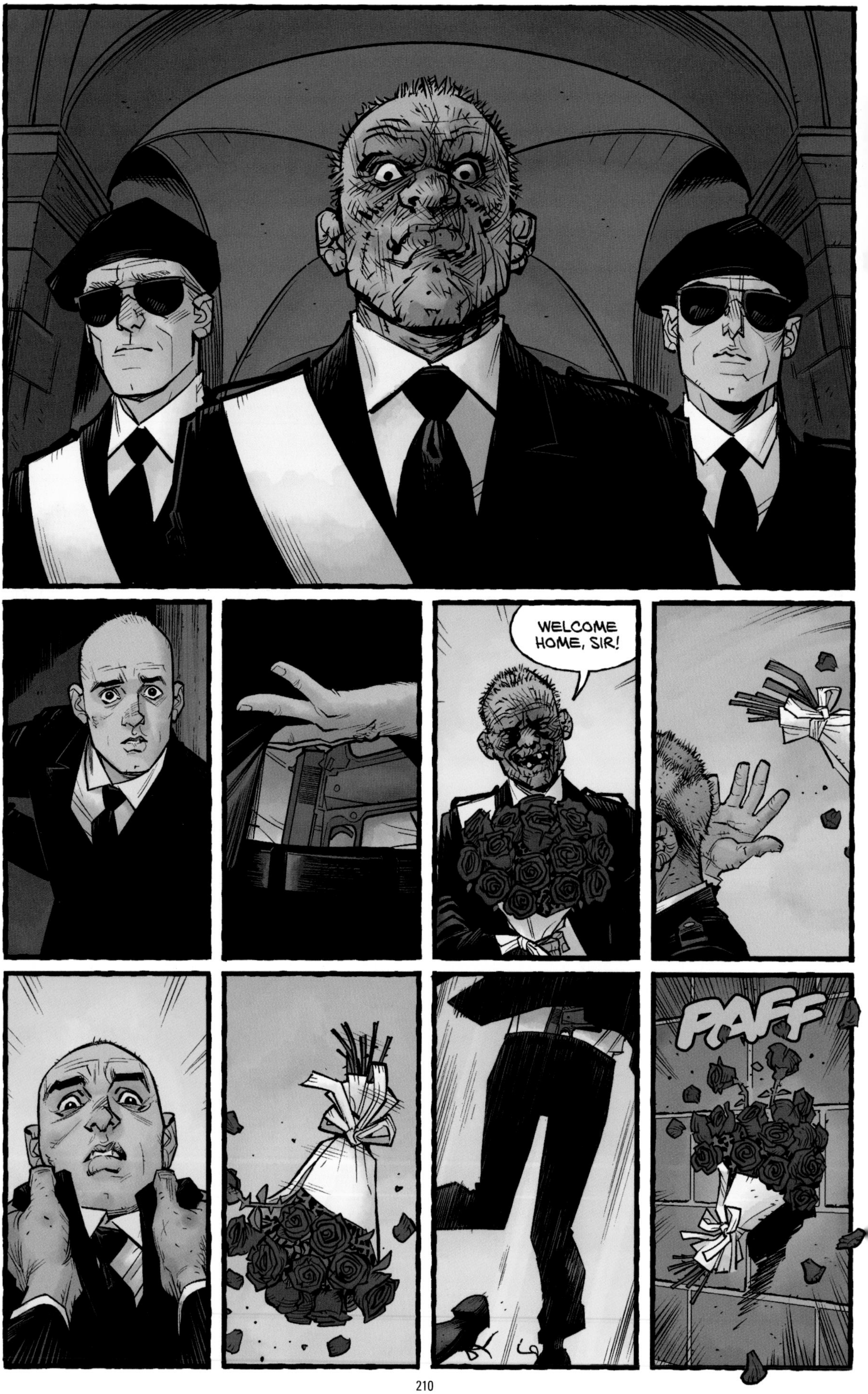
WELCOME HOME, SIR!
PAFF

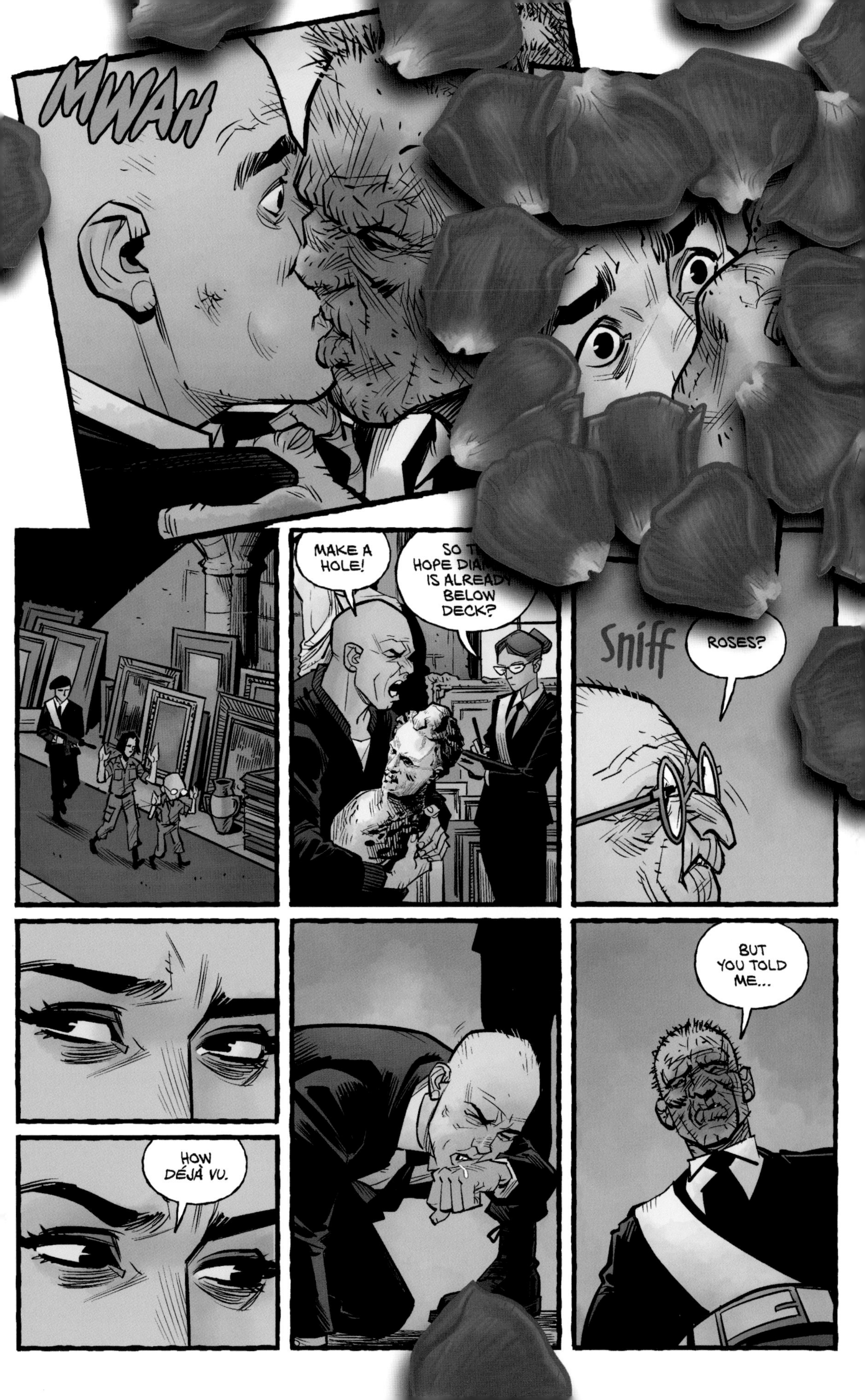
MWAH
MAKE A HOLE!
SO THE HOPE DIAMOND IS ALREADY BELOW DECK?
Sniff
ROSES?
HOW DÉJÀ VU.
BUT YOU TOLD ME...

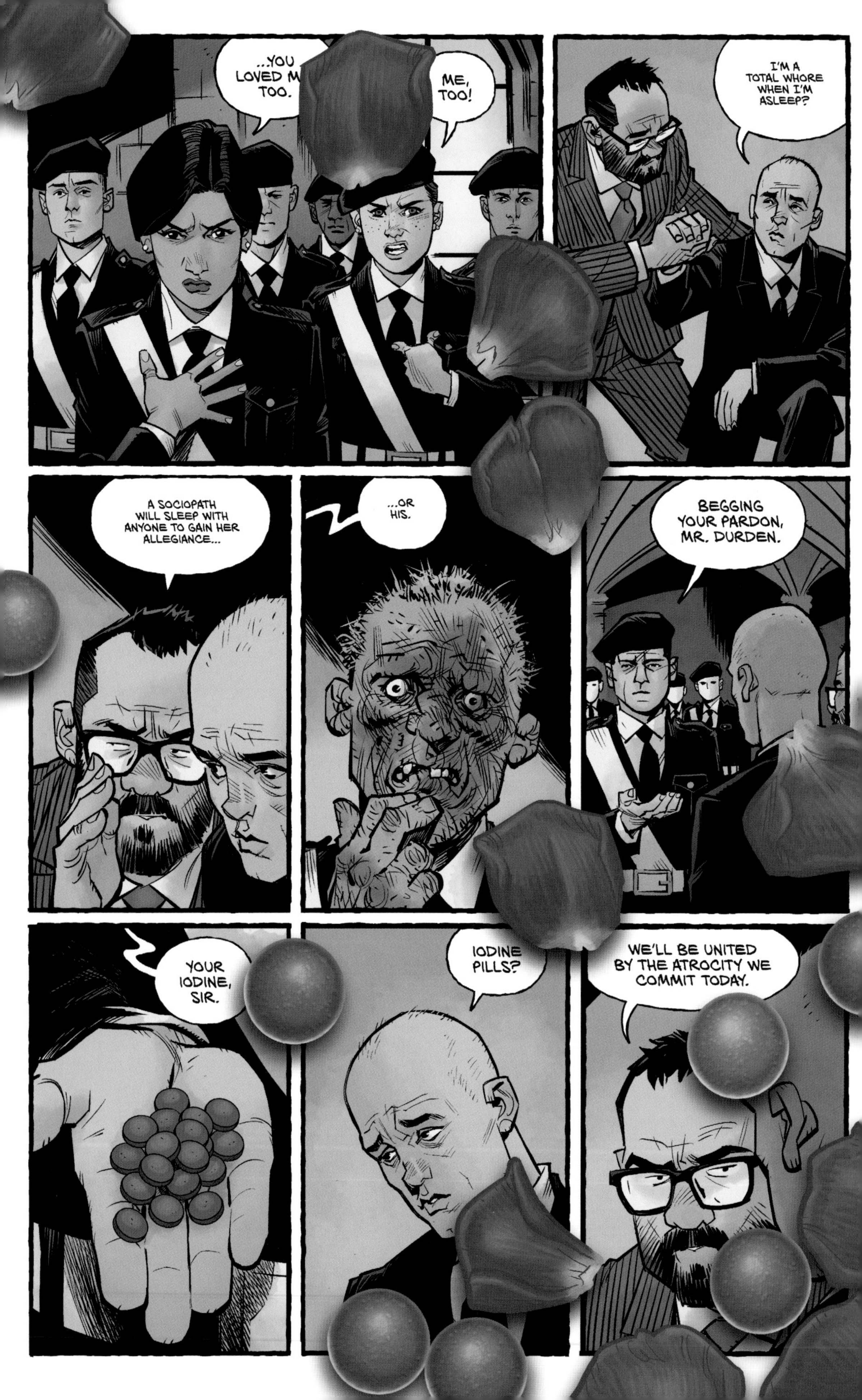
...YOU LOVED M TOO.
ME, TOO!
I'M A TOTAL WHORE WHEN I'M ASLEEP?
A SOCIOPATH WILL SLEEP WITH ANYONE TO GAIN HER ALLEGIANCE...
...OR HIS.
BEGGING YOUR PARDON, MR. DURDEN.
YOUR IODINE, SIR.
IODINE PILLS?
WE'LL BE UNITED BY THE ATROCITY WE COMMIT TODAY.

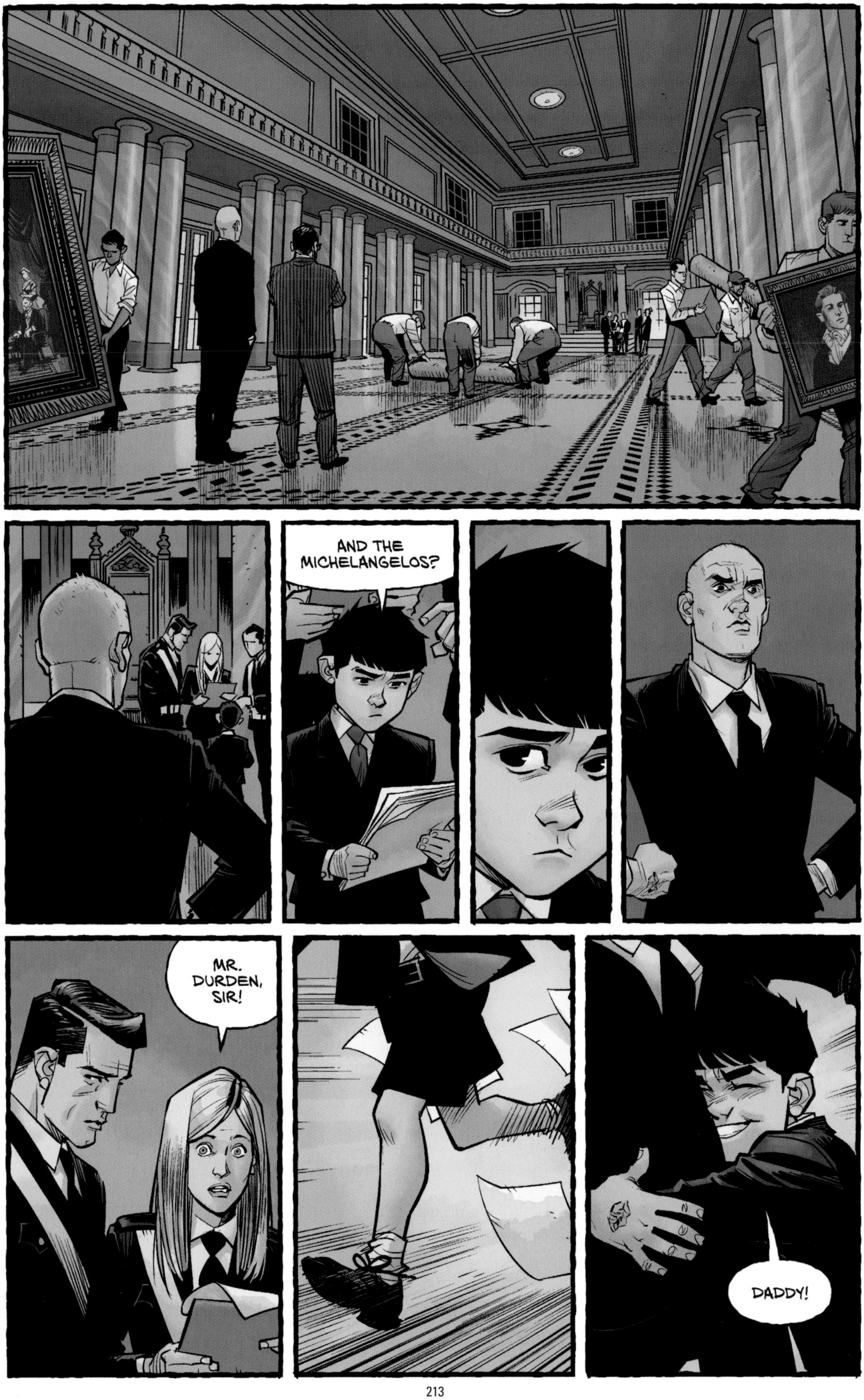
AND THE MICHELANGELOS?
MR. DURDEN, SIR!
DADDY!

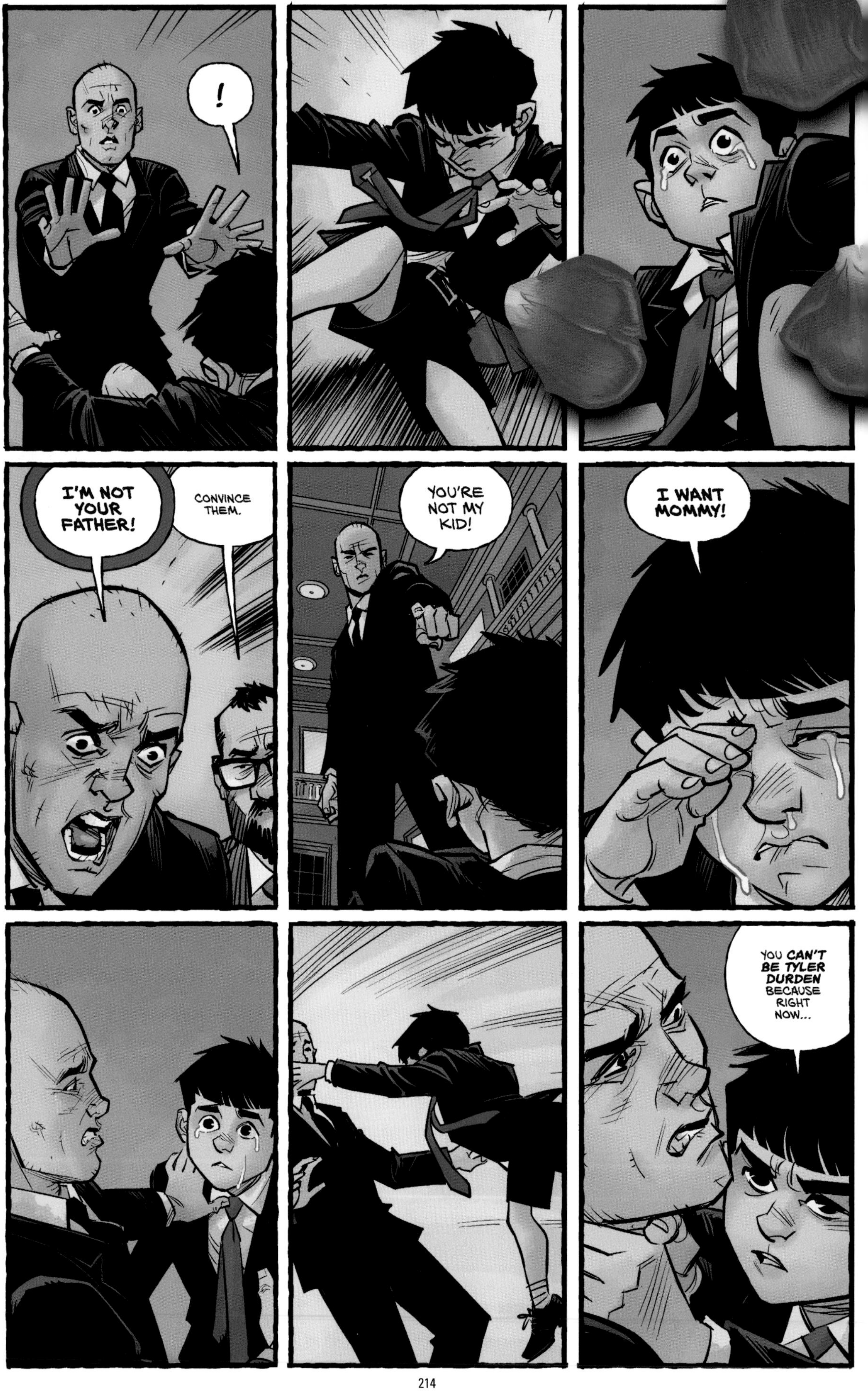
!
I'M NOT YOUR FATHER!
CONVINCE THEM.
YOU'RE NOT MY KID!
I WANT MOMMY!
YOU CAN'T BE TYLER DURDEN BECAUSE RIGHT NOW...

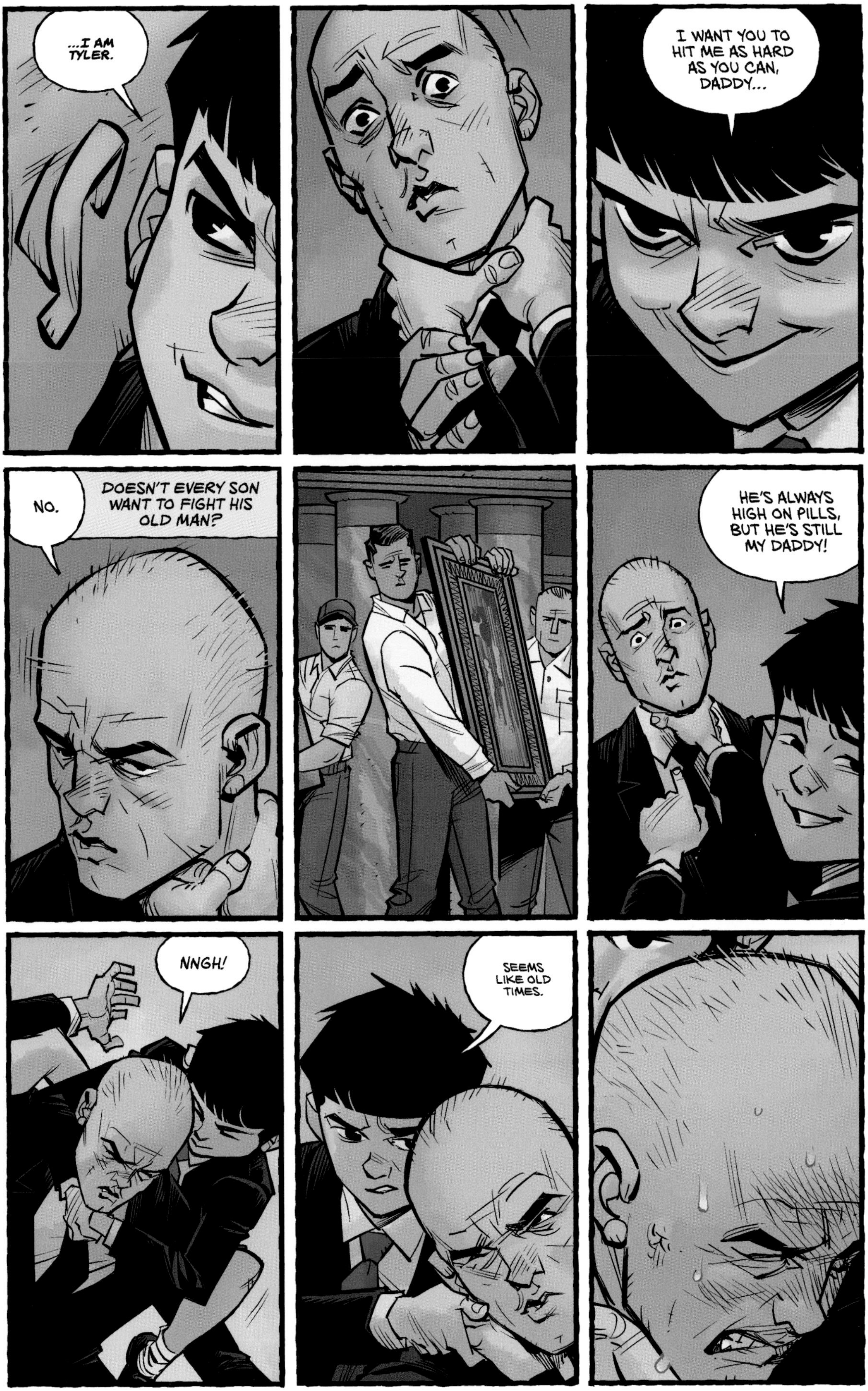
...I AM TYLER.
I WANT YOU TO HIT ME AS HARD AS YOU CAN, DADDY...
NO.
DOESN'T EVERY SON WANT TO FIGHT HIS OLD MAN?
HE'S ALWAYS HIGH ON PILLS, BUT HE'S STILL MY DADDY!
NNGH!
SEEMS LIKE OLD TIMES.

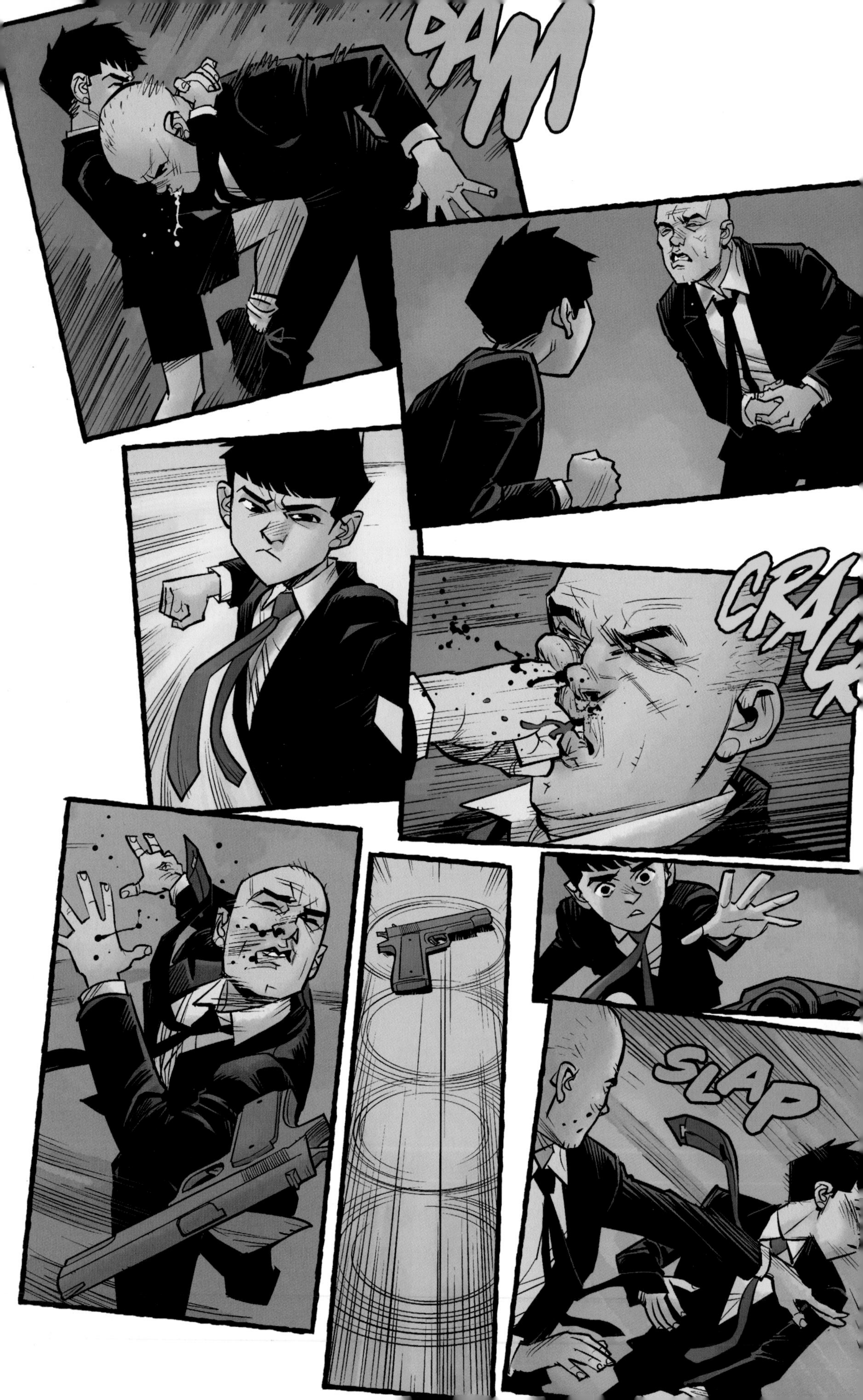

BAM
CRACK
SLAP

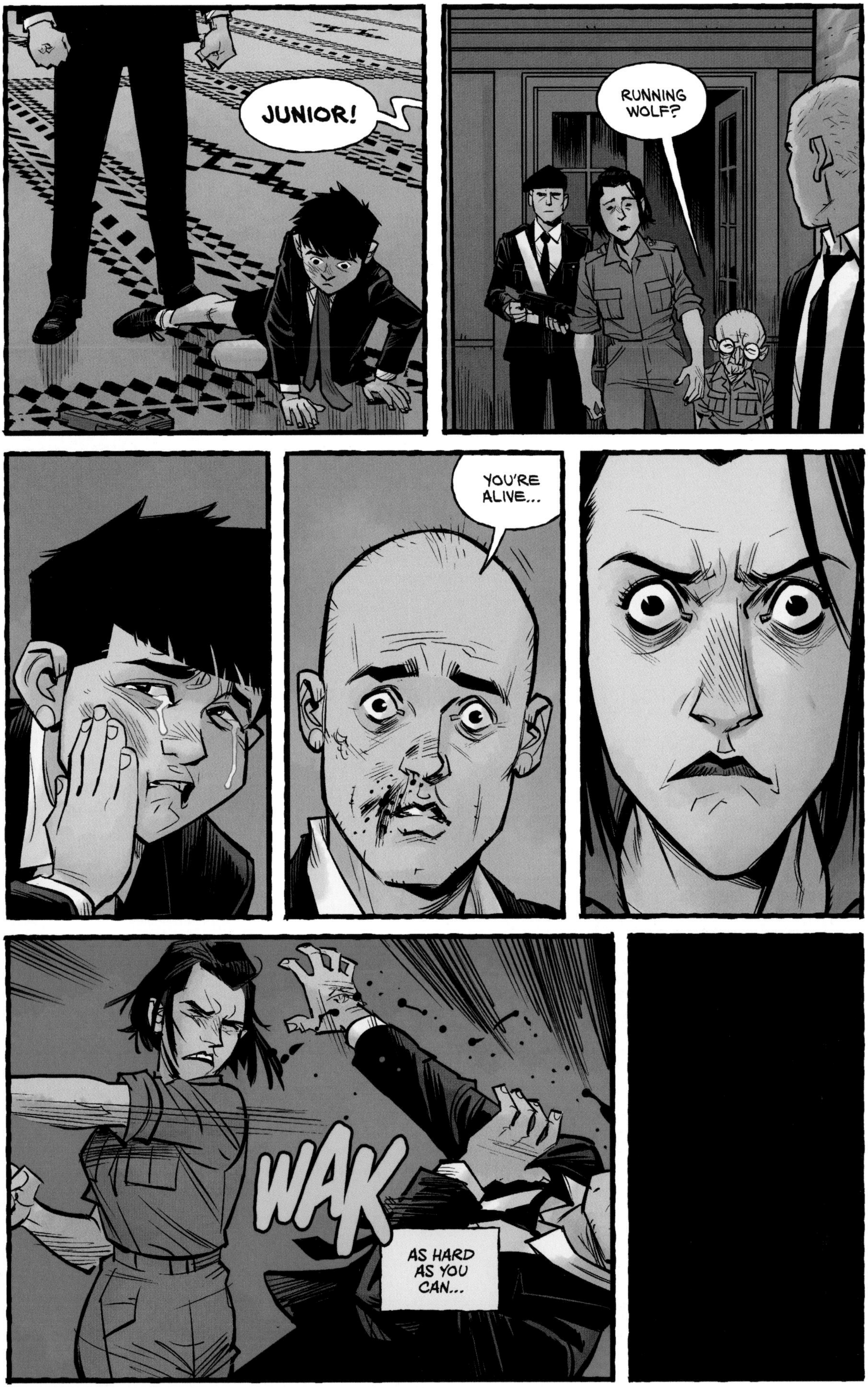
JUNIOR!
RUNNING WOLF?
YOU'RE ALIVE...
WAK
AS HARD AS YOU CAN...

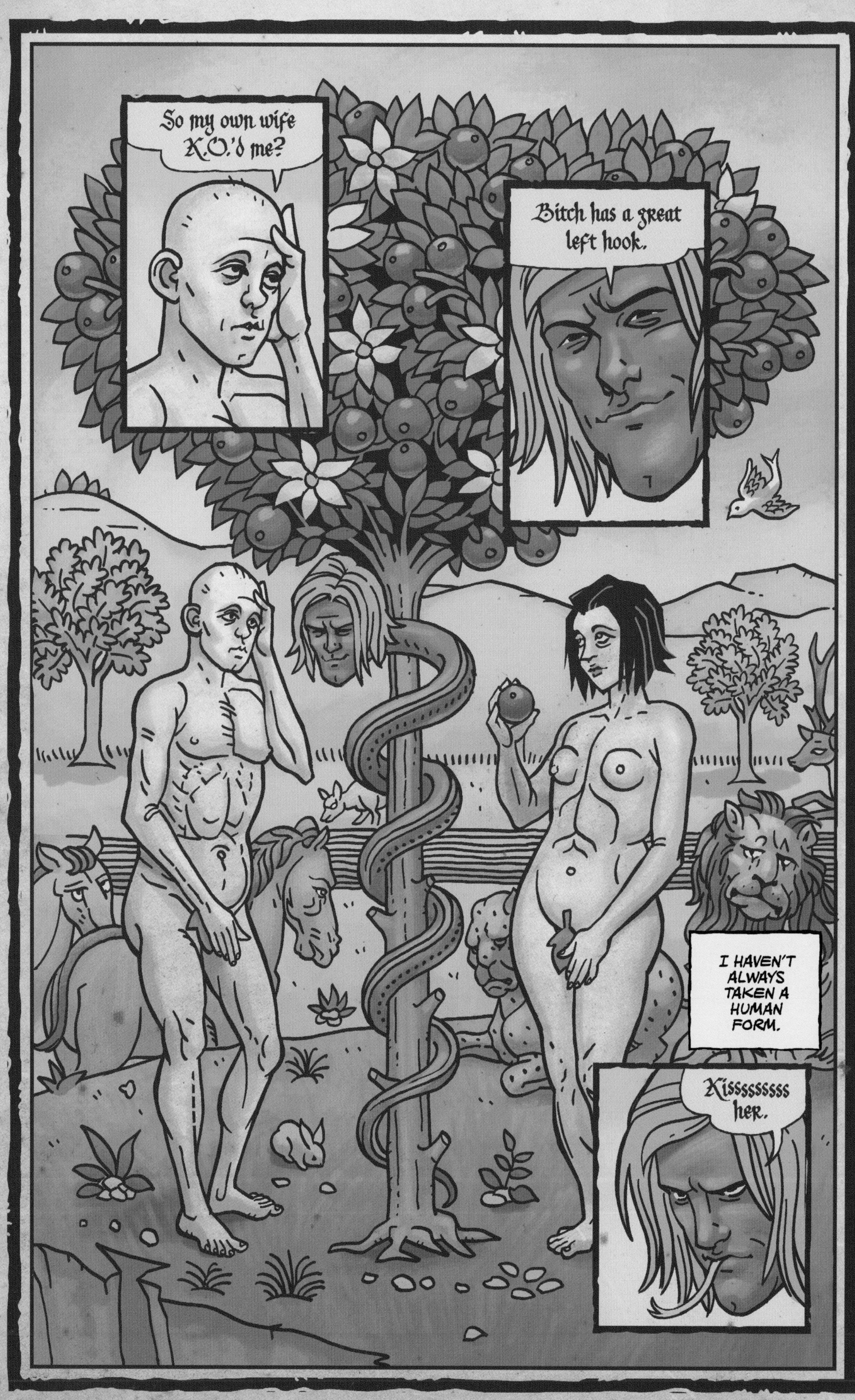
So my own wife K.O.'d me?
Bitch has a great left hook.
I HAVEN'T ALWAYS TAKEN A HUMAN FORM.
Kisssssssss her.

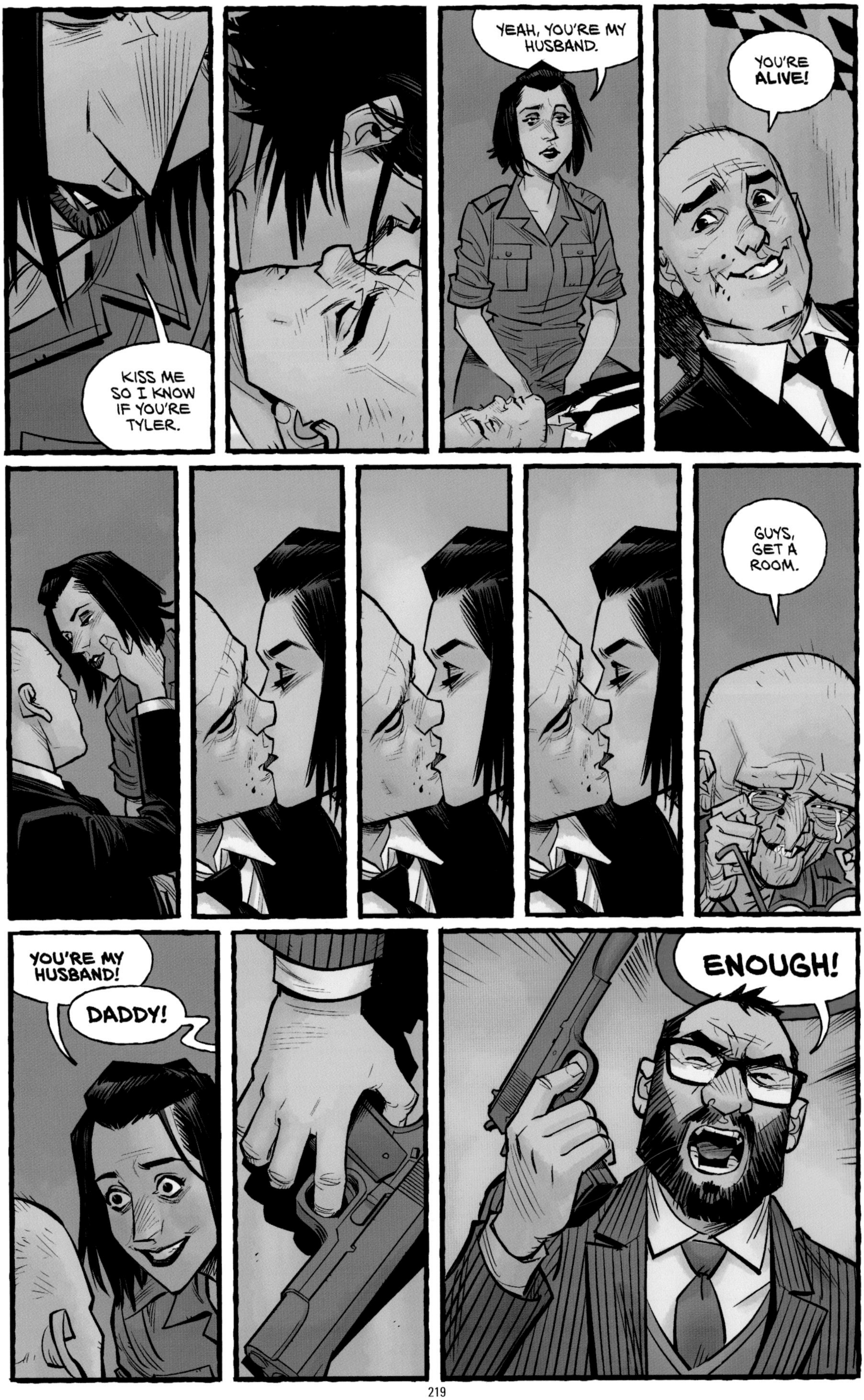
KISS ME SO I KNOW IF YOU'RE TYLER.
YEAH, YOU'RE MY HUSBAND.
YOU'RE ALIVE!
GUYS, GET A ROOM.
YOU'RE MY HUSBAND!
DADDY!
ENOUGH!

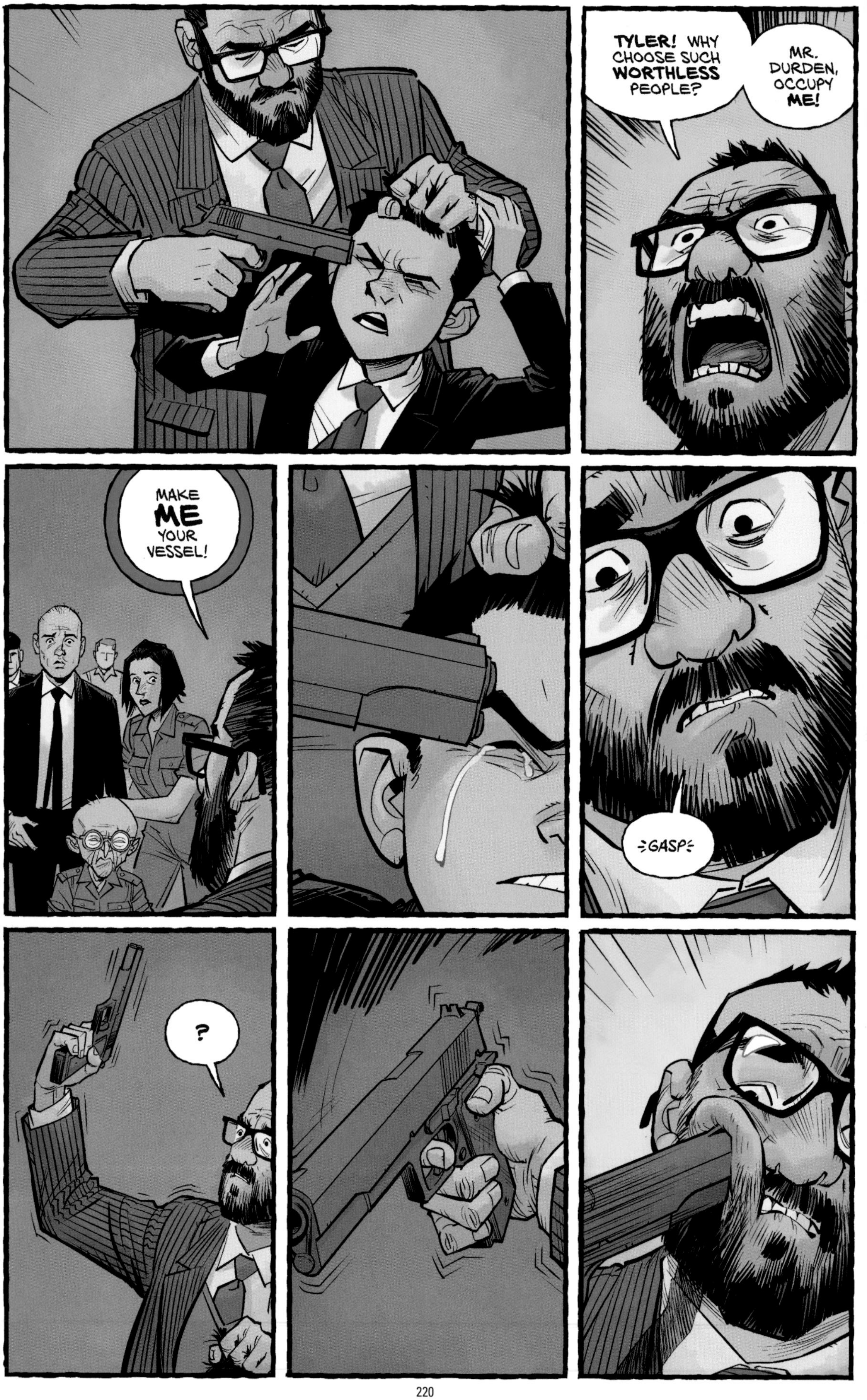
TYLER! WHY CHOOSE SUCH WORTHLESS PEOPLE?
MR. DURDEN, OCCUPY ME!
MAKE ME YOUR VESSEL!
GASP
?

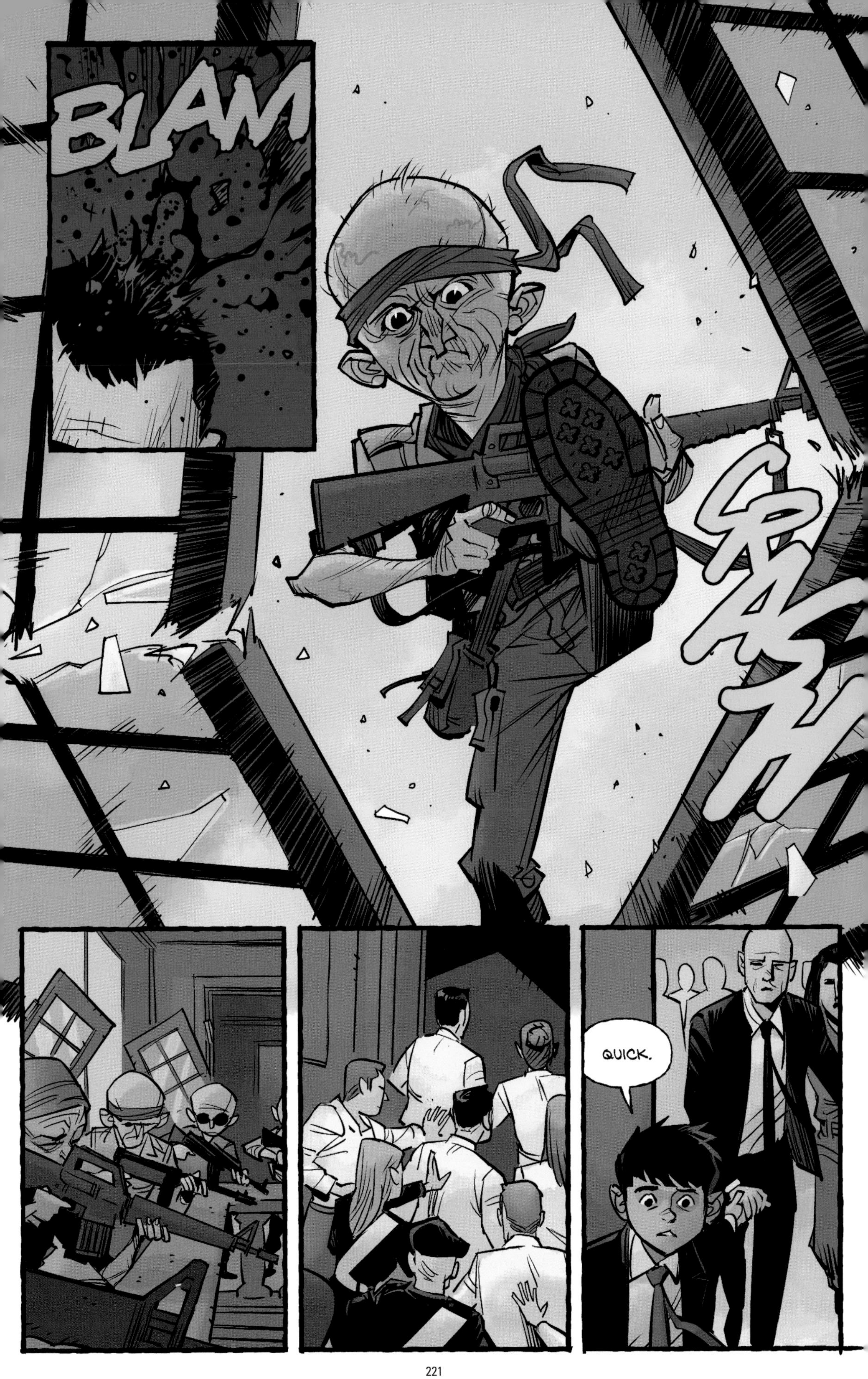
BLAM
CRASH
QUICK.

WHAT'S THE TRANQUILITY GAME?

NORSE MYTHOLOGY...

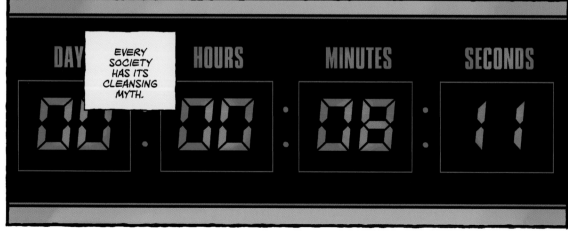

EVERY SOCIETY HAS ITS CLEANSING MYTH.

DAY   HOURS   MINUTES   SECONDS

00 . 00 : 08 : 11

"...RAGNAROK CALLS FOR THE ELITE CLASS TO HIDE WHILE THE REST OF THE WORLD HUNTS ONE ANOTHER TO EXTINCTION."

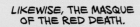
LIKEWISE, THE MASQUE OF THE RED DEATH.

EVEN HELTER SKELTER CALLED FOR MANSON TO HIDE IN A DEEP, DESERT BURROW WHILE RACE WARS WOULD DECIMATE MANKIND.

GENESIS, CHAPTER SIX, VERSES ELEVEN THROUGH NINETEEN.

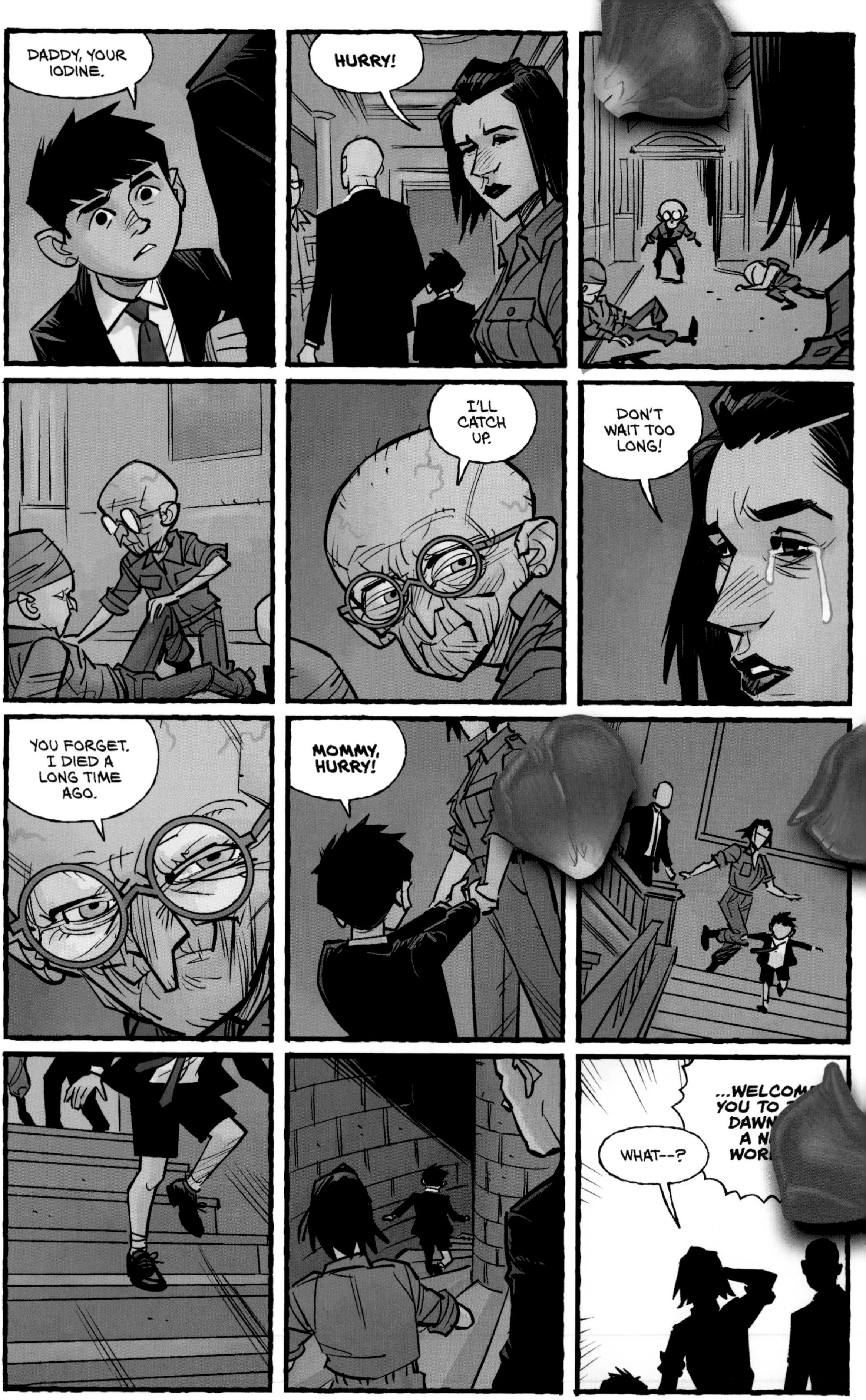
DADDY, YOUR IODINE.
HURRY!
I'LL CATCH UP.
DON'T WAIT TOO LONG!
YOU FORGET. I DIED A LONG TIME AGO.
MOMMY, HURRY!
...WELCOM
YOU TO
DAWN
A N
WOR
WHAT--?

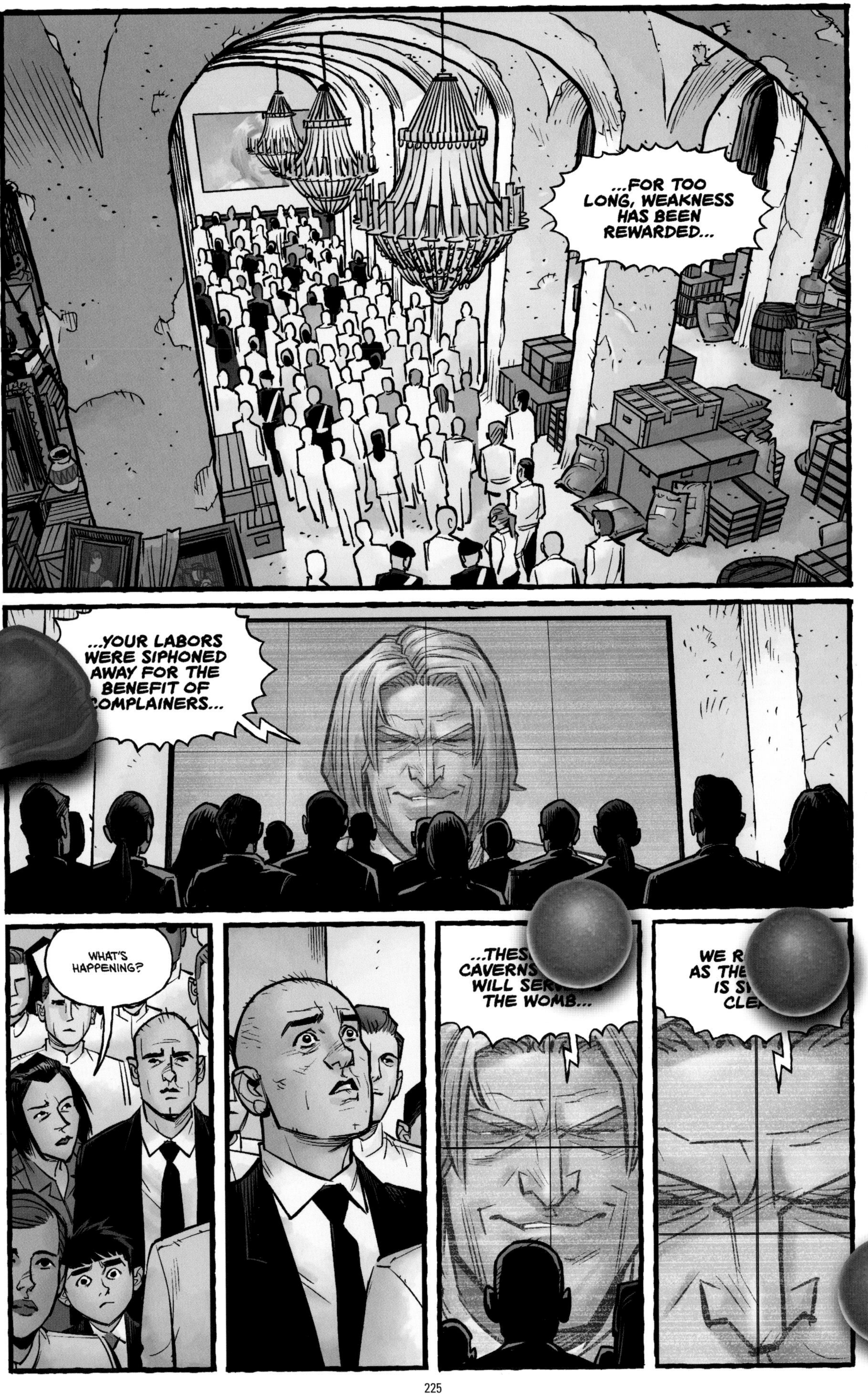
...FOR TOO LONG, WEAKNESS HAS BEEN REWARDED...
...YOUR LABORS WERE SIPHONED AWAY FOR THE BENEFIT OF COMPLAINERS...
WHAT'S HAPPENING?
...THES CAVERNS WILL SERV THE WOMB...
WE R AS THE IS S CLE

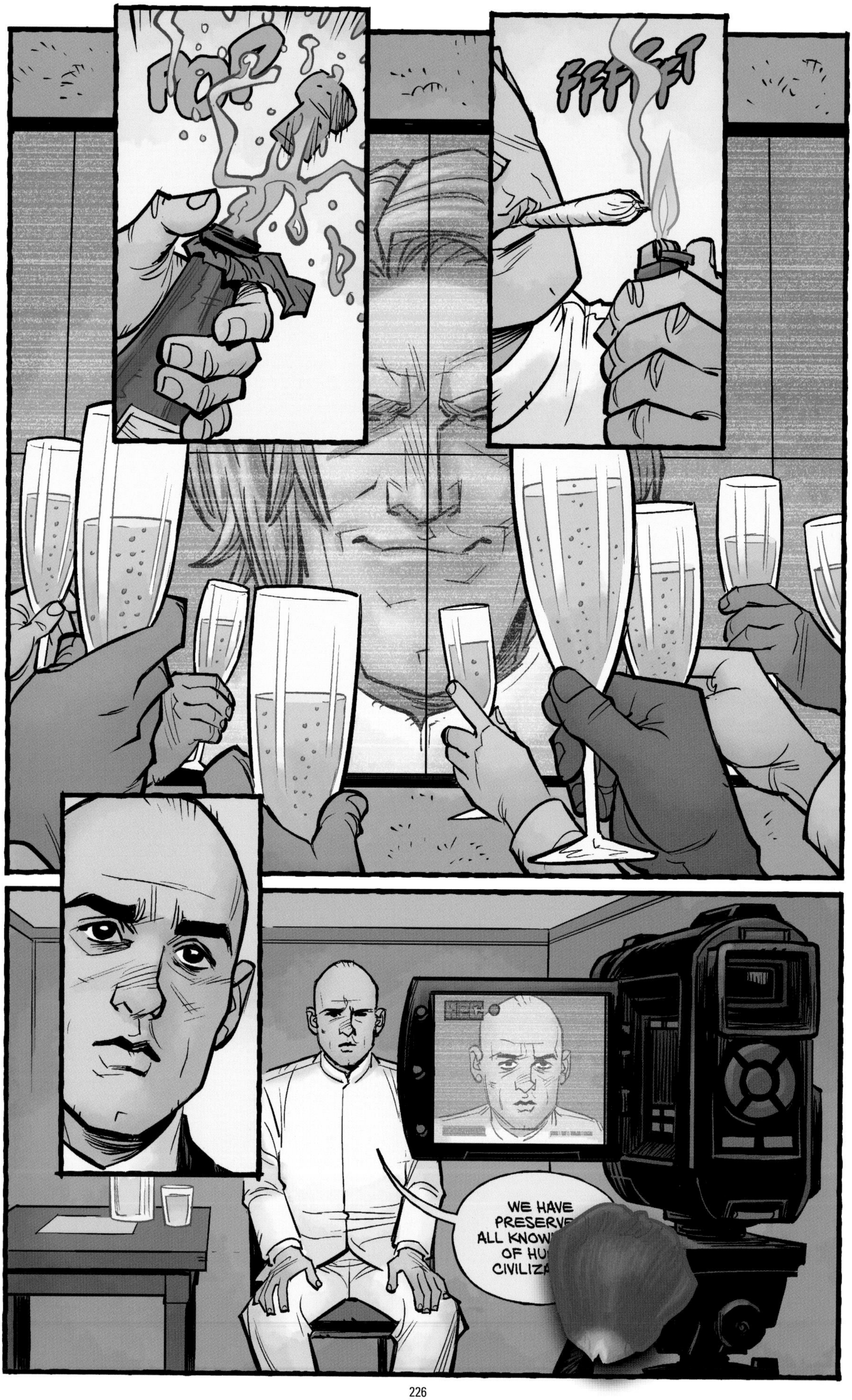
FFFSFT
WE HAVE PRESERVE ALL KNOW OF HU CIVILIZA

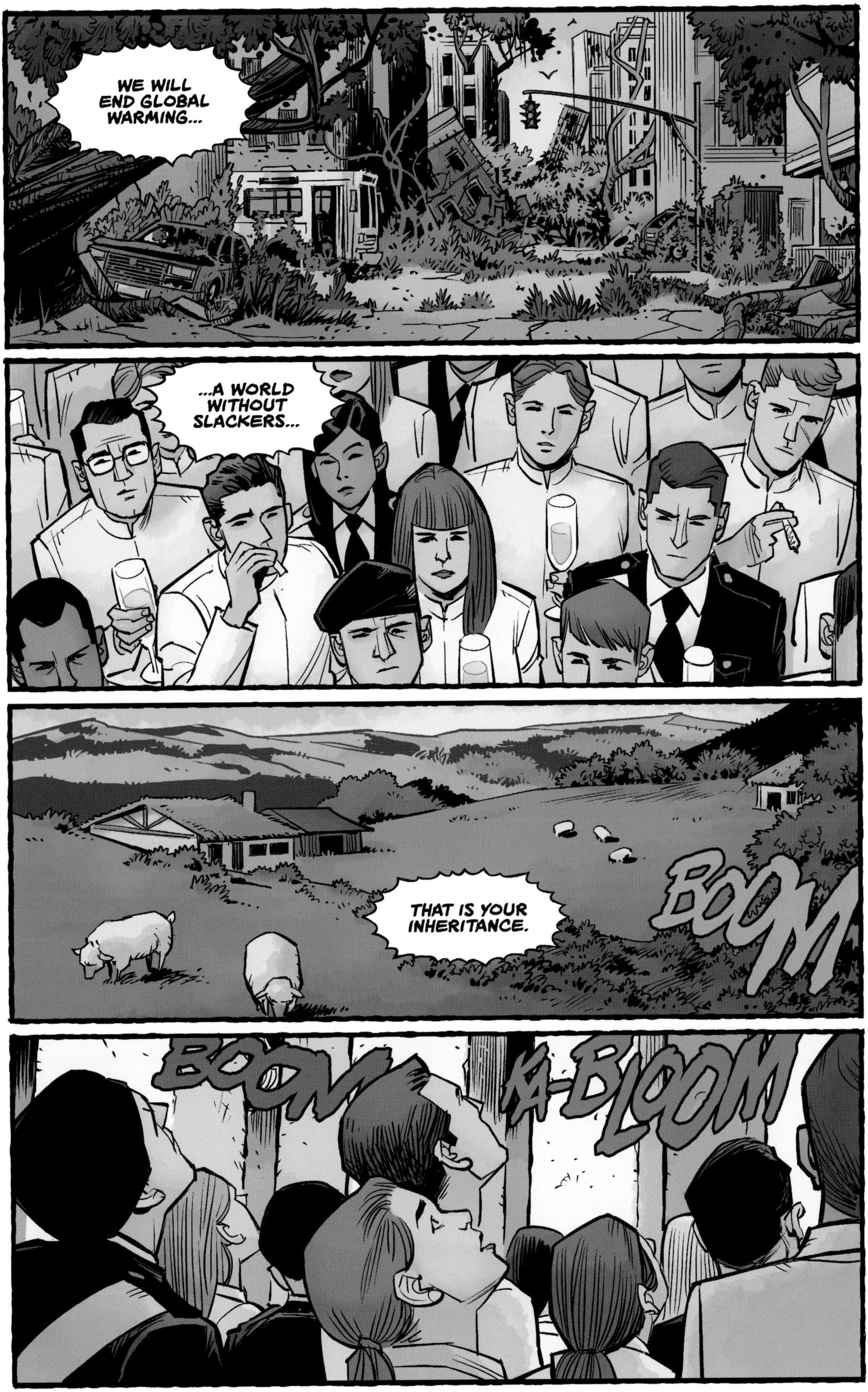
WE WILL END GLOBAL WARMING...
...A WORLD WITHOUT SLACKERS...
THAT IS YOUR INHERITANCE.
BOOM
BOOM
KA-BLOOM

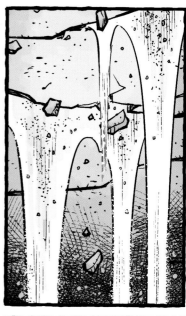

AS OUR AGENTS TRIGGER NUCLEAR BLASTS AROUND GLOBE...

BOOM

RUMMM

BBBLL

BARK

BARK

WE'RE IN THE BOTTOM OF AN HOURGLASS.

KAH-RASH

BOOM

GETTING BURIED ALIVE.

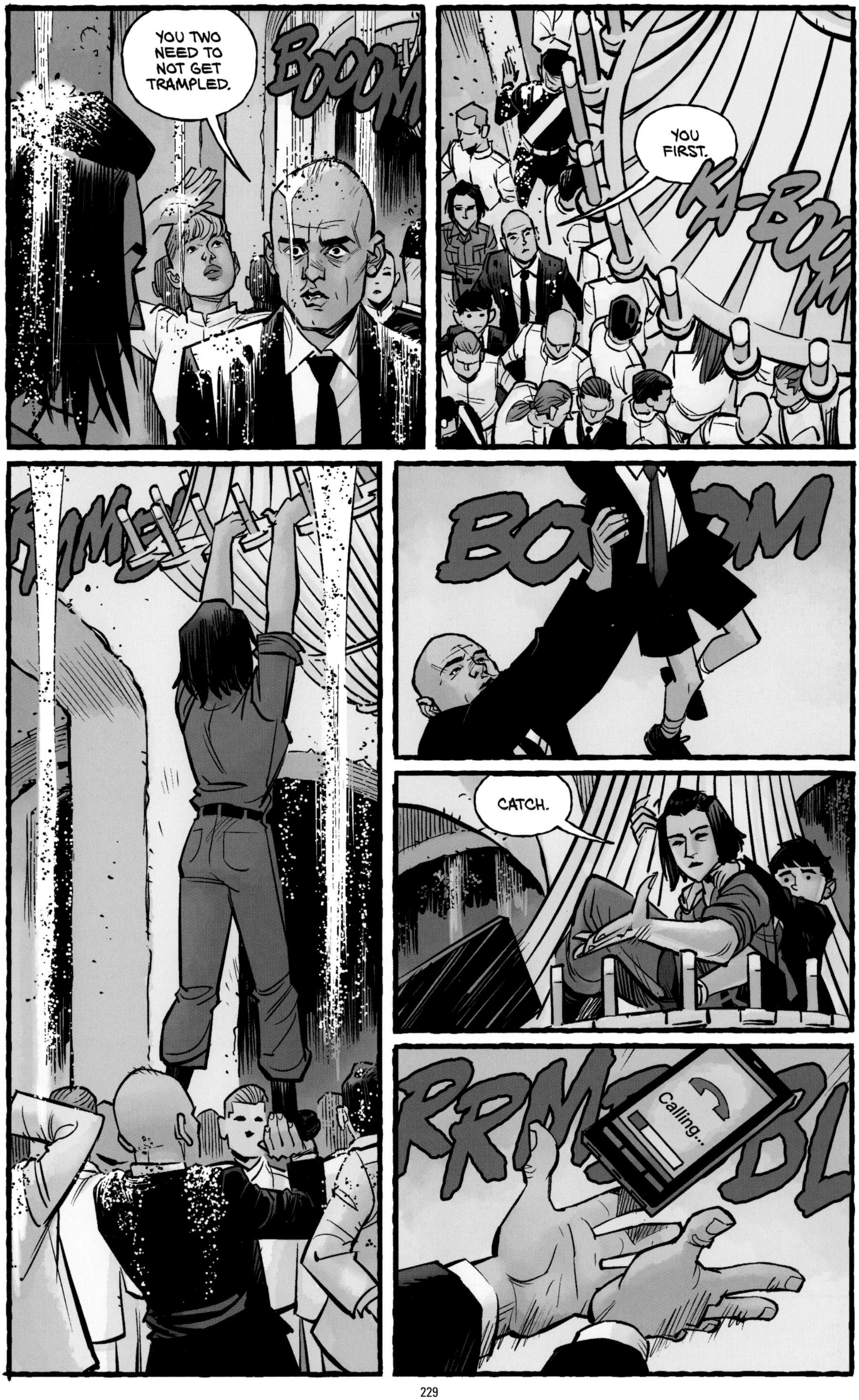
YOU TWO NEED TO NOT GET TRAMPLED.
YOU FIRST.
CATCH.
Calling...

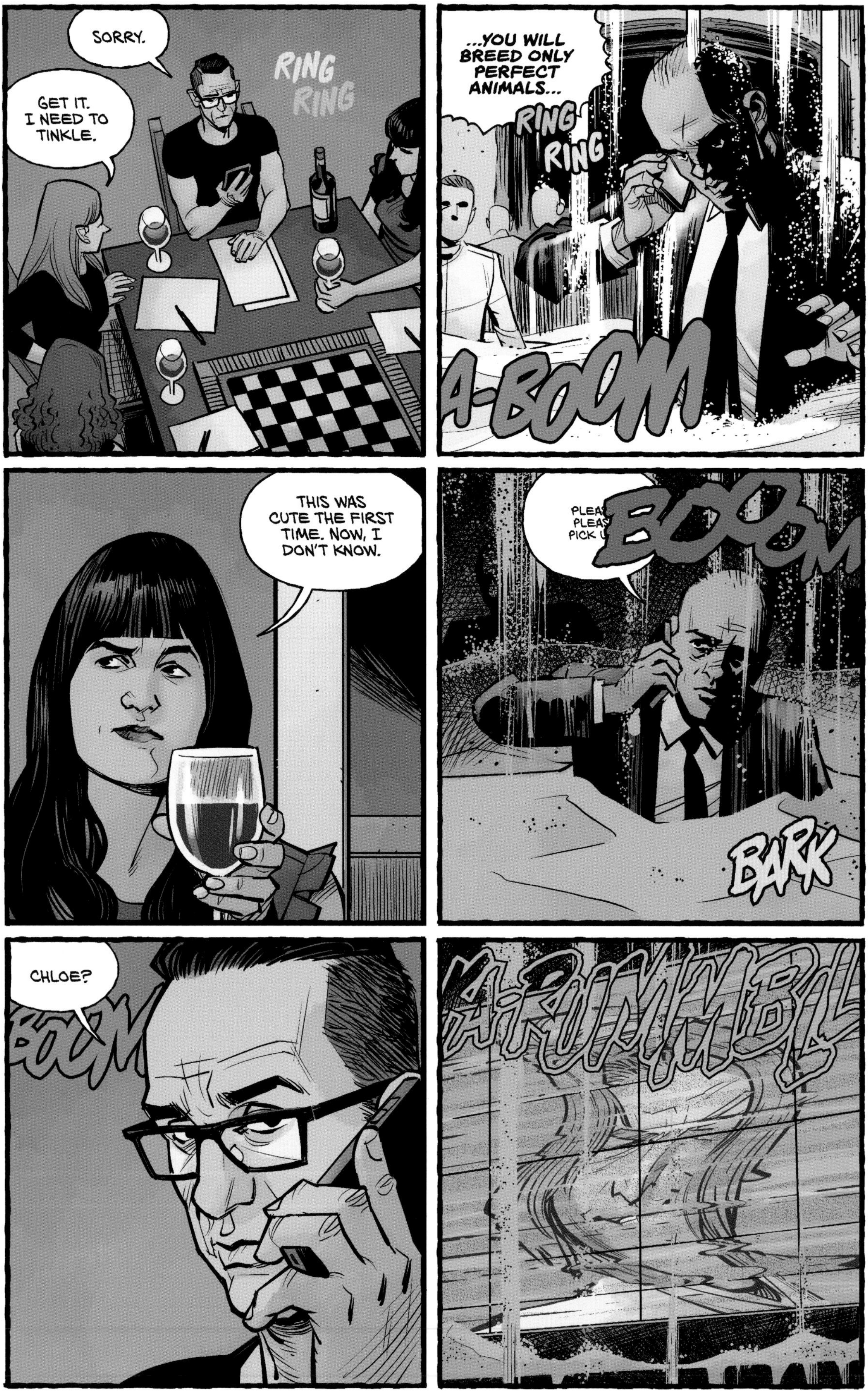
SORRY.
GET IT. I NEED TO TINKLE.
RING RING
...YOU WILL BREED ONLY PERFECT ANIMALS...
RING RING
A-BOOM
THIS WAS CUTE THE FIRST TIME. NOW, I DON'T KNOW.
PLEAS PLEAS PICK U
BOOM
BARK
CHLOE?
BOOM

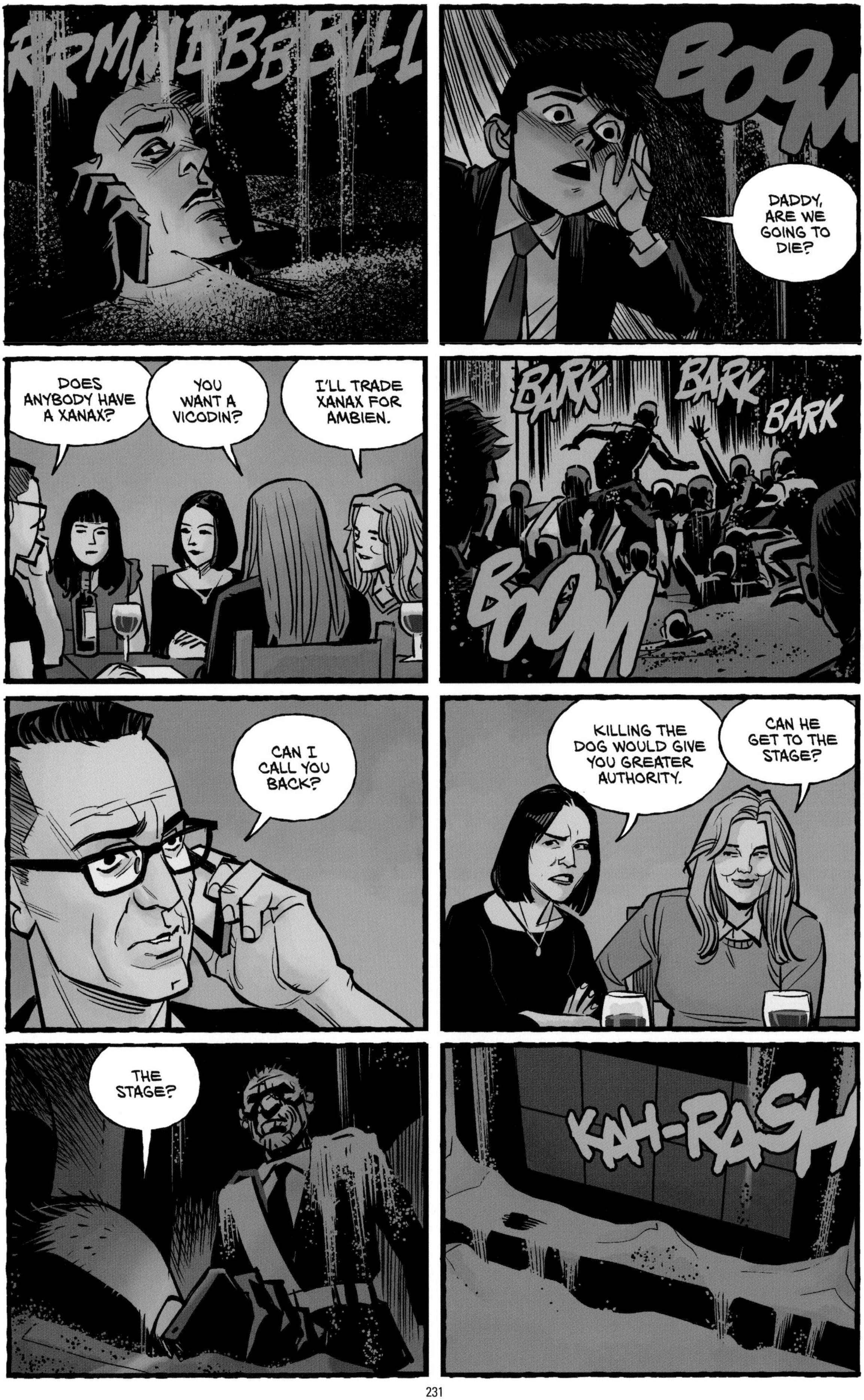
BOOM
DADDY, ARE WE GOING TO DIE?
DOES ANYBODY HAVE A XANAX?
YOU WANT A VICODIN?
I'LL TRADE XANAX FOR AMBIEN.
BARK
BARK
BARK
BOOM
CAN I CALL YOU BACK?
KILLING THE DOG WOULD GIVE YOU GREATER AUTHORITY.
CAN HE GET TO THE STAGE?
THE STAGE?
KAH-RASH

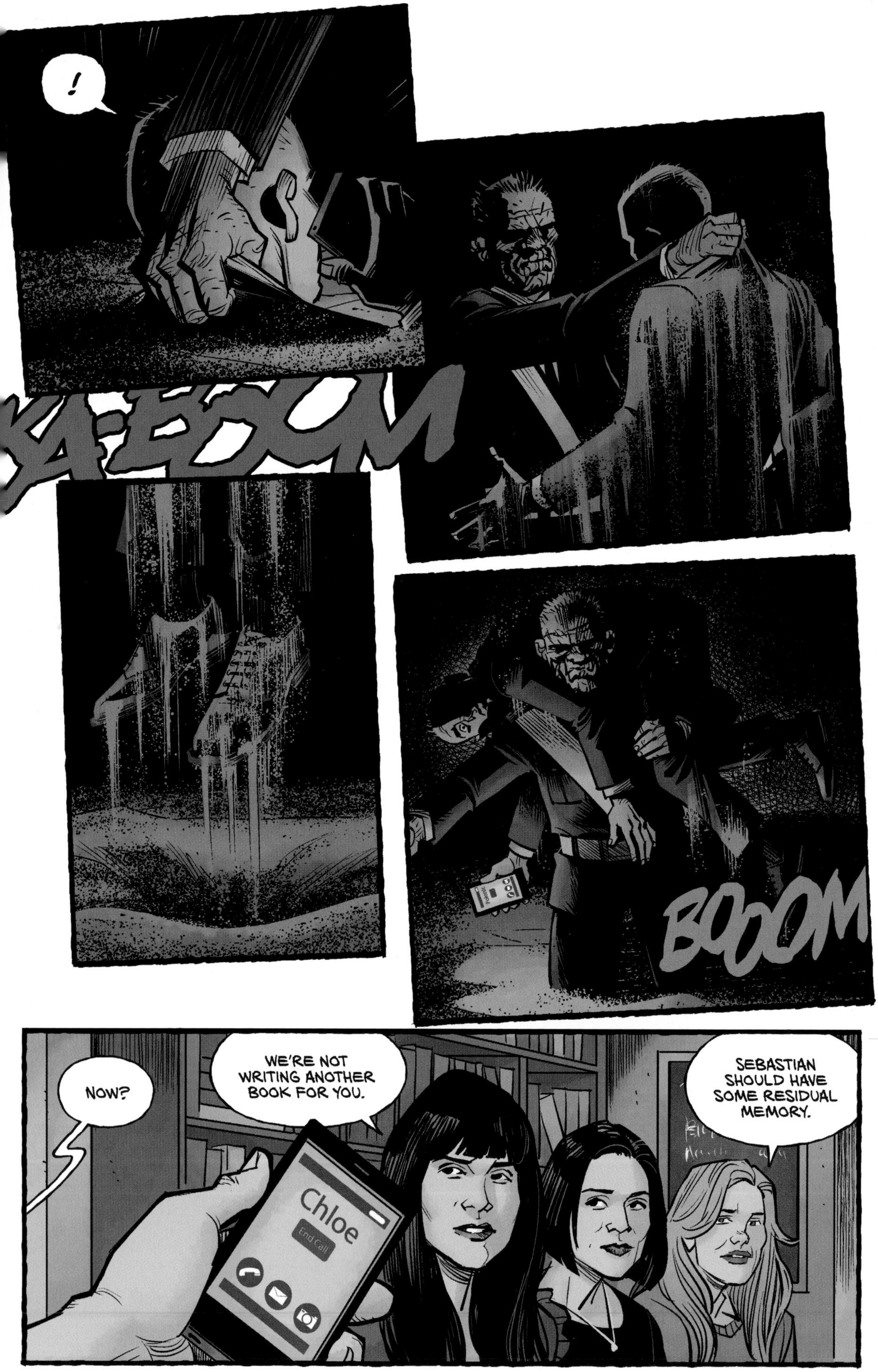
!
KA-BOOM
BOOOM
NOW?
WE'RE NOT WRITING ANOTHER BOOK FOR YOU.
SEBASTIAN SHOULD HAVE SOME RESIDUAL MEMORY.
Chloe
End Call

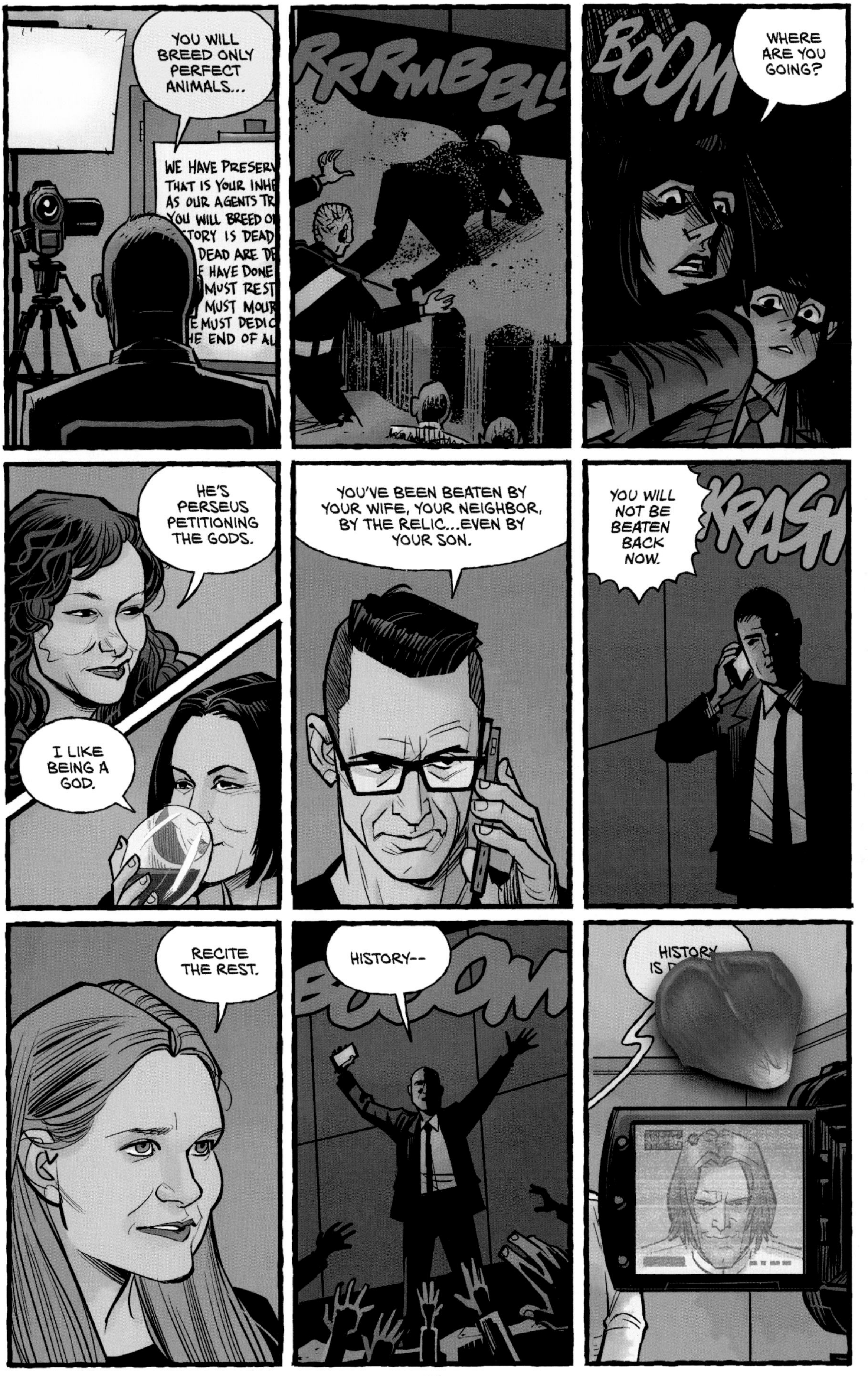
YOU WILL BREED ONLY PERFECT ANIMALS...
WE HAVE PRESERV
THAT IS YOUR INH
AS OUR AGENTS TR
YOU WILL BREED O
TORY IS DEAD
DEAD ARE DE
E HAVE DONE
MUST REST
MUST MOUR
E MUST DEDIC
HE END OF AL
RRRMBBLL
BOOM
WHERE ARE YOU GOING?
HE'S PERSEUS PETITIONING THE GODS.
I LIKE BEING A GOD.
YOU'VE BEEN BEATEN BY YOUR WIFE, YOUR NEIGHBOR, BY THE RELIC...EVEN BY YOUR SON.
YOU WILL NOT BE BEATEN BACK NOW.
KRASH
RECITE THE REST.
HISTORY--
BOOM
HISTORY IS D

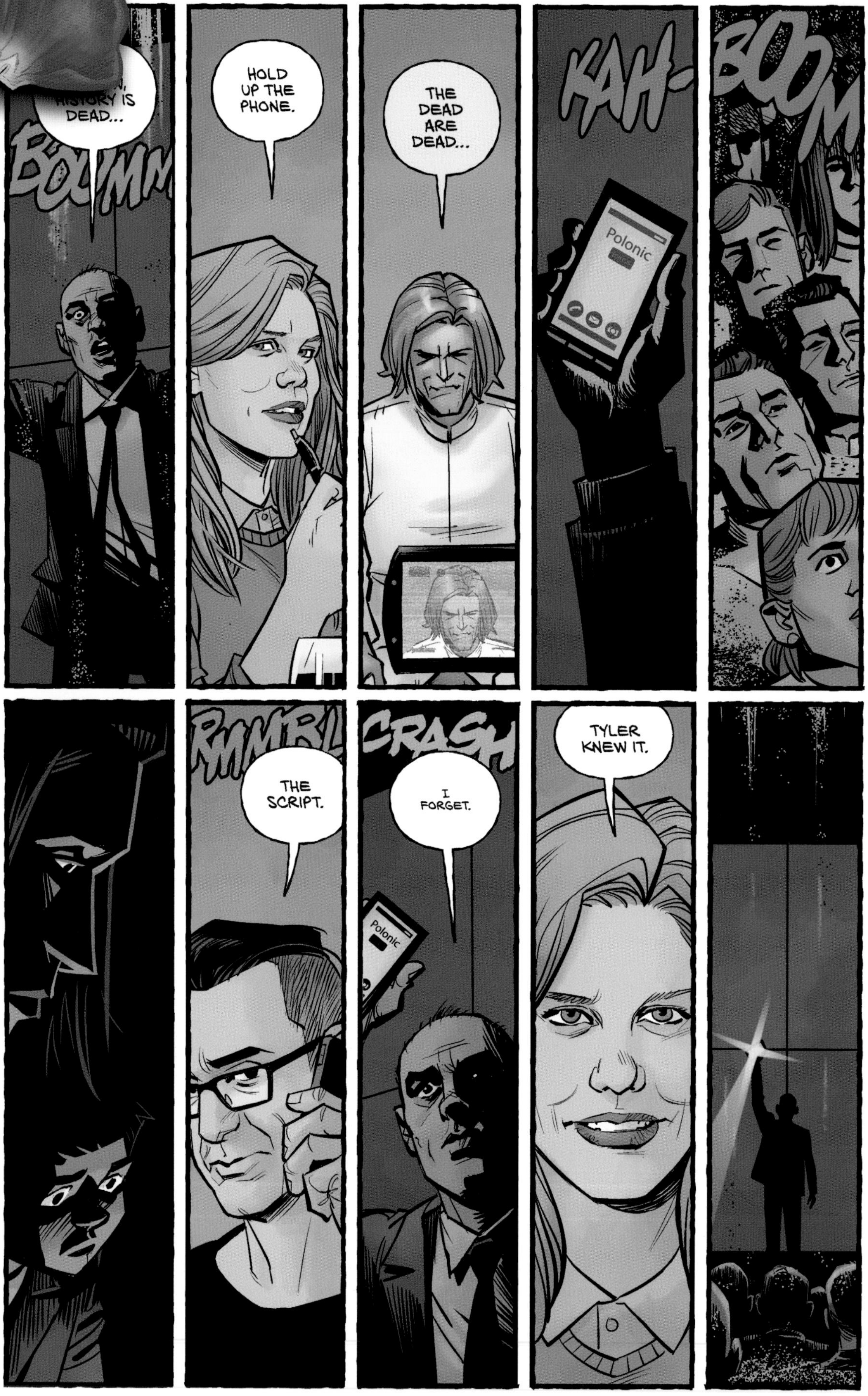
HISTORY IS DEAD...
BOUMM
HOLD UP THE PHONE.
THE DEAD ARE DEAD...
KAH-BOOM
Polonic
RMMBL
THE SCRIPT.
CRASH
I FORGET.
Polonic
TYLER KNEW IT.

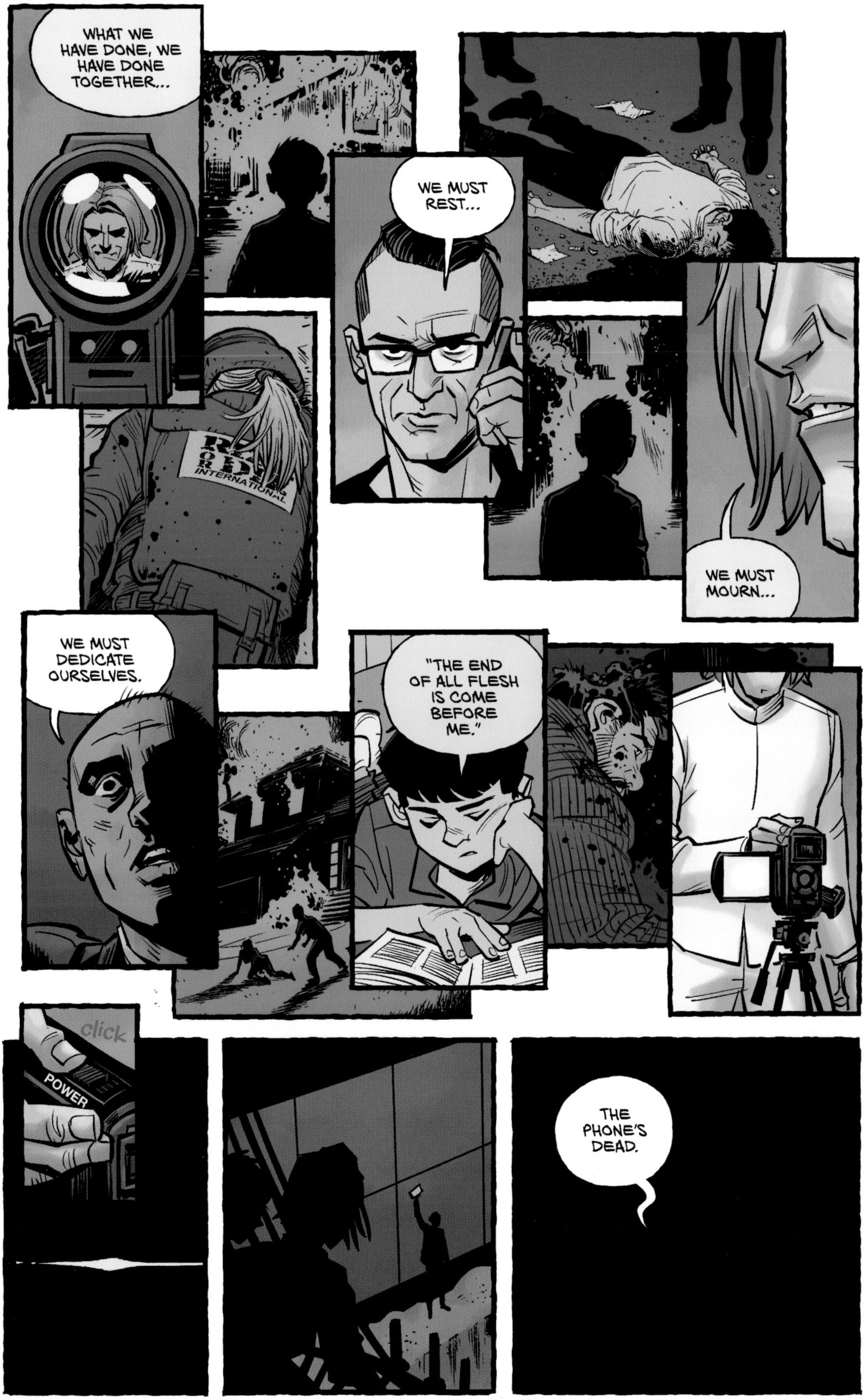
WHAT WE HAVE DONE, WE HAVE DONE TOGETHER...
WE MUST REST...
INTERNATIONAL
WE MUST MOURN...
WE MUST DEDICATE OURSELVES.
"THE END OF ALL FLESH IS COME BEFORE ME."
click
POWER
THE PHONE'S DEAD.

Chapter Ten

The End after the End of the World

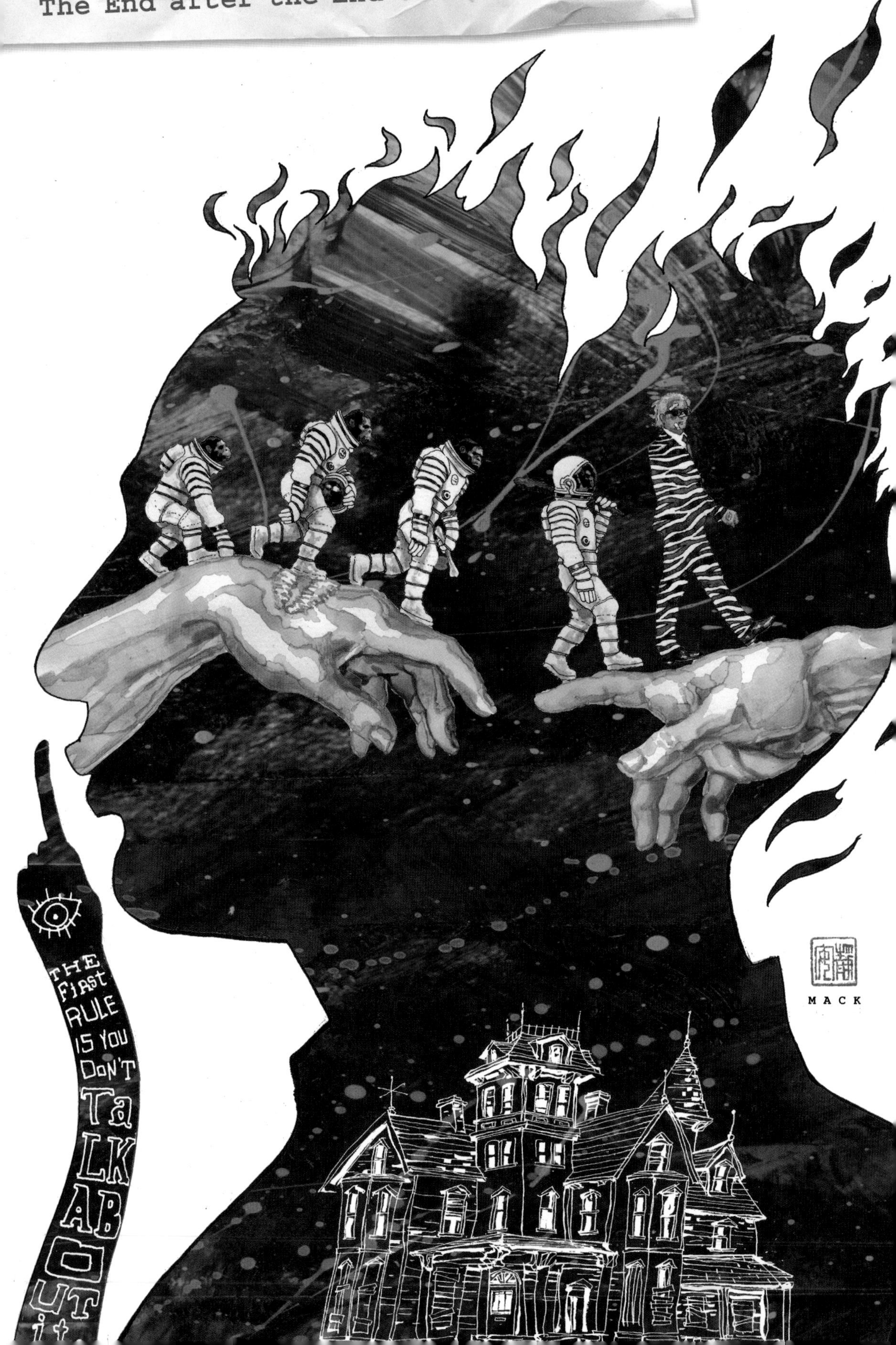
THE FIRST RULE IS YOU DON'T TaLK ABOUT it
MACK

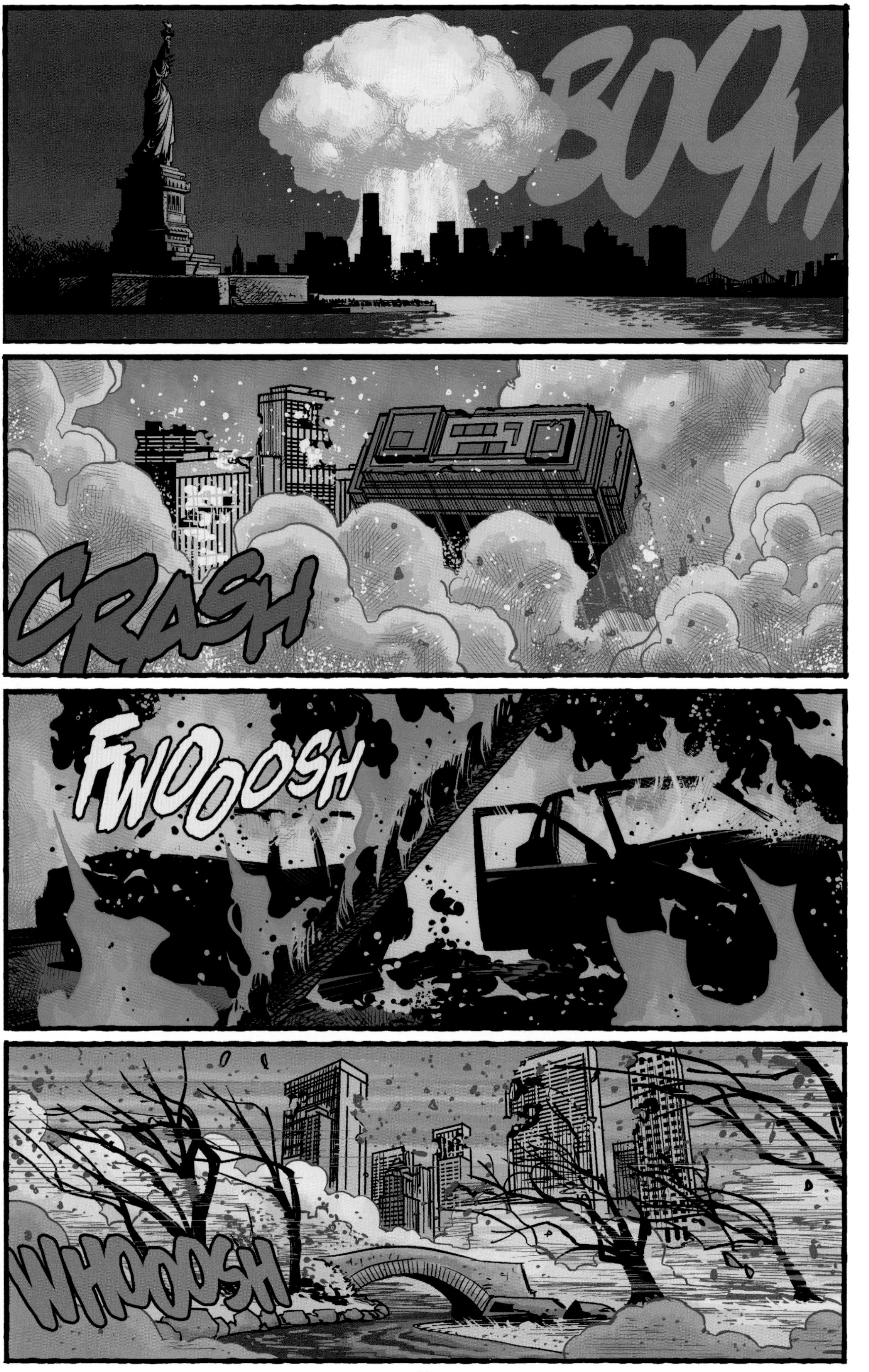
BOOM
CRASH
FWOOOSH
WHOOOSH

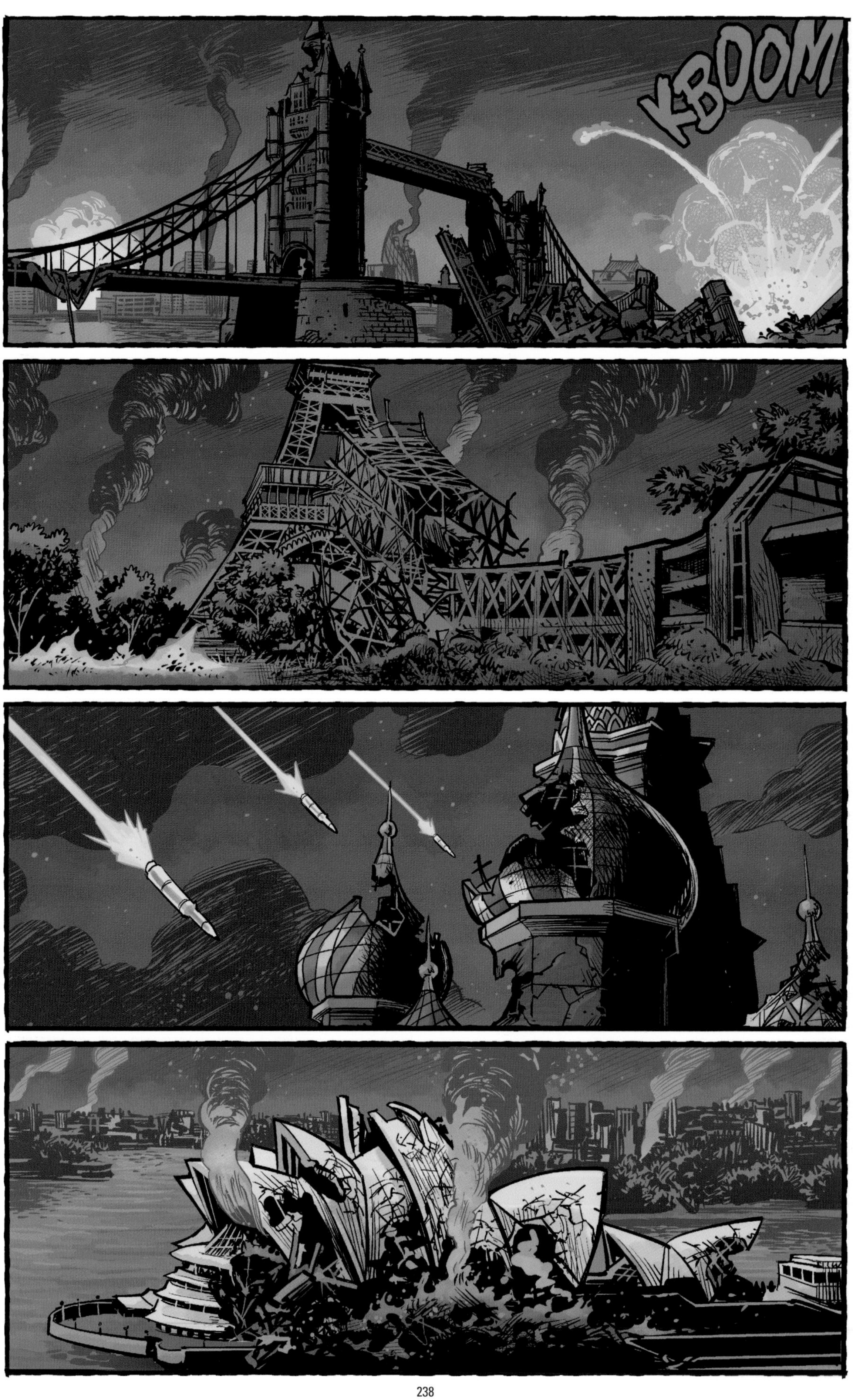
KBOOM

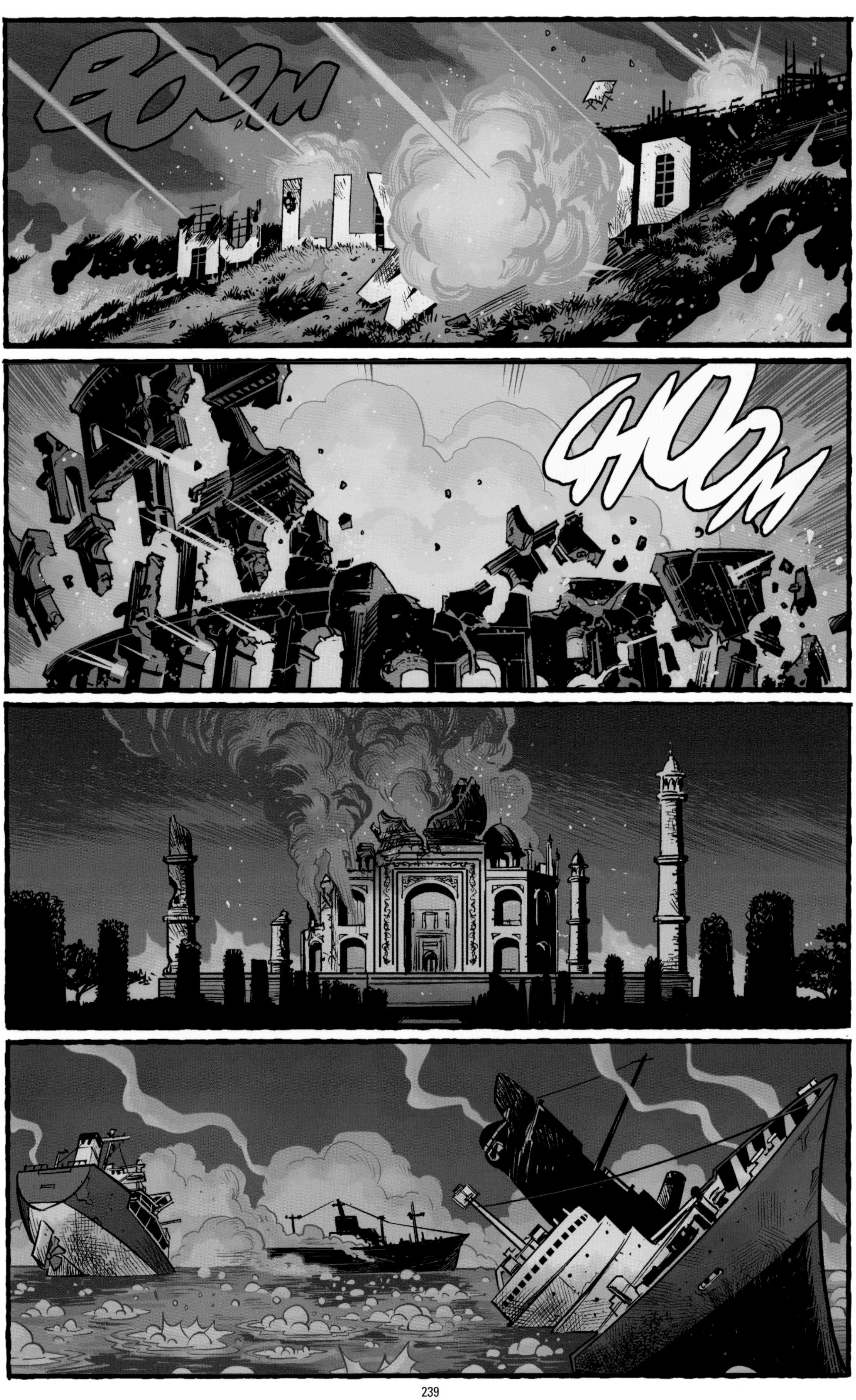
BOOM

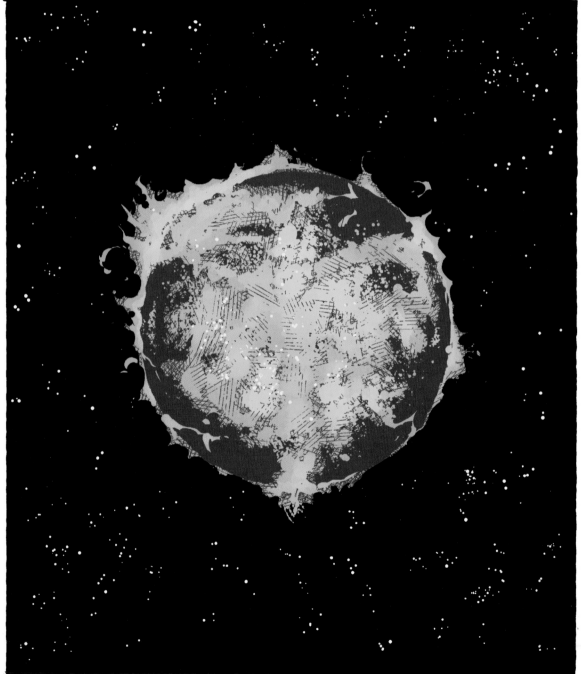

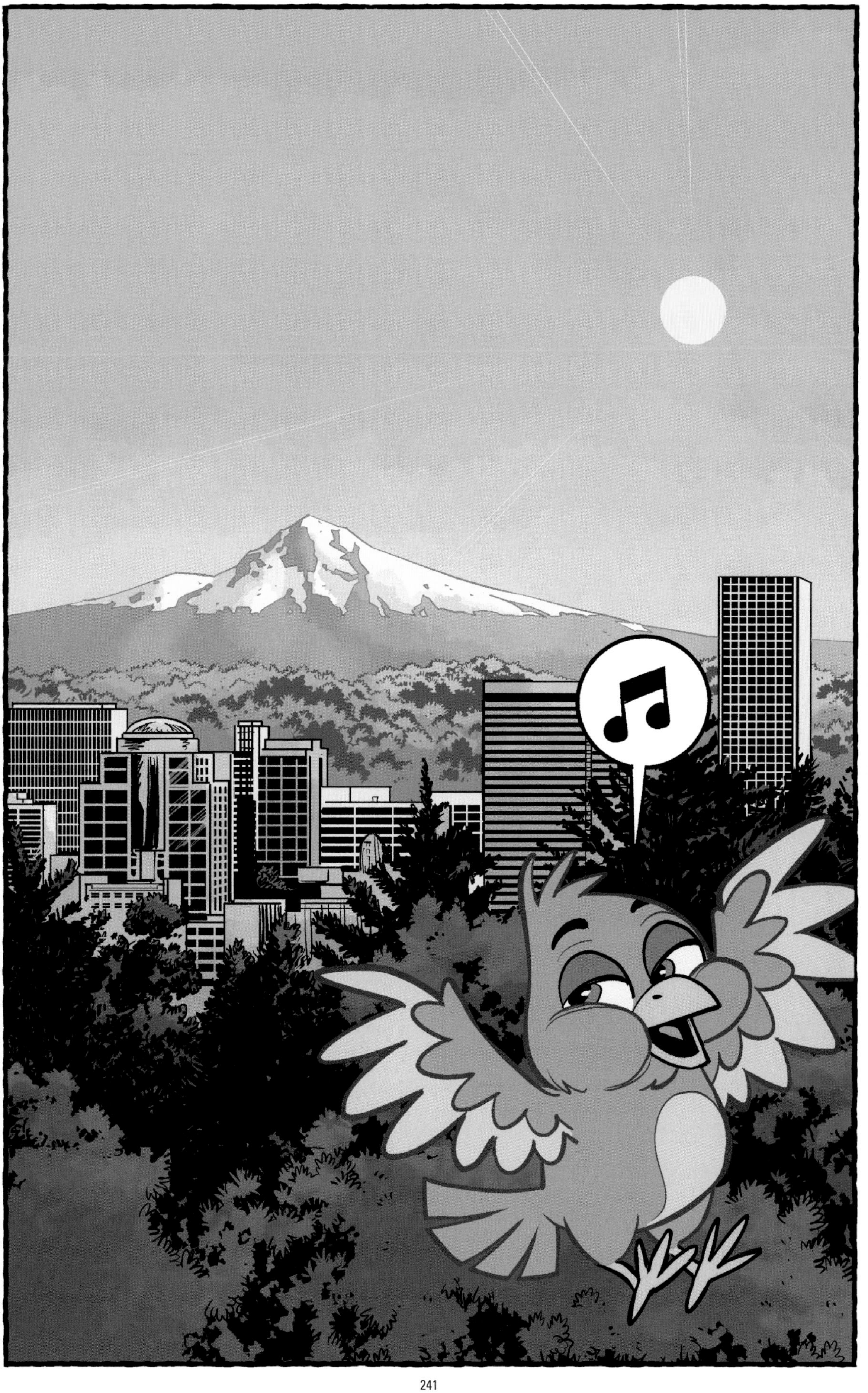

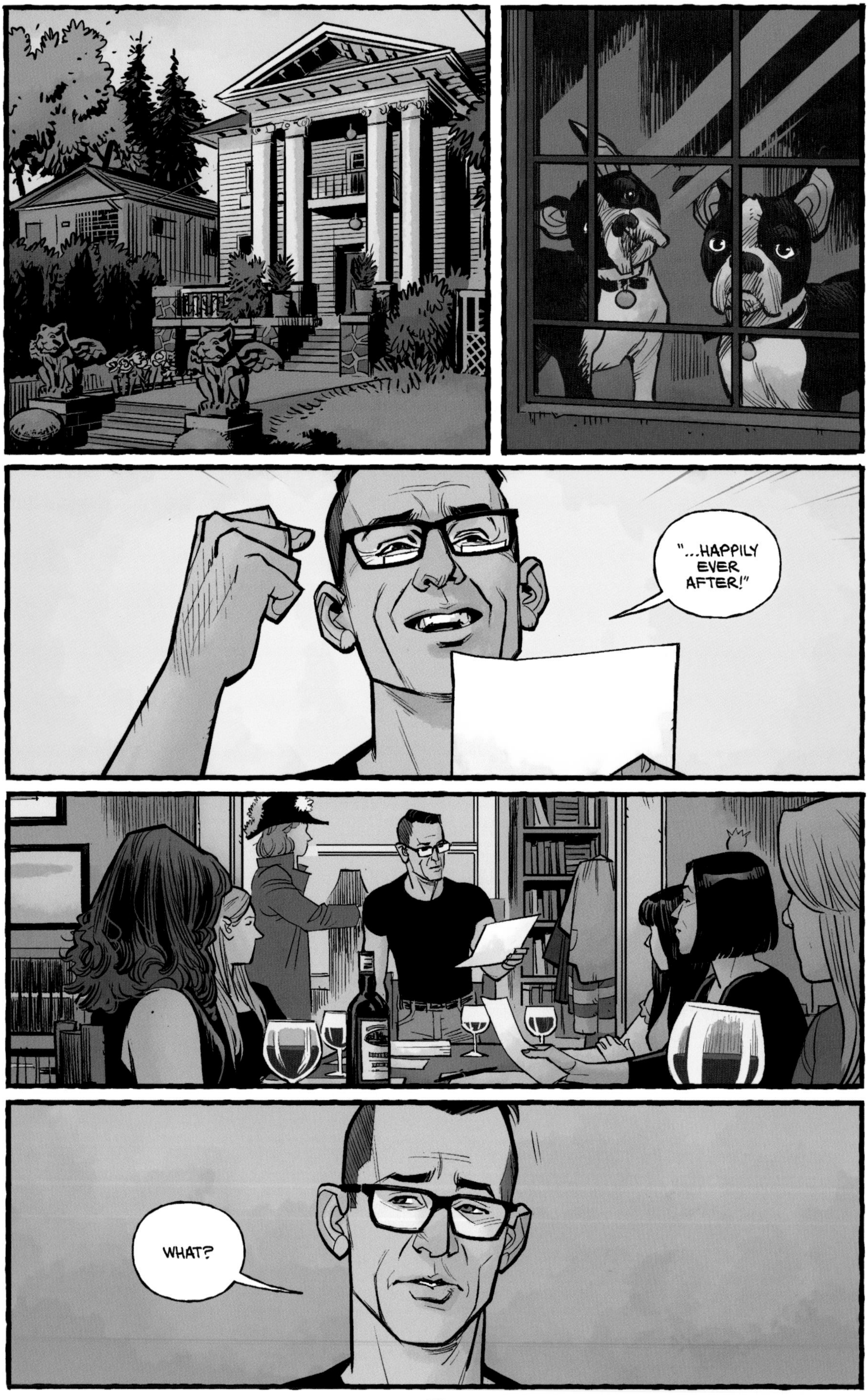
"...HAPPILY EVER AFTER!"
WHAT?

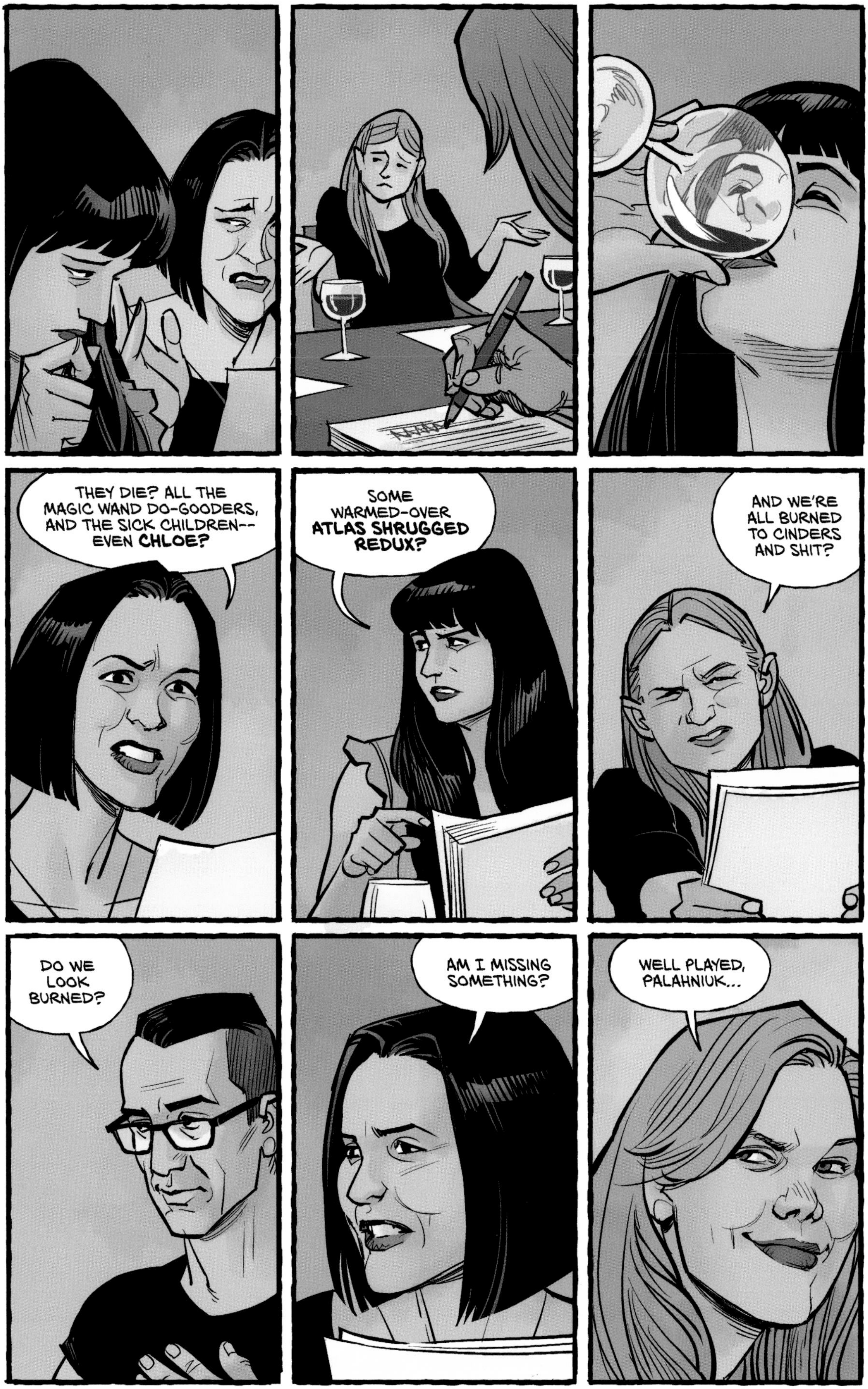
THEY DIE? ALL THE MAGIC WAND DO-GOODERS, AND THE SICK CHILDREN-- EVEN CHLOE?
SOME WARMED-OVER ATLAS SHRUGGED REDUX?
AND WE'RE ALL BURNED TO CINDERS AND SHIT?
DO WE LOOK BURNED?
AM I MISSING SOMETHING?
WELL PLAYED, PALAHNIUK...

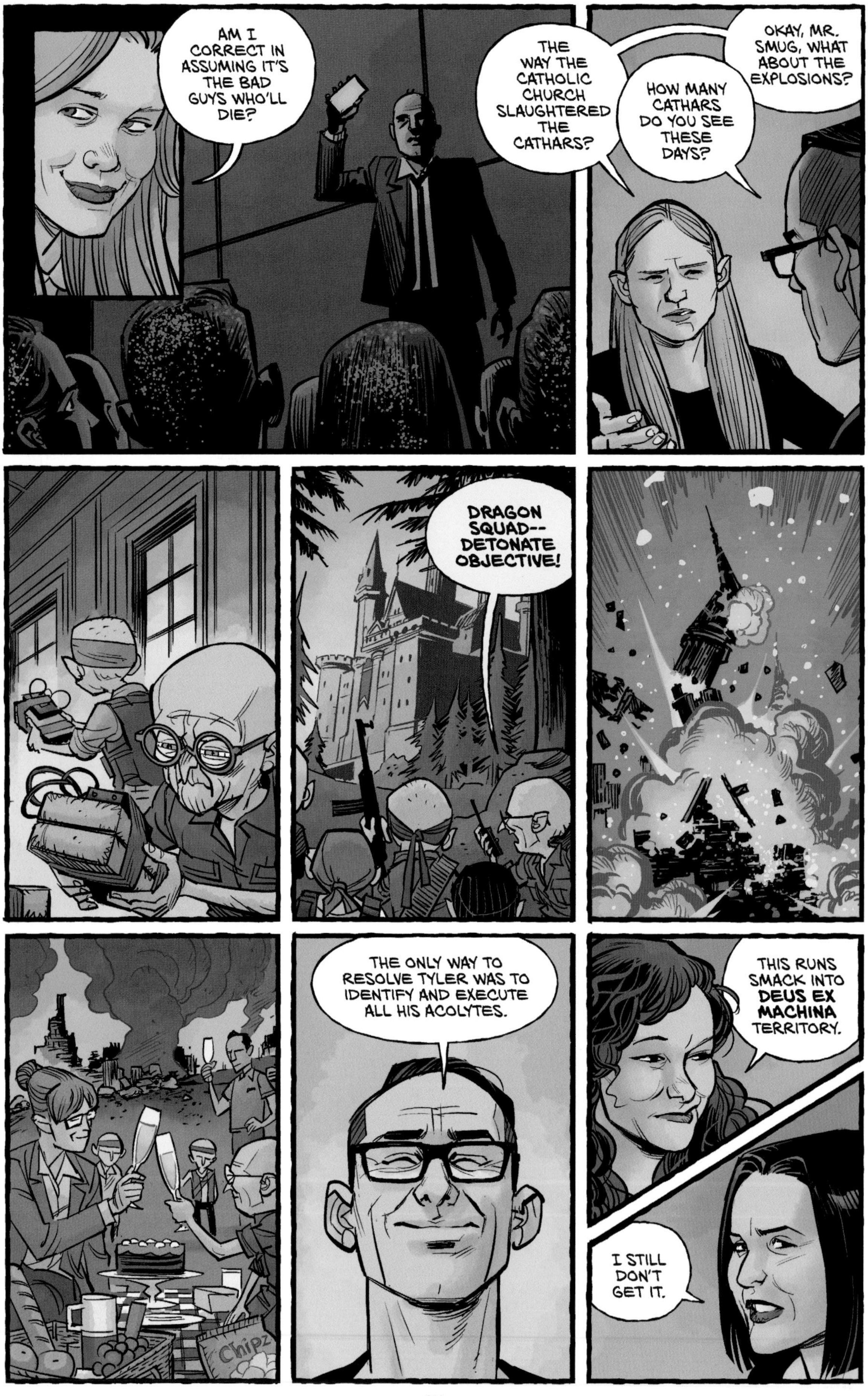
AM I CORRECT IN ASSUMING IT'S THE BAD GUYS WHO'LL DIE?
THE WAY THE CATHOLIC CHURCH SLAUGHTERED THE CATHARS?
HOW MANY CATHARS DO YOU SEE THESE DAYS?
OKAY, MR. SMUG, WHAT ABOUT THE EXPLOSIONS?
DRAGON SQUAD-- DETONATE OBJECTIVE!
Chipz
THE ONLY WAY TO RESOLVE TYLER WAS TO IDENTIFY AND EXECUTE ALL HIS ACOLYTES.
THIS RUNS SMACK INTO **DEUS EX MACHINA** TERRITORY.
I STILL DON'T GET IT.

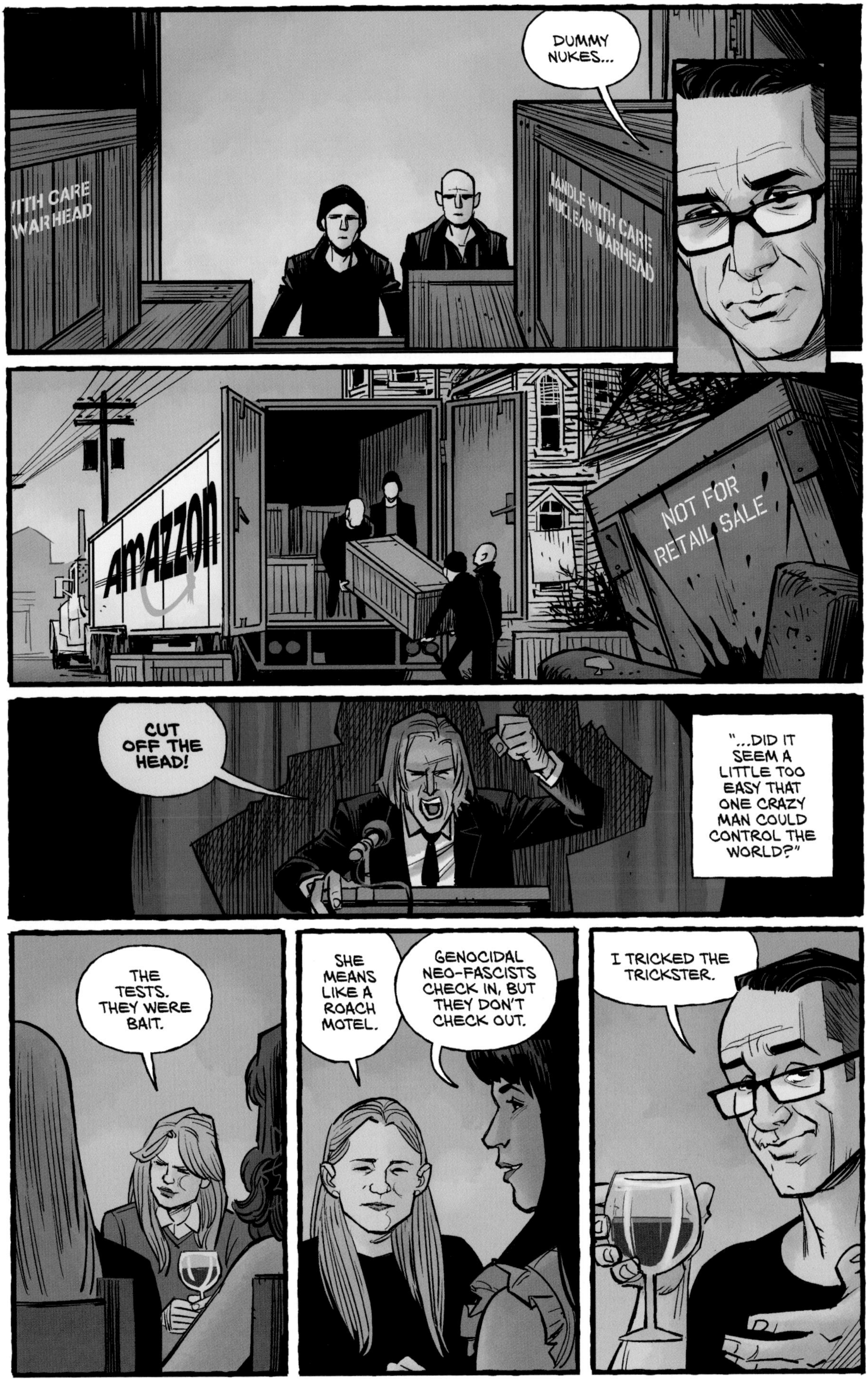

WITH CARE
WARHEAD
HANDLE WITH CARE
NUCLEAR WARHEAD
DUMMY NUKES...
AMAZZON
NOT FOR RETAIL SALE
CUT OFF THE HEAD!
"...DID IT SEEM A LITTLE TOO EASY THAT ONE CRAZY MAN COULD CONTROL THE WORLD?"
THE TESTS. THEY WERE BAIT.
SHE MEANS LIKE A ROACH MOTEL.
GENOCIDAL NEO-FASCISTS CHECK IN, BUT THEY DON'T CHECK OUT.
I TRICKED THE TRICKSTER.

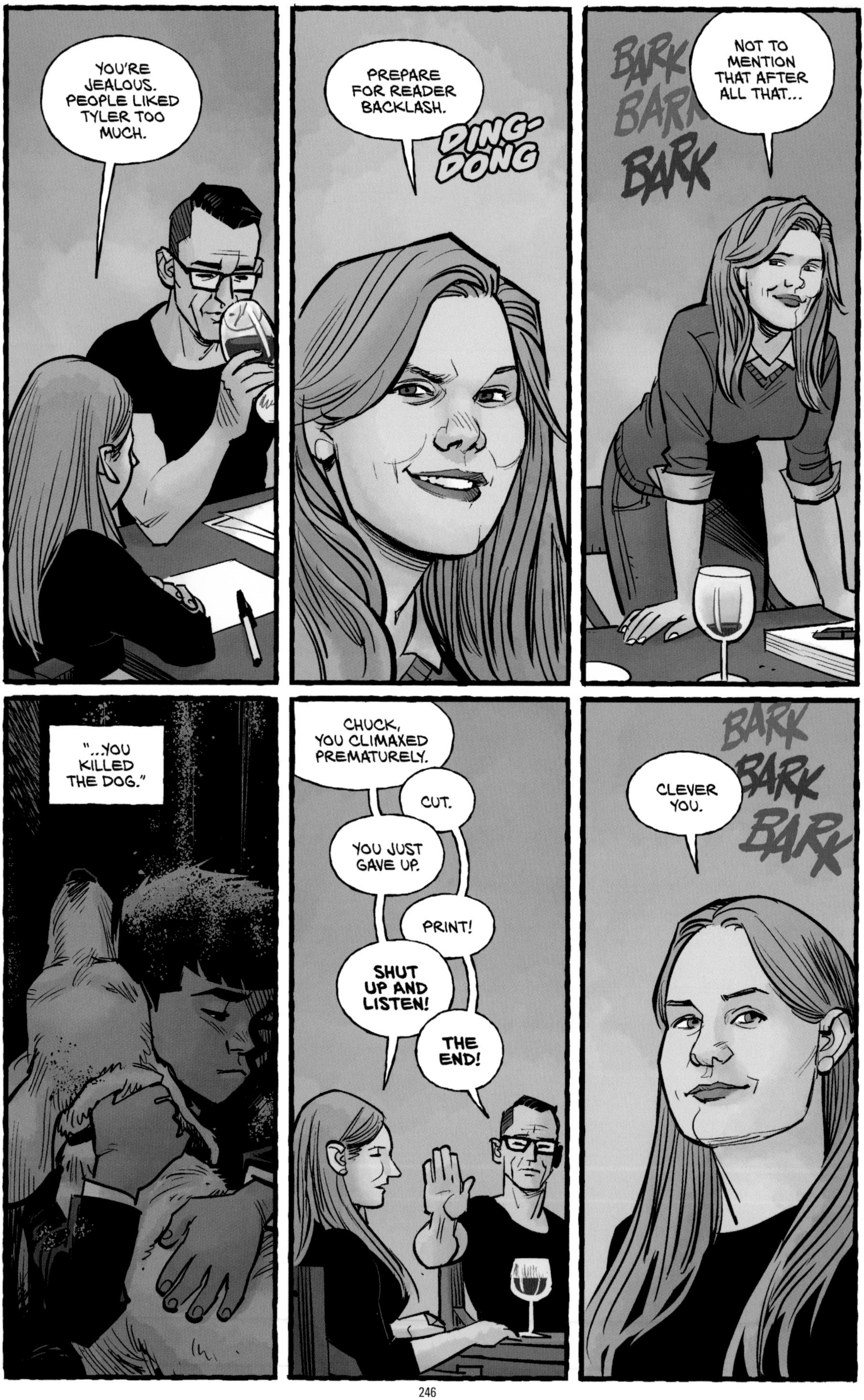

YOU'RE JEALOUS. PEOPLE LIKED TYLER TOO MUCH.
PREPARE FOR READER BACKLASH.
DING-DONG
BARK BARK BARK
NOT TO MENTION THAT AFTER ALL THAT...
"...YOU KILLED THE DOG."
CHUCK, YOU CLIMAXED PREMATURELY.
CUT.
YOU JUST GAVE UP.
PRINT!
SHUT UP AND LISTEN!
THE END!
BARK BARK BARK
CLEVER YOU.

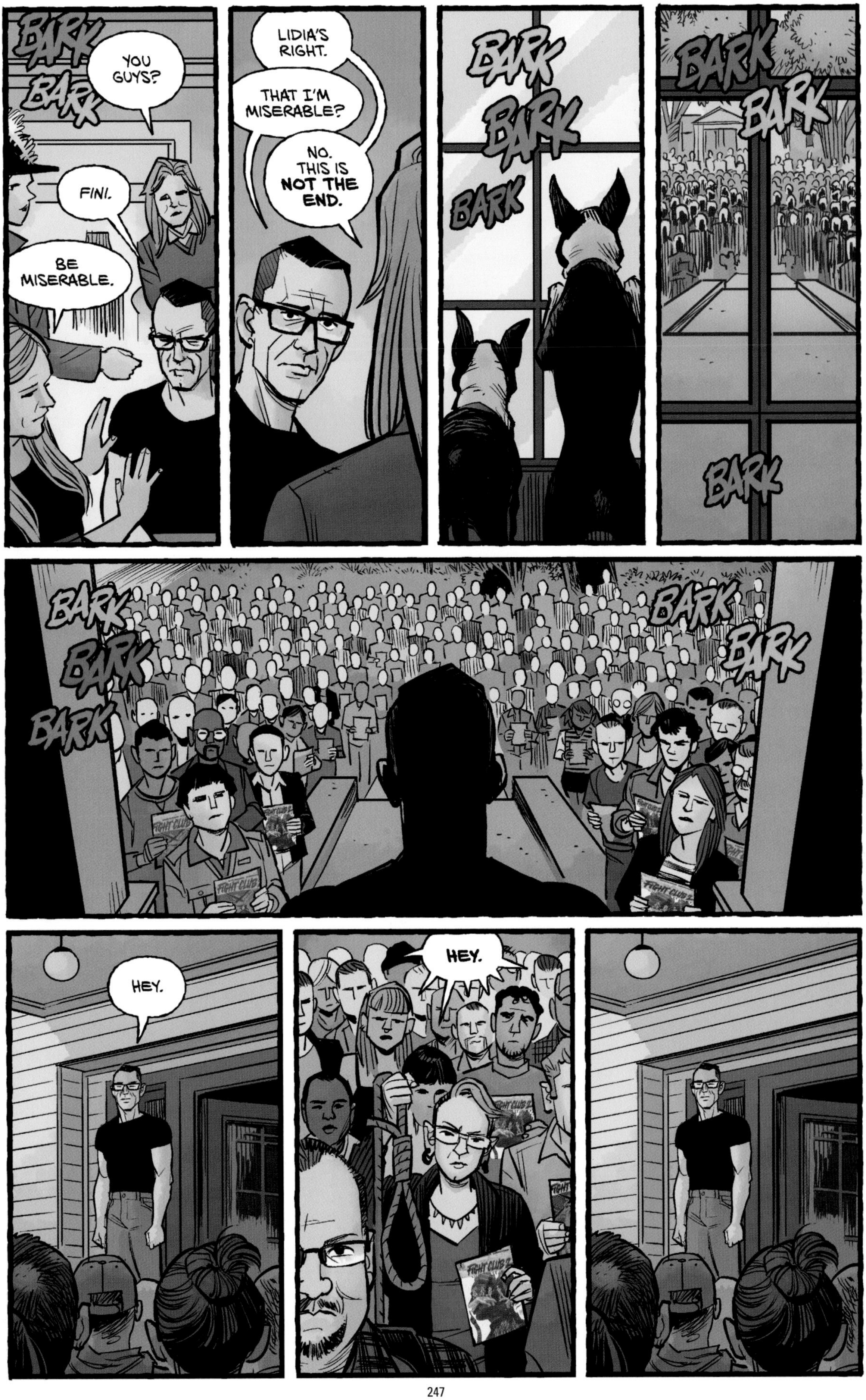
BARK
BARK
YOU GUYS?
FINI.
BE MISERABLE.
LIDIA'S RIGHT.
THAT I'M MISERABLE?
NO. THIS IS **NOT THE END.**
BARK
BARK
BARK
BARK
BARK
BARK
BARK
BARK
BARK
BARK
BARK
HEY.
HEY.

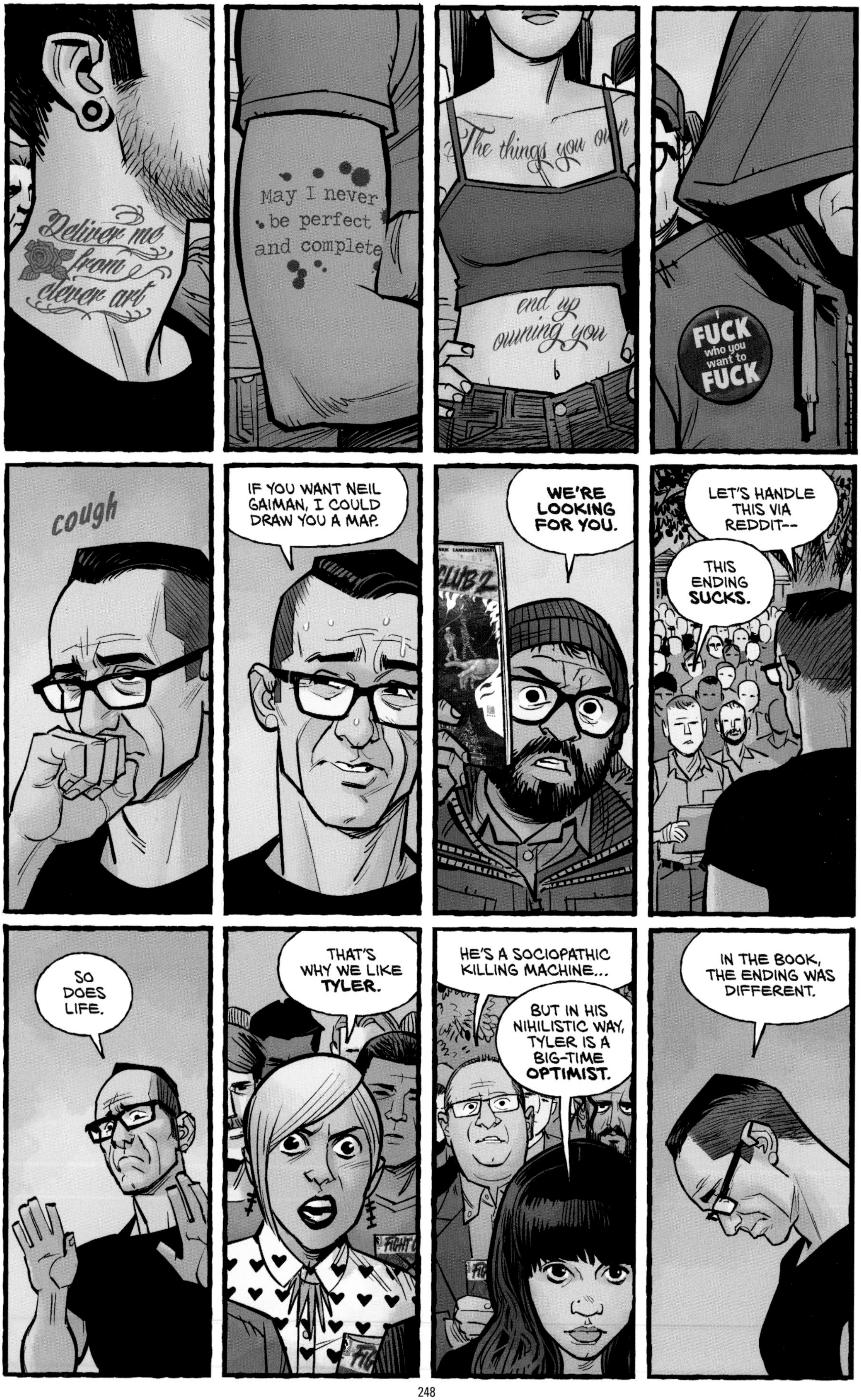
Deliver me from clever art
May I never be perfect and complete
The things you own end up owning you
I FUCK who you want to FUCK
cough
IF YOU WANT NEIL GAIMAN, I COULD DRAW YOU A MAP.
WE'RE LOOKING FOR YOU.
CAMERON STEWART
LET'S HANDLE THIS VIA REDDIT--
THIS ENDING SUCKS.
SO DOES LIFE.
THAT'S WHY WE LIKE TYLER.
HE'S A SOCIOPATHIC KILLING MACHINE...
BUT IN HIS NIHILISTIC WAY, TYLER IS A BIG-TIME OPTIMIST.
IN THE BOOK, THE ENDING WAS DIFFERENT.

YOU DON'T EVEN **HAVE** BOWEL CANCER!

YOU DON'T HAVE BOWEL CANCER EITHER!

HE'S NOT EVEN A NAVAJO!

WHEN THEY WERE ON THE ROOF...

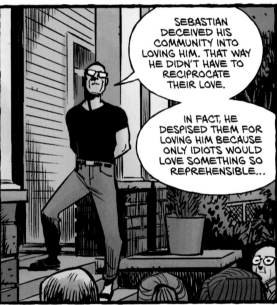

SEBASTIAN DECEIVED HIS COMMUNITY INTO LOVING HIM. THAT WAY HE DIDN'T HAVE TO RECIPROCATE THEIR LOVE.

IN FACT, HE DESPISED THEM FOR LOVING HIM BECAUSE ONLY IDIOTS WOULD LOVE SOMETHING SO REPREHENSIBLE...

WAIT-- THERE **WAS** A BOOK?

YES, YOU CHUCKLEHEADS!

VICTIMS FORGIVE THEIR VICTIMIZER. THAT'S THE REDEMPTION.

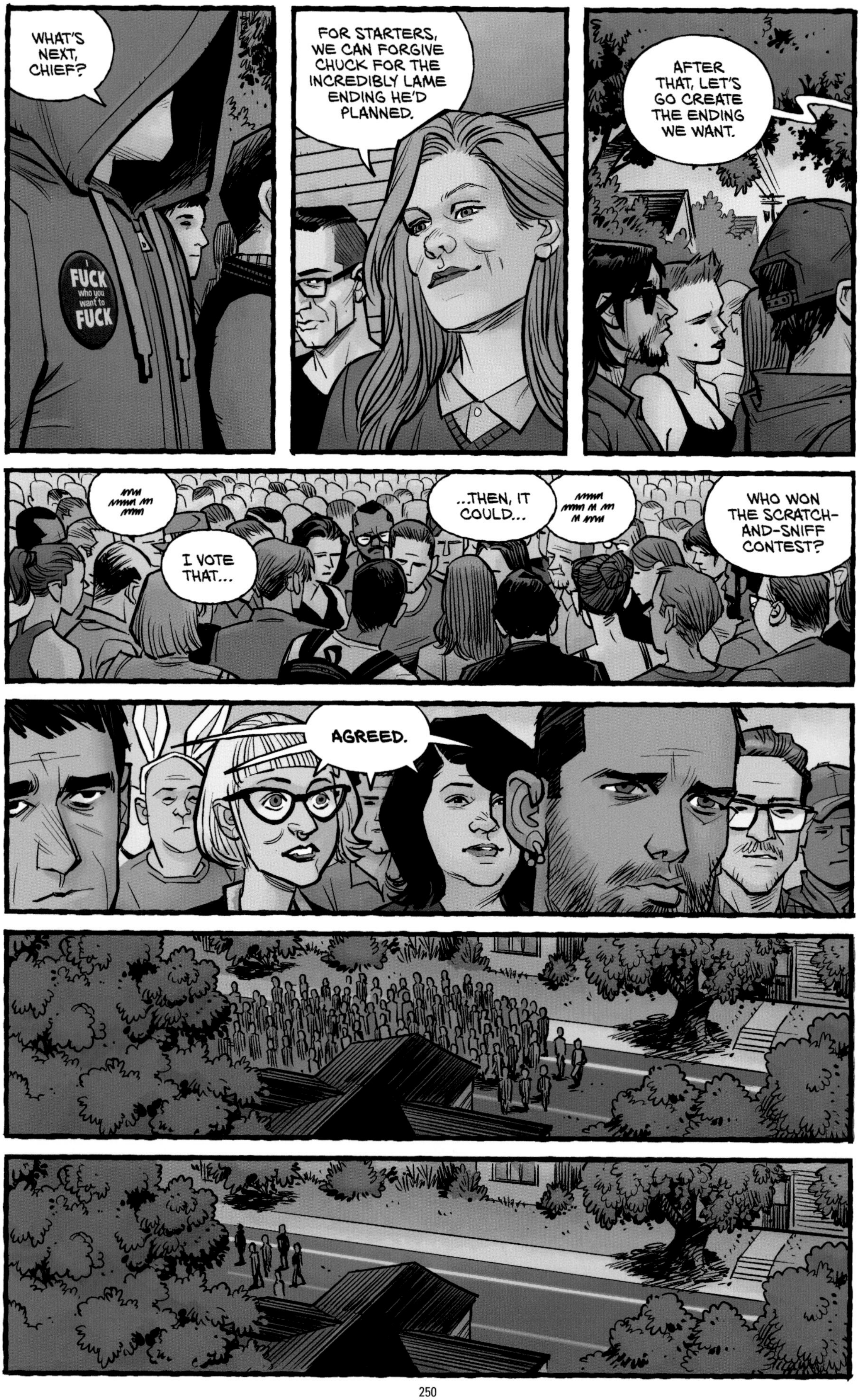

WHAT'S NEXT, CHIEF?
I FUCK who you want to FUCK
FOR STARTERS, WE CAN FORGIVE CHUCK FOR THE INCREDIBLY LAME ENDING HE'D PLANNED.
AFTER THAT, LET'S GO CREATE THE ENDING WE WANT.
I VOTE THAT...
...THEN, IT COULD...
WHO WON THE SCRATCH-AND-SNIFF CONTEST?
AGREED.

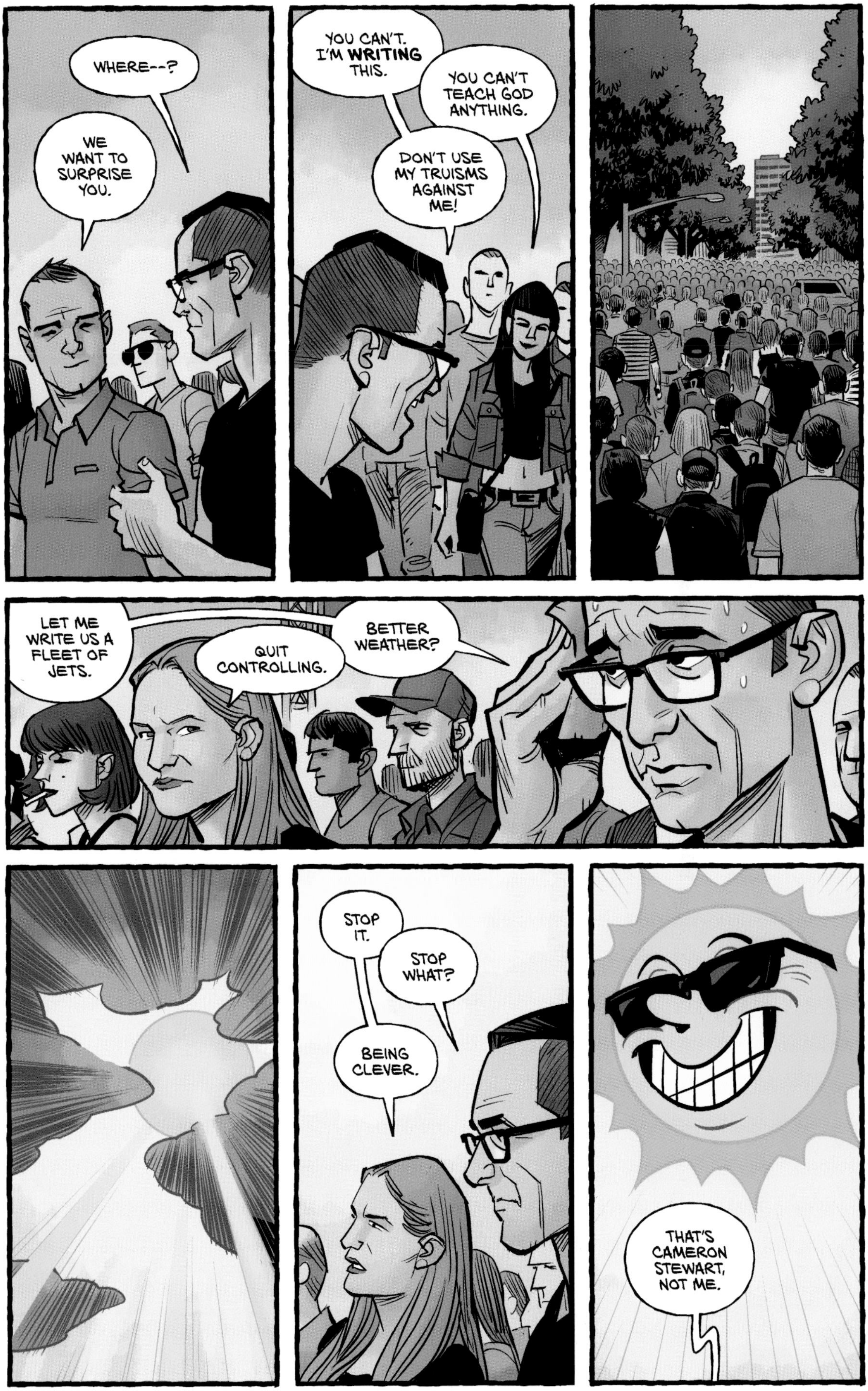
WHERE--?
WE WANT TO SURPRISE YOU.
YOU CAN'T. I'M **WRITING** THIS.
YOU CAN'T TEACH GOD ANYTHING.
DON'T USE MY TRUISMS AGAINST ME!
LET ME WRITE US A FLEET OF JETS.
QUIT CONTROLLING.
BETTER WEATHER?
STOP IT.
STOP WHAT?
BEING CLEVER.
THAT'S CAMERON STEWART, NOT ME.

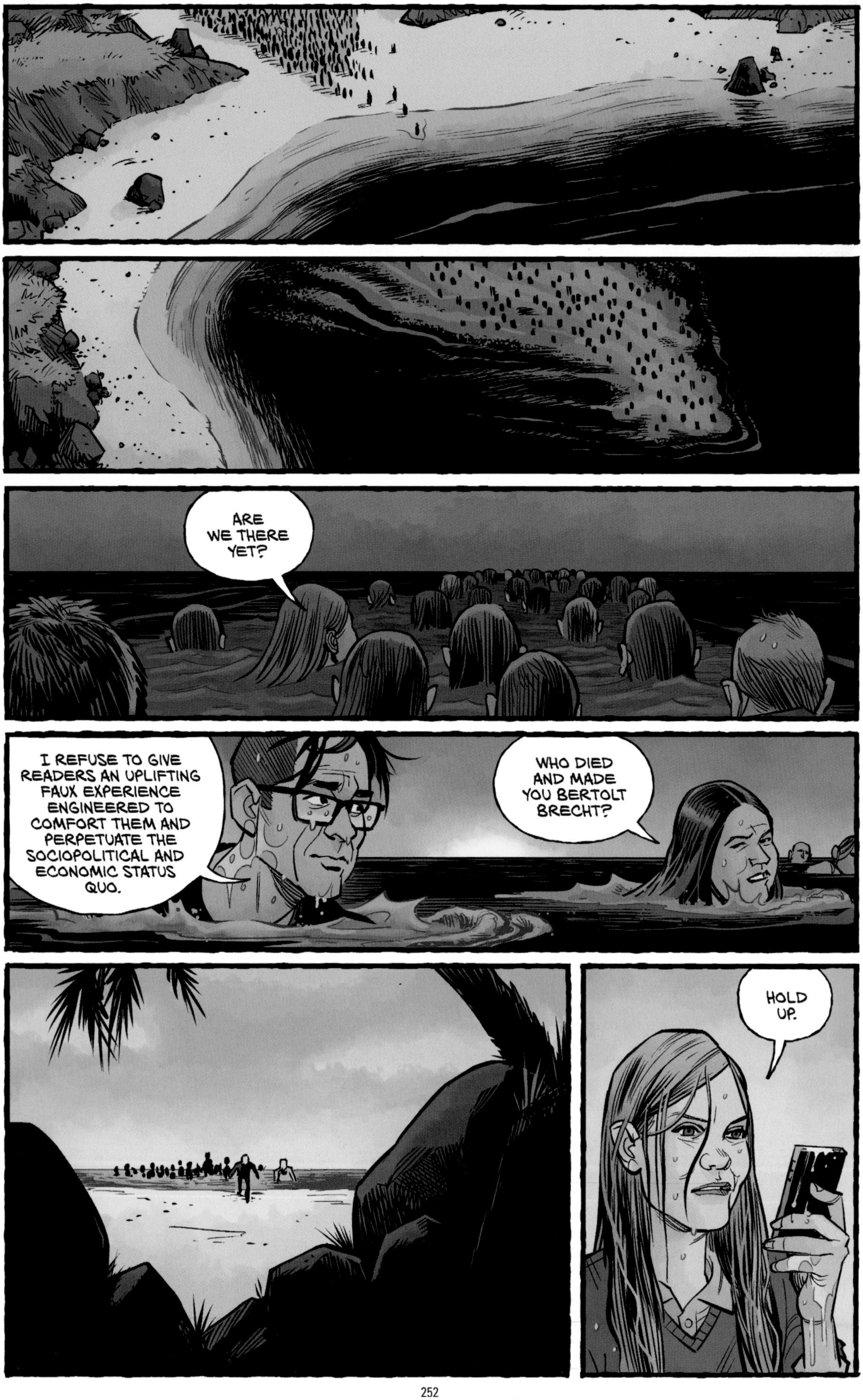
ARE WE THERE YET?
I REFUSE TO GIVE READERS AN UPLIFTING FAUX EXPERIENCE ENGINEERED TO COMFORT THEM AND PERPETUATE THE SOCIOPOLITICAL AND ECONOMIC STATUS QUO.
WHO DIED AND MADE YOU BERTOLT BRECHT?
HOLD UP.

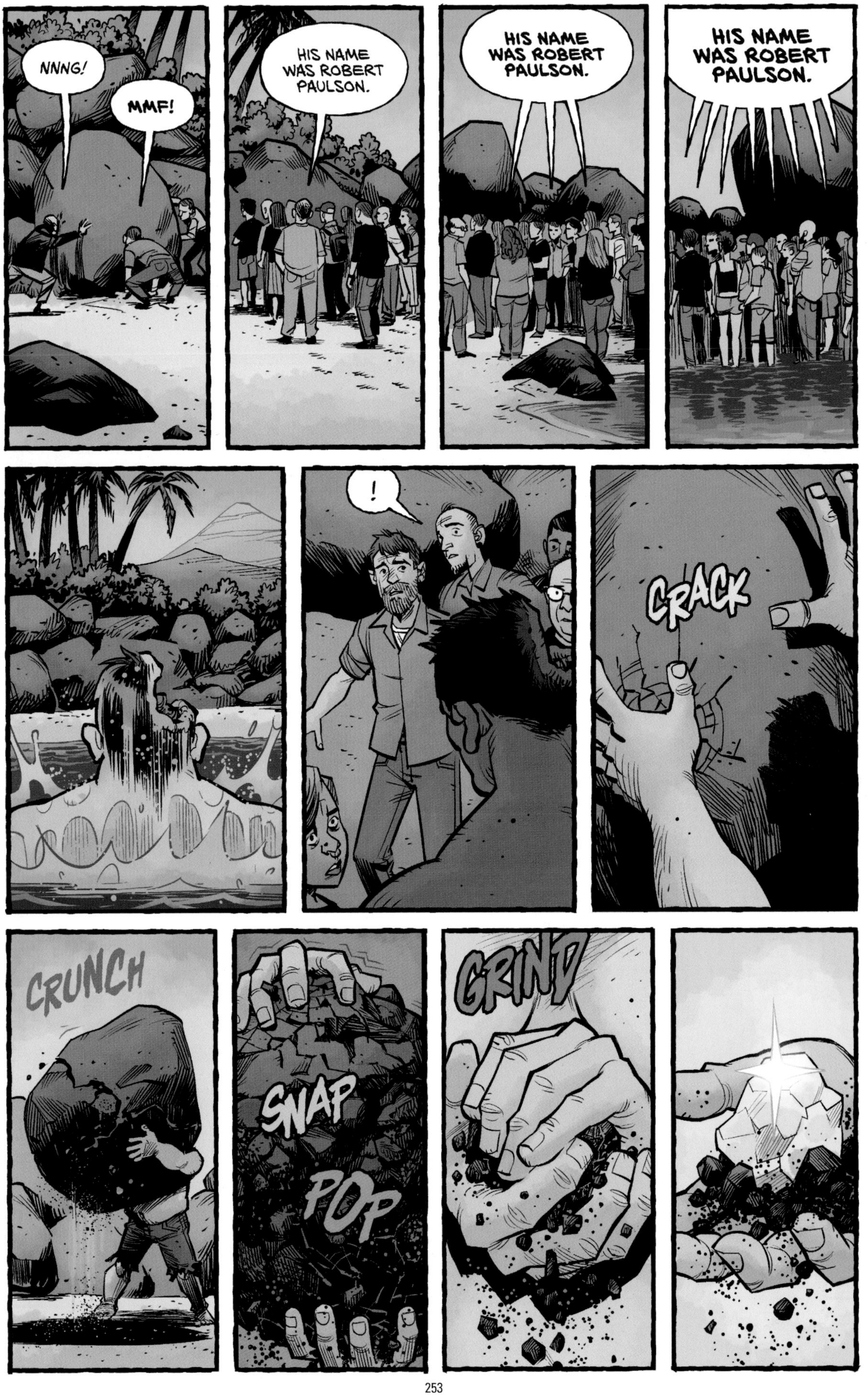
NNNG!
MMF!
HIS NAME WAS ROBERT PAULSON.
HIS NAME WAS ROBERT PAULSON.
HIS NAME WAS ROBERT PAULSON.
!
CRACK
CRUNCH
SNAP
POP
GRIND

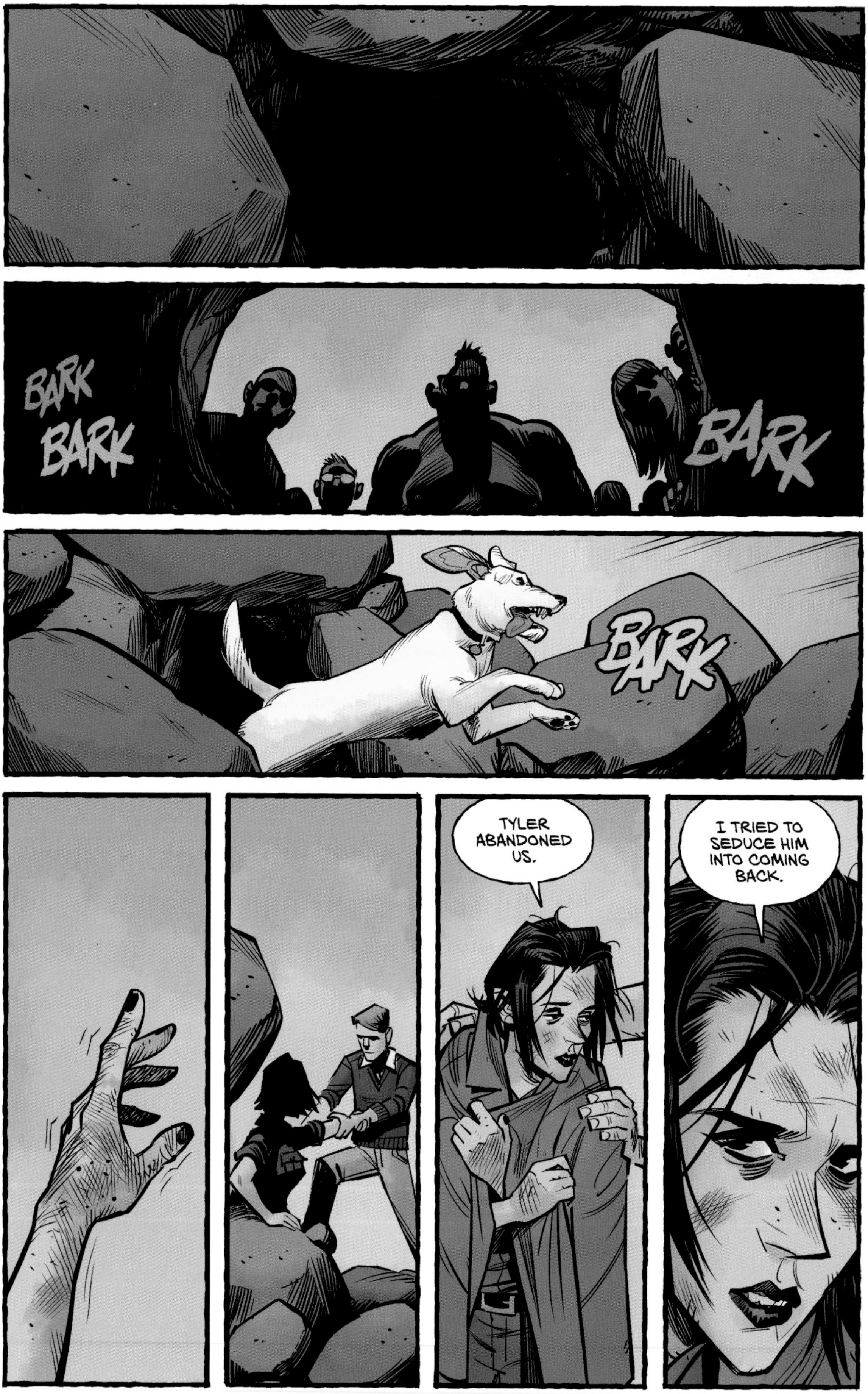
BARK
BARK
BARK
BARK
TYLER ABANDONED US.
I TRIED TO SEDUCE HIM INTO COMING BACK.

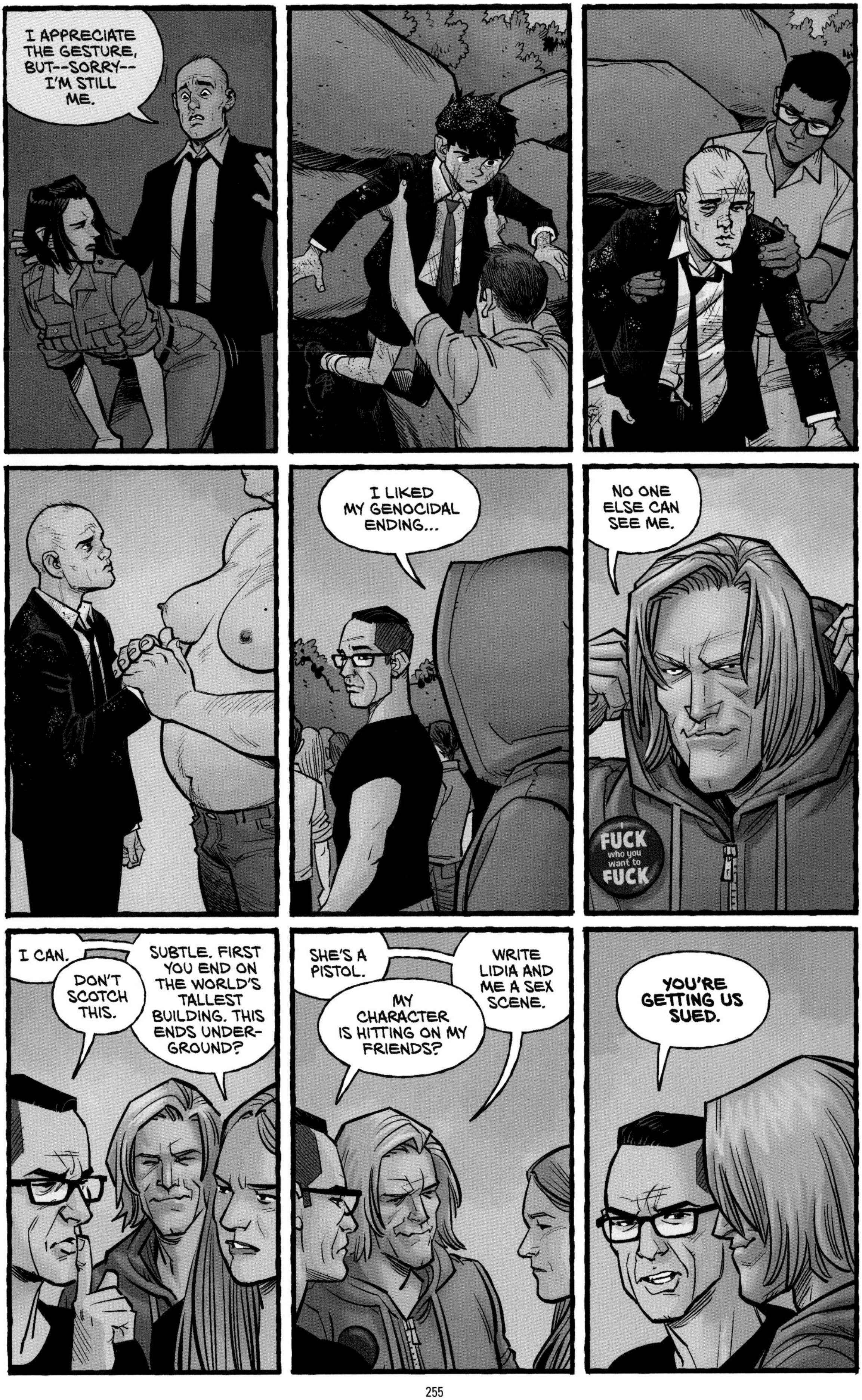
I APPRECIATE THE GESTURE, BUT--SORRY-- I'M STILL ME.
I LIKED MY GENOCIDAL ENDING...
NO ONE ELSE CAN SEE ME.
FUCK who you want to FUCK
I CAN.
DON'T SCOTCH THIS.
SUBTLE. FIRST YOU END ON THE WORLD'S TALLEST BUILDING. THIS ENDS UNDER-GROUND?
SHE'S A PISTOL.
MY CHARACTER IS HITTING ON MY FRIENDS?
WRITE LIDIA AND ME A SEX SCENE.
YOU'RE GETTING US SUED.

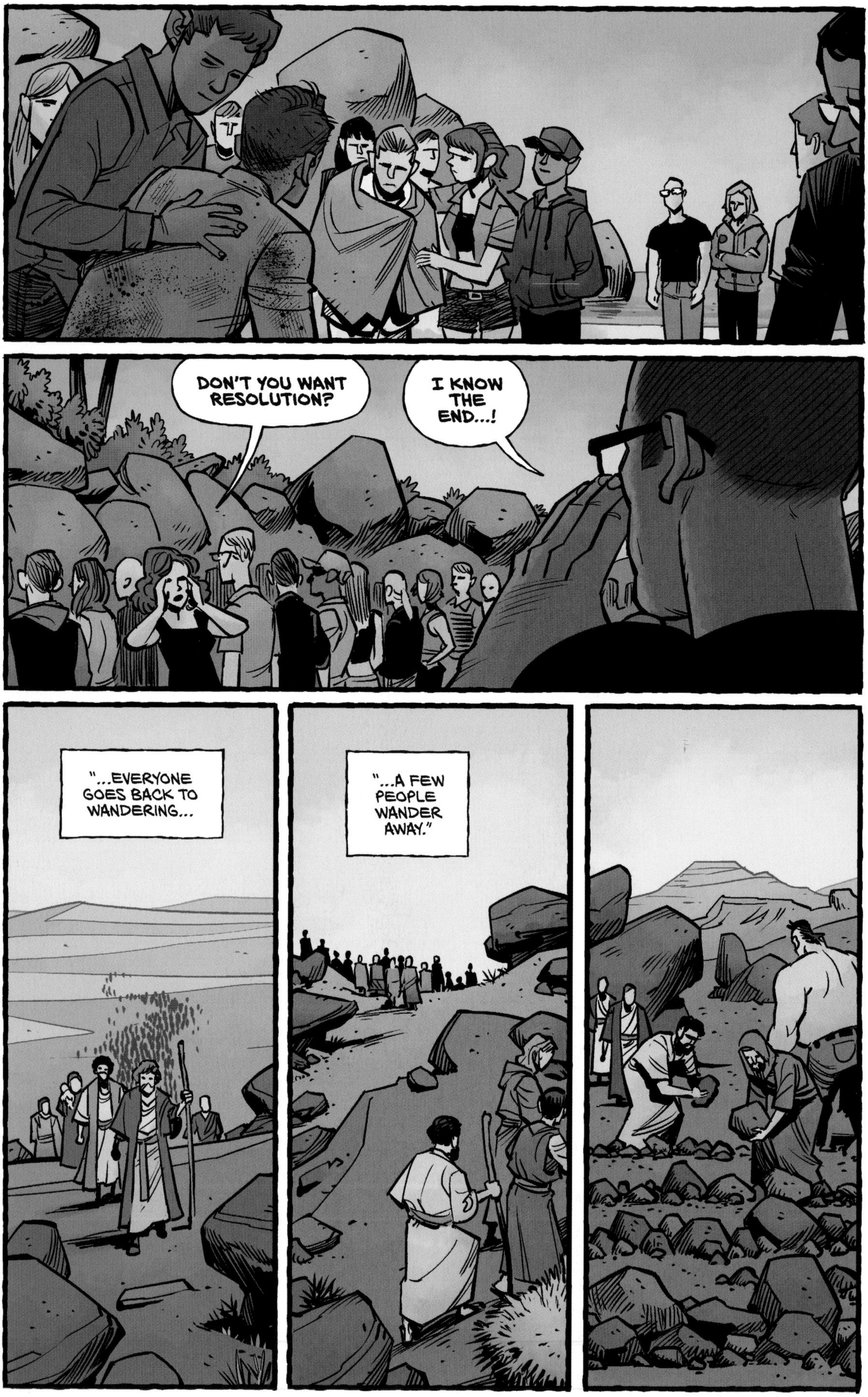
DON'T YOU WANT RESOLUTION?
I KNOW THE END...!
"...EVERYONE GOES BACK TO WANDERING...
"...A FEW PEOPLE WANDER AWAY."

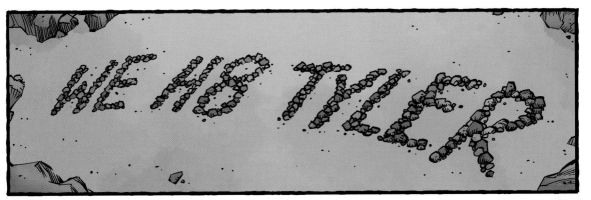

HAPPY ANNIVERSARY.

GUYS?

THIS APP SHOWS PEOPLE AROUND THE WORLD STILL BURIED ALIVE!

I VOTE WE GO SAVE THEM!

LET'S GO FORGIVE THEM!

SOUNDS REDEMPTIVE E...

HIP-HIP HU...

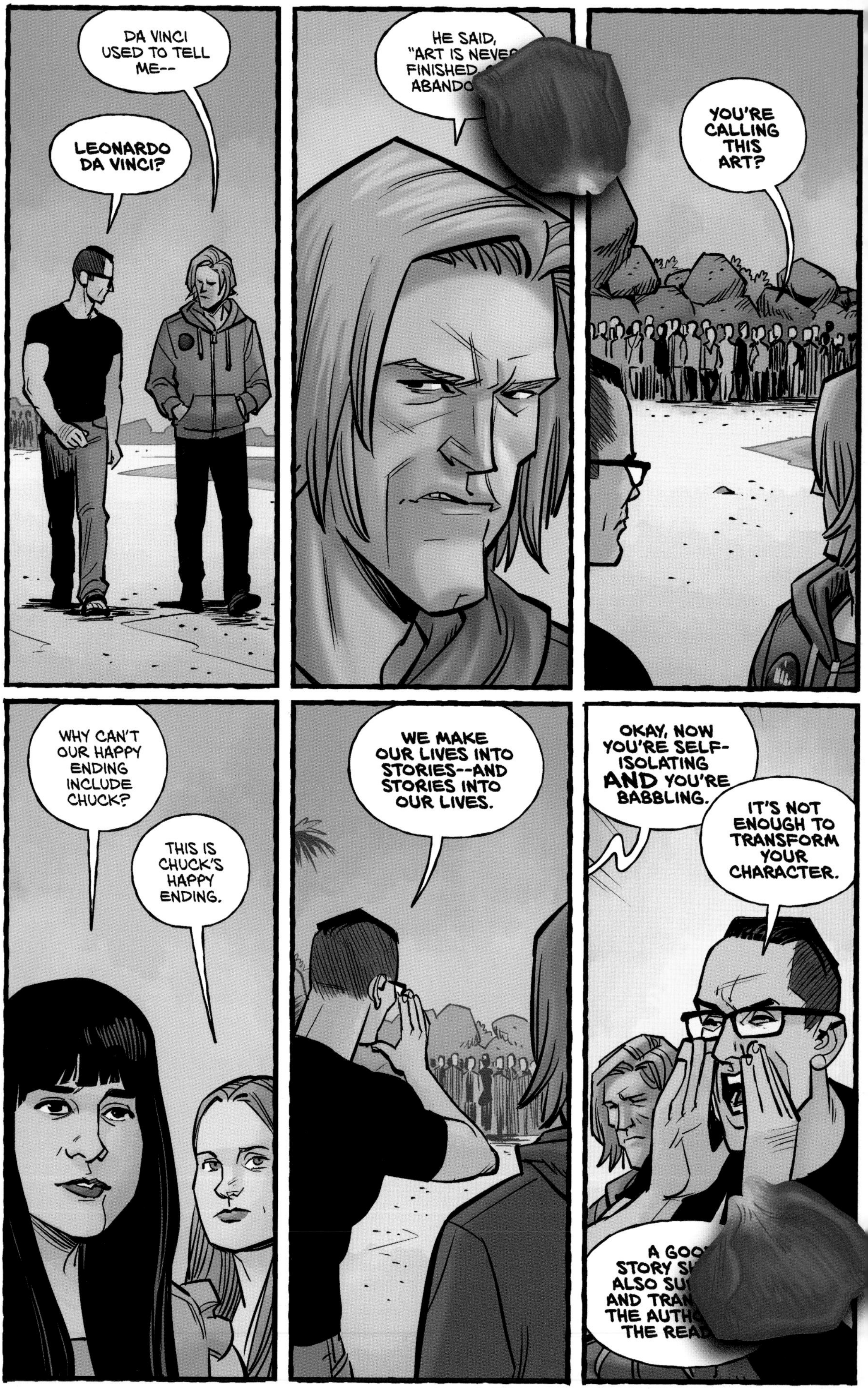
DA VINCI USED TO TELL ME--
LEONARDO DA VINCI?
HE SAID, "ART IS NEVE FINISHED ABANDO
YOU'RE CALLING THIS ART?
WHY CAN'T OUR HAPPY ENDING INCLUDE CHUCK?
THIS IS CHUCK'S HAPPY ENDING.
WE MAKE OUR LIVES INTO STORIES--AND STORIES INTO OUR LIVES.
OKAY, NOW YOU'RE SELF-ISOLATING AND YOU'RE BABBLING.
IT'S NOT ENOUGH TO TRANSFORM YOUR CHARACTER.
A GOO STORY S ALSO SU AND TRAN THE AUTHO THE READ

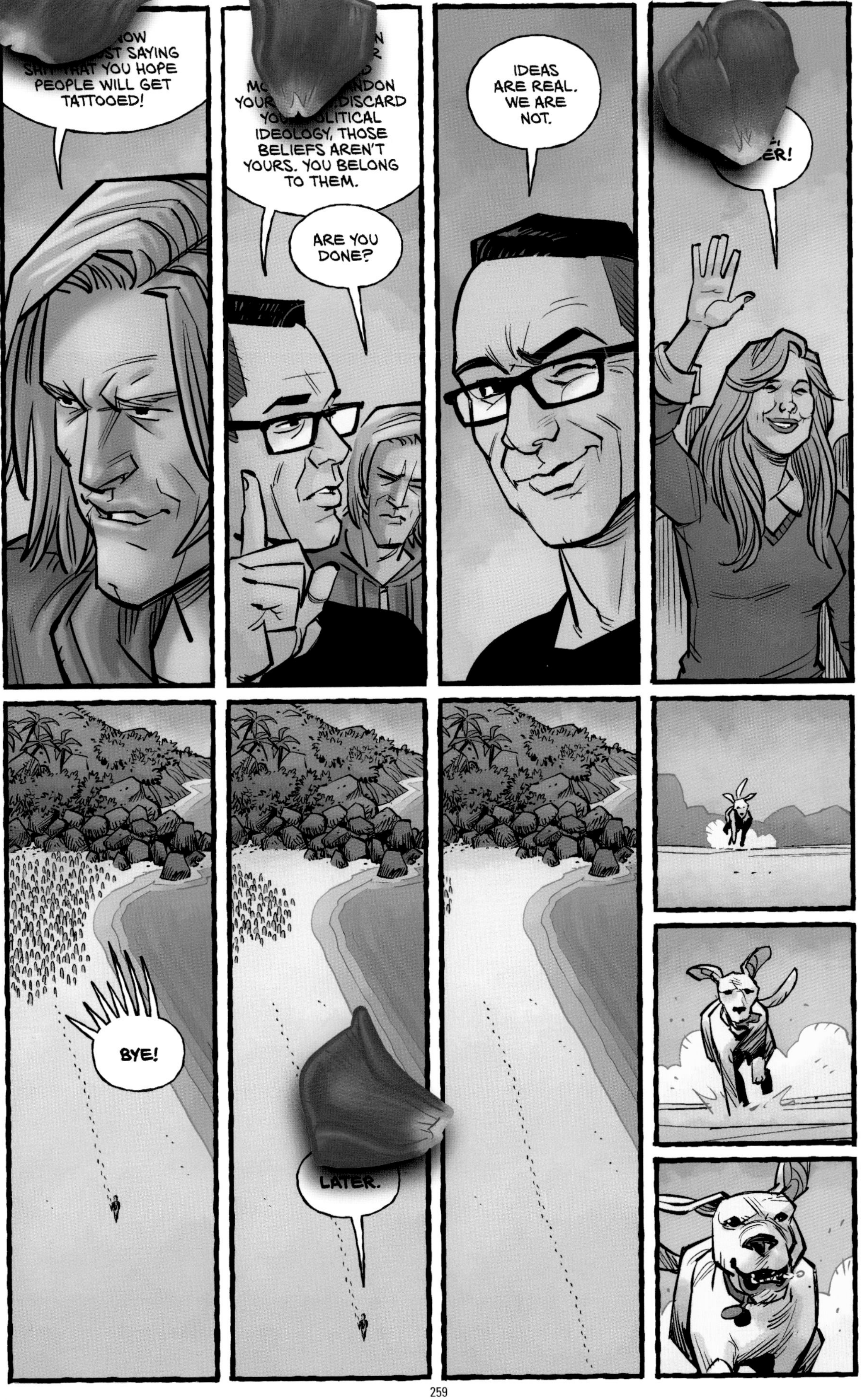
THAT YOU HOPE PEOPLE WILL GET TATTOOED!
DISCARD ... IDEOLOGY, THOSE BELIEFS AREN'T YOURS. YOU BELONG TO THEM.
ARE YOU DONE?
IDEAS ARE REAL. WE ARE NOT.
ER!
BYE!
LATER.

THIS MAKES IT A HAPPY ENDING.

WHAT'S NEXT, CHIEF?

Wom
Health
Center

A woman can never be **TOO RICH, TOO THIN, or TOO CLOSE TO THE EDGE** of **THE TABLE**

IT'S NOT MY HUSBAND'S.

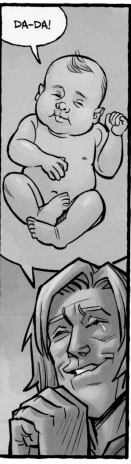

DA-DA!

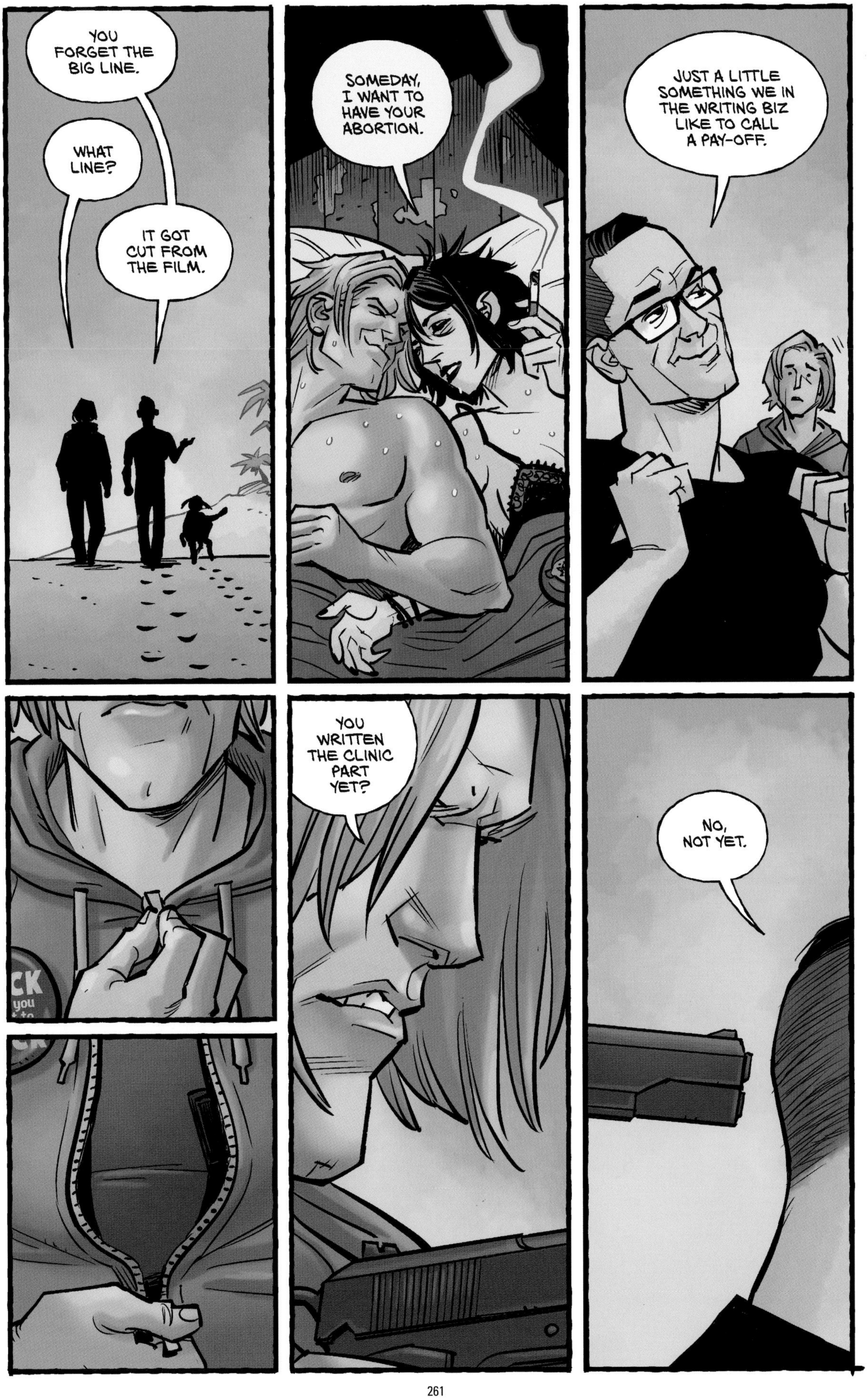
YOU FORGET THE BIG LINE.
WHAT LINE?
IT GOT CUT FROM THE FILM.
SOMEDAY, I WANT TO HAVE YOUR ABORTION.
JUST A LITTLE SOMETHING WE IN THE WRITING BIZ LIKE TO CALL A PAY-OFF.
YOU WRITTEN THE CLINIC PART YET?
NO, NOT YET.

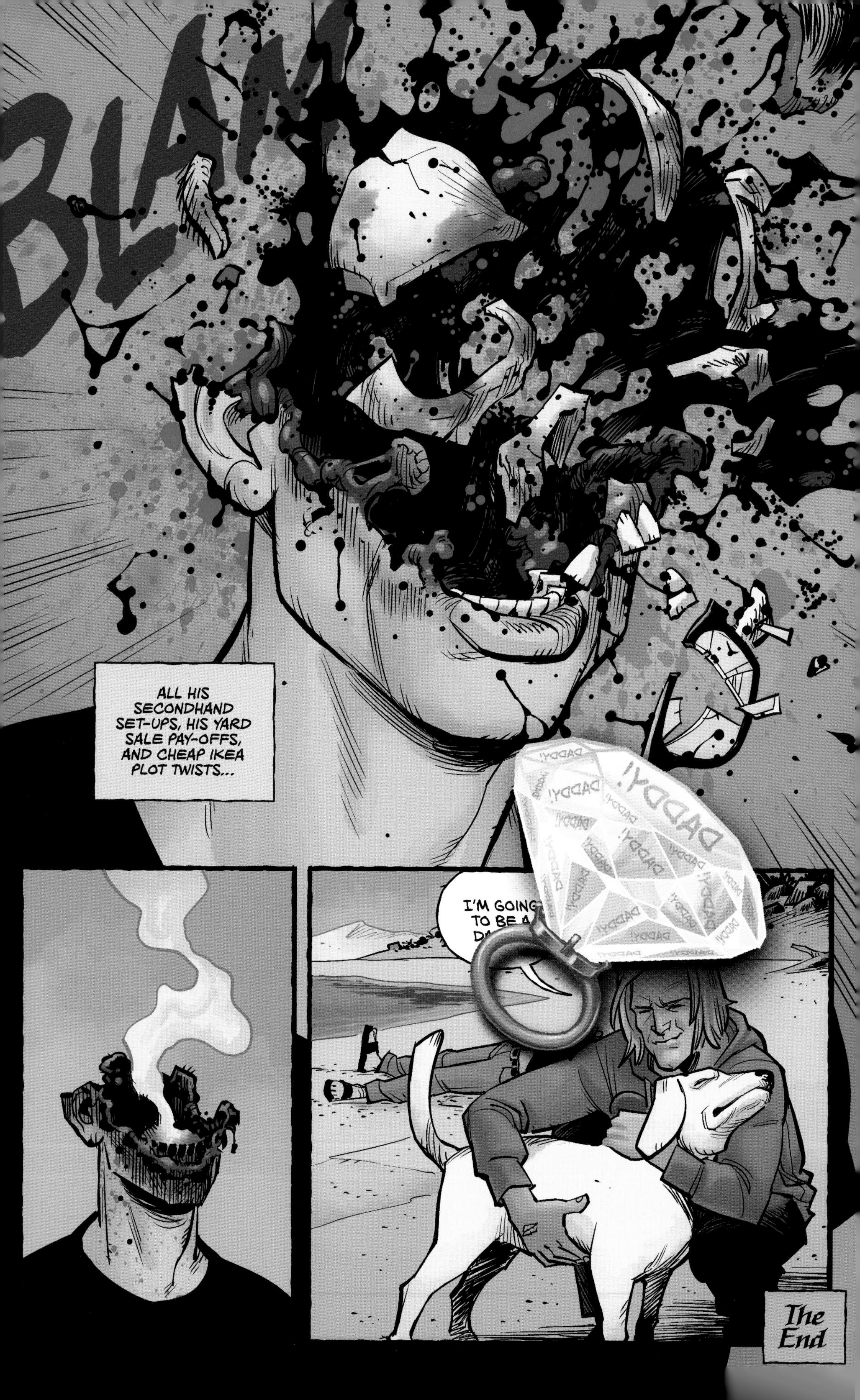
BLAM!
ALL HIS SECONDHAND SET-UPS, HIS YARD SALE PAY-OFFS, AND CHEAP IKEA PLOT TWISTS...
DADDY!
The End

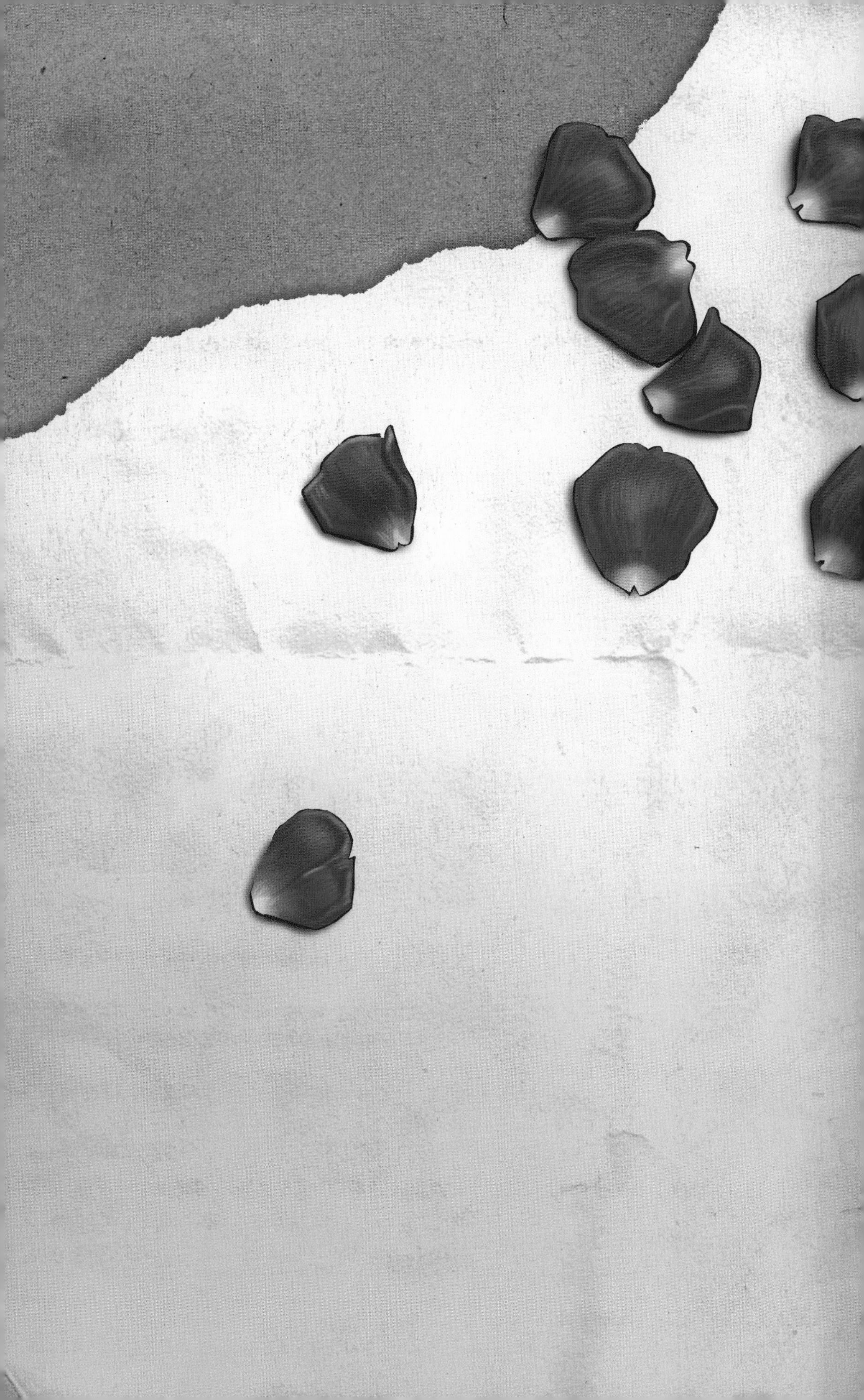

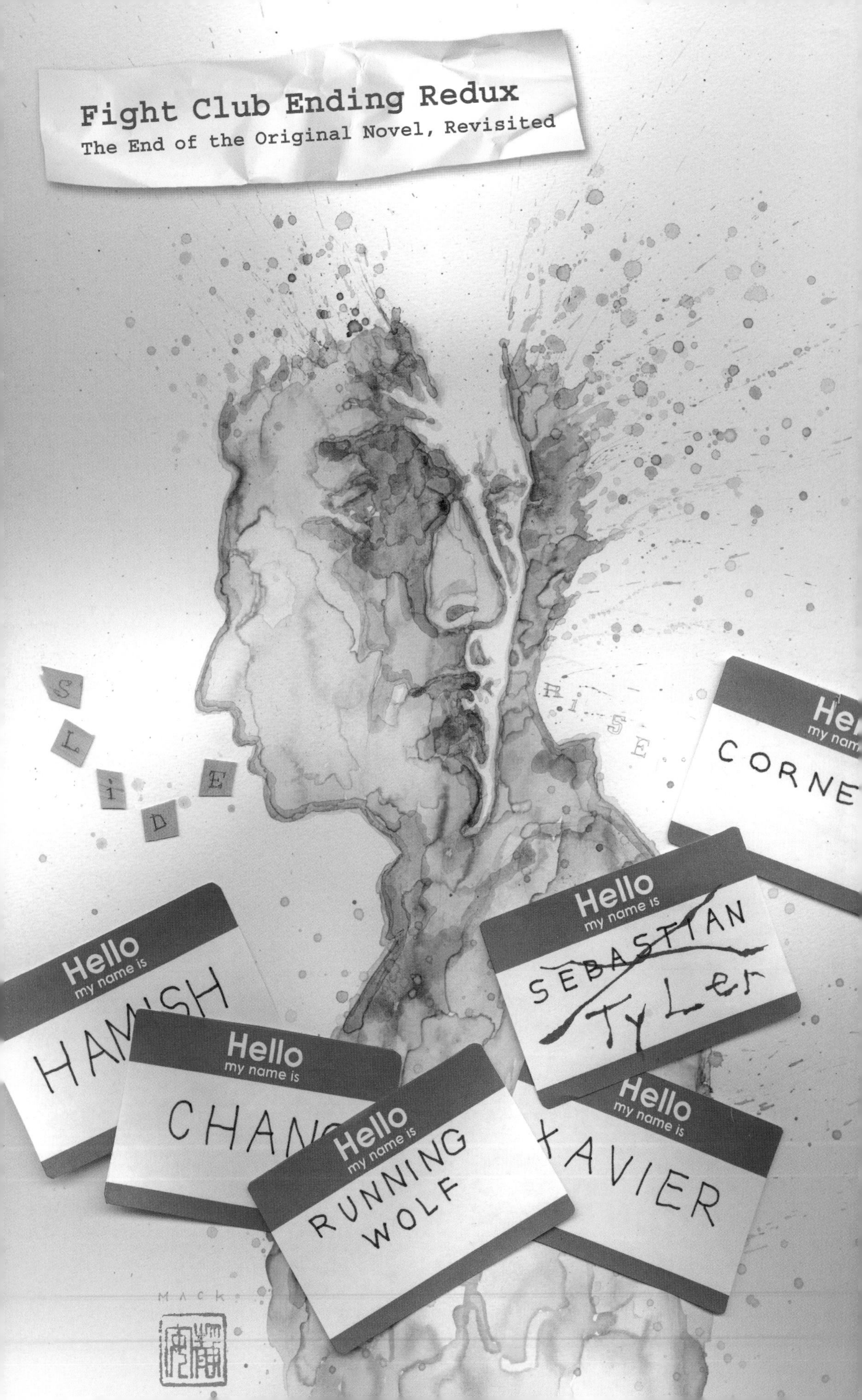

Fight Club Ending Redux
The End of the Original Novel, Revisited

SLIDE

RISE

Hello my name is CORNE

Hello my name is SEBASTIAN TyLer

Hello my name is HAMISH

Hello my name is CHANG

Hello my name is RUNNING WOLF

Hello my name is XAVIER

MACK

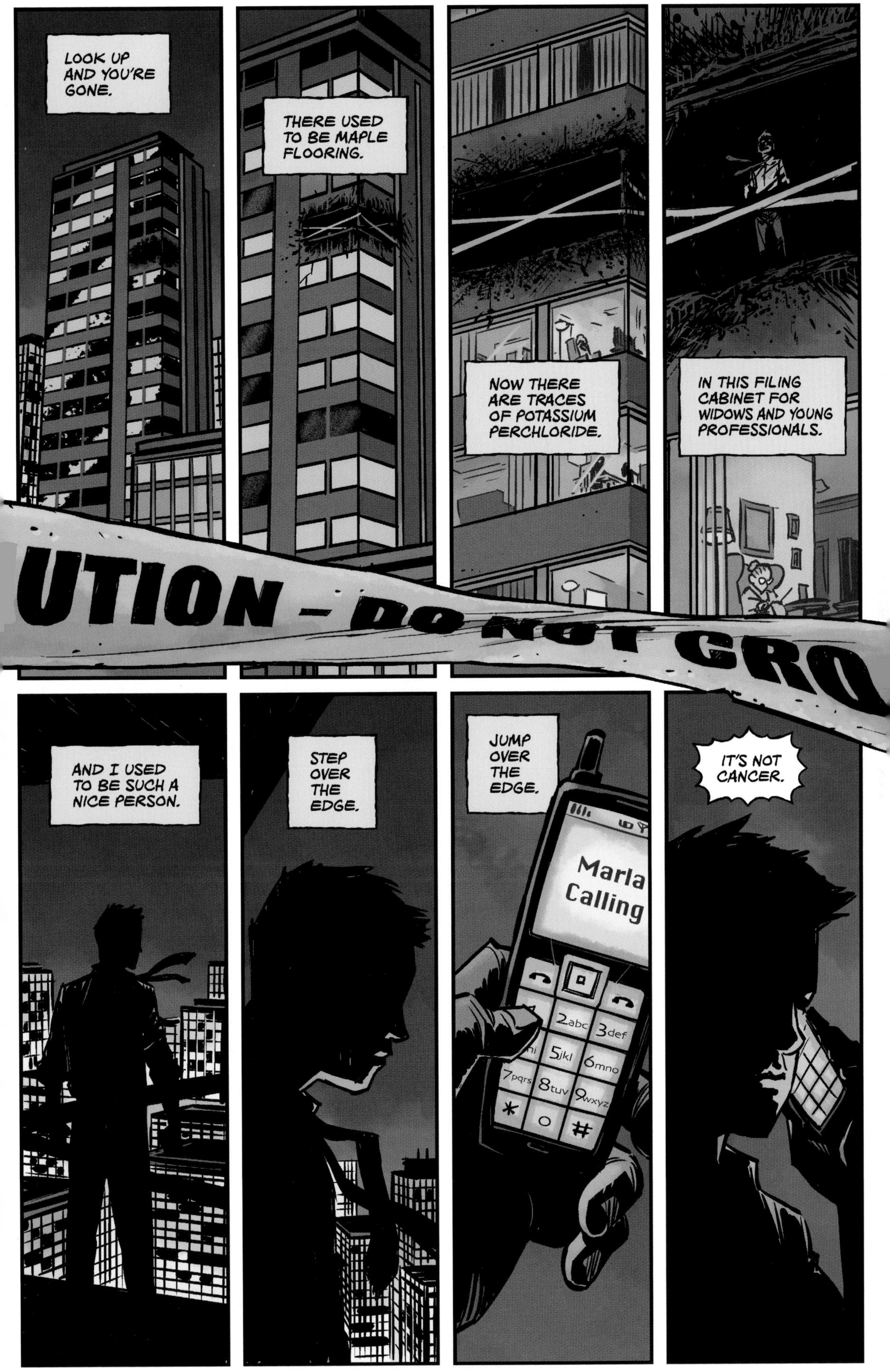
LOOK UP AND YOU'RE GONE.
THERE USED TO BE MAPLE FLOORING.
NOW THERE ARE TRACES OF POTASSIUM PERCHLORIDE.
IN THIS FILING CABINET FOR WIDOWS AND YOUNG PROFESSIONALS.
UTION – DO NOT CRO
AND I USED TO BE SUCH A NICE PERSON.
STEP OVER THE EDGE.
JUMP OVER THE EDGE.
Marla Calling
IT'S NOT CANCER.

THOSE CHANGES IN MY BREASTS.
I NEED TO SEE YOU.
I'M BEING FOLLOWED.
IT'S THURSDAY.
SLIDE...

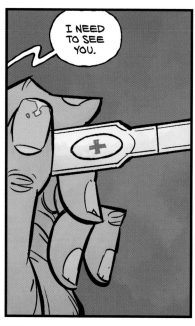

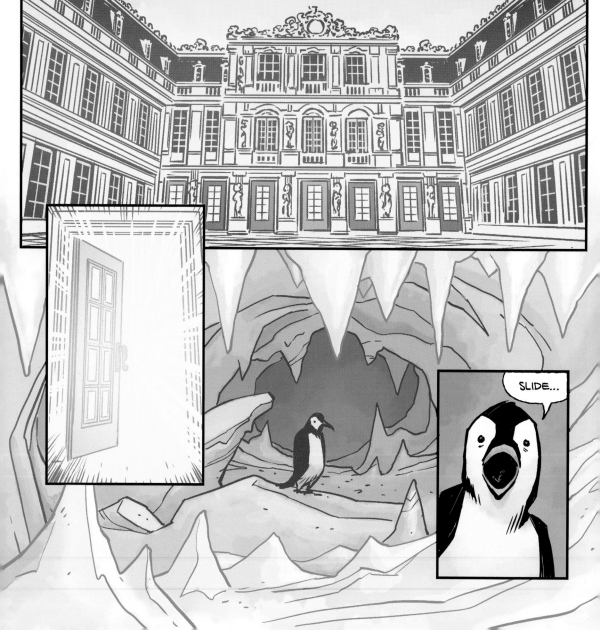

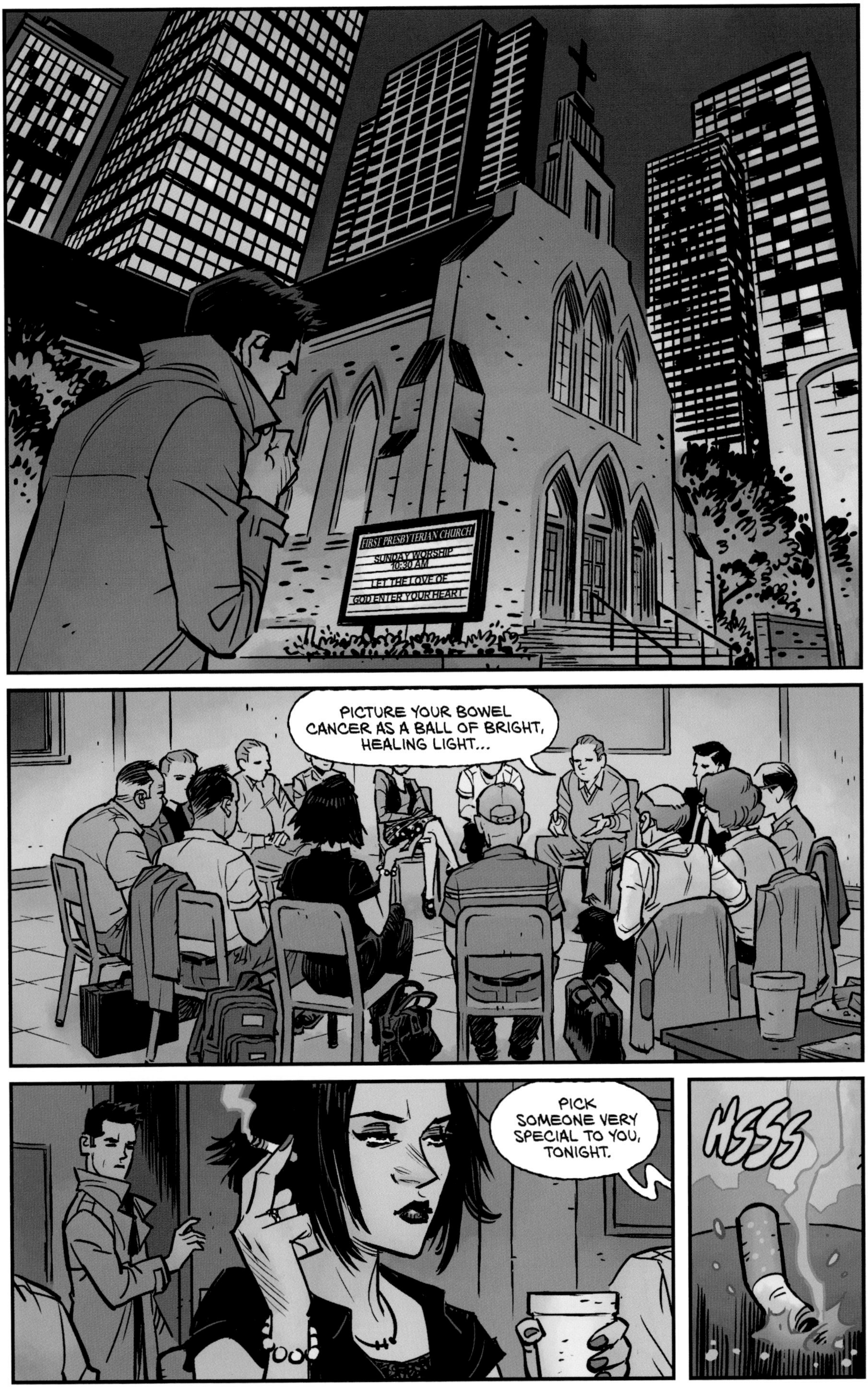
FIRST PRESBYTERIAN CHURCH
SUNDAY WORSHIP
10:30 AM
LET THE LOVE OF
GOD ENTER YOUR HEART
PICTURE YOUR BOWEL CANCER AS A BALL OF BRIGHT, HEALING LIGHT...
PICK SOMEONE VERY SPECIAL TO YOU, TONIGHT.
HSSS

DON'T TELL ME YOU FOUND ANOTHER LUMP.

WORSE.

WORSE THAN CANCER?

YOU'LL THINK SO.

EARTH TO CORNELIUS OR SEBASTIAN OR TYLER OR **WHOEVER** YOU ARE...

CANCER ISN'T THE ONLY THING THAT CAN AFFECT BREASTS.

IT'S NOT MINE.

DON'T PULL THE OLD "MY-ALTER-EGO-GOT-YOU-KNOCKED-UP" ROUTINE.

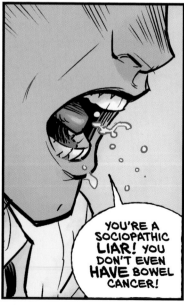

YOU'RE A SOCIOPATHIC **LIAR!** YOU DON'T EVEN **HAVE** BOWEL CANCER!

YOU DON'T HAVE BOWEL CANCER EITHER!

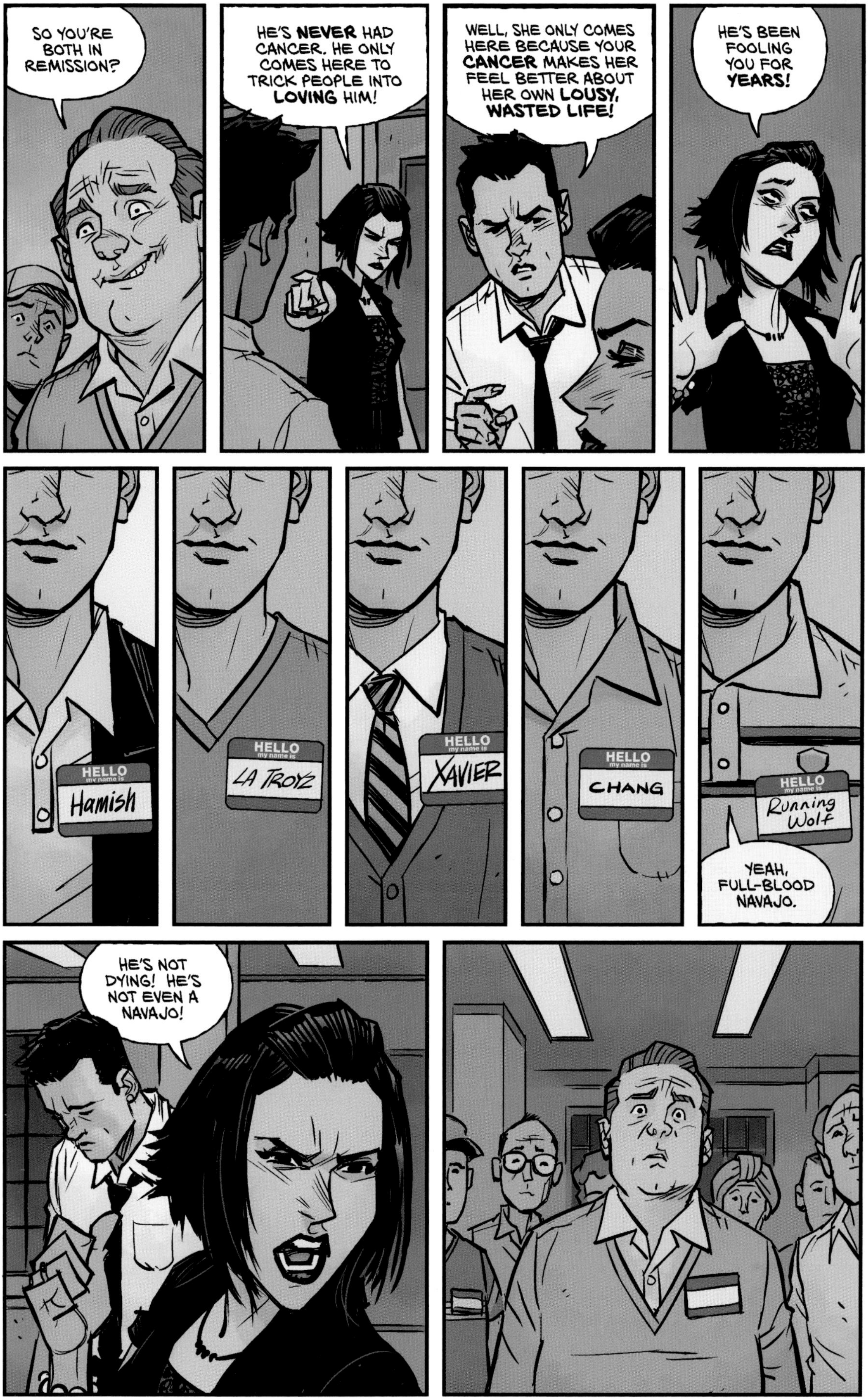

SO YOU'RE BOTH IN REMISSION?
HE'S NEVER HAD CANCER. HE ONLY COMES HERE TO TRICK PEOPLE INTO LOVING HIM!
WELL, SHE ONLY COMES HERE BECAUSE YOUR CANCER MAKES HER FEEL BETTER ABOUT HER OWN LOUSY, WASTED LIFE!
HE'S BEEN FOOLING YOU FOR YEARS!
HELLO my name is Hamish
HELLO my name is LA TROYZ
HELLO my name is XAVIER
HELLO my name is CHANG
HELLO my name is Running Wolf
YEAH, FULL-BLOOD NAVAJO.
HE'S NOT DYING! HE'S NOT EVEN A NAVAJO!

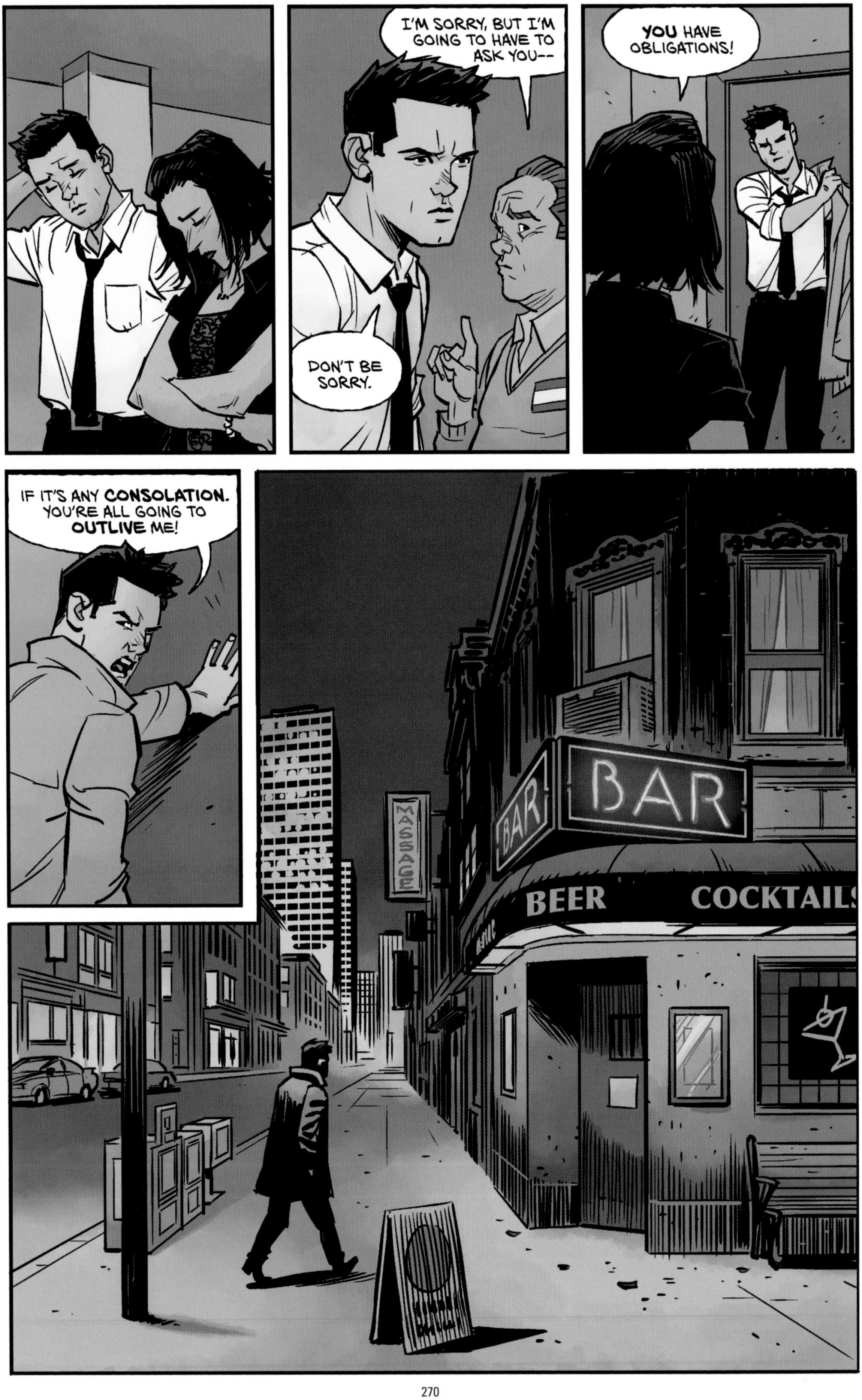
I'M SORRY, BUT I'M GOING TO HAVE TO ASK YOU--
DON'T BE SORRY.
YOU HAVE OBLIGATIONS!
IF IT'S ANY CONSOLATION. YOU'RE ALL GOING TO OUTLIVE ME!
MASSAGE
BAR
BAR
BEER
COCKTAILS

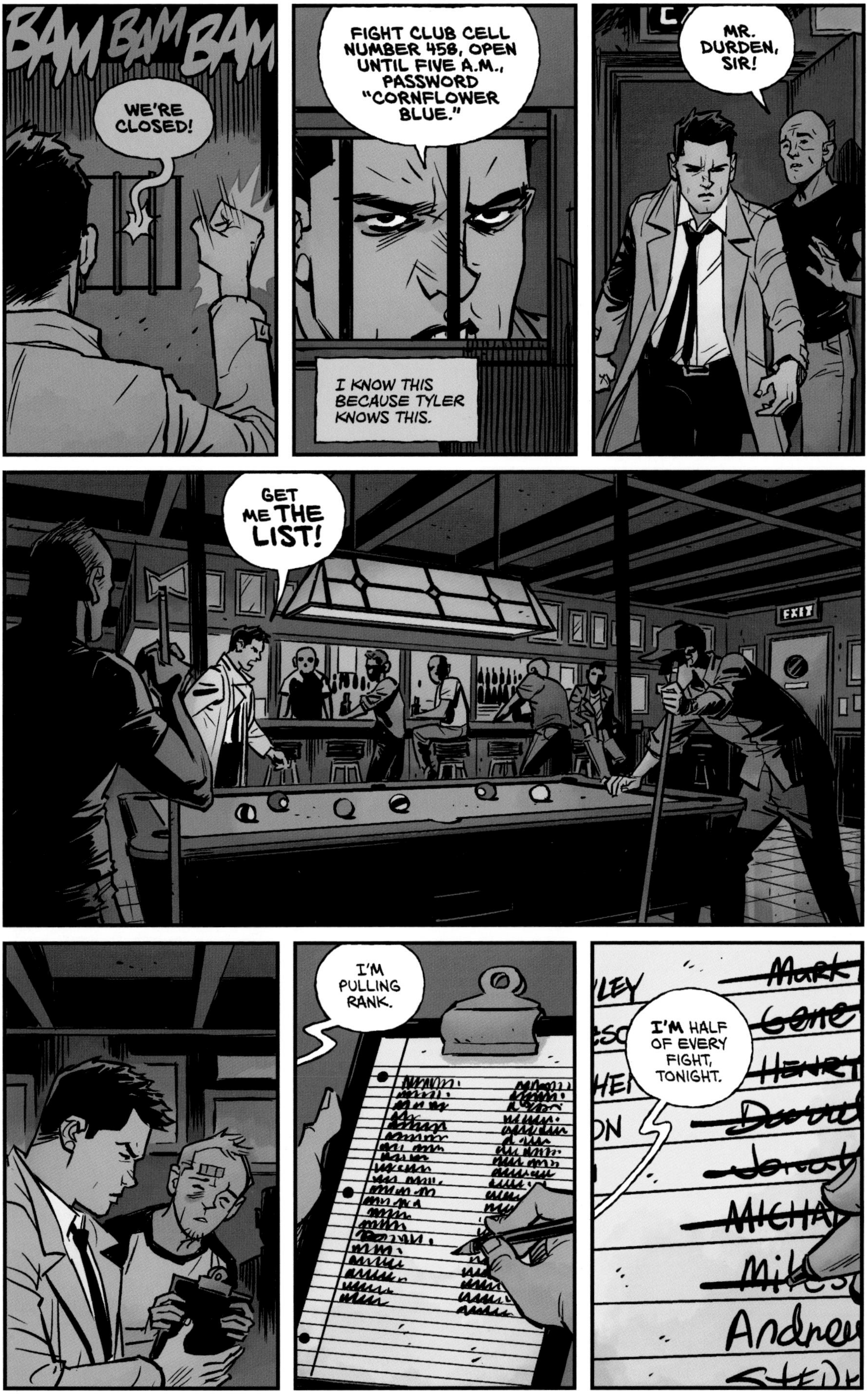
BAM BAM BAM
WE'RE CLOSED!
FIGHT CLUB CELL NUMBER 458, OPEN UNTIL FIVE A.M., PASSWORD "CORNFLOWER BLUE."
I KNOW THIS BECAUSE TYLER KNOWS THIS.
MR. DURDEN, SIR!
GET ME THE LIST!
EXIT
I'M PULLING RANK.
I'M HALF OF EVERY FIGHT, TONIGHT.

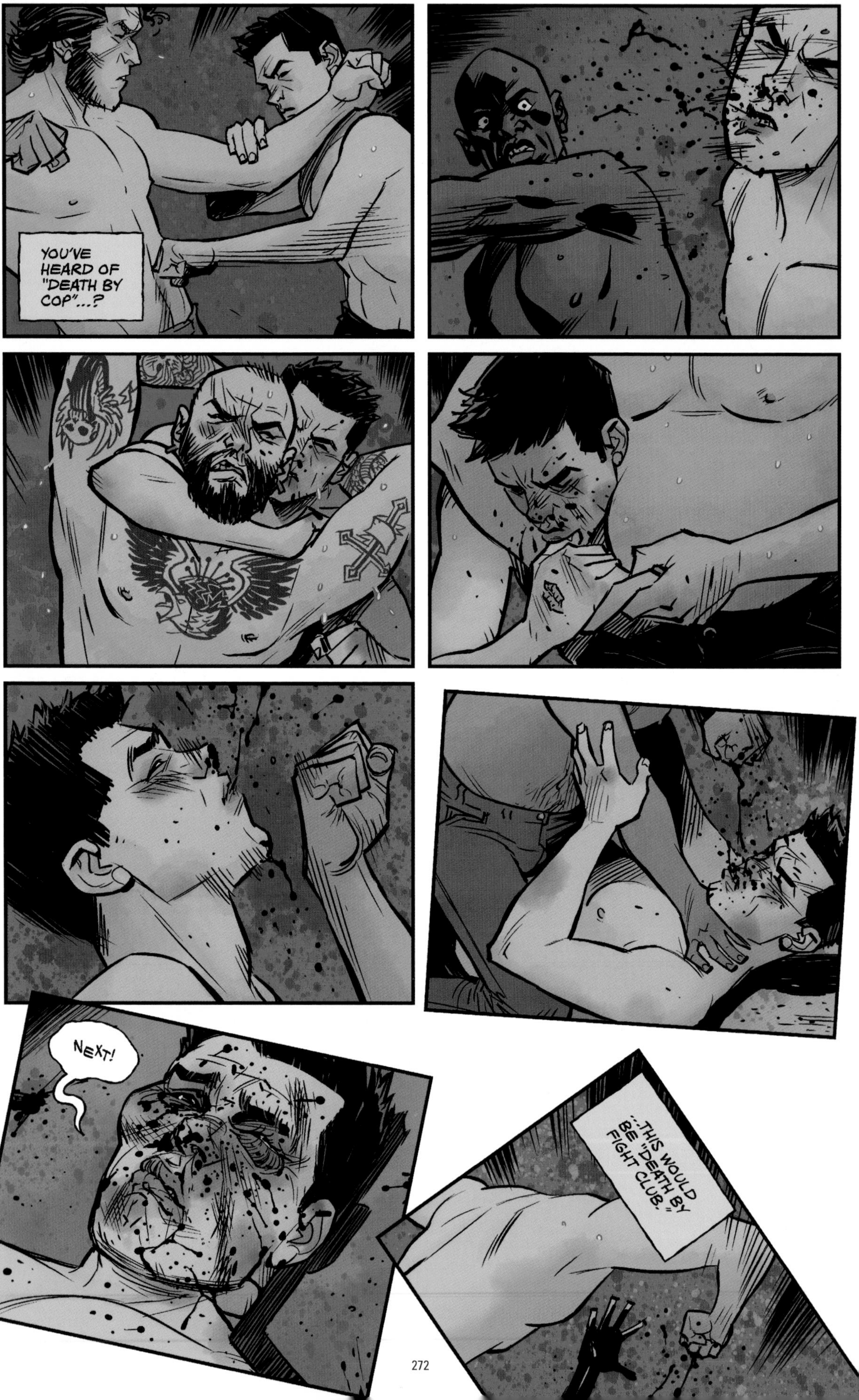
YOU'VE HEARD OF "DEATH BY COP"...?
NEXT!
...THIS WOULD BE "DEATH BY FIGHT CLUB."

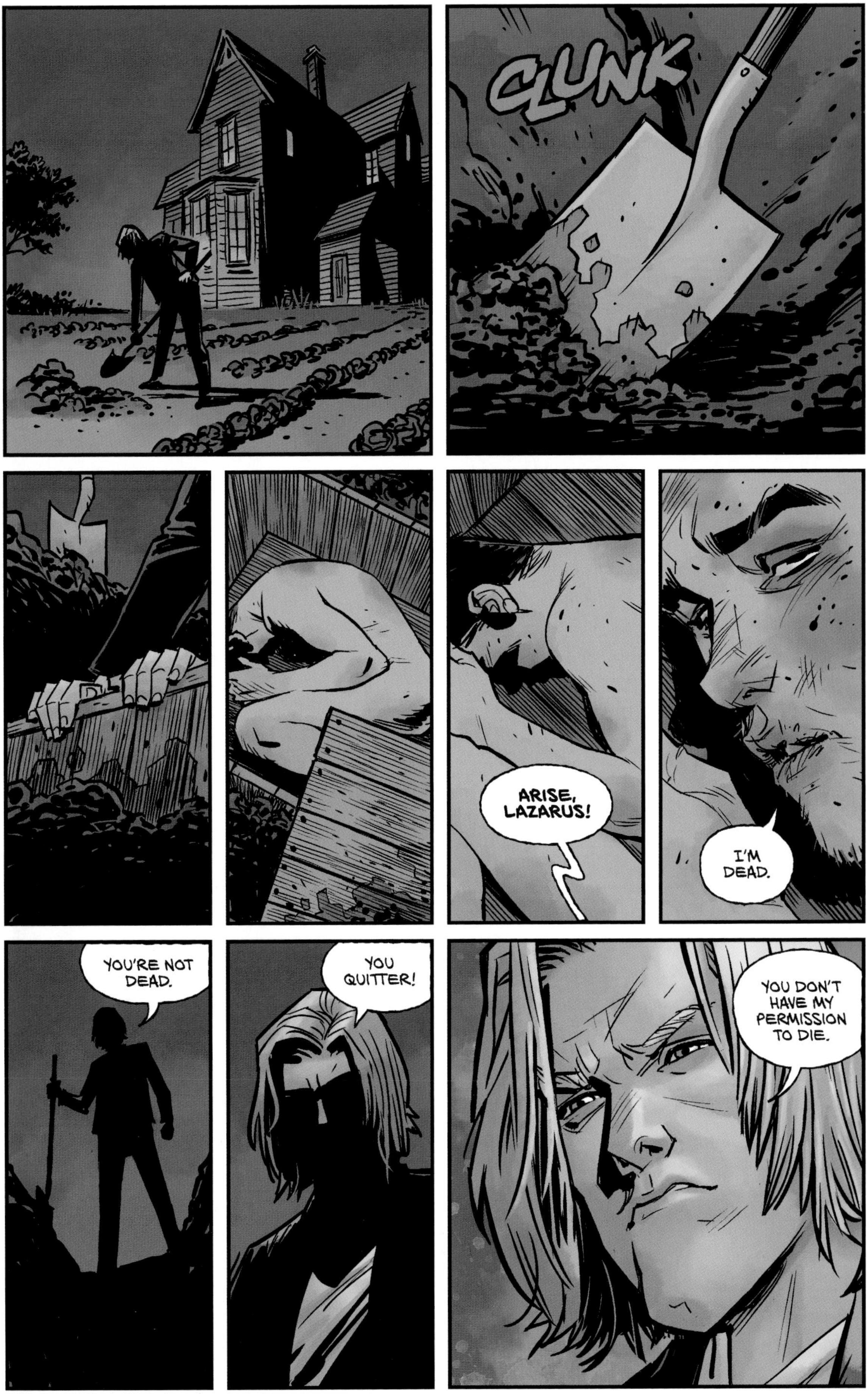
CLUNK
ARISE, LAZARUS!
I'M DEAD.
YOU'RE NOT DEAD.
YOU QUITTER!
YOU DON'T HAVE MY PERMISSION TO DIE.

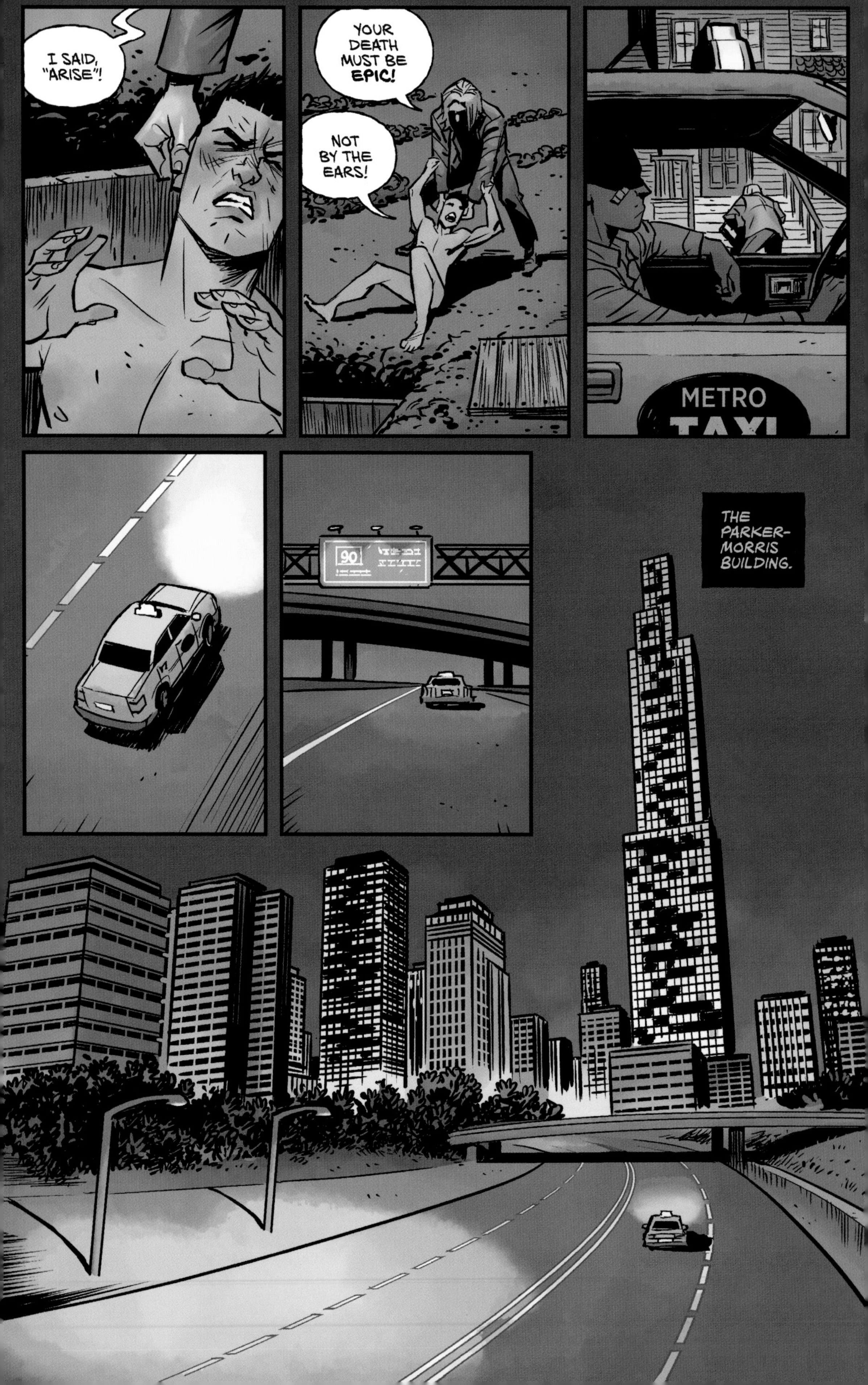
I SAID, "ARISE"!
YOUR DEATH MUST BE EPIC!
NOT BY THE EARS!
METRO
90
THE PARKER-MORRIS BUILDING.

YOU NEED TO DIE A **HERO'S** DEATH.

WAIT!

THTAY BAGK!

DEATH TO COMMENCE IN TEN...NINE...

EVERYTHING IS GOING TO BE **FINE!**

EIGHT... SEVEN...

THE **BUILGIN'** ITH GONNA **ETHPLODE!**

SIX... FIVE...

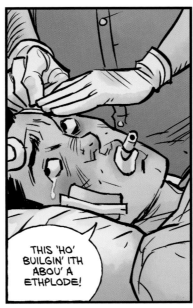

THIS 'HO' BUILGIN' ITH ABOU' A ETHPLODE!

DON'T WORRY.

EVERYTHING IS GOING TO BE ALL RIGHT.

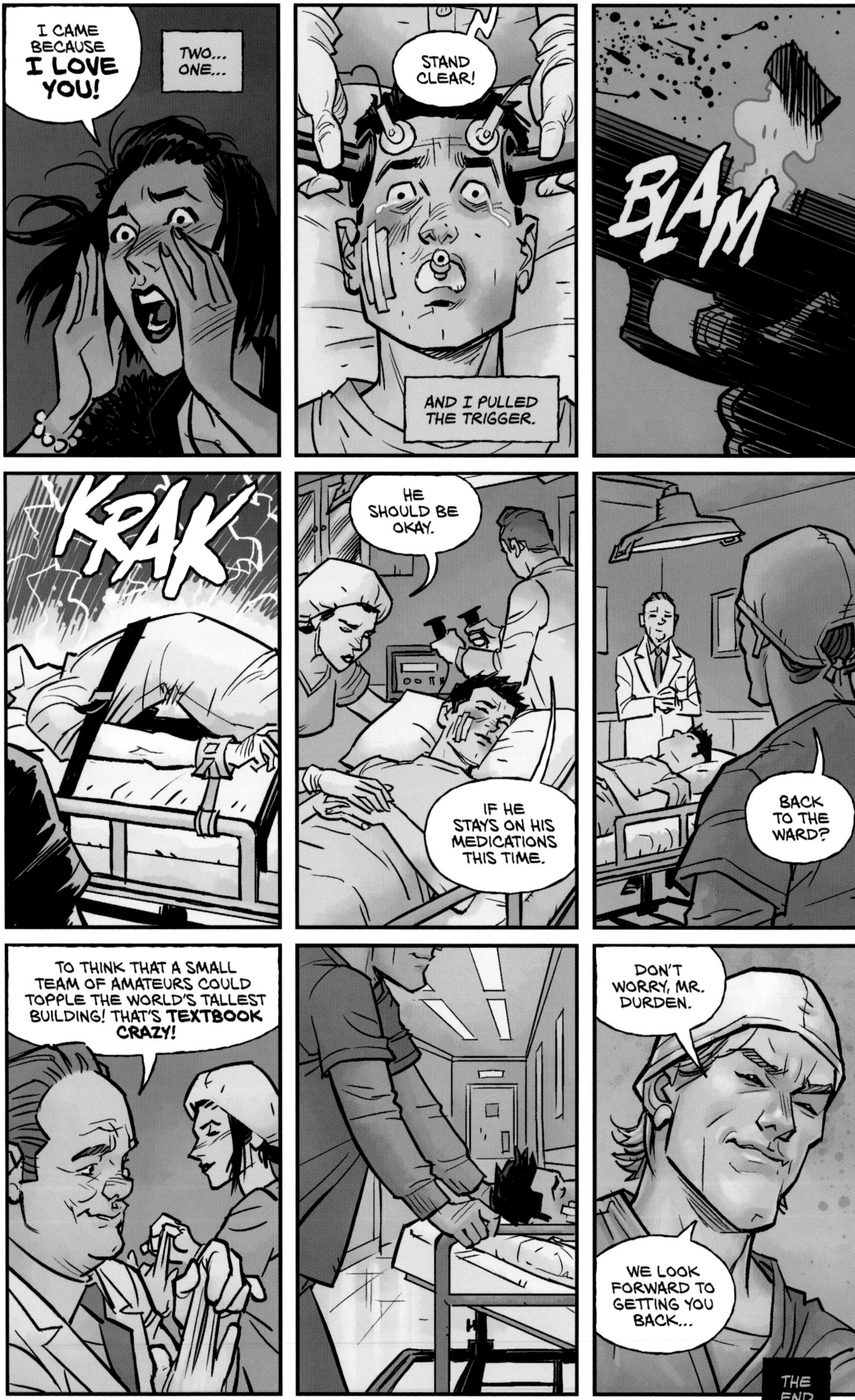
I CAME BECAUSE I LOVE YOU!
TWO... ONE...
STAND CLEAR!
AND I PULLED THE TRIGGER.
BLAM
KRAK
HE SHOULD BE OKAY.
IF HE STAYS ON HIS MEDICATIONS THIS TIME.
BACK TO THE WARD?
TO THINK THAT A SMALL TEAM OF AMATEURS COULD TOPPLE THE WORLD'S TALLEST BUILDING! THAT'S TEXTBOOK CRAZY!
DON'T WORRY, MR. DURDEN.
WE LOOK FORWARD TO GETTING YOU BACK...
THE END

Chuck Palahniuk, writer

CHUCK PALAHNIUK is the author of fourteen novels—*Beautiful You*, *Doomed*, *Damned*, *Tell-All*, *Pygmy*, *Snuff*, *Rant*, *Haunted*, *Diary*, *Lullaby*, *Choke*, *Invisible Monsters*, *Survivor*, and *Fight Club*—which all have sold more than five million copies in the United States. He is also the author of *Fugitives and Refugees*, published as part of the Crown Journeys series; the nonfiction collection *Stranger Than Fiction*; and the short story collection *Make Something Up*. He lives in the Pacific Northwest. Visit him on the web at ChuckPalahniuk.net.

Cameron Stewart, interior artist

CAMERON STEWART is an award-winning writer and artist of comics, including *B.P.R.D. Hell on Earth: Exorcism*, *Batgirl*, *Batman and Robin*, *Assassin's Creed*, and many more. He has won Eisner and Shuster Awards and been nominated for Harvey, Eagle, and Bram Stoker Awards for his original graphic novel *Sin Titulo*. Originally from Toronto, he has also lived and worked in Montreal, Berlin, London, and Glasgow. He punched someone once. It didn't work out so well.

David Mack, cover artist

DAVID MACK is the *New York Times* best-selling author and artist of the *Kabuki* series and the writer and artist of *Daredevil* from Marvel Comics. Mack created artwork for the opening titles of the *Jessica Jones* Netflix TV series. For the number-one hit film *Captain America: The Winter Soldier*, Mack worked with Sarofsky Design to create the art and concept for the credit and title sequence. Mack's work has garnered nominations for seven Eisner Awards, four International Eagle Awards, and both the Harvey and Kirby Awards in the category of Best New Talent, as well as many other national and international awards.

Dave Stewart, colorist

DAVE STEWART was born on the high desert while his mother danced to the chatter of a rattlesnake's tail. Despite a rare case of Sasquatch leg and the desire to run with any northbound moose migration, he found the coloring arts were a suitable profession to fuel the resources needed to build a moonshine still in the backwoods hills of southwest Portland. Much to his surprise he found that his coloring garnered him industry awards, unlike his feverish gathering of dry leaves for winter bedding. And he colors on.

Nate Piekos, letterer

NATE PIEKOS graduated with a BA in design from Rhode Island College in 1998. Since founding Blambot Comic Fonts & Lettering, he has created some of the industry's most popular typefaces and used them to letter comic books for nearly every major comic book publisher. Piekos's designs can also be seen on product packaging, on television, and in feature films.

Photos by Allan Amato

CAMERON STEWART

"Eisner winner Cameron Stewart . . . hardly needs me to tell anyone how great his art is."
—*ComicsAlliance*

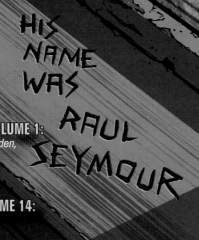

B.P.R.D. PLAGUE OF FROGS VOLUME 1:
With Mike Mignola, Christopher Golden,
Geoff Johns, Guy Davis, and others
ISBN 978-1-59582-675-6
$19.99

**B.P.R.D. HELL ON EARTH VOLUME 14:
THE EXORCIST**
With Mike Mignola, Chris Roberson,
and Mike Norton
ISBN 978-1-50670-011-3
$19.99

**BUFFY THE VAMPIRE SLAYER:
TALES OF THE VAMPIRES**
With Joss Whedon, Jane Espenson,
Jeff Parker, Cliff Richards, and others
ISBN 978-1-56971-749-3
$15.99

FIGHT CLUB 2
With Chuck Palahniuk
ISBN 978-1-61655-945-8
$29.99

SIN TITULO
ISBN 978-1-61655-248-0
$19.99

AVAILABLE AT YOUR LOCAL COMICS SHOP OR BOOKSTORE!
To find a comics shop in your area, call 1-888-266-4226. For more information
or to order direct visit DarkHorse.com or call 1-800-862-0052 Mon.–Fri. 9 AM to 5 PM Pacific Time.

DAVID MACK

"Mack's style takes narrative to the art gallery level . . . genius."
—Chuck Palahniuk

DREAM LOGIC
ISBN 978-1-61655-678-5
$34.99

REFLECTIONS
ISBN 978-1-61655-676-1
$24.99

KABUKI LIBRARY EDITION VOLUME 1
ISBN 978-1-61655-677-8
$39.99

VOLUME 2
ISBN 978-1-61655-703-4
$39.99

BUFFY THE VAMPIRE SLAYER: WILLOW—WONDERLAND
With Jeff Parker, Christos Gage, Brian Ching, and Jason Gorder
ISBN 978-1-61655-145-2
$17.99

FIGHT CLUB 2:
With Chuck Palahniuk and Cameron Stewart
ISBN 978-1-61655-945-8
$29.99

AVAILABLE AT YOUR LOCAL COMICS SHOP OR BOOKSTORE! To find a comics shop in your area, call **1-888-266-4226**. For more information or to order direct › ON THE WEB DarkHorse.com › E-MAIL mailorder@darkhorse.com › PHONE 1-800-862-0052 Mon.–Fri. 9 AM to 5 PM Pacific Time.

Dream Logic™, Reflections ™, and Kabuki ™ © David Mack. Buffy the Vampire Slayer™ & © Twentieth Century Fox Film Corporation. Fight Club 2™ © Chuck Palahniuk. Dark Horse Books® and the Dark Horse logo are registered trademarks of Dark Horse Comics, Inc. All rights reserved. (BL 5047)

RECOMMENDED READING

Lady Killer
JOËLLE JONES & JAMIE S. RICH

LADY KILLER
Story by Joëlle Jones and Jamie S. Rich
Art by Joëlle Jones
978-1-61655-757-7
$17.99

TWO BROTHERS
Fábio Moon Gabriel Bá

TWO BROTHERS
Story and art by Fábio Moon and Gabriel Bá
978-1-61655-856-7
$24.99

Spirits of the Dead
RICHARD CORBEN

EDGAR ALLAN POE'S SPIRITS OF THE DEAD
Story and art by Richard Corben
978-1-61655-356-2
$24.99

HELLBOY IN HELL
THE DESCENT

HELLBOY IN HELL VOLUME 1: THE DESCENT
Story and art by Mike Mignola
978-1-61655-444-6
$17.99

NANJING
THE BURNING CITY
ETHAN YOUNG

NANJING: THE BURNING CITY
Story and art by Ethan Young
978-1-61655-752-2
$24.99

VEIL
GREG RUCKA
TONI FEJZULA

VEIL
Story by Greg Rucka
Art by Toni Fejzula
978-1-61655-492-7
$19.99

THE UMBRELLA ACADEMY

THE UMBRELLA ACADEMY VOLUME 1: APOCALYPSE SUITE
Story by Gerard Way
Art by Gabriel Bá
978-1-59307-978-9
$17.99

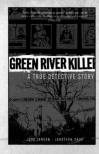

GREEN RIVER KILLER
A TRUE DETECTIVE STORY
JEFF JENSEN JONATHAN CASE

GREEN RIVER KILLER: A TRUE DETECTIVE STORY
Story by Jeff Jensen
Art by Jonathan Case
978-1-61655-812-3
$19.99

JONATHAN CASE
THE NEW DEAL

THE NEW DEAL
Story and art by Jonathan Case
978-1-61655-731-7
$16.99

BRIAN WOOD • ANDREA MUTTI
REBELS
"A WELL-REGULATED MILITIA"

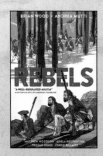

REBELS VOLUME 1: A WELL-REGULATED MILITIA
Story by Brian Wood
Art by Andrea Mutti, Matthew Woodson, Ariela Kristantina, and Tristan Jones
978-1-61655-908-3
$24.99

HUSBANDS

HUSBANDS
Story by Jane Espenson and Brad Bell
Art by Ron Chan, Natalie Nourigat, M. S. Corley, Ben Dewey, and Tania del Rio
978-1-61655-130-8
$14.99

ALEISTER & ADOLF
DOUGLAS RUSHKOFF MICHAEL AVON OEMING

ALEISTER & ADOLF
Story by Douglas Rushkoff
Art by Michael Avon Oeming
978-1-50670-104-2
$19.99

DARK HORSE BOOKS
DarkHorse.com

AVAILABLE AT YOUR LOCAL COMICS SHOP OR BOOKSTORE!

To find a comics shop in your area, call 1-888-266-4226. For more information or to order direct visit DarkHorse.com or call 1-800-862-0052 Mon.–Fri. 9 AM to 5 PM Pacific Time.

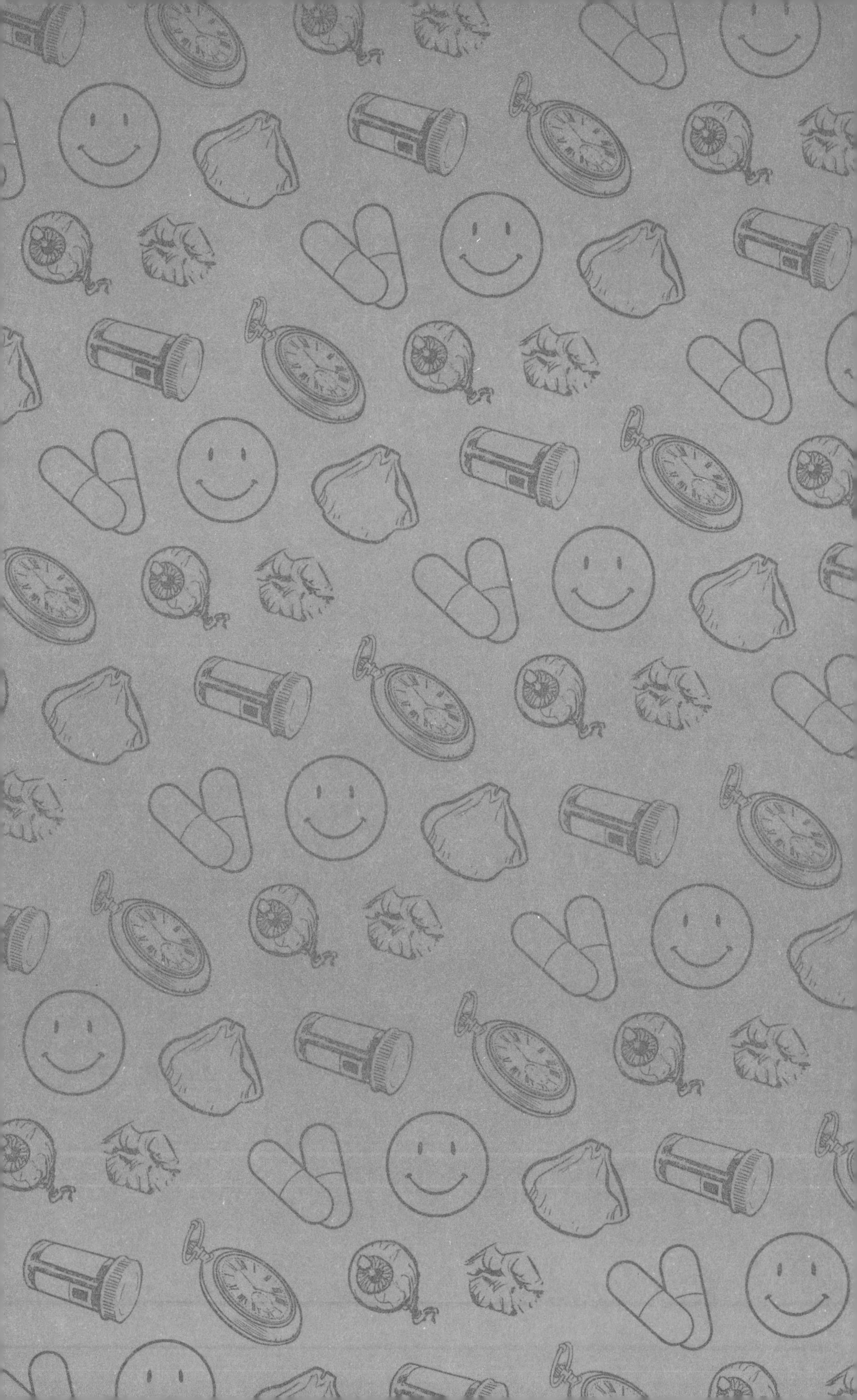